DR

BY THE SAME AUTHOR

Freud's Women (*with John Forrester*)
Memory and Desire
Simone de Beauvoir
Cabaret: The First Hundred Years
Femininity and the Creative Imagination:
A Study of James, Proust and Musil
The Rushdie File (*edited with Sara Maitland*)
Dismantling the Truth: Reality in the Post-modern World
(*edited with Hilary Lawson*)
Postmodernism (*editor*)
Ideas from France (*editor*)
Science and Beyond (*edited with Steven Rose*)

DREAMS OF INNOCENCE

Lisa Appignanesi

HarperCollins*Publishers*

HarperCollins*Publishers*
77–85 Fulham Palace Road,
Hammersmith, London W6 8JB

Published by HarperCollins*Publishers* 1994
1 3 5 7 9 8 6 4 2

A catalogue record for this book is available
from the British Library

ISBN 0 00 224164 1

Photoset in Linotron Galliard by
Rowland Phototypesetting Limited, Bury St Edmunds, Suffolk

Printed in Great Britain by
HarperCollinsManufacturing Glasgow

For John
Who Still Does
and
For Tilman Spengler Who Helped

'Nature is always valueless, but has been given value at some time, as a present – and it was we who gave and bestowed it. Only we have created the world *that concerns humans*!'

Friedrich Nietzsche, *The Gay Science* (1887)

'Don't you find it a beautiful clean thought, a world empty of people, just uninterrupted grass, and a hare sitting up?'

D. H. Lawrence, *Women in Love* (1920)

PROLOGUE

1985

FOR THE LIVING, death is always an unfinished business. Like a telephone conversation cut off in mid-sentence. Or a lovers' parting of the ways.

Anger and longing follow, a gritty residue of frustration and sorrow. Not to mention a labyrinth of imaginings.

When Helena Latimer found herself falling prey to these excesses, she was quick to chastise herself. She was neither a widow nor a bereft child – nor even an abandoned lover. She was, in fact, wonderfully fortunate: a young woman in her prime, with good friends and a profession she was committed to.

Yet since Max Bergmann had slipped from her life, she had begun to understand why Orpheus had dared to traverse the shades of memory to rescue his lost one. Any action, it seemed, was preferable to the raging and tearful impotence – the howling *why*? – of mourning.

Perhaps her condition was made worse by the fact that she wasn't even certain of the death.

The letter with the tell-tale script had arrived that very morning. Its presence, so casual amongst the bills and junk mail, had filled Helena with disbelief – an uncanny sense that a dead man had just stepped over the threshold.

It was the letter which had propelled her so quickly to this city she had never before visited.

> Helena, my dear,
>
> The whiteness here is a glare inviting shadows. The hills have the plump smoothness of down, but the mountains betray their crags and crevices . . .

So it had begun. And so it had gone on for three pages, dense with description of awesome mountains and lofty woods, of pure rushing streams and icy skies, of a village, a house. But that was all.

There had been no hard news, no address, not even a signature. There had been no explanation of why Max Bergmann had vanished without trace some two months back, no indication of his state or what might have led to his death.

It was in fact only when Helena examined the blurred stamp on the envelope that she realized it postdated the press announcement which had flung her into despair: the notice of Max's presumed death.

Thoughts as frenzied as circus acrobats had tumbled through her.

Max was alive. That date proved he was alive. The man, whose disappearance had thrown her into such tumult that she was forced to acknowledge he was the single most important being in her life, was alive. She must go to him, find him. He had written to her at last. She had felt so lost without him. But where was she to go? The letter must be in some kind of code, which meant Max was in trouble. He needed her. At least there was the postmark, the minute detail of a landscape, to go by. She would trace him. What was the skill of an investigative journalist but the ability to follow up clues? She was, at least, good at that.

And so she had picked up the telephone in the kitchen of her Kensington house and made the first in the series of calls which had landed her here.

MÜNCHEN 8KM the Autobahn sign announced and already the lights of the city played through the misty darkness.

Helena sat back in the seat of the cab and looked out of the window. A domed elephantine building loomed pale against the sooty night.

'*Was ist das?*' she queried the driver.

'Garching. The Max Planck Gesellschaft nuclear trial plant. They're testing thermo-nuclear fusion.'

Helena stored the facts for future use. She had rung the Green Headquarters in Munich before leaving to get a sense of what, if any, actions were being planned, to see if anything might tally with Max Bergmann's presence in the area. She knew it was a long shot. If Max was covering his tracks, then it would take more than a telephone conversation to discover why, let alone to find him. Yet find him she must. If he had written to her, then it was because he needed finding. By her. On the flight from London she had had wild visions of him held hostage in some dank room, his letter screened so that he could write only the most innocuous of messages.

She had long suspected that aside from his management of Orion Farm, aside from his writing and ecological campaigning, Max Bergmann had a secret life of covert action in the Green cause. He always knew the smallest detail about any radical venture in America – whether it was to do with liberating laboratory animals or perching atop a crane about to start digging a dam which would pervert the natural course of a river.

Then about eighteen months ago, without Max admitting it in so many words, Helena had had her proof. He had asked her whether, in the course of her research on toxic waste, she might sniff out a little information for him – to do with the relocation of a plant. She had done so and a few weeks later she had read of an action at the plant's proposed site.

After that, at irregular intervals, Max had given her little tasks to perform, never directly implicating her in any resulting action, never making anything explicit since that would have jeopardized her position. But Helena had known, and had been happy at their unspoken complicity.

It was because of Max's involvement in covert action, she sensed, that his deputy at Orion Farm had only made discreet enquiries of the police when Max had gone missing.

Yet when she had spoken to James Whitaker this afternoon and read him Max's letter, he had said without the least trace of irony, 'It sounds as if the great man has taken himself on an extended solitary holiday.'

'He wouldn't do that – without alerting you.'

'No, perhaps not. But then again . . .' She could almost hear James shrug. 'Well, let me know what you find.'

'I'll find *him*.' Helena had put more certainty in her voice than she felt.

'Yes, if anyone can, you will.' He paused. 'You know, Helena, someone else could have posted the letter for him, after . . . after . . .'

'His death,' she had finished for him, adding quickly, 'I don't, won't believe that.'

'No, of course not.'

James had sounded strained, strange. But then she felt strained as well, abandoned; had felt strange ever since Max's disappearance, as if gaping cracks had opened in the solid ground beneath her feet. With the notice of his presumed death, they threatened to swallow her. It was only with a great effort of the will that she could maintain even a precarious balance.

The cab driver was chatting away, giving her a guided tour of the Munich sights now that she had prodded him. Her German was rusty, but she could understand him well enough. She had Emily to thank for that, as for so much else. Emily with her old-fashioned button-up dresses and hand-knitted woollies; Emily the headmistress with her kind eyes and understanding smile. Emily who had taken her in, adopted her when she was a miserable twelve-year-old, saved her from the chaos of the foster family she never liked to think about. Emily who had given her everything – languages, an education, a sense of her own beauty, the book-lined house with too many rooms in a Kensington that was far too good for the likes of a Helena. And love.

Sometimes she thought it was for the love of Emily that she had done everything that she had done.

But Emily was dead now, had died five years ago. It was soon after her death that Helena had met Max Bergmann, had written the profile of him which had been instrumental in her getting a job with the paper. In a sense Max had replaced Emily as the stable, guiding force of her life. And that was the horror of it all. Without Max she felt utterly alone.

They had reached the town centre now. Elegant facades shone pale in the lamplight. Despite the lateness of the hour, the wide avenue swarmed with people. In the labyrinth of narrower streets into which they turned, the taxi could barely inch its way forward.

It was just as Helena noticed that the crowds were in part composed of masked revellers, that the driver announced, '*Fasching*. Carnival.'

A white-faced Pierrot, arm-in-arm with a scarlet Columbine, came towards them. Helena could see from their mouths that they were singing, but the noise of the streets transformed song to grimace.

A rap on the window opposite startled her. Helena turned, only to see a leering death's head.

She started back, terrified of the apparition, as if it were an omen.

'Your hotel is only two streets away.' The driver looked round at her. 'It'll be quicker for you to walk, if your case isn't too heavy.' He pointed beyond a tall gaily striped maypole, across a teeming market square.

'Yes, all right.' Helena felt a little unsure. But she paid him, hoicked her bag over her shoulder, felt herself propelled by the noisy crowd.

An arm groped its way round her back, prodding her to one side, moving her towards a door. She found herself in a huge *Bierkeller*, throbbing with sound.

'Nein,' she protested to the Harlequin at her side. 'I need to go the other way.'

'A drink first.' He didn't seem to hear her, and that arm still gripped.

She struggled away, dropping her bag in the process. Someone tumbled over it. There was a huge raucous laugh from the crowd, as if some deliberate trick had been performed. She felt utterly unnerved. And then someone planted a beery kiss on her lips.

'Eine süsse Ausländerin.' The figure grinned grotesquely from a pink-painted face crowned by a plaited peasant-girl wig.

Without thinking, Helena slapped the man fiercely across the face.

For the briefest moment, there was silence around her as the man glowered.

'Here, let me help you.' A tall figure in motley emerged from the crowd, picked up her bag and manoeuvred her swiftly back out through the door.

'Where are you trying to get to?'

Helena suddenly felt limp. 'Falkenturmstrasse, Hotel An der Oper,' she mumbled, registered that she was looking into the masked face of a fool, a veritable medieval fool with cap and bells.

'If I take your arm, will you bite?'

She shook her head, felt shamefacedly grateful to be able to lean against his bulk. He led her through cracks in the crowd, moved with the surge of it, then at last turned into a quieter street, and opened a door to the relative stillness of a lobby.

'It's carnival, you know, a pagan free-for-all. No good trying to fight it.'

He bowed slightly, the bells on his cap tinkling, and before she could thank him or protest that she had merely been taken by surprise, he disappeared through the doors and was lost in the crowd.

Helena looked after him for a moment. Then, with a shrug, she proceeded to the desk. She was, she realized, exceptionally, unusually tired. The strain of these last months had certainly taken its toll if she couldn't even negotiate her way through a boisterous crowd. Her friend Claire had been right to intimate that this whole matter of Max's disappearance had exerted a disproportionate hold on her. It was the passive waiting. That was the worst.

Tomorrow things would be better, Helena consoled herself. Action at last. But first, bed. And some food. She hadn't eaten since that morning. In fact a snack in bed with the television flickering her to sleep would be ideal.

The bed was deliciously cool, crisply white. Helena stretched out on it with a sigh, before forcing herself to sit up and munch at the salad, pick at the cheese, the thick hunk of dark bread. She sipped the fragrant white wine and watched the images on the screen. But she couldn't focus on them. Instead the lines of Max's letter, all but memorized now, replayed themselves in her mind together with the progress of their relationship. Trying to penetrate the mystery of the first had in the course of the day become fused with understanding the second.

Despite the state that had taken her over since Max's disappearance, Helena was not by instinct or inclination a navel-gazer. In fact her one longer-term relationship with a man had teetered on that very fact. She didn't particularly want to know the whys and the wherefores of her own choices and movements nor those of anyone else. There was far too much to accomplish in the world: endless interrogation of the psyche's meanderings was an idle luxury, a waste of valuable time and energy. Either one knew things instantly or one didn't. In the first case, one acted. In the second case as well, though momentary confusion might entail a slightly more rigorous pulling up of the proverbial socks.

She had known about Max instantly, had recognized that he was someone special as soon as she had heard him speak at that environmental congress in New York all those years ago, when she was just a stripling of a girl struggling to find a voice and a job. Max had stood tall behind the podium, a big man with a noble white head and austere features. His eyes beneath the shock of white hair were fiery, his spare movements tautly athletic. His voice, when it emerged, seemed to come from a deep well of silent reflection. This, together with the authority of his words, had made her suddenly think that she was in the presence of that rare being, a sage.

He had evoked the fragility of a planet subjected to rapacious marauders, an ancient precious earth, vastly rich in the variety of its species. And now it was being despoiled, transformed into a dusty desert. At the end of the speech, it was as if she had experienced a revelation – her hands were trembling, her mouth dry.

Helena had managed to persuade him into an interview, had travelled with him to the Farm in the hills of New Hampshire, and had interviewed him there. She was tongue-tied, shy, in awe of his presence, but in the course of the two days she had spent there, Max had filled her with confidence. It was as if his own zeal, his own absolute integrity, flowed into her, making her strong, aware.

He had shown her round Orion Farm himself. It wasn't the usual sort of farm, but a breeding station for species that were dying out, shunned or killed off by the ardours of agro-business with its reliance on chemicals. Variety and purity, Max told her, were his key words. Variety, applied to the plants and the seedlings that were nurtured in greenhouses and on open ground, to the rare old breeds of cows and sheep. Purity, to the methods used. And, Helena had grown increasingly to think, to the way of life Max encouraged here. It was almost monastic in its simplicity and discipline.

Apart from the core farm workers, there were twenty youths who were gathered together each summer for a kind of ecological camp. They worked the dairy and the vegetable gardens, and studied, under Max's strict tutelage. Some of these youths returned in subsequent years, went on to spread the word, or begin their own enterprises. It was these, Helena liked to imagine, though she had no tangible proof, who formed the crack forces of an underground ecological army. That wasn't simply wild conjecture on her part: she had met one of Max's youths working for Greenpeace, another in the Sea Shepherds.

The youths were housed either in outlying cabins or in the rambling main house, where meals were taken in unison. At the crack of dawn there were gymnastics; in the evenings, music or storytelling, when weather permitted, around a bonfire.

It was sometime in the course of that first visit that Max had fixed her with his soothing gaze and said, 'It is young people like you, Helena, who are needed. Young people to prevent the apocalypse which is creeping up on us in the very midst of our plenty.'

The words had fired her work ever since, her journalistic campaigning on Green issues, her investigations into pollutants and pesticides, into sulphur emissions, the course of acid rain and the dying forests of Europe; into the export of fertilizing chemicals to the third world and the decimation of the rainforest; into cycles of flood and drought, into the breakdown of traditional communities. Most recently she had reported on the Bhopal disaster. Her work had won her prizes and a reputation as well as a post at the *Sunday Times*, which gave her a great deal of freedom and a regular outlet. But it was Max she had learned from, been inspired by. In face-to-face meetings, telephone calls, letters.

Her visits to the Farm became as regular as pilgrimages.

Helena would always go there for at least two weeks sometime in early summer, and again in winter, to recuperate from the hurly-burly of her increasingly successful journalist's life. She thought of it as her retreat. There was a room which became hers, an attic space under the eaves of the house at a slight distance from the others. She was left largely to her own devices, to ramble and swim or ski and read, though Max always set time aside to talk to her.

It was on the first of those longer summer visits that a strange incident, which she now saw as a turning point in their relationship, had taken place. She was swimming in the small lake behind the main house when her watch strap broke and, noting it only after a few moments, she dived down to try and retrieve it. She was a strong swimmer with no particular fear of the depths, but after she had come up for air and plunged down a second time, Max was suddenly upon her, forcibly tugging her back to shore, his arm under her chin, as if she had narrowly escaped drowning.

'Are you all right?' he had asked her with something like panic in his eyes. And concern. The concern had stopped her from protesting that she had been in no danger, and she had simply nodded. Then too, the sensation of his arms around her made her hold her breath. It was the first time he had touched her. With most men that first touch would have led to another. She was used to that, used to the fact that the accident of a harmony of features, long legs and corn-gold hair led to a flurry of advances from men of whatever age.

Not with Max. He released her almost instantly and she thought she was grateful for that. But he had continued to look at her with a particular intentness as she had rubbed herself down, pulled on clothes, reassured him again that she was fine.

From that moment, a palpable bond seemed to form between them – one based on more than simply her admiration of him. The bond was all the stronger, Helena thought, because, for all their closeness, it carried no taint of carnality. With Max, there was no prying, no delving into areas best left untouched, no questions which couldn't be answered. He gave her peace.

During the quiet winter months, Max used the extra space in the house to provide a writers' retreat, a colony which had gradually gained in fame. The monastic calm was still there, perhaps even more so, but the faces were older, though they nonetheless looked to Max with something like worship. It was on one of her winter visits that Helena dared to ask him why there was never a woman amongst those faces. That was the one thing about the Farm which troubled her.

He had looked at her solemnly then, considered as he always did before answering, though this time she thought she saw something like a twinkle in those clear eyes.

'You know, Helena, I haven't known many women. I'm not very comfortable with them. I'm a solitary by nature, I guess. And if there were women here, well, the atmosphere would be altogether different. Sometimes, even with you – and you're special, we have an affinity – I feel it, that distraction in the boys' faces, that preening and forgetfulness.' He shrugged. 'Anyhow, it seems to me that given how important women are in most men's lives, it's good for them to have some time on their own, away from all that, in nature, an opportunity to explore something else in themselves, something even deeper than the sexual challenge.'

She hadn't argued with him, had taken it, had carried away with her his sense of her own specialness, the affinity between them. Like a love affair raised above the norm by its purity. Something they could both treasure.

And that, Helena thought, already more than half asleep, perhaps accounted for why Max had written to *her* and not to his deputy, James Whitaker. Or did it? She switched off the light. If she were lucky, tomorrow might bring some answers.

She woke to find pale sunshine curling round the heavy curtains. For a moment, she was uncertain where she was. As memory flooded through her, she leapt from the bed and dressed quickly. Barely seven o'clock. She had a good long day in front of her to reach the town on the postmark and to explore its surroundings.

The hotel dining room was already crowded. Whatever revelry the evening's carnival antics may have entailed, the dark-suited men trailing briefcases and the scent of aftershave seemed to have had nothing to do with it. They looked as orderly and as affluent as the pristine office buildings which had dotted the route from the airport.

Helena took her first cup of coffee with the *Süddeutsche Zeitung*, her second with the maps she had purchased, then put both aside to dig out Max's new collection of essays from her bag. She glanced at the inscription he had written for her: 'To Helena, a staunch battler and as pure as the mountain air'. With a flush in her cheek, she turned to the essay she had begun re-reading on the plane. 'Homecoming' it was called, one of Max's more philosophical pieces, and she wasn't sure she altogether grasped its intent. But the language spoke to her almost as poetry might, a language of digging in dark loamy soil and walking in shaded woods, of coming upon hidden violets and daisy-strewn meadows, of the interconnectedness of things and an at-homeness in nature.

She had first read this essay when Max had given her the book in Norway, at the environmental conference just outside Oslo. She had gone there specifically to see Max, needing to see him after those days in Bhopal. The foul scent of the blinding methyl isocyanate gas which had leaked from the chemical factory was still in her nostrils. The grim sight of those streets in which bodies lay dead and dying beneath a sky reddened by hundreds of funeral pyres pursued her. Only Max could provide some smattering of comfort, pull threads of direction from the disaster. And he *had* helped. Only then to vanish.

Helena shivered, forced herself to concentrate on the essay. She had read it in Norway, because Norway was Max's childhood home and she had thought that the essay would tell her how he felt about returning there after all these years. Now it suddenly occurred to her that some of the images here were similar to those in his letter to her. She filed the thought for further reflection. It was time to set off.

The Munich streets were unrecognizable now, somehow magically clean after the fervours of the night. Cyclists rode untroubled in their specially designated pavement lanes, as certain of their place as the brisk pedestrians and the gleaming cars.

Helena crossed the imposing Marienplatz, paused for a moment in front of the twin-towered bulk of the Frauenkirche to read a plaque announcing that the Messerschmidt firm, the famous arms manufacturers, were now patrons to the upkeep of the ancient ornate tombs which lined its brick walls. She smiled at the fittingness of it.

At the car rental office, she found to her consternation that only the BMW range was available. She hated these rampant agents of pollution. But she settled for a discreet navy blue model and, with a sigh, familiarized herself with gears and dashboard. Then she spread Max's letter and her maps out on the seat beside her. She was a born map-reader, the lines and curves and marks on the sheet of paper transforming themselves in her mind with easy fluency to the three dimensions of streets and roads and surrounding terrain.

A little bemused to find herself on the right-hand side of the street in this fat smooth car, Helena drove slowly through the morning traffic, heading south. When suburbs gave way to countryside, she relaxed. On the left-hand side of the Autobahn, she noted a large industrial complex, smiled when she saw the logo of Deutsche Aerospace on the main building: she had arrived at the precincts of the keepers of the Frauenkirche tombs. Could Max have had any interest in the workings of the firm?

Towards Sauerlach, she headed off the Autobahn on to quieter roads. It was beautiful here, the meadows still flecked with white, the covering of frost on the serried ranks of fringed pine giving them the aspect of hoary, bearded regiments. In the distance the mountains with their snow-capped peaks were already visible.

She stopped the car in a lay-by to have a proper look, breathed deeply of the cold morning air, and then headed off again. More alert now to descriptions which might tally with Max's letter, she travelled south east over gently rolling hills, past lumber mills and farmhouses sporting bright traditional figures and intricate painted scenes. Astonishingly fat sheep grazed in the meadows between the wayside crucifixes.

She reached Wolfratshausen well before noon. Suddenly nervousness coursed through her. She had arrived at her first destination. A stamp on an envelope had become a handsome Bavarian market town, complete with creamy yellow and green houses, an onion-domed church, and a lazy river swarming with ducks and plump swans. Her task now was to do the round of hotels and guesthouses and ask for Max Bergmann. Not that she expected, though she hoped, to find him, but she needed to pick up his trail.

She started with the nearest hotel, just doors away from the onion-domed church.

A sturdy woman with thick sausage curls smiled at her from behind a gleaming counter.

'*Ich suche einen Herrn Max Bergmann*. I believe he's staying with you.'

Helena was grateful for the growing smoothness of her German. Again she thought of Emily, who had encouraged her to learn the language, not because Em had an Austrian grandmother, but because, as she had insisted, 'If you understand German, you'll understand a good deal about this century of ours.'

The woman looked up from the register and shook her head. '*Nein, ich kenne ihn nicht*. There's no one here by that name.'

Her accent gave Helena pause, but she plunged on after a moment. 'That's strange, I had a letter from him saying he was here. Perhaps you might check back in your register, see if he left a forwarding address.'

The woman looked at her sceptically now. 'I don't remember anyone by that name. Bergmann . . .' she turned a page, ran a blunt finger cursorily down it, shook her head again.

'You're certain? He's a tall man. Looks about sixty, very handsome, with white hair, speaks English. Perhaps he used a different name . . .'

Suddenly the woman's face was all suspicion. 'We check all passports,' she said huffily, closing the register with an audible slam.

'Well, thank you for your help.' Helena smiled brightly, but she could have kicked herself. She would have to modify her questioning technique so as not to arouse undue suspicion. Of course identities would be checked. Still smiling, she said goodbye and on her way out picked up a little brochure about the town.

There were five other hotels and guesthouses listed. It wasn't a big town. She tried one, then another, and another, and cursed herself for not having thought in her hurry to bring a photograph of Max. Her hopes dwindled as she approached the last address.

There was no one behind the counter here. The single flowery sofa in the reception area looked worn. With a shrug, Helena pressed the desktop bell and waited. At last a youngish man appeared, his face visibly lightening as he looked at her.

'A room for you, Fräulein?' His eyes skimmed over her.

'Perhaps.' Helena was never averse to using any methods she could muster, including her charms. 'But first of all, I'm looking for a Herr Max Bergmann. I believe he may be staying with you.'

The man's face fell a little. He glanced at the register quickly, then shook his head.

'He's an old man, tall, white-haired, speaks English,' Helena lowered her voice confidentially, 'my father, in fact.' Her voice caught as she said it. Why had she said it? She put the question aside, raced on. 'He's been ill, I'm afraid he may have given a false name. Perhaps . . .'

The young man chuckled. 'You mean he may be here with someone else.' He glanced at Helena meaningfully, turned the register towards her. 'These old ones, eh? Some of them know how to live.'

Helena blanched. It wasn't what she had meant at all. But perhaps the man was right. That hadn't occurred to her. No, Max wouldn't disappear because of a woman. She looked through the register, tried to see a signature which might match Max's, whatever the name. But there was none she could be certain of.

'Nothing?' The young man was leaning nonchalantly towards her. 'I know, let's ask Berta in the restaurant. She keeps an eye on everyone.'

He ushered her towards a door and suddenly Helena found herself in a largish, slightly gloomy restaurant with thick oak panelling and chequered green tablecloths. The place was all but filled with lunchtime customers digging into heaped plates.

A blowsy middle-aged woman with bright rosebud lips greeted them.

Helena began her description again. The woman looked into the distance reflectively. 'Let me think now, rather gaunt, with deep-set eyes that stare right through you. Walks very straight. Does that sound like him?'

Helena took a deep breath, nodded. 'Could be.'

'Well, if that was the man you're looking for, he hasn't been back here for some three, maybe four weeks. I noticed him because he sat so quietly. Lost in thought, he was. Yes, that's it,' she preened herself a little at the description, 'lost in thought.'

'That's him,' Helena said. For a moment she didn't know whether to be thrilled or disappointed. So Max had been sighted here. But she had already known he must have been here from his letter, unless someone else had posted it for him. With a sigh, she tore a piece of paper from her notebook and wrote her name on it, handed it to the woman. 'If you see him again, will you ask him to leave a message for me? I'll come back and get it. Perhaps tomorrow.' She paused, added, 'By the way, was this man alone?'

'Oh yes.'

Strangely relieved, Helena looked towards the hotel assistant.

'And that room?' he prodded her.

'Not straight away.' She gave him her most brilliant smile. 'When I come back.' She waved at them both.

Outside, she paused for a moment. What next? The Post Office: there must be a poste restante and some directories. The slope-roofed building was a block away. She stood in a queue for a few minutes only to be met by a blank stare when she asked if there was any post for Max Bergmann.

It had been a stupid thought, she realized, as stupid as her search of hotel registers. If Max had deliberately disappeared, he could hardly have done it under his own name. The telephone directories were more promising and at the same time more distressing. There was a rash of industries Max might have been interested in: fertilizer factories, timber firms, power plants. Where to start? With no particular guide, except the size of the entry, Helena wrote down some addresses.

She got into the car reflectively, started to drive south, randomly following side roads which might take her to the sites Max had described. His letter had given her the sense that he was in trouble. But what kind of trouble could there be in these ancient Bavarian villages, sitting astride hilltops or nestling in quiet valleys? She passed a sleepy little town, a monastery with bulbous spires, saw the craggy peaks looming in the distance.

She had said to that man that Max was her father. It was an odd thing to have come to her lips. Helena suddenly shivered despite the warmth of the car. She switched on the radio. A Schubert sonata, wistful, lulling.

It was her American friend Claire who had put the suggestion into her mind. She had rung Claire just before leaving London to tell her she had heard from Max, that she was off, was finally going to have that holiday her editor had been urging her to take ever since she had come back from the harrowing trip to India. She had asked Claire if she would once again look after cats and plants and check through her post.

Claire didn't approve of her going, didn't altogether approve of Max. They hadn't got on when they had met. And yesterday, she had chided Helena for wasting a holiday and setting off on a wild-goose chase. 'Max isn't your responsibility,' she had said. 'He's neither your lover nor your father.'

No, Helena had no father. No mother either, for that matter. She was a free woman, a woman without progenitors. It was an idea of herself she had grown to like, to cling to even, ever since Emily had looked her straight in the eye and pointed out to her the wonderful liberty it gave her. But now, the notion that Max Bergmann could well be her father suddenly played havoc in Helena's mind: why else had she always been so strongly drawn to him? Why else had she been so distressed, at once angry and desolate, when he had vanished without word? Why else was she here speeding through this alien countryside?

Max her father. Max, who had singled her out.

She told herself some stories, tales of lost children, people misplaced and displaced.

Suddenly Helena veered into an opening on the road and turned round to retrace her route. She was letting her imagination run away with her again. The fog which had settled over the hills and was now closing in to obliterate everything but the taillights in front of her didn't help matters. It induced dream.

What she needed to do was to head back to Munich and go to Green Headquarters, sift through files, perhaps check the names of the factories she had listed in this vicinity, get a sense of what had brought Max to this corner of the world. Then tomorrow, she could come back to the Wolfratshausen area again and try to trace the descriptions in Max's letter.

The fog and the gathering darkness slowed her return to the city and it wasn't until the next morning that she got to Green Headquarters. Once it was clear who she was, they were helpful. Though they knew nothing of Max Bergmann's presence in the area, Helena did learn that there was a big anti-nuclear demonstration planned. She also learned there was a chemical plant and a timber firm near Wolfratshausen whose environmental policy they had doubts about. It was a long shot, but she rang both, was put through to a PR man with a smooth American accent in the first company who agreed to see her two days hence, and an assistant manager in the second who reluctantly agreed to an appointment on the same day.

Impatient with newspaper clippings, she set off again to Wolfratshausen towards midday, stopping to have a late lunch in the guesthouse where the blowsy woman had seen the man of Max's description. She knew it was a stupid hope, but she hoped that Max would suddenly appear, that he would materialize from the doorway and she could run into his arms. At least Orpheus had known where Eurydice was when he had gone in search of her. No sooner had the notion taken shape, than she answered it herself with one short word. 'Dead'.

Helena got up hastily and glanced around her as if afraid that the desultory customers had been able to read her mind. It was maddening how her thoughts these last weeks seemed always to be out of control.

The break-up with Andy had occasioned nothing like this, only a flurried sense of insult overridden by relief.

'Möchten Sie heute das Zimmer haben?' The man who had helped her yesterday was suddenly beside her.

Helena tried a smile. 'Later, perhaps. I'm not sure. I may have to go back to Munich tonight.'

She sped away, headed off into the countryside.

It was brighter today, the air so crisp that her nostrils tingled with it. The distant mountains were clear, the dark granite visible at points beneath the snowy caps. She tried different routes, narrow curling roads, flanked now by dense woods, now by fields. She came across a bank of reeds. Marshland. She must be near a lake.

She wasn't concentrating on her map, but on Max's letter, its words engraved on her mind now, so that she could almost chant them like a prayer against the recurring tides of despair which threatened her. She followed the rise and fall of the road, saw the lake glistening in the distance, the jagged mountains. It was a magical terrain.

Suddenly she jammed on the brakes of the car, almost skidded off the icy road. She had seen something out of the corner of her eye. What was it? A house, a row of chestnuts, the crest of a hill. She started up the car again, drove slowly until she found a point where she could turn, retraced her path. Yes, that grand house with the twin domes just visible through the bare trees, the lie of the land – it was just like the description in Max's letter. She hadn't imagined it.

With a surge of excitement Helena turned the car into the drive, stopped a little way from the house to dig out the letter, re-read the passage. She wasn't wrong. It was as he had detailed it, the two wings, the wide double door, the curl of the ironwork, and then to one side, the expanse of the lake.

Heart in mouth, Helena lifted the big brass knocker and let it fall, once, twice, a third time. She waited. Eventually the door opened. A dark-eyed face peered out.

'Ja?'

Helena put on her pleasantest smile.

The door opened a little further and she saw a broad-faced, curly-haired young woman, a girl really, in a loose flowered frock, half covered by a smudged apron. She was holding a mop in her hand.

'Ich suche einen Herrn Max Bergmann.' Helena carried on smiling.

'Kenne ich nicht.' The woman looked at her obtusely, and mumbled something Helena couldn't make out. Her vowels and consonants were all in the wrong places.

Helena made a quick decision, stepped over the threshold. 'Perhaps someone else in the house might know him.'

'Niemand daheim.' The girl shrugged.

'May I wait? I've come a long way.'

The girl looked around her uncertainly and finally opened a door on the left of the wide entrance hall.

As she walked towards it Helena noticed a blue leather spectacle case lying on the hall table. She started. It looked so like Max's case. Could it be? Her pulse quickened tangibly. She picked it up, put assurance into her voice.

'I believe this belongs to Herr Bergmann.'

The girl gave her that obtuse look again and then burst into excited speech, incoherent to Helena's ears, something about the glasses being on the floor. Lots of pieces.

She grabbed the case from Helena's hand, opened it, showed her the spectacles. They were remarkably like Max's, but the left eye had been shattered. It came to Helena that the girl thought she was being accused.

'I'll keep them for him, shall I?' Helena smiled, took the case back from her. 'I'll explain to him.'

The girl gave her a flicker of a smile in return, gestured her through the opened door, then looked up at her curiously.

'Amerikanerin?'

Helena nodded. If it made the girl happy to have her American, she was all too pleased to play the part.

She was rewarded with a giggle, an offer of coffee.

'Yes, please,' she said in English.

The girl trundled away.

Helena took a deep satisfied breath. She was on the right track. If Max himself was not here, the owners of the house would be certain to lead her to him.

She opened the spectacle case again and gazed once more at the fractured glass. Suddenly a shudder went through her. It would take a violent gesture, a punch, a kick, to create this web-like splintering. Had someone hurt Max, struck him? Was he lying imprisoned somewhere in this house?

Was she being stupidly naive in her open enquiries? Would the young woman now be running to fetch her masters?

Helena stilled herself, looked around her. She was in a spacious high-ceilinged room, every wall of which was covered in thick, leather-bound tomes with a dusty air about them. In one corner, by the window, stood a large desk, heaped with papers, manila files, a profusion of books, some of them open, others with an abundance of little sticky yellow markers protruding from their pages.

She edged towards the desk, started to read in an open file.

> The adepts of the Free Spirit were believers in free love. Just as the deer uses grass, the fish water, the bird air, so the holy man uses woman. By such intimacy she becomes chaster than before. There is a transcendental value to the sexual act here: it is a sacrament. For the adherents of the Adam-cult, ritual nakedness was an assertion of the natural, the unashamed innocence of Adam and Eve before the Fall . . .

So startled was Helena by what she read that it took her a moment to realize that the script was in English, another to hear the clatter of dishes. She looked up to see the young woman gazing at her suspiciously.

'Oh, thank you.' Helena hid her confusion, followed her to a polished mahogany table at the other side of the room where she deposited her tray.

'Thank you,' Helena said again. She sat down at the table and poured herself a cup of coffee, made a great show of installing herself before those watchful eyes, pulled out a book from her bag to cement the effect.

The girl seemed to relax, babbled something Helena couldn't make out.

She would have to be wary, Helena thought. She didn't want to be caught snooping and thrown out before she had at least had the chance to assess the owners of the house. She would have to proceed cautiously. But a trip to the toilet could cause no suspicion and it would give her a chance to get more of a sense of the place. If Max were being held in any of the rooms along the way, she was sure she could sense it.

Unfortunately the girl led her, not up the stairs, but towards the back of the house. Helena paused at an open door and peeked through.

'*Wie schön*. How lovely these old German houses are.' She opened the door wide. But there was nothing there beyond a confirmation of her words.

'*Ja, ja,*' the young woman mumbled, then pointed her towards another door.

She was waiting for her when Helena came out, led her back to the library.

Helena thanked her effusively, watched her leave and close the door behind her.

She sighed, gazed at the table. Mahogany. She didn't approve of mahogany. All those ancient trees in the dwindling rainforest hacked down to embellish the houses of the rich. For this was a rich house, despite the slight air of shabbiness, the cold. Run down, no longer in its prime. Why had Max described it in such detail? She didn't think he was actually here. The young maid didn't look like a jailer.

There was nothing for it but to sit and wait until the owners came back.

Her eyes fell on a tome propped on a bronze reading stand in the middle of the table. Odd the way it was so prominent, almost a centrepiece in lieu of fruit or flowers. Perhaps it was a bible, the bible of some Adam cult; she remembered the notes she had read.

Helena glanced towards the door, listened for footsteps. But surely there was no danger in looking at a book so obviously on display.

She lifted the heavy tome, opened it.

On the inside front cover someone had hand-printed a title: *Die Besessene – Das Buch von Anna.* The Possessed – Anna's Book. After that there was page upon page of light fluid script. Strange to find a hand-written volume like this bound in leather. Helena leafed through the pages. Suddenly the name 'Max' leapt out at her.

Perhaps this was it – the key to Max's disappearance, his whereabouts.

With a shiver of apprehension, Helena turned back to the beginning and began to read. The first page was brief, like an envoi:

> A story for you, my son. The story of our lives as I understand them now. What I couldn't have known, I have imagined. But it is true. More true I suspect than you would wish to know. Forgive us.

Helena read.

PART ONE

The Possessed

ANNA'S BOOK

ONE

1913

THE CHILDREN in that house were always conceived when a second man was present.

Now that she had learned a little more about the byways of life, Anna could wonder whether she had here arrived at the basis of a universal principle. A supplementary male presence, preferably real, perhaps imagined, was essential to the act of creation. For the dreaming woman, of course. But more particularly for the man.

But in those days, before the absurd clash of the world's armies had robbed them of their innocence and they still had to lift their skirts to run up the curved staircase of the house, she was more prone to talk than thought. They all were. Words had to stand in for so many gestures they weren't permitted. And such large words they were too: soul and spirit, struggle and transcendence, justice and morality. Words that muddled and confused, but in their ponderous way breathed a hope that some lack they all felt though couldn't precisely describe might be filled.

Only the house was silent. Yet, with its eccentric mingling of stately austerity and mannered grace, it alone seemed to have the wisdom to reflect on their actions.

It stood on the edge of a small hamlet resting peaceably in the foothills of the Bavarian Alps. From its rear windows one could see across the mirror stillness of a lake to slopes thick with blue-green pine. Beyond, there was the cold immovable granite of the mountains.

That summer of 1913, when the din of battle only sounded at the outer edges of the Austro-Hungarian Empire, Anna preferred to keep her eyes on the middle-distance. She had no interest in nationalist struggles in the South Balkans, or in the fact that the Austrian parliament had been indefinitely suspended. Nor did she care that the Prussian military was flexing its muscles in affairs of state or even that suffragettes were on the march in Britain. At home in Vienna, ladies in silk frocks chattered gaily beneath the graceful baroque arches of a thousand and one salons or listened dreamily to the vaulting sounds of the world's best orchestras.

And here, in Seehafen, things were even better. Here, she could ride or wander aimlessly through the capacious gardens, pausing to feel the morning moistness on an elm's bark. She could gaze on the fluttering dance of the daffodils or the slower swaying of the willows reflected in the indigo depths of the lake.

At such times she would hum little snatches of a Viennese waltz to herself and move in rhythm to the trees until her accelerated twirling brought her inevitably to a fence at the edge of the property. Then, with a surreptitious glance over her shoulder, she would hoick her dress above her knees and clamber across, running wildly up, up over the crest of a little hill and when breathless, throw herself face down on the grass amidst clusters of primrose and sweet-smelling celandine. Hands clasped under her chin, she would gaze through the grass at the plump brown and white of the cows in the valley or at the red-tiered steamer lolling across the lake; or turn herself over to muse at the tufted clouds ambling in acres of blue, until the height of the sun told her it was time to make her way back.

Or so it had been for almost two weeks of this holiday. But today was different, as her sister Bettina had been at pains to point out. Today Bruno would be arriving. Herr Bruno Adler. To be duly inspected by Bettina and the gathering circle of her friends. And soon she, Anna von Leinsdorf, would be Frau Bruno Adler.

Anna tasted the name as she had done almost daily for the last few months. It brought a little giggle to her throat and she stilled it with a mouthful of poppy-seed roll smothered in butter and a gulp of the coffee which Dora, the little dark-haired maid, had unobtrusively placed in her room just moments ago. For two weeks, when she wasn't more gainfully employed, Bettina had done little more than point out to her that now she must make an effort to put on a more serious demeanour. As if marriage were a corset which constrained; and movement and laughter were soon to be things of the past. But Bruno, with his warm chocolate eyes and that drooping moustache which tickled her forehead when he kissed her, wasn't like that, Anna thought.

It had been one of her father's last acts before he died to sanction their engagement. He had called her to his rooms in the Hofburg to relay the news – a certain sign of the event's significance. She had only been there once before and the Imperial Palace, with its endless plumed and helmeted guards and footmen, its succession of corridors and near-empty rooms, dismayed her. A grey chill pervaded everything and the awesome height of the rooms dwarfed even her aunt Hermine's magisterial girth – since of course she had accompanied her.

Her father had looked ancient, bowed by the weight of the Palace. Only his voice, as he conveyed to her from behind his vast desk that he had accepted on her behalf the marriage suit of Herr Bruno Adler, still carried that authority and clipped rectitude which in her mind she always associated with him. The careful marshalling of words, the listing of Herr Adler's attributes, largely financial, as if they were a catalogue of provisions for a distant Balkan regiment, had all passed over Anna's head into the windy distance of the room. All she could think of was that her father looked dreadfully ill. And when he had finished his speech and had at last fixed his monocled eye on her and said, 'I trust you are pleased,' she had nodded unthinkingly and then blurted out, 'I wish you would come home with us. This place can't be good for you.'

Her aunt had glanced at her severely, but her father's thin lips had after a moment crinkled into a smile. His dry cold hand had squeezed hers. 'I'll try. But I'm needed here for the time being.'

They were perhaps the last words he had spoken directly to her. Three months later he was dead. 'In the service of the Emperor,' her aunt pronounced to anyone who would listen, while Anna remained convinced that it was the draughty weight of the Palace itself which had killed him. She developed a visceral distaste for everything Imperial and the very sight of the letters K & K, the pervasive emblem of the monarchy, would make her shiver. Indeed, after that visit to the Palace, she had even grown to like her aunt's cluttered, somewhat oriental interior, with its Japanese vases, its great sprays of peacock feathers, its Persian carpets burdening the walls. At least there was the semblance of life here and from the windows one could see the sweep of the woods.

Then, too, though she never thought of it as her own, it was the only home she had known for the last seven years. Ever since her mother's death. Her mother, with her tawny eyes and her curling smile, whose portrait still graced Anna's room. When she thought of her first, her real home, it was her mother's laughter she remembered, and a sense of space. Nothing else. After their mother's death, Bettina had insisted on going off to study in Zurich. Since nothing ever stood in the path of Bettina's insistence, ten-year-old Anna had been moved in with her aunt. And her father had been free to dedicate himself increasingly to the service of his Emperor. 'A service which clothed him in honour', her aunt was wont to say and then murmur irascibly in the next breath, 'and not much else'.

It was when her aunt intimated to Anna that only her father's knowledge of his imminent and penniless death could have led him to accede so readily to Herr Adler's suit, given the vast distance between their respective families, that Anna began to pay Bruno Adler any significant attention. Before that he had simply been one of the many men, brightly uniformed or sombrely suited, to appear at her aunt's gatherings. Even after Bruno had been accepted as a suitor, with the proviso that no marriage was to take place until after Anna's eighteenth birthday, still over a year and a half away, she had been too shy to meet his many glances or engage in more than cursory conversation.

But her aunt's intimations, coupled with the cheerful prattle of her French governess, Elise, had fired Anna's imagination. It was not Bruno's wealth which impressed her: never having known lack, she was not interested in plenty. It was his difference. He was quite clearly not 'in the service of the Emperor'. Nor did he seem to come from anywhere. What a relief not to have to engage in a repeated litany of grands and greats which had paraded through too many centuries only to become like the tattered court cards in an ancient deck.

One day Anna casually asked her aunt, 'Is it true that Herr Adler is Jewish?'

Tante Hermine turned towards her with such a commotion of black satin that one of her Japanese vases teetered dangerously. 'Who told you that?' she asked, dark eyes narrowing.

'Oh, I heard it somewhere.' Anna smiled sweetly, her voice trailing off.

Within a week, Mademoiselle Elise had been seen tearfully off the premises.

Not that Bruno wasn't Jewish. It was simply that in the anti-semitic reaches of Viennese high society, such prattle was not permitted.

The day after Elise had left, Anna had allowed her engagement to Herr Bruno Adler to be announced.

She still missed Elise, missed her tinkling voice pouting risqué songs at the piano, missed the bubble of her conversation, her disquisitions on men's eyes and the fineness of Bruno's. Now there was only Miss Isabel with her volumes of Mrs Gaskell, her soulful renditions of the *Lyrical Ballads* and her constant news of the imprisonment or release of one militant suffragette or another. Anna liked her well enough, but hankered after Mademoiselle Elise's gossiping playfulness. She would particularly have liked to have had her at her side now to hear her impressions of Bettina and her husband, Klaus Eberhardt, and this curious house.

The wing Anna was in was as graceful as a Mozart sonata, all pale creamy hues and surprising ornament, right down to the airy rose and blue drawing room with its lightly gilded cupola and high windows overlooking the mellowness of lake and gardens. To walk across the hall to the opposite side of the house and its brother wing was to enter a different, darker world of heavy mahogany tables and gothic candelabra, of wainscoting and worn leather. Under the twin cupola here, bookshelves reached from floor to ceiling, broken only by the gleaming wood of fireplace and mantelpiece above which hung an old oil depicting a landscape not unlike the rugged peaks visible through the windows.

Anna would have liked to say to Mademoiselle Elise, 'I suspect Klaus's parents, who built this as their country house, couldn't agree on decor and split the place in two, one for Monsieur, one for Madame.' And Mademoiselle would have offered one of her mischievous chuckles and spiky comments before tying the sash on Anna's white linen dress just so.

Anna struggled with the bow now and tried to catch a glimpse of the effect in the looking glass above the painted chest. Then she straightened the white stockings once more and looped her long hair up as neatly as she could, fastening it with the two mother of pearl combs. Little tendrils still curled round her face. There was nothing she could do. Bettina would disapprove, as she had disapproved the night before when she had gone through Anna's wardrobe.

'Doesn't Tante Hermine realize you're no longer a child?' she had groaned. 'Mean old crow. When we get to Munich, I shall order some clothes for you. What must Herr Adler think – his bride-to-be still prancing around like a twelve-year-old?' At last, Bettina had pointed to the white dress and proceeded to lecture Anna on her behaviour for today, as if Anna were indeed still the child she had been on their mother's death, when the eighteen-year-old Bettina, her head held high in her grey-striped travelling suit, had set off for Zurich.

'Above all, don't run about and get covered in mud and grass.' Anna could hear her sister's resonant tones echoing in her mind as she looked longingly out of the window. And she could recreate the unspoken part of her lecture: 'Frau and Herr Trübl, let alone Dora, have enough to contend with without caring for your clothes. And you know I don't believe in working the servants. And I wouldn't have any at all here if this house weren't so big. And . . . and . . .'

Anna giggled. It was always the same. Her sister believed in this but didn't believe in that. For instance, she now didn't believe in governesses, but she did believe in education, in the value of books, in hard work. Bettina had beliefs and she, Anna, had none. Unless it were the belief that the grass was so green and the sky so blue that they were both beckoning to her. And if she went down the stairs very very quietly and clutched the book Bettina had given her to her bosom like a prayer, she might just escape outdoors without bumping into anyone.

Anna grabbed the apple from her tray and raced lightly down the stairs. Holding her breath, she made her way through the doors and ran towards a little gravelled lane where the shrubs shaded her from the house's view. She would be good today. She wouldn't stray from the paths. Nor would she tarry in the stables and end up smelling like the horses, as Bettina had once told her she did. With a happy crunch, Anna bit into her apple and as the sound rebounded through the air, tried to chew more delicately.

The path led her into Klaus's rhododendron grove. She called it by his name, because he had told her in his halting way one day that he had planted it himself. His eyes had played lovingly over the thick glossy leaves with their bursts of purple and pink and white blossom and, taking encouragement from her questions, he had told her of the origin of the plants, each one slightly different from its neighbour. She had never heard Klaus speak at such length and so passionately before. Her curious glance had brought a distinct flush to his cheeks above the curling bristle of his beard.

A sudden rustle from a corner of the grove had allowed him to turn away. She had followed his eyes and seen a little humped prickly form struggle unevenly across the ground, and freeze into a ball of stillness. Klaus had put a finger to his lips. They gazed at the tiny creature as it began to move again somewhat precariously. Then Klaus bounded silently down the path, a tall, loping, awkward figure. Within minutes he was back, bearing a can of milk, a saucer, a splint, a bandage.

With deft, gentle movements she had never seen in him before, he poured milk for the hedgehog, waited patiently for the creature to drink, picked him up in his large ungainly hands and quickly tied the splint round its injured leg. Anna marvelled. Perfect communion seemed to exist between the animal and this ordinarily clumsy, nervous man. Since that occasion she had begun to have a new sense of Klaus and even some inkling of what had always seemed his utterly incomprehensible union with her sister.

Anna crossed the grove, scanning it for signs of the hedgehog and then, turning into a lane which led alongside the little orchard towards the lake, she broke into a run. Where the path twisted and sloped, she suddenly tripped, only just catching herself before she stumbled to the ground. Neither twisted roots, nor loose branches had created the obstacle, but a pair of trousered legs stretched across the path.

'You should watch where you're going,' their owner muttered, barely glancing up at her. He was leaning against a tree, his attention wholly on the ground, while his pencil skimmed over his sketchpad.

'Sorry.' Years of ingrained habit spoke in the word. But she was angry. There was a grimy mark on her stocking. 'You should watch where you put your big feet,' she said under her breath. The man didn't look up at her again, didn't seem to have heard. With a scowl, Anna moved away, her pleasure spoiled. Who was this man? She hadn't heard any of Bettina's many expected guests arriving.

She had reached the rim of the lake when his voice called her back. 'You must be Bettina's sister, Anna, the one who's getting married.'

The nakedness of the description made her twirl round. He was coming after her with springy athletic steps, a battered straw hat raised in greeting. 'You shouldn't. Shouldn't get married. Turn yourself into a man's property. Become a slave to a corrupt system.'

Anna looked at him incredulously. A young, tautly handsome, clean-shaven face dominated by deep-set clear blue eyes in which the pupils were strangely large, fierce. They fixed on her.

'Who *are* you?'

'Johannes Bahr.' He bowed slightly.

Anna waited. There was nothing more. 'Johannes Bahr?' she queried and laughed suddenly. 'And that alone gives you the right to advise me on the course of my life?'

'This is the twentieth century.' It was at once an impersonal statement and an injunction heightened by the intimacy of his gaze.

'I know.'

'Do you?' He shrugged, lifted the battered hat again, to reveal a springy mass of chestnut hair. He seemed about to go, then added as an afterthought, 'You have a fine laugh, a free laugh. I wonder if one could paint a laugh,' he mused, as if he had already forgotten her presence.

And before Anna could respond, he was off, vanishing into the shrubbery.

Discomfited, Anna set off again, following the lakeside path past the boathouse. If all of Bettina's guests were like Johannes Bahr, she thought uncomfortably, this glorious weekend would be ruined. Yes, Bettina's friends would be just like her, always telling her what to do, what to feel, what to think. At least this Bahr had the advantage of youth.

In an effort to deflect her mood, Anna shifted direction and ran, ran back towards the house and the spreading copper beech she loved. Hanging from one of its thick branches, there was a swing. It was Anna's secret delight. Sheltered by the canopy of branches, she would sit or stand on the weather-beaten board and swoop through the air, higher and higher till her hair flowed in the wind and her feet all but touched the canopy of leaves.

It was when she had reached this dizzying height that Anna heard the single blare of a car's horn, heard the crunch of tyres over gravel. Through the greenery, she caught the glow of sunlight on brass. She jumped from the swing and raced towards the drive, arriving just in time to see the chauffeur open a gleaming door to a still begoggled Bruno, a bulky giant in the one-piece mechanic's suit he liked to don over his clothes when he chose to do the driving. Anna watched for a moment as he whipped off goggles and gloves and bent to kiss Bettina's hand. Watched his lips beneath the thick moustache as he mouthed, 'Frau Eberhardt, a pleasure. I hope I'm not too early. This new Mercedes model eats up the kilometres.' He laughed a boy's excited laugh, which sat oddly with the serious cast of his features.

'Not at all, not at all. Some of our number have already arrived.' Bettina was all charm. 'But I'm afraid I have no idea where Anna is. My sister *will* choose to disappear.' She threw up her arms in mock despair.

'Here I am.' Anna walked towards them with her light tread and heard her name emerge simultaneously from the lips of them both, her sister's in admonition, Bruno's in delight. Following the line of Bettina's exasperated gaze, she lifted one hand to her hair and tried uselessly to tuck fallen strands behind a comb, and the other to Bruno to accept his kiss. She noticed, with sinking heart, that the hand was far from clean and covered it swiftly with her words.

'Will you take me for a drive?'

'Anna! Herr Adler has just arrived and will want to wash and stretch his legs before lunch.'

Bruno's eyes smiled. 'Later, my dear. Frau Eberhardt is right.'

He looked from one sister to the other, both beauties, but in such disparate ways. Bettina, whom he had met only once before briefly in Vienna, was, in her stiff high-necked white blouse and crisp blue skirt, a model of queenly rectitude. Tall, willowy, she confronted you with clear grey eyes, her smooth dark head always poised at a slightly questioning angle. She had, Bruno thought, the slightly irascible smile of an intelligent woman who, knowing her own beauty, has to forgive the poor, superficial male, for always and inevitably thinking of that first.

Anna, his beloved Anna, was a little smaller than her sister, a little rounder, and as yet wholly unaware of her attractions. The delicate oval of her face lit up with her emotions; her smile puckered and teased deliciously, her nostrils flared with her temper as flagrantly as her pale gold hair fled from whatever its arrangement. And in the midst of it all, there was the watchful stillness of those tawny eyes, golden like some forest creature. Sometimes those eyes frightened him.

At the age of forty-five, Bruno Adler considered himself a supremely fortunate man. He had travelled a long way from that timid and tearful five-year-old who had watched his grandfather knocked off a Vienna pavement to a flurry of anti-semitic imprecations, a grandfather who had then wordlessly brushed off his hat, taken his grandson's arm and walked stoically away. It was the one childhood memory imprinted indelibly in his mind.

The rest was a haze of repetitive habit: the family dinners turned into gruelling examinations under the strict tutelage of his disciplinarian father; the clandestine visits to the tiny synagogue, thick with the smell of huddled male bodies and his mother's fear as she dragged him and his sister into the realm of what his father deplored as superstition. All remained a blur until his escape at the age of eighteen to America, where he had worked and learned and worked some more to emerge by the time he was thirty with his first fortune, reinvested now, increased fiftyfold, in industries which spanned the corners of the Austro-Hungarian Empire. Only one gross misfortune darkened this trajectory: his wife, Elisabeth, whose fate it had been to die, taking their firstborn with her.

But all that was in the past. Now there was Anna. He glanced at her, saw her impatience as he carried on a polite exchange with Bettina about the eccentricities of the house, the marvels of the site. He had not been certain that old von Leinsdorf would accept his proposal. Some of these ancient families held on with their fingernails to the teetering pinnacle of their nobility. But the old man had been amenable enough, given a little wait – long enough for him to die without having to confront the shame of the event itself.

Bruno had few illusions. He knew he had been accepted not for himself but for his fortune – something the von Leinsdorfs now sadly lacked. But then, he *was* his fortune. He had made it with his energy, his intelligence, his will, his perspiration, and it had made him. He would not be the same Bruno Adler without his wealth, his factories, his gleaming car and now his Anna, his own von Leinsdorf. And just as they had made parts of him, so would she.

Then, too, he loved her. There were half a dozen young women of equally high rank to whose families his fortune would not have come amiss. But he was honest enough with himself to know that he would have been distraught if the old man had refused him Anna. He could put a precise date to the moment when he had begun to love her. It was in her aunt's salon which he occasionally frequented, since it was useful to have friends amongst those dusty title-holders who made up the top echelons of the vast Austrian bureaucracy.

Anna had appeared amongst them that night like a ray of golden light. She had stood casually by the side of the grand piano and in her rippling melodic voice had sung one of Schubert's Lieder. He could hear it now. It was neither a particularly rich nor particularly fine voice; Bruno, whose dedication to music came second only to his work, knew that. But it had a purity, a clarity that spoke to him. And then just when the melody rose to a peak, her voice had cracked, gone slightly off key. Instead of blushing or showing any dismay, Anna had simply smiled mischievously, as if the fault were a quirk of style, and carried on triumphantly to the end. It was from that little moment of dissonance that he dated his love.

And he had not been wrong about her. He sensed that whatever the familial pressure, she had, like the free spirit she was, accepted his proposal in herself as well. As he looked back over the progress of their courtship, he realized that what most stirred her were the very points at which he strayed from what she expected. The periodic and repeated glow of her admiration had fanned what had begun for him as a loving curiosity into a veritable idolatry. Now, on those rare occasions when he didn't fall into an instant and exhausted sleep at night, and he thought of her, he sometimes shivered with a fear he didn't altogether recognize. The colour of that fear was not unlike the colour of Anna's eyes.

Those eyes, over lunch, moved around the table with growing, if secret, excitement. They were gathered in the arbour. The assembled company included two of Klaus's colleagues from the university, stern bearded men, and their soberly clothed wives; the raven-haired actress Camille Rang and her dramatist husband Emil Nussdorfer; Dr Petra Fluss, whom Anna had already heard Bettina describe as her dearest friend – a tiny woman with quick bright gestures and a surprisingly deep voice. She had brought along with her Johannes Bahr, whose presence, Anna gathered, had been unforeseen. In the midst of the general flurry, she had also learned he was an artist.

Bettina presided over a linen-covered table heaped with cold fish in creamy dill sauce, an array of smoked meats, crisp red radishes, moist black bread, an assortment of cakes and fruit, chilled wine.

'I hope you don't mind the picnic.' She gestured at the spread, smiled with particular warmth at Bruno. 'It saves labour. And food, after all, is for us only an inducement to conversation.'

'Quite so, quite so.' There was a general murmur of agreement, during which Anna gazed covertly at Johannes, noting his sullen air, wondering why, when he had been introduced to her, he had failed to acknowledge that they had already spoken. But that, she was soon to realize, was only the first oddity.

'Johannes Bahr?' Bruno queried, while helping himself to some pike. 'Aren't you the son of the jurist Karl Gustav Bahr? Fine man. Brilliant legal mind.'

There was no answer from Johannes, except for the brazen crunch of white teeth on radish.

'So he is no relation of yours?' Bruno unaccustomed to rudeness, raised his voice. Attention focused on them.

After too lengthy a pause, Johannes uttered, 'I have no relations with the law. It is not possible to have relations with the enemies of life.'

Bruno guffawed. 'So he *is* your father.'

'Have a little more of this sauce, Herr Adler.' Bettina, sensing trouble, tried to deflect it. 'My husband grows the dill himself.'

Bruno persisted. 'Come, come, Herr Bahr. The law is not an enemy. If I were to steal one of your canvases, would you not have recourse to the law?'

'If you were to steal one of Johannes's pictures, he would sit back in delight at the knowledge that you wanted it enough to steal,' Petra intervened tartly.

'I shall have to make the attempt then,' Bettina laughed.

'Take me with you.' Camille seconded her.

Johannes's features warmed as he looked at Petra, at Bettina, and then slowly one by one at each of the women at the table. 'The women have it, Herr Adler. They're the only ones to listen to these days.'

'Yes, yes.' Bruno bowed slightly in acknowledgement to the women. 'But, I insist that we need the law. It . . .'

Johannes cut him off. 'The law is only another name for power. The corrupt power of corrupt old men. The only power I believe in is this.' He held up his hands in front of him, turned them slowly. They all gazed at those long-fingered, oddly delicate hands, starkly white except where the paint showed its dark traces.

'And the power of women.' He gestured dramatically towards each of them in turn, stopping at Anna.

Her breath caught.

Bruno hid his mounting anger. 'I see we have a revolutionist in our midst,' he ironized, hummed a few bars of a satirical ditty that was making the rounds – the sad tale of a radical lamp-lighter whose revolutionary ardour was great, so long as his beloved lamp-posts were treated with due propriety. He saw an answering smile tugging at Klaus's lips.

'You are not in the revolutionary camp, I take it, Herr Eberhardt?'

'Klaus's only camp is somewhere in the garden, Herr Adler.' Bettina was quick to retort.

'Ah, but that too is a revolutionary camp these days, my dear.' Klaus wiped his lips with his napkin. 'The *Wandervögel* are showing us just that. A life in nature as an alternative to our increasingly corrupt and moribund social selves.'

Bettina seemed about to contradict him and then stopped herself just as Johannes burst in, his face suddenly animated. 'Yes, I approve of your camp, Herr Eberhardt. Come, let me tell you all a story about revolution.' His voice grew low, intimately seductive, drawing them all in, even Bruno, persuading them into unity.

'It's a true story, I'm told, insofar as stories can be true. And it took place not so many years ago, nor so very many kilometres from here,' he pointed towards the distant mountains, 'in one of the remoter valleys of the Southern Tyrol or perhaps the Dolomites.'

He looked at them each in turn, making certain of their attention, wooing their interest.

'You know the poverty of those places. The men leave their smallholdings to their wives, strong, resilient women with large hands and wintry eyes which look right through you. Yes, the men go off, off to America, to earn a bit of extra. Well, one summer, one of these peasants, who had been gone for years, returned home, asked after his cow, asked after his dog, asked after his child. He didn't bother to ask after the new children. Years had passed, after all.'

Camille tittered.

Bruno cleared his throat, threw a glance at Anna. She was utterly still.

'His wife took him into her bed. If little else, she remembered the milky smoothness of the skin on his back. A year passed. His money ran out. He set off. Off into the next valley, where,' Johannes paused, 'he came home to another wife. And then another, and another. Each welcomed him into her bed. In each house, he knew the name of a cow, a dog, a woman. Each recognized him and didn't recognize him. But wanted him nonetheless.'

The last sentence was uttered almost in a whisper. Johannes's gaze lingered on Bettina as silence settled around the table.

'You do talk waffle, Johannes,' Petra said in a husky voice.

'And *this* is your revolution?' Bruno broke in. 'The revolution of a scoundrel who seduces women away from their marriage vows?' He scraped his chair abruptly back from the table. Anna shouldn't be listening to this rubbish. 'Come, my dear. It's time for that drive I promised you.'

'No, no, you mistake me, Herr Adler.' Johannes stopped them. 'It is the *women* who are the revolutionaries in my little story. Women who are free, unmastered. They accept men as they accept the change of the seasons. With such women, there can be no law. No tyrannical law of the father, no crushing weight of deadening regulations. No Prussian master state.'

Anna suddenly laughed. 'And no property, of course.' She saw Bettina's startled look, felt Bruno stiffen. Now why had she said that? She hadn't understood a fraction of what Johannes was on about. She was merely parroting him, reminding him of what he had said to her earlier.

'Let's hurry, Bruno.' She moved eagerly away from the table, broke into a run.

Bettina gazed after her sister in astonishment. What had induced Anna's sudden outburst? Herr Adler would be upset, was probably already upset by Johannes Bahr's behaviour. And she liked Adler, was impressed by this large dark confident man with lively eyes who would soon be her brother-in-law. She chastised herself for not having stopped Bahr's story sooner. The arrogance of the man to lead them on in that way! It was after all a totally unsuitable narrative to recount in the presence of a young girl. But she had been captured by his words, by his oddly hypnotic presence. Yes, hypnotic.

Johannes Bahr was not in the least distressed by the commotion his little story had provoked amongst his listeners. There was nothing quite like a little disruption to allay the tedium of these lunch parties amongst the supposedly refined classes. In any event, he had come to believe that it was precisely for this that they invited artists to their tables. Though he sometimes wondered why he bothered to accept, since he far preferred the charged atmosphere of his studio.

He was a man who in his twenty-seven years had developed three distinct passions. The first was a passion for painting, which he pursued almost addictively.

The second was an overweening hatred for his father, who, in his pride and pomposity, his disciplinary zeal and overbearing humourlessness, represented for Johannes everything that was wrong with the current state of Germany. In his eyes, his father was a man who perverted natural impulse, who instantly converted all feelings into impersonal edicts of a turgid banality; the standard-bearer of a society gone wrong. He was also the man who, with his gross insensitivity, had beaten Johannes's mother into the ground, so that she had died when only thirty-three, a poor silent broken shadow of a human creature. Johannes, thirteen at the time, already hailed as an intellectual prodigy by his teachers, had never forgiven his father his mother's death.

This, he was astute enough to realize, had in part fed his third passion:

his love of women. It was a strangely democratic passion, for Johannes was capable of finding something to love in any and every woman. It could be the slant of a nose, the particular way a glove was stretched over a hand, the lilt in a voice. It could even be something others considered ugly: a voracious movement of the jaw; the crepe of powdered wrinkles.

When Johannes desired a particular woman, he was utterly possessed by this desire. This communicated itself to the woman as an attention, so total, so powerful, that it was almost impossible to resist. The very force of his attention convinced them that something magnificent was at stake, not merely a louche little encounter of the everyday kind. And indeed, for Johannes, it was never that. For only when he was lost in love-making could he replicate the sensation he had when he had been painting for hours: the sensation of being thrust on to a new and vaster plane. Only then did he feel himself transported away from the long tentacles of common cares which seemed to shadow his every move and drag him down to the abyss of the ordinary.

Johannes's zest for women found a convenient home in his beliefs: each woman was after all the embodiment of Woman, that principle which would save them all from the death-dealing world of the fathers and their soulless machine morality. Women's hold on that morality was freer, looser than the man's. They were closer to the hoary wisdom of the body, to their own sexuality, to the counterreason of passion. And that was a force which could disrupt the moribund order – of the family, the military, the state.

If Johannes sometimes saw himself as the male who helped to unleash this triumphant natural sexuality in women for the good of the world, he preferred to see himself as chosen for the task by the women themselves, a mere Adonis in Aphrodite's thrall.

As the guests began to disperse, Bettina Eberhardt found herself staring at Johannes, noting a diffidence which sat oddly with his bursts of intensity. She forced her look away. He had made her forget her sister. Forget everyone. She would have to question Petra about him. Was Johannes Bahr her lover, she suddenly wondered? An uncustomary flush rose to her face. Uncomfortably, she thought of Adler again, of Anna, and shrugged inwardly. Anna had to be exposed to such things sometime. To be so attractive and so innocent was a parlous condition for a woman. And their aunt seemed to have managed to raise her in supreme ignorance. Adler was, after all, a man of the world. He would expect his wife to have some knowledge.

Knowledge, for Bettina, was a greater good than almost any other, perhaps with the exception of talent, or what she would have preferred to call genius. She was of that generation of women who had first fought to have access to ideas on equal terms with men. Only education, universal education, would free the world from the shackles of prejudice and superstition. Only when women were educated would that crucible of humanity, the nursery, cease to be a chamber of horrors where the devils of ignorance perverted the child's impressionable mind. Social justice would dawn with the bright clear light of educated reason.

If such was the core of Bettina's beliefs, it was in part because nothing thrilled her so much as the free and supple play of a fine mind which briskly swept out the Augean stables of convention. One particularly dank and musty corner of those stables, where the cobwebs, she felt, were particularly thick, was that occupied by the body and sexuality. Even she, Bettina recognized, since she was nothing if not honest, was as yet a little afraid to enter there. In her mind, sex was mixed up with enslavement. Why else should some of the more remarkable women she had known in Zurich have dissipated their talents in the service of altogether mediocre men?

She had chosen to marry because it had become evident to her in the course of things that the life of an unmarried woman was paradoxically far more constrictive than that of one who was coupled. She had chosen Klaus Eberhardt: not the most eminent nor the most attractive amongst the various men who paid court to her in Zurich, he was the only one who gave her a sense of unrestricted freedom. And this she valued above all else. When he settled his loose-limbed, slightly ungainly figure into a chair and fixed his gentle eyes on her, she felt a kind of attentive repose emanating from him, which fuelled her mind, made it soar, gave her an energetic brilliance.

As a result, though people wondered at the marriage of the witty and resplendent Bettina von Leinsdorf and the shy Klaus Eberhardt, Bettina was fiercely protective of Klaus.

But now, as she looked at the solid figure of Bruno chasing after her sister as if she were a rare and precious butterfly, saw him stop her, tuck a loose strand of hair gravely behind her ear, heard Anna's carefree laugh, she suddenly felt nettled, angry at Klaus. Angry, too, at Johannes, at Petra, who were still lounging around the table and making desultory small talk.

'I'm going to do some work.' Bettina's voice carried her disapproval.

'You work too hard, Bettina,' Petra drawled. 'Isn't that the case, Klaus? Tell her. What with organizing her nurseries, her women, her writing, she'll run herself into the ground.'

'Bettina is at her happiest when working,' Klaus smiled. 'If a report on the nurseries of Munich calls, anything else is out of the question.'

'Even swimming?' Johannes queried.

'Bettina is not one of your sporting kind, Herr Bahr.'

Had she heard a note of irony in his voice? Bettina bristled and then was soothed.

'You should read her report. It's a fine piece of work. An important piece of work.' Klaus stoked his pipe with a characteristic gesture.

'I'd like to.'

The direct, assessing look Johannes gave her was one which in less liberal company might have been considered offensive.

It was that offensiveness which troubled Bruno, as he sat rigidly and at an appropriate distance from Anna, in the back seat of his car. He would have liked to have been behind the steering wheel himself, feeling the machine respond powerfully to his gestures, goading it to greater strength. As it was he could only sit stiffly and fume.

Anna shouldn't be allowed to spend time in the company of that young man. Hear such outlandish stories. Why, it was as if he had with one blow cut through all those wonderful ruches and pleats and puffs and lace and draperies which made women and courtship civilized, to expose the shivering white animal beneath. Bruno frowned. If Bettina sanctioned his particular variety of artistic licence, that was fine. But it was not for Bruno. Nor for Anna. And in his own home it would not be allowed. In his youth, it would have been unthinkable to speak that way in front of women. But things had changed. Vienna, Munich, they had both become nervous cities where anything was permissible and whole hosts of crackpot notions held sway.

It was hardly that Bruno was old-fashioned: indeed, he counted himself and was counted amongst the progressives. But there were things . . . He looked at Anna. She seemed wholly unmoved by the incident, utterly enveloped in the motion of the car and the splendours of the landscape around them. Perhaps it was only to his experienced ears that Johannes's little story conveyed its full meaning. Perhaps he should trust a little more to Anna's innate tact. For she had that. Nonetheless, since Anna was to spend the remainder of the summer months with the Eberhardts, he would have a word with Klaus.

Bettina restlessly scanned the pages of the books piled high on her desk, her thoughts inevitably winging their way back to Johannes's peculiar narrative, the sway of his voice, the dreaming clarity of his eyes, those quick white hands which seemed to fashion visions. She imagined the swing of his shoulders as he sauntered down an incline, the set of his clean features as he knocked at the door of one of those mountain houses half propped on stilts. Saw a woman with roughened hands opening the door to him, smiling a little at this stranger, unperturbedly welcoming him as her husband.

She leapt up from her desk and her thoughts. It was no use pretending to work. She might as well seek out the others.

It was from the midst of a little copse at the crest of the hill that she suddenly heard Johannes's voice.

'These flowers, so lovely. But remember, they are nature's sexual parts. Beautiful. Like woman's. Like man's.'

Shocked despite herself, Bettina stopped, waited.

'Yes, one can almost feel it here on this hill, among these old trees, these uncurling ferns. Right here. Nature's soul. Feel it. Touch. Smell.'

Swayed by the urgency of that voice, Bettina sniffed.

'Can you feel it? That primeval time before the god of obedience and disobedience covered that ancient couple in shame. A time when women and men walked with heads high, and followed only the rhythm of the earth, their bodies, their passions, unconstrained by fear. And now look at us, shackled by false gods, deadened by destructive notions of virtue, unless we can reawaken those rhythms in ourselves, be alive to them.'

Bettina burst upon the group. Klaus was leaning against a tree trunk; the others were sitting, Johannes holding Petra's hand to the ground. Seeing Bettina, her friend edged away from him.

'A fine little sermon from one of our new sexual theologists, if I'm not mistaken. Do you count yourself amongst the believers then, Herr Bahr?

How very advanced of you to replace one theology with another.' Irony dripped from her.

There was a moment's silence before Johannes turned cold eyes on her. 'And you, my dear Frau Eberhardt, seem to me rather more advanced in your ideas than in other parts . . .' He paused.

Petra laughed. 'Bettina is nothing if not well read.'

Bettina looked at her friend askance, saw a curious glance pass between Klaus and Johannes and then before she could resist, felt Johannes's hand encircle hers.

'May I?' He pulled her gently to the ground and pressed her hand to the gritty earth. 'Close your eyes. Rid your mind of its chattering monkeys. Touch. Simply feel.'

What Bettina felt rather more closely than the earth between her fingers was the pressure of Johannes's hand. She pulled away from him abruptly, brushed her dress into smoothness. 'I am not one of your peasant women, Herr Bahr,' Bettina began imperiously. 'And as for what we need to revitalize our tired empires, I very much doubt that it is the power of the erotic. A little more social justice would stand us in better stead.' Her voice had risen a little too high. She turned on her heel with a swish of skirts. 'Klaus?'

But it was Petra who leapt to her side. 'I'll stroll with you. We haven't had a chance to chat for a while.'

'Don't be angry, Bettina,' her friend cajoled as they followed the path towards the lake.

Bettina was silent for a moment, stilling her temper. Then she asked, 'Who is this Johannes Bahr you've brought us?'

'He's very talented.'

'He's very rude.'

'Only superficially.'

'You don't say.'

'Don't be ferocious, Bettina.'

They walked without speaking, paused to gaze at the sun's resplendent dip behind a granite peak.

'Has he replaced Olaf?' Bettina asked softly at last.

Petra shrugged, offered no more.

Bettina stopped herself from prying. Petra would tell her when she was ready.

For a year now her friend had been trying to extricate herself from a long-standing passion for a politician, some fifteen years older than herself. A charming, serious man, he was continually on the brink of leaving his wife for Petra, but had never quite managed to. And Petra, who had for years swung between hope and despair, had in these last months finally distanced herself from him. Bettina was proud of her. Proud of the strength of will she had shown, no less a strength, she imagined, than that which had led Petra successfully to complete a medical degree when the odds were so severely stacked against women. She smiled as she remembered Petra's tale about her finals, when one of her examining professors had refused to acknowledge that it was a woman sitting before him and insisted on calling her 'Herr Fluss' throughout.

Bettina's pride swelled to extend to all the members of her circle, the artists and writers and thinkers who frequented her home, men and women who knew that the world must be changed. She loved the sense of adventure which bound them together, the intoxication of risky ideas – so risky that her friend, Frank, had recently been arrested on a charge of *lèse-majesté* for one of his more outspoken ballads.

If such people frequented her salon, it was not only because of her and Klaus's generosity, of an atmosphere which permitted and fuelled the outspoken exchange of the new. It was also because they found in Bettina both a superb listener and a severe judge, a charming yet critical intelligence who could sift the wheat from the chaff.

This severe Bettina had not yet arrived at a judgement on Johannes Bahr. She would, she thought as she strolled with Petra, bide her time, still her suspicions, at least until she had seen his work.

Where Bettina's moods swung between critical severity and generous approval, Anna's, later that evening, fluctuated between curiosity and boredom, finally to rest in the latter. She had long stopped listening to the endless flow of words which drowned the air in the rose and blue drawing room and when she noted that even Bruno's attention was wholly engaged elsewhere, she stole quietly out of the house.

It was a mellow evening. A fat moon hung lazily in the sky, shedding its glow over the gardens. Anna took a deep breath and meandered happily along the path which led through the rhododendron grove to the lake. She had enjoyed the afternoon, had loved racing along the twisting road in Bruno's car. She had been triumphant when she had elicited from him the promise that he would teach her to drive. Tomorrow. They would begin tomorrow. Her hands clenched an imaginary steering wheel in excitement and she ran to recreate the sense of wind streaming through her hair.

The resonant sound of a splash made her stop short. Without quite knowing why she hid, she edged behind a shrub and peered out at the lake. There was someone swimming. Clean hard strokes cutting the water. Anna watched, saw the swimmer clamber ashore.

Moonlight glistened over a wet naked body, a man's body, tightly muscled. She closed her eyes, then quickly opened them again. Saw him bend, stretch, bend, stretch in a rapid graceful succession of movements, each of which seemed to etch itself indelibly in her mind.

Only then did she take in that the man was Johannes. And that recognition made her shiver oddly. She felt herself freezing into position, utterly unable to move. And she had the sense, though it was hardly possible, that he was returning her gaze. Why else was there that sudden smile on his face, a smile she felt she could touch if she only stretched out her hand?

He was bending towards the lake now, helping another swimmer, one she hadn't seen, ashore. A woman, Petra, her white chemise clinging wetly to her. He drew her towards him, into his arms, shielded her with his body. They kissed.

Anna had the distinct sensation that a slow-motion spectacle was being acted out for her eyes alone. A laugh broke from her, a cool unearthly laugh which released her limbs into motion. But Anna wasn't too sure whether the run she burst into took her in his direction or towards the safety of the house.

TWO

'WE SHALL WAIT right here.' Miss Isabel waved her neatly furled umbrella and motioned both Anna and the blue-uniformed porter authoritatively towards a bench in the Munich station.

Clamour covered everything except her gesture. The place was alive with voices, bustle, the din of engines and the more distant jangle of tramcars. Anna, who had spent the last four weeks in the countryside, felt as if she had suddenly been shaken from the dreaming heat of a long August sleep.

In that sleep two refrains had mingled, two goodbyes. Bruno's basso profundo, murmuring 'Only a few more months now'; and Johannes's mellow baritone, 'We'll meet again, I'm sure.' For the rest, after Bettina had suddenly decided that she needed to be back in Munich and had dragged Klaus with her, there had only been the returned Miss Isabel, whose chatter had become indistinguishable from that of the crickets and jackdaws.

But now, all at once everything was briskness and sharp punctuation, from the hurrying clack of heels to the raucous calls of the conductors. And here were Klaus and Bettina already, guiding them through the station to a waiting carriage, taking them through the busy Marienplatz, pausing to admire the gothic excesses of the Town Hall and, since two o'clock was striking, the enamelled copper figures of the Glockenspiel perform the miniature tournament which rang out the hour. All the while Bettina flung questions at her, interspersing them with comments on the city streets through which they passed – the southern quality of the buildings, their pastel yellow and ochre hues, the charms of the Residenz, of the lofty churches, of the Prinzregentenstrasse, of the English Gardens.

'Half way between Berlin and Rome, isn't that what they say about Munich?' Miss Isabel intoned, holding her Baedeker to her. 'A marriage between the disciplined Prussian male and the feminine Italianate.' She suddenly blushed scarlet.

'I prefer to think of it as half way between Vienna and Paris.' Bettina's tone was dry.

'In the middle, in any event,' Klaus reassured.

'I've almost learned to drive,' Anna said in a half whisper for Klaus's ears.

'That's good. You could do with a few more accomplishments.' Bettina pre-empted his response. Then, realizing she was hardly being fair, she smiled at her sister to lessen the impact of her words.

She had, in the time they had spent in the country together, recognized that she was increasingly taking on the tone of a deriding and critical mother with Anna. Anna's dreamy laziness, her ability to squander time, filled Bettina with a barely containable irritation. It was one of the reasons she had decided to cut short their stay in the country. It wasn't fair to Anna, she repeatedly told herself. If Anna was the way she was, the blame was as much Tante Hermine's and her own as it was Anna's. After all, she had abandoned her sister to Tante Hermine's care.

She had determined to try to make good her sisterly shortcomings over the time remaining until Anna's marriage. But no sooner was she confronted by her sister than she grew impatient again. And at the moment, there were other things which concerned her more nearly.

'Bruno put a car at my disposal. Every weekend. And a chauffeur to teach me,' Anna giggled. 'We had great fun, didn't we, Miss Isabel?'

The two women shared a conspiratorial smile.

'Miss Isabel was making fine progress, too, until . . .'

Isabel gave Anna a stern look and finished her sentence for her. 'Until I had a little run-in with a haycart. Nothing serious, mind. Do you drive, Frau Eberhardt?'

Bettina shook her head and gazed out of the carriage window. They were passing a café where she had once spied Johannes. She scanned the tables uncomfortably and then turned back.

'Tomorrow we go and see my dressmaker first thing. And then I hope you'll take in the Pinakothek. You're interested in art, of course, Miss Isabel?'

'Of course.' Miss Isabel patted her Baedeker as if the question itself were an offence.

'And we can visit Herr Bahr's studio.' Anna intervened. 'Perhaps you can take us, Klaus, if Bettina's too busy.'

'I don't know if . . .' Bettina murmured, stopped herself at Klaus's, 'Certainly, certainly.'

They crossed the Isar and turned into Bogenhausen with its gracious candy-colour residences set in ample gardens.

'Here we are.' Klaus leapt from the carriage and opened the door to the pale amber house in which he and Bettina had settled some three years before.

'How lovely it all is,' Miss Isabel crooned. 'And one can see the river.' She all but twirled round the rooms of the parterre. 'So ample and yet so spare. How perfect. And all these books.' She looked at the massed volumes lovingly.

'If Bettina has children before me, perhaps you can come and live here, Miss Isabel.'

'Anna!' both women uttered her name simultaneously, Miss Isabel flushing, Bettina in consternation.

'What have I said now?' Anna looked at them both in amazement. In the last month, she had grown fond of the thin Englishwoman with the equine features who, away from Tante Hermine's abrasive eye, had taken on an attractive coltishness; and she knew that Miss Isabel, with Anna's wedding pending, was worrying about her next place of work. 'I haven't said anything wrong, have I, Klaus?'

Klaus patted her shoulder reassuringly. 'Nothing at all, little one. It's a fine idea.' But his gaze was fixed on Bettina, who turned brusquely away.

It was Klaus who two days later accompanied them to Schwabing, the site of Johannes Bahr's studio.

Schwabing was to Munich what the Latin Quarter was to Paris. In the first decades of the century, its narrow streets teemed with artists, writers, and revolutionaries of a hundred persuasions. It was from here that the Blaue Reiter group sprang its bright frenzied canvases on the world; from here that *Simplicissimus* aimed its satirical barbs at the hypocrisies of contemporary life. Behind the thick frieze curtain of the Café Stephanie, Schwabing's unofficial headquarters, a thousand ways of attacking the bourgeois order in paint or print were ardently discussed over chess or billiards or coffee or SEKT. Sometimes, paint or print spilled over into life and utopian visions became actual experiments.

Anna, Miss Isabel, and Klaus made their way through the leafy English

Gardens, across the Leopoldstrasse and into a maze of little streets. In one of these, Klaus led them through a portico, and up an uneven staircase.

On the second landing, a clash of angry voices confronted them, closely followed by the dark-suited figure of a man, pulling a plump woman behind him. She had not had time to don her hat and its feather tickled Anna's hand as the couple brushed past them. From the top of the stairwell an amused voice called down, 'Do come back when you're in better humour.'

'A different kind of tournament,' Anna heard Klaus whisper.

When they reached the attic level, they saw Johannes leaning over the bannister, a large smile on his face. But his eyes were angry.

'You have just witnessed the retreat of a dissatisfied client.' He ushered them into an ample, well-lit, untidy space. 'I apologize for Signor Fanfani. He wasn't pleased with my rendering of his beloved.'

'I'm not surprised, if this is it.' Klaus was looking at the painting on the easel which showed a woman with a garishly bright mouth, her torso bare but for the shade provided by the single sunflower she held in her hand.

The lines of the painting were strong, simple, almost as a child might do, Anna thought. The colours fierce. 'I like it,' she murmured.

'There you are. A woman of taste.' Triumph rang in Johannes's voice. 'The lady of the laugh approves.'

Anna met his eyes. He remembered. She hadn't been sure that last time they had met in the country he had known it was her. Suddenly instead of the crowded studio, all she could see in front of her was his naked figure bending, stretching, on a moonlit night. She averted her gaze, but said softly, 'I should like to be painted like that.'

'Anna, really!' Miss Isabel reprimanded in English.

'Perhaps it would be better to wait until you are Frau Adler,' Klaus suggested. He folded his long body into a rickety wooden chair, and lit his pipe.

'I'm sure Bruno would love a portrait of me.'

'I'm not,' Miss Isabel muttered.

Johannes picked a mottled rag from the floor and all at once flung it forcibly on to a paint-laden table, so that the assortment of tins on it clattered. 'I'm tired of commissions. No more for a while. Not until I'm desperate again.'

The outburst seemed to have rid him of his anger, for he now began to turn canvases which had faced the walls round for them, so that the room took on a wild brilliance.

There was silence as they gazed at the images: mythological figures parading in rain-dark forests; couples entwined; a strange Pietà in which Mary had all the trappings of a circus performer; portraits, one unmistakably of Johannes himself, his neck elongated, the chin protruding aggressively; other portraits, mostly of women with lush hair and eyes that stared directly out at the viewer, sometimes wary, sometimes regal, animal-like – all executed with those brazen colours, those simple lines.

Anna felt she had stepped into a dangerous, unrecognizable world. She made her way slowly twice round the room, noted an assortment of coloured bottles, bric-à-brac gathered in corners, gourds, dried flowers, a coat rack of motley velvets and chiffons. Then she peered into a dimly lit second room. Here, amidst the clutter, she spotted an unmade bed, a sink piled high with chipped crockery, and pinned to the walls a variety of sketches, half executed. In a few of them, she recognized Petra; in one, she was almost certain, Bettina.

'So you're painting my sister.' Her voice fell oddly into the silence.

Klaus leapt out of his chair.

Johannes cleared his throat.

'Show me.' Klaus lumbered towards the small room.

'No, no.' Johannes barred Klaus's way. 'Not yet. It's just a sketch at the moment. An idea. I was thinking of using her for a study of a modern Athena.' He gestured Anna away from the door. 'What's in there is still private,' he said sternly.

'Sorry,' Anna winced.

Their eyes met.

This young Fräulein von Leinsdorf, Johannes thought, had all the trappings of a trouble-maker. No, that wasn't quite right. It was something else. Something about the way she looked him directly in the eyes, fearlessly, without coyness. Something in that fresh, but uncanny, laugh of hers, which bounced off social proprieties. He watched her cross the room: light steps, an unconscious swing to her body, a natural grace. And that rich hair, refusing order beneath the not-all-together balanced hat. Yes, that was it. She was an innocent. It was such a rarity in the circles in which he moved that it had only just come to him. A pagan innocent.

'Is Bettina sitting for you?' Klaus interrupted his musings.

'No, no,' Johannes demurred. 'Nothing like that. Though I'd like her to.'

Klaus's frown evaporated into a sudden chortle. 'She might not like the result.'

'No, I imagine not.'

After they had left, Johannes looked after them for only a brief moment. Then, with an almost savage gesture, he lifted an unfinished canvas on to his easel and began to dab at it furiously. The activity wiped all thoughts from his mind and all sense of time. The world had become simply a particularly brilliant hue of red. And that red eluded him.

When Bettina arrived at Johannes's studio towards the end of the afternoon, she noted that slightly out-of-focus cast to his face which she had begun to recognize. It signalled that he still inhabited the world of his canvas.

'Shall I come back later? Tomorrow?'

'No, no, stay. I'll just be a few minutes.' He glanced at her gratefully as she perched herself on a chair at a respectful distance from him, removed her sensible hat and picked up a stray newspaper.

From the corner of her eye, however, she looked at Johannes, saw the tensed muscles of his shoulders, the leap of that white hand on the canvas, the total concentration, which he might soon turn on her. It was that, above all, which transfixed her, that ability he had of losing himself while in the presence of another. It gave her the sense that she was in the proximity of genius. She held herself very still, only momentarily chastising herself for having abandoned the nursery so early. It was unlike her. But then everything she had done this last month, she readily acknowledged, was unlike her.

A few days after her return from the country, she had written Johannes a note to invite him to one of her Friday evenings. It was the quiet season; few of her friends were in town and it would be interesting to thrust Johannes with his odd fluctuations between uncouthness, impassivity and urgency amongst them. Then, too, Bettina told herself, Petra would be there and she would appreciate it.

Rather than posting the note, she decided to drop it round herself. She was curious to see how Johannes lived; curious, too, about his work. And time was short.

Happily, he was in and urged her to stay for a moment, turned canvases round for her to look at.

Though she was loath to admit it, Bettina had little sensitivity for the visual. She could see the strength of Johannes's pictures, but she was rather shocked by what she registered as their crudity. Her face must have betrayed it, for he quickly turned the paintings back to the wall. But then with something like a grunt, he positioned a particularly graphic rendition of intertwined bodies on his easel and proceeded to lecture her on the use of space, on colour, on classical allusion, as if she were a stubborn and ignorant child.

To escape him, Bettina turned towards the table, and picked up a copy of Nietzsche's *Thus Spake Zarathustra* which lay there. 'I suppose this is where you get your inspiration,' she said, with retaliatory zest. 'It's rubbish. The worst book he ever wrote.' They argued vociferously, with growing heat on both sides. Until suddenly he kissed her. Kissed her hard on the lips. Too hard.

She didn't struggle. Only looked at him incredulously and then turned on her heel and left.

She did not allow herself to think about it except to say, 'So that's that for Herr Johannes Bahr'.

But contrary to all her expectations he had arrived at the Eberhardt home in Bogenhausen the following evening, had even donned a stiff collar and cravat for the occasion. Bettina was both amazed and singularly nervous. Her laugh pealed too high, she lost the thread of her sentences. Johannes, by contrast, was all complaisance and rectitude. In his evening clothes, even his face had taken on a strangely aristocratic cast. When the time came to leave, he held her hand only a fraction longer than might be necessary. Or so she had chosen to think. And he extended an invitation to her and to Klaus to drop into the studio at their leisure.

The next day Bettina had sought out Petra. Over a lunchtime cup of coffee between Petra's hospital rounds, Bettina had probed, albeit casually. Her curiosity about Johannes had reached a new peak. She discovered from Petra that Bruno Adler had indeed been right: Johannes was the son of the famous jurist Karl Gustav Bahr, that relations between them were particularly tense.

But she learned little more than that. Because she had suffered over the years from scandalmongers, Petra shunned gossip. That day, she was even more than usually reticent. She also evaded any questions about her own involvement with Johannes.

Then, just before they parted, Petra sighed a little mournfully and apropos of nothing, suddenly said, 'I'm getting a little too old for Don Juans, don't you think?'

Bettina had immediately interpreted this as a reference to Johannes. Alone again, she had been filled with a profound sense of injury and a mounting anger. That kiss. Merely the trifling gesture of a Don Juan. She determined to put all thoughts of the scoundrel out of her mind.

But it had not proved so easy. That very evening over dinner, Klaus had said, 'I was browsing in the bookstore and what do you think I found? An article in a 1909 issue of *Future* by our new friend Johannes Bahr.'

'Interesting?' Bettina had scalded her tongue over too hot a spoonful of soup.

'Quite, I think. More your sort of thing.' Klaus had shrugged. 'On the liberation of women, though he doesn't focus on your particular question of mothers. I suspect he's more interested in having women independent so they can liberate men.' He had paused then, an odd smile on his face as he waited for her response, and when it hadn't come, he had gone on, 'I may drop round and look at his paintings tomorrow. Would you like to come?'

'Not this week. I'm too busy.' Bettina had kept her voice resolutely even.

For the next three days, she managed to drown herself in work. A crisis had helped. One of the mothers of the nursery children had failed to pick up her little one at the requisite time, had seemingly abandoned him. Arrangements had to be made, the mother found. The crisis contained, Bettina's thoughts had willy nilly reverted to Johannes.

The importance Johannes and his kiss had taken on in Bettina's busy life was due to the fact that it was only the second kiss of that kind she had ever received. The first had long since ceased to have any meaning for her, though it had effectively helped to shape the direction of her life and her ideas. Its bestower had been her philosophy tutor, a man whose rooms she had gone to regularly and at her own insistence once a week during her sixteenth and seventeenth years. The philosophy lesson was the most exciting event in Bettina's calendar. She worshipped the bearded middle-aged man who was her tutor, loved his learned disquisitions which treated her as an equal and enquiring mind. She grew breathless with the mental effort he demanded of her as they read through Kant and Hegel and Schopenhauer and even, dangerously, a little Nietzsche. Beside that struggle for understanding, everything else in her life seemed pallid, frivolous.

The eruption of physical passion one early spring afternoon, in the midst of what was for Bettina fervent intellectual speculation, had shocked and stirred her intensely, before turning to a nausea which rose in her throat and blocked her speech. She was disgusted by the beseeching look in the eyes of the man who had seemed a giant; disgusted by the rapid rise and fall of his breath, by the quiver in the moist hand he had placed on her arm. She had fled, taken to her bed for a week, and another, refused food. She had never returned to the tutor again.

Her mother had died shortly after. This death somehow became entangled with her own moment of blinding physical passion, with her tutor's disgrace and disappearance from her life. In determining to go to Zurich to study, Bettina left all this behind her.

In Zurich she devoted herself ardently to her studies. She had a bottomless hunger for learning and she fed it not only with books but with friends. Men and women alike were drawn to her, to the energy she radiated. Amongst the latter, were a number of older, emancipated women who took her in as one of themselves. They shaped her interests and her understanding. She began to nurture a half-formed and magical notion that virginity was the very stuff of a woman's independence. The inner armour of a Joan of Arc. To have no unseemly and overwrought ties to a man was to enable one's soul to soar freely in that higher sphere that great minds inhabited.

It was not that Bettina did not like men. Indeed, she worshipped them, when their qualities made them worthy of her worship. She could sit for hours at the feet of some aged professor and with her judicious queries, her empathy, transform the merely talented into geniuses. For this characteristic, her attentions were much sought. If any admirer should overstep the bounds of propriety, one freezing look from the lofty Bettina was always enough to cool any unwelcome ardour. In the small Zurich world, she developed a reputation for brilliance, which followed her to Germany and grew with her well-penned articles.

When she had accepted Klaus's marriage proposal four years ago, in part to assuage her father's earnest imprecations and the interference of her aunt and other well-intentioned friends, it was on a single condition. She would maintain her freedom: she would not sleep with him. Nor would she welcome any advances of that sort until she signalled her readiness. And that day might never come. She couldn't promise. If necessary, she had intimated with slight distaste, he could satisfy his desires elsewhere. *They* would be companions, loyal partners in the adventure of life.

All this she had made amply clear to Klaus and cautioned him to think over.

Klaus, who had been devoted to Bettina for over two years and was as deeply in love with her as he was in awe of her, would have agreed to almost any conditions. He was a man with only a modest sense of his own worth. At the university, his innovative work in pathology had assured him a respectable place – but one which over the last ten years he had been too unassertive to capitalize on.

His passions, apart from Bettina, went into collecting. He was fascinated by plants and particularly flowers. Their intricate detail, their endless innovation, it seemed to him echoed the complex and mysterious changes wrought by disease in the human tissue he examined under the microscope. On their extended honeymoon, when they had travelled to the Far East, he had filled sketchbooks with precise and beautiful drawings of thousands of species new to him. In the country, he had a roomful of books with exquisitely detailed illustrations of the flora of different lands. His garden and conservatory gave physical existence to a smattering of these specimens, all tended as lovingly as his work of cataloguing.

For the rest, Klaus was happy simply to be part of Bettina's life. He was proud of her accomplishments, pleased to be able to put his wealth at her disposal either for the benefit of any number of projects or simply to create a home in which their many friends – drawn as he well knew by her flame – could gather.

As for that other side of life, he had begun by thinking that Bettina would as a matter of course, once they lived side by side, retract her condition. At first, he had set aside one evening a month when in the subtlest way he knew, he played court to her. Gradually, the periods between such evenings lengthened. He began to think that he no longer knew how to make any approach. It saddened him, since he would have liked to have children. But after a time the situation between them began to take on the guise of normality, as if all married couples lived this way and no other was imaginable.

It was Klaus Bettina was thinking of as she sat tensely waiting for Johannes to leave his canvas. She had told Klaus nothing of her six, or was it now seven, visits here, except once to mention casually and rather deprecatingly that she had been to see Johannes's paintings.

'Oh? I'm considering buying one,' Klaus had replied. He had lately begun to purchase the work of young artists, and Bettina, knowing that his eye was far better than hers, rarely interfered. On this occasion, she simply let the remark pass with a half-voiced, 'That's nice.'

But the situation was becoming intolerable. In her own eyes she was above lying. But how to tell Klaus of that first kiss, now repeated severalfold? How to tell him that she had begun to feel that her internal vow of virginity was foundering? For tell him she somehow must. And love Johannes, she had begun to think she must as well.

Johannes turned to her now at last.

'Thank you for waiting.' He took her hand, stroked it, let his fingers caress just beyond the point where her starched cotton blouse met her wrist.

Bettina sat still for a moment, meeting the intensity of his gaze, and then wrenched her hand abruptly away. 'I've read your article on women.' She rose from the chair, turned her back on him, played with the assortment of brushes on the table. 'It's all wrong. Wrong, I tell you. A ministry dedicated to the liquidation of the bourgeois family! Ha! Pleasure as the only source of value! What rubbish!'

He laughed. 'So you don't agree that self-sacrifice and self-denial are simply part of the moral corruption of patriarchy?'

'Self-denial is essential or we would have anarchy.'

'A little anarchy might be a blessing.' He was rueful. 'You haven't questioned enough, Bettina. What is this self-denial but a postponed selfishness in the name of a promised greater good which never comes and deadens us in the process? So that we cease to be able to desire.' He paused for a moment. His voice grew lower. 'It is feeling, pleasure, passion which will save us.'

She veered round to face him. 'Passion is not a salvation.'

'No,' he half-conceded, looking at her intently. 'Not if it's a guilty secret torn from the tyranny of marriage. Though, even then, perhaps . . .'

'Nonsense. Just look around you. Look at those poor single women, abandoned women, who bring their illegitimate waifs to our nurseries.'

Johannes's eyes gleamed. Bettina's attacks excited him even more than the way her neck curved long, stem-like from her tensed slender shoulders. It was a new form of excitement for him and it had taken him over quickly. The quickness had surprised him: she was not, with her studious seriousness, his type of woman. Yet the fury with which arguments he couldn't always counter leapt from those delicate lips so roused him that he had lost interest in all others. As always, he was torn now between taking her into his arms, feeling the oddly animal nervousness of her proud body, and prolonging the stimulation of the verbal duel.

He hesitated. 'They are victims. Victims of a male order in which women have been coerced into bartering their bodies, their pleasure, in the hope of security. But for us, who breathe a different air, who are stronger . . .'

'What different air?' She began to pace away from him. 'More nonsense. I breathe the same air. I . . .'

He put his arms around her, embraced her tightly from behind, his lips in her hair. 'Sniff, Bettina. Smell it,' he whispered in her ear. 'The air of freedom. High. Pure. We shall bask in it. Be reborn out of our tawdry little everydaynesses.'

'Mine are not tawdry.' She continued to resist him, though she could feel the pressure of his body beginning to confuse her.

'No, perhaps not.' His voice was husky. 'That is where you will save me.' He turned her within the circle of his arms. She looked into those wintry blue eyes almost on a level with hers, felt the force of his kiss, of his hands, so that her body in its quivering response became a stranger to her. 'Yes, you'll save me,' he murmured. 'Transform me. Fuel my work.'

She was lulled by his voice, as much as she was impelled by the sensations he roused in her, stronger each time she saw him. 'Save him,' she thought dimly, 'saved by him.' The words spoke to her, released something in her, as if a residual guilt had been cleansed, as if the animal act could be transfigured into an angelic mission.

'Speak your desire, Bettina. It's important to me that you speak it. Especially you who live so much in your words.' He was holding her so tightly now, she could hardly breathe. 'Tell me. Tell me, not like some chaste little virgin, who's frightened of her desire, but like a free woman, boldly. Tell me when.'

With a violent movement, Bettina broke from his arms. Summoning all her dignity, she looked at him coldly. 'But I am a chaste little virgin, as you so blithely put it.'

Johannes stared at her, comprehension coming only slowly to his face. 'I see.' He paced towards the window, looked out on the hot roofs of houses.

'I see. I'm sorry. I didn't know,' he muttered after a moment.

How could he have known? She spoke so openly, so familiarly about things, about sex. He recalled his first impression of her, an intuition of a woman who was more advanced in her ideas than in her body, his inclination to paint her as Athena. It was as if since that first intuition he had been led astray. Damn it, what human misery these bourgeois marriages hid. Not only his parents' generation, but his own. Yes, under the shelter of all those roofs he could see before him, crippling unnatural distortions of intimacy were being played out. And they were at the source of the general social distemper. He was right. Only a sexual revolution, a revolution in personal relations, would alter things. Even for Bettina. He should take her here, now, ground those airy, if bold, notions of hers in some material knowledge.

He turned back to look at her. No, she was too proud, too fine. She would run. And he wanted her. Yes, he suddenly realized, he wanted her even more now, the challenge, the strange rectitude of her, wanted to see how she would come to terms with her passion, understand it.

He moved towards her. 'It doesn't change anything, Bettina,' he said softly. 'Nothing in the way I feel. Each time is always the first time. For me too. When you're ready. Soon.' He clasped her hand.

She pulled it away abruptly, feeling humiliated, feeling for the first time that her chosen virginity was a failing, like a revelation of some secret ignorance. 'I must go,' she said icily. She lifted the briefcase she always carried, and brandished it on her breast like a shield as she fled down the stairs.

Johannes was left with a greater sense of uncertainty than any he had ever experienced about a woman he desired.

In an effort both to entertain and educate her sister, Bettina decided later that week to take her along on one of her nursery visits. She had an ulterior motive. With Anna and Miss Isabel present, there would be no temptation to drop in on Johannes on her way home; she had decided not to see him until her thoughts had assumed some semblance of order.

One of the two nurseries whose work she coordinated and helped to sponsor was located in a poor north-western corner of the Schwabing district. It, like its sister establishments, was based on a double premise. Bettina firmly believed that if one kindled the taste for education at as early an age as possible, it would blaze more strongly later and produce better individuals. She was also convinced that the impoverished mother's lot had to be eased for her own as well as the child's good.

Most of the mothers of Bettina's nursery children were effectively unmarried, either because their husbands seemed to be constantly absent or because they had never existed. In print, Bettina argued the case of unwedded mothers, urging that these women were as moral as their married sisters, that the reproaches society covered them with were hypocritical, part of an entire edifice of double standards which sheltered men while humiliating women. There was something severely askew in the morals of a city where as many as forty per cent of children were born to unmarried mothers, who led abject lives as a result.

With the mothers themselves, as well as their children, Bettina was sympathetic but firm. The children loved her for it; the mothers, though generally grateful, were less certain. With her clear sense of priorities, Bettina had a way of tackling what she saw as the disorder of their lives and introducing a structure they were not sure they could live up to.

Anna had been markedly tentative about accompanying Bettina to her nurseries. Things were not easy between the sisters. They had already argued once at the dressmaker's, where Anna, thinking she could at last give vent to her own taste, had pined over the newest oriental fashions, flowing trousers and loose gowns in wondrous tints of lemon yellow and orange crepe de Chine; whereas Bettina had insisted on practical needs, a tailored travelling suit which seemed to require a maximum of stays, a heather evening dress with a minimum of ornament, and so it went on, until Anna lost all interest and began to resent the countless visits to the dressmaker all this would require.

She would have been perfectly content to while away the hours until her return to Vienna by losing herself in a maze of streets with Miss Isabel or by watching life go by from the tramcar on which Klaus had readily acquiesced to accompany them. Happier still, to sit in Johannes

Bahr's studio and glimpse the magic by which paint became image, had her sister not firmly quashed that notion.

But Bettina was not to be deflected from her plan to have Anna accompany her to her nurseries. And when the day of the visit finally came, Anna was pleasantly surprised. The nursery hall was brightly painted. Large fairy-tale figures paraded round its walls. The children, in their blue smocks, had freshly scrubbed impish faces. As they painstakingly traced letters or animals or played with blocks, laughter would suddenly erupt from them. It was all quite unlike the grey constricting atmosphere Anna had imagined.

Having introduced them to the two young women who had regular care of the children, Bettina left Anna and Miss Isabel in their hands. It was her afternoon for reading with the older children and as Anna watched her, she noted that Bettina performed this task with particular relish. It struck her as wholly unexpected that Bettina should be so at ease with the children.

She continued to observe her sister with growing interest. What she saw filled her with a rare admiration. For the first time perhaps, she also found herself genuinely liking Bettina. The thought that it might really be the first time astonished her. But this was not the moment to pursue it, for suddenly there was a commotion at a far corner of the room and one of the teachers came scurrying up to Bettina, whispered in her ear.

Bettina gestured to Anna. 'Here, you take over. This is Eva and she's going to read *Little Red Riding Hood* to you, best she can. Miss Anna will help you out with the difficult words, Eva. All right?' Bettina patted the little girl's head and strode off. 'Hans is next, Anna,' she called over her shoulder.

Anna concentrated on her task, but from the far corner of the room, she heard a wail, 'It's true, they did', followed by a burst of tears and Bettina's severe, 'Now come with me, Maria'.

'No, I won't. You'll hit me.'

'Have I ever hit you?'

From the corner of her eye, Anna saw Bettina tugging a small tow-haired child along with her.

It was the end of the afternoon before she had an insight into the cause of the commotion. Mothers were coming to collect their children, heavy sullen women with tired eyes, chirpy girls, hardly older than herself, with spry hats and shop assistants' manners. Each of these women was politely greeted by the teachers and Bettina, who also enquired about their health, before turning a child over and occasionally reporting on progress.

One woman, however, was quietly taken aside and asked to wait. 'Frau Eberhardt would like a word with you.'

Anna positioned herself so that she could clearly, if discreetly, hear that word. At the other end of the room, little tow-haired Maria stood cowering by one of the teachers.

'Frau Keller, Maria has been at the centre of a disturbance today,' Bettina began.

Plump, large-featured, Frau Keller shot a hostile glance at the little girl, who turned to face the wall.

'She described to the children in great graphic, and I must say, somewhat violent detail, a scene she witnessed between you and your "boyfriend" last night.'

'Why, the little vixen. I'll smack her bottom, teach her some manners, teach her what comes of lying,' the woman scowled.

'No, no,' Bettina interrupted, 'I am not asking you to smack her. What I am asking you is, if the child has not imagined the whole thing,' Bettina drew herself up to her full height and took a deep breath, 'that you not conduct your sexual relations in front of her. If you must . . .', she waved her hand vaguely, 'then go to another room. We cannot have such goings-on discussed in the classroom.' She looked at the woman distastefully.

'Another room?' Anger mixed with contempt spread over Frau Keller's features. 'Do you think we live in a palace? There is only one room.' She flushed suddenly, realizing what she had admitted.

Bettina's colour, too, had risen. 'Yes, well then,' she said quietly, 'restrain yourself, Frau Keller. You don't want another child to look after single-handedly, do you?'

The woman seemed to have shrunk. Her face sagged. With a visible effort, she squared her shoulders. 'No, no, it's not like that. Fritz and I are to be married. As soon as we have saved up enough money for a bigger flat. As soon as . . .'

'Yes, yes, but meanwhile,' Bettina was crisp, 'I don't want Maria observing you and reporting to the children. I shall be forced to ask you to take her away.'

'No, no.' The woman was pleading now, and then with a burst of rage, 'I'll teach her, I'll . . .' She waved her fist at the child.

'Maria is not to blame,' Bettina said sternly. 'If we have any inkling that you have punished her wrongly . . .' She let the threat hang and called the little girl.

'Off you go now, Maria. Remember what I told you.'

The child nodded, frightened, as she took her mother's hand. The woman gripped the little girl fiercely and then, mindful of Bettina's gaze, smiled at her in exaggerated fashion.

'Poor little thing.' Miss Isabel broke the silence. 'She's going to get it when she gets home.'

Bettina shrugged.

'Why?' Anna intervened. 'What did she see?'

'Anna, really!' Bettina looked at her aghast and marched out of the door.

Anna noticed that her sister was shaking. Perhaps she would be too, she thought, if only she had seen what little Maria described. But no one, no one would tell her. It was as if there were a conspiracy formed with the particular aim of keeping her ignorant.

Bettina continued to shake in the carriage on the way home. To lighten the weight of her sister's mood, Anna sang the praises of the nursery, said she wanted to return.

'Really?' Bettina relaxed into cushions, considered. 'Perhaps it would be something for you to do in Vienna. I know there's a similar project just beginning. I could find out more.'

Anna nodded. Then, looking out of the window, she suddenly exclaimed, 'Oh, there's the Café Stephanie. Let's stop and sit, Bettina. I still haven't been there.'

'Bruno wouldn't approve,' Bettina murmured.

'Of course he would. As much as he would of nurseries,' Anna smiled. 'Please. Please, Bettina. Miss Isabel wants to as well.'

Bettina sighed as Miss Isabel looked demurely away, but she instructed the driver to pull over. The three women made their way, Bettina hoped unobtrusively, past the noisy billiard room, past the chess players rapt in concentration, to a corner table. She kept her eyes down, made certain that she and Anna faced away from the milling crowd in the room: it really didn't do for a respectable young woman of Anna's age to be seen amongst the motley regulars of the Stephanie, whatever Anna thought.

But no sooner had they ordered than a familiar voice addressed them from behind.

'May I?'

Without waiting for a response, Johannes Bahr pulled a chair up to their table.

'Decidedly a pleasant surprise.' He leaned lazily back into his chair. 'What brings three such charming ladies into this smoky den?'

'I had to visit, just once,' Anna beamed, and babbled on. 'We're on our way home from Bettina's nursery. And what a time we've had.' Before Bettina could stop her she had recounted the highlights of the afternoon up to and including Bettina's confrontation with Frau Keller.

A frown darkened Johannes's face. He gazed at Bettina. 'You shouldn't have reprimanded the child. Made her think she had seen something evil, said something bad. Surely you know better.'

Bettina bristled at this public reproof.

'What do you know about the education of children, Herr Bahr?'

'Frau Eberhardt behaved with absolute correctness,' Miss Isabel intervened loyally. 'I can tell you if it had been one of my charges, I would have . . .'

Johannes cut her off. His eyes blazed. 'The child had seen something absolutely natural, was naturally curious, naturally excited. Why distort it all by punishing her? Aren't sexual relations between men and women something natural? Don't we all partake of them?'

Anna held her breath.

'Herr Bahr, really!' Miss Isabel exclaimed.

Bettina's voice when it came was cold but even. 'I did not chastise the child for what she had seen, but her mother for allowing her to see. Nonetheless, the girl had to be told that it is not permissible to recount such things in public. It disturbs the other children, disrupts the class.' Her head high, she turned to Anna and Miss Isabel. 'I think we had better go.'

'Disturbs the children? Disrupts?' Johannes's lips curled in irony. 'Isn't that precisely what we need? A little disturbance, a little disruption, to break the stranglehold of hypocrisy.'

Bettina rose imperiously. 'Good day, Herr Bahr.'

'Yes, perhaps,' Anna murmured, as she followed her sister.

He gave her a quick questioning glance and then turned to block Bettina's path. 'You don't understand. I need to make you understand.' He lowered his voice. 'Come tomorrow, Bettina. It's important.'

Bettina flounced past him. Only in the carriage did she speak and then simply to utter a scathing, 'Artists!'

'Yes.' Miss Isabel filled in for her. 'One has to forgive them a great deal.'

Beneath the show of imperturbability, however, Anna noticed that there was once again a quiver in the gloved hand Bettina raised to straighten her hat.

When Johannes answered the knock at his door the following afternoon he fully expected to see Bettina. But it was the younger von Leinsdorf sister who confronted him, her cheeks glowing pink, a wildness in her eyes. His first impression was that something dreadful must have happened, that Bettina was sending him a messenger. But Anna conveyed nothing of the kind.

'Will you invite me in?' she asked softly after she had denied being sent to him. She was filled with the excitement of her adventure. She had stolen away from the house when the others thought her resting and made her way swiftly through grey drizzle, oblivious to anything but her destination.

Johannes stood back and let her pass.

She threw a lingering glance at the canvas on the easel and then confronted him.

'I wanted to speak to you. Speak to you alone.'

'Oh?'

'Yes. You see, I'm so ignorant and you, you know so much about things,' she finished a little lamely.

Johannes was aware of a sense of mounting discomfort. 'What things?'

'Things.' Anna gestured abstractly. 'You know, things we were talking about yesterday.' She turned away from him, unsure now, and then suddenly, as if a momentous decision had been taken, turned back, blurted out, 'Do you know, I saw you that night, by the lake, naked?' Tawny unblinking eyes gazed at him.

'I know,' he murmured, recognizing he would have preferred not to. He felt strangely reticent with this beautiful young woman, for she was beautiful, he acknowledged, but still just a slip of a girl. A sense of foreboding passed through him. He shook it off. 'Please, will you sit down?' He pulled up a chair for her, pausing for time, watching the unconscious seductiveness of her gestures. What did she really want of him?

'I wasn't intending to be seen,' he shrugged.

Anna laughed, filling the room with a throaty sound.

'I know. But now you must tell me.'

'Tell?'

She nodded. 'Yes, I'm to be married soon, you see, to become someone's property,' she laughed again, quoting him, 'and . . .'

'Then your husband will tell you, show you rather. The showing will be more effective.' His voice was cold. It was as if Bettina stood at his shoulder.

Anna looked crestfallen.

'You, yes, particularly you, will learn very quickly. Now, I think you should go.'

Johannes hadn't intended to sound so cruel. Her candour moved him. But words would never do for her, he realized. And he wasn't prepared, here, now, to give more, to take what she perhaps didn't know she was offering. It troubled him a little – as if he had suddenly become the living disproof of his own ideas. A hypocrite, like the rest, but in reverse.

'What will I learn?' she murmured.

He tried to keep his voice even. 'You will learn about passion,' he said lightly, softly. He touched her brow where it had furrowed, smoothing it. Warm, silken skin. 'If you're lucky.' He smiled suddenly. 'If not, we may still meet again. Now you must go.'

The brightness had gone out of her. She had the air of a forlorn child, reluctant to move from a place of warmth.

'Will you paint me?'

Then he remembered. That was what was at the base of his hesitation, not Bettina. Johannes shivered. It was long ago now. He had been young, a mere twenty, just beginning his life as a painter. The girl had wanted him to paint her, had offered herself. Their love had lasted as long as the time of the painting and then, by mutual agreement he had thought, it was over. But it wasn't. She had written to his father, talked of broken promises, a child pending, demanded money. His father had intervened, apportioned blame while sneering at wild oats, paid money, assumed power. That was what he couldn't forgive – the paternal assumption of power, the making ordinary, the tidying away. The woman pretending meekness, running to the man with greater power, complicit with him. There had been no child. Only a woman calling a father into existence, activating him.

He looked at Anna, her youth. No, he would have none of that any more. Experienced women were the ones for him. And that usually meant married women. Women who had known the price of chains knew the value of freedom. Their fathers were close at hand in the person of their husbands. They didn't need to call any others into existence.

'Will you?' Anna repeated.

He gazed into those thick-lashed animal eyes. 'Perhaps. One day.' He took her hand to lift her from the chair, to signal that it really was time to go. A surprisingly firm hand it was, yet soft. Was he wrong about her?

He didn't have time to consider it. There was another knock at the door. He was sure, in the way that he sometimes knew things with certainty before they happened, that it would be Bettina.

That elegant, intelligent face met his with a question, then looked beyond him. There was an audible gasp.

Johannes stood back, an initial foreboding quickly replaced by a sense of exhilaration in what would inevitably be a dangerous moment.

'Come in, Frau Eberhardt.' He pronounced her name with added formal emphasis. 'I have a guest, as you can see.'

'So this is where you are.' She addressed only Anna.

'This is where we both are.'

Johannes could only admire the younger one's courage. There was not a trace of guilt on Anna's animated features.

'And what, may I ask, are you doing here alone?'

'I'm not alone,' Anna smiled, 'as you can see.' She almost skipped with delight at her own impudence as she came towards her sister. 'I hoped Johannes might paint me. A wedding present for Bruno. Don't you think it's a lovely idea?'

Johannes chuckled. The girl had flair. He had to give her that. 'I have told Anna Herr Adler might not think it appropriate.'

Bettina scrutinized them both. '*I* don't think it's appropriate. What can you be thinking of, Anna?'

The girl shrugged and then said with a petulance, the reality of which he couldn't be quite sure, 'But *you're* sitting for him, aren't you?'

'Certainly not. In any case it would hardly be the same.'

'Oh well.' Anna held out that firm little hand of hers. 'I guess we have to go. Goodbye, Johannes.'

Bettina's gaze as she approached him covered him with contempt. He had the distinct sense that he might have lost her. And he didn't want that. No. She was too fine. He squeezed the hand she gave him. 'Anna has reason, you know, to suspect you might be sitting for me. I've done a little sketch. You might want to see it.' He said it as a last resort. He never showed his work, unless it was finished to his satisfaction.

He felt her stiffen with that nervousness which also signalled her arousal. But she cut him.

'Another time, perhaps.'

He bowed uncharacteristically. 'Perhaps when I come back, then. I'm away for a few days. An exhibition opening in Vienna.'

There was momentary confusion in Bettina's face. Then she caught herself. 'Perhaps. Come, Anna. The carriage is waiting.'

'Vienna?' Anna held back. 'Oh, do come and call on us.' She beamed him a parting smile.

Johannes, gazing after the two sisters, wished that he could invisibly perch between them and listen to the dialogue which would ensue. He smiled to himself, had the sudden and now rare urge to write. A little story about two women. It tickled his fancy.

But he set the wish aside as a whim, a mere indulgence. Instead, as if he had suddenly been jolted by an electric current, he picked up a sketchpad and with thick, rough strokes mapped out an idea for a painting: two women wandering in opposite directions, lost in a wood where bare trees were just curling into bud. For the time being, he utterly forgot their living incarnations.

THREE

Bruno Adler had long imagined for himself a triumphant social moment exactly like this one.

A gracefully arched rococo hall, resonant with the sound of violins, its gilded mirrors lit by a bevy of crystal chandeliers. Women swirling in clouds of silk and satin and tulle, their smiling faces arched towards the immaculate men who held them in their arms – but turning, when they saw him, to deepen their smiles and gesture their appreciation. The dowagers in heavy velvet keeping the waltzes' time with their ornate fans, nodding their approval as he passed the stiff chairs on which they rested their bulk. The cream of Viennese society, all bows and charm and courtesy. And all put in motion by him. For him, because he had made his way into the inner sanctum. Because he had married the daughter of Count von Leinsdorf: Anna von Leinsdorf, from today, Anna Adler.

He looked at her now, twirling in the arms of a young uniformed lieutenant, the creamy white train of her dress of old lace in her gloved hand, her eyes sparkling with the animation of the dance. So beautiful, like a porcelain figure fashioned by a master craftsman. His palms grew moist, but he stopped the urge to break in on them, to put his arm round her. There would be time, plenty of time now. She was his.

He continued his stroll round the vast room, making small-talk, reaping congratulations, assuring himself that all was as he had ordered it – from the footmen in their braided coats to the discreet waiters, to the crystal glasses, fruit-laden bowls and platters of fanciful miniature pastries on the long marble table. It was a stroll not unlike the tours of inspection he regularly carried out in his factories: like any good general, Bruno knew that attention to detail was as important as the grand plan. He saw his reflection in one of the many mirrors, noted the gleam of his white shirt, the smile beneath the heavy moustache.

'You look like a happy man.' Bettina caught him unawares.

'Not smug, I hope.'

Bettina smiled. It was not the first time Bruno had startled her with one of his leaps of intuition. 'No, never that,' she demurred.

He laughed. 'Only a little perhaps. And only for a little while.'

'You leave soon?'

Bruno glanced at his watch. 'Half an hour.'

'I envy you Paris.'

'Sometimes I envy myself. All this.' He made a sweeping gesture. 'Anna.' He watched Bettina carefully. Despite the smooth coil of her coiffure, the elegant lines of her lavender dress, she seemed ill at ease, preoccupied.

'Yes.' She made a little *moue* in which he read her slight distaste for all this splendour, for the empty civilities of the old Empire. Almost, he wanted to lecture her, to say, 'If I had been born to it, I might share your contempt, but you see, for me, it has a different meaning.' But he kept his counsel. Instead, he said, 'Perhaps, on our return, you'll come and stay a while.'

'Perhaps.' She smiled a little vaguely and then lifted her grey eyes to his. 'I've never said it, you know, but I'm very happy to have you as a brother-in-law.'

'Thank you.' Bruno bowed, grateful, feeling blessed. 'And if I might return the compliment.'

'Bettina.' Tante Hermine was upon them in a rustle of brocade. 'You must come and say hello to old Stallenheim. He hasn't seen you for years. He's talking to Klaus now. Excuse us, Herr Adler.' She deigned to turn her powdered jowls in his direction. 'I will only steal Bettina away for a moment.'

Bruno bowed. He had over the months grown accustomed to the venerable Hermine von Leinsdorf's manner towards him: a canny flattery barely masking a prickly disdain. The woman was like an old war horse who had unwillingly had to learn new circus tricks. He rather enjoyed seeing her perform them.

Bettina turned a rueful face to him. 'You see, Herr Adler, Vienna for me is a persistent round of duties.'

'And not of the kind you prefer.'

She had the grace to meet him on it. 'Not of the kind either of us prefer, I imagine.'

He laughed, liking her, worrying a little over the trouble behind those eyes. But only a little, for there was Anna, twirling past him on her light feet, stealing his attention. He watched her, as if mesmerized by her movements. Confronted by the glow of her youth, the perfection of that golden skin, the certain knowledge that she was his, he felt something akin to awe. For a moment, he couldn't move. Then, remembering himself, the time, the journey, he approached, beckoned, tentatively put his hand on her shoulder. Such a large hand on such a small shoulder, he almost drew away. But she turned laughing eyes on him.

'Is it time?'

Bruno nodded, not trusting his voice.

'Oh good.'

The sound of her eagerness disturbed him.

'Haven't you enjoyed your wedding party?'

'Oh yes.' She was startled by his question. 'We could get married every year. But . . . but now. I've never been to Paris, you see.' Her words came out all in a rush.

Bruno smiled. He was never altogether prepared for her exuberance, her sheer love of life, a sensuous exultation in the changing, the new. It was something the long years of struggle and achieving had almost wiped out in him. He would recapture it now with her. And show her so many things. Teach her. Yes. He folded her arm tightly through his and prepared his face for the barrage of goodbyes.

The Orient Express nosed its way through tunnels, sped westward across valleys and over bridges. Anna, too excited to sleep, turned the little knob on the bronze lamp and watched the shadows play across the train compartment. Then she wiped the condensation from the window and tried to peer out at the darkened world. It returned only her own image and she sighed, wishing for daylight.

Bruno had left her over an hour ago. He had placed a moist kiss on her lips, stroked her hair gently and whispered, 'Tomorrow. We will begin our married life properly tomorrow. In comfort.' She had looked up into his warm eyes and nodded with a mixture of relief and disappointment. Of what it was exactly that would begin their married life, she had only a hazy notion, though she knew whatever it was would begin with a kiss – as it did in the novels her governesses had given her to read – and end in bed. In her mind, that bed was covered in obscurity. The little girl in Bettina's nursery knew more than she did, though that knowledge hadn't served her very well.

Anna fingered the lace on her new nightgown reflectively. She had been happy to take off her wedding dress, much as she loved it. It was odd wearing a garment which belonged to a mother she could hardly remember. But Tante Hermine had insisted and after all the nips and tucks, it had looked wonderful, as Bruno's eyes had testified. But still, she was pleased to be rid of its weight, a weight which seemed to have pressed down through the years to envelop her, to disguise her as this different being, a married woman.

It was too bad that the new Bohemian maid whom Bruno had insisted they take with them spoke so little German. She would have liked someone to talk to. Never mind. When they got back to Vienna, there would be Miss Isabel. Bruno had said she could stay on with her, as a companion, and to improve her English. Anna sighed. Her stay with Bettina and Klaus had left her with a profound sense of her own ignorance. But over dinner, Bruno had complimented her on her French. She was pleased about that. Anna looked at the gold band round her finger, next to the clustered diamonds of her engagement ring, took them both off for a moment to move her fingers round freely and then hastily donned them again. She liked having Bruno's approval. And tomorrow, tomorrow there would be Paris.

Paris meant first of all the quiet luxury of the Ritz, then a leisurely stroll around the austere elegance of the Place Vendôme up to the Opéra, which with its lushly curving statuary reminded her of nothing so much as Vienna. To one side of the grand staircase, obscured by its mass, a couple stood clasped in an embrace, kissing. Bruno hurried her away. Under his vigilant eye, she glanced into jewellers' boutiques, read titles in a bookshop window. But she was more interested in the people, the quick-paced women with their vast hats, the small darting men, all in so much more of a hurry than at home. Except for that twosome by the Opéra staircase.

As they made their way back into the hotel, she noticed a slow-moving couple walking towards them: a striking dark-eyed man in a handsome grey coat with an astrakhan collar, firmly guiding a smaller woman, a hat perched somewhat precariously on her blonde head. Anna laughed.

'Look, Bruno, what a funny couple we make.'

He stiffened.

'There, look.' She pointed towards the mirror. 'Bettina's choice of suit does nothing for me.' She made a comical face, laughed again.

He relaxed a little, thinking that she was probably right, though to him she looked delightful, wondering at her lack of vanity. 'We'll set that right tomorrow,' he said, wanting to ply her with presents. 'But first there's a question of dinner.'

Dinner, in the Ritz's famous restaurant, was for Anna an event of such marvels that it almost made her forget the next step on the marital agenda. Until these last months, she had led such a sheltered life, with her aunt and her staid guests, her piano, her governesses. And now the spectacle of the Ritz played itself out before her like a glittering opera. Perfumes, each one more exquisite than the next, wafted off women's gleaming shoulders. Hair shone, jewels glistened, eyes sparkled in animated faces from which the chatter tumbled to the dramatic motion of hands. And she too was on the stage.

For a bare moment, she didn't know whether she was up to the part, but then she threw herself into it, returning men's lingering glances, as she crossed the room, sipping her wine, experimenting with the French Bruno had admired. Over a dinner of lemon-scented oysters, tender quail and the lightest of crêpes Roxelanes, Bruno outlined their itinerary over the next few days. As he detailed sights and museums, expounded on the history of the city and the current offerings at the Comédie Française, Anna thought to herself that he might prove even more exacting in his tourism than Miss Isabel. For a moment, her concentration lapsed and her eyes roamed around the room.

'Anna.' Bruno caught her up short. 'Am I boring you?'

'No, no,' she protested. 'I was just thinking how mournful that grey-haired man over there looks, sitting all alone in the midst of this gaiety.'

Bruno followed the line of her gaze.

'Perhaps his wife has died, perhaps she's abandoned him, perhaps . . .' Anna embroidered her fantasies.

Bruno looked at her strangely. 'You have a very ripe imagination, my dear, but apt, in this case.' He didn't have time to continue, for suddenly the man was upon them, shaking Bruno by the hand, bowing to Anna.

'Monsieur Adler, *quelle surprise*. How astonishing to find you here. And this is?'

'My wife,' Bruno confirmed. 'Of almost forty-eight hours.'

'Ah, what a beautiful woman. *Mes félicitations*. May I join you for a short while?' He pulled out a chair, and gestured to the waiter. 'Frédéric, Frédéric, *une bouteille de votre meilleur champagne pour mes amis*.'

Anna let the champagne tickle her throat, smiled at Monsieur Landry's compliments, his chatter, at once comic and heart-rending.

'Yes, yes, love, marriage, how wonderful it is, for I can see you love each other. You must enjoy it, enjoy it while you can. I was in love, too, once. But then . . . Perhaps you have heard, Monsieur Adler, my wife left me.' His face took on an air of utter incomprehension. 'Yes, left me. For a circus performer.' A sound half way between a laugh and a cry escaped him. 'Can you imagine?' He gazed into the middle-distance for a moment. 'But I musn't bore you with my little tragedy. No, no. You have everything in front of you.' He smiled winsomely at Anna.

'You will excuse us, Monsieur Landry,' Bruno rose. 'The journey, you know. We're a little tired.'

'Tired, after only forty-eight hours? *Ah non*.' He winked playfully at Bruno. *'Mes félicitations, mes félicitations.'*

'Poor man,' Anna murmured, as they made their way towards the lift.

'Yes, yes. But no dignity.' Bruno shook his head. 'These French, with their displays of emotions . . .'

'Who is he?'

'He owns a steel mill in Alsace. Used to be a fine upstanding man.'

Bruno's face registered distaste.

'And his wife?' Anna prodded him.

He shrugged. 'She was a . . . He should never have married beneath him. But no more of that.' He turned the key in the door of their suite, looked at her with warm eyes. 'Now we must concentrate only on us.'

'Yes,' Anna murmured. But as she followed Bruno through the thick-carpeted salon with its richly tapestried sofa and chairs, its highly polished secretaire, the story of Monsieur Landry haunted her. 'Poor man,' she breathed again, as Bruno held the door of her bedroom open for her.

'Soft-hearted Anna.' He raised her hand to his lips, and then whispered, 'I shall join you soon.'

She flinched and then remembered herself. 'Yes, soon,' she said nervously.

Lucy, her new Bohemian maid, was waiting for her. Anna let her uncoil her hair, pull the white nightgown over her shoulders and then dismissed her. She realized, as she stretched out on the cool sheets and closed her eyes for a moment, that she had had far too much to drink. A hundred images swam before her eyes, strange images of the massed dancing women in front of the Opéra encircling the embracing couple with their stony laughter, of a garishly painted circus troupe carting away the dark obelisk in the Place Vendôme, of Monsieur Landry, white-faced, like a clown, a single tear moistening his cheek. Images to fill the mysterious obscurity that followed the kiss.

'Asleep already?' Bruno stood above her, a vast figure in a burgundy dressing gown. He sat on the bedside, stroked the fan of her hair spread golden on the white pillow. 'You look like a Bernini angel,' he murmured, his chocolate eyes glimmering in the lamplight. She watched his lips move towards her, plant a moist kiss on her forehead.

'I hope I don't hurt you too much, my dear.' His breath was warm in her ear.

She felt the reassuring tickle of his moustache and smiled, as he moved to turn the light out. Almost, she stayed his hand, wanting the comfort of his eyes, but she felt awkward, unsure.

He stretched out beside her. 'Dear, sweet Anna,' he whispered, and she echoed him, 'Dear Bruno.'

She thought she heard him say, 'No, no, don't speak', though she couldn't be certain. His breathing had grown so noisy in the dark, punctuating the movement of his fingers as he slipped her nightie up her legs, touched her bare skin. His hand felt big on her breast, warm. She would have liked to keep it there, but he moved it away and then he was on top of her, a great weight, bearing down on her, something nosing between her legs, like that train they had been in, chugging through the tunnel, whistling, hooting in her ear. But the train was derailed now, tearing, heaving against a wall, pushing, pushing. She screamed.

'I'm sorry, my dear, so sorry.'

He was still for a moment. She tried not to move, to ease the searing inside her. But he was pushing against her again. And again, his breath sharp in her ear, rasping.

It hurt him too, she suddenly thought. She put her arms around him, wanting to assuage the sounds of his pain, the indignity of it. He let out a groan, a gasp, muffled in her shoulder. Then he lay very still, so still that she was afraid something had happened to him.

'Bruno, Bruno, are you all right?' Her voice felt so strange, too high.

He stirred, eased himself off her. 'Fine, little Anna. Sweet Anna.' He kissed her forehead gently. 'Goodnight, my dear. You must rest now.' She heard the soft padding of his feet, the sound of the door.

She lay there in astonishment. He was gone. Why was he gone? She wanted to call after him. There was a sticky wetness between her legs. Her body felt as if it had undergone a pummelling that had left an odd scent in the air. She turned on the bedside lamp, saw the rumpled sheets, the trickle of blood. Was it his? Hers? She leapt up, touched herself. What had happened to her? What had he done?

In a wave of anger, she threw her pillow on the floor. Oh, if only someone had told her, had spoken to her. Bettina, Miss Isabel. Her mother. Her mother would have told her, had she been alive. Explained what it all meant.

Suddenly, she thought of Johannes – he could have explained, she was certain of that, but he had refused. Ever and always this silence, this ignorance. And even now, she didn't understand what she knew.

With a sense of desperation, she ripped off her crumpled nightie and examined her body in the mirror. Like a Bernini angel, he had said. She had never really looked at herself naked before: the pale body, the full round breasts, the taut belly, the golden triangle above the shapely legs. She ran her hands over her skin and shivered. 'Frau Bruno Adler', she said out loud to her image. A wild laugh burst from her. Was this what it meant to be Frau Bruno Adler?

Tears streaming down her cheeks, Anna bent to wash.

Bruno, in his room, contentedly puffed at a rare cigar. It was done. He had had a moment's doubt that he would manage it when he had seen her lying there so still, so pure. Like an angel. And so achingly beautiful. His wife. He hadn't wanted to hurt her, sully her. But it was done now. And if he kept the light off and thought of other things . . . He grimaced inadvertently. Yes, he could do it again. And again. There would be children. Children who lived. She was strong, his little Anna, not like his first wife, poor Elizabeth, too frail for the weight of a man, the weight of a child. He shivered, sat very still for a moment, then puffed deeply again of his cigar. Yes, it would be all right. All right.

Thinking of other things, that was the key. Other things. Red lips. A tongue flickering over red lips. A wrist covered in bracelets.

Bruno felt a tingling at the base of his spine, felt his penis growing erect. He scowled, waited helplessly for it to pass.

And then with a grunt of something like despair, he rapidly pulled on his suit, his coat, and left the hotel.

Outside Rosa Mayreder's Vienna house, Bettina hailed a fiacre. It had been a good morning. The older woman had been in top form and had talked passionately about her work in the Austrian Women's Union. A thoroughly admirable person, Bettina thought, and a fine writer as well. And one who had greatly influenced her. She could still remember the impact of her book on femininity, that crystalline sentence – 'One will only know what women are, when what they *should* be is no longer prescribed to them.' Rosa had refused the prescriptions, as Bettina hoped she had as well – the prescriptions which ordered that woman was and therefore must be made to be weak-willed, second rate, ignorant. Rosa had succinctly shown how all this was only part and parcel of the game of sexual power, the man's sexual ideal foisted on women. Yes. And Bettina had refused the ideal as she had refused the sex.

Bettina avoided this corrosive train of thought, looked instead at the familiar cobbled streets, the *Fiaker*'s rounded hard hat and ample whiskers. It was strangely pleasant to be in Vienna again, to pause at the crowded thoroughfares where the cars whizzed noisily by ahead of the clattering trams. To recognize the familiar.

What had struck her as less familiar after her long absence from her native city was the extraordinary diversity of Vienna's population – Magyars, Slovenes, Croats, Czechs, Ruthenians, Italians, Poles, and more, alongside the Germans. To walk along a Vienna street was to travel thousands of miles and cross countless linguistic and cultural borders. The notion pleased her as did the magnificent curl of the Ringstrasse, its imposing public buildings, the stretches of park, the pervasive sounds of military bands rehearsing or playing in their pavilions. Perhaps, now that her family had less hold on her, she and Klaus ought to consider moving here.

To avoid temptation. The thought suddenly crystallized and she shook it away.

Yes, Vienna was a truly cosmopolitan city, teeming with ideas, with writers, philosophers, musicians, artists, with political dreamers and doers of all casts. There was, of course, the drawback of its decaying monarchy with its manifold lunacies which her father had so adhered to. But even that had its charm. She smiled to herself.

Where was it that she had read that hilarious list of Austria's contradictions? A country where the parliament made such liberal use of its liberties that it was usually kept shut though, by an emergency powers act, it was quite possible for the Emperor to manage without it, as he was doing now. But no sooner had the public begun to applaud absolutism than the Emperor determined that it was once again time to return to parliamentary government. And so it went on, in its own inimitable way.

She had arrived. The gilded laurel dome of the Secession Gallery was before her, its iron weight sitting heavily on the graceful white of cubes and cupolas. And the inscription on the door, 'To the Age its Art, To Art its Freedom'. She could still remember the stir the building had first caused all those years ago, the great generational battle between the artists.

And there was Klaus, waiting for her, tucking his copy of Karl Kraus's satirical mag into his pocket, striding in his loose-limbed way to pay the *Fiaker*.

'A pleasant morning?' He helped her down the step.

Bettina nodded. 'Very.'

'I've been through the exhibition once already. It's good. And there are three fine works by our new friend.'

Bettina swallowed hard. 'Really?'

'Come and see for yourself.'

As they made their way through the gallery, Bettina forced herself to listen to Klaus's words, his enthusiasm for various works and denigration of others. All of which led inevitably to their 'new friend'.

'You see how much finer, bolder these are than their neighbours.' Klaus stroked his beard thoughtfully. 'I have great hopes of our friend. In fact I have suggested a little scheme to him.'

Bettina made a great play of examining the pictures. One showed a woman decked out like some exotic plant in a lavish dress. Visible through its ornate flounces and drapings was a pale stalk of a naked body. Nervousness coiled inside her.

'I'll tell you about the scheme later.' Klaus looked at her closely. 'You do like his work, don't you?'

'Yes, yes,' she said as evenly as she could. 'But the brushwork seems a little lurid.'

'No. No, that's exactly it. That's where his genius lies. He has a great feeling for nature, its turbulence, its darkness. Like the best German romantics, but translated into a modern idiom.'

Klaus had his solemn air. It was one she rarely argued with and she let the subject pass now, worrying, as canvases and sculptures slid past her, about his latest scheme.

For old times' sake, Bettina had suggested that they lunch at Demels. They decided to walk, strolling through the crisp autumnal air down the narrow Augustinerstrasse, past the Hofburg and into the Kohlmarkt. In the café window, the finely decorated gateaux sat invitingly displayed and for a moment Bettina wondered at the oddness of a nation which liked to see its monarch's head on a cake. The thoughts that must pass through the mind as one cut into it. Another Viennese lunacy.

Inside, the café was just as she remembered it from Sunday outings with her father and mother: racks of newspapers, great globed chandeliers, cool marble-topped tables, formal waitresses in monastic black; and walls of arched mirrors which induced a madcap sense of vertigo as chattering faces, including one's own, were reflected ad infinitum.

Her mother had loved it here, her pretty empty-headed mother. Cafés, music, the opera, theatre, a joy in spectacle – they filled her life. And she had spoiled them, succumbing to their every whim, particularly little Anna's, letting her run wild.

'Shall I tell you about my scheme?' Klaus broke into her reminiscences.

'Do.' Bettina rifled in her bag for a handkerchief and pretended only a minimum of interest.

'You know I've been thinking of adding on an extra wing at Seehafen, just a few rooms for my library, the collection.'

Bettina nodded.

'Well, I've suggested to Johannes that he might design it, go and stay there for a while – as long as he likes, really. Oversee the work. Perhaps paint a few murals. Use one of the outhouses as a studio.'

Bettina gazed at him in astonishment. She searched for an argument, found one. 'But does he know anything about architecture?'

'Enough.' Klaus shrugged. 'And he has ideas. A master builder can do the rest.'

'I don't know, Klaus. I . . .' Bettina felt she was about to utter something irrevocable.

Klaus lit his pipe nonchalantly, then met her eyes, examining them.

'He's in a bit of a precarious financial position, you know. Some terrible row with his father. I can't quite make out whether he disinherited him or Johannes simply refuses his money. In either event, life can be hard for artists.'

'When did you find all this out?' Bettina was suspicious.

'Oh, just before we left. I bumped into him at the Stephanie. He was a bit the worse for wear. His electricity had been cut off. The landlord was threatening him.'

'I see.' Bettina looked away, caught her reflection in the mirror, the worried eyes. 'I . . .'

He stopped. 'I believe in him, Bettina. He has something. It might even be genius.'

'I know,' she murmured. She felt as if she had been brought to the edge of a precipice and Klaus were forcing her to plunge. 'But I'm not sure. Johannes is so . . . so . . .'

'Unpredictable?' he finished for her. He toyed with his pastry for a moment, didn't look at her. 'I think I understand, Bettina, understand your difficulty.'

What did he understand? Bettina sat rigidly in her chair. What had Johannes said to him? She felt suddenly as if she had become a pawn in the hands of the two men. It made her rage.

'What difficulty?' she said stiffly, barely containing herself.

'You know.' Klaus fluttered his long fingers vaguely in the air, then paused, smiled, suddenly excited. 'I thought we might both go down there next week. Talk it through with him. Then I'd have to get back. My course starts. But you could stay on a while, work on your book. Make sure things were going according to your taste.'

He met her eyes, but she couldn't decipher their meaning.

'I'll see,' she said as casually as she could. She buried her face in the copy of the *Neue Freie Presse* she had picked off the rack and she started to laugh. 'Listen to this, Klaus. From the classifieds: "Young lieutenant wishes to meet girl in pale pink dress and grey hat seen waiting in front of Hotel Sacher and sitting at performance of 'Madame Butterfly' with father and mother . . ."'

For the remainder of their stay in Vienna, Bettina was on tenterhooks. She couldn't settle to anything. All her conversations with new and old friends seemed to be taking place in the past, while the future was rushing towards her, threatening to obliterate her. At moments panic overtook her, as if she had been making her way carefully along some steep embankment only suddenly to slip on a sheer icy slope where there were no footholds. And she was falling, down, down, into a gully that rushed inevitably to meet her, but was still invisible. For a woman who had always foreseen and thought and controlled, it was a terrifying sensation.

She had not been back to see Johannes after that afternoon when she had stumbled on Anna in his studio. The arrogance of him to think that she would. In a sense Anna had saved her by her very presence: Bettina had been filled with shame, a sense of wanting to be anywhere but secretly, deceitfully *there*, in Johannes's studio. But Anna had not been able to save her from thinking about him.

And then that strange letter had come from him, more like a document, or a manifesto, than a personal letter. A sequence of dark musings linking Henry Ford's unveiling of a moving assembly line at his American plant to the war in the Balkans; evoking a bleak machine man, soulless, the fruit of centuries of reason. A man as expendable as the machine. Calling on some irrational life force to turn it all round before it was too late. Calling on her to understand. She *could* understand. She was one of the few.

In the experience of reading it, the letter had made sense. She had felt its plea as well as its evocative force.

She should go and see him, she had thought. Perhaps they could simply talk. He *needed* someone to talk to. But she had put it off. And off. Then Anna's wedding had intervened.

Placing a physical distance between herself and Johannes had given Bettina a semblance of control. And now, here was Klaus undermining it all, setting up schemes, throwing the two of them together. What had he deduced? What had Johannes said to him? She couldn't bring herself to ask, though the presence of the unspoken topic in her mind foreclosed the possibility of any other subject being raised with ease.

As a result during the remainder of their stay in Vienna, when they were alone, Bettina was unusually quiet. The quiet persisted through the journey home to Munich. She kept her head buried in a book, pretending that she couldn't feel Klaus's eyes on her, querying, trying to probe, ever so gently.

They were to leave for Seehafen a mere two days after their return to Munich.

'Is Johannes accompanying us?' Bettina asked that morning, needing to know.

'Oh no. Didn't I say? He was scheduled to go down a few days ago. Wanted to get a feel of the place, jot down some ideas before we arrived.'

'I see,' Bettina murmured. 'So you were only informing me of all this when we spoke. The crucial decisions had all been taken.'

Klaus shrugged. 'I didn't think you'd have any objections. And the plans are all still to be made.' He smiled in his slightly lopsided, endearing way. 'I won't go ahead with anything you don't approve of. You know that.'

She held back the arguments that were on the tip of her tongue. Perhaps she was simply imagining a greater knowledge on Klaus's part than he had. After all, it was quite in character for him to want to support the work of a young artist. She returned Klaus's smile as equably as she could. 'I know,' she said.

Seehafen, when they arrived, was unseasonably warm, bathed in a mellow autumnal light. Trees and shrubs glowed russet and golden, darkening into ruddy bronzes, burgundy reds, crimsons. The house in their midst emerged startlingly white. Klaus's pleasure at returning here, Bettina noted, was palpable. No sooner had he greeted the housekeeper than he was bending to check on the condition of a plant here, a bush there, letting the soil trickle through his fingers. She was a little in awe of him when he was like this, not understanding in what language the plants spoke to him.

'Do you know where Herr Bahr is?' Bettina asked Frau Trübl.

The woman shrugged, shook her head. 'We hardly see him,' she was a little disapproving, 'except for dinner. Will you be needing Dora?'

'No, no, we'll manage. It's only for a few days.' She glanced at her watch. 'But perhaps some lunch, in about an hour?'

They found Johannes just outside the boathouse. He had set up a crude trestle table and was mixing colours on a palette, colours which echoed the crimsons and russets around them. He seemed startled to see them. There was a strange gauntness to his face.

'Hello, hello.' He wiped his fingers hastily on a rag, stretched out a hand to Klaus. 'I'd lost track of time,' he murmured apologetically, bowed to Bettina.

She averted her eyes.

Klaus laughed. 'It's easy to do here. Have you made yourself comfortable?'

'Oh yes, yes.' He pointed to the boathouse. 'I've set up in there. I hope you don't mind. Herr Trübl helped me move some things and there's plenty of room.'

They followed him in, saw a camp bed, a rough table strewn with papers, a chair, one stretched canvas untouched, an easel.

'But surely, you'll sleep in the house. It will soon be far too cold out here,' Klaus protested.

'No, no,' Johannes demurred. 'There's the little stove.'

'And the light? There isn't enough light. I'll have Hans cut another window.'

'No, really.'

There was something very wrong, Bettina mused. She had never seen Johannes like this, so self-effacing, almost subservient. It couldn't last.

She found her voice. 'We'll discuss it over lunch. But I think Klaus is right. If you're to stay for any length of time, it can't be in here, in winter.'

From beneath the darkly arched brows, eyes of midnight blue met hers for the first time. 'Whatever Frau Eberhardt determines.'

She could almost hear him click his heels, so stiffly formal was the voice. She wanted to shout at him, 'Don't be ridiculous, Johannes.' Instead the flush rose to her face.

'And the plans? Have you made any headway with the plans?' Klaus asked.

Suddenly Johannes was electrified. His features took on a mobility, his eyes glowed. He moved swiftly to the rough table, picked up a sheaf of papers. 'Shall we look at them now? Back at the house. I want to show you.' He almost flew over the paths, talking exuberantly, hands waving, telling them how he had contacted various architect friends in Munich, spoken to some local builders. He had even received some rough estimates.

When they had arrived at the back of the house, he began to describe an outlying structure, all undulating curves and horseshoe arches, but using trees in their pristine form as columns; a structure which brought the outside in, which defied the break between interior and exterior, a space which played with the colours of the seasons, was a temple to nature. Bettina stopped listening to the waves of words and simply watched Johannes. It was hard to imagine that this man in the grip of a vision was the same person who had spoken so stiffly to them such a short time ago. His excitement caressed her, enfolded her, so that she felt herself once more in thrall to his presence. As she could see Klaus was.

Johannes's magic saw them through lunch, through a lecture on the current state of architecture, through sheafs of doodles and a few more careful drawings. It was only when he had left them, saying that he must just jot a few more things down on paper, that Bettina realized that he had not addressed a single word to her directly.

'What do you think?' Klaus quizzed her.

'It sounds wonderful,' she replied, but her tone was hesitant.

'It will be. But he'll need help. The organization.' Klaus was drawing her out.

'There'll be builders,' Bettina shrugged, refusing to commit herself, wondering again what Johannes had told him, why Klaus wanted her here.

Later that afternoon, she built up enough courage to seek Johannes out. As she could see through the partially opened door, he was hunched over the small table, an oil lamp already burning in the dim interior. She knocked cursorily and stepped in.

He leapt up. 'What can I do for you, Frau Eberhardt?'

His cold punctiliousness filled her with disbelief. He was behaving like a hired man who resented the hiring. She fumbled for words, blurted out what was on her mind more quickly than she had intended.

'What have you told Klaus?'

'Told Klaus?'

'About us.'

An abrupt laugh escaped him. 'Is there anything to tell?'

The hurt showed in her face. 'I see,' she said softly after a long moment, then turned to go so that he wouldn't notice the leap of tears.

'Bettina,' he called after her, put a staying hand on her shoulder. 'I didn't think there was anything to tell.' His voice was gentle now, the intimate, suasive voice she remembered so distinctly. She turned to face him, meeting his eyes. They were no longer distant, unresponsive.

'You didn't write, made no sign, didn't come,' he shrugged, surveying her. 'I thought it was finished. I almost didn't accept Klaus's offer because of that, but it was too tempting. In any event I would never speak.'

'He wants me to stay here. With you. For a while. Why?'

Johannes took her hand, smiled dreamily. 'Perhaps he understands. Klaus is a man who understands more than he speaks. Understands about art, too. That's why I wanted to do this, to come here. Though I don't like being beholden, as you've perhaps noticed.' His face was suddenly boyish. 'It's difficult for me to be grateful, to accept Klaus, you, as my benefactors,' he laughed. 'You *will* stay, Bettina?'

She turned away from him. 'I don't know. I have to think.'

'You think far too much,' he murmured. 'You'll have ample time to think, once you've lived. And it will give you something to think about.'

She almost rose to the bait, almost started to argue with him about his singularly reduced idea of life, his arrogant equation of it with passion. But she stopped herself, knowing by the quivering of her lips where it would end.

'I have to think *now*,' she said as forcefully as she could, and fled.

Looking after her, Johannes felt the grey listlessness which had trailed him for weeks, the sense of working against the grain, miraculously vanish. He hadn't realized she had gained quite so much power over him. But now he felt drunk, vigorously alive, as if the world had suddenly regained its vibrant iridescence.

Later that evening, over dinner, they argued heatedly, with the old zest, Klaus strangely taking Johannes's side. Johannes had been to the Freideutsche Jugend mass gathering at the Hohe Meissner, the mountain to the south of Cassel where all the various branches of the ramblers' associations, the *Wandervögel*, had gathered to celebrate the centenary of the battle of Leipzig on 13 October.

Bettina couldn't believe her ears. 'You there?' she snorted. 'I don't believe it. You, suddenly transformed into a parochial patriot!'

'Now, Bettina,' Klaus chided her. 'You know very well the *Wandervögel* are nature lovers, not blatant militaristic patriots.'

'That's just it.' Her eyes gleamed. 'They haven't a clue as to *what* they are. One minute their leaders are blathering on about a greater Germany, more nature to ramble in. The next they're meek pacifists digging up folklore and singing songs to the hills. Woolly rubbish, all of it.'

'You don't let yourself understand, Bettina. Feel,' Johannes murmured. 'They, these young people, we', he turned to Klaus for confirmation, 'we're looking for something new, something authentic, an openness to a way of life which isn't just the arid intellectualism or the endless mechanical production of the city.'

He stared at her as if she had suddenly become its spirit incarnate. 'Lifeless repetition in the service of an empty progress which only produces more machines. We need a regeneration, to be reborn in body and soul and imagination. The formulas don't come ready-made. We don't know what's on the other side. So the ideas are woolly. But the feeling is real, strong, pure.' He brought his fist down on the table.

Bettina snorted again. 'Yes, very real feelings.' Her voice rose in contempt. 'Very real anti-semitism. Why, I just saw one of these *Wandervögel* magazines and I can tell you it gave me very real feelings.' She made a violent ripping gesture with her hands.

'The Jews are charged with exploiting the German people, corrupting German culture, seducing German virgins,' she gave Johannes a mocking look and hurried on, 'organizing white slave traffic, running everything from the press to the department stores and, no doubt, the art galleries. The stupidity of it is unbelievable. And then on top of it, all this waffle about the demon drink, about vegetarianism. The only feelings these people have are those of blaming others for their own lacks. It's no different from the state itself, just clothed in sandals and dirty hats and stupid little songs.'

'Yes, yes, of course that side of it is all rubbish.' Johannes waved dismissively, but his eyes blazed at her attack. 'They don't know how to express their dissatisfaction, so some of them find these ridiculous arguments.'

'It's simply that they haven't found their Nietzsche yet – a poet to translate them into language.' Klaus was solemn.

'Nietzsche had some pretty scathing things to say about the common herd, as I remember it,' Bettina muttered.

Johannes fixed her with his blue gaze. 'When they're out there, Bettina, wandering with the sky above their heads, the earth beneath their feet, pitting their bodies against the elements, what they experience is far truer than words, than anything else. It lifts them, frees them.' He paused, glanced at Klaus, added more softly, 'If you had tried it, you would know.'

'Yes,' Klaus murmured.

A short sharp laugh emerged from Bettina. 'Tried it? Did I hear Johannes Bahr, champion of women's freedom, saying that? Is he suggesting I change my sex? You do know that in Bavaria, women are not allowed into these groups?'

The two men exchanged an uncomfortable look.

'Catholic Bavaria.' Klaus raised his arms in despair.

'It will change. All soon change. It has to,' Johannes added emphatically.

Bettina lifted a sceptical eyebrow. 'Wandering in the hills won't change it. Which is why I need my rest. Goodnight, gentlemen.'

The two men watched her leave.

'My wife is an altogether remarkable woman,' Klaus said softly.

'Yes,' Johannes echoed him.

'And when it comes to argument, she is right about almost everything,' he laughed.

Johannes heard the odd emphasis on 'almost'. He didn't respond, but let Klaus refill his glass.

'I sometimes wonder why it was that she acquiesced to my marriage proposal.'

'I find it hard to imagine Frau Eberhardt *acquiescing* to anything,' Johannes found himself saying, then corrected himself hastily. 'What I mean is that I can only imagine her actively accepting your proposal.' He met the older man's eyes, saw an odd light in them. 'If you'll permit yet another boldness,' he chuckled now, 'I imagine Frau Eberhardt actively approved of the quality of your appreciation, which I have reason to know is as remarkable as her intelligence.'

Klaus bowed slightly, stoked his pipe. 'But whereas I take great pleasure in purchasing your pictures, Johannes – pictures I appreciate – I have always,' he cleared his throat, 'given my wife the freedom that is her due.'

Johannes looked at him in surprise, but there was a candour in Klaus's expression, and he seemed to be waiting for a response.

'In that too, I can only say you are as remarkable as she is,' he offered after a moment.

Silence ensued. Within it, it occurred to Johannes that Klaus was telling him to take Bettina. Odd, he thought. It wasn't as if he were making him a gift of her, nor granting permission. Johannes would have despised both, as well as the giver. It was more as if Klaus were uttering a plea. A plea from a brother.

He was a rare being, this Klaus. Johannes had always known it, recognized it in that first moment when Klaus had sat quietly in front of his pictures. And now it seemed that the bond which had begun to take shape at that time was being wordlessly sealed between them. Yes, a bond between brothers.

It was the next evening, as the three of them sat sipping their after dinner coffee, that they saw in the distance a stream of torches cutting a swathe through the night.

'Look.' Johannes pointed. '*Wandervögel*.'

'There must be some sort of reunion tonight.'

'Let's follow them.' Johannes had already got up. 'You'll see, Bettina. It's not what you think. The experience is quite different.' His eyes skimmed over her, rested defiantly on hers.

She turned towards Klaus, who nodded at her with a strange eagerness.

'All right then.' Her manner was diffident. But as they hurried out into the cold hushed night, that little voice which had begun to claw at her ever since her first meeting with Johannes took up its refrain. What if he was right? What if Johannes was right and she was blind to something essential?

A tangy fragrance of pine mingled with wood smoke filled the air. On the winding road they became one with the stream of youths. The shadowy play of the high-held torches irradiated the curves of the road, falling here and there on dreamy young faces. Eyes aglow beneath their battered hiking hats, voices raised melodiously, they moved in trance-like unison through the crisp starlit night, until the hill appeared, braziers and a bonfire illuminating its crest, a setting for the enactment of some ancient ritual.

As if by a sign from above, the songs died out and an expectant hush filled the air. Then a disembodied voice came through the night, evoking the enchantment of the nature of which they were part, the running streams, the dense woods, the primeval mountains, this land, this earth, this mother which was theirs, so much purer, grander, more vital than the cities with their bilious smoke-stacks, their soul-destroying industries, their empty artifice. This, this glorious nature each particle of which was in sympathy with them, was their home, their origin and their resting place, was the true Germany. They had only to open their eyes to see what it offered, to build upon its example for the future.

Without knowing how it had found its way there, Bettina felt Johannes's hand wrapped round hers. The residual doubts that booming voice had left in her vanished in the pressure of that hand. She had a sudden certain sense, so strong, so new, of the utter naturalness of that hand on hers.

She walked home dreamily, in step with the two men, one on either side. They spoke little, as if words could only spoil what each had separately felt. Their goodnights were cursory. But as they separated in the garden of the house, Johannes whispered, 'Perhaps not the common herd, Bettina, but the exceptional individual, the one who laughs at danger, despises easy comforts, challenges limits. You?'

In bed, she lay awake for a long time, unable to sleep. At last, she got up again, went to the window, pushed aside the heavy curtains and peered out. The night was black now, but she had an eerie sense that at the edge of the lake she could see a lamp burning, Johannes's lamp. Was he waiting for her?

She shivered, clasped her arms round herself, felt, in doing so, that strange ache rising in her. Was she to remain eternally ignorant of what Johannes valued so highly? With a muffled cry, Bettina tore a coat from her closet and rushed silently down the corridor. She paused at Klaus's room, half wishing he would come out, stop her, and then hurried again, down the stairs, out into the cool night air.

Her nightgown whipping against her bare legs, she ran wildly until she reached the lake. Here, she stopped for a moment to catch her breath, to look round. Panic filled her. There was no light. She had imagined it. He wasn't waiting for her. She would have to go back. A pounding sounded in her head, accompanied the bitter taste of disappointment. She was a fool.

Johannes, watching her, had a sense that he had willed her existence from the shadowy play of starlight on shrubbery. He hadn't expected her to come. She had eluded him for so long: it was like a wound which sapped at the very source of his energy.

One day in September, when he had heard nothing from her in weeks, he had wandered in the Munich streets near her nurseries, followed the trajectory she might take across the river, had even rung the bell of her house, in the hope that he might catch hold of her. It was as he retraced his steps that he had suddenly remembered himself as a small child, evading his nanny's hand, chasing after a carriage which had taken his mother away, running after her, calling, crying. Later, when his nanny had found him and dragged him home, his father had berated him, told him roundly that boys didn't cry, sent him to his room for punishment. For weeks, no one would tell him where his mother was. He had surreptitiously searched the house for her every day, hiding from his father when he was there. And then, when his mother had at last come back, a new regimen was in place. He was only permitted to see her for half an hour in the morning, and then again for half an hour in the afternoon. She was making him soft, his father proclaimed. Soft.

'Bettina. I was waiting, hoping.' He touched her cheek. Soft. So soft. So unlike the hardness of her will, which resisted him. But as she turned to him now, she gave him her lips, moved against him.

'At last,' he murmured into her hair. 'At last.'

Bettina felt his hands reach beneath her coat, move over her, hold her tightly, more tightly than she had ever been held. In the circle of his assurance, in the blindness of night, her body seemed to develop a life of its own, pressing against him, swaying to the motion of his hands, reaching out, touching, the firm angles of his face, the hard, tensed shoulders. The adventure of it filled her, made her breath come fast.

Suddenly he drew away a little, held her still.

'You're brave as an eagle tonight, Bettina.' His words rustled into her ear. She could feel his surprise, a little like awe. She could only feel. Everything else was mere shadows. She touched his hand, arching her fingers through his, wanting his kiss, again and again, those fingers on her breast. And then his voice was trembling through her, the words of a half-remembered poem.

> 'See how everything's unfolding; so we are,
> For we are nothing but such blissfulness.
> What was blood and darkness in an animal,
> That grew in us to Soul and howled,
>
> Howled again as Soul. And it howled for you.'

'Rilke,' she murmured. 'The song of the women to the poet.' She felt his nod, the pause.

'Will you speak now, Bettina? It's important to me, to you too, I think, that you speak it.'

She knew exactly what he meant. Her throat felt dry, but when she brought the words out, they were firm. 'I want you, Johannes.'

He clasped her to him, kissing her, kissing her so that her limbs seemed to give way. Then, he lifted her into his arms and carried her to the little copse where he had first pressed her hand to the earth. 'The temple of our love,' he whispered. At the foot of the gnarled oak, he took off his coat and spread it like a blanket over the fallen leaves. They crackled as he crouched, crackled as he pulled her down beside him.

When she tried to remember the scene, the next day, it was the crackling of the leaves she remembered best. The rest was only a trace of the strange indescribable sensations he had roused in her, an ineffable mixture of pleasure and pain and then pleasure, so intense that she could not recapture any of it, short of the act of repetition. And she was bent upon that. Any sense of transgression she might have had was now inextricably fused with a sense of the inevitable naturalness of her actions.

There was only one other memory. His voice murmuring, 'Blood, your blood, in the soil. As it should be.'

The women howling, Bettina mused, howling for you.

FOUR

1914

ANNA ADLER STOOD on the terrace of the house in Neuwaldeggerstrasse on the outskirts of Vienna and wondered if she was happy. It was April. The trees were apple green in their budding freshness. A lingering morning mist gave a softness to the air. In the grounds, which she might later inspect, she would find the crocuses in full array, the first daffodils opening to the sun.

But now, she returned to her piano.

She had taking to playing for hours at a stretch, Mozart, Schubert, Wagner, of late mostly the latter. Bruno said her playing had become magnificent. But then, he seemed to admire everything she did or attempted, even her untutored watercolours. Except one thing.

She passed her hand over the gleaming wood of the grand piano. It looked so beautiful here against the long windows which gave out on the woods. Everything about the house was beautiful. They had taken such pains in choosing and arranging, Bruno acquiescing to her taste, allowing her her little experiments in simplicity, allowing the single stark sculpture which drew the eye to the other corner of the room so that from the piano she could rest her eyes on its subtle curves. But now it was all done, from top to bottom, from one end of the grounds to the other, and time rested heavily on her hands.

Anna struck a chord, let her fingers ring out the overture to 'Tristan and Isolde', lost herself in its waves of longing. Then with a burst of impatience she leapt up from the piano. Bruno wouldn't be home until the weekend. Increasingly it was the only time she saw him. There were problems, she knew, in various branches of his industrial network, nationalist demands, strikes, and he was always travelling. She had asked once whether she might accompany him, but he had said no. The word so rarely passed his lips in response to her requests that it took on an unquestionable force. But she had asked again and this time he had given reasons, told her he needed to concentrate himself wholly on his work when he was there – and the presence of his lovely little Anna would hardly permit that, would it?

It was the same reason, she knew, which lay behind his insistence that once the new house outside Vienna was ready, that would be their principal residence, rather than the spacious apartment in town they had first inhabited. Though she loved the house, she had liked being in Vienna, closer to people, to concerts, to cafés. Perhaps she would stay in the apartment tonight, take in a concert after the doctor's visit. Yes. Anna was suddenly filled with energy.

Sometimes, when she stayed here for too long alone, she had the strange sense of being imprisoned in a castle, like some fairy-tale princess. Oh, everything was wonderful and just as it should be and Miss Isabel was there with her and the singing tutor came regularly as did the guests at the weekend. But nonetheless, she occasionally felt trapped, like a singing bird, its wings clipped, unable to leave its gilded cage.

Silly, she thought, as she walked along the flowerbanked paths. So silly. She bent to look more closely at the little gossamer webs which sparkled through the greenery. Bruno was so good to her. There was only one other thing he had said no to. Just after their honeymoon, on Bettina's urging, she had asked him whether she might work at one of the nurseries her sister had recommended. About that he had been adamant. No wife of his could work, however charitably. He would donate funds, of course, but her labour, no. In any event, and his tone had grown softer, there would soon be children of their own.

And there was the rub. Anna lifted her too heavy skirts and broke into a run, stopping only when she was breathless. There were no children yet. That was why Bruno had arranged for the specialist to come to see her this afternoon. She wondered whether she would be able to speak to the man. But what would she tell him? That her husband spoiled her, that he brought her too many presents, that she had wardrobes full of dresses, boxes of rings and pearls and pendants. Yet in that one little corner of her life things, she suspected, were not as they should be. Or perhaps they were. How was she to know?

She remembered their honeymoon, that first night, then the second, when she had put her arms around him, wanting to touch him, asking him to leave the light on, so that she could see. It was perhaps the only time she had seen him angry. He had left her only to return later when she was already half asleep and to press himself wordlessly inside her. It had hurt a little less then, but increasingly over the weeks, when the strange rite was repeated, she had felt herself suffocating, drowning. Sometimes to avoid it, she said she felt ill. He didn't take it amiss. Perhaps he hated it too.

So though she missed him when he was away, loving his glowing eyes on her, enjoying his conversation, she was also sometimes relieved when that nighttime act didn't have to be undertaken. She wondered whether Bruno too had been to see a doctor. She didn't dare ask.

It was strange how marriage had made her timid, had turned her into a liar, making her suppress what she would otherwise have spoken, forcing her to pretend. Were all adults like that? Was her sister? She thought of the people she knew and supposed that probably most of them were.

Some weeks ago at one of their Sunday lunchtime parties, she had met the wife of an acquaintance of Bruno's, a dark-eyed, vivacious woman, glamorous, whom she thought she could discuss this with. Frau Hofer was in her late twenties, perhaps thirty, only a little older than Bettina. They had been engaged in a little tête-à-tête in the far corner of the drawing room, when Frau Hofer had announced that she was seeing Professor Freud.

'Oh?' Anna had looked at her in something like confusion. Though she had heard the name Freud two or three times, she had no clear idea of the import Frau Hofer seemed to attribute to her statement. 'What does he do?'

The woman had been a trifle taken aback at her naivety, but had then said with a wicked gleam in her bright eyes, 'He makes you see what you don't know about yourself. And believe me, my dear, there is a lot one doesn't know, a great deal one represses.'

Anna had mentioned Frau Hofer to Bruno, saying how much she liked her, casually asking him about Professor Freud.

'Ha!' Bruno's reaction had been instantaneous. 'A charlatan. Talks smut while pretending to cure. Why, one might as well go to a prostitute.' He stopped himself, realizing what he had said, coughed. 'I'm sorry, my dear, I didn't mean to offend you, or insult Frau Hofer.'

Anna for once had laughed her old buoyant laugh.

* * *

'Anna, Anna!' Miss Isabel was calling her from the terrace. 'Lunch, we'll be late.'

'Let's have lunch in town.' Anna came towards her with her old impetuous manner.

'But everything's ready. Frau Gruber will . . .'

'I'll speak to Frau Gruber. And I'm going to invite a friend to join us.' Anna picked up the telephone. 'Though it's probably too late.'

It was. Katarina Hofer was just on her way out, but she invited Anna to come to her at five, for a late tea. And then if she liked, she might join herself and a young cousin at the opera. They had a box.

'Oh yes.'

Sitting next to Miss Isabel in the car, Anna felt she had suddenly come back to life. All her trepidation about facing the doctor melted away in the excitement of the proffered outing with the glamorous Katarina Hofer.

Poor little Anna, Miss Isabel thought, happy to see her smiling for once.

Miss Isabel had very decided views about Anna's marriage. She was grateful to her employer, of course, who was a generous, honourable man. But she was angry at a state of things which had made her radiant, kind-hearted Anna so listless. She had caught Bruno's frequent glances at Anna's waistline. What madness it was to try to chain a mere child of eighteen, to yoke her into being a dynastic breeder. Miss Isabel shook her trim head. Why, even at her ripe age, when she had learned the difficult virtue of patience, such a way of life would seem utterly distasteful.

But for the moment, Anna was happy. So happy that she sailed through the horrid examination.

The doctor was a sweet, rather dapper old man, who kept making little clucking maternal noises as he tapped and prodded at her stomach, poked his cool instruments at her chest and, with more clucking noises, into her. When he had finished and she had smoothed her skirts, he looked at her with a kind smile.

'So what is the problem, Frau Adler?'

Anna giggled nervously. 'Babies. There don't seem to be any.'

'Well.' He stroked his beard, pronounced his verdict. 'You are perfect. A fine young woman.' He polished his glasses for a moment, settled them back on the tip of his nose. 'Perhaps your husband . . .' he gazed at her thoughtfully, then seemed to change the course of his question. 'You and your husband sleep together regularly?'

She nodded, then shook her head. 'Well, not exactly sleep.'

'No, not exactly sleep,' he smiled. 'But I know the answer already from my examination.'

'And so?' Anna looked at him warily.

He threw up his arms. 'And so nature must be allowed to take her course.' He shut his black bag emphatically. 'I will speak to Herr Adler. If I can find him. He is a man who is always in something of a hurry. As we are of the same people, he will not mind my telling him.'

Anna was tempted to embrace him. Instead, she walked him to the door herself. 'I love Bruno very much, you know,' she murmured. 'It's just that, about that . . .' She shrugged.

He patted her shoulder. 'These things take time, my child. Don't worry too much. Sometimes the worry is what makes it all so difficult.' He bowed to her. 'Please telephone me yourself if I can be of any further assistance to you.'

Anna felt a vast burden lift from her shoulders. Cheerfully she surveyed the few gowns that she kept at the Vienna apartment and chose a poppy red that Bruno had found a little too flamboyant. Then she dismissed Miss Isabel, telling her that she would stay over in the apartment tonight. Karl, the chauffeur, could drive her companion back home after he had dropped her at Frau Hofer's. If Bruno were to phone, Miss Isabel was to tell him that the doctor had said she was perfect and that she was celebrating.

Frau Hofer's home, a beautiful *hôtel particulier* near the Augustinerkirche, was as bright and modern as she was herself. The furniture was the spare, simple product of the Wiener Werkstätten school; the ornaments were few. But the walls were wild with the colour of contemporary art. There were several Klimts, their jewelled surfaces sparkling as brilliantly as her hostess's dark eyes.

'So you recognize me,' Katarina laughed. 'Kurt didn't. He's blind. He has the Berlin blindness,' she teased her cousin, a slender young man with a mop of curly hair. 'But I'm teaching him.'

Kurt laughed easily, not in the least taken aback by Katarina's tone. 'Tell her, Frau Adler. Tell her it's nothing like her.'

'Anna, please. Call me Anna. Well,' Anna inspected the painting in question, 'to be perfectly honest . . .'

'She hadn't noticed,' Kurt finished triumphantly.

'But I see it now,' Anna laughed.

'And I can see I am going to have to teach you, too.' Katarina's mobile face twisted into mock disapproval.

'Please,' Anna said softly. 'I know that I'm dreadfully ignorant.'

'Hush, child. That's the kind of thing husbands make you believe.' She smiled kindly and then paced, taking on a stentorian air, as if she were the stiffest of schoolmarms. 'You hear that, Kurt. This young woman who is probably your age has been browbeaten into thinking she's ignorant. You don't feel you're ignorant, do you? Not even when I point it out to you in black and white. You must take care never to do this to your women friends. Or, many many years from now, to your wife. Otherwise . . .'

'You shall travel all the way to Berlin simply for the satisfaction of hitting me over the head with a rolling pin,' he roared with laughter, fell cowering into a sofa.

'He's not stupid. He learns quickly.' Katarina winked at Anna. 'Here, Martie, put the tea things here,' she gestured at the maid who had just come in, 'and bring us a little wine and some cold meats. Otherwise my young friends will starve through "Die Fledermaus".'

Anna looked again at the splendid images on the walls. Suddenly she decided. 'Do you know the work of Johannes Bahr by any chance?'

Katarina's red lips settled themselves into a curious smile. 'Definitely not ignorant,' she murmured. 'Come, I'll show you.' She stretched out her hand companionably. Cool soft fingers enfolded hers, led her. She opened a door.

Anna saw a study, sparsely furnished, but feminine, a pink chaise longue along one wall, above it a picture by Johannes, the very one she remembered had been poised on his easel the first time she had visited him.

'I bought this not so long ago. I haven't quite decided where to put it. It's strong, isn't it, not altogether friendly to my other pictures. Horrible woman. But I like her mouth. And that flower, as if it were growing out of her.' Katarina looked at her reflectively. 'So you know Bahr's work?'

'I met him,' Anna stumbled. 'He's a friend of my sister's and her husband. In Munich.'

'Not altogether an easy man, I hear. But then none of these artists are if they're any good. So full of themselves, so prickly.' She laughed her tinkling laugh again. 'I guess they have to be. The world isn't always kind to them. And then too, we demand it of them. How else would we know they had genius!' Her animated eyes twinkled ironically. 'A little like Jews, really. The same dynamic.'

Anna started.

Katarina laughed. 'Don't stare at me like that. I should know. I am one.'

Anna followed her back to the drawing room. She felt lighter, more alive than she had in months. She could watch and listen to Katarina for hours.

But, all too soon, it was time to leave for the opera; time, as Katarina proclaimed, to make their grand entrance amidst *la toute Vienne*, to wave their fans, bat their lashes demurely from the splendour of their box. 'Bow, cousin. There's a sweet young thing I know, making eyes at you. Come on, Anna, like this, you're a married woman now.'

For a brief moment, Anna thought of Bruno, so far away. She wished that he could share her pleasure, wished that he took her more often to the opera. Then, as the music embraced her, she forgot about him altogether.

Bruno Adler was not as far away as Anna imagined. He had finished his business in Brno early and had decided to drive back to Vienna. Once there, a mild depression tugged at him – the reports, the columns of figures, the sheaves of foreign newspapers to catch up on. Rather than carrying on home, he determined on a different trajectory. It was a familiar one.

He parked his car near St Stephansdom and walked in leisurely fashion down the narrow cobbled streets which bordered the cathedral. Lotte. She would not mind a surprise visit, had not minded once in what was now nigh on eight years. He had never found anyone else with her, though he knew there were others. Usually he telephoned, or sent a message, just in case. He almost stopped now to do so. But no, the very thought that there might be someone else there with her now, doing those things, whet his appetite, so that he began to hurry, his steps echoing through the narrow street.

Eight years. Soon after his first wife had died. He frowned into the night. That horrible death which had robbed him of her and his firstborn. He had been desolate for months. Then one night, wandering randomly as he was wont to do in those days to eradicate his sorrow, he found himself near the Prater.

In the gaslight a young woman had approached him – a perky face, an upturned nose, button eyes, all beneath an outlandish hat from which a lank feather curled. What was it that she had said to him in that low husky voice of hers? He could still almost recall it word for word. 'You can hit me, you can screw me. Backwards, forwards, upside down. I'll sing for you, dance,' she did a little pirouette, 'but I'm cold and hungry and it's starting to rain and I need a bed for the night. I'm not begging, mind.' She had looked him straight in the eye. 'I give value.'

He had not often been with prostitutes. The occasional shop girl, yes, a maid, here and there, like every man of his class, a dancer for a while. But this one had done something to his entrails. She wasn't pretty – quite the opposite. But she was so young, so pert, exuded an almost febrile energy. He had taken her to a hotel and she had been as good as her word. Better. She had a sense of humour, was a sparky little vixen. With her boldness, her hard, foul-mouthed chatter, she seemed to release him. Two weeks later he had set her up in her own apartment.

Bruno hadn't wanted to know too much about her; certainly not for her to know anything about him. The anonymity was what drew him: he had never even told her his real name. But gradually over the years, he had learned things about her terrible early life – the dank-infested two rooms in which six of them lived, the dead older sister, the father who abused her, hating her in his drunken state for not being her lost older sister; the mother, distraught, beaten, kind, who tried to protect her, who earned what little money they had. It was not, he knew, an untypical story, but it wrenched his heart, and he had given her money, generous sums which monthly found their way into the bank account he had opened for her, money too for her family, so she could be as benevolent to them as she wished.

There were periods over those years when he hadn't seen her very much. But then, in the last while, since Anna, and more often since his marriage, his hunger for Lotte with her foul mouth and cocky ways had seemed to treble. It was as if confronted with one woman, his need for the other escalated. He didn't know why, had ceased to question it, though when he was with Anna, he was burdened with guilt. Yet he knew, and the shame of it hurt him, that without the darkness in which he could think of Lotte, he could never get hard for his wife. It was as if her very purity, her very innocence, overpowered him, frightened his manhood into nonexistence.

But he was hard now. Bruno shuddered, turned his key in the lock, climbed the three flights, rang. She was there, her face visible behind the latch.

Lotte opened the door, passed her tongue against her red lash of a mouth. 'Make yourself comfortable. I'll be with you in a tick.' She vanished into her bedroom, but after a moment poked her face out at him. 'Don't be afraid to touch it, you silly old thing,' she ordered him saucily.

Bruno smiled, took his jacket off, and poured himself a glass of whisky from the fine decanter he had given her. Then he relaxed into the sofa, looked round him at the familiar objects, the helter skelter of the space she had created, the mirrors, the feathers. Only when he had looked, sipped, did he let his hand fall to his groin, touch. A jagged breath escaped him.

She was with him in a moment, her brown hair pinned up loosely on her head, that gamine face rolling its eyes at him, her silk negligée open, falling around her. From its midst, she brought out a stockinged dancer's leg, touched her toes to his groin, softly, and then with firmer movements.

He gasped.

'Oh,' she chortled, 'so far gone there's nothing left for me to do.'

'Almost nothing.' He pulled her down backwards on his lap, revelling in the waggle of those hard buttocks, placing his hands on the bare skin above her frilly black garters, stroking, stroking, while she moved against him.

'Now, Lotte, please now.'

She rolled her eyes at him, then slowly, her fingers lingering, she unbuttoned his trousers.

'The bear is growling tonight,' she murmured, her mouth plunging down on his swollen penis.

Bruno buried his face in her hair, breathing in her sharp perfume. The pleasure of her tongue working against him was unutterable. He pressed his hands into her shoulders, felt for her small taut breasts, then leaned back into the sofa, feeling the pressure rise from the base of his spine, mount, mount, until he burst, groaning, 'Lotte, Lotte, Lotte, Lotte.'

She placed herself delicately on his knee, snuggling against him, fondling his hair. 'Still the best in town, eh? Say it, tell me.'

'The best,' he murmured.

She had the ability to rouse him, again and again. Her ingenuity was endless. Sometimes he wondered where she came up with those countless little tricks, those tantalizing little stories.

And now she had one of her wicked, teasing looks. 'I want to dance. With you.' She pulled him up, carefully buttoning his trousers, patting them straight with her nimble fingers. He felt a tremor. 'Not yet,' she admonished him severely. 'I've learned a new song, just for you.'

She took his hands and placed them on her buttocks. 'Comfortable?' She gyrated slowly against him, waited for his response, then put her arms round his neck. She began to croon, in her cracked unmelodious voice, more speech than song, moving all the time against him.

'Brown-eyed Bertie
You know the one I mean
He's keen on the ladies
Particularly the ones of eighteen.'

She winked at him. He took a step away from her, not liking what he heard.

'And what he likes best
Are the parts that are obscene
You know the very ones I mean.'

She was taunting him. Her dark button eyes took on a malicious look. Suddenly he knew what was coming and he didn't want it. No, not tonight. All tenderness left him. He pulled her arms off his neck, felt cold.

'Brown-eyed Bertie
You know the one I mean
He's a sentimental man
He does for a woman what no other man can
Particularly the ones of eighteen.'

Her voice rose emphatically.

'So young and green
They make him steam
You know what I mean.'

Bruno reached for his jacket. She had deliberately made him think of Anna. He should never have told her about the marriage. Now, when the malice took hold of her, she would refer to his wife in one way or another. Deliberately. He knew why. He had only discovered it in these last few months. She liked to rouse him to anger, liked him to hit her. Taunted, insulted, he had done so once, a second time, and had found her molten, on fire, all the masquerade of hardness gone. But it was not what he came for, and he hated himself for doing it. He wouldn't do it now.

'Don't go.' She drew him back. 'I'll stop. Promise.'

He met her eyes. 'Why do you want that, Lotte?'

She understood what he meant, shrugged her thin shoulders, seemed confused for a moment. Then she looked at him brazenly. 'Reminds me of dear old Dad, I guess.'

'Oh, Lotte.' He put his arms round her.

Her slender fingers burrowed beneath his trousers, pressed, moved. He grew hard again, despite himself. She wound her legs round his waist, like a child, rocking herself against his hardness. 'Take me to bed, Bertie.' She licked his ear.

He carried her into the next room, placed her gently on the wide bed.

'Undress, Bertie. Tonight is special.' Her quick fingers worked at his shirt, his trousers. He didn't like being naked. It made him feel unnatural, powerless, the sight of that ridiculous cock, jutting in front of him, searching for release. But he let her, let her find his skin, stroke.

'You've forgotten, haven't you?'

He gazed down at her pert face uncomprehendingly.

'It's our anniversary,' she laughed, snuggling her face into his waist.

'I'm sorry,' he murmured. 'How inconsiderate of me.'

'Silly Bertie.' She pounded his bare chest. 'But still a handsome man, after all these years.' She began to kiss him, quick little biting kisses, all along the length of him until he moaned with the pleasure of it, wanting her so much it shamed him. She lifted a leg astride him, touched herself, rubbed, rubbed, her face a mask of lewdness. Then she took his penis in her hands, began to hum, stroking to the rhythm of her hum, her eyes glinting, wicked. 'Brown-eyed Bertie . . .' She let the words shape themselves in his own mind. He sat up abruptly, responding unthinkingly to her attack, taking her loosened hair in his hands, tugging, tugging, until her eyes glowed with tears and she was down, down beneath him. 'Yes, yes, Bertie,' she whispered, 'put it in. It's a red letter day. Now, now.'

He plunged inside her savagely, punishing, rubbing out the melody, pressing again and again. 'Brown-eyed Bertie, it makes him steam.' She writhed beneath him, brought his mouth down to her nipples, wanting him to bite. She dug her nails into his back, finding the point just there between his buttocks, so that when he came to her cries, her song, he felt utterly emptied out, devoid of worries, blissfully spent.

He left her asleep, her body spread wantonly over the bedclothes, but her face in repose was strangely innocent. Bruno looked away, suddenly hating himself. He would send her flowers tomorrow, dozens of roses, put a little extra in the account. For a moment he wondered how she would spend the day, but no, that was nothing to do with him. With a feeling half way between disgust and desire, he put her firmly out of his mind.

At the apartment in Alleegasse, he let himself in quietly, poured a drink. He felt wide awake. He would work, read through one of the reports from the Lemberg factory in Galicia. He was worried about the progress of things there. There had been a strike, nothing serious, part nationalist protest. But he preferred his workers to be content. He thought for a moment again of Lotte, then, with a sigh, picked up his briefcase.

As he walked down the corridor to his study, he was startled to see a light glimmering from beneath a door. Anna's room. Strange. They must have forgotten to turn it off after the examination. Yes, that had been today. He should have telephoned her. He felt guilt rise painfully inside him. Poor little Anna, to be subjected to such things.

He opened the door. She was there. She must have been too tired to return home. He gazed at her for a moment in the soft lamplight, the shining hair spread out on the pillow, that pure golden face, the arm curved softly over the duvet. How beautiful she was. For a moment, as he watched her utter stillness, his pulse quickened. But then she moved, murmured something, seemed troubled. The quickening died away. He stroked her hair tenderly. Poor little Anna, poor little wife, to be subjected to all this. Perhaps – the thought suddenly presented itself to him – perhaps he didn't really want the children. With a shudder, he remembered his first wife, the pain, the terrible awesome sight of that tiny blue creature.

Bruno turned away, not wanting to contaminate her with that vision. Softly, fearfully, he stole from the room.

Anna woke early, thrilled to find Bruno ensconced at the breakfast table, his head buried in the newspaper. She kissed him daringly on the hair. 'Surprise, I'm here.'

Bruno smiled at her. 'I know. I paid you a little visit last night.' He looked at her questioningly.

'I went to the opera.' She misinterpreted his gaze. 'To treat myself. On Frau Hofer's invitation.' She babbled gaily, recounting the evening. 'We must go more often, Bruno.'

He took it as a criticism, was stiff in his reply. 'Of course, my dear. If that's what you'd like. When there's time. Which reminds me, there's a note in the post again from your aunt. She insists that we come on Friday, particularly you.'

'Why not?' Anna, having originally refused the invitation, now acquiesced quickly. 'And I . . . we might just as well stay on here until then, mightn't we? I'm so enjoying being here.'

Her tawny eyes were brighter than he had seen them in months.

'Of course, my dear, whatever you choose.'

'Oh good.' She clapped her hands in a wave of exuberance.

How easy it was to make her happy, Bruno thought. But he had to ask her. He broached it delicately. 'And was there anything else yesterday?' He sipped the bitter-sweet coffee.

'The doctor, you mean?' She laughed again, utterly untroubled. 'He pronounced me perfect.'

'Which you are.' Bruno was quick to confirm the verdict. 'Altogether perfect. But . . .'

She made a little *moue*. 'But he said he would try to speak to you, said you were a man who was always in a hurry.'

'Yes.' Bruno allowed himself a chortle. 'In too much of a hurry. It's my ripe age, Anna. So much riper than yours.'

Their eyes met. Of course, Anna thought, she had never considered it before. His impatience had to do with his age. How stupid of her not to realize.

In that bright look, Bruno shivered as if an icy hand had suddenly caressed his spine. No, perhaps he didn't have much time. He sprang into action to eradicate those thoughts. Work called. His office. He frowned, pulled his watch out of his pocket. 'I musn't keep Herr Gellner waiting. Goodbye, my dear.'

Anna followed him to the door, watched him don the hat and coat the butler proffered. 'You're very handsome, Bruno,' she said timidly.

He had already half forgotten her, but his face softened as he looked at her now. He paused. 'Perhaps I'll arrange for a concert tonight. You'd like that, wouldn't you?'

Anna nodded.

'Wear that pale green dress I like so much,' he smiled, marking a decolletage in the air with his hands. 'Show everyone how very perfect Frau Adler is.'

Anna lazed away a little of the morning and then, feeling the hours until evening beginning to weigh on her, she picked up the telephone without thinking and rang Frau Hofer: Katarina, she schooled herself. She would ask her advice on what exhibitions to see.

'Why, come with me instead, if you like.' Katarina's voice was warm on the telephone. 'I was thinking of seeing what some of the students at the Akademie are up to. Let me think, first there's the Professor. Then . . . about two, say. I'll collect you.'

Anna broke out into a merry whistle. That was all that was wrong with her. She was lonely. She needed a friend.

Never having been to school, she had never had many friends of her own age or otherwise. But somehow at her aunt's she hadn't noticed, had been happy enough with the routine of governesses and crowded evenings, interspersed with plenty of daydreaming. But now, now that she was married, the daydreaming didn't seem enough. Katarina would be a friend. Anna felt it.

The two women, as they paraded through the Akademie's atelier, had something of a disruptive effect on the young men who were meant to be concentrating on an exercise in still life. Katarina, striking in a tight-bodiced rose dress which emphasized her dramatic colour, spoke in low tones, but was not averse to waving her parasol to stress her points. Anna, light on her feet, quick to respond, was as enthralled by her friend as by everything she saw before them. She realized that it was only because of Katarina's friendship with the master that they had been permitted entry.

'I wish I could do something like this.' Anna stopped behind one of the students and waved her hand at the canvas.

'Why, I'm sure you could.' Katarina grimaced a little. 'No, no, I'm serious. They've started a class for women now. We could ask about it.'

'Bruno would never allow it.'

Katarina looked at her strangely. 'My dear, there is nothing husbands will not allow, as long as one knows how to ask.'

'Perhaps for you,' Anna murmured.

'For any woman,' Katarina laughed. 'I think you and I need to have a little talk. About husbands. About marriage.'

She said it so lightly, but Anna felt that she had nonetheless been disloyal to Bruno. Back in the carriage, she turned to her new friend. 'It's not that Bruno isn't good to me.'

'Of course not.' Katarina patted her hand. 'He's a fine man. Charming. Clever.'

'Yes,' Anna murmured.

'It's just that all marriages go through a few teething problems.'

'All?' Anna echoed.

'Don't look so surprised.' Katarina chortled. 'Show me ten happy young marriages in all Vienna and I'll show you ten liars.'

Anna's face fell.

'Don't look so heartbroken, my dear. It all improves, the edges soften. In time.' She took her hand again, squeezed it, met Anna's eyes with her own dark ones. 'But we'll talk again.'

They had arrived at Alleegasse.

'Come and see me on a quiet afternoon. Next Wednesday, perhaps?'

'May I?' Anna gazed up at her new friend. She could already hardly wait.

Tante Hermine's salon was, as always, as crowded with ferns as it was with people. When Anna and Bruno arrived, the venerable woman was holding court in her great Biedermeier chair, her corseted girth swathed in reams of dark satin.

She waved them over to her. 'So you've come, good, good. There's someone here who particularly wanted to meet you.' She tapped Anna on the shoulder with her fan. 'Stand up straight, girl,' she whispered and then in her normal resonant tones added, 'An old friend of your mother's. From England. She married into the Beauchamps.' Tante Hermine gestured for Bruno to help her up. She moved heavily, refusing his arm, leaning on her cane, guiding them towards the other end of the room.

Anna, somewhat taken aback, wondered what on earth she would say to the woman. She tried hard in those few moments to remember her mother, but all she could come up with in certainty was the portrait. It had displaced the living presence.

'Why, it's uncanny,' she heard a tall erect woman with dark hair murmur in English. She was standing with her back to the window, gazing at her as if she had seen an apparition.

'Lady Charlotte, this is Anna, Lisabeth's younger daughter.'

'You hardly need to tell me.' The woman kissed her on both cheeks.

'And her husband, Bruno Adler,' Tante Hermine added as an afterthought.

'A pleasure, Lady Charlotte.' Bruno was punctilious.

There were tears in the woman's eyes. 'You'll excuse me, but it's as if time hadn't passed, as if Lisabeth were standing here before me.' She dabbed at her eyes. 'Come, tell me about yourself.'

What Anna wanted more than that was to hear stories about her mother. And at last, after her aunt had left them, after the string quartet had finished its performance, they came. She and Lady Charlotte and Bruno sat in a little group facing out towards the woods.

'I left for England, just after Lisabeth was married to your father,' Lady Charlotte began. 'We corresponded, of course, but it wasn't the same. Before that,' her eyes grew misty, 'we saw each other almost every day. We lived next door to each other, you know. She played the piano so wonderfully, even then. I sang. We used to fantasize about running away from home and becoming artistes.'

Anna laughed.

'Yes, yes, we were quite serious, tried dressing up as boys to see if we might pass, found out how much it would cost to travel to Paris.' Lady Charlotte smiled. 'Silly, schoolgirl whims. It never came to anything, of course. Lisabeth got married instead.' A shadow passed over her face. 'And then Bettina came along. I left for England, but that's another story.'

Anna was touched by the sadness in her face. 'Please will you come and visit us while you're in Vienna?'

'I'll try,' Lady Charlotte promised, composing her face. 'And you must both visit me in England. But first, I'm going to Munich. I shall call on Bettina, of course.'

Leaving her, Anna felt tearful, she didn't quite know why. She so rarely thought of her mother and her life. At least now she knew that her mother had had one real friend.

And it was friendship which preoccupied her until Wednesday arrived at last and she rang Katarina's bell.

Vibrant in a flowing lemon yellow tea gown, Katarina opened the door to her herself. 'I've given Martie the afternoon off, so we can have a proper tête-à-tête.' The word on her lips took on the sound of high intrigue, so that Anna felt excitement war with her shyness.

This time Katarina ushered her straight into her study. On the table stood a bowl of pale peach roses surrounded by smooth ceramic coffee cups, biscuits. Katarina poured, motioned Anna towards an armchair, served coffee, sat opposite her. Her eyes were warm, expectant.

'So, my newly married young lady, tell me all about it.'

Awkwardness came over Anna. She searched for words, couldn't find her tongue, finally simply shrugged.

Katarina's laugh tinkled musically. 'It isn't that bad, is it?'

'No, no,' Anna murmured. 'Not at all.'

'Well then?' Katarina paused, put a cigarette in a long golden holder, waited. 'Perhaps it will prove easier if I tell you about my marriage first?'

Anna nodded.

'Well, mine is a fine marriage, a typical marriage, let no one say otherwise.' Her eyes twinkled. 'A perfect social contract. I brought the culture, Hansel brought the money. I run the house, organize the higher things in life, provide society, entertainment. And he pays. A better ordering of things one couldn't imagine. He is a happy man.'

'I never thought of it like that.' Anna was lost in her friend's irony. She felt miserable, stumbled for words.

Katarina leaned forward and took her hands. 'Everything is simplified, my dear, if you choose to understand marriage for what it is.'

'And the more intimate things?' Anna asked softly. 'Where do they come in?'

'Ah, there's the rub.' Katarina swung her long legs on to the chaise longue and leaned back. 'A social contract can't cover everything.'

Anna hesitated. 'You don't have children?'

'No.' She faced her again, a little rueful. 'But luckily for me, Hansel has two boys. They're already in their twenties. We get along quite well now. And of course it means there's no pressure on me.' She looked at Anna expectantly but Anna avoided the question. Instead she asked, 'And love?'

Katarina burst into laughter. 'That, my dear, is a very large subject. I love Hansel well enough.'

'But do you . . .' Anna gestured vaguely, not knowing quite how to broach the subject.

'Do we have sexual relations?' Katarina put it for her blatantly.

Anna flushed.

'That is really what you want to talk about, isn't it?' Her voice was soft now.

Anna turned her eyes away, nodded.

Katarina paced for a moment. Anna could hear the swish of her dress behind her. Then came a cool hand, stroking her hair, gently, soothingly.

'Is it so very bad then?'

She felt the tears leap to her eyes. The sympathy in that murmuring voice, the caress in her hair, that delicate scent propelled them. Something, some image rose to the cusp of her mind, then vanished.

'It's . . . I don't know how to describe it. I feel so reduced. It's always so dark and I feel suffocated and . . .' She put her hands over her face.

'Poor Anna.' The hand stroked her hot temple. 'No pleasure.'

There was silence for a moment. Then Katarina moved round to face her, lifted her chin, so that Anna had to look at her. Dark eyes examined her, probed. Only after what seemed a very long time did she speak, and then her voice had a husky ring to it.

'Would you like to learn about pleasure, Anna?'

Anna hesitated, then nodded, swayed by the voice, uncertain of its intent.

'Come then.' Katarina smiled a different smile, took her hand, led her upstairs. 'This is to be just between us. But I think, I have a sense, that a little lesson in pleasure won't go amiss.'

'My bedroom.' Katarina opened a door. 'Look around, make yourself comfortable.'

Anna looked, saw a bed covered with a coral spread, a vast mirror which reflected another Klimt, its lavish central figure decked out like some ceremonial peacock, a chaise longue covered in striped satin. She perched on it.

Katarina walked over to her boudoir, dabbed a little perfume behind her ears. Then, slowly, she unpinned her thick dark hair, and began to brush it rhythmically.

Anna watched, mesmerized by her movements.

Katarina caught her gaze in the mirror, chuckled throatily. 'The first part of the lesson, Anna, consists in seeing just how very beautiful we are.' She pulled her up and positioned her in front of the mirror. 'You'll tell me if I do anything that displeases you,' she murmured.

Slowly, with intense care, she began to unclasp the many hooks and buttons of Anna's dress. The air around them grew still, expectant, broken only by the sound of Anna's sudden intake of breath as cool fingers found bared skin. The dress fell to the floor in a heap.

Katarina smiled dreamily, busying herself with Anna's bodice, smoothing the lace, inadvertently touching her breast. Anna stepped back.

'No more?' There was a challenge in Katarina's dark eyes.

Anna didn't answer, waited, unsure, wanting that tingle again, that unknown leap of her flesh, not wanting it.

Katarina took her hands, 'You do it. Watch,' she whispered. Standing next to her, her eyes on Anna's in the mirror, she shed her tea gown in one swift gesture. Beneath, she was wearing only a silk chemise and Anna could see the outline of her long legs, the full breasts. She lifted her hands to them, moved fingers in a slow circular motion. Her back arched, her lips curled into a smile. 'Don't be shy, little Anna. Here, I'll help you.'

Quickly she loosened Anna's stays, folded her arms round her so that her hands encircled her breasts, pressed, moved. Anna felt a strange tugging sensation in her loins. Without thinking, she covered Katarina's hands with her own, squeezed them closer.

'Yes, that's good,' the older woman murmured. In the mirror Anna could see that Katarina's eyes were half closed, her lips moving towards her ear. She whispered, warm breath, tickling, tickling, 'This is how we begin to prepare ourselves for our husbands. So easy. So easy to have pleasure.' She guided Anna's hand downwards, down to her own mound, the same sure circular motions. Anna's breath caught. Two hands, her own, Katarina's, she could no longer tell them apart, touching, teasing, delicious waves lapping at her, lips on her neck, light, light as feathers. And then that hand guiding, allowing her to touch, the silk of a chemise, another fuller breast, the tautness of a stomach, round, firm, the fragrance. Anna leaned against her dizzily.

'Yes, we'll lie down a little now.' Katarina led her to the bed. 'But just to rest. This is perhaps enough for a first lesson.'

Anna placed her head on Katarina's lap, soft. Felt those cool fingers gently stroking her hair again, her temples, thought of wide lawns, moist in morning freshness, breathed in green scent. And then suddenly she remembered. Another lap, other hands, but the same, stroking, consoling. A tearful child. Herself. In her mother's lap. A blonde head, looking down at her, worried, tender. 'Poor Annerl. A nasty fall. That naughty horse. There, there.' The tears pricked at her eyes again.

'Will you come for another lesson, Anna?' Katarina roused her from her reverie. There was a new note of urgency in her voice.

'If I may.'

'You may,' she said with mock imperiousness, then laughed abruptly. 'The Professor won't be happy.'

'Why do you go to him?' Anna asked.

Katarina rose, slowly pulled on her gown, pinned up her hair, shrugged. 'Because he's interesting. He teaches me things, though I think he thinks he's trying to cure me.' Her face grew mischievous, animated. 'It's like a little chess game, but played out on me.'

'Cure you of what?'

She laughed again. 'Why, of this.' She waved her arms theatrically. 'My pleasure. For my own good, of course.'

Anna, not certain she understood, wanted to ask more, but Katarina was in full dramatic flood. 'Do you know what he said to me the other day? It's a gem. Perfect. He said, probably thinking of our husbands, "There where men love",' her voice took on a deeper register, '"they rarely desire; and where they desire, they do not love." Now that will give you something to think about until we meet again.' She hugged her. 'Next Wednesday?'

'And women?' Anna asked, already half way down the stairs, not wanting to leave her, gripped by this turn in their conversation. 'What does he say about women?'

Katarina arched a single dark eyebrow. 'I shall ask him tomorrow. But the Professor isn't always quite so good on women.'

Over the next weeks, Anna sought out her new friend whenever it was possible. They went to galleries together, to the theatre and sometimes to that bedroom which had taken on for her the aura of an enchanted cave filled with a treasure trove of delights. She had learned to be bolder in her caresses, to chart the ebb and flow of Katarina's pleasure as well as her own. The thought of it all when she was outside that magic space made her heart beat secretly faster.

But perhaps more than anything, she liked to rest in Katarina's arms and listen to that animated voice telling stories, revealing the world. It was while they were lying together in this way one day that Katarina once again took on the Professor's voice to relay that women blossomed on secrets.

Anna wondered. She thought sometimes that she would like to tell Bruno what she had learned, to show him. But ever since the doctor's visit, he had not come to her room at night, as if he had taken advice, were under orders not to hurry. Sometimes, without thinking, because she was so full of Katarina's witty voice, she would begin to repeat to him some saying of hers. But the repetition inevitably brought a flush to her face, made her voice thick, so that she would find herself giggling stupidly. Bruno didn't seem to notice. He was being kind to her, so kind that she sometimes had the impression he was treating her as a convalescent. She didn't mind. Her life had taken on such an amplitude of late that even her dreams seemed richer. And in the morning she woke to the heady scent of Katarina's perfume.

Then, on a warm Friday evening in early June, the bubble suddenly burst. Bruno and she were having dinner together on the terrace when he cleared his throat in a way Anna had come to associate with an announcement she might not altogether like.

He folded his napkin carefully. 'Anna, there's something we must talk about. Your friend . . .'

Anna had an intuition of disaster. She dropped her spoon with a clatter. 'Sorry. Yes?'

'I want you to stop seeing Frau Hofer.'

Something snapped in her. 'Whatever for?' Her voice was strident, unnatural.

'Because. You must,' he said firmly.

So they had been discovered, she thought. In herself, in the magic of that room, she had never felt they were doing anything wrong. But, imagining Bruno spying on that scene, Anna shivered.

'I know you've grown close to her. She's a fine woman.'

Anna looked up at him, confused now.

'But her husband,' Bruno continued, shook his dark head, 'he's got himself mixed up in some shady dealings. With some Croatian nationalists,' he scowled. 'It's bound to hit the papers soon. There's been embezzlement.'

'But that's no reason for me to stop seeing Katarina. It's not her fault. She'll need her friends.'

Bruno's large face took on a ferocity she rarely saw. He rose to his full height, his eyes glinting. 'You are my wife, Anna. And as such, my representative. Neither I nor you can be seen to be having any dealings with the Hofers. That's final.'

With a scrape of her chair, Anna rushed from the table. For the first time since her marriage, she locked the door to her room.

The next morning, she stole downstairs early, hoping that Bruno might still be asleep and that she could telephone without him knowing. What a nuisance that it was Saturday and that he would be here all day.

On the breakfast table in the morning room, there was a letter lying next to her place. She tore it open. Katarina. The note was all too brief.

> The news may already have reached you of Hansel's difficulties. We shall be leaving Vienna tomorrow for I don't know quite how long. I'll write when I can. And miss you.

Anna trembled. She slowly folded the note back into its envelope. But then, with a sudden burst of decision, she ran from the room. Karl would drive her. She would go to Katarina now.

At the foot of the stairs, she almost bumped into Bruno. He blocked her way.

'Good morning, Anna. I hope sleep has restored your reason.'

She avoided his eyes.

'A letter from someone?'

Anna knew he was asking to see it, but she sheltered the note in the folds of her skirt.

'From Frau Hofer, is it?'

She nodded, unable to lie in response to a direct question.

'Fine. You must answer it straight away, on both our behalfs, and say how sorry we are about her situation, but how she must understand it is impossible for us to see her.'

He took her arm, gently enough, and guided her towards the secretaire in the library. 'I'll wait, Anna.'

The tears rose in her eyes. 'There's no point. They're leaving Vienna tomorrow.' She turned to him, stubbornly confronted him. 'I want to see her.'

'That's not possible, my dear, as I've explained.' He scrutinized her as if seeing something in her he had never noticed before. Then, in a softer voice, he said, 'I shall ask Karl to deliver the letter to her as soon as it's written. There. Will that make you happier?'

Anna felt that a little piece of her was dying forever.

FIVE

THE SHOT that was fired at the Austrian Archduke in the small Balkan town of Sarajevo and which marked the beginning of a war the dimensions of which the world had never known, also marked the end of Bettina's love affair with Johannes. She was not unaware, in retrospect, of the irony of this linkage of dates, of the triviality of her little personal moment in comparison with the movement of history. But so it had been. On the very day she read of the Archduke's assassination, she had woken with the sense of an imminent ending. Indeed, in the very act of reading the papers, the phrases she would use in her letter to Johannes were forming themselves in her mind.

The decision, the determination to make a break had been shaping itself within her for some months. She had begun to hate, not Johannes himself perhaps, but his need of her, this dark, insistent, inexorable need which acted itself out in their meetings in what were now almost ritualized ways. It would always begin with an argument, friendly enough at first, in which they exchanged views about this or that. Then something she said would unleash a vituperative barrage from him, her fairly innocuous words acting as a catalyst to a destructive torrent of nihilist utterances – about a person, an idea, a way of seeing, a movement.

The content was almost irrelevant in the face of that destructive emotion, so that by the end of it she felt flayed, the very fabric of her rent. And only then would he make love to her, slow, worshipping, mounting in passion, higher, ever higher, until she thought she could bear it no more. And then at the apogee, his lips buried in her tangled hair, he would whisper, his voice uncanny in its need, 'Save me, Bettina, save me.'

No. She could endure it no more. Confronted by that endlessly repeated need, she felt spent, exhausted. She was haunted too by the sense that he was cracking, that she could do nothing for him, that she had to flee before the crack widened to swallow her as well.

It had not always been like that. No. At the beginning, in those first months of discovery, it had been unutterably beautiful. Bettina had understood then what he had meant before their coming together, when he had talked of inhabiting a purer air, the transport out of the ordinary bounds of identity into a different keener self which was at once part of everything. She had felt free, powerful, alive to the movements of her newly awakened body, to the world. And alive to him, the taut energy of him, the beauty of his limbs, his eyes, the layers and depths of them, like the sea, the caress of his voice, his hands. Alive too, to his canvases, seeing them as if for the first time.

And there had been so many canvases those first months, as many, she sometimes thought, as the occasions and sites of their couplings. Every time she returned to Seehafen from the city, there were more as if while the world turned icy and white, snowbound around them, he had frenziedly to replenish it with the colour it had lost.

The work on the extension had had to be postponed until warmer weather. Only the foundations were in place when the first snows came. None of them, innocents that they were, had considered this eventuality. Or perhaps Klaus had, but had wanted to seize the moment, had wanted to help Johannes all those months ago. Help her. For she was still convinced that he had intended it all.

Bettina had told him, of course. Told him right after that first night. Had walked into the conservatory where he was tending his plants and simply stated it. 'I have slept with Johannes.'

'Oh?' He had looked at her for a moment. She couldn't read his face, didn't want to then.

'I simply wanted you to know,' she said and then turned and left him. She couldn't have borne questions, wouldn't tamper with the sense of magic in which she floated.

She had stayed in Seehafen for that whole first week, and then after that returned every week for a few days. She had a vague sense of Klaus's approval. He didn't speak to her about Johannes and she did nothing to disrupt the companionable order of their married life together, except to change the day of their at-homes to Wednesday. In fact, in those first months, she had worked with a new energy, written a dozen articles, made plans for a new nursery, addressed women's meetings. She felt exhilarated and the climax of that exhilaration as well as its fuel was the time she spent with Johannes.

Klaus would sometimes accompany her on the journey to Seehafen. The first time she had been nervous, but he had been easy with Johannes, had behaved like a benevolent, even indulgent host or father, who turned a blind eye to the personal affairs of his guests, his children. Sometimes indeed, on those weekends, she had felt jealous of the time Johannes spent with him. The two men seemed to have so much to say to each other: Johannes passionately evoking visions of a new art, the vanguard of a new world order, in which the creative spark in each individual would ignite, burn; Klaus listening, occasionally questioning, assenting.

It was on the anniversary of their wedding in February that she had had a sudden insight into Klaus's deeper thinking about her. They had been to the opera and then to dinner. At home, at the door of her room, he had taken her hand, held it. 'Bettina, now that you are so changed,' he looked away, too delicate to make any specific reference, 'would you consider . . .' He made a vague gesture, looked at her with eyes full of longing. 'I would so like a child,' he murmured.

Out of compassion, out of her new freedom, she had put her arms around him, felt moist lips seeking hers. But her stomach heaved at the touch of this different, this alien male body. She drew away, trying to find words that wouldn't come.

'I can't, Klaus.'

He looked so sad.

'Not now,' she added, trying to make it easier. 'But I'm loyal to you, loyal to the terms of our contract. I shan't leave you. Unless you want it.'

'No, no.' His voice was strangled. 'I don't want it.'

Only as she said it did she first recognize that indeed she had no desire to leave Klaus, to live with Johannes. There was something too wild about him, too unstable. Klaus was her home, her life as she believed in it, with all its projects, all its ideals. He had taken a risk on her and Johannes, gambled, perhaps lost. She respected him for the risk.

It was in March or April that things began to change, after Johannes had been to Berlin for his exhibition. She knew that he had seen his father, though he refused to speak of that, only fumed about the hideousness of life in that city, of the stupid burghers with their functional briefcases, their officiousness, their watches, their blindness to the misery around them, their equal blindness to beauty.

Bettina knew too that the reviews of his work had been scurrilous. She had read only two – one that spoke of the crass indulgences of inebriated youth; another that spoke in soaring generalities about decadence and disruptive elements, the lack of respect for aesthetic order. Johannes would not talk about this directly either. But the change in him was palpable.

As the leaves burst from their buds and the flowers began to scent the earth, he seemed to lose all interest in his work. There were no new canvases to meet her visits. He spent his time with the builders, happy enough in their presence, but scathing as soon as they had gone about the actualization of his own plan, daily changing his mind about details, paring them away, so that the structure which took shape was far simpler than what he had originally conceived.

Then he lost interest in that as well. He began to spend time in Munich, rented a new studio, started to call on her at home, telephone at work, disrupting the order of her life with his exhortations, demanding to see her at impossible times.

And then there was the uncanny frenzy of his love-making. It frightened her, left her feeling obliterated, used up. What had started as liberation had begun to have all the characteristics of destruction.

She would try, Bettina thought, to express some of this in her letter. But not all. No. Some things were better left unexpressed. She would simply tell him that she still believed in him, had faith in him, but felt her own life was at stake. And she had to make use of that.

Of the baby she had discovered in this last month she was carrying, she would make no mention.

Johannes sat in his studio reading and re-reading Bettina's letter. On the table in front of him one bottle of wine stood empty, the second well past the half-way mark. He poured himself another glass and downed it as if the thirst of the desert were upon him.

So she was casting him off, without even doing him the honour of telling him so to his face. Sending him a letter instead, like that she might write to a merchant whose goods were no longer required. 'Thank you dear sir for the fine services you have rendered in the past. Unfortunately of late they have not been quite of the quality one might desire. Therefore I regret to tell you, etc. etc.'

With a savage gesture, Johannes stood and flung his chair across the room. It split one of the canvases lodged against the wall and in fury he walked over to it, kicked it, made the rip larger.

Then he laughed. Yes, it was all there in that neat orderly script of hers, in each turn of phrase which spoke of a duty to herself, to her work, to the struggle for existence. The platitudes at every turn, positing the general, higher good against the particular, the bright spark of individual life. Not unlike his father, really. Why, her husband was better, understood more.

He laughed again uproariously.

Yes, if the truth were known, Bettina had resisted him, almost from the first. Even when she had begun to allow him to take her clothes off, to gaze on that fine slender naked body, to explore its coolness with his lips, she would instantly clothe herself as soon as or even before the last amorous caress had reached its destination, arm herself with her petticoats and her ideas. All his words, which she had begun to echo, about the force of the erotic, about the salvation of the sexual body, had done nothing to counter that resistance. It was unnatural. Each week, she returned dutifully to her husband, never later than the preappointed moment, never forgetting her books, her papers.

Johannes slumped into his one dusty easy chair. Yet, if he were honest, it was that very resistance which had first stimulated him, that coupled to a sense of her fineness, that statuesque grace of hers – only sculpture could render it. The delicacy and susceptibility of her body – so unlike her mind – never failed to surprise him and to rouse him to almost violent passion. At first when she had come to him, he had felt a rare ecstasy in her shy touch, as if together they might relearn the world. And ideas, work had poured out of him, almost as offerings to mark her weekly return.

Then it had all suddenly changed, after Berlin. He had sold every single painting in that show, apart from the ones he had given Klaus in repayment for his generosity. Yet the notices and slander had disheartened him. Why couldn't they understand? Why were they so blind? As blind as his father who had appeared the day before the opening.

Johannes rubbed his eyes, not wanting to remember.

He hadn't seen him at first. They were busy hanging canvases, talking. Then that cavernous voice had boomed out, so that everyone could hear, 'So this is how you spend your time. Painting disgusting filth, splattering it on the walls.'

He had ushered the gallery assistants away, faced his father's jowly face, hidden by the ever-trim beard, the hard yet watery eyes beneath the shaggy brows.

'I didn't invite you here. Please go,' Johannes had begun with steely politeness.

'Didn't *invite* me? As if I needed or wanted an invitation. I just came to check what uses my name was now being put to. And it's as I expected. Utter filth, underwritten by the authority of my name.'

'Fine. I'll change it.' Johannes had felt hatred beginning to choke him. 'I'll take Mother's name,' he had spat out. Their eyes had locked. He could see the twitch moving in his father's cheek, the guilty lowering of the lids which always accompanied any evocation of his mother.

'No, no, that won't be necessary.' His father had crumpled and Johannes had felt his spirits soar.

'Go now. Please.'

Then there had been that note of pleading, that lying whine. 'You could do better, Johannes. You were so brilliant once. A worthy son. You could have made a fine lawyer, an estimable citizen in this great nation of ours.'

Johannes had walked away, sickened by the repetition of that old saw. But the voice had followed him.

'I hear you've taken up with one of the von Leinsdorf daughters. If she weren't married, she would make a good match. Even now perhaps. I would welcome some grandchildren.'

Johannes stopped in his tracks. He felt sick. Bettina's name on those dry, lying lips. How could his father know about her? They had almost never been in public together. He must be spying on him as he had once done in the past, sending out his minions, shadowing his movements, so that he had begun to feel as if he were incarcerated in some boundless prison. Either that or Bettina had spoken.

He left the gallery without looking back. If he had, he felt he might at last have pummelled the man, as he had so often wanted to do before – ever since as a small child he had first become aware of that voice, chiding, ordering, delimiting every step of his and his mother's existence, so that everything from the colour of his suits to the books he read was under his father's rapacious control. If only that fat, blubbery body had breathed its last. If only it were stretched out on a slab of marble, then he, Johannes, could breathe at last.

That evening, despite himself, he had described the first part of the encounter with his father to one of his oldest Berlin friends. Gert had laughed. 'Jealous. The old man is jealous. He knows he's being displaced, in the eyes of the world as well as his own. So he wants to eradicate you, take away your name. As simple as ABC. Forget about him.'

But Johannes found it hard to forget, particularly in relation to Bettina.

When he had returned to Seehafen and seen her again, he had been haunted by a sense that she had somehow betrayed him, that she now belonged to his father's camp. As they talked and argued, he began increasingly and irrationally to feel that she shared the general estimation of his work, that she was only just holding back from criticizing him. His love-making became frenzied, as if he were looking in her body for a confirmation that couldn't be found.

The harder Johannes searched, the more it eluded him, just as his painting had begun to elude him, had begun to seem an activity undertaken in vain. He spent hours walking around in a daze, feeling watched, trapped. And when she came to him, he would lash out at her. She was resisting him, she had so much to give and wouldn't part with it. He would make love to her savagely, wanting to possess the secret she was hiding, unable to attain the transport which had once so easily been theirs, thinking that what she held back was the very secret of life.

He began to do what he had rarely done in the past: to seek out women in the streets, to find easy comfort with one of the artists or performers in the Stephanie circle. What he really sought was not a woman, but oblivion.

And now Bettina had given him up. He was expendable.

With the glimmer of irony that comes from the bottom of a bottle, he saw his whole life as a series of futile lies, the last of which was that it was possible sincerely to hail Woman as a supreme sexual and revolutionary force and to emerge from that personally unscathed.

Why, Bettina was no better than his mother! Johannes stared dizzily into his empty glass, trying to trap the thought that had swum hazily to the surface of his mind. Yes, in essence just like his mother. She, too, had betrayed him, turned him over to his father, remained utterly passive when the man brayed at him, fulminated, struck him. He could still hear the hiss of that strap, feel it welting his skin, his teeth on his lips holding in the cry, holding it in until he could taste blood.

After that first remembered punishment, he would never shed tears in front of his father. Had never done so, not even after the severest beating – that time when he was eight and his father had tied his hands behind his back, sat him at his little desk, and kept him there for a day and a night, watching him, preventing sleep, until he had exhorted a promise from him that he would never draw a naked body again. Ha! It was then that he had learned that there was no reason to tell the truth if it was to one's advantage to tell a lie. But never to oneself. No.

And throughout all that his mother had never intervened, only looked on with compassionate eyes. Suddenly, he hated her for her compliance, her passive wretchedness. That was one lie he had told himself, it now came to him. The lie that his mother couldn't have saved him from his father's clutches. Like Bettina. A betrayer. With a violence he didn't know he possessed, Johannes grasped his glass and crushed it between his fingers. Blood trickled down from his thumb where a sliver had embedded itself.

Barely five weeks later, Johannes Bahr was one amidst a horde of young men who volunteered to fight for their various nations. It was not patriotism that drew him. Johannes – and he was not alone in this – wanted nothing more than to see with his own eyes that destruction which would once and for all signal the death of the old world, which would inevitably turn it upside down. Whatever emerged from the fires of that destruction, it could only be an order better than the one that had come before.

As he donned the rough, ill-fitting uniform which conferred on him a welcome anonymity, a thrill ran through him. To confront death, to risk death heroically was a greater adventure than any he had ever undertaken. And despite the tedium of those weeks of basic training in Munich, the drills, the standing to attention and the standing at ease, the endless goose-stepping, the blaring voices of the NCOs, he felt himself being cleansed, the seeds of a transformation taking root.

It was in this spirit that, just before leaving Munich, he went to bid goodbye to Bettina and Klaus. He had not seen her since the day her fateful letter had arrived. He had not even bothered to respond to it. But now, with the whiff of gunpowder already in his nostrils, he let the large brass knocker clatter on the door of the house in Bogenhausen for what might be the last time.

Bettina experienced his unexpected arrival as something of a shock.

She had willed herself during these last weeks not to think of him – there was so much else to think about.

The world had suddenly been thrust into turmoil, from one day to the next, with no intervening logic, like one of those abrupt jumps in the moving picture she had been taken to see. Her body too seemed to be subject to those same radical shifts. So that it was quite easy to pretend to herself that in the midst of all this she hadn't even noticed Johannes's silence.

But now, confronted by his physical presence, she had a sudden desire to fling herself into his arms. He looked so spare, strong, utterly self-contained and in his eyes there was that faraway gaze which she always associated with his genius. She wanted that gaze focused on her, wanted his body pressed against hers, his hands sensitive to the life growing within her. She shivered, forced herself to keep still, let the men talk, only half listening to their words – male words, about postings and units and guns. Klaus looked sad. He had been declared not fit enough, too old. She had been relieved, but she worried about his despondency. She would tell him about the baby now, soon, when Johannes was gone. Perhaps it would cheer him.

Suddenly Bettina found herself speaking, her voice odd in her own ears, 'So the old pacifism is gone now. It's off into the world of machines and flags held high, Johannes. The shift in you has been rather swift, hasn't it?' There was a savagery in her tone she hadn't altogether intended.

He focused on her for the first time, his gaze dark, bitter.

'New strategies for new times, Frau Eberhardt. One cannot stay in the same place too long.'

He bowed, as if they had never shared a bed together, lain in each other's arms. So be it, Bettina thought. She held herself tall.

And then he added, 'I was helped towards the light by someone near to me.'

But his eyes were already elsewhere and she wasn't certain he meant her, had intended it as a final attack. She refused the guilt.

'Lights are a little dim these days,' she murmured, letting him take her hand, noting that he barely touched it with his lips.

And then he was saying goodbye to Klaus and was gone, leaving her with a sense of loose ends, with a dejection echoed in Klaus's entire demeanour.

Without pausing to think, she confronted Klaus. 'I'm expecting a baby, Klaus,' she said in as even a tone as she could manage.

Emotions fluttered in rapid succession across his face. He looked at her, hesitated, began to pace the extent of the room, back and forth, back and forth, like a caged creature.

Bettina grew increasingly uncomfortable. She hadn't prepared for this moment, had refused to think about it. She wasn't ready for the pain, the fear, the confusion she read in Klaus's face. Why hadn't she thought about it more? At last, to fill the unbearable silence, she said softly, 'It will be your child, Klaus, if you want it. And mine. But if you don't, I'll go. I'll manage on my own.'

Klaus stopped in his tracks. He looked at her in utter astonishment. 'But Johannes? I thought you would want to be with Johannes.'

'No, that is finished.' She turned away from him, watched the sluggish movement of the river through the long windows. 'Quite finished.'

'I see,' he breathed. A slow smile began to spread over his features, stopped at his eyes. 'And Johannes?'

'I shall never tell him.' Bettina spun round to face him. Her fists were clenched. 'His going makes it easier.'

'Bettina, the poor man. If it's his child . . .'

'It's my child.' She was adamant. 'If you don't want it to bear your name, share in its upbringing, then I'll go.'

He put a staying hand firmly on her shoulder, as if her departure were imminent. 'No, Bettina, it's not that.'

'I thought you wanted a child.'

There was a plea in her eyes and voice, such as he had never experienced before.

'I do. Very much.' His tone was warm. 'It's only that Johannes . . .' He shrugged.

'Johannes has no interest in paternity, except to loathe it,' Bettina said acidly, only realizing as she did so that she could not, however hard she tried, imagine Johannes as a father. 'It will be ours, if you want that,' she said fiercely. 'Yours and mine. And I shall never tell. You can trust me.'

'I always trust your word, Bettina. That always.'

She smiled. With a completely uncharacteristic gesture, she took his hand and placed it just below her waist. She held it there, feeling suddenly safe, but as bewildered as he was, by the implications of what had just passed between them.

* * *

Neither Klaus nor Bettina was amidst the throng who gathered at the station the following day to wave and cheer and shout as the latest group of volunteers, Johannes in their midst, made their way to war. Squeezed amongst his fellows, festive garlands brightening their uniforms, he too waved from the train window, blew kisses at women and children, raised his voice in song.

The display of patriotic fervour induced a state of exhilaration: they were all suddenly heroes, larger than life, pitiless soldiers standing apart from the common fray. And as the train lurched into motion, Johannes, for perhaps the first time in his life, felt at one with his select group of fellow men.

It was a feeling which stayed with him through the journey, through the stops and starts of the train, through the weeks spent at the rain-drenched training camp in Pfalz. It persisted despite the corrosive smell of the old chemical factory in which they were quartered, despite the increasingly sodden straw and slimy blankets in which they slept, despite the growing, almost sadistic, severity of the drills to which they were subjected.

Fitter than most because of his long-time interest in the well-tuned body, unafraid of officers or circumstance, always willing to speak out if he saw injustice being done, Johannes soon drew round him a small band of younger men, boys really, who hung on his every word and gesture. He found strength in their admiration and over the weeks felt a growing sense of responsibility towards them.

He was particularly fond of Hans, a stocky blond youth of eighteen, son of Bavarian peasants. There was a sensitivity around his mouth which belied his stolidity, a stubborn resistance in the depths of his blue eyes when the NCOs called for greater and greater exertions. Like Johannes, he always performed as if he had just risen from a soft feathered bed and had eaten a luxuriant breakfast, instead of the stale bread and lumps of fat which formed the basis of their diet.

When, in the few brief moments of respite they were given, Johannes pulled out the paper and pens and colours he had carefully packed in his sack, and began to sketch, Hans would look on with something akin to awe. A bond, at first largely wordless, grew between the two men. Johannes began to count on Hans's steadfast presence by his side, to think of him as the younger brother he had never had.

What fuelled Johannes through the repetitive tedium of those weeks in Pfalz was the certain sense that soon they would see action, would be in the line of fire. But by the middle of November, gloom had begun to cut swathes into his expectation. Men who had arrived after him had left for the Front, while he had to wait and wait: he could bear the waiting no longer. During the Commanding Officer's next visit to the camp, before he had a chance to make his rounds, Johannes broke regulations, marched up to him, saluted and announced, 'It must be my turn. Now. Today.'

The officer looked at him queerly, turned to the Sergeant Major with a question.

'Private Johannes Bahr, Herr Kommandant.'

'Ah yes.'

Clever little eyes seemed to examine him intimately, take the gauge of him. The man coughed. 'A message has made its way to me from your father, Herr Dr Professor Karl Gustav Bahr.' He coughed again. 'It seems you are not an altogether stable element.'

Johannes barely managed to contain his clenched fists. His eyes bored into the officer's. With an effort of the will, he kept his voice even. 'As stable as the next man, I can assure you, Herr Kommandant. Try me.'

The man turned to the Sergeant Major. They exchanged words Johannes couldn't hear. Then he looked at him again, a sly smile forming in his swarthy cheeks. 'The Sergeant Major tells me that the only untoward thing he has been able to distinguish is the fact that you draw.'

'Yes, sir, it is my work.'

'Your only work here is to be a soldier. To fight for the Fatherland,' the CO barked.

'It has hardly affected my soldiering,' Johannes muttered. 'As for fighting, I have yet to see any. Which is why I am standing here.'

'Sir.'

'Sir.' He paused, met the man's eyes.

More murmuring between the two men. Johannes waited. To be followed, pursued, even here. He wanted to shout. To jab his bayonet into a body, watch it squirm. His father's fat persecuting body.

'All right, Private Bahr, you leave tomorrow morning. Together with four more men from your troop.' The CO's tone was clipped. Sly eyes probed Johannes again. 'You will bring your drawings to Headquarters straight away, for my particular attention. Dismissed, Private Bahr.'

'Yes sir, thank you sir.' Johannes saluted.

'Thank me at the war's end, Private.'

Johannes had a distinct sense that the man was laughing soundlessly.

It was only after the train had rumbled through a darkened Metz that Johannes knew for certain that he had arrived at the Front. They could see nothing but the shadowy outlines of blasted trees. Yet the din was overwhelming, a thunderous, persistent clamour, which pummelled one, anaesthetized the mind, annihilated thought.

The train stopped in the middle of nowhere. Their packs heavy on their backs, their boots caked with mud, they were marched through the wet night, until they reached what had been a French village. The streets were pitted with shell holes. Around them stood the skeletons of houses, their walls blackened, their windows shattered.

They were led into a church, their stumping boots echoing oddly on its stone floor. Here they slept, huddled near the altar. A Madonna, pitted with shrapnel, her nose and arms missing like some antique goddess, watched over them with a smile of unearthly calm. When dawn glimmered through the splintered colours of the windows, Johannes quickly sketched her, Hans and the others at her feet. For the briefest of moments, he thought of Bettina. Then the day took over.

Later Johannes would think of it both as the first and the last day of his life.

From the battery with which they were stationed, they could see the Moselle, its waters swirling with autumn rain, winding its way through the landscape. Closer to, there were the French trenches, their soldiers almost visible on a clear day to the naked eye.

But it was not what he could see that first imprinted itself on Johannes's mind. It was the smell, the smell of his own dug-out, a vile odour of putrefaction, of rotting bodies, of blood, of stale human sweat. Of fear mingled with the high whiff of disinfectants, of chloride and creosote. Only the whistle of bullets, the rattle of machine-guns, the burst of fire which sent the earth flying could wipe out that smell which permeated the very bread they ate.

On his first day in the sodden mass of the trench, Johannes sank back during a lull in the firing, only to find that his hand was resting on the remains of a corpse, its limbs being gnawed by an army of fattened rats.

The bile rose in him. He retched. The soldier at his side, seeing his white face, laughed eerily. 'You'll soon get used to that. Too soon.'

He proved right. The din of bombardment, the explosions, the uproar, were such that they numbed one into a leaden stupor. Johannes began to think that the only difference between himself and the dead was that *he* was impelled to scratch. He was suddenly prepared to do anything to avoid remaining for too long in this open grave. By the end of his fourth week, he was volunteering for each and every action, no matter how perilous. Action swept the mind clear of all reflection, obliterated the vermin, the slugs and beetles and lice which fed on living and dead alike. It worked as an intoxicant, produced a waking delirium which became for Johannes the very condition of war.

The battery commander had noticed Johannes's keen eye, and had seen the quick drawings he executed during the lulls in battle. He sent him to the observation post, situated in a little pocket near the crest of the hill above their trench. Field glasses glued to his eyes, Johannes would bark out any movements he saw in the opposite line, or in the devastated French town beyond.

On his third day, he saw a company of French soldiers moving through the town towards the front line. 'Range twenty-three hundred,' he cried to the telephonist, heard the number echoed, then within seconds came the zing and whine of cannon and artillery. A cloud of dust obstructed his vision. When it cleared, he saw the commotion of scattering soldiers, the dead and wounded on the ground, faceless. The enemy.

'Direct hit,' the telephonist shouted. The men cheered.

Johannes heard his own voice raised in a triumphal cry. His heart was beating wildly, his palms were moist, and as his fellows thudded him on the back, he felt the thrill of a hunter who has found his prey. Intoxicated.

But it wasn't enough. He wanted more. Thoughts still occasionally rumbled at the back of his mind, of home, of Bettina, his father, of injustices suffered, of the living beings who were now corpses. The thoughts had to be wiped out.

He told his sergeant he spoke French, volunteered for a reconnaissance patrol. He could understand, see, report. Hans and two other men came with him. They stole out in the dead of night across no man's land through a recent break in the barbed wire, flattening themselves into the mud when the flares burst and illuminated the ghostly stretch of land.

In the light of one of these flares, he saw an arm by his side – just an arm, with a German eagle tattooed on it.

They rushed on, on into the shelter of a little wood, skimming soundlessly between devastated trees, bayonets at the ready. Where the trees cleared into meadow, they heard voices. They stopped, held their breath. Automatically, Johannes registered the words. Ammunition was being moved. When? The men had grown silent. He could feel their wariness. A twig cracked. They had been heard. Johannes raced forward, Hans just behind him. A bullet whistled past them, then another. Two men. Mere shadows. Johannes lunged his bayonet into the first, twisted it. Flesh resisting, giving way. He fell with the effort, his limbs entangled with the Frenchman's. For a split second in the dim light he made out the outline of a face, eyes wide, curly-haired, delicate. Like a woman.

He shivered, registering the fact. Then he leapt up, pulled his bayonet from the dead body. His senses felt almost painfully alert. A wonderful clarity filled him, an electric stillness not unlike that which followed the act of love.

He saw Hans standing over the second splayed body. He clapped him on the shoulder, pulled him away. They ran, their feet slipping through the mud, back into the shelter of the blasted wood.

As the weeks grew into months, Johannes became known as a man without fear. He threw grenades with deadly accuracy, getting as close to the enemy as possible. Twice, after raids, bathed in sweat and blood, he carried wounded mates back to their camp. He was promoted to corporal, awarded medals, became something of a local hero. There were many like him: men who seemed not to understand danger, who took on perilous missions as if they were going out for a loaf of bread. Death drew them like its warm smell.

Johannes understood nothing of it, didn't question it, didn't think. Action was like an eagle's flight in high mountain air. Intoxicating, yet strangely peaceful.

In the gaps between action, he played tarok with his mates, jotted random undated notes in his diary. Time had ceased to exist, apart from the routine of the trench. He also drew, painted small chaotic images in livid colour, violent forms which replicated the splintered life around him, the explosions, the shell bursts, the fractured bodies. And exorcized them. Anything to escape that smell, that sense of slow decomposition, or the tedious hours of respite spent in those concrete underground shelters as close and airless as tombs.

Later, when his ordinary mind began to work again, Johannes would think that he painted to exorcize war itself.

From home, he had had almost no correspondence – a note from Klaus wishing him well and carrying Bettina's best regards; a letter from his friend Gert in Berlin. He looked at them blankly and then crumpled them up, turning to smile inchoately at Hans, to exchange a few words. The two of them spoke little, but were always together, the tall agile corporal always shadowed by the stockier youth.

Sometimes the latter, when they were back at the rest camp, would hum slow melodious wordless songs, while Johannes drew. In his jacket pocket, next to his chest, Hans kept a stark jagged image Johannes had pencilled of him. Johannes began to think of him as the only aspect of Germany worth saving, a wild forest flower, simple, modest, almost hidden by the rampant, more aggressive vegetation, but so pure in form and detail and colour that it far outvalued the rest.

They took their ten-day leave together, not enough time to go home where Johannes in any event had no desire to go. Instead they travelled to Ludwigshafen, tramped along the borders of the Rhine, gazed at fairy-tale castles, ate bread and cheese in fields so peaceful they seemed to belong to a different world. A small riverboat took them slowly to Mainz, meandered along the graceful curves of the river.

The wonder Johannes read in Hans's eyes made him feel mellow, gave him a hope he couldn't quite name, as if here lay the proof that the cut and thrust and noise of what he had always acerbically understood to be male relations were not the norm, but merely a distortion. With Hans, Johannes grew kind. Even when they returned to the Front, that kindness, that mellowness, persisted.

At the end of February in the midst of a freak snowfall, they were moved further up the line. Johannes didn't know why. None of them had much inkling of the direction the war was taking. Life – and death – centred in their own little sector. Days passed, distinguished only by the disappearance of men and the arrival of replacements. He had stopped reading the newspapers. The print, with its blatant talk of victories, its crass disparagement of the enemy, bore no relation to what he experienced.

To arrive at their new position, they had to plod for miles through a communication trench. Then they were out in the night air, tramping through a wood, stumbling over tree stumps, avoiding the pools of boggy water which filled the shell holes. Thin flakes of snow had covered the earth with spots of eerie white. Johannes was mesmerized by the filigree delicacy of that whiteness. He stooped where it had gathered more thickly to feel its coolness, picked up a handful. And then in front of him, he heard the blast of an explosion, shouts.

He fell to the ground, pulling Hans down beside him, shouting to the others. Clods of earth fell on their heads, rubble, the whip of a branch. Then silence. He looked up. In front of him the mine had deposited a boot, thick with fresh blood, a foot still trapped within it. He leapt up shuddering. So much death – he had thought himself inured. But the lace of the snow against that reddened boot filled him with horror. He met Hans's shocked eyes, stumbled on, a cloud of despair suddenly settling on his shoulders like an evil omen.

In their new dug-out, he was moved to machine-gun duty, Hans at his side, tending to the gun, to the flow of ammunition. The action of the machine-gun dispelled his despair. Corpses became impersonal again, distant targets in a boy's game. Battle seemed as natural an occurrence as the rising and setting of the sun.

On four panels at his post, Johannes painted a detailed rendition of the lay-out of enemy territory. The painting made it real for him. It also provided his fellows with a constant source of amusement. A map for idiots, they termed it, but it was a gentle form of teasing. One by one they would come to him during rest times and ask for a drawing of themselves for girlfriends or mothers. Sometimes, Johannes complied.

The seasons passed: summer increased the stench but was preferable to the mud of winter and spring. The back-up trenches grew more sophisticated, complex rabbit warrens of concrete, where the officers would occasionally ask Johannes to paint a replica of some dreamt-of natural world on their walls. Each move to a new location, each brief leave, was a relief, breaking for a short while the repetitive motion of the machine-gun which had begun to monopolize even his sleeping hours.

In the early spring of 1916, the site of their newly extended line was even more oppressive than usual. There were no hills, only flat barren fields growing an excrescence of barbed wire between themselves and the enemy. On their first night in their new position, Johannes, Hans and two recent arrivals were ordered off into listening posts amidst the barbed wire of no man's land.

They set off through the darkness, two by two in separate directions, running, crawling, zigzagging, cutting their way, the shells whizzing over their heads until they took shelter in one blasted hole and then another, ever closer to the enemy line.

At last, when they found a hole so close that they could see the French rifles, they leapt into it, waited. The explosions grew less frequent, the night quieter. They listened.

And then the howl came, an agonized cry of pure pain, drilling into their souls. The youth beside Johannes trembled. He put a hand on the boy's shoulder to calm him. But the howl returned, naked, piercing, reproaching them all with its agony, marking the hours of the night like a discordant church bell. It turned everything about them to stillness, so that its pain was uncannily audible, unique, individual. By the time the sky began to lighten, Johannes could bear it no more. The cry was an indictment of them all, of this whole wretched war, of the system that had brought it into being.

Leaving the youth, Johannes ran in the direction of the injured man, easily tracing his cry in the ominous quiet to a position in the field some hundred metres back. As its tones grew closer, there was a sudden burst of shell fire: his own movement had broken the hypnotic spell the howling voice had cast.

Johannes started to zigzag wildly. Sweat poured out of him. And then he saw him, saw the man hanging on the barbed wire, as if on a crucifix, pinned to it by the force of a blast, blood draining out of him. Johannes felt an answering howl rising in him, his voice becoming a sheer jagged edge of pain. 'Hans, Hans, Hans.'

His friend's face was a pale mask, already a death's head. Then, his eyes fluttered open. The horror in them burned into Johannes's entrails. 'Hans, Hans,' Johannes murmured now, soothing his friend, himself, 'it'll be all right.' He started to clip wildly at the wire, trying to cut him free, cutting a portion of the wire with him, the tears clouding his vision. Finally, he managed to heave Hans on to his shoulders. Stumbling, tripping, he pulled him along, the battle now blaring over their heads, the shells coming from all directions. And then there was a blinding flash of brightness before his eyes, like fireworks exploding in uncanny profusion, blue, yellow, green, red.

And then nothing.

* * *

Out of that nothingness, gradually, only very gradually, vague pale shapes began to emerge as if all his powers of perception were glued behind a milky screen. Fluttering ghostly forms came towards him and then swam away into a dreamy vastness. Sometimes their lips moved, but he couldn't distinguish their sound.

Then the sounds came into focus, saying incomprehensible things, but soothing in their tone. Once he thought he might be in heaven, a creamy distant place of gently floating images. But then there were other sounds, not soothing these, but moaning, crying, like children in the dark, yet still distant. He couldn't touch them. He tried, reached towards them, but the effort was too great. He was bound, tied to a smooth boulder, his legs and arms splayed. His father's face railed at him, punishing, spitting out shells which exploded inside him, burning, painful, leaving the odour of charred flesh.

On the day when Johannes realized that his limbs wouldn't respond to his command, everything else suddenly came into jarring focus. He was in a hospital ward. The walls of vomit green were flanked by beds, each of which held a grey-blanketed moaning figure. He was one of them. One of his legs was in plaster; bandages covered his chest and one arm. He couldn't move his head. There was an acute pounding at his temples, behind his lids when he closed his eyes.

He smelled her before he saw her, the lulling fragrance of ferns, of apple-green soap. A woman. Bettina, he thought dimly. How long had it been since he had felt a woman, heard that soft rustle of a skirt? His eyes fluttered open.

'Good morning, Corporal Bahr. A very good morning. We *are* better today, aren't we?' A hearty, cheerful voice. Not Bettina, no, but cool fingers on his wrist, and when he looked up, grey eyes, a curling smile.

He tried his disused voice. 'Where am I?'

'You *are*, that is the first thing.' A laugh. The delicious sound of crystal tinkling. 'And very lucky you are to be, too. Another few millimetres, and the shell would have travelled into that main artery there,' she pointed to his neck, 'and my voice would have come to you to the trilling of harps.'

She waited for her words to take effect and then hurried on. 'Where you are is the military hospital in Strasburg. And what you are is a hero, like all my boys here.' She made a sweeping gesture with her hand. 'Now, in a few moments, the doctor will be round and we'll see to that dressing.

And if the pain is too bad, we'll give you a little more morphine, so you can just rest and get better. All right? Just call for Matron Kanzel.'

Johannes smiled, his face aching with the effort. She looked like an angel, he thought, with that stiff blue dress and that funny little hat perched on her smooth blonde head. He closed his eyes.

And then with a sudden stabbing pain it all came back to him in a swift series of unrelated fragments, things he didn't remember registering, things he didn't want to remember. The trench with the rats rustling through it, the dead resting in its niches; the thunderous din, a clamour of screams and shells; his bayonet piercing that resisting flesh, pushing, pushing; the massed mutilated bodies by that concrete bunker, like so many dismembered dolls, piled up one on top of the other in their different uniforms, their limbs intermingled in a parody of love. And that scream . . . No, no, Johannes opened his eyes abruptly. The doctor, the relief of a living presence.

Johannes stayed at the military hospital in Strasburg for some three months. For a good half of that time, he had no clear sense of what was dream, what was memory, and what was the passage of the present. The morphine deadened the pain, but induced a state of such heightened cerebral sensation that life needed little of the stimulus of actuality to take on a hallucinatory acuteness.

The merest pressure of the matron's fingers was enough to induce a sense of bliss; the disappearance of the man in the next bed, a state of panic, in which the figure of Hans, pinned to barbed wire, loomed larger than life. Days and nights rolled into each other in a time out of time which was not unlike what he had experienced at the Front.

As his wounds began to heal, the plaster come off, and the doses of morphine grow smaller, an empty depression set in. The only talk in the ward was of the movement of troops, of victories and heroism here, of defeat and scabrous cowardly enemies there. He learned of the sinking of the *Lusitania*, the Zeppelin raids in Britain, the Austrian victory at Lemberg.

But what did these victories mean? It should now be clear to everyone, he thought, that Germany was nothing other than a bloated octopus, its rapacious tentacles grasping for power, in Europe, in Africa, obliterating its young in its blind pursuit. Like all the other states engaged in this war to end all wars. And it had gone on for almost two years already. He had a sense of utter hollowness, a lack of purpose which nothing seemed to fill except a hatred for his own febrile body, the dizziness which still overcame him when he walked, the wretchedness of his weak flesh.

One day when a blaze of sunshine illuminated the ward, the matron brought him his sack. In it he found his diary, his colours, pens, a sheaf of drawings which he could not remember executing. He gazed at images of frenzied excitement, gathered troops, men with guns, barbed wire, dismembered and wounded bodies, bloody. The energy of the images filled him with incredulity. How could they have risen from his hand? Hurriedly he put them away. Then, balancing a piece of paper on his tray, he began to sketch unthinkingly, automatically: the men in the beds around him, their sallow, shocked faces, their stumbling gait, like blinded creatures, whom gravity had betrayed. He tore the paper up, covered his eyes, rubbing them, rubbing.

He tried again, blotting his gaze to the torment around him. When he saw what his hand was executing, he crumpled the piece of paper bleakly. Hans, trapped on the wire, his mouth round with his cry. No, he would draw no more. The next afternoon, when Matron Kanzel, thinking to busy him, brought him fresh paper, he looked at it with a kind of terror and turned his face to the wall.

A few days later, a figure he only half remembered appeared by his bedside.

'Corporal Bahr.' The man saluted.

Johannes took in a thin, ascetic face, a fine arched nose, fair hair. The features swam into place.

'Lieutenant Schrader.' Johannes didn't return the salute, though he had nothing against the man who had always treated him fairly.

'I thought I would try to see you during my leave. It occurred to me that no one might have told you what happened.' He paused, looked Johannes in the eyes.

'Hans, Private Müller. Is he . . . ?'

The man shook his head, 'Died before we could get the medics to him. After the men dragged you back into our trench. Apparently you keeled over just metres from it.' Admiration flashed across his features. 'Broken leg, apart from the shells, the shrapnel.' He gestured vaguely to his neck, chest, arm.

'And Private Müller?' Johannes insisted, saw the man's face grow grim.

'The men said they had to pull you apart. The wire, you know, the blood.' He looked away. 'He spoke your name before he died. I thought you might want to know. You were friends, weren't you?'

Johannes nodded, trembling.

'The men were much relieved that the howling had stopped. It ate its way into them. Morale was low.' He stopped himself, realizing that he had transgressed the bounds of what should pass between officer and soldier. 'Still, you'll be pleased to have this,' Schrader smiled thinly and pulled a letter from his jacket. 'Two months' leave. After you're released from here. Not bad, eh.'

Johannes stared blankly at the piece of paper.

'Maybe by then it will all be over.'

Johannes didn't answer.

The lieutenant shuffled uncomfortably in front of him. 'Well then.' He raised his arm in salute, preparing to go.

'And Private Müller's things?' Johannes suddenly asked.

'They've been sent to his parents. Perhaps you might like to visit them. They're not too far from Munich.'

He looked up at the man, something coalescing in him.

'Yes, I might.'

'I'll get you their address. A rapid recovery then, Corporal Bahr.'

Johannes nodded, a distant but kindling sense of destination beginning to form in him.

On the day of his release from hospital, for the first time since his hospitalization Johannes studied his reflected image in the small glass. He saw a sallow haunted face, eyes that had lost their vivacity. His uniform was huge on his shrunken frame. The warm glances of the matron and the other nurses had not prepared him for this: they had returned to him a sense that, for all his inner torment, he was still a man. In his morphine-induced state, he had even dreamt that they desired him – Johannes, the man who had always believed that the body must be brought to a state of physical perfection in tandem with the soul.

The story the glass now told him was different. It spoke of a fractured creature, too poor a male specimen to bring to any woman. Johannes shuddered. Better not to think of that, or of anything else.

It came to him that throughout these last years all he had done was attempt to avoid thought, first after the fiasco with Bettina, then throughout the endless months of war.

When thought pounced on him unawares, he was filled with desperation. All his dreams, all his hopes of a changed world in which people lived freer lives, were closer to their bodies, their impulses, less constrained by hypocritical regulations and self-regulations, had shrivelled, taking him with them, leaving a mere husk.

And war, which he had conceived of as the great catalyst of the new, the great event which would tear apart the old, moribund civilization – what was it but an infernal and excessive perpetuation of the status quo, where all the disciplinary institutions of the state and the self-discipline of its people were unveiled for what they truly were: infernal machines of death. Or so it had proved thus far.

Sometimes, in these last weeks, he had wished again for the relief that morphine brought, that floating distance between himself and the world, himself and himself. He had even once, pleading pain, asked Matron for a dose, but she had refused him roundly.

But where was Matron now? Johannes looked round the ward, made his last goodbyes. He learned that she was off-duty. That saddened him. He wrote a hurried note of thanks, then, his sack over his shoulder, he slowly left the hospital building. His legs felt awkward and ungainly as he stepped on the gravelled path. There was altogether too much air, too much sky. He felt a return of dizziness, stumbled and then, ashamed of his own weakness, hurried on.

Where the public road intersected with the path, a large car blocked his crossing. Its door opened. A woman gestured to him. He looked at her unseeingly.

'Corporal Bahr. Don't you know me?'

The voice woke him. He saw a large blonde woman with grey eyes in a neat tailored suit.

'Matron?' he asked uncertainly.

'Yes,' she laughed at his confusion, 'though when I'm not wearing blue, you can call me Hilda. Come, come,' she patted the seat next to her, 'we've been waiting for you. You need a good meal, or what passes for such these days.'

He slipped in beside her, relieved to be in an enclosed space again, to allow his will to slip away.

The car rolled smoothly forward. He saw the city streets pass before him, strange and yet ordinary – undamaged buildings, shop fronts, people, women. Yes, that was part of the strangeness, so many women in the streets, brisk-paced, determined.

Matron followed his glance. 'Yes,' she said ruefully, 'a great deal has changed.' Suddenly she took his hand and placed it firmly on her leg so that he could feel the silk of her stocking beneath the thin fabric of her skirt. She moved a little closer.

Johannes closed his eyes, letting the warmth of her permeate him. He sniffed in her fragrance, felt lulled, heard her laugh as if at a great distance, 'Anything to heal the soldiers of the Fatherland.'

The words jangled, but he let them pass, unwilling to rupture the warmth that engulfed him, the soft roll of the car.

'And here we are,' she said brightly after what seemed to him far too short a time. 'A little good food, and then you'll see how much better you feel.'

'Yes,' Johannes murmured vaguely.

In the restaurant, there were far too many people about, their voices rushed, guttural. He let her order for him, watched her bright, calm, ageless face. She radiated health. He ate slowly, not tasting the food, but wanting to do it justice to please her. She chatted cheerfully, untroubled by his lack of response. But he was glad when the meal was over, in a quandary when she met his eyes and asked him whether he wanted to catch the three o'clock train or leave the following morning.

'Is there a hotel near the station?' he asked. He suddenly felt weak, unable to imagine how he would find a hotel, the train.

Her lips curled. 'I'll take care of everything, Corporal Bahr.'

They were in the car again; the clustered apartment blocks gave way to peaceful leafy expanses, and then an ornate iron gate, a tree-lined drive, a large house.

'Is this the hotel?' Johannes asked, liking the quiet, wondering that it could still exist.

'A kind of hotel.' She smoothed her skirt and led him towards the door. 'But my very own. You can spend the day here, the night. It will make a change. From all that.' She waved vaguely into the distance.

The house had a hush about it. Its heavy furniture and rich brocades seemed to have remained unchanged for centuries. The room she showed him to looked out over calm gardens, where a hammock swung between two young oaks. She followed the direction of his eyes.

'Perhaps you'd like to rest a little?'

He nodded gratefully, followed her down to the gardens. In the leafy shade of the hammock, for the first time in months, the closing of his eyes did not signal the return of battle. Instead, in that half-state between dream and waking, he saw female forms, Matron amongst them, supple, swaying in a slow archaic dance. He remembered a time which now seemed aeons ago, when he had dreamt of women as strong recuperative forces, maternal icons, embodiments of nature's saving grace.

He dozed peacefully.

But later that night when she came to his bed, offered red lips, skin fragrant with soap, he felt no answering stir in his body. It was as if some fire in him had died, obliterated by that greater conflagration. None of her gestures could kindle it. And her repeated attempts only awakened those other images, so that her red lips became a bloody gash, her rounded stomach poured out entrails, until Johannes pushed her away.

Despair bit at him, bringing with it a new emotion: shame.

'It happens sometimes, you know.' She was kind. 'The war, the shock . . .'

When she had left him, Johannes wept for the first time. Wept for Hans, for the curly-haired French youth, for the dead, for himself. When he woke, it was as if from a great distance. He couldn't place the room, read his identity from the blue-curtained window, the ornate lamp. Where was he? Who was he? Strangely, the questions induced no panic. He felt calm, so calm that he wondered if perhaps he had died in the night.

He only stopped at Munich to change trains. There was no one he wanted to see or to be seen by. The sight of so many young crippled men, walking on sticks, their eyes glazed, was oppressive. It was like the hospital ward without the moaning. He fled the city.

By the time he reached Weilheim, it was dark. He sat on a bench in the station, exchanging desultory comments with other soldiers, dozing. In the morning, light came with the newspaper headlines blaring German victories in Poland, Russian retreats.

Around the kiosk, people cheered. 'It will all soon be over,' they congratulated each other. One old man in a farmer's cap slapped him on the back. Johannes managed something akin to a grin. He profoundly wished he could share their optimism, but all he wanted was to get out of there, to create the greatest distance possible between himself and the war.

He asked the man if he knew a way to get to Rottenbach. 'Try the market,' the man advised him. 'One of the farmers is bound to be going that way.'

The lavish colours of the market set up a hum in Johannes. Heaped greens, lush golds, fiery reds, muted purples, fruit, vegetables, buckets of dahlias. His sight was riveted, seemed to take on sharp focus for the first time in months. He fingered an apple.

'Take it, take it. Eat,' a voice from behind the stall ordered him.

He looked up to see a tiny grey-haired woman with the kindly face of a garden gnome. Johannes searched for some change in his pocket.

'No, no.' She shooed the money away. 'We have enough here.'

He tried a smile, a thank you, his lips again feeling stiff.

'Do you know anyone who might be going towards Rottenbach today?' he asked her.

She pointed, 'Three stalls down. Ask for Otto. Going to visit the girlfriend, eh?'

He didn't gainsay her.

Otto turned out to be a farmer with bandy legs and a dour, weathered face.

'Yes, I can take you. If you help me load up. About half past one.' Shrewd eyes examined Johannes suspiciously. 'You're not deserting, are you?'

Johannes shook his head. 'No. On leave.'

'Too bad.' The man looked at him slyly. 'We could use some extra hands on the farm. You can pay, yes?

Johannes reached into his pocket.

'Later, later.' The man looked round him furtively. 'Come back at half one.'

Johannes was punctual, helped load the cart, though his shoulder ached with the weight of crates. He sat next to Otto on the rough wooden seat, watched the horses straining. Otto chatted and was surly by turn. He complained about having to leave town so early, without his lunch, unheard of before the war, but now there was only his wife and himself, and too much to do. Even his daughter had gone off, to work in a munitions factory. He scowled. The boys now, that was different. They had to do their duty. On the Russian Front. His voice was a mixture of resentment and pride.

Johannes offered little, answering only direct questions. But slowly a picture of what the war had wrought even so far from the Front, even in these peaceful hills where the sun shone with a moist brilliance, began to build up in his mind.

Otto dropped him at a fork in the road. In response to Johannes's profuse thanks and the notes he pulled from his pocket, he offered a set of complicated instructions, turns here, a field to be crossed there, another road, and he should arrive at his destination.

Johannes walked, two kilometres, four, five. Slowly. Distance was irrelevant, punctuated only by the wayside crucifixes with their carved weather-beaten saviours, mourning over the countryside. He stopped at one, a rough-hewn figure who had fallen from his lichen-covered post and was swinging erratically in the wind. An upside down Christ, dangling from his nailed feet. He was tempted to rectify him, but no, Johannes smiled bitterly, his present posture was far more apposite.

He walked on past stretches of waving corn, then wheat. A heavy physical heat suffused everything. Only gradually did his ears grow attuned to the sound of birds, bees straying through the fields, corn rustling in the breeze, so different from the clamour of the battlefield. He had forgotten.

Towards sunset, he learned from a boy who was leading some dappled cows across the road that the Müller farm was just past the next village.

'Have you got any empty cartridges?' the boy asked him excitedly.

Johannes shook his head.

'Too bad. What about a grenade? Could I see a grenade?'

He shook his head again. Dimly he remembered his own excitement when he had first handled the weapons of war. Could it have been only two years ago? Others still longed for that thrill.

He ruffled the boy's hair. 'They kill, you know. Have you ever seen a dead animal, a blasted animal?'

'Yes.' The boy hopped about from foot to foot excitedly. 'Bam bam bam, there goes a Russkie.'

'Switch the uniforms and your Russkie's just a German,' Johannes murmured.

The boy looked at him queerly, edged away.

Johannes heaved his sack on to his other shoulder and continued on his way. Gloom covered him again. Scratch the surface, lift away the thin restraining veneer, put them in a group, and men were all murderers. He suddenly recalled his last conversation with Bettina, her surprise at his sudden lust for battle. Johannes laughed out loud, painfully. He had set off to be transformed. And now he was, into even less of a man than he had been then.

The Müller farm stood on the edge of a deep valley. It was a modest affair. In the receding light, Johannes saw the gathered hay peeping out of the upper storey windows and behind the stone house, a wooden barn. There was no sign of any inhabitants but two window-boxes were bright with a profusion of geraniums. Johannes squared his shoulders and knocked at the door.

It was opened by a woman, a square, lined face topped with streaked grey brown hair. But the blue eyes gave him a start. They were so like Hans's.

'Frau Müller?' Johannes queried softly, his cap respectfully in his hand.

She looked at him uncomprehendingly, edged away from the door.

'Frau Müller, I am a friend of your son's.'

Tears leapt into her eyes. 'Corporal Bahr?' she asked softly, her voice filled with disbelief.

Johannes nodded.

The tears began to stream copiously down her leathery cheeks. She brought out a large man's handkerchief to wipe them, apologized. 'Do excuse me. Please, please come in. Karl, Karl!' She rushed past him out of the house, down the slope to the barn. 'Come quickly,' she shouted, her words swallowed in a rush of dialect Johannes could barely make out.

He sat down at the heavy oak table which took up a good part of the kitchen in which he found himself. Tiredness suddenly overwhelmed him. He was here. And now what?

But he had no time to think. A spare stooped man had come into the kitchen, was wiping his hands on his trousers. 'Corporal Bahr, Corporal Bahr. We are honoured by your visit.'

Schnapps found its way rapidly to the table. An oil lamp was lit.

'Hans wrote to us about you, told us how much he admired you.' Frau Müller spoke slowly as if each word was a pellet to be clawed from her innards. 'Father Josef read the letters to us. Hans wrote very beautifully,' she said proudly. The tears glistened on her leathery cheeks again. 'Look, look what they sent us.'

He followed her. In a dim recess of the room, pinned to the wall, he saw the quick sketch he had made of Hans. It was grimy, the paper wrinkled, but they had placed it above a little shelf on which a wooden Madonna, a candle and some trinkets stood, making a shrine of it, a shrine to Hans. Johannes looked at the image and shivered. It was strangely alive: there stood Hans in all his stolidity, with his full lips and oddly sensitive eyes. He had loved him.

They all gazed at the image silently for long minutes. Then Herr Müller mumbled, 'Tell us about him. Tell us about the Front.'

Johannes told them, starting slowly and then waxing warm with descriptions of Hans's exploits, his bravery, his fearlessness. He created a battle front of giants, an aura of heroism which was at once truth and illusion. The illusion, he realized, was essential for solace and in the telling, he tasted some of its consolation himself. He stopped short at describing the death. Some things did not need to be spoken. He simply told them that Hans had died as he had fought.

A supper of cabbage, potatoes, thick bread and cherry tart had come and gone. 'You will stay in Hans's room,' Herr Müller said. It was an order, not a question, and Johannes found himself in a tiny chamber right at the back of the house where one room opened on to the next in a sequence of doors. The narrow straw mattress creaked as he turned on it. The small flickering candle showed white-washed walls, a wooden crucifix. On the window ledge, there was a single book, a worn volume of Goethe's poems.

Johannes slept dreamlessly.

He stayed on with the Müllers for over two weeks, acting as a surrogate son, paying a kind of penance. He wore Hans's trousers and shirt, learned to milk the cows, scythe and bundle the hay, dig potatoes. They talked little, but he helped the old man repair the barn, brought water from the well, busied himself with a hundred small jobs. Between tasks, he took off his shirt and lay in the fields, listening to the sounds of the dry earth, breathing in the sleepy scent of the tall grass.

Flesh crept round his ribs. He grew brown, stronger, felt his scars heal, his feet tread the ground more firmly. The smell of warm creamy milk, hay and wild herbs suffused him, muting the stink of corpses. But at night they rose again in his dreams. Mutilated figures clawed at his body, demanding that he join them, Hans's voice loud in their number.

Johannes wondered whether it would ever be possible again to dream the dream of a natural life, a symbiosis of earth and sky and love and community, an unhaunted eternity of sowing and harvesting, of animals and people and work and rest, all in one.

On Sunday he went to the lofty white church in the hamlet with the Müllers and watched the solid, slow-moving peasants kneel, bend their heads beneath a baroque ceiling so encrusted with ornament that it seemed the image itself of the distance between them and heaven. Nonetheless, he listened silently to the soothing tones of the Mass. Perhaps a kind of comfort could be found here. He spoke to Father Josef, a gaunt giant of a man whose face was a mass of ridges which seemed as ancient as the hills.

But still at night the dead returned.

When Frau Müller began to talk as if he would still be there with them in the autumn, Johannes realized it was time to go. On a Tuesday morning, hot in his heavy uniform, his sack laden with the bread and fruit and sausages Frau Müller had insisted he have, he took his leave. He promised he would write, and return to see them when the war was over.

But as he clambered up the hill and waved, he wondered whether the war could ever end. Even if the guns on the Eastern and Western Fronts were to grow silent, how would it be possible to still the dead that each and every one of them now carried within him?

SIX

1916

'LIKE THIS, FRAU ADLER.' Old Trübl, the Seehafen caretaker, crouched between the rows of feathery green leaves, gently loosened the loamy earth with his fork and tugged. 'You see, perfect.' He held up the long plump carrot and turned it slowly in his hand. 'Now you try.'

Anna imitated his actions exactly and pulled.

'Fine,' he grumbled, looking not altogether pleased. 'When you've filled the barrow, call me. I'll be in the orchard.'

Anna worked, as she had worked throughout that summer of 1916. Yesterday it had been the marrows and beetroot, the day before beans, next week it would be the potatoes and turnips, not to mention the apples and cherries and the plump greenhouse tomatoes. She smiled as she pulled up a stubby carrot and flicked the earth from it. The Seehafen grounds had certainly undergone a radical transformation over this last year. Lush lawns were now neat rows of vegetables, flowerbeds thick with berries. Chickens wandered behind the kitchen doors, pecking incessantly. There were even two goats, tethered to their separate trees at the very back of the estate, far from the stables where the horses she so loved were lodged.

Klaus had instigated it all, seen the food shortages winter had brought and feared the worst for the following year, should the war go on interminably, as it seemed to be doing. And now the Seehafen gardens helped to feed the ever-growing numbers of children in Bettina's nurseries.

Anna stretched and looked with satisfaction at the half-filled barrow. How pleased Klaus would have been to take part in this first harvest. But his turn had come and he was now away on the Eastern Front working at a field hospital. So it was left to Anna and the Trübls.

Her sister, Anna decided, had a genius for organization. It had been Bettina's idea that Anna come here; it was she who had squared it with Bruno, she who had pulled strings and arranged for twice-weekly deliveries from Seehafen to Munich. Anna sometimes thought that if it had been up to Bettina to organize the war effort, the whole miserable business would already have been over.

And she did it all despite little Max, or perhaps fuelled by him, Anna wasn't sure which. When she had come to visit Bettina and Klaus for Christmas, just after the birth, she had been amazed to see the ease with which Bettina handled the wrinkled little bundle of a baby. When Anna had taken him cautiously into her own arms, unsure how to hold him, Bettina had laughed, 'Don't worry, he won't break. He's a sturdy little chap, with impressive lungs.' She had looked up at her curiously then. 'You know, I remember you like this. A tiny mewling thing. I minded the squawling rather more then.'

Perhaps that accounted for Bettina's ease, Anna thought now, wiping her brow, lodging the straw hat more firmly on her head. She already had some experience of babies. Not like her. Max's helplessness had frightened her, those wise old eyes poised in that infant body. She had been relieved to return him to his mother's arms.

Klaus too had looked on Bettina admiringly, though they had argued about how soon she could take up her duties again. For, of course, no sooner was Bettina up and about than she was off to work, sometimes taking Max and the nanny with her.

Anna lifted the wheelbarrow and manoeuvred it carefully back towards the shed. There was no point disturbing old Trübl. She was quite capable of managing and there was still much to do before the light gave way.

She had been sorry to go back to Vienna after that visit. The city had lost its lustre. Perhaps it was the omnipresence of those tired-looking men in uniforms or the depression that had set in when it was clear the war wouldn't be over by that first Christmas. Perhaps it was also that she still missed Katarina. There had been cards from her of course, from Prague, then Lyons, Paris, and finally just this spring one from London, written in French, a grim little note bemoaning how much they were hated there. War – it infiltrated all relations, distorting them.

By the first week of August, days after war was proclaimed, Miss Isabel was off. They had both cried. But Miss Isabel was adamant that they would meet again before the year was out. Meanwhile, she had to serve her country. Women would be needed now that the men were at the Front. Her eyes had sparkled. Perhaps she could work in a hospital, or even as an ambulance driver. They had both laughed at that: Miss Isabel's driving was still somewhat erratic. But her determination had fed Anna and she had worked on Bruno, finally convincing him as the fateful month neared its end that she would be far better off being gainfully employed than pining away in the vast house outside Vienna and far from everything. On top of it all, there were rumours that petrol would soon be rationed, and then how would even he manage the comings and goings?

So Bruno had acceded, promised that he would make enquiries, find something both suitable and useful. In a celebratory mood, Anna had had a special dinner prepared and they had clinked champagne glasses laughingly in a toast to her new life.

And then it had all changed.

Anna didn't like to think about it any more.

She busied herself unloading the carrots into the crates in the shed, noticed a broken one and tucked it under her shirt. The goats would appreciate that.

With a sudden flurry of movement, she raced towards their corner of the grounds. She could really run now, unhampered, ever since she had taken to wearing the battered trousers she had found in the house. Anna laughed, suddenly feeling her old self again, yet a new self. A photograph in the newspapers had given her the idea: a picture of women munitions workers, sensibly dressed with their shirts and trousers and boots. Why not her? So she had cut the trousers down and taken them in and could now run and ride and bend and lie in the grass with a wonderful liberty. Even if old Trübl didn't approve, as his disdainful looks indicated.

The goats gobbled down her offering in a trice, then looked at her with their stark lidless eyes, asking for more. 'Later,' she told them. Pan, the male, snuffled in her hand, then jutted his head, horns at the ready. She was never too sure of the male. Something about his face, the beard, reminded her of that Pole. That's what it was.

Anna sat down by the tree and leaned back, staring at him. She shuddered. There was that scene again, the event that had shattered the cocoon of her life, invaded the safety of her home, made the war more immediate than any number of newspaper headlines. It still made her tremble, despite the passage of time, despite her new existence at Seehafen.

It was evening. Anna had been sitting by the fireplace in the salon of the big house outside Vienna. She was trying to knit, not something she was particularly skilled at, but the word had gone out that woollies would be useful for the men on the Eastern Front. Suddenly she had heard the French windows opening behind her. The wind, she had thought, and decided to finish a row before bothering to get up.

But before she could do so, they stood in front of her. Two men: one, the thin one with the pointed beard, wielding a gun, thrusting it aggressively at her; the other, more stolid, with a square, drowsy face, clamping a hand over her mouth, choking her.

'Don't scream,' the bearded one ordered, 'just tell us how many others are in the house.'

Anna stared at the man in incomprehension. She was shaking.

'How many?' The man jabbed her with his pistol.

She lifted a trembling hand, showed two fingers.

'Adler?'

She shook her head.

'Servants?'

She nodded.

'Good.' His lips formed into a thin smile. Hot beady eyes assessed her. 'She won't be any trouble.' He gestured to his mate, who removed his hand from her mouth.

'Who are you?' Anna stammered. 'What do you want? How do you know my husband?'

'It is for us to ask the questions.' The man waved his pistol in her face. 'But since you ask, Frau Adler,' he spat out her name and then threw his shoulders back proudly, 'we are the vanguard of the Lemberg Patriotic Front.'

'What?' The words made no sense.

'She's never heard of us,' he said to his friend, laughed brusquely. 'But you will, you'll hear a lot more of us. When is your husband back?'

Anna stared at him, murmured, her lips dry, 'I'm not sure. I don't know. Tomorrow night. Perhaps the next. What do you want?'

He didn't answer her. 'We'll just have to make ourselves comfortable and wait then. Now let's go and get those servants in here, and they can bring some food while they're at it.'

She thought of the kindly Grubers, their fright. She straightened her shoulders to protest, 'But they're asleep.'

'So they'll wake up to a surprise.' He prodded her up with his pistol, marched her to the door.

For the first time, the other man spoke. In Polish. She couldn't understand, but he seemed to be querying something. The two of them argued for a moment and then the bearded one said: 'If the phone rings, you pick it up. Speak naturally. If it's your husband, make sure you tell him how you're longing to see him. Now move.'

Bruno wouldn't ring again tonight, Anna thought. But if he should, how would she communicate anything to him? She shivered again. What did they want with him?

It was only after they were back in the salon, with the Grubers and a tray of food, that Anna noticed how young the two men were. They ate ravenously, looking up every minute, like stray dogs whose meal might be nabbed from them at any second. When they had finished, the bearded one walked round the room, touching objects, inspecting, like a prospective buyer.

'Look at it, Stephan, look. See how this Jewish filth lives, while we, eh, our people struggle,' he spat. 'And look at this. This is what they call art.' He pointed at the stark figure which was Anna's favourite sculpture and seemed about to strike it with his pistol.

'Stop it,' she screamed. 'Stop. You have no right.'

His arm faltered in mid-air. 'Right?' he lurched towards her, changed his mind, brought his gun down over the sculpture, chipping away a piece of it. 'You'll see where right is.' He lifted his arm again to repeat the gesture.

Anna ran towards him, stopping his hand, struggling with him.

The other man interceded, pulled Anna away from his companion. There was a rapid exchange between them and the bearded man sat down in a chair near the door, his pistol resting in his lap. 'Another little move like that and you'll have to contend with this.' He pointed to his gun.

Anna gave the Grubers what she hoped was a reassuring look. She picked up her knitting, but she couldn't make the needles work, her hands were shaking so much. What did these men want? Would they kill them, kill Bruno? The needles dropped out of her hand.

They sat there through the night, dozing fitfully, and through the next morning, only moving to go into the kitchen as a group, to eat furtively. Anna was worried about Herr Gruber. He hadn't been well and now his skin had a sickly pallor to it. She addressed Stephan. 'At least let the old man lie down, you have nothing against him. You could lock them both in their room with some food. They won't do anything.'

Again there was that exchange in Polish. Then they all marched to the Grubers' room.

'And if we need . . .' Frau Gruber mumbled, looked at Anna beseechingly.

The bearded man was suddenly magnanimous. 'We'll come and check on you every few hours. Never let it be said that the Lemberg Patriotic Front has anything against servants. Even the servants of Jews.'

Frau Gruber looked away.

Anna suddenly wanted to hit him. But she walked quietly ahead of them, back to the salon, sat, sat interminably through the long hours of the afternoon, into the evening. They had started to talk again, more nervously now, arguing. The bearded one waved his gun about. And then she heard the car. She stiffened. Had they noticed it? If only they kept on talking, if only she could distract them. She started to scream, yelling at them, telling them they were fools.

The bearded one jabbed his gun into her ribs, wrapped his hand round her mouth.

And then Bruno was at the door.

'Anna, what on earth? Grotowski, Haller, what are you doing here? Put down that gun, you fool.' He was brusque, commanding, walking straight towards them.

Anna felt the gun moving away from her back, as if the man could not help but respond to the order. But then he was pointing it at Bruno, waving it.

'Don't move another step closer, or I'll shoot.'

Bruno stopped, looked the man in the eye. 'What are these antics about, Haller? What do you want?' He turned towards the other man, 'And you, Grotowski, I expected better of you.' He shook his large head sadly. 'Anna, my darling, go and sit over there, while I deal with these two.'

'None of your smooth Jewish words, Adler.' The bearded man waved his pistol again. 'The Lemberg Patriotic Front wants the factory. We'll run it. For the good of Poland. For the good of our people. Not so that you can sit here reaping profits, eating the sweat off our backs.'

Bruno stood to his full impressive height. 'And if you shoot me, you think someone will give you the factory. The Galician authorities perhaps. Ha!' A loud growling laugh boomed out of him. 'And how many of you are there in this new Lemberg Patriotic Front? Tell me, Grotowski. You're not a liar. Ten, twenty, thirty? And you'll learn to run that operation in a day and pay your workers? After you've been arrested for my murder. You remember our mutual friend, the Chief of Police, Demowski? I think he remembers you.'

Bruno suddenly stopped laughing. 'Now if you want to negotiate about something, then you put down that infernal gun and tell me what it is that you want, calmly, if that's possible. And I promise not to ring the police as soon as you've stepped out of my door. Grotowski, speak to him. You're an intelligent man.'

There was a burst of Polish again. Bruno joined in. Then Grotowski took the gun from Haller's hand and put it down on a table at the other end of the room.

'Fine, gentlemen, now come with me.' Bruno turned back to look at her. 'I'll be with you in a little while, my darling,' he murmured.

A little while. How long was a little while? Anna sat and stared into space, counting the seconds of a little while until time became merely a hiatus between the moment Bruno had stepped from the room and the moment when he would come back.

When he did, she could only gaze at him.

'It's all right, Anna, poor darling, it's all over, they've gone.' He hugged her, patted her gently on the back, fetched her a large glass of cognac, made her drink. 'How long were they here?'

Anna told him.

He clenched his fist and banged it down on the table, so the glasses danced. 'Damn them. Damn this madness.'

'The Grubers,' Anna suddenly remembered. She raced up the stairs. The two old people were sitting upright in bed. Frau Gruber had her rosary in her hands, and murmured, 'Thank God', over and over as Anna reassured them, Bruno brought food and drink.

When they were alone together again, sitting opposite each other at the little breakfast table in the morning room, Bruno told her that he knew the men quite well, that Haller had long been a trouble-maker in the works. He laughed harshly. 'I gave them the factory, told them they could run it for a trial period of a year.'

'Oh.' Anna's eyes opened wide.

'What I didn't tell them is that Lemberg has been captured by the Russians. Our forces are in retreat.' Bruno suddenly slumped down on the table, covered his eyes. Anna put her hand gently on his shoulder and he folded his round it. 'They can negotiate with the Russians,' he murmured at last.

It was only that night that the crying took hold of her, wouldn't release her until morning came, choked her at random moments for days afterwards. She knew that it was as much because of the crying as because of the event itself that everything then changed.

She was still, Anna thought now as she returned to her digging, full of admiration for the bravery Bruno had shown at the time. She had never seen him like that, never taken the full measure of his strength, his confidence, his skill at managing people. But it was there, there in his large capable hands – an authority which could always arrange things the way he wished.

Yet over the next weeks he had been sullen, depressed. She knew there were problems he would not discuss with her, terrible difficulties because of the war. She knew, too, though he didn't tell her, that he was worrying over financial losses.

They had closed down the big house. She wasn't safe there now, he thought. Anything could happen in these times of madness. They had moved into the Vienna apartment, found a small flat nearby for the Grubers. Bruno was solicitous, worrying over her, treating her like a fragile doll. There was no longer any question of her going out to work. And to tell the truth, for the first weeks, she hadn't wanted to. She was shaken by that strange eruption of violence in her own home. When she left the house, she always looked over her shoulder.

The Christmas trip to Munich had come as a godsend. On her return, she felt freer, less under threat. The injunctions about engaging in patriotic work had grown louder and Anna wanted to do something, anything. So she had begun to take part in voluntary efforts – a day in an orphanage here, another in a women's charity there. But Bruno was still concerned. So many of his holdings were in territories where nationalist feeling ran high. And she was known as his wife; that fact couldn't be disguised. He hired a bodyguard to look after her. And so it had gone on for over a year – a year which had brought them closer, despite or because of its pressures.

It was the following January, when she told Bettina about Bruno's necessary and increasing absences, that Bettina had come up with her wonderful plan. She must go to Seehafen in the spring. No one would trace her there and she would be far more useful than in Vienna. Bruno could come and stay whenever he wished.

And so she was here. Anna finished loading another barrowful of carrots. It was almost, she sometimes felt, like the days before her wedding. She was free to do more or less as she pleased, and now that she had done with the garden, what she felt like, more than anything else, was a little session in the boathouse.

When she had first arrived she had discovered the boathouse was full of colours, inks, sheaves of paper. Johannes's, she knew. Bettina had told her of the time he had spent at Seehafen, the half-finished extension. Johannes, she thought, wouldn't mind if she made use of his things. And she had used them liberally.

She had started to dabble in Vienna. Katarina had always encouraged her and the drawing and painting had become for her a form of silent communication with her absent friend. In the boathouse, she gradually felt she was working under the aegis of Johannes as well. When it was raining, she spent hours on end here. Otherwise, she stole away when possible, sketching outdoors in the vicinity of the lake first and then coming in to undertake the more difficult task of colour.

Anna was never satisfied with anything she produced, but she loved the process, the adventure of it. She had no idea where the images she made sprang from. They were nothing like her, she thought, these heavy, weighted, iconic forms – grave primitive creatures with soulful eyes who bore the burden of the world, who had not yet learned to dance. But she made them nonetheless, thinking of each as a special friend.

Inspired by the local craft of painting directly on to glass, she had begun of late to try her hand at that too. She was mesmerized by the way the sun refracted through the painted glass. That was what she would do today.

Anna worked, mixed a deep red, and applied slow deliberate lines, humming silently to herself all the while. When she had grown hot with the effort, she rose and looked out of the door, listened. Not a sound. With a secret smile, she picked up the large towel she kept here and walked towards a little grassy knoll she had discovered which was sheltered from the grounds by scented shrubs of flowering hawthorn. In a few quick gestures she shed her clothes and lowered herself into the cool water. Then she swam out briskly towards the centre of the lake till, panting, she turned over to float lazily and gaze at the sky, the jagged expanse of the distant mountains. The cool lap of the water on her bare skin lulled her, never failing to bring back Katarina. And as she lay there in a state akin to sleep, she remembered little scenes with her friend, unsure whether what buoyed her up was the lake itself or memory.

When the cold of the mountain water began to chill her, Anna made her way back to shore. She dried herself slowly, relishing the light breeze on her skin, shaking out her hair so that it tumbled wildly about her. Then she started to dress.

'No, no. Not yet.'

The sound of a voice so startled her that, like a forest creature scenting danger, she froze into position.

'Not yet. Let me look at you.'

There was a rustle of branches and then a man appeared. For an instant she didn't recognize him – the uniform, the weathered leanness of his features.

Then she murmured, 'Johannes'. With a swift gesture, she bent for her shirt.

He stopped her hand. 'No, Anna, please. Let me see you.' There was a plea in his voice. 'You're beautiful. You've grown so beautiful.' He ran a finger gently down her skin. 'Unbelievably beautiful,' he whispered almost to himself, his breath catching.

Anna didn't know whether it was the unblinking fascination of his eyes or the sensation which his touch evoked in her, but for a split second, she was mesmerized, unable to stir. Then, with a shiver, she moved into action, forgetting her underclothes, tugging her trousers on, her shirt, edging away from him. He caught her before she had made her way through the break in the shrubs.

'Let me.' He crushed her in his arms, found her lips. She struggled against him only for a moment and then met his kiss, felt it leaping through her, felt the heat of his body. In that instant she suddenly remembered how once, so long ago, she had watched him from the shelter of the bushes, had seen that moonlit form. She broke away from his embrace, gazed up at him with frightened eyes. Then she bounded through the shrubbery, fleeing, her trousers flapping round her, her shoes left behind.

Johannes, looking after her, took a deep breath. How could he have been so blind to her before? Why, coming out of the lake then she had been like some apparition which had sprung from the hidden recesses of his mind, an incarnation of the very form of beauty. A woman of the future, all gold and sun and laughter and newness, free of the gloomy curse of chastity. Those smooth curves, wet, glistening, those pink-tipped breasts, the snaking hair, and that look in her eyes of pure unquenchable longing. Watching her he had felt something like awe, and then that stirring, almost painful, of his body coming back to life, rising from the dead.

Johannes stretched out on the grass. Wet. Wet with her. He fingered the droplets that had touched her body. Again that sensation at his groin, like an ache, a tugging at his unwilling flesh. How long it was since he had loved a woman. When, on his few brief leaves from the Front, his mates had vented their lust on haggard, exhausted prostitutes, Johannes had looked on, his flesh cold, only his eye alive and his fingers sketching, sketching. Examining those sketches again, he had seen that his depictions of the carnal coupling had transformed them into dances of death, cadavers intertwined on sheets become graves. His own lust had been vented in the perils of battle. Only there had he felt that arousal, that pounding of the blood, the surge of blinding ecstasy. And then death, that fear which had drawn him on, had killed him, leaving only a scarecrow with the taste of ashes in his mouth.

And now? He looked up through the dappled leaves and then suddenly turned over to rake his fingers through the grass, bury his face in it. Now that young woman had walked out of the waters like some pagan Venus to rouse him. He wasn't certain he wanted to be roused.

He had found his way to Seehafen blindly, unthinkingly, simply walking for days on end, sleeping in barns, only to find himself on the twisting road that led to the house. Seeing it, he had thought no one would mind if he camped out in the boathouse for a few nights. The place had seemed deserted until he had heard that splashing in the lake.

Johannes leapt up. Should he stay now? Go? He walked back to the boathouse. He had met with Bettina here. Where was she now? And Klaus? They seemed so remote, he could hardly remember them. And the boathouse bore no traces of them. But his narrow bed was still there, the little stove. And on the table, his paints, piles of paper. Johannes looked again. Not his work. He leafed through the stacked images quickly, saw the squares of painted glass. Anna. It could only be her.

He picked up one of his brushes. Suddenly he knew exactly what to do.

* * *

Anna stared through the expanse of windows at the back of the new extension. The sun was setting, a flaming ball between the cold craggy peaks. She had told Frau Trübl that she would take her supper here tonight, as she sometimes did, rather than with them. She needed to be alone.

She leaned against the naked tree trunk which formed one of the supporting columns of the room and breathed deeply. He had made this strange space, she reminded herself. It had become her favourite room, not quite finished and bare as it was, except for an assortment of Klaus's leafy plants and the small wrought-iron table in the corner.

'Frau Adler, Frau Adler.'

The sudden voice made Anna leap.

'Look who's here, Frau Adler. Isn't it splendid. Herr Bahr is on leave from the Front.'

The pleasure in Frau Trübl's voice made Johannes smile. It was wonderful the impact a uniform had on some.

'Anna.' He stepped forward, kissed her hand. The look he turned on her had a touch of mischief in it. 'What a pleasure it is to find you here.'

'You'll eat here with Frau Adler, won't you, Herr Bahr? It won't be long. And then you can come back into the kitchen and give us news.'

'Yes, yes,' Johannes smiled. He sat down opposite Anna. She *had* changed, he thought. Those lowered lids, that movement of shyness.

'I *am* pleased, so pleased that you are here,' he murmured.

Tawny eyes met his with a startling directness. 'I'm married now, you know,' she announced.

He laughed, the sound burbling inside him and then rising with a richness he had forgotten. The laugh swept her up so that she joined him in it.

'I know,' he said, when the wave had subsided. 'But I've never been a respecter of property.'

She considered him. 'But you're altered in other ways.'

'Inevitably.' He looked grim for a moment and then waved his arm, as if putting all that behind him. 'You'll restore me.'

'How?' She met him on it.

He wanted to take her hand, feel its softness, but Frau Trübl had come in, balancing a large tray.

'Everything is so fresh here, you must eat and eat, Herr Bahr. Even the bread. I baked today.' She fussed over him, heaping his plate with a thick fragrant soup, cut thick slabs from the loaf, waited for him to taste.

'Delicious, utterly delicious, Frau Trübl,' he thanked her.

'Not like the Front, eh?'

'No,' he said flatly. 'Nothing like.'

'Perhaps you could bring Herr Bahr a bottle of wine, Frau Trübl,' Anna intervened. 'From the cellar. Herr Eberhardt would wish it.'

'Yes, yes, of course.' The woman scurried away.

Johannes looked at Anna gratefully, but she averted her gaze. They sat quietly for a moment, toying with their food. The atmosphere between them grew dense.

Anna was trying desperately not to think of the sensations he had aroused in her. She kept calling forth the figure of Bruno, a staunch bulwark, to stand between her and Johannes, but as soon as he spoke or she met his eyes, Bruno vanished.

'You've started to paint,' Johannes said now.

Anna felt a flush creeping up her cheeks.

'Yes, just to pass the time.' She shrugged away any serious intent.

'I like what you've done. It's fresh, distinctive.'

'Really?' Pleasure suffused her. 'How kind of you to say that.'

'I could help you, give you a few pointers while I'm here.'

'Would you?' Her face had a look of pure delight.

Johannes nodded, gazing at her. He drank in her pleasure, feeling like a parched man who had arrived at an oasis after a long trajectory through the desert. He felt he had never seen such a look of spontaneous joy on a woman's face before.

'We could start tomorrow if you like.'

'Oh yes,' Anna breathed.

'Perhaps I could paint you, while we work. You wanted me to, once, do you remember?' He laughed a little bitterly.

She nodded.

'Though I'm not sure that I can any more. Paint, that is.' He turned away from her, stared into the shadowy darkness beyond the glass. The massed trees seemed to turn into ranks of clamouring skeletal figures, their gnarled branches coming towards him with howls of pain.

'Johannes, Johannes, are you all right?' Anna placed her hand on his shoulder. 'You've turned ashen,' she murmured.

He gripped her hand, holding it tightly as if it would save him from the encroaching ranks.

'One can't forget.' She was adamant. 'Of course, you can still paint.' Tawny animal eyes looked into his, unblinking. Her face seemed to share his pain.

'You. Perhaps if I gaze only on you.' He smoothed her hand, buried his lips in her palm. Peaches, she tasted of ripe, sun-warmed peaches.

Anna drew slowly away. 'You can paint me, Johannes, but I think you mustn't touch me,' she said earnestly. 'It makes me forget who I am, makes me forget Bruno.'

'I'll try,' he whispered.

It wasn't altogether clear to her whether he meant the painting or the touching.

The next day Anna rose at dawn. Sleep had evaded her and now she wanted to clear her mind. Silently she stole down to the stables and saddled her favourite horse, a young golden mare who went by the name of Fanny. No more side saddle for her, since she had donned her trousers, though she had carefully considered whether she should wear them again today, now that Johannes was here. But the thought of riding had swayed her.

Anna led the horse out towards the gravelled drive and then, mounting, cantered towards the road away from the estate. In the wooded bridle path opposite, she gave the mare her head, exulting in the animal's energy, the whip of her own hair in the wind. But thoughts of Johannes wouldn't leave her. They had taken a short stroll together after dinner the previous evening, and had hardly spoken; yet the sense of his presence by her side had been so acute that it was as if her senses were alive to his every footfall, every change of expression, to the point where she thought she could see a smile shaping itself on his face when an owl hooted directly above them. She had asked him about the war, about his posting, but his voice had been so grim, his response so brusque, that she hadn't pressed him. But he *had* told her that his leave would soon be over.

Anna dug her heels into the horse's flanks and pressed her to greater exertion.

When Johannes and she had made their way back to the house, she had told him that Frau Trübl had prepared the second bedroom in the left wing for him. He had turned to face her so abruptly that she had jumped away. His laugh had been a little bitter. 'If I'm not to touch you, Anna, it's better that I sleep in the boathouse.' With a single finger, he had slowly traced the line of her cheek, then nodded and set off across the grounds.

It was strange, Anna thought, turning the horse back towards the house, but she could still feel the imprint of his touch. Why? Why should it be so? Yes, it was true she liked the way his nose flared at the base, liked the clarity of his eyes with the dark rim round the centre, liked the set of his jaw and his lithe, easy walk. But she liked so much about Bruno too, his handsome solidity, his chocolate eyes. Yet his touch . . . Anna slowed her horse as they approached the house. It was madness to think this way. She must stop.

There was great activity in the stables when she arrived. Trübl was spreading fresh hay and for once his truculence seemed to have deserted him. 'Fine morning, Frau Adler.' He took the reins from her. 'It's good to have one of our boys back with us, eh?' He patted the horse's rump.

Anna turned to see Johannes carrying a large bale through the doors. She greeted him, nonetheless averting her eyes. What if he could read her thoughts?

'Riding early?' He looked at her.

She smoothed her shirt, nodded.

He smiled, a wide easy smile which made her pulse leap. 'And I like your riding outfit.'

'It's easier to work in this,' Anna mumbled.

'You tell her, Herr Bahr,' Trübl intervened. 'It's not right for a young lady to be going around dressed like that.'

'Nothing's quite right these days, Trübl.' Johannes winked at her. 'And I suspect Frau Anna's garments are the least of our worries.'

'Yes, yes, of course, but . . .'

'Here, let me help you with that.' He stood on the other side of the sweating mare and started to brush her down, keeping time with Anna's movements.

They worked silently. The smell of the fragrant hay coupled with the heat of the animal rose to Anna's nostrils. A dreaminess pervaded her, a slowness of time, so that she felt she had been standing here, brushing rhythmically, the man opposite her, since the world began. Trübl's voice, when it came, startled her.

'I'm off to the orchard now. Are you coming? Remember, Frau Adler, the pick-up comes this afternoon. And there are still the potatoes to do.'

'I'll help, of course,' Johannes offered.

Having Johannes alongside them meant that by the time the sun was high in the sky, they were well ahead in their work. Frau Trübl set out a picnic lunch in the arbour and, once they had eaten, Johannes suggested in a completely matter-of-fact voice, that Anna come to the boathouse now for her painting lesson.

'We'll be back in good time for the afternoon shift,' he reassured Trübl.

'No need.' The old man waved them off. 'She deserves a break and I'm certain you do as well.'

'Are you sure?' Anna was hesitant.

'Off with you.' Trübl was genial after his beer. 'I'm going to have a little nap myself.'

In the boathouse, Johannes selected one of her pictures and stood it on the easel. Cocking his head, he looked at it first from one position, then another and yet another. Only then did he turn to her. 'Now, Anna, whatever I say, you musn't take offence. I'm just going to try and make you see certain things about composition.' He took a sheet of white paper and covered up a portion of her painting, then drew a triangular form on it. 'You see how if I place this here, it changes the entire weight of the painting. The pull of the eye is in the opposite direction. Now, watch.' He turned the paper over and traced a free hand circle, covering another portion of the painting with it. He repeated this several times with different shapes.

Watching what at first she thought of as incomprehensible antics, Anna gradually began to discern a dynamic tension at work between weight and proportion and line.

'I see,' she suddenly breathed excitedly. 'I see, so if I had taken the hat off her head and instead painted a basket here,' she gestured swiftly at the canvas, 'then the whole thing would have been far more satisfying. And the mood different.'

'Got it in one,' Johannes nodded. 'You learn quickly.' His eyes grew dreamy. 'Now let me show you something else.' He started to draw quickly. A forest took shape, dappled light through trees, falling on bracken, darkness beneath. 'What do you see, Anna?'

She told him.

'Look again.' His hand traced out a pattern at the base of the picture.

Where she had previously seen trees, she now saw fawns, their hides dappled, growing out of bark.

'You see?'

She nodded.

'This is what I love about drawing, painting, when it works. The interconnections of things. A world of correspondences.' He smiled a little bitterly. 'But now I rarely see them.' He shrugged. 'Let's go out and try some sketching.'

Anna followed him out of the boathouse.

'Right here will do. You see those shrubs, that hawthorn, the taller tree behind. See what you can do with that.'

Anna started sketching busily, only realizing after some minutes that Johannes had thrown his pad to the ground and was walking about restlessly.

'Don't you want to draw, too, Johannes?' she asked softly.

He gazed back at her. 'No.'

She thought she saw a tremor pass over his lips.

'But you said, said you would paint me,' she murmured.

'Will you swim with me, Anna?'

She looked at him, aghast. 'No, no, I couldn't.'

'Please, Anna, no one will know. And I need to see you, want to see you.' He rubbed his hands over his eyes abruptly. 'I need to forget, Anna. I can't paint until I forget.' There was a tortured look on his face. 'Yesterday, I thought you helped me . . .' He stopped in mid-sentence, shrugged, began to walk away listlessly.

Anna, watching him, felt tears bite at her eyes. She shivered, despite the warmth. Seemed to reach a decision. Slowly she walked towards the sheltered grassy knoll, stepped out of her trousers, began to unbutton her shirt, thought better of it, and jumped into the water.

It was only when she was some way out that she heard him and then before she could turn, a sleek head came out of the depths beside her. There was a rapturous smile on his face.

'Thank you,' he mouthed. And then he dived below the water, sending waves round her, only to surface again at a distance, wave and disappear again. In a moment he was back at her side. 'Race you back?'

She nodded, responding to the impish challenge, the childlike glee in his face. She pounded through the water, keeping pace with him, the exertion wiping away residual worries until, breathless, they reached the shoreline together. Only as she clambered up the grassy knoll ahead of him did it occur to her that he might be as naked as that day when she had first observed him.

Anna flung herself down on the ground and clenched her eyes shut. Above the sound of her own breath, she was acutely aware of the swoosh of the water as he lifted himself ashore, the sway of the grass as he moved through it. Then nothing, except the rustle of the grasshoppers in the tall grass, the chirrup of the birds, the buzz of a plump bee nestling into a poppy. Anna lay there, hardly daring to breathe, letting the earth's warmth seep into her, the sun burn into her back. Drowsiness overcame her.

And then, she felt fingers at her neck, gently lifting her damp hair, the flutter of lips. A tremor ran through her. Fingers, lips, as delicate as Katarina's, she thought sleepily, only remembering when she arched her shoulders in response that there was no Katarina here.

'Please don't touch me, Johannes, please,' she murmured. 'You promised.'

He let out a short sharp sound, not quite a laugh. 'Once I thought I was capable of the superhuman,' he muttered, 'now I'm not always even sure I'm a man.'

Anna lifted her head to look back at him. He was sitting at her side, his chest bare, a sketchpad balanced on his trousered legs.

His tone changed as he met her gaze, 'Please turn over, Anna,' he said softly. 'Your eyes will remind me.'

'Are you drawing me?' she asked.

'I'm making a beginning.'

She bent to look at the drawing, but he sheltered the page with his hands. 'No, not yet.'

Anna lay back, balancing her head on an arm, looking at him through lowered lids. Below his right shoulder, she saw the thickened ridge of flesh, the blue-black pin points. She winced. He hadn't told her he had been wounded.

'What is it, Anna?' He noticed her disquiet.

'Nothing.' She closed her eyes, listening for the scratch of his pencil. It came, but then stopped after a moment.

'Just this, Anna, for the composition.' His tone had a light irony and before she knew what he meant, he was unbuttoning her shirt, pushing it back so her breasts were half-bared. She heard his sharp intake of breath, her own. He caught her lifted hand, met her eyes. His gaze burned into her, stopping her motion.

'Please, Anna,' he repeated. 'I know, pretend you're someone else. We don't know each other. You're a model I've hired,' he laughed, 'yes, my model.'

The notion tickled her. To be someone else. Yes. She lay back, tasting the sun on her bared flesh, feeling his touch even though it was no longer there.

'You know,' he said after some moments, 'there is no shame in the body, Anna. How could there be any shame in such beauty? A little modesty perhaps, but no shame.'

She sat up abruptly. 'I'm not ashamed,' she said adamantly.

He looked at her oddly. 'No, perhaps not.'

'It's just that . . . you know, Bruno. It's not right.' She moved to pull her shirt round her.

He stayed her hand. 'You're not Anna, remember,' he laughed.

'No, not Anna.' She joined him in the game. 'Not Anna.' She lay back, stretching out, luxuriating in the feel of the grass, the whisper of the breeze.

She didn't know how much time had passed, but all at once the scratch of the pencil was gone. 'Am I Anna again?' she asked, raised herself on an elbow, saw him stretched out beside her.

'Yes.' He turned glowing eyes on her. 'Anna again,' he smiled lazily.

She looked at him, the face relaxed, boyish again, as she first remembered seeing him, the long graceful neck, the bunched muscles at his shoulders, the tufts of curling hair at his chest, the taut skin where the trouser belt played loosely at his waist. Suddenly she murmured, 'May I touch you?' She didn't wait for an answer. Her hand rested on his warmed skin, smoothing, skimming.

Johannes, letting her, felt the rush of wings over his body and then the blood pounding through his veins with a heat he didn't remember. He stayed her hand. 'Anna,' his voice cracked. 'If you touch me, I must touch you.'

Her eyes looked down into his, dark now, flecked with yellow. 'Just this once,' she whispered, lowering her lips to his.

He folded her in his arms, tasting her kiss, moist, fragrant, like peaches again, feeling the silken skin of her back, so firm, yet soft, her weight on him, the rounded breasts, taut against his flesh. She seemed to purr, like a supple cat. He groaned, arching against her, despite himself, feeling that mound.

She edged away from him, her mouth open, panting a little, pouting. 'That's enough, Johannes. I shouldn't have.' She pulled on her rough, shapeless trousers. 'No more touching Anna,' she smiled dreamily. 'But you can paint your model.'

The next days took on a recurrent pattern. They woke early, working with Trübl until lunch; then, having eaten together, they went down to the boathouse, swam or rowed out to the centre of the lake. Afterwards on the grassy knoll, Johannes drew her. He worked his way from pencil to a variety of inks, to pastels, learning the shapes and curves of her body, the sudden impulsive changes of mood, the play of expressions on her face as she buried her nose in a hawthorn blossom or couldn't bring her pencil to capture the form she wanted. For often she worked beside him, taking his suggestions in good stead, laughing that wild laugh of hers, concentrating herself totally.

'You're not a model, but a muse,' he told her, and she smiled radiantly. He didn't touch her, keeping to his side of their bargain, but sometimes his fingers would skim her skin, as he moved her heavy hair back from her face, or guided her pencil.

In the late afternoon, if there was no work to be done in the gardens, they sometimes rode or walked, exploring the countryside. And in the evenings, after dinner, they would return to the boathouse and Johannes would give her lessons in the application of oils. Or they would simply chat.

As the days passed, Johannes felt the memories of war receding, a kind of inner healing taking place. Of the future he refused to think. It was as if time had stopped, here in this garden, their own little paradise. He was slightly in awe of Anna. Not a fear, but a respect for her beauty which she seemed wholly unaware of, almost a greater respect for what he named her naturalness, her impetuosity. It was as if she had been unspoiled by social graces and everyday hypocrisies. She had an inner integrity, unrelated to any spoken principles and he always took what she said to be what she meant.

Sometimes he thought that what she had above any person he had ever met was a gift for life itself.

He would have given anything to make love to her, to learn the inner recesses of her pleasure, the secret motions which made her what she was. But he had too much respect to force her. And nothing, he sometimes thought dismally, to offer. When she was sitting for him and his desire for her grew too great, he would lope off across the grounds, and run, run until the moment had passed, coming back to her like a chastened schoolboy. He wondered if she had any idea what was going through him. Though he knew, not only from the time she had touched him, but from a hundred other little indications, that his desire was returned. That fuelled his work, making his imagination and his fingers leap in unison with an energy he had thought he would never experience again.

In the early morning hours of a Friday some twelve days into his stay, Johannes woke from sleep to the sound of rumbling thunder. He looked out of the boathouse's small window to see lightning forking out of the dark sky. The rain would come pounding down soon, and perhaps if he were lucky would continue at least until mid-afternoon, so that Trübl would not need his services.

Bright-eyed, Johannes quickly gathered a sackful of colours and brushes, and a large rolled drawing which had been lying in wait. Then, with a bound, he rushed towards the house, depositing his materials in the extension, before running to the shed, where he knew the sacks of plaster had been stored since before the war. Two trips were necessary to cart the materials and the ladder into the house, but he managed it, just as the first drops of rain came pelting down.

As night receded, he had applied his first coat of plaster to an area just beneath a curving arch.

By the time Anna came down to breakfast, a stretch of wall was covered in drawing of a reddish-brown colour. She looked at him in amazement.

'What are you doing?'

Johannes smiled down at her from the top of his ladder. 'I had once promised Klaus a fresco and at last, I'm ready to do it. I can't stop – I have to work while the plaster is wet.'

She left him only to come back minutes later carrying a bowl of warm milk and some rolls. 'Breakfast?'

'In a moment.'

She placed the tray on the table and sat to watch him. The energy of his quick fierce strokes fascinated her, the certainty of his movements.

As he stepped down from the ladder to gulp his breakfast, he asked,

'Like it? It's you, you know. You'll see it in a little while.' He clambered back up the ladder.

She watched him for the length of the morning, saw the sinopia take shape, herself stretched out on a grassy slope, flowers wreathing her, her hair growing into the ground. And then Johannes covered over part of the drawing with another thin coat of plaster.

'And now for colour, I should get at least this section finished by tonight.' He rubbed his shoulders, moved his head round in a circle. 'Almost as hard as digging,' he smiled at her. 'Let's just hope the weather doesn't mean the whole thing flakes off by next week.'

He applied the colour, greens, swirling, almost blue and then brashly yellow, the ripe peachy hues of skin, poppy-red flowers, and stark brilliant whites, hawthorn on a late afternoon. After a while, tears leapt into her eyes, she didn't know why.

'I'll be back soon,' she said softly. 'Just want to check on the grounds.'

The rain had stopped, but the sky still swirled with dark clouds, and the ground sloshed beneath her steps. In a daze she couldn't fathom, she fed the goats, brought the horses a fresh bale of hay, and then walked out towards the lake. There she stopped, aghast. The tears she had held back now poured down her cheeks. A bolt of lightning had split an old oak. A vast branch and part of its trunk had toppled through the cluster of hawthorn bushes right into the midst of their secret knoll. It was ravaged now, exposed, like the pale splintered wood of the tree. She touched its bark, shuddered. Slowly she walked back to the house. It was like a sign, she thought. She had been too carefree, too happy.

She didn't want to disturb Johannes, but she couldn't restrain herself from telling him.

He glanced down at her. 'I'll be through in an hour or two. We'll go and see about it then.'

'All right.' Her voice cracked.

'Anna, Anna,' he clambered down the ladder, 'what is it?' He had never seen such anguish on her face.

She rushed into his arms, wept, the sobs shaking her frame. He stroked her hair, kissed her tears, asked her over and over again, 'What is it, Anna? Tell me.' But she was mute. He held her tightly and as he held her, the passion rose in him, so fiercely that he thought it would smother him. He looked into her brimming eyes. 'I don't know if I can go on like this much more, Anna. I'll have to leave.' He edged into a corner of the room and turning away from her covered his face with his hands.

It was then that they both heard it, the sound of a car hooting through the stillness.

'Bruno,' Anna murmured. Her face white, she rushed away from him and fled to her room.

Twenty minutes later, she was down in the pretty pastel drawing room. Her face scrubbed, a fresh high-collared muslin blouse neatly tucked into her full trim skirt, her hair pinned up, she put her hands out to her husband.

'I'm sorry to have kept you waiting, Bruno. I wanted to tidy up for you. We get a little sloppy in our ways with all the work here.'

'You look lovely, Anna. A relief for tired eyes.' He drew her into his arms, kissed her hair.

She rested against his solid mass. Bruno, she thought, a bulwark between me and Johannes. She lifted her face to him, examining him. 'You do look tired, Bruno.'

He smiled. 'It's been a long drive. The rain was dreadful. And the road was littered with soldiers. There seem to be as many of them on leave as at the Front,' he chuckled a little grimly. 'At one point I had four of them in the car and it didn't seem right not to drop them where they wanted to go.'

Anna sat down beside him. 'Johannes Bahr is on leave too. He was wounded at the Front. He's staying in the boathouse.' She said it as casually as she could, happy that the words had tripped off her lips without stumbling.

'Oh?' Bruno leaned back into the sofa. 'Poor man. Still, he's lucky to be alive. There were more Germans killed in those first months of battle than they like to tell us.' He stared bleakly into the middle-distance. 'But we don't want to spoil our few days together by talking about the war,' he smiled at her. 'How have you been, my little one? You've grown even more beautiful, I think.'

Anna laughed. 'It must be the work.' She counted on her fingers. 'Carrots, beets, beans, marrows, potatoes, apples, we've harvested them all. But Bruno, how terrible,' she leapt up, 'we haven't even offered you a drink, and you so tired.'

'A schnapps, my dear, would be very nice.' His gaze followed her. Yes, he was tired, he thought, tired to his very marrow. Tired of the endless and probably fruitless attempts to save his remaining factories, tired of the bravado of the war, the emptiness of the patriotic sloganizing of the press, tired of the hatreds. While war raged on the outside, the various nationalities in the Hapsburg Empire raged against each other on the inside. There was a tide of pan-Germanism spreading through the country, with its rhetoric of superiority and purity. Where did that leave him as a Jew? He had once been proud of his native city, whatever its problems, had thought of it as an international capital, with its mixture of peoples, its lazy tolerance, its fine newspapers, its bubble of art and ideas. But now, two years into this blasted war, everything was hatred and pettiness.

He drank down the proffered schnapps in one mouthful and smiled unseeingly at Anna. Yes, he felt almost too tired for any of it now. He forced himself to focus on her lovely face. Perhaps he should ask her to come back to Vienna with him. She would cheer him. No, he thought, remembering how pinched she had looked in the winter months. That would be too selfish of him.

'Perhaps you'd like to have a wash and a rest before dinner, Bruno. Frau Trübl is fluttering round the kitchen like a hen gone mad, not knowing quite what to do to welcome you. I should go and help her.'

'Yes, perhaps that would be best.' He patted her hand, downed a second schnapps.

'Your room's all ready. She's seen to that.'

Bruno climbed the stairs tiredly. He already felt himself drifting off to sleep.

The table was set in the formal dining room. Frau Trübl had insisted on that and on the large candelabrum and the best silver. Meanwhile, old Trübl had gone to warn Johannes in the boathouse that they had a guest and that they would be eating punctually at eight. Anna didn't stop him. Nonetheless, Johannes appeared a little late. She averted her eyes, not certain how to greet him. But Bruno was welcoming. He stretched out his large hand and grasped Johannes's warmly.

'It must be a relief to be here away from the Front. Like a little bit of paradise.'

Johannes looked at him queerly. 'Yes, it is that,' he acknowledged.

'I was sorry to hear from Anna that you had been wounded.'

'Oh.' Johannes shrugged it off. 'I fared better than many.' He glanced at Anna. She was crumbling a roll in her plate, her eyes downcast. The perfect wife. His heart felt as if it were seizing up. But he couldn't bring himself to hate Adler. He didn't know whether it was the other man or himself who had changed, or simply the blunting effect of the war, but he felt less hostility than he remembered feeling towards him. He was talking about the Eastern Front and the Austrians now.

'Yes, I've just come back from Lemberg. It's sheer chaos. Did I tell you, my dear?'

Anna shook her head, her nervousness growing at the very mention of that name.

'Well, as you know the Austrians took it back again from the Russians. And now my factory has been turned into a barracks. You'd think they'd want steel. But then, efficiency was never high on my country's list of priorities. And it's true, the place was a shambles and there's only women and old men to do the work now, and nobody wants money. Only food.' He shook his vast head grimly and threw back half a glass of wine. 'Still, what was I saying, oh yes, the barracks. Well, the chaos. Half the soldiers can't understand the officers and vice versa.' He lowered his voice confidentially. 'While I was there, a lieutenant shot himself after his ranks had failed to follow orders. He simply couldn't bear it any more.'

Johannes found himself warming to the man's garrulousness.

'Not like that in the German army, is it?'

'No,' Johannes agreed. 'We understand each other perfectly well. When we can hear each other, that is.'

Bruno laughed, stopped himself. 'It is important still to be able to joke, isn't it?' He looked at them both questioningly. 'Sometimes, with some of my acquaintances, I find myself laughing alone. And they give me such severe looks.'

'I know what you mean.' Johannes laughed with him. They clinked glasses, tossed back the wine.

Bruno chewed reflectively on what passed for beef. 'Whatever the outcome of the war, I don't think the old Empire will last, you know. Perhaps it's for the best. When it takes twenty-three bureaucrats to process a single tax payment, something has gone seriously wrong, don't you think?

Johannes chuckled, nodded.

'And when a country has three million civil servants and spends far more money on its bureaucracy than its army, it shouldn't really go to war!' Bruno downed the rest of his wine, poured more for all of them. 'Still, I'm overstepping myself. Far be it from me to tell my betters what to do.'

'Sometime we'll have to tell them.' Johannes sounded a new note.

'Still a revolutionary, eh, Johannes? I may call you that, mightn't I? God knows, I might even be on your side if this war ever ends.' His face suddenly grew tense. 'But I'm not sure about revolutionaries. Their manners are terrible. Did Anna tell you about our little escapade? She was heroic, truly heroic.' He looked at his wife appreciatively and raised his glass to her. 'To Anna.' He gestured to Johannes to do the same and, a little shakily, Johannes did so.

'To Anna,' he murmured. 'What happened?' he asked.

'So she hasn't told you? She doesn't like to remember her bravery.'

Anna flushed. 'You were the brave one,' she mumbled.

'Pah, I had the measure of those scoundrels.'

Bruno proceeded to recount the story to Johannes, who looked at her oddly throughout.

'Of course, within months the two wretches were conscripted and now they're bravely serving their emperor and using their guns to better purpose, no doubt.' Bruno finished with a flourish just as Frau Trübl walked in with a large cherry cake.

'Oh my good woman, you've outdone yourself. I haven't enjoyed a dinner so much in months.' Bruno was effusive.

'Yes, Frau Trübl.' Anna echoed him. 'And you must both join us now for dessert.'

The woman flushed.

'Yes, yes, we insist,' the two men chimed in.

As they chatted, Johannes tried to catch Anna's eye. He met with no success. She was being resolutely the wife, avoiding him.

So that was that, he thought. He would leave tomorrow. He felt as if another part of him were dying. Too bad. He would have liked to have finished that fresco.

With an effort he rose to his feet. 'I had better get back,' he said, mustering his voice to politeness.

'Let me walk a little of the way with you, Johannes. I need some air. Anna, will you join us?'

She shook her head. 'No, I'm a little tired now.' Her laugh was brittle. 'We wake so early here.'

'Not tomorrow,' old Trübl grunted. 'Tomorrow you are not to get into those trousers. Not with your husband here.'

Anna flushed. 'No, of course not. Goodnight.' She walked slowly from the room, only breaking into a run when she reached the stairs.

Bruno left Johannes half way to the boathouse and then strolled in the opposite direction. He had drunk too much and talked too much. It wasn't dignified. But it was happening to him more and more these last months. He kicked the loose gravel on the path. He was being infected by the general madness. Still, this evening had been a pleasure. It was always such a delight to be with his darling Anna. And that young Bahr hadn't turned out to be such a bad fellow, a little surly at times, but then they all had good reason for surliness these days.

Bruno walked. He wasn't in the least sleepy now. Perhaps he should go to Anna. No, he would wait a little, until she was asleep. Then he could gaze his fill of her. She grew more beautiful each time he saw her. Then perhaps . . . but no. There was really no need of that. The idea of a child had ceased to drive him. It was as if the war had eaten up the future, along with his will. Yes, that was it.

A light drizzle began to fall and Bruno hurried towards the house. He would sit in the library for a while, find a little Schnitzler story of a shop girl or a de Maupassant to tickle his fancy, something quite removed from the war. He let himself into the library and gazed at the shelves. Simmel, Weber, Bölsche, a host of naturalists. Didn't his in-laws have any light reading at all? Finally he found a volume of Balzac in French. He eased himself into a leather chair and began. But the words didn't hold him and when he closed his eyes, the world spun. Restlessly he got up. He would go into that oversized extension that Anna so loved and examine Klaus's rare species. Perhaps they were faring better through this war than he was. Bruno chuckled to himself.

He opened the large double doors to the room and searched for a light, tripping over something before he found it. A ladder. There was work going on here. He looked at the tins of colour on the floor. Perhaps that Bahr fellow was finishing up what he had left incomplete. Bruno's eyes travelled up the wall. A mural. Unfinished, that too. He gazed at it and then his fists clenched. Anna. It was Anna.

He sat down heavily in the nearest chair and stared at the image in disbelief. She was naked, her bosom barer than he had ever seen it, covered only by swirling grass. It was all so vivid, he felt she would move if he touched her. Bruno rubbed his eyes. She must have posed for him, naked, like that.

Rage flooded through him. He bounded up from his chair, looked more closely. No, there was more to it than that. That face, the throat flung back, the fanning hair, the half-closed eyes. That look of ecstasy. Pain gripped him, clutching at his throat, making him dizzy. That look could only mean one thing. He had seen it on Lotte's face. But never, never on his wife's.

His wife had coupled with Bahr. Bruno let the thought sink in, paced like a caged animal. The slut. Suddenly, he gripped a tin and threw it violently at the image. Red paint splattered over Anna's breast, like blood. He watched its progress. A mere slut, he repeated to himself over and over. And he had thought her so pure, so innocent, had never wanted really to touch her, to sully her.

With a wail which seemed to split him in two, Bruno lumbered up the stairs. How could she? His Anna with another man. His mind was in turmoil as if the very foundations of his life had been shattered and columns were tumbling round him. He could hardly breathe, was blinded by the dust. All he could see was that look of ecstasy on her face. His Anna, his angel, a whore. He slammed his fist on the bannister.

He would show her, show her how one treated whores. He opened the door to her room. Dark. Perhaps she was with him right now, out there in the grass. He would find her, both of them, tear them to shreds. No, no, first he would tear her clothes, those frivolous little bodices, those nightgowns, with which she sheltered herself from him. Shakily, Bruno lit the candle on the nearest table. No, she was here, turning over in the bed, her eyes fluttering open.

'Bruno.' She stretched her arms out towards him.

A real slut. She would have anybody. Everybody. Two at once. His breath came in gasps. In a step he was beside her. He slapped her across the face, watched her recoil. But she didn't make a sound. Yes, she knew her guilt. A guilty whore. He ripped the blankets off the bed and with a savage gesture, split open her nightgown. There they were, the breasts that other man had painted, fondled. Perfect. He saw them through the other man's eyes, saw the taut stomach, the golden skin. Suddenly he felt himself grow hard, so hard his trousers rubbed harshly against him.

'Bruno, what is it?'

That voice again, so caressing, but she was trying to hide herself from his gaze, pulling the nightgown round her.

'Slut!' The word that had been swirling round his head at last found release on his slurring lips. He repeated it again and again as he shed his jacket, his trousers, forced her hand round his jutting penis, gripping it there with his own. The sensation of her fingers round him, so gentle, almost made him swoon. But he didn't want that, didn't want that lying gentleness. His hands bit into her shoulders, pressing her down, down on her knees. 'Take it,' he groaned, 'take it in your lying mouth.' She bent her head back to look up at him, but he wouldn't meet those deceitful eyes. 'Take it.'

Her hand curled round his penis and then he felt her lips closing round him, so moist, so soft. He moaned. Yes, she knew what to do, the slut. His eyes closed, he pushed against her, heard her sob, felt the lips drawing away. No, not yet. Not yet. She had leapt away from him, up on to the bed. He caught her hands, pulled her down, forcing her legs apart. How soft she was, compliant really. A true whore. He thrust into her again and again, painfully, so that the punishing hurt him, covered her breasts with his hands, bit at them, bit hard, found her mouth, probed, probed. The liar. His hands circled her throat. How easy it would be to snap it. But her arms were round him now, pummelling his back, and there was a tremor inside her he had never felt before. And then the pressure rose from his spine, rose, rose, burst through him, making him helpless. With a sob, he heaved into her, pushed, pushed, moaning, 'Slut, slut.'

His eyes were suffused with tears. Stumbling, his limbs numb, he found his clothes. He wouldn't look at her, even though he could hear her as if from a great distance calling his name. Somehow, despite the overwhelming dizziness, he found his room. He sat on the edge of his bed and wept silently into his large hands.

Anna too was crying, her body racked with sobs. Why, why had he done that? She felt humiliated. Shamed. Her body bruised, debased. He was drunk, she knew. She had never seen him drunk before. He was always so kind, so considerate. Drink. Perhaps that was all it was and the strain he was under. But why had he called her a slut? Why wouldn't he meet her eyes, answer her?

She cried until she had no more tears. Then she got up slowly to wash, her legs feeling odd, flayed. She shakily poured some water from the jug into the bowl. In the small mirror above the dresser, she caught her reflection. Her eyes looked bruised, her face ghostly. But there was something about her sore parted lips. She looked at the tear-stained face more closely. And then she saw it. The mural. He must have seen the mural. She should never have let Johannes do it. But strangely, when she had watched the image emerging from the wall, she hadn't thought of it as herself, only as something beautiful. Yet to Bruno it would seem as if . . .

Anna began to shake uncontrollably. An image from 'Otello' leapt into her mind. She had seen the opera not so long ago, seen Otello's hands encircling Desdemona's neck, like Bruno's had encircled hers. She could still feel the imprint of his fingers. But she wasn't Desdemona. She was still here to tell the tale. Nor was she, Anna realized, as innocent, certainly not in Bruno's eyes. And he had found a form of punishment to fit the supposed crime. A humiliation of the flesh for a supposed sin of the flesh.

How cold she felt, as cold as a dank tomb. She drew the blanket over her. Johannes had said there was no shame in the body, but she felt shamed now. Horribly, radically shamed. She would never be able to face Bruno tomorrow. Perhaps never be able to face him again.

Anna curled herself into a small ball and wept silent tears.

Dreams besieged her, a plague of images: her own figure floating on a curving wall, no, no, on the grass, the tree split by lightning falling towards her. No, not a tree, but Bruno, his face huge amidst the spikes of branches, the chocolate glow of his eyes turned stony, granite-cold. That face was coming towards her, she had to move, run, or she, too, would be turned to stone, but she couldn't. Her limbs were like concrete, fixed in fear to the ground. 'Stop, Bruno, it's me,' she was shouting, but no sound came to her lips, already stone, and he was falling, coming towards her. Bruno.

But by the morning, Bruno had vanished. She found a note from him slipped under her door. A cryptic, terse, bitter little note. 'Goodbye, Anna,' it said. 'Should you need ever to come back to Vienna, you will find me satisfactorily gone.' She shuddered. As simple as that, the end of her marriage. She looked out of the window on the rain-swept grounds. He was driving through that rain now, hunched at the bleary windscreen. Driving away from her. Bruno, her bulwark.

An uncanny laugh formed inside her, echoed through the room. Suddenly, with a fierceness she didn't know she possessed, she pulled the sheets from the bed, bundled them into a heap, went to find new ones and made up a fresh white bed. Then she crawled into it, drawing the blankets up over her head, thinking, though she knew it was childish, that perhaps if she lay still long enough, slept for a hundred years like some fairy-tale princess encased in stone, everything would have changed.

She didn't know how much later it was that a knock roused her. She felt leaden, drugged. Frau Trübl, she thought, and murmured, 'Come in'. But it was Johannes who confronted her. He was wearing his uniform and she knew instantly what he had come to tell her.

'I couldn't find you anywhere.' His voice was cool. 'Or anyone else. So I thought I'd come up.'

'To say goodbye.'

He nodded.

Anna laughed that uncanny laugh. 'Two in one day.' She burrowed under the blankets, hiding. 'Goodbye, Johannes,' she murmured, heard the door close. The tears again. She let them fall.

'What do you mean, two in one day?'

He was still there. She gulped down her tears.

'Bruno's gone,' she mumbled.

He pulled the sheets away from her face. 'Gone where?'

Anna shrugged. 'Left me.' She buried her head in the pillow.

He took her hand, stroked it gently. 'Why, Anna?' he asked after a moment. 'Was it the mural?'

'I don't know.' She looked at him, shivered.

He folded her into his arms. 'I looked for you in there, saw it. Someone threw red paint at it. Poor Anna. All my fault.'

She snuggled against his rough jacket, wanting his warmth.

'And you mind terribly, don't you?'

'I mind,' she said, meeting his eyes, unable to lie.

'I'll write to him. A convincing letter. Perhaps it will help.' His voice was flat. He rose.

'Don't go, Johannes. Please don't go.' She stretched out her hand to him.

He took it. 'But if I stay . . .' His eyes burned into her.

'Stay,' she said softly.

He turned towards the door and for a moment, her heart stopped. He was going after all.

Then she heard the click of the key and he was back at her side.

'Anna, my Anna.' He buried his face in her hair, kissing her gently, stroking, finding her lips. She gave herself to that gentleness, her body humming to his touch, returning his caress, urging him as he urged her, helping him undress, touching, touching, gazing at his limbs, seeing, feeling his joy in her flesh until she thought she would faint from the pleasure of it. And then, as he came into her, slowly, so slowly, tantalizingly, that she felt herself melting against him, she whispered, 'I think I love you, Johannes, I think I know what it means.'

He smiled, his eyes so clear above her that she felt she was looking into the bluest sky. And then he covered her lips, pressing more deeply into her, probing, probing, rubbing, until she cried out.

'Love me, Anna, love me like you did that day on our knoll,' he whispered into her ear, his breath warm on her, tickling. He turned her over, so that her weight rested against him, her lips found his chest. He arched against her, arched so high, that she felt as if her body were opening, flowing into him as he flowed into her, calling her name, calling his, Johannes, Johannes, Anna, Anna.

Later she lay in the circle of his arms, feeling his moistness, gazing out at the patches of blue in the clearing sky.

'I could love you forever,' he murmured.

She turned to him, stroked his face, his chest, the scar. 'But . . . ?'

'But I only have ten days,' he smiled, his lips quivering.

'We will have to make ten days forever then.' She looked up at him, her eyes serious.

'Yes, my Anna. We will have to do just that.'

SEVEN

THERE WAS NO WELCOMING PARTY to meet Anna when she returned home that afternoon late in November 1916. Under a slate-grey sky, Vienna was shrouded in mourning. Only a thin mewling kitten patrolled the pavement in front of the house. It followed her through the doors, tucked itself snugly between her cases in the lift and preceded her into the empty apartment.

As she looked round, Anna resisted the tears which these days sprang too readily to her eyes. Ghostly white sheets covered sofas and chairs. Dust was gathered everywhere on the once-gleaming furniture. Stately palms had turned a mottled desert yellow, monuments to their own past life. Anna lifted the little kitten into her arms and stroked it absently.

'We'll have to make do somehow, won't we,' she murmured.

Not that she had expected a welcome. But she hadn't known that Bruno had closed down the apartment altogether. Perhaps she should never have left Seehafen, though there hadn't really been much choice now that winter had set in and there was so little work to do.

As it was, she had outstayed her time there. Bettina had sensibly said well over a month ago, when the fogs had obliterated the mountains and everything else, that soon they would have to close up the big house for the winter. Fuel was too precious a commodity these days to be squandered. Not that Anna had had any of the big tile stoves lit; she simply wrapped up in old coats to face the cold evenings. Frau Trübl had begun to give her strange glances, even once asking her whether she would like to join them in their snug little cottage beside the stables.

Three months had passed and there had been no word from Johannes. This time the tears did fill her eyes. He might be dead and no one would think of telling her. No, she wouldn't even consider that. He had warned her that he wouldn't write. On that last night they had had together, he had said – she could remember his words precisely – 'I won't be able to fight if I think of you, Anna. I'll be afraid of dying. And the fear brings on the death. I've seen it. It's those who have too much to lose who go first.'

Anna swallowed hard. She had thought of him, of course, thought of him all the time. No, not thought. Thought was the wrong word. She had felt him in the lapping of the lake against her body, in the rustle of the high grass, in the tug of the wind on her hair. He was everywhere during those first weeks after he had left – in that house, in those grounds, in her, so that she didn't feel her separateness. And then with the first chill of winter, he was suddenly gone, so that she was half a person, bereft, meagre. A hole seemed to have formed inside her and the hole bore the name of his absence. But it was a secret space, and with her everyday mind she worried about other things. Central amongst them was Bruno.

Gently Anna lifted the little cat from her lap and began to put things away, pull the sheets from the sofas, search out dusters. How little she knew about the running of this place. It was a distressing incompetence, one that would make Bettina laugh. Bettina.

Anna had resented her presence when she had come down to Seehafen for those few days with little Max. She had wanted Johannes to herself in the brief time they had together. She still wondered if Bettina had noticed anything between them. No, perhaps not. She had been so engrossed in tugging every particle of Johannes's war experience out of him that there was hardly time to notice anything else. And she had learned more in those few days than Anna had garnered in weeks. Johannes had spoken easily enough, ruffling little Max's hair unseeingly while he did so, getting down on all fours to find lost toys.

It had all made Anna just a tiny bit jealous, but at night, lying in his arms under the stars, she had forgotten.

Anna watched the kitten nibbling at the cheese she had brought from Seehafen. She would have to buy food and that, too, was a problem. She had so little money. She hadn't dared tell Bettina. Hadn't dared tell her about Bruno either.

She had heard nothing from him in all these months. She had written, of course, to say that she was coming back. Perhaps the letter hadn't reached him. The post was so bad these days. Then, too, he might not even be in Vienna. Whether Johannes had ever written to him, she didn't know. What could he say, in any event, after everything that had transpired?

Anna roused herself. The first thing to do was to phone Tante Hermine. Then tomorrow, she would start looking for work.

She tried the phone tentatively, heard the signal with relief. At least that hadn't been cut off. And her aunt's voice when it came was as scolding and blustering as ever.

'Why have you been away for so long?' Her aunt didn't wait for an answer. 'I'm getting old and things are really too difficult these days. You *must* visit me more often. But you'll come tonight, at least. And make sure that husband of yours comes as well. I've been trying to reach him for weeks, left messages in his office. At seven. Promptly.'

She rung off, before Anna could get in a word. Anna laughed and looked at the buzzing receiver: at least there was still one unchanging point in her universe.

She left in good time, taking a tram to conserve her money, and walking the rest of the way, despite the light drizzle. Everything looked bleak. Vienna, she had to remind herself, was in mourning. Franz Josef had died and though many may have thought or wished him dead before, the city wore a shroud of intractable melancholy. Some of the familiar cafés had shut their doors. People hurried brusquely through the streets, avoided each other's eyes. There was a dankness in the air, a smell of creeping poverty which emanated from the beggars and rose to enfold them all.

Anna, too, hurried, her eyes on the cobblestones. Even at her aunt's house, things had changed. There was no longer the familiar footman at the door, only a maid to take her coat.

But her aunt still presided in her favourite corner chair.

'Anna, at last.' She proffered her cheek. 'Let me look at you, girl. Hmmm, a little pale.' She held her pince-nez to her eyes and examined her niece critically, her gaze travelling down her form. 'And still not producing any children.'

Anna gulped, happy that the room was still almost empty.

Her aunt caught her glance. 'Not many of us tonight. My officers are all busy elsewhere,' she laughed raucously, 'except old von Effinghen. He's been retired. Got too deaf, I guess.' Her powdery face crinkled. 'That's what I need to see Bruno about. Where is that husband of yours?'

'I'm not sure,' Anna murmured.

'Eh? Speak up, girl, I'm not as young as I used to be. Ah,' her aunt looked beyond her, 'there he is now. Why didn't you say so, girl.'

Anna blanched, not daring to turn round. As if in silhouette she saw Bruno kiss her aunt's hand, turn stiffly to her. She stepped back, her heart rising in her throat. 'Hello, Anna,' he said softly. She couldn't believe the change in him. It was as if he had shrunk into a spectre of himself. His hair and moustache had turned grey. The lustre had gone from his eyes; the skin sagged, loose round his features.

'Hello, Bruno,' she whispered, tears tugging at her eyes. She had done that, she with her callow unthinkingness. She wanted to take him in her arms, comfort him, but he was already edging away from her, sitting down by her aunt's side, listening, his eyes elsewhere. How would she speak to him? He wanted nothing to do with her.

The room was beginning to fill up. Anna moved into the fray. She must mingle, listen. Perhaps someone would know of a job for her. She greeted some old acquaintances, tried to accommodate herself to the chatter she had forgotten how to make, heard endless catalogues of Franz Josef's sixty-eight years of glory, gloomy speculations about the end of Empire, of Poland's new nationhood, of more food riots in Berlin.

And then he was beside her, this ghost of Bruno. 'I'm leaving now, Anna.'

'May I come with you?'

'If you wish.'

He was looking through her to something at the other side of the room.

'Thank you.'

She said goodbye to Tante Hermine, promising to return within the next few days, got her coat, and climbed into the car beside him. Then the silence mounted with the passing streets until she could bear it no more.

'Bruno, will you come back home with me?' Her voice broke.

'That is no longer my home,' he said tersely.

She took a deep breath. 'I . . . I would like to speak to you, Bruno.'

'I don't think we have much to say to each other, Anna.'

Silence again and that tension. It was unbearable. Anna opened the window.

Then he cleared his throat. 'I would have had the apartment ready for you, but your letter only arrived today. I shall send someone round tomorrow.'

'There's no need.'

'I shall provide for you while I can, Anna.'

There was something so grim in his voice that the tears leapt into her eyes.

'You don't have to provide for me,' she murmured.

They were turning into their street.

'I will be correct. You are still my wife. Technically. There is an account open in your name.'

'Please come up, Bruno. Please.' The tears were streaming down her cheeks now. 'I . . . I'm afraid to be alone.' It wasn't what she had meant to say. 'It's . . . it's just that I want to speak to you.'

They pulled up in front of the house. He glanced at his watch. 'Frau Gruber might still be awake. I could send a fiacre for her. We could talk over a bite of supper somewhere.' His voice was so cold it chilled her.

'You don't want to come up to the apartment then,' she said bleakly.

'No, Anna, I don't.'

She put her hand on his shoulder tentatively.

He shrugged it off, as if she had burned him, but he met her eyes for the first time. The pain she read there frightened her almost more than his coldness.

'Please don't touch me, Anna. As you well know, that is all over between us.'

'I know,' she mumbled. 'But Bruno, please, I must talk to you, make you understand. It's not what you think.' Again her words had carried her where she didn't want to go.

'Understand!' The word was strangled in his throat. 'I understand too much.' He started the car and pulled off abruptly, veering round the corner, going much too fast. 'Sacher's,' he said, stopping short. 'They should have a table for us.'

He ushered her into the dining room, left her at the alcove table while he went for a messenger. Chandeliers, silver, white cloths, the light dazzled her. She escaped to the powder room, tried to blot out the signs of her tears, took several deep breaths. He was waiting for her when she returned, still avoiding her eyes.

'Look at me, please, Bruno. I haven't changed that much.'

'I have,' he murmured, examining the menu.

She let him order for her, waited, no longer knowing how to begin.

'I had a letter from that man,' he said at last. He was pushing his food round his plate. She had never seen him do that. 'I didn't believe a word of it.'

'No,' she breathed. 'What did he say?'

He laughed bitterly. 'Haven't you worked out your stories together?'

'All right, I'll tell you, Bruno. It's like this.' Her eyes suddenly blazed. 'When you did to me whatever you did to me that night, nothing had happened between Johannes and myself. No, don't look so disbelieving. Yes, yes, he had seen me. But so what? He's an artist. He's painted hundreds of women. It doesn't mean anything.'

Anna could hardly believe her own ears. She had never told the story to herself like that. But it had truth. Yes, as she said it, she realized just how much truth.

'My wife,' Bruno murmured.

'Yes, your wife. But simply a woman. Me. Anna von Leinsdorf, Anna Adler. A woman with a body. Like any other woman.' She stopped, sipped some wine. How was she going to go on? She took a deep breath. 'And I was there. And he needed to paint again. See something other than dead bodies.' Did she know that was true, Anna wondered? Where was she finding these words? But he was looking at her now, looking at her directly. She plunged in again.

'And then, after that evening, after . . .' She stopped, unable to go on.

'After that evening.' He was prodding her now.

'After that evening, everything changed. In me. I felt dirty, shamed.' She laughed suddenly. 'You wanted to shame me, didn't you, Bruno?'

He flushed, the colour coming back into his face making him look more as she remembered him. 'One can't talk about these things,' he muttered.

'No, perhaps not. But I'm talking now.' She drank some more wine. 'And Johannes helped me to overcome it. He made me clean.'

He looked at her uncomprehendingly, 'Clean? How, clean?'

'I don't think you want to know, Bruno. I don't think you'll understand.' Suddenly she lost her impetus. No, he wouldn't understand, she knew that. But she had said it. Now there was only one more thing. And she couldn't lie to him about that either. How much easier it would be anywhere but this room, or even if he let her touch him. 'You didn't protect me, Bruno. With all your wisdom, you didn't protect me.' She saw the pain shoot through his eyes. 'No, that's not fair. I shouldn't have said that. What I did I wanted to do more than anything else I've wanted to do in all my life. Except cause you pain, Bruno.'

He rose from the table. 'I . . . I have to leave you for a minute, Anna.' He moved clumsily away, almost running through the vast space of the dining room.

She waited. Waited. He wasn't coming back. She shouldn't have spoken. She should simply have told him what needed to be said – that last thing. The tears came back again. Anna hid behind the menu. If he didn't come back, she wouldn't even be able to pay. She waited. No one. She told the waiter she had to go. Did Herr Adler have an account? Yes? Then please tell him when he returned that she had to get home, a visitor, yes. No, the housekeeper.

Anna walked blindly through the streets. Perhaps she should write to him. But she was so bad at words. Didn't even always know what she wanted to say except once she had said it. And writing was so final. Anna stumbled over an uneven cobblestone, leaned against a wall to regain her balance. The street was deserted. Cold heavy rain fell mercilessly. She hadn't even noticed how wet she was. She went on. At the crossroads, a car skimmed past her so quickly that she had to leap back on to the pavement.

'Anna!'

It was him coming towards her. Of course, his car. She hadn't noticed. Perhaps he wanted to kill her. She squared her shoulders.

'You didn't wait.'

'I thought you had left.'

'No, no. I wasn't feeling well.' His voice was hoarse. 'I'm sorry.'

She looked into his face, sallow in the lamplight. And those eyes. She turned away, unable to face them.

'Come into the car. I'll take you back.'

It was only a few blocks more and they didn't speak. But when he stopped the car, Anna said again, 'Will you come up, Bruno. Please.'

'I'd rather not.' He was looking grimly into the rain-covered windshield.

'Tomorrow, then,' she sighed. 'There is something more I need to say.'

'All right then, now. Let's get it over with.' He slammed the door hard behind him.

They went up in the lift, silently, like strangers, looking straight at the wrought-iron grilles which marked the floors. Anna waited for him to open the door of the apartment, then realized he didn't have the key. That distressed her almost more than anything else. She fumbled for her own.

The hall light was already on. Frau Gruber was there. She came towards them slowly, welcoming them, excited. She had found a black kitten in the apartment. Look, there he was now.

'Oh, I'd forgotten.' The kitten pawed at Anna's skirts and she picked him up, stroking him. 'He followed me home. He must be starving. I didn't have anything to give him, except some cheese.'

'I fetched a few scraps,' Frau Gruber smiled. 'There are so many of these strays around these days.'

'I think he wants to stay,' Anna murmured, carrying the cat with her into the salon. The lamps were lit, the place looked less forbidding than when she had arrived.

'Shall I prepare you some tea? I think there's some left.'

'Yes, thank you, Frau Gruber. And thank you for coming at such short notice. I'm grateful.'

The woman beamed. 'And shall I prepare your room, Herr Adler?'

'No, no, that won't be necessary.' Bruno shrugged her off. 'I won't be able to stay for more than a moment.'

She left them in the room they knew so well, but in which they were now so awkward. They didn't speak until the tea was on the table. Anna noticed that Bruno's hand shook as he held his cup. She steeled herself, paced for a moment and then turned back to him. She had to see his face. She clenched her fists.

'I'm having a baby, Bruno.'

He put his cup down with a clatter, his face as white as the porcelain.

'Yes, I didn't think you'd be pleased.' There was no irony in her voice. 'I'm not certain it's yours, but it could very well be.' She looked at him earnestly. 'I have no way of knowing.' She turned away now, picked up the little kitten and fondled it. Waited. Bruno didn't move.

'I'm sorry these are the circumstances under which I have to tell you. But I thought you should know.' The tears, the tears again. 'Once you would have wanted to know.' Suddenly she could bear it no more, that motionless face, that lack of response. She fled from the room, heard the splintering of glass behind her.

'Anna!' He called her back. He was standing by the fireplace. In the unlit coals, she saw their shattered wedding portrait.

'What is it that you want of me, Anna?' His voice was bitter.

She sank back into a chair. 'I don't know,' she murmured. 'I just knew that I had to tell you, that you had to know. And from me.' She averted her eyes. 'I haven't told anyone else yet.'

'And you've told me, because you're afraid he'll be killed,' he hissed.

'Perhaps, Bruno.' She met him on it. Then she stood up. She was shaking, her legs barely able to carry her. 'But that comment wasn't worthy of you,' she said in a low voice. 'I'll leave tomorrow. That will be best.' She walked towards the door, afraid she would fall, holding her back straight.

'Anna.' He gripped her shoulder, forcing her to turn back, then instantly released her. His face was in turmoil. He passed a shaky hand through his heavy hair, dishevelling it. 'I'm sorry. I didn't mean . . . didn't mean for you to go. Of course, you must stay. I shall take care of you, take care of everything. I'll have the doctor come round tomorrow. But I must go now. I must.' It was a plea.

She tried to take his hand, but he pulled it away. 'No . . .' His voice cracked. 'Please understand, Anna. It hurts me to be here. This place,' he waved his arms wildly, 'I haven't been here for months. And it hurts me to see you.' The words seemed to tear out of him. 'Perhaps it will get better.' He tugged on his coat.

She watched him, her heart breaking. 'I care for you very much, Bruno. I don't know how to show it.'

Bruno stumbled down the stairs, clutching at the walls. Outside he breathed deeply, heavily, for some minutes, unable to move.

Why had she come back? It had almost got better and now her presence confronted him with it all again. He had hated her, how he had hated her, convinced himself that she wouldn't come back. Had barely been in Vienna fearing to see her, to bump into memories of her. Outside, in Galicia or Moravia, he could breathe more freely, even though everything else was terrible. He had travelled, from office to office, factory to factory, seeing the worst, seeing the women working, the old men, the growing poverty, the hungry children, the encroaching chaos. What profits he hadn't lost, he had given away. Why not? There would never be children of his own now and there were so many others. He had refused, despite the money to be made, to convert his factories into munitions works. He preferred to throw his fortune to the winds, or to invest patriotically in those much vaunted war bonds, which he sensed amounted to the same thing. It made him feel lighter, lifted some of the burden which pressed him into the ground.

In Vienna, he stayed at the Sacher Hotel. It suited him, the anonymity of the suite, the lack of questions. He shouldn't have brought her there. It was stupid of him, but she had taken him by surprise, repeating over and over how she wanted to talk to him. And she looked so pale, so small, no more than a child. A child who had betrayed him but who was kind to him, who spoke with such directness in her tawny eyes.

The kindness made it worse. God, how it shamed him.

Bruno stared through the car window, unable to summon the energy to start the motor. The shame had eaten at him for months, nibbling away at his own idea of himself, crushing it, until there was nothing left.

It wasn't simply the shame of her preferring another man. He fought to control the jealousy that gripped him again, even now. That had been partly his own fault, in any event. He shouldn't have left her alone so much. There was a far greater shame, the torment of his own behaviour. There were ways of dealing with wives who betrayed one, after all. Civilized ways. But he, he had behaved like an animal. No, like a deranged ripper, some demented brute raised in a hovel. Attacking her, hitting her, forcing her, his own wife.

And there was worse still, what he hated to admit, what he had only admitted to himself after the scene had played itself over and over in his mind obsessively with never lessening force until he felt he was going mad: he had enjoyed it. Yes, had lusted after her while hating her, hitting her. Anna. Little Anna. The woman he adored.

He hadn't been with a woman since. He no longer trusted or recognized himself. Bruno Adler, that upright man, honest, dignified, civilized. The shame of it, the guilt gnawing at his entrails.

And now he was no longer himself. All his ideals had toppled, his dreams. He had loved her so much, had cherished her, wanted to protect her, to build a life together. Even after the war had eaten away at things, she still represented a purity, a hope. Perhaps his only one. And he had destroyed it with his own mad bestiality.

What was it that she had told him over dinner, that had made him gag, started that terrible churning in his stomach so that he had to flee to his room? 'You didn't protect me.' He certainly hadn't protected her. He had attacked her himself, a ravaging unforgivable brute.

And now? Bruno felt the sickness rising in him again, that dizziness which took him over from time to time and left his mind blank. He fought it back, started the engine, drove to the hotel, too fast, the pain blurring his vision as much as the pelting rain. He lay down on his bed and stared bleakly at the ceiling. Now there was to be a child, the child he had once so wanted. No, not that child, but a creature conceived from either his own savagery or another man's. God, how that hurt, like a knife slowly twisting in him.

Yet he would try to behave well, redeem a tattered shred of his dignity, care for her. As long as he didn't have to see her too often. Have those eyes look at him, remind him, reflect his guilt, his shattered pride.

As long as he didn't have to come too close to her so that he was tempted to fold her in his arms.

With a sob, Bruno turned over and covered his face in the depths of his pillow.

The baby grew inside Anna, making her sick in the mornings. But by midday she was better and she went off to work in an orphanage where she helped delinquent boys with their reading. It paid little more than self-respect, but that was important to her and the few shillings went into her rainy-day box. Bruno had been as good as his word. The bank account was there, the apartment taken care of.

He came to see her only irregularly. He hated her, she knew, wanted to avoid her. She prayed he would get over it. She so wanted him to take an interest in the child he had once avidly desired. And she missed his presence in the apartment. From Johannes there was still no word and with each passing week, the idyll of Seehafen receded, so that even though she still dreamt of him, she began to think in the bright light of day that the whole episode had been a dream conceived of her own longing. The baby she convinced herself must be Bruno's, though in truth she knew that she would only be sure when she saw it.

On the last day of January, by which time she had had to have her dresses let out to accommodate her new girth, she rang Bruno. She rarely dared to. But this time was different. Saturday was his birthday and she wanted to invite him over, for a drink, perhaps dinner. It had been some weeks since he had visited. Bruno, located, agreed, if a little stiffly.

Anna was pleased. She went to do the shopping herself, collecting together the ration cards she had saved, thinking that if she protruded her belly a little further, some of the merchants might take pity on her and give her a little extra. Everything was so scarce, but she managed to find a scrawny chicken, some vegetables.

After having helped Frau Gruber with the cooking, she dismissed her, and laid the table herself with the best silver and the Sèvres china she had inherited from her mother. It looked so pretty, she thought, and she too would make an effort today, with a blue dress he had chosen for her himself, now suitably adjusted; a little rouge on her cheeks; her hair freshly washed. And the present. It wasn't much, since she had wanted to use her own money, but cigars were hard to come by at the moment, and she hoped he would be pleased.

They sat opposite each other in the dining room, candlelight glowing over the table. They were a little on edge and Anna covered over the silences by babbling about the orphanage, telling him stories about the boys. From time to time she caught him glancing at her stomach.

'He's growing,' she said on one of those occasions.

Bruno swallowed hard. 'Why do you say "he"?'

She shrugged. 'That's how I feel.'

He looked away, that strange ache she didn't recognize in his eyes again.

'Bruno, do you remember, in Paris, on our honeymoon, that man whom we met, whose wife had left him?'

'Why do you bring that up?' he asked fiercely.

'I don't know, I think about it from time to time,' she mused. 'I . . . I didn't run away.'

He grimaced. 'Only because there was no one to run with.'

'You would have wanted me to?' she said quietly.

'Perhaps.'

The kitten, sleekly plump now, leapt into her lap. She stroked it slowly.

'Don't hate me, Bruno, please don't hate me. I'll try to make it up to you.' The tears formed in her eyes.

He winced.

'The kitten likes the baby,' she said after a moment. 'It kicks now. Here, feel.' Suddenly she was by his side, lifting his hand to her stomach. He could feel the warmth, the small movements. Like the tug of his own mortality. A child to judge the wreck he had become, to hate him as he had hated his own autocratic father, as he loathed himself. Bruno sobbed, buried his face in her belly, and then leapt back blindly, pushing away his chair.

She pressed herself against him, her arms round his neck, wanting the shelter of him. 'Oh Bruno, I do care for you.'

'Please, Anna.' He drew away, hurried into his coat, thanked her for his present.

'Will you come again, next Saturday, it means so much to me,' she asked softly.

He fled. But he came back, drawn to her, to that swelling mound, as if to his own death. He had even managed to find her some flowers, two orchids like the memory of a time which would never be again, and chocolates, rich, dark.

'Like your eyes,' she said, laughing up at him, grateful, fluttering around him, making him comfortable, disappearing into the kitchen. He leaned back into the sofa. 'Like a wife.' The thought formed itself. Perhaps he could come back, here, to her. He was so tired, always so tired.

He stirred himself, gazed round the room, went slowly into his old study. Nothing had been touched, but the wood shone, as did his leather chair, his desk with the embossed paperweight and the row of antique figurines. He fingered them, moved slowly into the morning room where they used to have breakfast. She had made it her room now, he could see the signs of her, the basket of wool, the imprint of her weight in the flowered chair. He sat down in it. On the table beside it, there was a sheaf of papers. Drawings. He looked at them. Pictures of war, macabre bodies, flayed, arched, mutilated. His temples began to pound. Brothels, women with sagging breasts, wearing officer's caps, men on their knees. A letter in the pictures' midst. He couldn't stop his eyes from perusing it.

From him.

> Dearest, I try not to think of you. If you need money, send these to Fischer in Berlin. He'll help. Everything is rightfully yours.

A dizziness overcame him, blurring his vision. He closed his eyes, rubbed, rubbed. An image of Anna came to him, so real he could almost touch it. Anna punished. Anna stretched on a white bed, flayed, mutilated, a dead baby beside her. Like his first wife, Elisabeth. He leapt up, trying to rid himself of the vision, scattering Johannes's pictures on the floor. Stumbling.

She stood in front of him. 'You've seen the pictures,' she mumbled.

A strange hollow laugh burst out of him. 'Yes, a patrimony for the baby.'

She stared at him, those tawny eyes so direct. 'Johannes doesn't know about the baby.'

'No, no, of course not.' Bruno didn't want to look at her, but those eyes held him, not a trace of shame or guilt in them, only a widening of the pupils in, what was it, fear, yes, like on that night, when he had despoiled her. He turned his back on her, picked up the pictures with clumsy fingers. 'They're good. They should bring in something. If it weren't a little redundant, I would buy them myself.' Again that hollow laugh coming from he didn't know where within him. He handed them to her. 'He'll make a far better father for the child than I will, Anna,' he said, his voice breaking.

He walked away. She stopped him at the door, blocking his exit, throwing her arms around him, her head in his shoulder, crying, 'Bruno, please.' He held her, breathed in the perfume of her hair, felt her softness. He could die here, in these arms. His loins quivered. And then the baby kicked against him and he saw the image again, the dead woman on that slab of a bed, the child beside her. Like an image of his own mortality.

His head throbbed painfully. 'Goodbye, my darling,' he murmured, 'forgive me.' He looked at her for a moment as if imprinting her living form on his mind and then fled into the wintry night.

Thick wet flakes had covered the ground and were still falling in abundance. Bruno lifted his hot face to the sky and let the snow settle on it. He watched the play of those pure flurrying shapes. Yes, he would drive out to the hills. The white expanse would eradicate those seething images, those demons which warred within him. He didn't dare close his eyes, though he wanted above all to sleep, to rest. He drove, fast, too fast, the conflicting emotions tearing at him, his pulse racing as quickly as the car. By the time he reached the hills, his arms had grown numb with the effort of concentration.

The air here was cold and hard and pure. He breathed in deeply, his nostrils tightening with the effort, and walked. The whiteness of the snow illuminated the night. Ahead of him, at the top of the slope, the high wolf-like pines rose into the sky. He could hear the wind whistling through them. He would go there and rest. He moved slowly. With each heavy step a weight seemed to drop from his soul, so that as he climbed he began to feel light, emptied out. When he reached the first trees, pain forked through his breast. Sharp, clean. His face grew contorted and he laughed that strange, hollow laugh. Then he slumped against a tree. 'Goodbye, Anna, forgive me,' he murmured. The wind swallowed his words.

They brought Anna the news of Bruno's death two days later. A prim little man came from his office, a black armband round his coat. His moustache moved over his lips like a clown's as he spoke. Yes, a stroke, they thought. A dog and a boy had found him. A mastiff, he added, as if the difference were impressive.

Anna stared at him and slumped into a chair. It would take some time to sort out the business side, of course, it was all so complicated, made more complicated by the war, he continued.

But Anna had stopped listening. She sat in the chair in the morning room where he had last sat. Sat for she didn't know how long, gazing into space. She sat there while Frau Gruber placed milk into her hands, forcing her to drink, leading her to bed, and then sat there again while the phone reverberated with Tante Hermine's voice, other friends, acquaintances.

The obituaries had appeared, lauding Bruno as a great man, extolling his virtues, his entrepreneurial skills, his gifts to charities. Visitors appeared, uninvited, and still she sat unmoving, listening and not listening, staring into space. Only one thought went round and round in her mind: she had killed him.

Anna told Bettina when she arrived, summoned by Tante Hermine to help with the funeral. They were the first words she could remember speaking.

'I killed him.'

Bettina gazed at her oddly, stopped compiling lists. 'Don't be ridiculous, Anna. You're just distressed. He died of a stroke. Tante Hermine told me he hadn't been well for some time, had had dizzy spells.'

'I killed him,' she repeated again.

'Silly girl,' Bettina breathed, adding a little harshly, 'We all have to contend with death these days. You're not alone. And you'll have his child.'

'I'm not certain it's his,' Anna said flatly.

Bettina's eyes widened. A hush fell over the room. 'You mean . . . Johannes?' she said softly after a moment.

Anna looked at her and nodded slowly. Then she turned away, tears filling her eyes for the first time since Bruno's death. 'I don't know. That's why he's dead,' she cried, 'I killed him.'

'Nonsense.' Bettina was sharp.

'I never should have told him I didn't know,' Anna moaned, rocking herself backwards and forwards, her hands folded round the baby.

'You never should have slept with Johannes,' Bettina said tersely.

'You don't understand, Bettina,' Anna murmured. 'I love both of them.'

'Don't I?' Her sister looked at her a little forbiddingly and then stood to her full height. 'Might as well make the best of a bad thing, Anna. If Johannes makes it through the war, you'll be free for him.' She laughed queerly.

'Don't be so callous, Bettina. It will never be the same.'

'Nothing is ever the same, my dear.' Bettina tried a kinder tone. 'Time doesn't stand still. And now unless you want to go to bed and cry privately, I suggest you give me a hand. Frau Gruber can't do everything and we have a lot to prepare for tomorrow.'

Anna helped, an automaton to Bettina's instructions. But everywhere she moved in the apartment, she bumped into Bruno. The content of their last meeting, previous meetings over these winter months, played themselves over and over in her mind, following her to bed, raging through her dreams, waking with her, so that her first thought was always, 'I killed him.'

Bettina's stern presence kept her upright through the funeral. But when she saw the coffin being lowered into the cold earth, she had a mad desire to throw herself in after it. Poor, poor Bruno, she thought. So alone. She could keep him company now.

Only her sister's hand on her shoulder restraining her, gripping hard, kept her from taking that little step over the edge.

When she looked up from the grave at last, her eyes met those of a woman standing opposite her. Under a hat that was far too elaborate for her thin but dramatic features, her face was stricken, contorted, wet with tears. For a moment Anna felt she was gazing into the mirror of her grief. She stared. Who was this afflicted double who shrunk into the crowd and disappeared, never to offer her condolences? Those weeping eyes haunted her.

But Bettina pulled her away, saw her firmly through the innumerable handshakes, the obligatory drinks. Then when it was all over, she tucked her into bed.

'I have to go back in the morning, you know that.'

Anna nodded.

'Would you like to come with me?'

She shook her head.

'Perhaps stay with Tante Hermine, then?'

'No.'

'You'll be all right? You won't do anything foolish? Promise me.'

'I won't.'

'Good.' Bettina smiled at her sister. 'You can phone me if you need anything, and I'll come back in time for the baby. Remember, Anna, you're only twenty-one years old, and your life is just beginning.'

Anna did not feel her life was beginning. She sat through the days, one much like the next, filled with memories she couldn't eradicate. They were all of Bruno. In these last months he seemed to have outweighed Johannes, and his death had obliterated him altogether.

Frau Gruber had caught a grippe and Anna was alone with the little cat, refusing all other company. She telephoned to say she wouldn't be returning to the orphanage. She forgot to eat, only remembering food when the cat's miaowls grew persistent, penetrated the fog in which she pondered Bruno's last words to her. 'Forgive me, Anna.' What had he meant? The question would persist in her as she walked coatless out into the streets, bought what food she could, thinking only of Bruno and the kitten.

One day, she was certain she saw Bruno sitting opposite her in what had been his favourite chair.

'Bruno, tell me what you meant?'

She rushed towards him, saw that he was about to speak, just when he vanished again.

Anna sobbed, 'Come back, Bruno, speak to me.' She sobbed through the night, unable to stop, and then in the morning, he was there again, his hand on her shoulder, stroking her hair, stroking. Like her mother. Her mother. Anna's tears stopped. Tentatively she put out her fingers to cover his. And then nothing, he was gone. Like her mother had gone.

The pattern repeated itself. She thought if she cried enough, if she were careful enough, then one day he would stay, would speak to her, forgive her.

When Frau Gruber returned to the apartment after some two weeks of illness, she found Anna in bed shaking, her face a spectral white, murmuring Bruno's name. She called instantly for the doctor, who could only diagnose a grippe, recommend a tonic, food, rest. Frau Gruber tended to her, tried to cheer her. 'It will soon pass, my dear. Soon you'll have the baby.'

Anna didn't seem to hear her. She cried the days away. Only when the old woman gently said to her one day that there was no more housekeeping money, that in fact she hadn't been paid for some months, did Anna's eyes come into focus. 'Of course, of course.'

She moved clumsily to find some clothes, forgot to comb her hair, forgot her coat, her hat. She walked heavily through the streets. A pale sun shone. The buds were plump on the chestnut trees. 'You should have waited for spring, Bruno, everything is better in spring,' she said to herself.

At the bank they looked at her strangely. A man came over to her. 'Frau Adler?'

She nodded.

'My condolences.'

Anna looked away. 'Thank you,' she murmured.

'I'm sorry there's so little money in the account. You see, our instructions were only to transfer a certain sum a month, and the first account is now frozen until your late husband's affairs are cleared. It shouldn't take too long, I trust, though the war measures slow everything. If you would like us to advance you a sum to tide you over . . .'

Anna gazed at him uncomprehendingly. 'No, no.' Then, thinking of Frau Gruber, she changed her mind. 'Yes, perhaps a little.' It was all too complicated. She sighed, took the money the teller handed her, said goodbye, didn't notice their eyes following her.

She got lost in the streets, didn't feel the cold, only the heaviness of her limbs. When she finally arrived home, she handed all the money to Frau Gruber and took to her bed. The little cat curled up next to her. 'You know,' she looked at him, 'we never gave you a name. I think we'll call you Bruno, now that he never comes back.'

The cat purred.

Stroking it, whispering, 'Yes, Bruno,' she felt a little calmer.

The next day the post brought a letter and a packet. She opened the letter first, from Bettina.

Dear Anna,

I hope you're not still being stupid and are eating properly and taking plenty of rest. Remember, first of all, that women on the whole do not kill men and are far more likely to be killed by them. Bruno was a strong successful man, old enough to be your father. You are not responsible for his death, however stupidly you may have behaved. Remember too, that guilt is not a useful emotion. Read some Nietzsche, avoiding what he says about women. About us he is very stupid.

The child is now the important thing. And your health. Take care of yourself.

As ever,

Bettina

Anna read the letter twice and laughed for the first time in months. Bettina was incorrigible. She would never understand how she felt. Never understand about emotions.

But Anna felt better.

She was more frightened of the second letter. It bore an official army stamp, and like the first packet she had received from Johannes, had made its interminable way to her via Seehafen. Again, this time, as she shakily unravelled the knot, she prayed that nothing had happened to him, that he was well. But she had a sense of foreboding which was entangled with an image of Bruno stumbling amidst Johannes's scattered pictures.

Dearest Anna

Here I am a hero again, though a minor one this time, since the wound is only deep enough to make me hobble on a stick, like some tired old Trojan for whom battle has gone on far too long. If I'm lucky they'll send me quickly back into the fray. At least there the bombers and the cannon drown out the moans of the ward.

Still there are compensations here. The morphine provides an ersatz bliss: painted flowers have a more vital scent than the remembered real. So too the painted corpses.

And then there are one's companions. There was a particularly entertaining young corporal here until a little while back. An artist, he claimed, like myself, though he was not particularly flattering about the enclosed. An excited little man with the staring eyes of a visionary, who harangued us for hours on end about the imminence of apocalypse. At times, I had the eerie sense that he might be my double, though the content of his lectures was thankfully different. He was obsessed with Jews, evoked multitudes of them – repulsive slackers, scoundrels all, the eternal mushroom of humanity – undermining the war effort, robbing the great proud German nation. He forgot to mention that this great proud nation eats its young at an unprecedented rate.

We have all gone mad, Anna, all apart from you, who are fresh and pure and alive like the jade-green waters of our lake, like the sleepy scent of the opulent earth on a summer afternoon. Only the memory of you gives me hope. If only I could take your life into me, be reborn in its fullness . . .

Be well. I hope Bruno has forgiven you.

And again, should it be necessary or possible, some pictures to sell.

Johannes

At a first cursory reading, the letter seemed cheerful enough, but as she read it again and again and tried to hear Johannes's voice through it, Anna was filled with apprehension. There was a note of cynical grimness between the lines which she didn't remember in him. And the hope he had of her seemed to be addressed to a different creature, not the Anna who sat here listlessly, resting the sheaf of papers on her bulging form. When she looked at the pictures he had enclosed, her despondency grew. Gone was the frenzied line of the earlier drawings, which in its feverish movement, whatever the content, had a stormy life to it. Here instead there was a clinical detachment, an anatomical exactitude which turned wounded men into ugly dead animals, their bodies so much meat exposed on slabs.

And then that reference to Bruno. Anna shivered. It was too close to the truth of what she felt. She stared blindly into space. She had a sense that she was being physically tossed between the two men each of whom held up a mirror to her, reflecting a different and vanishing Anna. And in between these two dim forms, she could no longer find herself, as if she had already disappeared.

In an attempt to shake off the depression she went for a walk. She sat in the Burggarten and watched the thick spring shoots poking their heads through the earth. If she watched closely enough, she suddenly thought, she might see them grow, catch the action of that force which propelled them upwards. A spring storm caught her unawares, soaking through her dress, and still Anna sat until night covered her.

The next morning she started to cough, a hard racking cough which shook her whole body uncontrollably. When she took the handkerchief from her lips, it was flecked with red. She looked at the red patches uncomprehendingly. They reminded her of something. Then it came to her. They were like the patches of red paint which flecked her bosom, after Bruno had flung paint at the mural. Johannes had tried to cover them up, but whatever his efforts the traces of that blood-red paint remained visible. Anna smiled and hid the handkerchief. When the little cat jumped up on her lap and poised himself there on top of the baby, she stroked him reflectively, 'Yes, Bruno,' she murmured.

The baby started to come early, after a particularly fierce bout of coughing. Frau Gruber called for the doctor who instantly had Anna sent off to the clinic in the Wienerwald. Of the birth itself, she remembered nothing except the flurry of activity around her and her shouts, as loud as the pain itself. And then there was that tiny form in her arms, its face wizened, troubled, frowning. Just like Bruno, she told herself. She gazed at it for the length of a day, heard it snuffling by her side at night. Just like Bruno, she repeated over and over in her half sleep, her body sore, stiff, too spent to twist and turn. And when the sun pierced through the shutters in the morning, she woke afraid. The tiny bundle was staring at her, judging her, accusing her. 'I never meant to harm you, Bruno,' she whispered into the emptiness.

The baby wailed. Anna looked at it helplessly, her fear mounting.

It didn't lessen over the days she spent at the clinic, mounted further when the child was put into her arms and attached to her breast. She felt as if Bruno was tugging at her, pulling at the little remaining strength she had. She looked away in fear.

The day she went home to the apartment in Alleegasse, Bettina arrived.

'You shouldn't have let him come so early,' she chided Anna, 'I couldn't get away.' But she smiled as she kissed her, picked up the bundle. 'And what's your name, young man?'

'He doesn't have one yet.' Anna looked at her beseechingly.

'Well, then? What shall it be?' Bettina cradled the child.

Anna shrugged tired shoulders.

Bettina looked from her sister to the child. 'You've exhausted your mother's imagination,' she made a great pretence of scolding the baby, 'so now we'll have to put our minds together and see what we can come up with. What about Leo, after your venerable grandfather?' She gazed at Anna, who didn't respond.

'Leo it will have to be, for the time being at least. Leo Adler.'

'Leo Adler,' Anna repeated and, turning her face to the wall, stammered, 'You have your baby now, Bruno, the boy you always wanted.'

EIGHT

1918

ON 7 NOVEMBER 1918, Bettina Eberhardt stood in the midst of an immense and excited crowd in Munich's Theresienwiese and felt a surge of rare elation as the mingled cheers swept over her.

She lifted her hands to applaud the crowd, clapped the women, old and young, the throngs of workers from the Krupp plant, the Rapp Motor and Bavarian Airplane Works, the soldiers, the peasants, the children, massed together across the vast stretch of the meadow on this glorious day in this glorious autumn which would see in peace and a glorious new order.

And she cheered along with them. Cheered their unlikely leader, Kurt Eisner, that shy, slight, grey professorial figure with straggling beard and eyes of unflinching integrity. Cheered the blind farmer Gandorfer, who had rallied the peasants, convincing them their best interests would be served by a Bavarian Free State, a republic in which their own Councils saw directly to their needs. Cheered the poets Toller and Mühsam. Cheered her own husband, Klaus, who had come back from the Eastern Front an adamant pacifist and had bravely called for the King's deposition in articles, meetings.

There had been countless meetings these last weeks, in halls, beer cellars, cafés, houses. Meetings she had addressed, making the case for women's suffrage. Meetings in which she had listened to speeches on the reorganization of housing, of food distribution; fierce debates on the economy, on justice. But also meetings in which she had listened carefully to the stumbling addresses of ordinary men and women recounting their experiences, voicing their needs. The massed resonance of these voices, the innumerable pamphlets and proclamations, had created an unprecedented electricity. One breathed it with the air. High tingling sparks of freedom which made one's head light after all those wearing, leaden, sepulchral years of war.

And the charge had reached a new pitch now as the crowd surged forward, marching towards Munich, towards a peaceful revolution.

Head high, Bettina marched in their midst. She couldn't see Klaus any more, but that didn't matter. They were all brothers and sisters now, united in purpose.

As if to reinforce that very fact, she felt a hand on her shoulder, turned to see a soldier's uniform, a worn but handsome face, crystal blue eyes.

'Johannes, you're back.'

His words were lost in the roar of the crowd, but he smiled a peculiar smile and then waved as he was propelled forward.

She hadn't known he was back in Munich. She would have to find out where he was living. Had he seen Anna, she wondered? But only for a moment. There was more urgent business at hand, that of creating a Bavarian socialist republic, of eradicating the blight of hunger and poverty, of setting up a decentralized society of self-managing communities, a responsible state which would never again lead them blindly into war.

Bettina marched euphorically into the future, and felt, as Eisner donned the mantle of President, that she had entered it.

Like all futures, this one too had a way of stumbling over its own present. In the various forums she attended over the next days, Bettina realized that a host of people had been foisted into positions of power which they had no idea what to do with. In the interminable debates in the Councils of the new independent Bavaria, as many cranks as sensible orators took the floor. When she presented her position paper on the organization of childcare to the education committee, the views that were expressed about women were prehistoric.

She complained of this to Klaus when they caught up with each other late in the small hours of the night.

'Freedom has a way of feeling like chaos to begin with,' he replied.

She hadn't seen him for a few days and he looked exhausted, his gangling form thinner than ever. But his eyes shone with a clear light, so different from the hopelessness she had read in them when he had first come back from the Front.

'Yes, I'm sure you're right,' Bettina concurred.

'How is Max getting on?'

'Fine,' she chuckled. 'He asked me today whether the President was going to live in the Palace, now that the King has gone. And whether he could visit him there.'

'No palaces for this lot,' Klaus smiled. 'Too expensive to run.'

'Shall we check on Max now?' Bettina asked, 'while the tea's brewing.' She could see Klaus was itching to.

They climbed the stairs to their son's room and looked silently at the small sleeping form. Klaus bent to kiss him. For a moment the thick lashes fluttered open, lips puckered into a smile, and then he turned peacefully away from his parents.

'He seems to grow by the hour,' Klaus whispered as they closed Max's door behind them.

'His will certainly does.'

'He takes after his mother.' Klaus looked at her whimsically. 'Which reminds me, I bumped into Johannes a few days ago.'

Bettina busied herself with the tea. 'Oh yes? I saw him at the march. Just in passing. Has he been back long?'

Klaus shrugged. 'Not very. He's sharing a studio with Ella Kessler. I co-opted him to work with us. He's going to make posters.'

Bettina stirred her tea nervously. 'Has he changed at all? At half-glance he seemed a little the worse for wear.'

Klaus gazed into the middle-distance. 'He has a severe case of nihilism. A common enough disease these days.' He smiled in that new determined way he had. 'But one we should soon be able to treat.'

'With posters?' Bettina was sceptical.

He was silent for a moment. 'I told him, Bettina.'

'Told him?'

He nodded. 'About Max.'

'You didn't!' She was incredulous. It was so long since any of all that had been mentioned. She had thought Klaus had almost forgotten.

'We have to be honest these days.'

'What did Johannes say?' she murmured, more distraught than she had been throughout these weeks of high excitement.

'He stared at me for a moment, a little strangely, aghast perhaps. Then he clapped me on the shoulder and said he couldn't think of a better father for the little chap than me, if that's what I wanted.' Klaus grinned a little. 'He went on to add that he'd never believed in human property, and now less than ever.'

'Good,' Bettina muttered, but she was worried. 'Will he shout it from the rooftops?'

'I don't think so. He told me it was between the three of us. He was comradely.' Klaus lit a cigarette. A pause grew into a silence. In it Bettina felt increasingly uncomfortable. Klaus was gazing at her so oddly. She averted her face. At last he said, 'Are you sure this is the way you want to continue, Bettina, the best way?'

'Oh yes.' She nodded vigorously. Her thoughts flew to her son. 'Max is so attached to you, so clever,' she looked unseeingly at her hands, 'it would upset him, confuse him if we were to say anything different.'

'And *you*, Bettina?' Klaus cut her off. 'What about you?' His voice had a slightly threatening, insistent note she didn't recognize. She met his eyes. There was anger in them and something else, an obliqueness.

A startling thought fluttered into her mind, flew into dark crevices, scattering light. 'You,' she stumbled, assembled courage, '*you* don't want to continue this way.' As she said it, it was no longer a question, but a flat recognition. She rose from the table. Its once-polished surface had lost its sheen. She hadn't noticed before. 'Is there someone else?' she asked, wishing as soon as they were out that the cheap words hadn't been uttered. But she plunged on, the voice no longer her own, 'Because if you want to go, you must. These are revolutionary times, after all.' She turned away from him.

He gripped her wrist. 'It's not like that, Bettina. Not altogether.'

'Not altogether?' She searched his face, saw a stranger emerge from the familiar features. There was something almost soldier-like in his stance, as if his avowed pacifism had given him a new ruggedness. The brown eyes beneath the slightly drooping lids had a startling brightness about them, and the lines which had etched themselves around his full lips emphasized a sensitivity which had once been half hidden by a beard. 'Not altogether?' she repeated, this time with a tremor.

Suddenly he kissed her, long, hard. The unexpectedness of the action took her breath away. She found her arms cleaving to his shoulders, her lips warm. 'Revolutionary times, indeed,' she murmured, drawing away, just a little.

'Yes,' he echoed and firmly led her to her room.

When she rose the next day, Klaus was already gone. But a secret smile played round her lips as she saw the indentation of his head on the pillow.

What strange times these were, Bettina thought, allowing herself the luxury of a languorous stretch. To be sleeping with one's husband. But this was not the moment to muse on her odd sense of having transgressed on the forbidden, nor to ponder the differences between Klaus and Johannes. She had innumerable duties to attend to, the first of which was her unbreachable hour with Max.

Contrary to all appearances and expectations, Bettina was an imaginative mother. While she was with Max, she gave herself up to him fully, playing madcap games, explaining the universe to him, her perennial rectitude only visible in the adult comprehensiveness of these explanations, so that the little boy often spoke things he didn't yet understand. Her time with him up, however, she would brook no pleas of 'just one more game', or 'another few minutes', but would simply hug him firmly and repeat, 'more is not better'.

As a result, little Max grew up with a pronounced if mysterious sense of the benefit of limits, which he applied to the world only to be shocked when it answered with unreasonableness the reasonableness which was his own. He was an altogether charming and lively little boy. And Bettina always took a deep and contented breath when she embraced him for the last time before setting off for work. That day she squeezed him to her with extra force and wondered for a moment what Johannes would think of him, now that he had been told Max was his son.

But in those heady post-war winter days when the difficulties of daily life – of food and fuel and influenza – were as fierce and numerous as the ideas which were espoused to regulate them, Bettina had little time for pondering her personal life. It was two weeks after the armistice was signed – and the right-wing rumblings about Germany, having been stabbed in the back by the socialists, the Jews, its own new governments, had already made themselves loudly heard – before she managed to see Johannes at all. And then it was hardly a satisfactory meeting.

Klaus had recommended that she stop in at an artists' soirée in Schwabing on her way home. He would try to meet her there.

Bettina easily found the designated warehouse. Inside, it was transformed by a cacophony of posters and banners. A carnival atmosphere prevailed. Streamers flew. Music blared. Huge balloon-like puppets, effigies of the old ruling elite, swung from the rafters. The walls shrieked with lettering and graphics, louder than the laughter and the voices. 'German Culture is Dead, Long Live German Culture!'

'Only money does not die', shouted the caption above an image of a mountain of corpses. A man, his face whitened to look like a death's head, stood on a chair and chanted savagely to a gathering group:

'DADADADA.

In the name of DADA, you are all indicted.

Hang up your hopes.

Hang up your paradises.

Hang up your idols, your heroes, your artists, your religions. They are all nothing.

In the name of DADA, I proclaim the beginning of year one of the reign of Nothing.'

He cackled wildly.

Bettina turned away in distaste, bumped into friends, couldn't hear their words over the hubbub, moved on, saw someone pouring water over what looked like a painting by a German romantic. And then Petra embraced her, swathing her in furs, laughing, 'Isn't it wonderful', before being swept away by a man in uniform. Bettina edged towards the opposite side of the room, where paintings were hung in more orderly rows and things were quieter.

'Like them?' a voice with the soft, precise inflections of Johannes's asked from behind her.

She swerved round, but all she could see was a tall elegant man in a frock coat and top hat. As he turned his face to her, she leapt back. There, where a face should have been, there was instead a pink snout and little piggy eyes.

The man laughed mischievously and removed his mask.

'Frightened you, did I?'

'This is childish nonsense, Johannes.' Bettina crinkled her face primly.

He bowed formally. 'You have it in one, Madame. Aggressive childish nonsense to cock a snook at authority.' He leaned back against the wall in a pose of dandyish nonchalance. 'It's good to see you, Bettina. Almost good to be alive. I hoped you might be here. Shall we take a little quiet stroll? I think you have something to tell me.' He put the mask to his face again and laughed.

She looked away from him, refused his arm. His manner irritated her. 'Why have you got yourself up like this, Johannes?'

'I told you.' He matched his steps to hers, bowed to people, making sure all and sundry realized they were together. 'It's a very simple statement, Bettina. Even you can understand. Men in wonderfully aristocratic frock coats are pigs. Aren't you amongst the revolutionaries?'

'But it cheapens everything. Makes a mockery.' She was talking so loudly to make herself heard above the noise that people stopped to listen.

'And that too is the point. Until we cease to respect the empty forms of authority, there will be no change. None.'

They had reached the door and he held it open for her. 'Anyhow, don't you think this is an accurate representation of the real me? A swine. The inner man writ large.' He laughed again.

'Take it off, Johannes.' She took a deep breath of the crisp night air and looked into his face, shadowed by moonlight. His eyes were as wintry as the night. She suddenly had a sense that those eyes which she had loved for the way they looked passionately forward to some imaginary future, now only looked coldly down on the mass of humanity.

'I think you have something to tell me, Bettina?'

She shivered and then squared her shoulders. 'Klaus has already told you. About Max.'

'Don't look so frightened, Bettina.' He dug his fingers into her shoulder. 'I won't file a paternity suit, in case that worries you. I won't breathe a word. I'm just rather surprised that you never felt the need to tell me yourself.'

'The need?' Bettina looked at him incredulously. 'Just remember what you used to say, Johannes. About woman being free. Needing to grasp the nettle of their own strength. About men being merely incidental. Servants to the great matriarch.' She let out a shrill laugh.

'Touché. The great Bettina unearths another internal contradiction.'

His face looked bruised now and she said more softly, 'I didn't think you'd want to know, Johannes. You weren't all those years ago interested in being a father, or so it seemed to me.'

Johannes smiled more gently now. 'Right as always, Frau Eberhardt. I'm not. Klaus makes a far better father. And little Max as I remember him is a fine chap.' He passed a finger down the curve of her face. 'I won't breathe another word about it. Ever. Promise. And I respect you for not telling me.'

She met his eyes. 'How are you, Johannes?'

Before he could answer, a police van swerved noisily into the street and came screeching to a halt in front of them. Johannes winked at her rakishly. From the depths of his pocket, he unearthed a monocle and screwed it into his eye, simultaneously drawing himself up to his full height in front of the warehouse doors. With his top hat, he towered over the approaching men and presented the quintessential face of aristocratic respectability.

'A problem, Officers?' He addressed the two uniformed men punctiliously.

The men looked uncertainly at each other. The first cleared his throat. 'Trouble brewing, we were told.' He gestured towards the doors.

'Trouble?' Johannes raised an eyebrow. His face took on an air of arrogant disdain. 'Really, gentlemen, I think you've come to the wrong place. The Countess von Leinsdorf and I have just come out of the exhibition and everything was as peaceful as it would be in a palace of culture. But see for yourselves.' He stood back and gestured them towards the door. The men shuffled uncertainly. 'My wife was particularly enamoured of a fine little Madonna, exquisitely rendered, the very essence of Bavarian art. Do look at it.'

'Well, if you're sure, sir,' the first man shuffled his feet and doffed his cap, 'that there's no trouble, I mean.'

'No trouble. But that little Madonna . . .'

The policemen backed away. 'We must have come to the wrong address.' They climbed hurriedly into the van, anxious to be off.

Johannes looked after them, smiling. 'There it is. The wonderful German respect for authority in action. Do you think if I'd been wearing a workman's cap I would have got away with it? I tell you, Bettina, in order to change anything in this country you'll have to get a signed and sealed statement from our absent Kaiser to sanction revolution.'

His hollow laugh echoed down the narrow street.

'I want to talk to you about something other than politics, Johannes.' Bettina was disgruntled. 'Is there anywhere we can go?'

'Yes, yes.' He looked at her questioningly. 'There's a place not too far from here. Serves foul beer, but it's clean.' He laughed that devilish laugh again. 'That's the real reason Bavarian socialism has got this far. The beer the Prussians have foisted on us is execrable. No one can bear it.'

'Stop it, Johannes. You've grown cynical.'

'And you've grown even more ravishing. It can't be the war. So it must be little Max.'

Bettina swallowed hard. They had reached the bar. It was almost empty except for some soldiers who leaned drunkenly against the counter. They found a scrubbed oak table in the dimly lit back room. Bettina sat opposite him on the hard bench and watched the shadows the tallow candle threw over his face.

'It's about Anna. Have you heard from her? Seen her?'

Johannes shook his head, avoided her eyes. 'You guessed then?' he asked quietly. 'Or she told you?'

Bettina nodded at the latter.

He gazed at her quizzically, then threw up his hands. 'The two von Leinsdorf sisters. The women in my life.'

'It's not a joke, Johannes.'

'No, no, of course not.' He paused, reached for a cigarette. 'How is Anna?' he asked softly. His eyes were suddenly dreamy.

Bettina shrugged.

'I would go and see her, but . . . She's not like you. She doesn't know how to deal with her husband. I worry about her.'

'So you don't know?'

'Know what?' He frowned.

For the first time she saw the exhaustion in his face, a weariness that had settled permanently round his lips when he was still.

'Bruno's dead.'

'I see.' He breathed sharply. 'You think I should go to her? In Vienna?' He leaned back against the wall. 'She may hate me, you know. I never knew even in those few weeks we had together, wonderful weeks, what she was thinking. She never spoke much. She's all feeling.'

Bettina felt him looking through her, over her shoulder, into another space. She didn't know whether she wanted to hear any of this.

'I would look at her. Touch her. She's so beautiful. And suddenly I'd have the feeling that I was seeing the grass moving, each blade, fine, distinct. At other times, it was like gazing into the lake. I would see myself, but purified, distilled, transparent. And then I'd sink.' He shook himself. 'How is she?'

'There's been a child, a little boy.'

He sat up stiffly. 'I see.'

'No, you don't see anything.' Bettina was suddenly angry. 'He may be yours.'

He looked baffled for a moment. 'Is that what she told you?'

'Go and see her for yourself. Bring her back here. There's work to be done. For both of you.'

Johannes burst out laughing, his old boyish laugh. 'Some things, Bettina, despite wars, despite millions of dead, despite revolutions, never change. And you are one of them.' He kissed her lightly on the cheek. 'You'll have to give me her address. I only ever wrote to her at Seehafen.'

'Other things don't seem to change much either, Johannes.' Bettina smiled with a wryness she didn't altogether feel.

The first thing that struck Johannes as he made his way towards the address Bettina had given him was that the old Imperial capital had lost its lustre. The elegant women with their playful eyes and soft, knowing smiles had disappeared. In their stead, there was greyness and pinched noses, a flurrying of old rucksacks and haggling voices. The rucksacks particularly struck him. It was like Berlin, he guessed. No one quite knew from where the next meal might be foraged, what item might be bartered, so one set one in readiness. He had stopped for lunch in one of his old haunts and been told there would be nothing on the elaborate menu until perhaps this evening. He had made do with a glass of foul wine and a list of complaints from the man at the next table followed by a plea for cigarettes.

Johannes let the ornate brass knocker fall and waited in front of the substantial house. A black-skirted maid opened the door, looked up at him queerly as he asked for Anna and then scurried away before returning quickly and inviting him in. The room he was led to had the musty clutter of a bygone era. He wouldn't have associated that particular suffocating taste with Bruno Adler, but then one never altogether knew what people were like when they were at home.

No wonder he had died, Johannes thought mischievously to himself. But for Anna to stay in this! For a moment he had a vision of the knoll at Seehafen, of Anna borne out of the waves. So palpable was it that it was as if he could smell the perfumed air, stretch out his hand and touch paradise.

Before the objects around him could take shape again, a commanding voice barked at him.

'Herr Johannes Bahr?'

A darkly swathed form wheeled its way towards him in a vast mahogany chair. A mottled hand was offered. 'Hermine von Leinsdorf. You are a friend of Anna's?'

Johannes nodded.

The woman held gilt spectacles up to her eyes and peered at him, seemed to decide that he would do.

'I'm glad you've come. She has too few visitors, and she won't come to my evenings. Stubborn girl. To carry on mourning this long is unseemly, don't you think?' She didn't wait for him to answer. 'And she works too hard. It's bad for her health. You'd think that Adler would have sorted things out better.' She sighed dramatically. 'But then no one could have foreseen this blasted war. Eh? Speak up.' Two bright little magpie eyes stared at him from layers of cheek.

'I asked where Anna was,' Johannes bellowed.

'She'll be back soon. Always punctual. Not for me, for that brat of hers. Imagine Adler dropping off like that, just before the child was born. Altogether inconsiderate of him, I say. Look at me. I'm far older than him. And it's not as if he was shot at.' She shook her head disdainfully.

A grandfather clock boomed the hour from somewhere in the midst of the house.

'Any minute now.' From somewhere in the heaped satin of her dress, Hermine brought out a gold watch and studied it. 'And what do you do, young man?'

'I was an artist,' Johannes said flatly. 'Before the war.'

'An artist?' She raised her spectacles to her eyes again, and paused. 'You didn't by any chance do those monstrous pictures Anna has put up in her room? It looks like a mortuary. Quite unpleasant. I refuse to go in there any more,' she sniffed at him.

Johannes shrugged, suddenly laughed.

'Well, it's best to be honest, young man. At my age there's no time for lying.'

'Johannes.' A faint voice startled him from behind.

He turned and saw a pale girl in a grey workaday suit. She was standing utterly still. Her skin was translucent, her eyes, wide in astonishment, too large for her face.

'Anna?' It was a question.

She raced towards him, a smile irradiating her features, and flung her arms round his neck, pressing herself against him as if to test his reality.

'So you are a *good* friend,' he heard Tante Hermine exclaim loudly.

Anna leapt away from him. 'The very best. I thought . . . I thought he might be dead.'

'He looks alive enough to me,' Tante Hermine grunted dourly.

'Yes.' Anna gazed at him, the colour flooding into her cheeks, so that she looked a little more like the woman he remembered. 'Yes,' she breathed again, her eyes not leaving his face.

'I gather you'd like to be alone.' Tante Hermine put her chair noisily into motion.

'Please,' Anna whispered, not taking her eyes from him.

Two days later, they were on a train together, bound for Munich. Johannes didn't quite know how it had happened. It was as if, ever since she had put her arms around him, had taken him to her room, loved him with a silent intensity which had made the space around them disappear so that they were back on the grass under a billowing sky and history had vanished, he was under the spell of her certainty. She had assumed that she was to come with him, that the child would come too. She had asked him nothing and told him nothing, simply put her hand in his as it was now and told him that today she would be ready to go.

Johannes watched her holding the pale drowsy child. It was odd the way she tended to him without looking at him, like some Madonna whose gaze was directed beyond the merely mortal particularity of the boy. Yet there was a strange efficiency about her dealings with the child, a note which was unlike any other she struck. So unlike the look which she now rested on him, so deep and golden and lavishly promising, that he was again lost in it, forgot the questions he wanted to pose about Bruno, about the child, about the past and the future. There was only the present, the rhythmic chug of the train, the splatter of raindrops over the misty window and the heat which came from her, warming him, abundant, swallowing him, like the earth itself.

'He came back to me.' Anna looked dreamily out of the window at the dark wintry waters of the Isar. Bettina placed a cup in her hand. They were breakfasting together in the morning room in the house in Bogenhausen.

'Good, that means you can get married and Leo can have his father.'

Anna put her cup down with a clatter and started up from her chair. 'Don't ever say anything like that again, Bettina. Leo's father is dead.'

She turned her gaze back to the window. 'As for marriage, you know Johannes doesn't believe in it.'

'What Johannes believes is neither here nor there.' Bettina was adamant. 'What do you intend to live on? Has Bruno's estate been settled yet?'

Anna shrugged. 'I don't know if there's anything there. The war, the government, they seem to have eaten it. But it doesn't matter. We'll manage.' She wouldn't let her sister spoil her happiness.

'Manage! Johannes hasn't got a mark to his name and paintings are rather less in demand at the moment than potatoes. Then there's the little question of housing. He's sharing a studio with a woman painter at the moment, you know that.'

Anna didn't allow herself the gasp she felt. She sat resolutely still and murmured again, 'We'll manage. He'll find another place.'

Bettina looked at her sister's frail form and stilled her impatience. Anna was too thin. With her aureole of golden hair and vast eyes, she had an ethereal quality. Bettina took her hand. 'You know Klaus and I will share everything with you, Anna. You can stay here, and Leo will be looked after with Max. But times are hard for everyone at the moment. Johannes should find a teaching post at the Akademie. Or something. So that he can look after you.'

'Yes, yes,' Anna mumbled, then met Bettina's eyes with a dreamy resoluteness. 'We'll manage, Bettina. I'll find a job. I'll start looking tomorrow. And then in the spring, I thought Johannes and I might go down to Seehafen. Like before. The country suits us. Potatoes *and* painting.' She smiled a brilliant smile and that old wild carefree laugh boomed out of her, too large now for her frame.

The weeks passed filled with the activity of setting up a new order. Johannes, without Anna's urging, found a new studio. It wasn't a space that would easily accommodate a family, but then neither of them really wanted that. Anna could come there, could stay, whenever she pleased. Leo, she felt, without needing to hear it from Johannes, belonged in a separate space. Nor did Johannes explain about any other women there might have been. And she didn't ask. There was really no need to.

When she was with him in that little room at the back of the studio which she had filled with bright things – a canary-yellow bedspread, a single vast sunflower she had fashioned herself out of some stiff material – they were so immersed in one another that the rest of the world ceased to exist. The play of their limbs, the satin caresses, the deep satisfying kisses, fed them both so generously that Johannes no longer had to perform an act of memory to see her as the golden Venus of their Seehafen idyll; whereas he took on a ruggedness, his eyes a clarity of sea and sky, that made the women turn to look after him as he walked down the Schwabing streets.

He experienced her as a drug that he couldn't name but could never get quite enough of, whatever the voluptuous excess of their encounters. If she arrived a few minutes after the regular appointed hour, if she were late back from work, a hunger had already begun to course through his veins that made him restlessly despondent. Or if a message came through the one telephone in the house to say that for some reason, she couldn't be with him, he felt a gaping emptiness within him which nothing else could fill. It was not rational. He knew with his mind that she would soon be there. There was no one to keep her from him, except the boy and daily duties, but nonetheless, the hunger would fill him, like a child for whom the breast is delayed.

He worked through those winter weeks with a clarity and energy which had rarely been his. A vast triptych took shape, Anna as a glowingly sensuous Madonna at its centre; beneath her and around her, a hell of mutilated bodies and skeletal remains which her radiant presence obviated, began to exorcize. For many years, people were to say it was his best painting.

Apart from the triptych, there was the work he did to order, the posters, and banners, and illustrations which were the graphic loudspeakers of the new regime. Sometimes, in the new emphatic idiom he had uncovered for this propaganda work, he went far beyond the regime itself and amused himself. One of his posters demanded a state ministry dedicated to the liquidation of the bourgeoisie, the bourgeois family and bourgeois sexuality: a postscript in compelling but minuscule red called for the destruction of the very ministry demanded above.

Another showed a naked man and woman, luxuriantly entwined, their only covering a floating fig-leaf in which the words 'Pleasure is the single source of value' were inscribed. He was particularly proud of this poster, as he was of one other in which a large toddler wearing only a delicious smile strode like a giant above tiny figures of stiff adults in frock coats, uniforms and judge's hat and gown. 'The child is a genius,' roared the lettering. 'Set the child free.'

The child in question bore no physical resemblance to either Max or Leo. With the children closest to him, Johannes played when mood or occasion took him, but the play always had something impersonal about it: it was an engagement with himself, not with the children. Or so Bettina thought she observed, adding to herself that they seemed to like him nonetheless.

For Christmas, at Anna's insistence, they all went to Seehafen. The grounds were covered in snow when they arrived and the children tumbled in it gleefully, while the men drew them on to greater and greater antics. Anna, a rapturous smile on her face, looked on with Bettina for a moment, and then left without a word. A few minutes later, she was galloping past them on her favourite mare. Her hair loosed in the wind, her face beatific, she waved to them and plunged on, scattering snow from the laden branches which arched the path.

Bettina saw Johannes look after her with an expression which was half way between wonder and pain. Then he too was off, repeating her gesture as he passed them, waving, urging his dark stallion across the trodden path.

In the evening they all sat in front of a roaring fire and roasted chestnuts. It was Klaus, a boy on each knee, who told the stories. Stories of old St Nicholas, who brought prettily wrapped presents to the good children and dark coals and old onions to the bad. It must have been the dramatic look on Klaus's face when he pronounced the word 'bad' which frightened little Leo, for the usually impassive child suddenly burst into tears and scrambled across the room to his mother's side. Her eyes abstracted, Anna cradled him to her, made soft cooing noises. Johannes, Bettina noted, averted his eyes, only to let them fall on Anna again, when Klaus had wooed the little boy back to his lap. She didn't have time to ponder it, for just then Max addressed them in his most serious voice, 'What's bad?'

Johannes laughed. 'Go on, tell him, Bettina.'

Bettina thrust back her shoulders. 'Bad is when you hit another child for no reason.'

Little Max's eyes grew dark. 'And if there is a reason?'

Now both Klaus and Johannes were chuckling.

'You'll just have to give in, Bettina.' Johannes urged her on. 'And tell him "bad" is what his parents say it is.'

Bettina threw him a fierce look.

'But they haven't said, Uncle Johannes.'

At this Johannes burst into gales of laughter, over which Bettina turned to her son and seriously explained, 'That's because the word has so many senses, Max. One sense is that we behave badly when we hurt other people, so that if you had hit Leo because you were annoyed at his interrupting Daddy's story, that would be bad.'

'Bravo, Bettina,' Johannes continued to ironize. The little boy looked from one to the other of them in evident perplexity and then sighed. 'Can we have another story, Daddy?'

'Yes,' Klaus smiled, planted a kiss on the dark, curly head. 'Have I told you about my visit to the Royal Palace?'

The little boy shook his head and looked at him wide-eyed.

'Well then, it was just last week. I went along with the Finance Minister because we had to decide what to do about the royal winter garden. The place was spooky, almost deserted. There were only roomfuls of Greek statues who stared at us from vacant eyes, hundreds of Chinese dragons billowing out of great vases. When we had climbed to the top, we saw a lush, gigantic garden, huge luxuriant trees whose tropical foliage hid the glass roof, lotuses, orchids, so that we thought we had travelled thousands of miles to some wonderful Amazonian forest and all in the space of a walk. And,' Klaus fixed the children with his gaze, 'in the midst of the garden, there was a waterfall, as big as the one I showed you last summer, Max, which sprinkled us with crystalline drops.'

'And?' It was Anna's turn to prod him.

'Well, we had to decide the garden's fate. There isn't enough coal to go around this winter, and the garden consumes a lot of our meagre supply.'

'So what did you decide?' Anna looked at him askance.

'It wasn't an easy choice, I can tell you. The garden is so beautiful,' Klaus said reverentially. 'But then the people need coal.'

'But you said coal was bad,' Max piped in.

Johannes and Bettina joined in laughter.

'You let it die,' Anna breathed, distraught.

'Of course they let it die,' Bettina murmured, 'people's lives are more important than plants.'

'It's horrible.' The tears rose in Anna's eyes.

Klaus gazed at her sympathetically. 'It is.'

Bettina fumed. 'Don't be ridiculous, Anna. Just think for a moment. Plants or people.'

'I leave the thinking to you, Bettina, I always have done. You've always thought better than I have,' Anna erupted.

Bettina rose to her full regal height, gathered Max in her arms. 'You make thought sound like excrement, Anna.'

The men shared a quick wary glance.

She nodded at them curtly and left the room.

Anna stared after her, indifferent to little Leo's tugging at her skirt.

It was only when Klaus gently mentioned that perhaps it was time for little Leo to be put to bed as well that she reluctantly left them. She was back soon after, sat down close to Johannes, took his hand, listened abstractedly to what the men were saying.

'You know,' she remarked after some time had passed, 'I still can't accept it.'

They looked at her questioningly. There was a remoteness in the tawny eyes.

'The winter garden, I mean. Killing all those plants. After all, they're alive too, just as the garden at Seehafen is alive, that hedgehog you once tended to, Klaus, is alive, the horses are alive. We're all part of the same life, the same living whole. Even the dead.' She shivered.

'It was an artificial garden, Anna. Man-made,' Johannes said gently.

She nestled against him, at a loss for the words which would express what she meant.

'I know how you feel, Anna, but it had to be done,' Klaus said quietly.

'Still talking about gardens, are we?' Bettina had come back in.

Johannes nodded. 'Anna is trying to tell us that our revolution is nothing unless it respects nature.' His tone was ironical, but he looked at Anna obliquely to test the accuracy of his words. She smiled at him gratefully.

Bettina sat down with a flurry of skirts. 'Soon she'll be counselling us all to go home and tend our gardens, a twentieth-century Candide.'

'Would that be so awful?' Anna challenged her.

'No, but a great many of us haven't got gardens to tend. And only after we've legislated for a little more equality, can we begin even to think of gardens.' Bettina grew vehement as she spoke. 'Don't be so naive, Anna. It begins to look like either stupidity or wilful selfishness.'

Anna flushed while Johannes guffawed.

'You know, Bettina, you remind me of something a corporal I knew during the war once told me. A great fat fellow, with a wart on his nose. He was always fulminating about this and that and one day he said to me, "Once this war is over, Bahr, I'm going to move to Brazil, better still the Yukon. You know why? It's these European women. They're all a bunch of frustrated soldiers. I want to marry a woman, not a spiritual sergeant." '

Bettina stiffened. 'And I'm the spiritual sergeant, I trust, not the fat corporal.'

'The General, Bettina.' He raised his glass to her.

It was the next day that Bettina told her. She was driven by she didn't know quite what demons, but convinced herself that now that Johannes knew, it was better that Anna found out from her than otherwise. They were in the kitchen preparing dinner, Bettina putting the finishing touches to the gingerbread house she had promised Max.

'There, do you think they'll like that?' Bettina examined her handiwork.

'It's lovely,' Anna exclaimed, and then added a little grudgingly, 'Where did you learn to do that?'

'From one of the women at the Schwabing nursery.'

'A few more raisins there and there would make the composition better.' Anna rapidly inserted the fruit in a new arrangement. It was strange how in these last weeks during which she had grown strong and sure in Johannes's love, she felt increasing resentment at the very skills and certainties she had once so admired in Bettina.

'Yes, that is better,' Bettina acknowledged. She sat down at the rough pine table and watched her sister's fluid motions. Even for someone like herself, who put a low value on things of the surface, it was striking how beautiful Anna had grown of late, almost like that idealized icon Johannes had made of her in his conservatory mural. Even in the shoddy trousers she had decided to don today. No wonder he couldn't keep his eyes off her. Or his hands. It made Bettina uncomfortable to see them both touching each other so openly. There was a palpable heat which came from them.

Bettina cleared the loose flour off the table. 'There's something I've been meaning to talk to you about, Anna, now that you and Johannes are so firmly together.'

Anna smiled secretly.

Bettina folded her white apron, paused, met her sister's radiant eyes. 'You know, Anna, Johannes is Max's natural father.'

Anna sat down heavily. An alien creature seemed to be tugging at her entrails, biting, chewing. She reached for the jug of water, shakily poured herself a glass and then looked at it without moving. Her mind recoiled from the images which bounded across it, images of Bettina in Johannes's arms, of lips not hers. In the distance she could faintly hear Bettina's voice.

'Of course he doesn't know. Must never know. It would confuse him.'

'Johannes doesn't know?' Anna heard her own taut voice.

'No, no, Max, of course.' Bettina gave her a strange look.

'And Klaus?'

'Klaus knows everything. And in all the ways that matter most, in all real ways, he *is* Max's father,' she added triumphantly. 'I thought it wasn't right, since you're not a child any more, since we're so much together, that you should be the only one in the dark,' she finished a little lamely.

'Of course. In the dark,' Anna echoed. 'Excuse me.' She rushed from the room.

'In the dark.' The words reverberated in her mind. Without thinking she flung on her coat and made for the stables. Astride her mare, she galloped down the path, didn't return the waves of the men and the children who were sledging down a small slope, made her way instead across the road and into the woods.

The snow was so bright here that it seemed to illuminate even the shadowy crevices of her mind, which she didn't like to visit. Stupid of her. She should have known about Johannes and Bettina, had known really, now that she looked back in the light of her new wisdom at events all those years ago before she was married to Bruno. She remembered that summer in Seehafen, the days in Munich. Yes, she was a fool. She should have known.

Anna urged the horse to greater speed. What a strange institution marriage was, just as Katarina had told her. Bettina and Klaus, both here with Johannes. She dug her heels into the mare's side. No, she musn't dwell on that. It was so long ago.

She and Bruno had been strange, too. Anna reined in her horse, leapt off, threw herself into a mound of untouched snow, felt its coldness permeate her, cool her heat. She didn't like to think of Bruno now. Not actively. Though with part of her – a secret part of her that she didn't like to acknowledge – she knew he was always there, a diffuse presence, watching her, watching over her, sometimes through his son's eyes. In the early days of the little boy's life, she had had an almost magical sense that Bruno was embodied in the child. Yes, it was still with her. Even though it was now clear Leo had her hair, her eyes, looked people said exactly like her. When Leo was happy, then she knew Bruno was happy. When he was fractious, then she felt that Bruno was admonishing her, that he still hadn't forgiven her, would never forgive her. It made her afraid of the boy, as if she had to tiptoe round him in order not to bring down his father's wrath upon her. Sometimes she hated him.

Anna brushed the snow slowly from her clothes. She hated thinking like this, hated Bettina for forcing her to think. She mounted the mare again, rode more slowly now, wanting to avoid her racing reflections, yet impelling herself to confront them.

Yes, and then Johannes had appeared, like some luminous figure back from the dead. She *had* thought him dead, convinced herself that he had to be dead as part of Bruno's retribution. But Johannes was miraculously alive. His return was a sign: in the smell and touch of him, she was filled with the blessed sense that Bruno had at last forgiven her. She was free to live. And how rich and joyous this new life was, as if all these last arid years in the wilderness had been merely a preparation for this bountiful flowering. She had been filled with a boundless energy, a sense of almost excessive health, and all because of the love of Johannes, sanctioned by Bruno.

She wouldn't allow Bettina's unearthing of the past to disturb the wonder of it all. It had to be over between her sister and Johannes, otherwise Bettina wouldn't have spoken. Would she? Anna urged her horse on again, faster and faster over the pristine white of the trail. Johannes and she would move away from here, away from all of them, move to a new life together. They wouldn't come back to this house, despite the fact that she loved it so much. *They* had probably been here together. And she didn't trust Bettina any more, she was too clever, much cleverer than her. And Johannes was her life, had given her life. She couldn't lose him.

Anna said it to him that night as they lay coiled in each other's arms, dreamy with the taste and smell and touch of each other. 'Johannes, let's go away together. Somewhere new, fresh, away from everything.'

He buried his lips in her neck beneath the heavy mass of her hair.

'When I'm with you, I am away,' he whispered, 'away in some lush tropical country where the tigers leap.' He raked his fingers over her arm, smiled lazily.

She curled closer to him, smoothed the warm skin of his loins, felt him stir. 'No, Johannes, I mean really away.'

He sought out her eyes, trying to read them in the shadowy darkness. 'Perhaps, Anna, when I've sold some pictures.' He stretched languorously against her.

She didn't mention what Bettina had told her, wouldn't utter her name between them for fear that it might darken their togetherness.

Over the following weeks, Anna spent fewer and fewer nights in the house in Bogenhausen, only dropping in after work, to see little Leo and put him to bed. Sporadically she searched for flats, where she and Johannes and the little boy could live, but there was so little time, less money, and she had convinced herself that they would leave the country imminently. Then too, Johannes seemed to have little interest in changing the present arrangement. He liked to live where he worked. So nothing was altered, except that Anna saw her son less and less.

Klaus remarked on it to Bettina one morning, after the nanny had whisked the children away.

Bettina looked at him in that new admiring way she had and said matter-of-factly, 'Anna and Johannes are much too immersed in one another to have room for another person.'

'But a child, Bettina?'

'There's no more place for children and erotic love in the same room than there is for the sun and the moon in the same sky. They may follow on from each other, but simultaneously . . .' She shook her head whimsically. 'Love, that kind of love, I've come to see is a very selfish emotion.'

'And us, Bettina?' He examined her fine-boned profile.

'Us? We're just an old, established couple,' she laughed gaily. But her face grew quickly serious again. 'I think Leo is quite happy here. He's such a quiet inexpressive child, it's not always easy to tell. But I think so. In any event, he's no problem and Max has rather taken to him, keeps wanting to make him smile.'

'Still, I think I'll have a word with Anna.'

'Don't, Klaus. Things will change of their own course, soon enough.

And she deserves a little happiness after all. The last years have been hard on her.' Bettina's tone was strangely rueful.

Things did change, too soon, and not in the way that either Bettina or Klaus could have predicted.

Soon after their talk, on the twenty-first of February 1919, Kurt Eisner, the socialist leader of the Bavarian Republic, the man alongside whom Klaus and Bettina had worked, was assassinated. The country was thrown into frenzy. The Workmen's, Peasants' and Soldiers' Councils proclaimed a general strike. A state of siege ensued. Various factions, anarchist, Communist, Social Democrat vied with each other for control of the government.

Meanwhile, right-wing militia groups, some in the pay of the Berlin government, some purely for their own sport, in a re-enactment of the excitements of the recent war, began to terrorize Munich as they had other cities. Amongst their triumphs, they could already count the murder of the Spartacist leaders, Rosa Luxemburg and Karl Liebknecht.

Munich's public spaces were aflame with pickets and debating voices, amongst them Bettina's, Klaus's and even Johannes's, for his anarchist and artist friends were now in the ascendancy and, for a brief utopian week mingling visionary proclamations and carnival, they took over the Munich government.

Johannes's more radical posters draped the walls. Outside his studio building, a vast one, showing a naked man and woman emerging hand in hand from a prison cell, urged 'Free Love'. A week later, leftist anarchists gave way to Reds of a deeper shade. Against the encroaching force of the Whites, as the central government troops were known, a Red guard was created. A red flag flew over the Wittelsbach Palace. There were eruptions of violence across the city, between left and right and left and left.

Bettina was frightened. Reform, yes, even radical reform, but not revolution, not violence. Klaus was not sure that the tide they had helped to let loose could now be stopped. They argued and he left without a word. Somehow in the midst of the growing chaos she managed to find a car which would take her, the children and their nanny off to Seehafen. She ordered Frau Trübl to say that they were her own grandchildren, if anyone asked.

When she tried to return to Munich the following day, her car was forced into a multitude of detours, and eventually she had to backtrack towards Seehafen. Berlin troops were moving towards Munich and on May the first, the day the workers should have been parading through the streets, Bettina discovered that it was the army which was doing the parading. Two days later, she finally managed to steal back to the city. There was no sign of Klaus, nor had there been since her departure.

She drowned her anxieties in work. The conditions in the nurseries were growing untenable. Apart from the shortages of every kind, there had been repeated instances in these last weeks of mothers urgently asking if the children could be kept overnight, or simply not coming to collect them.

Now matters were even worse: the teachers were exhausted, the children fractious. People were afraid to go out on the streets. Bettina rang colleagues, exhorted help, found a cabaret singer to entertain one group, an actress who would stay the night and help out with another; two mothers who would remain with a third. When she finally ventured out to go home, the streets were dark, deserted. There wasn't a cab in sight.

Bettina began to walk, her heels clicking ominously on the empty street. A military car tore past her forcing her against the wall. In the distance she could hear an alarm bell jangling menacingly from a church tower. She quickened her pace. Turning a corner, she heard a thud, grunts, the hollow sound of fists on flesh. Then she saw them, five of them, two in worker's caps, three in field grey, fighting, saw the rifle butt raised like a club, the unequal battle.

She screamed, screamed so that her throat ached, 'Why? Why are you doing this? Stop. Stop at once.'

The sound of her piercing cry echoing down the narrow cobbled street stopped them for a split second. In that moment, one of the men darted away. Shutters flew open; 'Go home,' a voice shouted from the top of a house.

'Red bitch!' one of the soldiers spat at her.

'How dare you!' Bettina said coldly, unaware that her lips had moved.

The other soldier heaved the limp form he had been holding against the wall. He too spat contemptuously at her feet. Then the three of them turned and loped away.

Bettina stared at them, stared at the motionless body. Tears gathered in her eyes. From somewhere within her, a voice battered at her eardrums, laughing, laughing, 'The future is a long way away, lady. A long way away.'

She shuddered, felt she might faint. Images of a battered Klaus, a wailing Max, danced before her eyes.

Then, with a sudden resolute stiffening of the shoulders, she banged at a door and demanded help.

NINE

1919

KLAUS EBERHARDT SHELTERED behind the thick curtain and gazed down on the patrol marching triumphantly up the street. It was all over. They had lost. Six months of hard work and dreams and the Free Bavarian Socialist Republic was at an end. It had begun in November and now it was May: Klaus counted the months on his fingers as if the clumsy childlike act would somehow clarify the lightning movement of events. Only May 1919 and hostile White troops were pouring into the city wreaking havoc with what had begun as innocent dreams.

The faces of the White soldiers, he thought as he peered down, looked no different from those of the Red. And was it that the same people who hailed them now and showered them with flowers had so few months ago gathered round his friend, Eisner, and hailed the advent of socialism?

Socialism. What was it but a name for a series of self-evident human needs which could not be disputed – a need for social equality, individual liberty, dignity and peace?

Yet it had been disputed. The words which encapsulated their dreams had been flung and bartered with increasing ferocity, and had gradually grown meaningless in the process, until finally they had become mere sputterings in a battle for power. And then the guns had come.

Klaus sunk into an armchair and buried his face in his hands. Five days ago he had shot a man. A gun had been thrust into his hand and he had been told to defend the revolution. And he had shot a man, had seen him fall, had seen the blood splatter, could almost make out the traumatic pattern in the tissue. An ordinary man, like himself. In all those years of war, he had patched and sewn and tended the wounded, hoped to save where he often saw die, had told himself that never again must this gross savagery, this wholesale murder, be allowed. Now when it was all presumed to be over, he, an avowed pacifist, had murdered. In the name of his dream of peace.

Tears moistened his hands. Through them he gazed at his fingers. Long, knobbly, familiar. Fingers which had stroked little Max's head. Fingers which had killed. He shuddered, felt his mind reel.

'Have a drink, Klaus.' A voice gently beckoned him.

He looked up confusedly at the woman. Who was she? Why was he here?

'Drink. It will do you good.'

He took the cup. Daphne, of course. He had come here not knowing where else to go, though he hadn't seen her for months, not since the time he had stumblingly told her it was over between them, and she had smiled and said it didn't matter, they were friends anyhow, weren't they?

Klaus gulped down the hot liquid. He hadn't dared to go back to Bettina. Not only because they would find him there. The word had gone out that the arrests had begun. Arrests of the traitors. He scalded himself thinking of the definition of that word.

'All right?'

'Thank you.' Klaus tried a smile.

'The news isn't good, Klaus.' She lowered her slight form into the chair opposite him. 'I've just come back from the Stephanie. It's almost empty. Karl told me they're rounding people up and shooting them on the slimmest of circumstances.'

'I'll go then. When it's dark. I don't want to get you into trouble.'

'There's no need.'

The doorbell rang and they both stiffened. Daphne gestured nervously to the bedroom. He crept towards it and hid unthinkingly behind a curtain. Through its folds, he heard a woman's voice.

'Is Herr Eberhardt here? I was told he might be.'

Bettina. Klaus took a deep breath. 'It's all right, Daphne,' he called softly. He waited to hear the click of the door and then stepped out.

'Thank God,' Bettina murmured. She stared at him for a moment as if she had seen an apparition, then turned to Daphne. 'Thank you for looking after him.' She gave the other woman a curious sidelong glance, before moving towards Klaus. 'I have a car waiting downstairs. Will you come?'

'Home?'

She nodded.

'No, it'll endanger you.'

He saw the flush at her temples which signalled anger. 'We'll see about that. Besides, you look ill.'

With the quick gestures she had learned from her brief nursing course during the war, she held her hand to his head and took his pulse. 'Definitely unwell, Klaus.' She gave him a worried glance and then, taking his arm, manoeuvred him out of the door, thanking Daphne again all the while.

The procession of troops had passed now. Only the leaflets the low-flying planes had dropped littered the streets. Klaus pulled the brim of his hat low, didn't look to see who was their driver.

'We'll be all right.' Bettina put more assurance into her words than she felt.

She had been worried sick since that night when she had seen the beating, and still there was no word or sign from Klaus on her final return home. More worried on the next day when it had become clear that violence erupted each time the city took a breath. She had rung everyone she could think of, gone to see Johannes only to find Anna alone in the studio, as nervous as she was. And then yesterday, she had seen Klaus's photograph in the paper, alongside a score of others listed as traitors. Rage at this travesty of truth had momentarily drowned her worry.

It was while she was pondering a plan of action, making a list of the ministers and professors she could contact to erase this ridiculous slur from her husband's name, that Johannes had rung suggesting three further places where Klaus might be, counselling her to lie low for a while. White justice consisted of trial by execution.

Lying low was not Bettina's forte. She had a crystalline certainty from she knew not where that Klaus would be in far greater danger without her than with her. It was his way, even in these last months, of listening too quietly to what everyone was saying, of seeming to acquiesce even if the speaker implicated him. As if an uncertainty about his own integrity – which she knew to be unimpeachable – always trailed him.

Klaus was silent in the car. He shrunk back into the seat and refused to meet her eyes. When they reached home, the silence continued. It was as if he didn't hear her. He simply stared out at the river vacantly, his fingers tremulous as he lit cigarette after cigarette. Bettina put him to bed, and after only a moment's reflection about the wisdom of the act, called their family doctor. He was loath to come out. It would be dark soon, the streets perhaps unsafe. She convinced him, said she would send a car for him; it would see him back.

When the old man emerged from his examination of Klaus, he stroked his beard nervously and looked askance at Bettina. 'Well, he's ill, a high temperature, but I'm not absolutely certain if it's influenza or not. Give him these every few hours.' He took some powders from his bag. 'Make sure he drinks as much as possible.' He paused, looked at her oddly and scratched his head. 'He told me he was a murderer, should be arrested, a long story, not quite clear . . .'

Bettina swallowed hard. 'His mind's wandering. It's the strain of these last months, these last years.' She smoothed her skirt. 'You know Klaus, he wouldn't hurt a fly.'

'Yes,' the old man murmured reflectively, clicking his bag shut. 'Perhaps . . . well, if he's not better in a few days' time, I might recommend a sanatorium.'

Bettina leapt at the word. 'Yes, yes, doctor. Could you put that in writing?'

She took comfort from the scratching of his pen, folded the note carefully and placed it in her secretaire.

After he had gone, she sat by Klaus's bedside. His eyes were closed, but his lips seemed to be moving ceaselessly – an incomprehensible mutter in which the odd word rang out clearly.

Bettina watched and reflected. All their hopes for a just democracy had drowned in a sea of violence. She had known in these last months since Eisner's assassination that they were trying to move things too quickly, these hotheaded men with their total visions, wanting everything turned topsy turvy instantly, when what was really needed was the slow, hard work of education, of reorganization.

Democratic ideas, new structures, the necessary responsibility of each individual could not be instituted in a month, all at once, forever. Particularly in a Germany where the power of the state – a state which was the mirror image of the Prussian army with its rigorous military hierarchy – had always taken precedence over any notion of individual rights. Not that it was any better in Russia; look at the chaos Lenin had wrought. No. She had argued with Johannes about it, as Klaus was arguing with himself now, she thought as she watched his murmuring lips.

And what was to become of them now? Patience and restraint were needed, clear thinking to separate the good from the bad; and instead they were in the midst of a civil war.

Bettina dozed, until the nervous jangle of a bell made her leap up in alarm. The ringing was accompanied by a banging at the door. She smoothed her hair. Through the shutters, pale slits of light announced dawn. She walked slowly down the stairs.

'What is this racket?' She pulled the door open abruptly and faced two policemen and a soldier. The latter held a gun at the ready.

'Klaus Eberhardt?' one of the policemen barked.

'Yes, this is the Professor's home.' Bettina drew herself up regally, remembered Johannes in his frock coat. 'There is no need to shout, or to wave that gun. I am Frau Eberhardt, Bettina von Leinsdorf.' She spoke slowly, enunciating each word. 'This is a quiet neighbourhood. What is it that you want?'

The soldier lowered his gun, but one of the policeman growled, 'His arrest.'

'His arrest?' Bettina lifted a contemptuous eyebrow.

The man tried to push past her, but she stood her ground, blocked the doorway.

'Have you a warrant? Professor Eberhardt is an important man and we will stand for no slapdash revolutionary nonsense here.'

The men exchanged a questioning glance. One of the policemen dug in his breast pocket and produced a tatty flier showing a series of ranked photographs.

Bettina flicked her eyes over it. 'Why, gentlemen, this is mere propaganda.' Her voice oozed scorn. 'No official seal. Not even a signature anywhere in sight.' She crumpled the flier and looked at them suspiciously. 'If you are really here as the representatives of the highest judicial authority, if you are really here to arrest my husband, then you must return with the proper documents.' She made to close the door in their astonished faces, only adding, 'And be sure to tell your superiors that my husband is seriously ill with influenza and can be moved nowhere except an infirmary without risk to his own life and those around him.'

Bettina slammed the door forcefully. She waited until she heard their footsteps receding and then slumped into the nearest chair. But there was no time to lose. Quickly she found the note from their family doctor and rang the clinic he had mentioned. It was full. They were taking no more patients. She tried another whose name she dimly knew. But here too, there were no more beds. She suddenly had an image of all Munich huddled in asylums or prisons. She telephoned Petra, relieved to find her in, explained her need. Petra had some friends in a small experimental clinic for nervous ailments, just on the outskirts of Munich. She would try to take Klaus there that evening.

'Now, Petra, please. This evening may be too late.'

She heard her hesitate, then her acquiescence. 'All right, as soon as I can.'

Bettina took a moment to think. It might be safer to disguise Klaus in some way, in case the car was stopped. She remembered that somewhere he had a white doctor's coat. With swift determination, she went to rouse him, to explain only the minimum, since his eyes were still not focusing. Then she found the white coat, insisted that he put it on, told him that at the clinic he would go under the name of Klaus Niemayer from Königsdorf. He had come to Munich deliberately because he had heard of the work of the clinic. She made him repeat the name several times, packed a small bag for him, and one for herself.

Petra arrived just as she was dialling the number of Johannes's house. No answer. She would have to go there later.

They managed to arrive at the clinic without being stopped and at Petra's insistence, a space was found for Klaus. Bettina explained to the doctor that she might not be able to visit Herr Niemayer for some days but that should she be needed, a message should be sent to Seehafen.

Yes, Bettina thought to herself. That would be best. She would go to the children and take Anna and Johannes with her.

But at Johannes's studio, there was only a tearful Anna.

'He's vanished,' she said. 'He wouldn't tell me where he was going. Said it would be safer.'

'I'm sure he's right. We'll go to Seehafen and wait until this has all blown over.'

'I can't leave.' Anna was adamant. 'Johannes may need me. May send a message.'

'And Leo?'

Anna looked at her stonily. 'Leo will be fine with you.' She turned away and began dabbing at the small oil painting on the table.

'I think it would be wiser if you came with me,' Bettina insisted.

Anna shook her head. 'You don't understand, Bettina. Johannes needs me. Needs me here. Yesterday the police came. I met them at the bottom of the stairs. They were taking away a friend who was camping out in the studio.' She hid her eyes. 'I won't let them take Johannes away.'

Bettina shrugged. 'When you find him, both of you make your way to Seehafen. You can stay in the boathouse. No one will think to look there. Don't go to Bogenhausen for a while.'

Anna nodded, looked up at her sister again. 'Is Klaus all right?'

'I don't know,' Bettina murmured. 'But I think he's safe.'

'I wish I thought Johannes was safe.' Anna shivered.

Suddenly she flung herself at her sister and began to sob. 'I don't think I could bear another loss, Bettina.'

Bettina cradled her in her arms for a moment and then kissed her lightly on the hair. 'We'll get through this too, Anna. We've been through so much already. Johannes will be all right. He can talk his way out of anything.'

Where Johannes was, words were not a primary asset. Handcuffed between two detectives, an officer with a revolver at the ready opposite him, he and two other prisoners were being driven through the streets of Munich. Behind them were the soldiers, their machine-guns poised as they joked about the rich picking of traitors this day had brought.

Despite himself, Johannes laughed. 'So there we are. Heroes of war become criminals of the peace in less than a year. Doesn't it strike you as odd?' He addressed the policeman on his left.

The man shrugged, while the soldiers behind him hooted and jeered. The officer opposite cocked his gun menacingly. 'Keep your trap shut, Bolshevik scum.'

'Yes sir, Herr Lieutenant.' Johannes made a great show of trying to salute with handcuffed wrists.

'Why don't you try and escape?' a voice from behind baited him.

Johannes twisted his head to see the man enact his murder by machine-gun.

'It's heartening to see the new authorities have even more respect than I do for the rule of law,' he muttered under his breath.

The officer lashed him across the face with his gun. 'I told you to keep quiet.'

'Yes sir, sir.' Johannes slumped back in his seat.

Minutes later they were shoved roughly from the vehicle. Dazzling sunlight bounced off heavy stone walls and prison gates. Johannes tried to shield his eyes, read the scrawls chalked on stone: 'Reds executed free of charge', 'Spartacist sausage factory.'

In a different spirit, he would have laughed away the crude threat of this right-wing humour. But he was suddenly frightened, more frightened than he had ever been throughout the war, he realized. There was a kind of individualized brutality at play here, a blind raucous hatred which would make killing him a vengeful pleasure to these men. And he didn't want to die. Not now. Here.

He walked obediently between the policemen, let himself be searched, pawed like one animal by another, said nothing as his clothes and few possessions were taken away, walked silently between two warders towards his cell. They passed through a bleak yard, a wall pitted with gun holes, at its base bloody shreds of what looked like dried human flesh.

Johannes shuddered. From somewhere, he heard men's voices jeering again, 'We'll have your brains splattered on that wall.'

Hoots of laughter.

'He's the artist, yeah.'

'We'll get him to paint with his own blood.'

He was relieved when the cell door clanged shut behind him and he heard the screech of the bolt.

Johannes looked around the tiny room, saw the narrow bed with its musty blanket, the reeking bedpan. He leaned heavily against the door and closed his eyes for a moment.

No, they wouldn't kill him, he told himself, not unless it could be classified as an accident. He wasn't important enough, not like poor gentle old Landauer, and that meticulous commissar Leviné he had taken such a dislike to.

But rumour had it that they were murdering indiscriminately. He could well believe it from what he had seen of those soldiers today, the blood on the wall. And so many of his friends had disappeared. It was lucky that they hadn't found him at home. They might have taken Anna then, too, out of sheer malice. Anna.

Johannes wiped his brow. The heat was overpowering. Anna. That was why he now cared about his life. He stretched out on the narrow plank bed and stared up into the glazed slit which passed for a window. It was Anna who had twice now revivified him, given him a sense of connection with the world.

Everything had gone dead for him in those last years, his own isolated life one of a series of equally isolated and meaningless fragments replete only with an absurd horror. And then through her, in her, he had felt a kind of visceral force; had an apprehension, however unprovable, of a vast pulse which throbbed through everything, regardless of his petty consciousness, a pulse which linked the colours he put on canvas with living beings, which made the shape of a bosom the curve of a mountain. It was as if she had given flesh and life to his boisterously voiced youthful beliefs in the healing power of the erotic. When he lay in her arms, the years in which so much blood had been senselessly spilled could almost be reimagined as a sacrifice to a bountiful nature.

And now, even now in the depths of this prison, if he visualized Anna, he could feel that pulse which made him hope.

Clothing that hope in words, however, as he had sometimes tried to do, seemed a near impossibility. Was he really trying to say that if only men could accept that they were a single element in a sympathetic universe in which everything was organically linked in an endless fertile cycle, they might still be able to salvage something out of the slaughter which the exploitative machine mentality had wrought?

Johannes scoffed at himself. To conjure pantheistic fantasies from this cell which spelled the end of his recent hopes was a crass bit of innocence. Yet when Anna's hands rippled over his body, he had the energy for a hundred utopias fashioned out of the lavish sensuality she gave him.

Johannes leapt up as the cell door clattered open. Two warders ushered him out along the narrow corridor with its blind doors, down a flight of stairs past another row of cells, this time barred. Someone shouted his name. He looked up to see an acquaintance from the Stephanie, then a fellow artist, another friend and another. It was as if all Schwabing were suddenly behind bars.

The guards hurried him along towards a room where his fingerprints were taken. Then, a number was stuck in front of him and a photograph snapped.

'I am an artist,' Johannes protested, 'not a common criminal.'

'We'll see about that,' a policeman sneered.

'See about what?' A man entered the room, an officious spring to his steps. He was small, beady-eyed. The public prosecutor, Johannes realized.

He was taken to an office where the charges against him were spelled out: conspiring with traitors to overthrow the Republic; fomenting public disquiet with revolutionary posters; sheltering traitors in his home. The list went on endlessly, as did the questions.

Johannes began to laugh at the warped logic of it all. Eight months ago, this very same man could have been charging him with the very same supposed crimes, but then he would have been speaking in the name of the Monarchy instead of the Republic. It was all as he had predicted in his bleaker moments. Nothing had changed in the structure of power, except a name.

He spent the night twisting and turning restlessly on the plank bed. From time to time the heavy silence was broken by the splatter of gunfire, the resonant wail of a voice. The next morning after a cup of gruel had been passed through the door, his warders arrived to take him to the exercise ground. He asked them about the shooting. They shrugged, refusing to meet his eyes, but one of them as they neared the door to the yard whispered, 'Careful out there, comrade.'

Johannes looked at the man in astonishment, but didn't have time to question him before he was pushed out into the glaring sunshine of the yard.

It was the same bleak rectangle he had passed through the day before. In a far corner, he could see a group of soldiers. Opposite him, alongside the bloodied wall, two prisoners walked listlessly.

Johannes didn't know what propelled him to shout out to them, 'Hello, comrades, fine day.' Perhaps it was only the desire to hear the sound of his own voice, to elicit some human response. One of the men waved back at him. Johannes smiled, made the sign of victory, broke into a sprint. From the corner of the yard, the soldiers began to jibe and hoot.

'It's the pig artist.'

'The one who paints the dirty pictures.'

'You gonna paint for us, Red scumbag.'

'No free love in prison, eh?'

'Look, he knows how to run.'

'Let's teach him to run faster.'

Johannes approached the grinning faces, wondered for a split second whether he should retrace his steps or turn to make his way across the yard, which would mean passing in front of them. No, he wouldn't turn back. He increased his pace, ran in front of the soldiers.

'He's making for the gate.'

'Trying to get away.'

'Stop him.'

Johannes tripped over a foot that had been placed in his path. He stumbled, fell to the ground, heard the whistle of a bullet past his ear. There were shouts, 'Stop, stop,' then the spatter of guns, a commotion, in which a single thought pounded through his mind, 'They're going to kill me. Here. Now. Like a dog.'

Anna confronted the thin-lipped man on the other side of the warped wooden desk.

'Why can't I see Herr Bahr?'

The man rose impatiently from his desk and flicked his nose with a tobacco-stained finger. 'You've already been told once by my assistant, Fräulein, visiting days are every second Wednesday. And then only for parents or husbands and wives. This is a prison, not a convalescent home.'

Anna looked at the man with barely concealed hatred. It had taken five gruelling days filled with nightmare fears to learn that Johannes had been arrested, another two to ascertain what prison he was in, only to be told that Johannes had been moved to the prison hospital. And still they wouldn't let her see him, nor even tell her what condition he was in. She was suspicious of the illness. So many ugly rumours had been making the rounds, of men being secretly executed, of accidents. She shivered, took a deep breath.

'I am almost Herr Bahr's wife, his fiancée,' she said coldly.

The man sniggered. 'These Bolsheviks always have any number of "fiancées".'

Anna glared at him.

'Though you're an exceptionally pretty one, I admit. Nonetheless, the category "fiancée" is not a permissible one. And now, young lady, I'm a busy man.'

Anna almost burst into tears. Then an image of Bettina flashed into her mind. Bettina would never take this kind of treatment sitting down.

Anna squared her shoulders, drew herself up to her full height, took on her sister's tone. 'I shall complain to your superior about this, Herr Brucker. The slight to the honour of a von Leinsdorf is not to be taken lightly. And Herr Bahr is a respected artist. Whatever your own views may be, he has patrons in the highest places.'

As she flounced away from him, she saw the startled look on his face.

It almost made her laugh. Being Bettina had distinct advantages. Anna turned back for a moment for a parting shot.

'Should you decide to make a special exception in my case, you can reach me here.' She wrote her number on a sheet of paper, making sure that she signed it 'Anna von Leinsdorf', and placed it emphatically on his desk. 'I expect to hear from you,' she said in Bettina's clear dry tones.

But by the time Anna had made her way out of the dank grey building, the momentary exhilaration had passed. Despondency trailed her. She had been haunted by a sense over these last weeks that Johannes had been returned to her only to be taken away, as if she had to be punished for her excessive happiness.

It was a ridiculous way to think, she chided herself. Johannes would be the first to laugh at her for her silly superstitiousness. It came of being alone too much. Alone and only half a person. Anna shivered despite the warmth. In those long nights spent without him in their bed, she felt as if she had been torn in half, her skin a scarred surface from which Johannes had been ripped.

She needed to take advice, to talk to someone about the best course of action. How long could they keep him in prison? Would there be a trial? She wouldn't go to Bettina again, be the eternal younger sister. Besides, for all her sensible advice, Bettina would inevitably make light of her desperation. As she had when they had spoken over the telephone yesterday evening.

Anna walked, forcing herself to think coherently above and beyond her fears. Bettina had suggested she might go and visit Klaus at the clinic to see how he was getting on. Klaus wouldn't make light of her worries. He would know about procedures.

Anna found a taxi, asked the driver to wait while she clambered up to the studio. She found the clinic's address, emphasized to her downstairs neighbour how important it was that any callers were to ring her back after five or leave messages. With a silent prayer, she hoped against hope that Herr Brucker might see fit to do something about her request to see Johannes.

The clinic was on the outskirts of the city on the road which eventually led to Bayreuth. Having asked the smiling receptionist for Herr Klaus Niemayer, Anna was promptly met by a plump woman in white who introduced herself as Dr Gerda Hilferding and who invited her for a stroll round the grounds during which she expounded the philosophy of the clinic, its concern with releasing the repressed forces in individuals, buried angers, hidden desires, as a way of reintegrating the patient's personality.

All of which Anna gradually realized was intended to pave the way to telling her that she might not find Klaus in quite the state she had last seen him in.

'He's of course still in the midst of his crisis,' the woman said casually, 'still obsessed with the notion that he's a murderer. But we've had several cases like this in this last year. They eventually mend. It's a question of accepting that in our imaginations, in our infantile state, we all harbour murderous desires. History has recently given us a little too much scope to live these desires out. There are those of us who can't put up with the enactment of buried fantasies.' She clucked under her breath. 'So, you'll wait here.' She motioned her towards a table and chairs in a little arbour.

Anna waited, worrying for Klaus, worrying too that this visit might have been in vain.

But when Klaus appeared, he looked strangely fit. His cheeks were ruddy, his embrace firm.

'Anna, how good to see you. Have they offered you coffee, a drink?' He was like a concerned host, fussing over her, hoping the drive hadn't been too long, hoping she wasn't too hot.

When she asked how he was, he returned her question instantly with his own, asking after her welfare, after Leo and Bettina and Max. Anna decided she had misinterpreted what the doctor had been trying to tell her and she plunged straight in with her immediate concern.

'Johannes has been imprisoned.'

Klaus put a finger to his lips, hushed her.

'I don't know what to do. They won't let me see him. What can we do, Klaus?'

He looked at her oddly for a long moment. The silence grew.

'Klaus,' Anna prodded him.

He seemed to recollect himself. 'Do, yes. Get a good lawyer. Let me think. Heilbron, Octavius Heilbron. He'll be sympathetic, but hasn't been implicated. Try to make sure there's a proper trial and soon. Otherwise . . .' He shrugged.

'Otherwise,' Anna felt herself blanching.

'I've heard that people disappear in these prisons,' he said with an uncustomary hint of relish. 'Yes, disappear.'

Suddenly he leapt up and executed an outlandish dance, as if he were being marched at rifle point by an invisible patrol. His legs flew out from his thighs, his back arched forward, his arms shot up over his head. 'Prison, prison, prison,' he chanted rhythmically, his eyes wide with fear. Then he stopped abruptly in front of her. His tone grew confidential again. 'That's where I'm going, Anna. Where I should be. Where we should all be. Inside. Awaiting proper trials. Who knows what crimes we're all guilty of, eh?'

His head jerked back as if he had heard someone spying on them. His voice grew lower, secretive. 'And the judgements have to be made, Anna, the sentences passed and served. But where shall we find the judges? Stern judges, virtuous judges with a real sense of right and wrong. Not just scoundrels on the payroll of power.' He suddenly laughed raucously. 'Eh, Anna? Hypocritically virtuous scoundrels like Johannes thinks his father is.' He slapped his thigh. 'What a way to pay back the old man. Get himself thrown into jail.' He giggled.

Anna looked at him in dismay.

'It would be wonderful if the old man had to pass sentence on Johannes.' He laughed uproariously again.

'What are you saying, Klaus?' Anna wanted to shake him. 'Stop it. There's nothing funny. Johannes is in prison. He might be killed.' She shivered. 'We have to do something.'

'Yes, to find an honourable judge. Like looking for a needle in a haystack,' Klaus muttered to himself, 'but if you find one, tell me. I'll walk up to the prison gates myself and bellow my crimes.'

'Klaus, Klaus, look at me,' she was shouting.

He looked startled, shivered. 'What were you saying, Anna?' he murmured. 'Little Max is well, is he?'

Anna nodded, the tears gathering in her eyes.

'I'll have to get back, Klaus. Are they treating you well here?'

'Oh, yes, yes, too well,' he said absently. 'You'll kiss Bettina from Herr Niemayer, won't you?'

She hugged him. 'Soon you'll be able to kiss her yourself. As soon as this is all over. The garden needs you.'

Klaus smiled. 'The garden, yes. I wanted to plant an oak for Max. You know, near the lake where lightning split that old tree.'

'Yes, I know.' Anna trembled, remembering. 'That would be a very good thing to do.'

* * *

On the journey home, Anna found herself in a state of even greater despondency than on her way to the clinic. But that evening, after she had spoken to Bettina and was once again replaying the troubling sequence of her encounter with Klaus, she was struck by an idea.

It quickened her pace as she made her way the next day to Octavius Heilbron's office, made her tone in speaking to him more certain; made her pick up the telephone to ring Herr Brucker and tell him that she had every reason to believe that he had thought over their meeting and that he would now grant her dispensation to visit Johannes at the earliest possibility. It made her pack a small case with alacrity and board the 19.07 to Berlin with a sense that she was acting with as much practical good sense as Bettina could have wished.

When she arrived in the city the following morning, she was initially weighed down by its grey heaviness, the dour facades of the stately buildings, the monumental statues. But keeping her purpose firmly in mind, she manoeuvred her way swiftly through the crowded streets and checked in at the Unter den Linden hotel, cheered by the trees and cafés which lined the avenue beneath her. Ten o'clock. She would telephone straight away. Octavius Heilbron had found the number for her in his directory.

A woman's clipped voice answered her. Yes, Anna was told, this was the residence of Geheimer Justizrat Karl Gustav Bahr, but Justizrat Bahr could not come to the telephone at the moment. No, nor could a meeting be arranged for the time being. Herr Dr Bahr was not well.

'But it is vital that I see him,' Anna pleaded. 'Tell him I have an urgent message from his son. I am certain he will want to hear it.' She gave the woman her number. 'I won't move until I hear from you,' she added.

Anna waited, pacing the small room. She looked out impatiently on the busy street below. A father could not but respond to a plea from his son, she told herself. An hour passed, and then a second. Despair began to gnaw at the edges of her hope. She stretched out on the satin-covered bed and closed her eyes, willing the telephone to ring. At last, through the rampant images of a dream, she heard it, playing in and out of the bells of St Hedwig's Cathedral as they tolled out the hour. She leapt up to reach for the receiver.

'Fräulein von Leinsdorf? Herr Dr Bahr will see you tomorrow morning at eleven. Please be punctual.'

'Yes, yes, of course, thank you, thank you.'
A silly girlhood hum set up a dance in her mind.

> 'Lucky day, lucky day. All the birds fly this way.
> Lucky night, lucky night. All the stars shine so bright.'

It was being called Fräulein von Leinsdorf again which had brought it back, Anna thought. She knew she had used the name out of sheer deviousness. People seemed to respond with greater attention when she used it. And that was certainly a good enough reason in this instance. Anna laughed. She was suddenly brimming with energy. She splashed some cold water on her face and raced down the stairs. She would make use of her day in Berlin to explore a little of the city. But first some food. She was ravenous. It occurred to her that over the last few days she had forgotten to eat.

She found a café near the Schauspielhaus and sat down at a terrace table which looked on to the handsome square. A small crowd had gathered near the statue of Friedrich von Schiller at its centre. In its midst, standing on some steps and declaiming, was a tall bearded man. He was oddly dressed in a ragged vest and tattered shorts, like some wild creature out of a romantic play. But with his shepherd's staff and rugged features, he had the aura of a biblical prophet.

'It seems that Graser's back,' the man at the table next to her said to his companion.

'I thought they'd locked him up for refusing conscription.'

'Guess they've let him out again. Or maybe he's been up in his mountain all this time.'

'His mountain of truth,' the second man chuckled.

'Maybe he's got a point. Anything's gotta be better than this dump. And they grow their own food.'

'Can't grow coffee in Switzerland.'

'You call this coffee,' the man spat.

'No theatres, no cabarets. The pure simple life.'

'Pure? With all those artists and dancers and vegetarian kooks up there?'

The second man grinned. 'I guess there are different kinds of purity. Graser's all right, you know. Our very own wild man. Better than a lot of the lunatics we get these days. Last week there was a messianic crank in the square, foretelling doom, unless we all gave everything up and flagellated ourselves daily with birches. As if we hadn't had doom already.'

'There must be money to be made in this business of saving the world. Everyone's doing it.'

'Shall we go and listen to Graser? I quite like some of what he calls his poems.'

The two men got up.

Anna, who had been eavesdropping with interest, hurriedly finished her sandwich and followed them.

The man they called Graser was declaiming in a low but resonant voice, something about mountains and clear skies and tall straight trees. But it was his presence which captivated Anna. He was completely at ease in his strange garb as if he carried his own place with him. And he was beautiful. There was a strength and a peace in his face that she had never encountered before.

'Where does he usually live?' she found herself asking the man who had been sitting at the table next to hers.

'Ascona. Unless it's your neighbour's spare room.' The man laughed again. 'These anarchists have little sense of private property.'

'Ascona,' Anna murmured. Suddenly she felt Graser's eyes on her and looked up to meet them. A clear blue gaze, like being washed by a lake.

'Come and join us, young woman.' Graser waved his staff at her.

Anna smiled and turned away.

'Geheimer Justizrat Karl Gustav Bahr' – the gold-lettered plate on the side of the wrought-iron gate glistened in the morning sunlight.

Through the arch of dappled leaves, Anna could only just glimpse a turreted house with an imposing stone facade. She wondered for a moment if this was the house in which Johannes had grown up, if it was over these little rounded hills and amidst these trees he had run as a child to fish in the shimmering pond in the distance, where two youths were now flicking their rods. Who would have thought that this vast sprawling city contained this quiet enclave?

But there was no time for dreaminess now. She was already late: Grunewald had proved further away from her hotel than she had expected.

A push at the bell elicited the sound of fierce barking, then a man's voice followed soon after by the man himself.

'Fräulein von Leinsdorf?' he enquired.

Anna nodded and the door at the side of the gate swung open. She followed the man up the path to the house, found herself ushered in by a hatchet-faced woman, who pronounced with grim disapproval that she was ten minutes late, and then whisked her unceremoniously into a large gloomy room. She motioned Anna towards a stiff-backed chair and closed the door firmly behind her.

Anna waited almost afraid to look round her. Then she braced herself, reminding herself that she came from a family who had spent its life in imposing governmental buildings. She had nothing to fear from a Prussian Justizrat, she who had wandered as a child in the Kaiser's Hofburg. Never mind that she had hated it all even then. She had never been afraid.

Karl Gustav Bahr startled her by emerging from a second door hidden by rows of leather-backed tomes. She rose abruptly, was surprised to see him wearing an ordinary suit. Somehow she had imagined a judge's cloak.

Watery eyes squinted at her from beneath bushy brows. 'Be seated, Fräulein von Leinsdorf.' The voice was deep, commanding, but his step as he moved behind his desk was uneven and his clothes hung round him as if they had once belonged to a far larger man.

'So. I gather my renegade son is in trouble again and has sent a woman as his emissary.' There was an unmasked bitterness in his tone alongside the blatant contempt.

Anna countered it hurriedly.

'No, no, Herr Justizrat. It is entirely on my own initiative that I have come here to entreat your help – as I would have entreated my own father's had he still been alive.' Anna gazed directly into his eyes, her own filling with tears.

He looked at her sceptically. 'You know that my son and I have had no communication since before the war. He has consistently abused me and made a mockery of the family name.'

'Surely not. I have never heard him do anything of the kind.'

'You have not known him long then.'

'Since before the war,' she countered him.

He made a scoffing sound from deep within his throat. 'It was before the war that we severed all relations.'

'Surely one cannot sever relations with one's own flesh and blood, one's own son.' She looked beseechingly up at him. She had the sudden sense that if she touched him, if she took that gnarled, blue-veined hand in her own, he would trust her. She moved her chair a little closer to the desk. 'Surely not.'

He laughed, a cold unnatural sound. 'You are a mere slip of a girl.

When you have lived as long as I have, you will learn that when honour is at stake, when the natural order of authority is deliberately flouted, it is as possible to sever all links with one's own flesh and blood as it is to do anything else in this world.'

He banged his fist on the table, rose to his full height. 'My son's continuous disobedience, his lack of respect for paternal authority, his immorality, is a direct challenge to the order of the German state. I have no more feeling for him than I have for a common criminal. Indeed, were he to appear in my court, I would pass the harshest sentence.' His voice boomed, his face grew red. Anna felt herself beginning to shake. 'Yes, like those deserters I condemned to death during the war.' His fist folded round a heavy glass paperweight on his desk and for a moment Anna thought he might crush it, as he so evidently wished to crush Johannes.

'But Herr Justizrat, please.' Her voice caught. The interview seemed to be at an end. 'Johannes needs you. You are the only one who is certain to be able to help him.' She took a deep breath. 'My father used to say that justice needs to be tempered by mercy, that Emperor Franz-Josef was so loved because he believed in mercy. I come to you as I would come to my own father.'

He was silent for a moment, contemplated her from his height. She thought she heard the word 'Catholics' issue from his thin lips. Then he scowled, sat down heavily. 'So what kind of trouble is Johannes in now?'

She opened her mouth, but he didn't let her answer, rushed on, his cheek twitching. 'You would have thought the war would have taught him. Apparently he performed credibly during those years. Oh yes, I have my sources. I know. Medals, the lot. I almost contacted him in November, to congratulate him, but then he got himself mixed up with those scurrilous Reds. Unpatriotic idiot. Ingrate. As if authority could rest in the mob!' A thick tongue passed over dry lips.

'And now I presume he's in prison, where he belongs.' The lips formed themselves into a malevolent smile. 'And you want me to move the earth to get him out. That's it, isn't it? I knew it all in advance.' He sat back smugly in the broad chair and blinked at her from hard eyes.

'Yes, Herr Justizrat. And I hope you will. My father would have,' Anna said quietly.

'Your father would have,' he echoed her. 'But then he had a worthwhile daughter. Two worthwhile daughters.'

'If Johannes survives,' Anna shivered over the words, 'I would be a daughter to you.' She looked at the gnarled old man's hand on the desk and folded hers round it. The hand was cold, lifeless, like a crinkled sheet of paper.

'So he has said he would marry you?' One shaggy eyebrow rose in scepticism.

Anna swallowed. 'We are married, sir. Were married in January. Quietly. Otherwise how would I dare to come and see you?' She raised modest eyes to him.

For a moment he seemed not to believe her. He surveyed her closely, then slowly he brought his hand to rest on hers. 'A von Leinsdorf for a daughter,' he mused, almost to himself. Then his eyes grew crafty. 'And you think if I bail Johannes out this one more time, you can bring him to order? Induce him to lead a respectable life?'

Anna drew her hand back, squared her shoulders. 'Johannes is an artist, Herr Justizrat, a fine artist. Even Prussians allow a little special dispensation for the conduct of artists. Frederick the Great . . .'

He cut her off. 'And you will provide me with grandchildren?' His eyes travelled over her, settling on her hips.

Anna swept back her instant rage. 'I will try,' she said softly. 'And as I said, I will be a daughter to you.'

'Yes, yes, one can only try.' He smiled perfunctorily, stood to his full height. 'Good, I, too, will try. Though it will not be easy.'

The way he said it left her in no doubt of his own certainty of his success.

As she rose to shake his hand, he stopped her for a moment. She could almost feel his mind racing, plotting.

'You will say nothing of this meeting to my son, of course. He needs to understand that I have done this for him out of sheer paternal duty. After all, in these times of disorder, with power dissipated at the centre, it has been difficult for young men to know how to behave. But now order is being restored. We must get back to the business of making Germany strong again, breathe new life into our nation.' A cavernous laugh boomed out of him, as he glanced at her hips again.

'Goodbye, Fräulein von Leinsdorf, or should I say, Frau Bahr. When we meet again, I shall call you Anna.'

'Goodbye, Herr Justizrat. Thank you.'

Leaving the house, Anna shook off the distaste which covered her like a foul odour. The man was despicable, as she now remembered Johannes had intimated all those years ago when they had first met. He hadn't spoken of him since.

But Karl Gustav Bahr's character mattered not a jot. Nor did anything that she had said. All that mattered was that he put in motion the forces which would return Johannes to her. And for that she would always be grateful to him.

By the time Anna had reached her hotel, she had convinced herself that soon Johannes would be with her again. Her spirits soared, matching the speed of the train which brought her back to Munich. Now, in the short term, all she hoped for was that Brucker had arranged for her to see Johannes. She raced from the station to the studio. But when she arrived the only message was one from the housekeeper in Bogenhausen. She was to come straight away.

Anna felt a shiver of panic. Had something happened to little Leo? She hadn't thought of him for days. No. She clenched her fist into a tight ball. Not that. Bettina would have contacted her herself. Anna quickly rang the Bogenhausen number and, getting no answer, asked the operator to connect her to Seehafen. Frau Trübl answered, told her Bettina was out in the gardens with the children. Yes, yes, everything was fine. Would she like Bettina to ring her back?

'No thank you, Frau Trübl, just give them all my very best and kiss the children for me.' Anna rang off and breathed a sigh of relief, before quickly dropping her case off at the studio and hurrying over to Bogenhausen. Perhaps the housekeeper had left her a message there. Perhaps there was something from Johannes who for some reason hadn't wanted to send anything through to the studio.

Assuming no one was in, she let herself into the house with her own key.

'Frau Anna, thank goodness you're here.' The housekeeper confronted her. She was unpinning her hat, and Anna realized she must just have come in. 'This came for you yesterday.' She scurried towards the hall table and picked up a large sealed envelope. 'A messenger delivered it and said I was to place it directly into your hands.' She did so now.

'Thank you,' Anna mumbled. She examined the bulky package suspiciously, gazed at the official seal without recognizing it. Slowly she walked towards Bettina's secretaire and sliced the seal carefully with her ivory paperknife. Inside there was a heavy sheaf of papers.

Anna glanced at the covering letter and sank down into the nearest chair. Bruno's estate. Bruno. Her heart raced with she didn't know what emotions.

'Are you all right, Frau Anna? You've turned all white.' The housekeeper gazed at her solicitously.

'Yes, yes,' Anna murmured. 'Do you think you could get me a glass of water?'

She drank it down thirstily and then forced herself to focus on the legal jargon.

Bruno's complicated estate had at last been cleared. It seemed that far from having left nothing but debts, which the sale of assets would cover, as the lawyers had originally intimated to her, he had before the war converted a substantial portion of his fortune into American dollars, treasury bonds, stocks. She was, it appeared, a relatively rich woman. The attached pages showed a breakdown of holdings once various taxes had been cleared. All Anna had to do was to instruct the executors on how she would like the capital handled, etc. etc.

Anna covered her face with her hands. She was trembling.

She felt as if a great weight was bearing down on her shoulders, constricting her chest – an unshakeable burden of gratitude she could never repay.

'It's too much, Bruno. This and Johannes, too. I can't.' She felt her lips moving against her hands, the tears moistening them. Then a fear spliced through her, becoming more actual as she formulated it soundlessly into words. Johannes wouldn't come back. That was what Bruno was telling her.

Anna gripped the arms of her chair savagely. No. That was madness. She was fantasizing. It wasn't Bruno's voice she was hearing, it was simply the voice of her own fear. Bruno was generous, not vengeful. How astute it had been of him all those years back to convert a part of his wealth into dollars. He had always been a man of forethought and he had acted for the future, for his heirs.

With a frenzied urgency, Anna shuffled through the papers again. Yes, there was the date on which Bruno had converted part of his estate into American currency. Just a month after their marriage. A thought for his children. The tears leapt into her eyes again. Leo. She must go to Leo.

Anna glanced at her watch. It was too late to phone Brucker. At best she couldn't see Johannes until next week. And perhaps by then his father . . . Anna didn't dare elaborate the thought. If she hurried now, she might catch a train to Seehafen. Yes. She must see Leo. Perhaps they could all travel to Vienna together.

Johannes opened his eyes and lifted his head slowly. The nightmare sounds and smells, the mangled bodies of the battlefield, were finally receding. The pain wasn't too ghastly now. Just a few surface wounds. Those ridiculous gangsters didn't even know how to shoot straight. And he was far better off in the infirmary here than in his cell. The little nun who tended to him was of an ethereal kindness, despite her admonishments that he must pray and her doubling of her prayers for him when he insisted that he had no one to pray to.

Johannes smiled with only a trace of bitterness. He felt like the proverbial cat with nine lives. How many had he used up now? Seven? Eight? How did one count lives? He might be able to count better if they had some morphine here to dull the pain and give him the necessary distance. But like so much else, that too was lacking.

He looked round the little room. No one to occupy the other two beds. Perhaps those gangster soldiers didn't always miss. Or have the bad luck to have the warders come running just as they were indulging in their morning sport – for that was what had saved him as far as he could make out. There had been a message that he be taken to the examination room again. Not the cemetery.

The little nun, Sister Thomasina, told him he had been here for nine days now. But it seemed an eternity. The world had grown opaque, remote, its circumference Sister Thomasina's soft comings and goings. Everything else was dream in which figures with no substance flitted. Even Anna had been reduced to a shadow, a golden blaze of hair, a scent of warmed peaches.

Here was Sister Thomasina now, her small face a perfect girlish oval beneath that great white headdress.

'A letter has come for you, Herr Bahr.' She smiled shyly. 'I was told to deliver it to you. Shall I read it or can you manage on your own?'

'Read it to me, then I can have the pleasure of your voice. Unless its contents embarrass you.'

'Nothing can embarrass me, Herr Barr.' She flushed.

'Go on then.'

She tore the letter open with slim fingers and then read in a clear schoolgirl voice:

> Johannes,
>
> I have arranged for you to be transferred to Schleierman's clinic where you will be under the care of the great man himself. The charges against you are being dropped. I have explained to the relevant powers that you have long suffered from bouts of mental disturbance and that your actions are therefore not always of your own responsibility. Given your impeccable war record, not to mention my own standing, the public prosecutor has agreed that a period of confinement will in this instance stand in the stead of the inevitable sentence. Your transfer should occur not much after this letter has reached you. I trust that as soon as your period of confinement – which will be as brief as your actions warrant – is over, you will come to see me. I am an old ailing man now and a visit from my son would not be amiss.
>
> As ever,
> Karl Gustav Bahr

Johannes all but tore the letter from Sister Thomasina's hands and read it through again. Only her presence prevented him from cursing.

'I am overjoyed to be the bearer of such good news,' she smiled at him with her sweet smile. 'My prayers have been answered.' She crossed herself and cast down her eyes. 'We must thank the good Lord.'

'I would like to be alone for a moment, Sister,' Johannes said as soon as she looked up at him again.

'Of course. I understand.'

He watched her graceful receding form and then lay back on the bed, his mind racing.

Good news, Sister Thomasina had said. Why was it then that he felt that any sentence would be better than this? To be branded a madman by his own father. To be engineered out of any responsibility for his own actions. To be made to feel after all these years like a delinquent five-year-old.

Johannes pounded his pillow, felt a blast of pain and relapsed into it. Only his father's death would put an end to this interminable dance. Or his own. Nine lives, he thought. There couldn't be many left. He would certainly not spend the last in any period of confinement designated by his father. There had already been far too much of that in his life.

Anna clasped Leo's small form to her and wept silent tears. She should never have left him for so long. He seemed not to recognize her, was distant, aloof, the thick-lashed tawny eyes above the smooth golden cheeks utterly self-absorbed, unresponsive. What would Bruno have said? Anna ruffled the smooth tow-haired mop and planted a kiss on it, but the child struggled against her. She let him go. He ran like a wild creature released from a trap, sped across the garden to Max's side.

'He'll come round.' Bettina had stolen softly to her side. 'Just give him time. They hate being left. And they make you pay when you come back.' She started to laugh, but stopped awkwardly when she saw Anna's stricken face. 'Really, Anna, just give it time.'

Anna nodded, gazed at the boys playing in the distance. When Leo looked up, she waved at him. He turned away abruptly and threw his ball into the copse, speeding after it.

'Will they be safe? Shall I go after them?'

This time Bettina allowed herself the fullness of her laugh. 'Really, Anna, first you pay no attention to the child at all, and suddenly you're worse than a hen with its eggs. What's come over you? It can't just be the fact of Johannes's absence.'

Anna looked askance at her sister. 'You have a way of reducing everything to such simplicity, Bettina, that I'm instantly lost. I don't know what's come over me. But I do have something to tell you.' She turned towards her and took both her hands in her own. 'It was too late to talk about it last night.'

Bettina examined her sister curiously. 'Well?'

'I've heard from Bruno's solicitors. Suddenly there's a great deal of money.' Anna paused. What she was going to say had only come to her last night, but then, and even more so now, it seemed to her the perfect solution.

'I want you to have it. Most of it. You and Klaus. What isn't put aside for Leo. I'll just take what I need for Johannes and me to move away from here. If that's possible.' Her face turned grim.

Bettina was silent for a moment. Then she burst out, 'But that's ridiculous, Anna. I know Klaus and I are a little short at the moment. But then so is everyone.' She paused. 'Anna, you're just feeling guilty. That's it, isn't it? About you and Johannes. It's no state to make decisions in.'

'I'm not feeling guilty.' Anna was adamant. She shook her head fiercely. 'It's not as clear as that. It's just that all this has brought Bruno back. I can feel him following me. It's as if, as if . . .' She shuddered and looked up towards the tree which had been blasted by lightning. 'One can't have everything. He's been too good.'

'We'll talk about it when Johannes is back.' Bettina squeezed her hand. 'You're overwrought. It's all these worries. Tell me about Klaus, now.'

Over the next days the sisters talked, slowly, cautiously, growing closer. A dreaminess that she always associated with Seehafen began to suffuse Anna, eradicating the anxieties which had pursued her during the last month. She learned that the charges against Johannes were being miraculously dropped, learned for the first time about the 'accident', that he was mending quickly and would soon be transferred to Schleierman's clinic.

As she basked lazily in the early summer sunshine, little Leo gradually began to tumble over her, take part in the games she invented for him, or in the hide and seek he adored – pretending not to see her or be seen when she was in full view and then launching himself at her with a giant hug. 'Mummy's not there', he would call out as she approached him and then scream with delight, 'There, there.'

Despite Bettina's evident disapproval, Anna took him riding with her, moving slowly over the well-known trails with him in her arms. To her sister's even greater disapproval, she also sometimes took him to bed with her at night. 'To make up for lost time,' she proclaimed laughingly.

On the tenth day of her stay, the telephone rang. Anna happened to be near it and picked it up only to hear Johannes's voice. 'At last,' she murmured. 'When can I come and see you?'

'I would rather you didn't come here, Anna.' His voice was strange.

'Please,' she begged him.

'It won't be long now. As soon as I'm able, I'll come to you.'

'Has it been too awful?'

He laughed oddly. 'Let's say it hasn't been as wonderful as the period which preceded it.'

'My poor Johannes.'

'You'll stay in Seehafen?'

'Unless you want me to come to you.'

'No, wait for me there. And then be prepared to go somewhere. Anywhere but Germany. I love you, Anna.'

Before she could echo his words with her own, the line went dead.

Replaying the conversation, Anna was suddenly filled with a sense of urgency. She sought out Bettina. 'We must go to Vienna tomorrow,' she told her with an unusual certainty in her voice. 'Everything needs to be in order. I think Johannes wants to leave Germany.'

'Given that he's been complaining about this place for years, I can hardly say I'm surprised,' Bettina said drily.

'Don't joke, Bettina.'

'No, of course, you must all go. If it's necessary.' She surveyed Anna critically. 'You *will* make him work, Anna, won't you? What's special about Johannes, important about him, is his work.'

'This isn't the time for lectures, Bettina.'

'No, perhaps not. But I worry about him, about you. If he isn't working, he's always so desperate, chasing something that isn't there. And when he finds that it isn't, he's devastated. It's as if he hasn't realized that the world outside his canvases is about half measures, little steps forward; as if he hasn't realized that paradise is always elsewhere.'

'Not for all of us,' Anna murmured. 'Some of us have tasted it right here.'

'And that undoubtedly is the difference between us.' Bettina was wry.

'One of them, certainly.' Anna smiled.

TEN

LITTLE TENDRILS of morning mist curled slowly from the lake, leaving its shimmering indigo surface exposed.

In another hour, if the sun were hot enough, it would gradually burn the mist from the hills and the mountains all around them. Then in the crystalline clarity, drooping palms with dancing fronds, lush, spreading magnolia and plump juicy cactuses, tall cedars and ragged firs would all rub shoulders and reveal themselves in their full splendour. Anna had never known such richness of colour and texture, as if this little remote corner of the Ticino had been singled out by some unseen presence as an experimental garden where the tropical and the alpine could mingle and flourish. No wonder people referred to it as paradise.

Anna sighed happily. It was in this light that she had first seen the village, over two months ago back in August. August 1919. She had thought of it then as the dividing line between the true end of war and the beginning of a new era of peace.

They had spent the night in a pension in Locarno and then early in the morning boarded the little boat which would take them further down Lago Maggiore. Ascona had gradually emerged from the mist: a cluster of red-tiled roofs, atop creamy-coloured houses with green shutters, behind them the graceful old campanile of San Pietro-Paolo.

As they had moved closer to the small wharf, she had spied a house perched on a stony precipice at an angle from the village. Its two wings met in an expansive curved and columned bay, glazed on the first floor, but on the top giving on to an open-air loggia. Looking at those columns, Anna had the sense that someone was looking back out at her. She glanced away but her gaze was drawn back to the house again. Her skin began to tingle strangely. It was as if the person gazing at her from the terrace were herself.

She had gripped Johannes's arm fiercely and pointed to the house. 'Isn't it beautiful? Wouldn't it be wonderful if we could live there?'

And now they were here. Had been here for some six weeks. And it was she who was looking down on the lake watching the little fishing boats hoisting their nets into the lake, watching the hills emerge from the mist.

Anna took another breath of the cool morning air and then rushed down the two long flights of stairs which brought her to the white-tiled kitchen. She would bring Johannes coffee in bed this morning, since it was she who was up first. Perhaps it would lift the ill-humour he had been in these last days.

She hated it when that blackness descended upon him. Over these last months she had grown so attuned to him, every nerve and vessel in her so exposed to him, that when he looked at her from those remote wintry eyes, it was as if there was nowhere she could run to shield herself, and she felt herself dying, turning to stone.

It had been like that when he had returned to Seehafen after his confinement at the clinic. She still shivered when she remembered that initial meeting.

She had been playing with Leo in the lake, trying to teach him to float and had then clambered up the little grassy knoll with him. They were tumbling about in the long grass, Leo hooting with laughter as she threw him up in the air and caught him in her arms. It was then that she had heard Johannes's voice. She rushed up to embrace him, throwing her arms round his neck. But he had only stood there stiffly in their circle, his face impassive, and kissed her perfunctorily on the cheek. Leo had started to whimper and she had picked him up gaily, pretending that there was nothing amiss in the way Johannes had greeted her.

'Hasn't he grown?' she had said proudly.

'Yes, quite the little man.' Johannes's voice was cold, his eyes averted.

And so it had continued for the next days, Johannes grim, refusing to look at her, refusing to sleep with her, refusing to talk about going away, telling her nothing about his incarceration, retiring to the boathouse, offering as his only excuses, 'I have to get used to the world again', or, 'Not with Bettina here'.

She had been hurt, distraught, afraid, doubly troubled, because any time Johannes was in their vicinity, Leo would cower and begin to cry. Johannes made no effort to make friends with the little boy, though he played well enough, if a little absent-mindedly, with Max, and on several occasions she caught him in deep conversation with Bettina. She felt frightened, excluded, and yes, jealous, all her certainties about Johannes crumbling, all her new warmth for Bettina evaporating.

At the end of that week, Klaus had come home. The panic was over: the government had at last forbidden the execution of prisoners without trial, and the wholesale arrests had ceased. It had taken the brutal and mistaken massacre of twenty-one youths from a Catholic Working Boy's Club to bring the government to reason.

Klaus was quiet, tearful. He jumped nervously when anyone entered the room. But he seemed to take sustenance from Max and Leo, and kept the boys busy from daybreak till sunset. Not knowing what to do with herself, Anna tagged along with them. On several occasions she and Klaus came across Johannes and Bettina engrossed in conversation. It was when she caught the look in Klaus's eyes, which she felt echoed her own, that Anna decided something had to be done.

Late that night she stole down to the boathouse and curled next to Johannes on the narrow bed. He was asleep, his breathing even, his naked body warm beneath the single sheet. She started to stroke him, a little surprised at the instant sensation the touch of him elicited in her, as if her body had been coiled in waiting for him without her knowledge.

She was surprised, too, at the immediacy of his response, the hardening of him against her, the gasp of his breath, as if it had only been a disciplined effort of the will which had kept him from her. As she kissed him, heard him murmur her name, she felt suddenly powerful. And then he was pulling her down on him, loving her as he had never loved her, as he had always loved her, making her senses sing his name, listening to him with her skin, seeing him with her fingers.

When they lay together afterwards, bathed in each other's moisture, he had whispered, 'I'm not worthy of you, Anna. Not worthy of your generosity.'

'Don't be silly, Johannes, it's the prison speaking,' she had replied after a moment, but his words had pained her. It was after that that she realized he had planned to leave without her, hadn't wanted to involve her in the necessity of flight.

'But I thought you loved me, Johannes, thought you wanted me with you.'

'I do, my darling.' He had clasped her to him. 'But I don't know where I'm going. Where I'll end up.'

'I want to be with you, Johannes. It doesn't matter about that. Tell me why you're so changed.'

He didn't answer and after a moment she said, 'I had this idea that we might go to Ascona. I heard some people talking about it.'

'Ascona . . . Mühsam's place, where Fanny went.' He looked at her strangely. 'A haven for Schwabing's criminal dreamers; the anarchist's Eden. That's not like you, Anna. Or is it?' he mused. 'Sun and nature worship, is that it? Would you really like to go there, Anna? Even without me?'

'I don't think I want to do anything without you, Johannes. Anything at all.' The tears had started to stream down her cheeks and he had kissed them away, loving her until the sun rose and she had forgotten there had ever been any question of them parting.

The bond between them had sparkled so brightly over the next days that it almost obliterated the need for speech, though she did want to know why exactly Johannes felt he needed to flee. She sensed that Bettina already knew, but felt it a humiliation to need to ask her. Johannes would explain in due course, she decided. And then just to have him near her, loving her, seemed such a precious gift that she didn't want to risk the possibility of his coldness again.

There was only one cloud on her horizon. Leo did not want to be in Johannes's presence. Every time Johannes was near Anna, the little boy would start to whine or cry or simply turn wooden, all expression leaving his face. It pained her, reminded her acutely of her debt to Bruno. He would want his son to be happy; but there seemed to be nothing she could do to cajole the boy in Johannes's presence. Johannes in turn was stiff when the little boy was there, abstracted.

It occurred to her that it would be better to leave the child here until they were settled in Ascona, until Johannes's spirits had lifted sufficiently. She talked it over with Bettina.

'It's true that children hate disruption,' her sister had reflected, 'but don't leave it for too long, Anna, for your sake as well as his.'

The parting had been difficult, but then once they were on their way, the sheer joy of being with Johannes, of seeing him so free and unencumbered and loving, had made her forget everything else. The days and weeks had fled by in a flurry of exploration. There was so much to see in Ascona, so many people: the colony of naturists on Monte Verità, who lived spare, simple lives, the saintly Graser she had seen in Berlin, amongst them; the dancers, artists and poets, the Russian émigrés all seeking to build better, richer lives, model communities, in this tiny idyllic corner of Europe nestling between Swiss and Italian Alps, though it felt as remote as the wilds of South America.

The house Anna had designated from the first as 'theirs' belonged to an Italian Count whose circumstances had been straitened by the war. Once contacted, he was only too happy to rent it out to them, in the first instance for a year.

And so they had moved in, had swept up cobwebs and whitewashed vast expanses of wall, ceilings, arches, had laughed at their grimy bespattered faces, and rolled on the large bed with its crinkly straw mattress when passion took them. They had bought odds and ends of furniture from local peasants and craftsmen to make up for any lack, had the old well renovated, begun to dig in the overgrown garden until the sweat poured from them.

The top floor with its central loggia had been designated as studio space. Johannes had insisted that they divide it equally, the right-hand room which gave on to hills and the lake for him, the left with its view of the village and harbour for her. In his studio, he had installed the habitual narrow bed, the rough table with its array of odds and ends, an assortment of pine cones, dried leaves, a goat's skull, tins, jars. Apart from the view, the room took on the semblance of all the other studios she had seen him in.

Her own stood empty except for a table and an easel. There was still so much to do before she felt she could settle and then she wasn't sure that that was what she wanted to settle to. She was concentrating on assembling a nursery for Leo, gathering wooden toys, intending to ask Johannes whether he would paint some animals on the walls for him.

A little over ten days ago now, he had started to work. He had barred her from his studio, but for the first few days, he was unchanged, cheerful, more passionate than ever, loving her rapturously under the stars. Then the coldness had begun to set in. He locked himself into his studio, wouldn't emerge if at all until she was asleep. Two days ago, when she had asked him how his work was going, he had lashed out at her, 'Don't ever ask me that. Ever.' She hadn't seen him for the rest of the day or the night.

Then yesterday, Johannes had been contrite, asked her if she wanted to walk up the mountain with him. Near the top, in a little shady grove, they had come upon a group of dancers, their thin toga-like garments flowing, their bodies writhing expressively in the afternoon breeze. They looked like wood nymphs moving to the sound of Pan's horn, figures from some antique frieze. Anna had found herself beginning to sway to their motion, had felt Johannes's eyes on her, seen them kindle. 'My child of nature,' he had called her last night, caressing her, but there had been no fire in his touch. And she was afraid that now, this morning, he would be remote again, coldly aloof, with that wintry light in his eyes which seemed to freeze her very life.

Anna arranged the earthenware cups, the coffee jug, thick slices of buttered bread on the platter, took a flower from the vase on the window-sill and placed it in their midst. Then she pattered up the stone stairs to their bedroom.

He was still asleep, sprawled amidst the bed sheets, his chest bare, one long leg arched. She could see the discolorations where his wounds had been. Too many wounds, she suddenly thought, and yet he looked so lean, so strong, his body so taut even in repose, that she sometimes forgot what he must have been through in these last years. She traced the arch of his bronzed cheeks, saw the thick lashes flutter open to reveal those eyes, almost too blue in the morning light. He looked at her dreamily. Her womb stirred, as it did so often at the sight of him, making her captive to his touch, wanting him inside her with a physical intensity which was like no other need she had ever known or could imagine.

'Little Anna,' he murmured, drawing her lips to his, kissing her lightly. 'As fresh as daybreak.' His fingers found their way through the loosely tied silk of her robe to her back, smoothing it, caressing, moving towards her buttocks, pressing her to him. She could feel him growing hard against her. She buried her lips in his neck, moaned softly, wanting him, craving.

'Not yet, Anna.' He lifted her away from him gently, untied the knot of her robe. 'Will you dance for me, like those women yesterday? I've been dreaming about it.'

She felt recalcitrant, confused, but he was already humming, a mournful little tune which she dimly recognized. She turned her back to him, looked out of the tall window which gave out on to the lake. The mist was still curling, but streaks of sunshine now played over the waters. She gazed out for a moment, taking solace from the beauty outside, finding inspiration in it. Then she crumpled down to the floor, buried her head in her lap, arched her arms loosely over it.

She listened for the call of his tune, then slowly she rose, curling, curving like the tendrils of mist, swaying her arms, her body, turning slowly towards him, stretching, sinuous, her arms high, her robe parting to reveal breasts, belly. His voice rose, the rhythm faster, she could feel his eyes burning into her. Shyly, she gathered the folds of the long robe round her, crossing her arms with its ends, so that her legs were bare, her feet skimming the polished floor. The wind is coming now, she thought to herself, blowing me away. She flew to the corner of the room, her arms stretched in front of her, reaching, reaching, for the sky, the sun which would burn her away.

And then he was behind her, his arms round her, his hands folded round her breasts, fondling, caressing, restraining her. And still she stretched away from him, reaching, her body taut, grasping for the sky, almost forgetting him, wrapped in her dance. She felt herself being lifted high, higher and then he was in front of her, holding her, carrying her, his penis rubbing between her legs, so that when he deposited her on the edge of the bed, she was already arched against him, so tight, so close, closer, his penis deep inside her, throbbing, hot, hungry, like his lips, drinking her in, scorching her, so that she disappeared. No more Anna. No more mist, just wave upon wave of sensation and the layered blue sky of his eyes.

Afterwards, they sat and drank cold coffee, their fingers entwined, both wondering at their passion, so unexpected after the aridity of the last days. Dimly Anna remembered that there was something she had wanted to talk to him about. What was it? Yes, Leo, the nursery. But it wasn't the time. This moment couldn't be ruptured. Later. She would do so later.

In fact it was three days later. She hadn't seen Johannes for a day and a night. He had been locked in his studio. She didn't know if he waited until she was out to come down and eat. But when she called him announcing lunch or dinner, all she heard was a cold muffled voice, uttering a polite, 'No thank you'.

The weather had changed that morning. The wind lashed fiercely against the window panes, thunder rumbled from somewhere in the mountains, and then the sky released an unstoppable torrent of water. Anna sat at the table in her studio and leafed unseeingly through a book she had picked out at the small library in the village. But mostly she watched the rain, the fat pellets falling heavily on the lake until it heaved and shuddered uncontrollably, the commotion of the trees which started at their uttermost tips and then moved down gradually until it startled the vegetation beneath.

She saw a solitary man in a dark bulky suit running along the harbour. A sodden newspaper covered his head. For a moment she thought he was coming towards her. With his heavy, solid steps, his stiff yet agile gait, he reminded her of someone. 'Bruno,' she said out loud, and shivered.

With sudden decision, Anna rose from her chair and went to knock on Johannes's door.

'Come and watch the storm with me,' she called to him.

He opened the door to her, then closed it rapidly behind him, as if he were hiding something within. He looked weary, unshaven, his eyes dazed beneath the tousled hair.

'I can see the storm from my window,' he murmured.

'Please, Johannes.'

He shrugged.

They walked through the loggia, the gusts of rain splattering them and then raced downstairs to the large glazed terrace which fronted the room they had made their salon. They watched the storm silently for a few moments and then Anna asked, 'Shall I bring some lunch up here?'

'I'll help.' He nodded.

They filled a platter with goat's cheese, tomatoes, slices of salami and bread. Johannes uncorked a bottle of wine and brought it all up on a tray. They sat opposite each other at the table in the bay and gazed out, Anna glancing at him surreptitiously.

'Don't look at me like that, Anna.' He ran a hand through his tangled hair. 'I'm not guilty of anything. You know I have to work.'

'You never had to work like this, secretly, interminably, before.' The words came out far more accusingly than she had intended them.

'You haven't known me very long, Anna,' he said coldly.

She willed away the gathering tears.

'I'm having difficulties. I can't share them.' He softened his tone. 'Perhaps it would be better if I found a studio elsewhere.'

'No, don't do that.' A yawning gap opened within her.

He shrugged. 'Then try to be a little more patient.'

She took it silently. Words were always such clumsy tools for her.

After a moment, she said, 'Johannes, I want to go and fetch Leo now. Bring him here. Bettina tells me he's a little sad. It would be far nicer for him with us. Will you come with me?'

He stared at her uncomprehendingly. 'I don't know why you want to inflict fatherhood on me when he's not even my child,' he muttered. 'He isn't, is he?' He eyed her with sudden suspicion.

Anna's mouth fell open. She looked at him aghast, then over his shoulder, beyond him, on to the street, as if she had seen a ghost. 'Don't say things like that, Johannes.'

He made a gesture of hopelessness and scraped his chair back from the table. 'Do what you must, Anna.'

She heard the studio door shutting behind him, the click of the lock.

Three interminable days later, Johannes was waving her off from the little harbour.

As he watched her standing on the open deck, her hair billowing in the breeze, her city suit trim around her supple form, he thought he must be mad to let her go like that. Already he could see the captain eyeing her, see the concupiscent bow with which he brought her a chair. For a breathless moment, he was tempted to run after her, go with her. Then the boat moved away and all he could do was blow her a kiss which strayed with the wind.

As he trudged back to the empty house, he was haunted by the sense that she wouldn't come back. Why should she? He had behaved abominably. But he had felt trapped, no longer a free agent. The tight fingers of domesticity had begun to close round him, choke him. There was always a time for everything, a time to eat, to sleep, to wake; always someone checking his comings and goings, asking questions even if they were not necessarily voiced. It was like being at home again, locked in the prison of the family, with Anna a more beneficent, a more attractive version of his father, but nonetheless clocking his moods, his actions, trying to penetrate their meaning. Soon habit would replace any intensity except the intensity of resentment.

Savagely, he kicked a stone from the path. It hadn't been like that in their months together in Munich. Perhaps because the space had been his, a slapdash studio, not a home.

Johannes opened the door to the house. It was a beautiful space, well-proportioned, gracious, with little architectural surprises. And it was filled with her traces, the potted lizzies still in full bloom, the lovely old Persian rug she had found and hung half way up the fresh white-washed walls of the broad staircase, the fragments of brightly coloured tiles she had arranged on the corner table. And her laugh, not so frequent now, that wild unbridled laugh, he could still hear it echoing. Johannes rubbed his eyes and retraced his steps. He needed to be outdoors for a while.

He walked up the stony path which led from the back of the house, past the tiny old peasant chapel, to the hills. Soon he could see the lake again, shimmering beneath him and in the distance, the receding boat which carried her away from him.

No, Munich had been different. Not only because the studio was his, but because they had all been engaged in the heady euphoria of overthrowing the old order and bringing in the new. Or, as he liked to think of it, dethroning the all-powerful father and instituting a world of brothers, a democracy of equals. In his wilder moments, he had suggested that it should really be a matriarchy, a different principle by which to chart the ways of the horde. But the brotherhood of equals would have done. Except that the brothers started to squabble amongst each other, and the fathers had come back into play, disciplining them, killing, incarcerating, reinstituting the old order in all but name. Only the figurehead of the king was gone.

Johannes smiled bitterly into the trees. The proof of it all was that his father still maintained his power, could still manoeuvre the thick cords of red tape only to bind him in them and manipulate his life. And the old man had done so to manipulate him out of prison – where had he managed to remain alive, he would at least have had the dignity of the political prisoner – into a punishment park of a more lethal kind.

Schleierman's clinic was a psychiatric hospital of the old sort, where once a diagnosis had been made, the fate of most was to spend the rest of their lives under mental arrest. But Schleierman was shrewd. For Johannes, he had diagnosed a case of mild paranoia, and decided to give him the run of the hospital, as long as he reported to him three times a week and to his nurses daily. 'So that you understand no one is against you and the only constrictions are the necessary ones made to fulfil the court order,' he had smiled crookedly at Johannes from beneath spectacles which perched precariously on his arched nose.

Johannes held nothing against Schleierman. It was what he had seen in the clinic that had so profoundly disturbed him. He was both fascinated by the abyss that the human psyche could reach and afraid that somehow he would be infected by this new world of suffering and sink irretrievably into it. So that at times he felt ready to bound madly over those iron gates even if it meant that he was impaled on one of their spikes.

Yet he had stayed out his term; had spent weeks observing the victims of schizophrenia with their vacant eyes, their varying paralyses, their delirious speech which made a kind of arcane sense to him as it poured out of their almost unmoving lips.

And then he had been freed, with the proviso that he check into the clinic twice a month at specified times over the next years. It was in a sense the final twist in the odyssey of humiliations his father had laid down for him, another cord with which to tie him and strangle him. It was why he had had to flee. But that was only the first of the reasons.

The second was crystallized for him in a chance meeting he had had in the streets of Munich, just after his release from the clinic. It was near the Marienplatz. He had been strolling, trying to come to grips with the sense that he was free but not free, trying to get the measure of the city's atmosphere. Seeing a small cluster of men in army uniform, he had stilled his instinct to turn the other way and instead had gone towards them. He was not a criminal, after all.

As he approached, he recognized one of the soldiers – the odd little corporal who had so impressed him with his strangeness when he was in hospital back in 1916. He had greeted him and the man had instantly drawn him into conversation. Though conversation wasn't quite the right word for the harangue he had then been treated to: a delirium of phrases about the cowardly traitors in Weimar who had betrayed the nation, humiliated the great German people by signing the intolerable Versailles Treaty, disarmed the Fatherland. The Weimar traitors, Jews and Reds to a man, with their contemptible and unGerman ideas of democracy, would have to go. No German could rest in honour until the greatness of the nation had been restored.

And so it had gone on, to Johannes's growing disbelief. For a split second, the idea had seized him that this crabbed, pale-faced corporal who proudly sported an Iron Cross was the comic incarnation of his father's Prussian narrow-mindedness, his relentless sense of patriotic duty. Then he had been overcome by a sense that he hadn't really emerged from the gates of the clinic, that war continued to rage, that its bloated jingoism pursued them everywhere, that its madness polluted the very air they breathed.

He had fled for his life, run away, come here.

Johannes neared the crest of the hill and looked back again at the expanse of the lake, its curves and bays and inlets all visible now in the clarity of the mid-morning light. He stretched out on the earth and gazed through the dappled trees. How to explain to dear, sweet, innocent Anna the tangle of reasons why they had had to flee Germany and why fleeing in itself was not enough, since some dreams could no longer be dreamt.

His first instinct had been right. He should have gone alone. He no longer had the kind of hope which made a union possible, and he wasn't worthy of her. Five years ago, before the war, before this last year of pyrrhic victories and incarcerations, before he had lost so many of his lives, she, this place, would have been everything he dreamt of: the magic of an unspoiled natural site; the eccentric mixture of idealists, mystics, anarchists, artists – practical philosophers all of them, trying to live out the model lives of their dreams; the villagers and peasants with their simple, uncorrupted ways. And Anna, that magnificent animal who gave and gave, gave him so much more than he could ever return to her, that he already felt his life trickling out through the hole she had made by her absence.

But half of him, he knew, desired that absence. He had realized it as soon as he started to work again. He had looked out of his window at the beauty all around him and started to draw a prison wall splattered with human remains, each brick bearing the hidden imprint of a dead man. He had torn up the drawing only to find that all his subsequent sketches were cold clinical depictions of the insane, faces from the madhouse. These, too, he had torn up, afraid that Anna would see them, despite the locked door. But whatever he tried, the results were always the same. Even his drawings of Anna had the same cold ugliness, as if it had taken on a permanent residence in his soul.

So that when he emerged from his studio, forced to see her, he sometimes felt he was performing in a masquerade, donning an identity that bore no connection to him. Or it was the other way round, he would come into the studio having left her arms and try to paint what was before him, only to find another Johannes wielding the brush. He was no longer capable of the natural. He would only soil it with the dirt of these last years. And then, when he was in the midst of the intense absorption which always characterized work, she would call him to order with her musical voice, and he would feel himself splitting apart. And trapped, always trapped.

It was better that she had gone.

Johannes rose to begin his descent. His eyes were wet. He hadn't realized he had been crying. Perhaps he would stop in and see Graser. The man might be able to convey to him a little of the peace he seemed to carry within him, though Johannes doubted that he was capable of receiving that any more. Paradise left him restless; just as all those ideals of model worlds he had once had filled him with black scepticism.

And yet everyone around him here in Ascona was imbued with these self-same ideals. Ascona – European capital of outcast dreamers; outpost of radical progress, where visions of free love, of natural and egalitarian communities, put on the flesh of everyday life.

So that now he felt doubly cast out – from the world and from his dreams. He scoffed at his own self-pity. There were two tragedies in life, he remembered some English wit having said. One is not to get your heart's desire. The other is to get it.

And he, Johannes Bahr, at the age of thirty-three, was in the position of having experienced both.

'You've arrived just in time.' Bettina hugged her sister. She had that excited look on her face which Anna always associated with the birth of a new project. And a new project for Bettina inevitably meant a series of tasks for those around her.

'In time for what?'

'In time to help look after the children for a few weeks,' Bettina laughed. 'We're moving. Munich is bad for Klaus. And the news has just come that he's got a post in Berlin, starting in January.' She was triumphant.

'But what about the nurseries?' Anna felt disoriented.

'They'll have to manage without me. And there'll be plenty to do in Berlin. Besides, I'm pregnant.' She patted her stomach.

'Oh Bettina.' Anna kissed her on both cheeks.

'And this time,' Bettina looked at her wryly and lowered her voice, 'it's Klaus's. Not that he seems particularly pleased. He's still in something of a stupor. Imagine that. Women have got the vote. I'm pregnant. And Klaus is still in a stupor.' She laughed with an undertow of bitterness and then was excited again. 'He'll snap out of it once we're in Berlin. We were hoping to leave on Monday to go house-hunting and now that you've arrived, I won't have to try and find a second nanny.'

'Is Leo asleep?' Anna asked.

'I'm afraid so. But go and have a peek at him while I make us some tea. Then you can tell me all about Ascona.'

Anna climbed the stairs and softly opened the door to Leo's room. He was sleeping peacefully, his little arms stretched above his head, his face angelic. She bent to stroke his cheek, saw him stir, half-hoped he would wake, but he simply turned over with a little snort. She left him quietly.

'But you'll keep Seehafen, won't you?' Anna asked Bettina when she returned bearing a stacked tray.

'In fact we were thinking of selling it. It's too far from Berlin to be all that useful.'

'Don't sell it, Bettina, please,' Anna cried out. 'Or sell it to me. I couldn't bear it going to a stranger.'

'I was about to say that there was no point selling anything now. Money isn't worth the paper it's printed on, except the American kind. Which is how, thanks to you, we're going to manage to move and not sell.'

Anna sank back into her chair, took the proffered tea. 'It's only that I'm very attached to Seehafen. It's like home.'

'More so than Ascona?'

Anna averted her eyes. 'So far, yes, it's early days.'

Bettina nodded sagely. 'How's Johannes?'

Anna forced a smile. 'Fine.'

'Just "fine"?' Bettina imitated her tone and examined her astutely. 'Is he working?'

Anna nodded.

'Well, that's the most important thing. It's when he's not working that you have to worry about the bouts of temperament.'

Anna, as always, felt ruffled at her sister's show of greater knowledge about Johannes. Yet the comment interested her. 'Do you think so?'

Bettina nodded, poured more tea.

'He wouldn't come with me, you know.'

Bettina looked up abruptly, eyebrows raised in surprise. 'He can't come here, Anna. Don't you know that?'

Anna gazed at her in astonishment. 'Can't?'

'He's broken the court order by leaving the country. He could be arrested. Really, sometimes I wonder what you two talk about.'

'Don't be horrid, Bettina.' There were tears in Anna's eyes.

Bettina squeezed her hand. 'Sorry.' After a moment, she added softly, 'I don't know where you've learned all these tears, Anna. You never used to cry as a child. Just run and tumble and laugh crazily. I used to be quite envious of your daring. It must be these men. They've made you too sensitive, all raw emotion. You'll have to grow a second skin.' She shook her head humorously and then looked her sister in the eyes. 'I did try to warn you that Johannes wouldn't be an easy proposition. But then, I guess he is Leo's father.'

'Bruno was Leo's father,' Anna said fiercely.

'You know that now, do you? How?'

'I just know, Bettina, leave it alone.'

They were both quiet for a moment.

'So you're asking Johannes to raise another man's child. There's a certain irony in that.'

'I guess so,' Anna said uncomfortably. She moved from her chair, started to pace tensely.

'Yes, an irony,' Bettina mused. 'You know, I've always had this notion that there are certain men who are eternal boys. Sons. They don't know how to grow up. Klaus and I talked about it once. He thinks a lot of artists are like that. It fuels them. All that rebellious energy.'

'Like Johannes, you mean.'

Bettina shrugged. 'Perhaps.'

'And you don't approve?'

'It's hardly for me to approve or disapprove.'

'I've never known you to be slow to judge, Bettina.'

She didn't take it amiss. 'I guess I'm improving with age,' she laughed.

Watching Klaus and Bettina depart the next day, Anna thought that she probably was. Difficulty made Bettina thrive. It did not seem to be that way for her.

Little Leo had turned away from her this morning, his body rigid, refusing to be touched, his face a sullen, unspeaking mask. She told herself it would get better, but it hurt nonetheless. Bettina was right: she must grow a second skin.

The bustling, competent nanny was preparing the boys for their walk now.

'Will you come with us?' she asked her.

'Do come, Auntie Anna,' Max piped up. 'You can watch us sail our new boats. See. They're just like real ones.' He came bounding up to her and proudly displayed the carved sailboat. 'Papa made them for us and they float ever so well in the wind.'

'I'd like that.' Anna smiled at him. He was a friendly, talkative child, full of words and experiments. Perhaps Leo would be like that in a few years.

But not yet, Anna reflected sadly as she watched him race over and try to grab the boat from Max's hand, punch it, pull. His battling rage transfixed her.

'Don't be silly, Leo, you have your own boat.' The nanny's voice was stern. She brought his boat to him, but he thrust it away and pulled again at Max's. 'Better boat, better boat,' he wailed.

'Here, take it.' Max passed it to him. 'I don't mind.' He looked seriously at Anna. 'Papa said they were both the same.'

'Thank you, Max,' Anna murmured.

She accompanied the children, allied her routine to theirs. But the days and particularly the evenings passed with increasing slowness. She missed Johannes with a visceral intensity. It was as if she was only half here, as if she could respond to nothing fully.

She imagined him in the house alone, pacing with that taut dark energy which had been his in those last weeks, that self-absorption which excluded her as effectively as a locked door. As he became more real to her than the present she now inhabited, she began to think that she had misunderstood everything. The door wasn't locked to keep her out, but to keep him in. The absorption was that same concentration he had always given his work, only now the subject wasn't her, so that she was a distraction. How selfish of her to suppose that she could always be at the centre, would always have an equal priority. She would never have dared to ask Bruno to forget his work for her.

The inadvertent comparison made her gasp. She pushed it away, focused again on Johannes. What had he said to her on one of those nights when she had melted in his arms? 'Laugh for me, Anna, the way you used to. I can never hear you laugh enough. I always wanted to find a way to paint that laugh.'

It was true. In these last years, her laughter so often seemed to have an undertow of desperation.

Leo. This human legacy Bruno had left her was part of it. The responsibility haunted her. She tried to imagine Leo in the house in Ascona, the garden, the bright nursery. And then she heard him crying, saw Johannes's dark look, their mutual stubbornness, felt herself being torn apart, her half presence unwanted by both. It was a terrifying image.

The days passed. Leo grew a little less sullen. From her corner by the fireplace, Anna watched the stubborn intentness with which he placed his bricks one on top of the other, higher and higher until, seeing that they were about to totter, he kicked them down first of his own accord and gave a little triumphant grimace before beginning the task again.

He also liked collecting stones, brought fresh ones home from the park daily and lined them all up in varying orders. If she offered him a stone, he would examine it critically, sometimes throw it away, sometimes keep it. The ones he kept were always arranged in a separate line.

She wasn't allowed to share in his play. It was always Max who approached her with queries or asked her to take part in a game. But she knew that Leo was keenly aware of her: it only took an approach from Max to bring him scurrying in her direction, his handsome little face taut with emotion.

One afternoon when he fell over in the park and began to cry, she ran to take him in her arms. He looked at her mistrustfully, his body stiff. 'Want Aunt Bettina,' he cried. 'Aunt Bettina.'

Anna tried not to let it hurt. But that night she left the children alone with the nanny for the first time. She went to Schwabing, sat in the Stephanie, looked round for acquaintances. There was a pall in the atmosphere, as if Schwabing itself had grown tired and needed to regather its forces after the excess of the last year. She sipped her *Sekt*, talked to a familiar face or two, was about to leave, when a big burly man approached her and threw his arms round her.

'The radiant Anna, muse of muses. Is that foul painter finally going to allow us to share you?'

'You're drunk, Gert.' Anna struggled from his arms.

'Nothing has changed *there*.' He laughed a big bellow of a laugh. Ordered another glass for her.

'Where is the foul rake? I haven't seen hide or hair of him in all the days I've been here. And no forwarding address. He's not still in jail, is he? Someone would have communicated that bit of news.'

Anna shook her head. 'We've moved.'

He looked at her astutely from small bright eyes. 'Still we, then, is it? And just a teeny weeny bit secretive?'

'Just a teeny weeny bit.' Anna suddenly smiled.

'Don't smile at me like that or friendship will be for nought, you Viennese heartbreaker.' He beat his breast with an air of mock frenzy.

Anna laughed. 'And how's Berlin?'

'A little less dull than this place at the moment, which is not to say a great deal. Come and visit.'

'I may just do that.'

'Did I hear that miraculous word, "I"?'

Anna flushed. 'You did.'

'A good word, a fine word. But tell that old rogue of yours something from me nonetheless. Tell him Seidermann's looking for some work for a Swiss gallery.' He winked at her. 'A few pennies never come amiss, eh, especially when they're in hard currency.'

'Thanks, Gert.'

'Just remember that you're eternally in my debt, oh muse of muses.'

On her way home, Anna reflected that she felt distinctly cheered by her little escapade. She must get out and about more, for Johannes's sake as well as her own.

When she arrived at Bogenhausen there was a telegram awaiting her. 'Come to Berlin as soon as possible. Bring everyone. Telegraph arrival time to Hotel Kempinski. Klaus.'

Anna stared at the words, uncertain as to what they signified. There had been no prior talk of her bringing the children to Berlin. But Klaus and Bettina must have their reasons.

Anna busied herself, alerted the nanny, checked train schedules, packed bags. The activity, she realized, did her good. There was a lesson in that, too. With a sudden sense of exhilaration she penned a quick note to Johannes. She hadn't written to him yet, hadn't known how to put into words her sense of desolation without him, her dawning recognitions. Now she told him of the changed plans, and about Seidermann being in Switzerland. Then she added, 'Miss you terribly, but not certain when I'll be back' – nothing more.

Klaus, his features strained, was waiting for them at the station in Berlin as they disembarked from the night train. He embraced the children, let them walk ahead with the nanny, while he took Anna aside.

'Bettina's lost the baby,' he said, his voice tense. 'I thought you might go to her straight away. In the hospital.' He wrung his hands. 'I thought she would like everyone with her when we brought her home.'

Anna felt he might begin to cry, right there in the station. She had an acute sense of his pain, of his need for support. She gripped his arm. 'I'm so sorry, Klaus. How is she? Of course, I'll go to her immediately. Where will you be?'

He was a little vague. 'The hotel. I don't know. Perhaps just for tonight. There's an apartment we could move into temporarily. The one house we saw that Bettina liked is really too unreasonable.' He stumbled over his words. Anna sensed that he hated making decisions without Bettina.

'An apartment would be a good idea. With the children,' she offered tentatively. She, too, was unused to decisiveness. But looking at Klaus's face, she realized it was essential. 'Yes, the apartment. As soon as possible,' she said firmly. 'Bettina will be more comfortable there. And she'll need to rest, I imagine.'

He nodded, tried a watery smile.

'Why don't you take the children to the zoo, so they don't have too much time to worry?' She said it as much for him as for them.

The hospital gave Anna the jitters. She remembered another hospital but with the same echoing corridors where heels clacked eerily and nurses smiled with official good cheer. She had been so frightened then, so certain, it now came back to her, that Bruno had been coming to take her away, whether in love or revenge was unclear.

She shook herself. She musn't allow herself to feel haunted, behave like a silly, superstitious slip of a girl. She could hear Bettina's voice saying that. She was a woman now, with responsibilities. And, perhaps for the first time in her life, the tables were turned and Bettina needed her. Anna's heels rang more firmly as she neared the ward.

Bettina's face was almost as white as the pillow it rested on. Anna took her hand, squeezed it.

'How do you feel?' she asked softly.

'Like an idiot.' Bettina's long lips curved into irony and then quivered. 'I guess Klaus's child was not meant to be,' she murmured.

'Now who's behaving like a superstitious fool?' Anna followed her own thoughts.

Bettina met them. 'Who, indeed?' A single tear rolled down her cheek.

Anna kissed her, sat quietly by her side.

'I had this sixth sense it was wrong,' she said after a moment. She looked into the distance, musing, refusing Anna's gaze. 'It was at Seehafen, you know, this summer, when we were all there together. I had this notion that Klaus was only making love to me to settle scores. With Johannes. Because Max was conceived there, when the three of us were together. A return match, so to speak. But Klaus was in such a state that I didn't like to say no.' Suddenly, she gasped. 'I'm sorry, Anna. I was thinking aloud. I shouldn't be saying this to you.'

'What are we sisters for?' Anna said ruefully.

'Yes.' Bettina held her hand more firmly. 'It's the loss of blood, you know. It makes your head light. I feel I'm floating all the time.'

They were silent for a while, then Bettina began again, 'You know, sometimes I have this strange notion that Klaus was more in love with Johannes than I was. Seduced by his passion, his rudeness, his genius, even his revolutionary fantasies. And Johannes was not in the least unhappy to have Klaus there. I was just a pawn in a little chess game between the men.'

'You've never been a pawn to anyone, Bettina.' Anna was adamant. 'It's just the momentary weakness speaking.'

'Perhaps. Perhaps not. In any event, I sometimes wonder whether all this sexual business is worth it for women.'

'Bettina!'

'Well, perhaps it's not the same for all of us. But for me . . .' She shrugged. 'The doctor said I shouldn't have any more children, Anna,' she blurted out, her face suddenly as fragile as a pale flower. The tears came again now, copious.

'I'm so sorry.'

'You musn't tire Frau Eberhardt out.' A nurse suddenly appeared from nowhere, her voice metallic. 'She should sleep.'

'Stay, Anna.' Bettina gripped her hand.

'But no more chatter.' The woman was firm as she handed Bettina a pill and a glass of water.

Bettina slept. Anna stayed by her side. She had never seen her sister look frail before, never seen her cry. It shook her, as did all those things she had said. Reflecting on them, Anna suddenly had the glimmerings of a plan.

Over the next days, she spent every afternoon with Bettina. In the course of those afternoons, she learned far more about her sister than she ever had before. And about Johannes. Some shift in the balance of power between them made her unafraid to ask Bettina questions about him, and all those little factual matters of daily experience which she herself was oddly blind to came clear for her.

The day before Bettina was due to leave the hospital, Anna said to her, 'Has Klaus told you? The apartment is ready to receive you.'

Bettina nodded. 'I can't wait.'

'I thought I'd stay on with you until Christmas or the New Year. Help out.'

'I'd appreciate that. The doctor says I'm to take things easy for a few weeks.' Bettina fidgeted.

'And we'll try to make sure that you do – though I hope that doesn't take up all our time,' Anna laughed.

Then, a little cautiously, she said, 'Bettina, after you're altogether well and settled in, I thought I might go back to Ascona and . . . and leave Leo with you for another while, if you don't mind, if that's not asking too much,' she finished all in a rush.

Bettina gave her a long scrutinizing look. 'I was wondering if you'd come round to that.'

'Is it too much to ask? Do you think it's wrong? It's just that I can't live without Johannes, and for the time being, I can't imagine Johannes living with him.' She was racing.

'It's not wrong, no,' Bettina said slowly. 'So many people do it. It's just that I can't conceive of leaving Max for more than a few days. But then,' she laughed, 'when I think of losing little Leo, I don't feel very happy either. I've grown accustomed to having him with us. And so has Max. And Klaus.' She suddenly laughed with a more bitter tone. 'And losing two in one throw would be altogether too many. So yes, he can stay with us for as long as you like.' She suddenly beamed.

'Thank you, Bettina.' Anna hugged her. 'And there's something else. You know that one house that you liked so much in Grunewald, the vast one. Klaus was telling me that he wasn't sure about it. That it was too expensive.'

Bettina's face fell. 'He didn't tell me that.'

'No, but listen, Bettina, it's beautiful. We've all been to see it together. And,' she paused, wondering how to phrase it, remembering how in

Vienna, when they had been to see Bruno's executors, Bettina had refused to take all but a tiny fraction of her legacy, and that only after Anna had insisted to the point of hoarseness, 'and I thought we might buy it together and one of the wings could be mine to use when I'm here. Please, Bettina.'

'Now that, Anna, sounds to me like a fine idea.' Bettina's cheeks took on some of their former colour. 'And if we put our energy together, perhaps we can even move in by Christmas. Yes, a new city, a new house, a new decade. The twenties. I've had enough of all this depression, Anna. All of us, mired in it. It's time to get back to work. No heroics, this time. War. Revolution. Men's antics. What we want is slow, steady improvement. I have this idea . . .'

'I can tell you're better, Bettina,' Anna smiled, cutting her off.

'And I'll be even better come Christmas,' Bettina said staunchly.

Looking at her, Anna felt more certain of that than of anything else in her universe.

ELEVEN

THE BELLS OF SAN PIETRO-PAOLO chimed out the notes of the Midnight Mass, each note as crisp and clear as the twinkling stars in the wintry sky above Ascona. Each, for Johannes, the bearer of an anticipated message. Anna was not coming back. Not coming back.

He buried his head in his arms to block out the sound. But it was not eluded so easily. Johannes leapt to his feet and ran, away from the bells, away from the house, away from the village, until the beating of his heart replaced all other sounds. When he stopped to gauge his whereabouts, he realized that his feet had taken him on to the only sure path of escape. Laughing at himself, he slowly began to make his way along a series of narrow uneven trails. Ascona's proliferation of communes marked his way: clusters of wooden cabins, more imposing establishments, housing groups of any and every variety of idealist. He pulled his jacket more closely round him as he neared the windy crest of the hill.

It was the second time he had been filled with this certainty that Anna would not return. The first had been all those weeks back when her brief note had arrived. Reading it, he had felt that he had lately misjudged her. In the note's terse wording, its lack of any overt emotions, he had seen again that Anna he had first loved in the war years, that fresh impulsive creature, who had followed her instincts straight into his arms only to take him over so rapturously that he felt he had stumbled upon the sensual goddess of his youthful dreams. This Anna, he had a sudden conviction, would find another man as certainly as she had found him. Had probably already found him.

This Anna was not like the second Anna with whom he had begun to feel enslaved. The second Anna he now dated from Bruno's death and the birth of her child. She was no less a sensual creature, but something in her had been wounded. She was in need. The passion she had elicited from him, had given him, had been if anything greater, but the emotional demand she made of him drained him.

Or so he had begun to see things in the great expanses of time he had spent alone since her departure. Too much time, in which he had considered and reconsidered their various lives and the ties which bound them. His own, in which all he could see to value were a few paintings, a wordless kindness to a dead friend, a few moments of passion which obliterated all the rest. Anna's – with its strange innocence, as if that long aristocratic line of decaying Viennese had suddenly, by some accident of nature, branched into a resplendent new tree, lush in its foliage but overly sensitive to wintry weather. Her husband, Bruno, who had appeared to him almost as a comic incarnation of Austria-Hungary, a man who had pompously married capital with culture. But he had done so with energy and he had had the taste to love Anna. Johannes still remembered their last meeting, the lost, slightly dazed quality of Bruno's eyes, as if he knew that the world he had aspired to, had striven to build on and extend, was crumbling at its very foundations.

Yes, it never ceased to surprise him, but he had liked Bruno then. As he valued Klaus with his embattled sincerity, his scientist's love of detail, not so unlike his own, but with a blindness, an inability, an unwillingness to grasp contradictions, to put philosophy in the place of catalogues. And Bettina, that other stray von Leinsdorf, with her principled high seriousness and quick wit, so that she put words to things even before he had grasped what he was thinking. Yes, he liked them all, damaged as they all were by a history they themselves had partly made. It was only himself that he hated, and the sordid canvases his imagination refused to abandon.

No, there was no reason for Anna, with her singular gift for life, to return to him.

Desolation filled him as he trod the remembered path. He had sought solace here before, when her note had first crushed him. But he hadn't been to visit Mario's little band of outcasts for a month now. After the initial series of visits, he had gone back to work, telling himself that his sense that Anna wouldn't return was a fabrication, that he didn't need to replace her either with communes or the artful hothouse flowers which bloomed there. It was true that before going she had been vague, but she had talked of the two of them and the child spending Christmas together. He would bide his time.

But now Christmas had come and hadn't brought her with it. What it had brought instead were incessant dreams of her and an inability to work. Johannes quickened his step, felt an unseen branch whip him across the face, heard the hoot of an owl. He hooted back. The sound freed him a little. He smiled darkly to himself.

They were probably all hooting at the dacha, drunk on wine and other kinds of drugs, drunk on their anarchist dreams, drunk on the communal freedoms Ascona permitted.

He could see the glow of the fire through the slightly crooked windows now, hear the bark of the mangy old dog they kept to alert them to intruders. The door opened before he could knock, and a small bearded man, almost a boy, in frayed shirt and trousers, confronted him.

'It's Johannes,' the man called out in his heavily accented French for everyone to hear, before patting him warmly on the shoulder. '*Entrez, entrez*, come in, comrade, good to see you again.' He restrained the dog forcibly.

Johannes could almost hear the groan of relief in the barn-like room behind him. 'Expecting a raid?' Johannes queried the younger man softly.

'Not really,' he grinned. 'But you never know. Last year, the Zurich police chose the day after Christmas to pay us a visit and take André away. So we're a little wary of seasonal cheer,' he laughed. 'But we've been good children this last month. Only one little trip to Spain and back.'

'Don't tell me any more.' Johannes stopped him. He preferred not to have too clear a sense of what the members of Mario's group were up to, what bombing forays or heists they might or might not have been engaged in, for the good of the cause. That wasn't what he came for. The last thing he needed was to find himself transported to Germany by the police and back into his father's clutches.

'Here, I brought you a small offering.' He handed Mario a hip flask of brandy and looked round the large musty room. They were a motley lot with their bright tattered clothes and thin faces, their mixture of accents and tongues, these young dreamers who refused nation states and family ties. Like so much flotsam and jetsam washed up on the mellow Asconan shore by the plague-ridden sea of capitalist civilization. And here they hoped their hopes of a purer morality, dreamt their dreams of a new form of community, of unhampered social relations, of an unconstrained sensual life in the arms of Mother Nature. Just like himself, Johannes thought, laughing soundlessly.

Now that he had been recognized as a friend, they had relaxed again, were reclining on blankets scattered on the floor around the blazing fire. They were smoking, drinking, talking desultorily. One couple were kissing. In a far corner of the room a pipe was being passed round a small group. Johannes greeted a few of those he knew by name, then sat down by Mario's side near the fire. He took a slug from the proffered bottle of wine. Then after a moment, he asked, 'Is Janine not here?'

'Oh, she's here all right. But she's in one of her states. So she's gone off to the little cabin. She's been impossible this last week. Won't have anything to do with anyone except Sophie.' He picked up a guitar and started to strum randomly.

'I'd stay right here if I were you. Want a smoke?'

Johannes nodded.

Mario gestured to the group in the corner. A lanky youth with vast dark eyes brought the ornate pipe to them. Johannes inhaled deeply, leaned back against the wall, listened to the words of Mario's song, inhaled again and again.

There was that welcome lassitude creeping up his body now, loosening his limbs. He stretched luxuriantly, felt himself beginning to float. Oh, that longed-for sense of disconnection. That was what he had come for. Nothing mattered now, not Anna, not that blasted painting he couldn't get right, not the lack of money. Only the blazing fire, each flame arching separately, its forked tip a pure wispy blue, the wood crackling so that he could hear its dismemberment, his legs stretching, stretching, until his toes reached the other end of the room. And the strumming in his ear, the strings resonating with an almost painful clarity through his veins as Mario's voice lamented, mourned, rose to an aching plea, soared, taking him with it, so that he was flying to its sound, carried by it over the hills of Castille, gently deposited on the plain, where the women with their sombre, melting eyes brushed his cheek with the tips of their fans and drew him on, on.

Johannes rose unevenly to his feet, nodded to Mario.

'Careful you don't get burned, friend.' He heard his voice from a distance.

'Burned?' Johannes pondered. He would like to burn. But the night air which lashed him as he opened the door was cold. So cold, he could feel his blood rushing away from it, hiding deep within him, frightened by that icy sliver of a wintry moon. The tall straggly pines would protect him. They brushed the star-speckled sky with their feathery branches, fractured the moon's cold light, spangled it in a hundred directions. He wouldn't step in that light.

Johannes trod carefully. But the cabin was already there, a candle glowing from its single window. He peered in. A slight woman sat at the edge of a narrow bed. Reclining on it, her long angular body tensed like a bow about to snap, lay Janine, raven hair pouring over wolf-like features, over bare creamy shoulders above the tightly draped blanket. Johannes tapped at the window, saw her snap, leap, shudder, saw the other woman's contorted face.

'*Qui est-ce?*' she demanded in that low, broken voice.

'Johannes,' his own answered from a great distance.

'Johannes,' he heard her echo and the door creaked slowly open.

She pulled him in, threw her arms round his shoulders, so that the blanket fell from her. He could feel the taut nipples of her breasts piercing his jacket, that hungry mouth searching for his, the musty smell of her invading his nostrils.

'Janine!' the second voice was stern, scandalized. He felt a form brushing past him in the small space.

'*Non, reste.*' Janine whipped away from him. Her hand fastened round the other woman's wrist. Then she pressed her naked body firmly against the closed door. 'Stay.' It was a command. 'Johannes is my friend. Like you.'

She turned to him, 'Aren't you, Johannes?' Slim fingers stroked his cheek. A red tongue licked curling lips. 'Let me take your coat. It's warm here.' As if unaware of her nakedness, she reached nimbly for his jacket, folded it neatly over the back of a chair, patted it, patted the small potbellied stove. 'Very warm.'

Johannes watched the long taut legs flick towards him, the dark crisp triangle at their arch. Quick fingers were unbuttoning his shirt, pulling it from his shoulders. Yes, it was warm. And the fingers were cool, dry, like the rustle of leaves, like that crisp triangle. He wanted to touch it. Touched it, his eyes seeing only the slow movement of his own hand on that parched grass.

'Stop it, Janine. Stop him,' a voice hissed.

For an instant, Johannes met troubled brown eyes in a pointed girlish face. Then they turned away and a laugh rumbled from deep within Janine's throat. 'No. No, come. Men are gods, Sophie. They can rise of their own will.'

Johannes felt two hands on his bare shoulder, one hesitant, moist; the other firm, dry, guiding it, moving it across his chest, down, down. How vast his body had grown, each nerve alert, but the voices were distant. He must touch her again, that dry grass on the little hillock, the smooth plain of her belly.

'It's just like my dream, Sophie. You see, like my dream. I dream the past and the future.' She kissed the other woman on the lips, but the hands were still on him.

'Shall I tell you my dream, Johannes? Lie down,' she propelled him towards the narrow bed, 'lie down and I'll tell you my dream.' The laugh rumbled inside her again. He could feel it rise and subside as she guided his fingers to her small pointed breasts. She leaned over him, dark like a vast bird, passed her beaked lips over his bare chest, her hair bathing him like feathers, lashing against him as she swung her head away to arch across him on the bed. He could see her toes rubbing against the other woman's legs.

'It was a long time ago. In another, a buried life. In England I think. I lived in a tiny cottage, at the edge of the village, just where the line of the forest began to grow dense.' Her voice dropped, secretive now. 'I was a witch,' she cackled, 'a witch.' She ran a pointed nail sharply across Johannes's breast, so that he arched abruptly, caught her hand. She looked at her finger. A tiny drop of blood. She smiled, put it in his mouth.

'The people would steal out to see me, so that I could brew potions for them. Potions for making babies, potions for getting rid of them.' She ran her hand over his groin, rubbed, rubbed. 'And the men would come, so many of them,' she laughed again, high like a bird's shriek, 'so that I could perform rites on them, strange erotic rites.'

Her eyes with their glittering purple lights flickered on his. And then she was kneeling astride him, his legs encased beneath hers. Slowly, she began to unbuckle his belt, flick open buttons, her pointed nails careful yet cruel, caressing, pricking. He could feel his penis, his, yet not his, growing vast, too big for him, other, heavy, wanting, wanting. The clutch of her hand. He heard the other woman gasp, or perhaps it was his own breath. He wound his fingers in Janine's long hair, pulled her closer, so that her lips brushed his, but she arched back, drawing him with her. He was facing her, his heavy penis between them, too heavy in her hand, like a mace, beginning to throb.

She pressed her taut breasts towards him, whispered secretively in his ear, 'I would have them ride me like a stallion.' Suddenly her long legs were coiled round him and she was edging herself over his penis, encircling it, slowly, the muscles so tight round him, clenching, clenching. He moved against her and she fell back on the bed, pulling him down with her. 'Yes, ride me like a stallion,' she crooned, 'sail me like a wave, fly me like a billowing cloud.'

Johannes rode, sailed, flew, her body tensed beneath him, and then supple, moist, so moist, wave upon wave of it and then insubstantial so that she seemed to slip from his grasp and reappear in another shape, a doubling of her, a small oval face with a spicy scent, above him now, next to the raven-haired witch's. And then he was holding air, his penis still too heavy, exposed to the elements.

He heard her laugh ringing in his ears in the distance, and then her voice, shrill now, 'And when their members stood raw, throbbing, for all my little black cats to see, only then would I take their love juice, distil it from their loins.'

He could see her now, too tall, kissing the other woman, rubbing against her. And then coming closer to him, closer, her hair lashing his groin, her nostrils arched. Her hands were on his penis, her tongue, her mouth, warm, soft, licking, sucking, drawing the juice from him, so that he arched, arched into that mouth, those hands, moaned, flowing into her, all of him, gone, spent.

With a triumphant smile on her face, she massaged herself with his sperm. 'Love juice,' she murmured, 'doubly strong. For my potions. Their power in my hands.' Her eyes flickered, darkly malevolent as she looked down on him.

He didn't know if he had slept for a moment, but suddenly she was cowering, huddled in a corner of the room. 'They're coming,' she whimpered. 'They're coming. Help me, help me, Sophie, Johannes, they're coming to burn me.' She shivered, leapt up, pointed through the small window. 'Look, it's there, the fire. Put it out, Sophie, run. With your tears. Run, quickly.' She propelled the woman through the door, bolted it behind her. 'Help me, Johannes, help me, cleanse me, please, please, wipe her out, the witch, rid me of her, I'll be good.'

She was kneeling by the bed now, her head bent, her hands raised in prayer, like a small girl.

He stroked her hair gently. 'It's all right, Janine. No one will burn you. It's all right.'

'You have to help me, Johannes.' She lifted frightened eyes to him. 'She's there,' she brought his hand down to her groin, 'there, inside me. The witch. Chase her out. Now, now. No, wait.' She splattered some water over herself, over him, began to lap at him, her tongue moving rough, then smooth, over his body, his feet, his legs, rousing him, urging him into her, pleading as she lay beneath him, 'Now, Johannes, quickly, wipe her out.' Her voice rose with her hips to meet him. 'There, there, chase her, faster, faster, Johannes, cleanse me of her, take her, yes, yes, there, you've found her, wipe her out, rid me of her.' She was crying against him, and as her legs pressed into the small of his back and he came into her with a great shudder, she began to shout over and over, 'Clean, clean, clean. Janine is clean.'

Then, her eyes luminous, she lay quietly beside him. She gave him a shy smile. 'Thank you, Johannes. You can leave me now.' She curled away to face the wall. 'I'm safe.'

A grey dawn had begun to glimmer as Johannes made his way unsteadily down the hill. He would have liked to have spent more time in that perilous country Janine and the opium took him to. The flickering hallucinatory drowsiness paradoxically allowed him to see more, see clearly, unhampered by the shadows cast by work, by Anna.

Anna. He suddenly felt soiled, broke into a run, headed down towards the lake, gazed at the mirror of the waters.

Men are like gods, Janine had said. Johannes laughed, averted his face from a passer-by. Once he too had believed that unleashed instinct, sex, marked men out as godlike. But now he was prone to think the opposite just as likely. Men were mere regular soldiers attached to a prick who was their sergeant. When the sergeant barked, they jumped to it! Wherever the prick pointed they ran. Tails wagging the dog. And if there was any time left over they might paint a picture or write a poem.

He grimaced into the wind. Whatever had happened to his ideas of sexual salvation? They had served him far better. They had brought him Anna. But he had botched that. He hurried on, taking the high path along the lake.

Yes, the famous masculine principle, the rising sun of Apollonian light and order, what was it really but, as Bettina might say, a usurper of power and privilege, cloaking its murderous lusts with the smile of reason. Even now, though he had lost his sense of holiness, Johannes still felt it was the women who might save them, the tortured Janine with her frenzies amongst them. If saving was possible.

He was suddenly in a hurry, his hand twitching, wanting to grasp his brush. He had an idea for a series of paintings, a grand idea.

As Johannes rushed into the hushed house, he only paused for a moment to remark on its emptiness. Then, with a sense of urgency, he doused himself in cold water, donned fresh clothes and climbed the stairs to his studio. No one saw him over the next few days.

On New Year's Day, the day that welcomed in the second decade of the century, Anna arrived back in Ascona. Berlin had been deep in snow, a dark, windy city. But here, despite the winter rain, there was a softness in the air. The curve of the hills, the clustered houses of the tiny village, the bright clumps of vegetation, all spoke to her in a welcoming voice.

Anna asked the driver to drop her assortment of cases and parcels at the door of the house. Then she took a deep breath before lifting the latch and letting herself in. She felt at once anxious, excited and shy, uncertain which emotion predominated.

'Hello,' she announced to the empty hall. 'I'm back,' she called up the empty staircase. There was a stillness about the house which suddenly made her shiver.

What if Johannes weren't here? What if he had gone? She hadn't written to announce her arrival. She raced up the stairs. 'Johannes, Johannes!' Her voice took on a note of desperation. She heard the studio door open and she stopped on the landing. He was coming towards her across the rain-spattered loggia, his face rugged, his eyes bluer than she remembered them, staring at her in disbelief.

'Anna,' his voice was hoarse, 'Anna, my Anna.' He lifted her off her feet into his arms, kissed her, kissed her so deeply that she was breathless with it.

'Let me look at you,' he murmured. He held her at arm's length, his head cocked, surveying her.

She felt herself flushing at what she read in his eyes. 'Oh Johannes, I've missed you so much. So much.' She pressed close to him, running her fingers through his tousled hair, feeling herself beginning to melt into him in that way she seemed to have forgotten but her body remembered all too vividly, no longer knowing why she had ever left him.

'And Leo?' he asked softly.

'He's staying with Bettina, for now.' She averted her gaze.

His eyes danced. 'So we can . . . ?' He lifted her in his arms, not waiting for her answer, and carried her down the stairs to their bedroom. It looked untouched, as if no one had passed over its threshold since she had left. Even the pillows and the silk feather comforter were plumped up as she remembered them.

'I love you, Johannes,' she murmured, tears tugging at her eyes.

'Do you, Anna?' He set her down on the bed. 'Despite everything?' His face suddenly looked dark.

'With everything.' She pulled him down beside her, hungry for him, the lean tautness of his limbs, the slight scent of linseed oil that emanated from his white hands, the bristle of his roughened face, the smooth silkiness of his haunches, all of him, so much that needed to be learned again, like a vast garden which in her memory had grown overhung with stifling creepers and branches, blotting out those miraculous secret bursts of colour beneath, violets and primulas, limpid pools of water lily, hidden corners and crevices teeming with life.

Loving her, being loved so ardently, Johannes felt again like a young man for whom the world of women had as yet unveiled few of its secrets. He had the sense, too, that he had been granted a reprieve. He clutched at it.

In the bed that had once again become their world, they drank in the new decade, watched a wintry sun rise in the pale sky, ate hungrily of the scraps of food Johannes had in the house and more ravenously of each other.

Then they walked, exploring new trails along the lake, stopping at various peasant houses, buying eggs in one, a string of onions in another, a slab of ham at the next, a bottle of rough wine, bringing home their purchases, only to let them lie on the scrubbed kitchen table while they gazed into each other's eyes, their hands beginning to touch, to stroke, the passion overtaking them before they reached the airy bedroom, so that they made love on the stairs, on the landing, filling the house with their ardour.

And so it continued for one week, then another and another, until Anna lost track of time altogether. When Johannes retreated to his studio, she retired to hers, and dreamily took up the brushes, which had lain largely unused for far too long; or sat at the piano filling the airy house with the vibrancy of chords and quick-fingered melody.

But as mild winter merged imperceptibly into early spring, her eyes were drawn increasingly towards the windows.

One day she rose with an eager mischievous light in her tawny eyes. Brushing Johannes's cheek briefly with her lips, she raced downstairs to brew some coffee before pushing open the heavy back door and gazing out reflectively.

There had been too little time in the autumn to work out here. Except where they had dug close to the house, the land was still largely covered in a thick tangle of undergrowth broken only by the traces of flowerbeds, the cracked remains of paths, a few trees. Anna fetched boots, a pair of gloves, and walked out, lifting tufts of branches to see what lay beneath, finding some piled stones in the distance, a half-hearted attempt at a wall, an abandoned nest filled with mouldy leaves. She prodded the earth with her boots, felt its textured moistness, looked round her dreamily.

It was thus that Johannes found her.

'You'll catch a chill, Anna,' he chided her, but smiled. She cut such a strange picture out there in the misty morning in her nightie and heavy boots, her pale gold hair tumbled from sleep, like a sleepwalking child, but caught in a frothy tantalizing dream, not a nightmare.

She came running towards him. 'And what, Johannes, if flowers and plants were my paint and the sky and soil my canvas?' she asked with no preamble.

He laughed, 'No larger, no greater.'

She clutched his shoulder, looked up at the sky as if in the grip of a vision. 'Do you think it's too early to start? I need to dig, need some help. Perhaps a boy from the village.'

He was entranced by her fervour. No sooner had they breakfasted than she rushed away, came back hours later, her arms laden with horticultural books, a copy of Blake's *Auguries of Innocence* somehow amongst them. There was an abstracted set to her face. She took the books up to her studio, leaving him musing at her slightly awkward secretiveness.

The very next day, their lives took on a new regimen. Instead of clutching at him, as she had done before her departure, holding him back at her side in the mornings, she would rise early and with Rinaldo, the dark-eyed, curly-haired youth she had recruited from the village, she would go out into the garden and begin the day's innumerable tasks.

Johannes would watch them from his studio window, or from the back of the loggia, and often abandon the work he had in hand to sketch them, then to paint them – the golden Anna, and the dark, sinewy boy who followed her like a shadow. Except when it rained, and she retired alone to her studio, emerging tired but buoyant to let him take her mellowly into his arms. Sometimes, after they had made love, she would read to him in her clear musical voice from the volume of Blake which seemed to speak to her.

> 'To be in a Passion you good may do.
> But no good if a Passion is in you.'

Days rolled into weeks. The expanse at the back and sides of the house was cleared except for the trees. Then, towards the middle of March, Anna announced that she was going off for a week, perhaps a little longer, to a place on Lake Como, another in Milan, where she had heard of a botanist, a nursery. Johannes wondered at her. She had not asked once whether she could come into his studio to see his work. It was as if she had taken an unspoken decision. He could not even feel a trace of her waiting for an invitation. He was relieved at that, if slightly puzzled, even perturbed, since he didn't know whether she would approve of what she saw.

When she returned, carried by a small truck laden with plants and packages, she was ecstatic.

'Just wait, Johannes, wait until you see the beauty of it.' Her lips trembled.

'Nothing could be more beautiful than you,' he murmured.

She met his eyes. 'Do you mean that, Johannes?' she whispered.

He looked at her. A new lime green dress which fell loosely from her shoulders only hinting at the suppleness of the form beneath, leaving her golden arms exposed, setting off that creamy neck and throat, the aureole of hair, the wide tawny eyes, the Grecian nose above the curling lips, slightly open now as she gazed at him. He nodded slowly. 'When you've been away, Anna, and I see you again, I can't imagine how I've ever let you go.'

Her eyes flickered. She ran into his arms, letting him kiss her, hold her, despite the glances of the man who trudged up and down the steps unloading her purchases.

That night, after they had made love and he was so suffused with the touch and scent of her that all the rest of the world seemed to have disappeared, he suddenly sensed her looking at him oddly. 'What is it, Anna?' The stars peeping through the vast bay window cast shadows on her face.

'I know you won't marry me, Johannes,' she said in a small, unfamiliar voice. 'You don't believe in marriage. But just once, I would like you to say if you love me. I would like to know.'

He tried to read her eyes, but they were opaque. 'We are married, Anna, in all the ways that matter,' he murmured. Lingeringly, he traced the line of her hip, her thigh, placed his hand on her mound, felt the curl of her body towards his, the inevitable longing stirring in his own. 'And sometimes I think that, whatever I may do, I love you far more than my own life.' His voice was hoarse. 'I didn't think the words between us mattered.'

'Oh Johannes.' She was crying, the tears moistening his face as she kissed him, covered him with her newly quivering body, flowed into him with such lavish generosity that despite his passion he felt almost unequal to her.

'What is it, Anna?' he asked afterwards. 'You're different. Something's happened.'

She shrugged, didn't answer, ran downstairs instead to come back with a bottle of wine she had brought home with her. She was laughing now, teasing, had donned a silk robe he didn't recognize, lavish white flowers on a red ground, that made her look like some transplanted geisha. He had a sudden inkling that all this time he had been a fool, that there *was* another man, that she had seen him in Milan, somewhere, that he had asked her to marry him. There was a new scent to the robe, too, one he didn't recognize. He grew tense, wary, waited for her to speak.

She curled next to him, proffering wine, sipping quietly. And then it came. 'I bumped into an old friend in Milan. Quite by accident,' she laughed, that wild laugh that seemed to come from some other place.

He hadn't known that there had been an old friend.

'Oh,' he said quietly.

'Yes, in the arcades near the Duomo. I thought I might do some shopping, that you might be growing tired of me in my garden rags.'

He didn't take her lead, negate her.

'An old friend.' Her voice grew dreamy.

'Who is he, Anna?' he blurted out despite himself.

She looked confused for a moment, then laughed again. 'Not he, she. Katarina Hofer, an old friend from Vienna.'

For a moment, Johannes didn't believe her.

'She gave me this. Do you like it?' She swirled round in front of him, holding the candle before her. 'I admired it so much. And she had only just bought it.'

Johannes relaxed a little. 'And was it she who asked you if you had remarried?'

Anna nodded, smiled. 'I invited her to come and visit us on her way home. I hope she'll come.'

'And is she "married"?'

'Her husband died last year,' she laughed, then rushed on as if to cover her tracks, 'he was old. She says she's a merry widow now.'

'Indeed. And is she? Merry, I mean.'

'Katarina is always merry.' Anna leaned back on the bedstead and clutched the pillow to her. She was silent for a moment. Then she said, as if speaking to the stars, 'You know, Johannes, before you, Katarina was the only one who made me feel things.'

He wasn't quite sure he had caught her sense. 'Feel things?' he echoed.

'Yes, you know,' she giggled, and passed her hand along his chest, down his groin, played with him, kissed.

He stopped her fingers. 'I see,' he breathed.

'Do you?' she teased.

An Anna he didn't know. The way in which it roused him was almost painful. He came into her too quickly with a shuddering violence. And still she laughed.

The image of Anna with another woman struck him with the force of a revelation. It began to obsess him in the course of that long sleepless night. A succession of scenes played before his eyes, each more painful and yet more fascinating than the next. Not another man, but a woman. A woman.

He was at once taken by the images and racked by an emotion which was new to him, but which he decided over the next days must be jealousy. Jealousy, that emotion he had always despised, a sign of pettiness, redolent of property values, beneath contempt. Jealousy, all the more insidious because it came to him that while at least with a man he would know the gestures of his competitor, with a woman he was on uncharted ground, unable to replicate or better the pleasure. How to master this gnawing jealousy became for him an obsession as strong as the jealousy itself.

He watched Anna, secretly now, from his window as she laid out her flowerbeds, pressed and prodded and sowed, humming to herself, imagining he didn't know what. Her presence taunted him and plagued him by turn, but grew more captivating with each new day.

Soon after her return, he decided one morning to invite her to his studio.

'Would you like to see my new work, Anna?' he said nonchalantly as they were breakfasting on the terrace.

'May I?' she asked, surprised. 'I didn't like to ask.'

'You may not like what you see.' He was wry.

She laughed. She was full of laughter these days. 'I'll take my chances.'

'Seidermann was here early in December. He took quite a few of them away with him. Said there was a museum which might be interested. I don't think I mentioned it. There was a cheque while you were away.' He was suddenly nervous, babbling, as if he were taking a potential new patron to see his work.

'That's wonderful, Johannes.' She squeezed his hand. 'I can't wait to see them.'

Anna, as she entered the studio, had a sudden sense of transgression. The atmosphere in the room was as charged as the wall racks Johannes had built to hold his canvases. It felt dense, dark, secret, despite the fresh spring sunlight which streamed through the window. It was the aura cast by the large paintings he had positioned against the wall opposite her. They ate up the light.

She didn't know quite what she had expected, perhaps the cold, clinical distance of his later war work with its maimed bodies and marionette-like figurines, though she had hoped for the warmth he had infused into the last images she had seen of herself, the wonderful triptych with its luminous colour. But this was something different again. A series of dark night works, thick with encrustations of oil and rampant suffocating vegetation. She shuddered involuntarily. It was like stepping into a hell which offered no exit.

'I call these three, "Inferno",' Johannes said, as if reading her thoughts.

She averted her eyes from his questioning gaze and sat in the chair he had put out for her. Now that she was appropriately positioned and could see the detail more clearly, she realized that they were forest scenes, each lit by some spectral bonfire made up of human remains. In the first, a woman danced, tall, sinuous, more angular than the trees, her face contorted, her eyes rapacious. She was surrounded by other women, dancing figures too, their movements wild, as they clung to each other, as in some medieval dance of death.

The second painting repeated the theme. This time she could see that all the women were really the same one in different postures. Here the bonfire burned more brightly and in its midst was the wreckage of the world, cannons, guns, blasted buildings. In the final picture, the woman herself was atop the flames, incandescent, and only the trees looked on, stately, slender. For a moment she thought the woman might be herself. The hair had caught a golden gleam.

Anna turned away. She wanted to ask, 'Who is the woman?' Instead the tears leapt into her eyes, and she murmured, 'They're too painful, Johannes, too painful.' She reached for his hand.

The look on his face made her feel she had failed some vital test.

'"Paradiso",' Johannes said. 'Though not quite complete. Perhaps He moved her to the other side of the room, began to draw out mounted canvases from their racks.

Anna looked and breathed more freely. She felt she had left a dark night of the soul for a glowing pagan daylight, a world overflowing with colour yet serenely classical in its composition, a tree always at its centre, two figures always somewhere in its vicinity. One golden, the other dark. Herself and the youth.

There was only one dissonant note in the canvases, but perhaps she only imagined it, a face hidden in the vegetation, peering out at the key players.

'"Paradiso",' Johannes said. 'Though not quite complete. Perhaps uncompletable.'

He laughed and she joined him, not wanting to confront what she thought she heard in his tone. They had been so happy, of late. Instead, she said lightly, 'Sometimes I think I'm not quite strong enough for your visions, Johannes.'

'Does it take strength, Anna?' He looked her intently in the eyes.

'A great deal more than the garden.' She kissed him playfully, whispered, 'Thank you for inviting me.'

* * *

Two weeks later, when the crimson pelargonium had already begun to overflow from the urns Anna had positioned on terraces and loggia and garden paths, and pink angel's trumpet swayed magnificently above more delicate spiraea, Katarina arrived. As Johannes watched the two women embrace, the sleek dark head above the tousled blonde, he felt the acid of jealousy tearing away at his veins. But he hadn't prepared himself adequately for the vivacious charm Katarina turned on him.

'Johannes Bahr.' She took his hand, clasped it warmly in both of hers. 'An honour. Has Anna told you that I have been an admirer of yours since well before the war, that I have one of your paintings, would have many more if life permitted? No, I can see by your face she has forgotten.' Her laugh tinkled, enveloping both of them.

Johannes bowed.

'How silly of me,' Anna smiled. 'I *had* forgotten. Johannes always makes me forget everything.'

'I can see why.' She gave him a swift, assessing look and then wryly, her dark eyes twinkling, addressed Anna as if he were no longer there. 'I did warn you about artists, didn't I, Anna?'

'Katarina's warnings are always like invitations,' Anna explained playfully to Johannes, then turned to her friend. 'But we must show you round, show you your room.'

'I can already see that you've decided to live in heaven.' Katarina gestured around her expansively.

'But you may find us a little dull.' Johannes lifted her case, took in the fashionable cut of her dress, the swinging loops of pearls, the satin ribbon that hugged her hips, the length of the silk-stockinged legs as she climbed the stairs.

'Dull?' Katarina gazed at him from beneath dark lashes as he opened the door of the guest bedroom to her. 'Dull, when I've rediscovered my darling Anna and am in the company of one of the great artists of his generation?' she chided him, putting an arm around Anna's waist.

'He doesn't know you yet,' Anna laughed happily. 'Katarina is never dull, Johannes, you'll see.'

'I think I already do,' he murmured, then, bowing a little stiffly, said, 'I'll leave the two of you to catch up on things.'

'Not for too long, Johannes.' Anna seemed to be teasing him.

'And if I may, I'd love to see your work.'

'Of course.' Johannes left them, torn between wanting to leave them alone and wanting to stay if only to see what they would do. Jealousy crackled inside him. He had a sudden shimmering vision of taking part in their revels, charting their pleasures. Only by kindling this jealousy, stoking it to explosive dimensions, he sensed, would he rid himself of the hold it had taken on him.

Anna was only liminally aware of his disquiet. The thrill of having Katarina at her side in her new home wiped away everything else.

'I was afraid you might not come,' she said to her when they were alone.

'And pass up the opportunity of seeing you again? And of inspecting the famous Johannes Bahr?' Katarina's laughter trilled merrily. 'Despite all the years, you're still sometimes a silly goose, my Anna.'

They strolled slowly along the lakeside path, Katarina keeping up a repertory of oohs and aahs as each new vista slid into sight.

'It's a veritable paradise here, Anna. A place to live out the good life.' Katarina stretched her arms high and performed a little pirouette.

'And many have tried,' Anna smiled wryly and pointed to a little break in the shrubbery.

'Ooooh,' Katarina giggled. 'A nudist enclave. But we musn't spy.' She tucked Anna's hand through her arm. They walked on, happy in each other's company. At the top of the incline, they paused for a moment to catch their breath.

'And what do you think of Johannes?' Anna now shyly voiced the question she had been wanting to ask ever since they had set out.

Her friend examined her from beneath the broad rim of her straw hat. 'I think what I thought when I first laid eyes on you in Milan. I think that he must love you very well.'

The way she said it brought a flush to Anna's cheeks.

'And that you need no more little lessons in love,' Katarina continued lightly, 'though the occasional refresher course in common sense might not be amiss.'

Anna smiled. 'You may not be wrong there, and I hope you'll administer it.' She put her arm through her friend's again. 'And you? You told me so little about yourself in Milan. I realized when I got back that I had babbled unstoppably about myself.'

Katarina chuckled, patting her friend's hand. 'You needed to.' She paused, took a breath. 'I, Anna, am in the bizarre position of finding myself attracted to a man who wants to marry me. Can you believe it?'

'Never,' Anna laughed. 'You'll have to rewrite your code book for young ladies. Who is he?' she asked, and then a little shyly added, 'Will you?' She gazed at Katarina, thinking again how little she had changed, how beautiful she was.

'Perhaps,' Katarina winked at her naughtily, 'but before I embark on long stories let's go to that little café you told me about in the village. I'm not a mountain goat and it would be nice to pretend we're in Vienna again. My memories of our past splendour grow warmer with the years. And I always omit our disgraceful leave-taking,' she added, almost to herself.

They sat in the warm spring sun on the café terrace, sipped strong bitter coffee, and looked out at the lake, Anna proudly introducing Katarina to any acquaintance who stopped.

'So,' Anna prodded her at last.

'So his name is Adam Mackenzie and he's a Scot and I met him in the way silly young girls are supposed to meet their saviours in Viennese novels. Utterly ridiculous. There was a Zeppelin raid and I was terrified, didn't know which way to turn and suddenly this rugged man appeared from nowhere, took my arm and led me to safety. Yes, that's just how it was.' She laughed at Anna's astonished face. 'Then, after poor old Hansel died, the heroic Mr Mackenzie told me he'd been in love with me for years and duly proposed to me.' Katarina's lips curled mischievously.

'And?'

'And I told him to wait a little longer for my answer. At least until after this trip, so that I had time to think.'

'You're very hard on your men, Katarina.'

'Am I? Well, he's very rich, three years younger than me, and he's in love with me. So I can hardly be certain there's a sound basis there for marriage. Think, Anna,' her dark eyes twinkled ironically, 'what would the Professor say?'

'He'd say you were a heartless wretch.'

'That, Anna, was hardly the language he used.'

Anna gazed at her speculatively. 'I don't know what he'd say,' she murmured after a moment, 'but I'd say you were afraid. Afraid to risk disappointment.'

Katarina looked at her askance. Slowly she lit a cigarette, puffed, gazed into the distance. 'That, Anna, is perhaps the most astute thing you've ever said to me.' She paused, scrutinized Anna's face. 'And I suppose that you know this because you, yourself, are always singularly unafraid.'

'So that's what you think of Johannes,' Anna said softly.

'A dangerous man? Yes, perhaps.' She took Anna's hand, stroked it slowly. 'And he makes you forget your child.'

A shadow passed over Anna's face.

'But then you too have always been a passionate creature.' There was a wistfulness in her eyes as she said it. Then she shook herself, smiled in self-deprecation. 'But I've barely known the man for five minutes, Anna, and here you are wanting great proclamations from me,' she chided her. 'All I know about Johannes Bahr so far is that he's very attractive, very talented, and that if we don't get back soon, he'll be running after you.'

It was Anna's turn to laugh, but the laughter quickly turned into a look of utter astonishment, for there, coming towards them across the harbour street, was Johannes.

Katarina winked at Anna in her old comic manner.

The days of Katarina's stay with them passed quickly. Johannes seemed to grow as fond of Katarina as she was, Anna thought, rarely leaving their side, particularly after Katarina had gazed raptly at his paintings and declared that if she had sufficient funds, she would buy two or three or even four of his recent pictures straight away.

To Anna's surprise, she was even enthusiastic about the Inferno sequence. If only, she wailed, she had the funds to commission a portrait of herself. Johannes asked her to sit for him one morning, in any event; gave her a charcoal drawing he had done of Anna in Munich. On the bottom, he inscribed it, 'For Katarina, who cares for her too', making Anna flush.

It had been months since she had seen him so witty and utterly charming. It made her think that the life they led together was too reclusive, that he needed people more than she did. She suggested to him that they throw a party on the eve of Katarina's departure. The weather was balmy; the garden with its bursts of flower beginning to take on a little of the hues of her dream.

Johannes responded with alacrity, telling her to leave everything to him. She saw him race from the house with a sheaf of drawings under his arm. Only later did she realize that he had used them to pay the restaurateur for his services, to induce a local accordionist to play for them.

Everyone she knew in Ascona and more seemed to be present on the night – artists and poets and writers and dancers and naturists speaking a multitude of tongues above the tones, mellow and brash by turn, of the tiny dark accordionist.

Torches played over the garden, on the terraces, in the loggia, casting strange shadows on faces known and unknown. Food was heaped on plates. Wine flowed. A woman burst into dance, rising from the ground like one of Anna's plants and twirling amidst the guests. Katarina in a dramatic silver sheath of a dress glowed like a moon goddess, turning her light on everyone. Amidst the growing hilarity of the evening, as couples began to twirl a little drunkenly to the music, she suddenly threw her arms round Anna.

'This is wonderful. I feel like a girl again.' She kissed her softly on the lips. 'And you look ravishing.' She touched the folds of Anna's amber dress where they gathered dramatically over her left shoulder, and gazed at her, her fingers smoothing her bare skin, her hips beginning to sway slowly in a dance. Anna followed her.

'I think I've decided to accept the redoubtable Mr Mackenzie,' she smiled dreamily.

'Because of Johannes's shining example?' Anna teased her.

'Perhaps,' she laughed. 'And yours.' She embraced her again lightly.

Over her shoulder, Anna spied Johannes, his eyes dark, glinting dangerously. He was dancing with a tall willowy woman with raven hair. She blew him a kiss, waved him over. He didn't smile, but a moment later, he was at their side, the dark woman on his arm. Gazing at her, Anna suddenly shivered, almost forgot what she had wanted to say.

'Katarina,' she stumbled, 'Katarina's going to get married. A toast is in order.'

She saw Johannes lift her friend in his arms and kiss her, saw Katarina's look of astonishment, saw a spasm pass through the dark woman, all in the space of the moment before Johannes's arm was round her shoulder and he was waving the restaurateur over, invoking the group to silence, raising his glass in a toast to Katarina.

Tears sparkled in Katarina's eyes. She, too, raised her glass in a toast of thanks to her dear, dear, old friend, Anna, and her new friend, Johannes, their hosts. There was a general round of applause, a burst of music and then, at a signal from Johannes, a sudden hush, as fireworks illuminated the sky.

* * *

The next day Katarina was gone. Anna, having accompanied her as far as Locarno, returned to a house which felt hollow after the night's celebrations.

The last guests, Anna realized, must have left at the crack of dawn. She and Katarina had retired to the latter's room at about three when the party was still going strong, and talked. At some point sleep must have overtaken them, for she had woken, still fully clothed, tangled in her friend's arms. Johannes had been asleep when they set off, was perhaps still asleep.

Shaking off the tug of sadness, Anna went upstairs to change into her gardening clothes. She opened the door to the bedroom softly, but Johannes was nowhere to be seen. Perhaps he was up in his studio. She wouldn't bother him. Things had been so good between them since she had made the vow not to infringe on his space, to interrupt. Though she would have liked to be with him now. Somehow, in these last days with Katarina here, she felt she had lost touch with him, even if he had been so much with them. Still, she was delighted by how Katarina had taken to him.

In the gathering heat of the afternoon the chirrup of the cicadas filled the garden. It looked slightly the worse for wear. Pebbles from the path were strewn on beds and lawn. Overhanging branches had been cracked, flowers and pale shoots trampled. With a little sigh which she knew was partly fatigue, Anna began to work, half hoping that Johannes would see her from the studio and come down to help. She wanted to ask him about the dark woman she had seen him with, the one in his paintings, though she didn't quite know how or what to ask.

At a rustle behind her, she looked up to see the very figure she had been thinking about emerge from the foliage. The woman held a small basket in her hand. Herbs protruded from it, bright green against her white slip of a dress. Anna stepped back.

'I hope I didn't frighten you.' The woman addressed her in French. 'Johannes said I could help myself,' she smiled absently, stretching out a hand. 'My name is Janine.'

Anna stared into dark, deep-set eyes, down at that long angular hand with the scarlet nails, didn't take it, then covered her rudeness by displaying the dirt on her own. 'I'm Anna,' she murmured. 'Do you live near here?'

Janine pointed vaguely up the mountain.

'I see.' Anna turned back to her clearing. She could feel the woman's eyes on her

'Can I help you?' she asked after a moment.

Anna shrugged. 'If you like.'

'I like.' Janine reached for a small rake, bent to a flowerbed.

Watching her, Anna wished she hadn't been polite, wished the woman would go, didn't know how to tell her so. How dare Johannes give this stranger run of the house? But not a stranger to him, no. Anger coiled inside her, as dark and sinuous as Janine's curved shape.

But as they worked side by side, clearing and patting, prodding and tying, it began to subside. Janine had a way with the plants, her hands quick, gentle, her eyes intent, a hum always on her lips. When she caught Anna gazing at her at one point, she smiled mysteriously, 'I talk to them, you know. They understand.'

'Yes.' Anna's voice faltered. She wiped the perspiration from her brow. Her anger was now all aimed at Johannes. Where was he? She gazed up at the house, towards the loggia where he sometimes sat sketching. Was it his shadow she saw there?

Janine's dark gaze was on her. 'You look tired. Why don't we rest for a while?'

Without waiting for her response, the woman sat down beneath the flowering cherry, patted the ground beside her in invitation. 'It's so hot.' Her lips curled whimsically and then in one swift gesture she pulled her dress off over her shoulders. But for a pair of briefs, she was naked beneath. 'You don't mind, do you?' She was rubbing the moisture from her long body, her small erect breasts. Then she stretched out languorous as a sleepy panther. 'Ah, that's better. You should join me.' She looked up at Anna from beneath long lashes.

She must have come from one of the naturist colonies, Anna thought. Yes, she could see Johannes visiting them, his eyes alert to the women. With sudden decision she slipped out of her frock, stretched out on the ground. A soft breeze tickled her skin. The warmth of the ground made her drowsy. She closed her eyes.

Suddenly she was aware of the touch of a strange hand, cool, long-fingered, playing over her body, circling her nipples. She stirred, looked up to see that sharp-featured face above her, the heavy flow of dark hair.

'Si belle,' the woman murmured. 'No, don't move. It's nice, *non*?' That rapt black gaze held her.

Then, behind Janine's raven head, silhouetted in the brightness of the sun, she saw tousled hair, eyes strange in their intensity.

'Johannes,' she breathed.

He was down on his knees at her side, his fingers following in Janine's trail. 'She's lovely, isn't she, Anna, almost as lovely as Katarina.' His voice was strained. 'Touch her.' He lifted her hand to the other woman's bosom, led it down to her taut hip. 'Soft, silky.'

Janine moaned softly, curled closer to her.

'What are you doing, Johannes?' Anna arched away from him, away from the woman who had now started to stroke him, to ease open the buttons of his shirt.

He didn't answer her, didn't seem to hear her, seemed to be in some kind of trance. But he pulled her back. 'Kiss her, Anna, you like kissing her.' His fingers traced the line of her lip. She shivered.

'Yes,' he murmured, 'kiss her.'

Anna met Janine's eyes, wondered for a moment if the woman understood German. 'It's not natural what you're doing, Johannes, what you're saying,' she hissed at him.

'Not natural, Anna?' He mocked her. 'Everything we do is natural. We're only animals, after all,' he laughed, pulling back her hair with a tug to stare at her from black eyes. 'Isn't what you and Katarina do behind locked doors natural?'

'Johannes!' A sudden horror of realization rose up in her, made her gasp. She leapt up.

'*Laisse-la.*' Janine had curled close to him. '*Elle n'a pas envie. Mais moi . . .*' Her long fingers flickered over his crotch.

He was kissing her. Anna leaned heavily against the tree, felt her legs giving way. They were rolling over and over on the ground and he was kissing her, had already done more than kiss her, had allowed Janine into her space, had painted her. Had manoeuvred her into approaching Anna. In revenge for Katarina. Not only that. For the first time, she noticed the sketchpad, the pens scattered on the ground at a short distance from them. He had watched them.

And now, because of her resistance, and not only because of her resistance, he would make love to Janine, right here, in front of her eyes. Deliberately in front of her eyes, to taunt her. In her garden. Yes, she could see his erection straining, see Janine beginning to writhe, those long legs wound round him. No, she couldn't allow that. Not that.

And if he wanted to see, she would let him see. Two could play at the manipulation game.

Anna laughed her wild laugh. What was it Katarina used to say to her, show her?

She bent to run her fingers through Janine's dishevelled hair, languorously smooth the skin of her back, brush the grass from it. The woman raised her head away from Johannes, looked towards Anna in surprise.

'*Nous sommes belles, nous les femmes,*' Anna murmured, slowly tracing the line of Janine's angular face, her long neck. 'We women are beautiful,' she repeated again. She cupped Janine's breast softly, saw her eyes flicker. She skimmed her lips.

Janine extricated herself from Johannes's embrace. 'Yes, beautiful.' She echoed Anna's gestures, gripped her hand.

Anna shivered. They were on their knees facing each other. Beyond Janine's shoulders, she was aware of Johannes's gaze, aware too of the white flash of her foot, still buried in his crotch. She pulled the woman towards her. 'Will you come with me?' she whispered, stroked, cajoled.

The smile Janine gave her had a girlish mischief in it, despite the dark drama of her features. 'I always prefer women,' she laughed, her face a little tremulous. 'Certainly in the daytime. Though sometimes at night, Johannes . . .'

Her voice trailed off as Anna tugged her to her feet.

'Come.' She wound her arm through Janine's, led her away from Johannes. Away towards the edge of the garden, where the old trees provided a leafy canopy.

Later that night, with the door of the room safely locked against him, and a chair propped against it for good measure, Anna lay in bed and wondered at the day's events. She had only a hazy recollection of the sequence of things after the two of them had left Johannes. She remembered stretching out on the ground, closing her eyes and imagining Katarina still with her, Katarina in Vienna, so gentle and witty in her touch. But this Janine was different: there was a frenzy about her, a fierceness which tore at her, forced her into a kind of excited awareness. And then at one point, she had seen Johannes standing over the two of them, his eyes black, raging; had seen him touch Janine who arched catlike at his caress.

Anna had been afraid then, afraid that the two of them would finish what they had begun earlier. And somehow, she had interposed herself between them and it was her, Anna, he had come into, whether by her stealth or his choice, she didn't know. Her he had shuddered into convulsively, telling her he loved her. But she had been angry at him, had veiled her anger as she saw a humming Janine off the premises, was angry again now.

Anna thrust his pillow on to the floor, curled into her side of the bed. Her eyes wide open, she dreamt. Dreamt of someone sucking at her, draining her life blood like those leeches she had once read about, no, seen, black, shiny, clamped to her mother's body.

In the morning, she could hear him knocking, his voice soft, asking to be let in. She lay very still. She didn't want to see him, wanted only to scream.

Later the knock came again, the soft voice followed by a rustling beneath the door. A piece of paper. She looked at it for a long time, before picking it up. A picture. A small boy weeping, the tears thick on his cheeks beneath the sad, lowered eyes, his shirt in disarray above short trousers. One sock had fallen to his ankle.

She gazed at the picture, fascinated by the thick whorls of the fallen sock. Then she let it flutter to the floor. It fell on the reverse side. There was a word, scrawled there. 'Sorry.'

She returned to her bed. Leo, she thought, she must go to Leo, though the picture wasn't of Leo.

The knocking, the soft voice, recurred throughout the day and into the night. It woke her the following morning and was followed again by the rustle of paper. An envelope. She tore it open, saw a strange spidery script. She read it three times before its meaning began to penetrate her anger.

> Dear Anna,
>
> You said I should call you thus, so I take the opportunity. You also said that you would be like a daughter to me. I have had no sign of this as yet and I hope this letter will provoke the first and certainly the last.
>
> I am on my deathbed. The doctors tell me I have some three weeks to live, four at the utmost. I would like to see my wayward son and yourself one last time. To make my peace.

Tell Johannes no harm will come to him in Germany.
I count on you.
Your father,
Karl Gustav Bahr

Anna stared out the window on to the glistening lake. A boat was just leaving the small harbour, its stern spreading a fan of waves in the still water.

Suddenly she was all decision and haste. She washed herself cursorily, brushed her hair, pinned it up, found one of the dresses she had bought in Milan, lemon yellow with a lime stripe. Its colours pleased her and she let her eyes rest on it for a moment. Then, hurriedly, she put on matching stockings, high-heeled shoes, packed a small bag. Finally, she pulled a soft straw hat down over her hair. She looked at herself in the glass. She was ready.

She pushed the chair away from the door, heard it rattle strangely, opened it to find Johannes perched there, a picklock in his hand. He stared at her, his face drawn.

'I thought . . . I thought you were unwell, I don't know what I thought.' He let his tools drop, embraced her.

She was moved at the pain she read in his eyes, but she held herself stiff.

'Forgive me, Anna,' he murmured. 'Forgive me. I don't know what came over me.'

Looking at her, Johannes was struck by how he had lost his way in the tangle of his own jealousy, his attempts to master it only breeding a forest of his own excess in which he had lost her as well.

She said nothing, started to move away from him.

'Where are you going?' he held her back.

She turned. 'To see your father. He's dying. You should come too.' Her tongue felt thick in her mouth.

'My father?' He was aghast.

She nodded.

'Why?'

'He asked me to.'

'That letter . . .' He scanned the room for it.

She gave it to him, watched the hostility and suspicion contort his features.

'When did you see him, Anna, when?' His tongue felt thick at her betrayal.

'While you were in prison.' She kept her voice calm. 'I told him we were married.' She laughed abruptly. 'I promised I would treat him as a daughter would treat him. I gave my word. I don't break my word.' She edged towards the door.

'Don't go, Anna.' He tightened his grip on her. 'It's madness. He's implacable, manipulating, controlling. He'll destroy you.' He was shouting.

'Madness?' She stood very still, stared at him. 'Manipulation, control? I should be inured to them now, don't you think, Johannes? I've lived with you for long enough.'

'What do you mean, Anna?' Horror filled him.

She wrenched away from his hand. 'Just think of that little episode with Janine, Johannes. Think of it. I'm sure your father couldn't have done any better.' Her voice rose and she struggled to control it. 'In any event, I'm going. I promised.'

He raced ahead of her, stopped her at the bottom of the stairs. She could feel his eyes boring into her.

Anna looked at him. 'You should come too, Johannes,' she said softly. 'I imagine he's asked you. Several times. In a way, it's your last chance. It's time you buried your father, put his ways to rest.'

'You're telling me that I'm like him, Anna, is that it?'

She shrugged. 'Not in any superficial ways, Johannes. Not in your ideas. But . . . Oh, I don't know. All I know is that there's a boat due to leave soon.'

She stood very still. 'You could catch it,' she murmured. 'With me.' Then she evaded him, closed the door quickly behind her, only looking back once for a last glimpse of the house, the garden, like a half-finished painting against a blue sky.

The engine on the boat had already started purring when she saw him, a tall man in a pale suit, his hair tousled, a small case under his arm.

He sat down beside her, took her hand. He didn't look at her.

'Will you marry me, Anna?' he murmured.

A laugh began to ripple through her, burst from her throat, 'I'll think about it, Johannes. How long do I have to think?'

'As long as you need.' He met her eyes, scrutinized her.
She squeezed his hand. 'I thought we already were.'

It was midsummer by the time they arrived in Seehafen. Anna had hoped to leave Berlin sooner – straight after the small wedding party which had followed quick on the heels of Karl Gustav Bahr's funeral. But there had been so much to catch up on in Berlin, so many people who wanted to see Johannes, that they had stayed on.

Johannes had behaved impeccably, if a little stiffly, with his father, as if he had pre-scripted his lines and couldn't allow himself to deviate from them. To her, he had been so tender, so solicitous, that she sometimes wondered whether she had imagined the entire episode with Janine. He had even made efforts to be friendly with her son, though so far these had done little to allay Leo's suspicious hostility. Distressed by this, Anna had told herself everything would be better once they entered the idyllic precincts of Seehafen. There they would be a family. A happy family.

She had come on ahead with Leo, while Johannes made a detour to Darmstadt where he had been invited to exhibit his work. The boy was easier when she was alone with him. He played quietly on the lawns of the house or scampered over fields while she looked on.

Anna took pleasure in his beauty, the soft sturdiness of his limbs, the downy curve of his cheeks, the clarity of that secret tawny gaze. But she couldn't read him, didn't know whether, when she embraced him, he would push her wilfully aside, or relax into her arms. Nor could she make him speak to her except in response to direct questions. He was silent, closed.

Soon, she thought. It was simply a question of time. And there were so many things in him to be proud of: his dexterity with his puzzles, his careful but outlandish drawings. He was even beginning to read. That was Bettina's doing, Anna knew. His second mother. She had begun with something of a shudder to characterize her sister as such.

That afternoon he was stretched out on the ground beside her on the little knoll which had once been her and Johannes's secret meeting place. He was prodding the earth with a stick, taunting a beetle, who clambered over it, only to be confronted by the stick again. Anna smiled, folded her arm round the child.

'We'll go in the water soon, Leo.'

The boy glanced up at her. 'Swimming.' There was a sudden stubborn expression on his face. 'Want to swim.' He pointed towards the lake. 'In the deep.'

'You will.' She ruffled his hair. 'Soon. You'll learn.'

Over this last week, they had created something of a family ritual over their bathing. Johannes would play with the boy in the small shallow strip near the shore, while she swam out, and he would swim while she played or tried to teach Leo. Yesterday the boy had started to protest, wanting to follow Johannes into the deep. She had laughingly cajoled him out of it, allowed him to flounder and then caught him in her arms.

'Swim *now*. *Now*.' Leo leapt up, started to race towards the water.

'All ready then?' Johannes appeared from behind the hawthorn and swept the child into his arms.

'More than ready,' Anna smiled, meeting his eyes. It was extraordinary the effect he had on her when she saw him here, in this place, this magic place, where she had first spied him. She wove her arm round his waist, needing to touch him.

He kissed her lightly.

It came to her now, as it had repeatedly in these last days, that they could stay here together, all three of them. *Should* stay here now that Johannes had been given a legal pardon. She already had a vision of the boathouse, enlarged into a proper studio; a bright nursery set up for Leo in the left wing of the house next to a room for a nanny. She hadn't talked about it yet to Johannes, but she would, perhaps tonight.

'Swim,' Leo repeated, tugging at her arm. 'Swim now,' he said more emphatically.

'Now, now, now,' Anna chuckled.

'Right.' Johannes leapt into the water with the child in his arms. He set him down in the shallows, began a splashing game.

Anna followed them, a little more slowly, relishing the coolness of the lake.

'Off you go.' She waved Johannes away, caught Leo from behind. 'Watch, Leo, Johannes is swimming. Now you kick your legs, kick, kick.'

The boy started to kick frantically while she held his arms, walked him to the height of her shoulders and back again. He began to shriek. 'Want to swim. Swim deep. There.' He lurched his arm away from her, pointed towards Johannes. 'There, there.'

She caught him just where the bottom plunged. 'It's too deep there.' She showed him, sank her head beneath the water, held him above it.

He paid no attention, struggled from her arms. 'There, out there.'

Johannes was back at her side. 'I'll take him out, Anna. It'll be all right. He's a brave little tyke. Aren't you, Leo? Now you just keep kicking and hold on to my hand. Understand?'

Leo nodded as Johannes gripped him around the back, set off with him.

Anna watched them, shielding her eyes from the sun's glare on the surface of the water. It seemed to swallow them, leaving only bobbing outlines in a bright haze. With a tremor, she headed off behind them, her eyes glued to her son's golden head.

They were already some fifteen metres from the shore, when she heard Johannes say, 'Good, Leo, now I'm going to let go a little, and you keep kicking. You'll swim.'

'No,' Anna shouted. But it was too late. Johannes had released the boy. He was floundering, his head going under, disappearing.

'Johannes!' she shouted again, just as he caught the sputtering child.

'That was good, Leo. Now shall we try again?'

There was a set look on her son's face as he nodded.

'No, Johannes!' She grappled with his arm.

He laughed at her. 'He wants to learn, Anna.' He let the boy kick for a few seconds and then released him.

The child splashed frantically only to sink again after a moment.

'Johannes, stop!' Anna was shrieking now.

'Well done, Leo.' He paid no attention to her, but swam away with the boy bundled under his arm, then after a moment asked, 'Again?'

Leo nodded.

Anna caught the grim set of her son's lips, the fear in his eyes. 'Stop it, Johannes, that's enough.' She swam up to them, tried to take Leo from Johannes's arms.

'No.' Leo kicked out at her.

'He wants to swim, Anna.' Johannes's look was implacable.

She let them go, watched from a distance, panic gathering in her as the intervals of kicking and sinking grew longer, until she could bear it no more.

She plunged towards them, 'That's enough, Johannes. You're mad. He's just a baby.' She was shrieking. She snatched Leo from Johannes's arms, saw the mute tears in her son's eyes, saw in the same instant Johannes's rage, saw him pound off towards shore, clamber on to it, walk away, his shoulders stiff. In that moment, while Leo pummelled her and grabbed savagely at her hair, she had a certain sense that Johannes would continue walking, would pack his bag, would leave, and she would be left here with this furious stubborn child, his face contorted with hatred.

She held on to him tightly nevertheless, dragged him back to shore. By the time they reached it, the tears were streaming down his face. With the ground firm beneath his feet, he started to blubber with stubborn determination, 'Swim. I want to swim.'

'You *can't* swim.' Anna was harsh. *'Can't.'* Her hands shaking, she wrapped him in a towel, carried him across the grounds, and deposited him unceremoniously with Frau Trübl just outside the stables, while she raced to find Johannes.

Leo stared after her, his eyes wide, unmoving. Continued to stare as she vanished from view. To gaze at the space where she had been.

At last, he announced to Frau Trübl, 'She gone. Gone 'cause I can't swim.'

For a long time, he was certain of that fact.

TWELVE

1925

CARS HOOTED AND BLARED their way down the Kurfürstendamm, their gleaming headlights illuminating the fauna and flora which sprouted magnificently in the Berlin night. Slender long-legged women as brightly apparelled as exotic birds eyed loose-suited young men affecting American ease. Rat-eyed pimps and prostitutes of any number of sexes jostled with plump frock-coated gents and elegantly furred matrons. Jewelled bands glittered on pale foreheads, long sparkling clusters fell from ears, lavishly feathered boas flew through the air. From the revolving doors of bars and restaurants and clubs, trumpets moaned, player pianos jangled, bands boogied.

As a large motorbike roared noisily past the taxi in which Bettina sat, she was reminded of a phrase she had recently seen in an English magazine: 'The roaring twenties'.

Yes, it was an apt term for the times. That was what lay at the heart of their epoch: a frenzied love affair with speed and sound. Speed enough to mark a rupture with the past, to escape into a new time zone. Sound enough to drown out its murmurings and some of the uglier rumblings of the present, the cries and moans which emerged from the squalid tenements of the city.

Bettina sighed, snuggled into the capacious folds of her fur and looked out of the window. But there was no cause for sighing, she told herself. Over these last five years, the first five of this roaring decade, dour, dark, Prussian Berlin had flowered into a city of noisy revellers engaged in a perpetual carnival. Even if their primary desire was for pleasure, their excitement had infected the very air they all breathed and created a new freedom, a new openness. It pervaded casual exchanges and intellectual debate alike.

She felt it in herself, too, in the length of stockinged leg she could show and shock only herself; in the words she could use. The horrors of the war years, the terrible plight of the inflationary period, were at last behind them. The blight of censorship both external and self-imposed was finally disappearing. In their place a joyous new Weimar democracy was being born in which everything was possible.

She had said as much to the women's meeting she had addressed this afternoon. True, there was still much to be done. One had only to go to the working-class quarters of the city to be struck by the blatancy of that. But now, at last, it seemed possible for reforms to bite. She had exhorted the women to make good use of their new short-skirted freedom, called on them to elect more women to the Reichstag so that laws which concerned them and their children would be passed, improvements made to the educational system, equal wages for equal work.

They had clapped her loudly and a voice had called out from the back of the room beseeching *her* to stand for office, asking who could be better placed than Bettina Eberhardt, who sat on innumerable committees, who edited a magazine?

That little moment was in part responsible for her high spirits, Bettina acknowledged, rebuking herself simultaneously for her vanity. But it was only one part. Bettina smiled again secretly.

Only Klaus remained untouched by the excitement in the air. She turned from the spectacle of the brightly-lit Ku'damm to look at his face, absolutely still except for the shadows of the street which played over it. Nothing seemed to stir him these days. He had become increasingly reclusive since his breakdown, rarely leaving the house except to go to his laboratory, sitting mutely though with seeming contentment through the many gatherings in their own home. An old man before his time.

She touched his arm. 'I'm so glad you decided to come tonight.'

He shrugged. 'It's not every day that a retrospective of Johannes's work opens at the famous Flechtheim Gallery. And for his sake, for old times' sake . . .' His thin, lined face was suddenly illuminated by a smile.

'And here I thought you were coming out to celebrate this great new year of 1925. And my new hairdo,' Bettina laughed, touching her hand to the short bristle at the back of her neck, the smooth sides. Her head felt so light.

'It suits you. Makes you look just like Max.'

'Are you sure? I let myself be talked into it by Maedi. She said it was the latest thing.' Bettina grinned ruefully. 'Now I feel like an overgrown schoolboy masquerading in his mother's earrings.' She shook her head so that the earrings jangled.

'It really does suit you.'

The car slowed as they neared the Gedächtniskirche. As always a small crowd in an outlandish mixture of garbs was gathered round its steps. Tonight there was a man with shaven head and flowing oriental robes addressing the group. A little further along, a salvation army band blared out a tune.

Bettina chuckled. 'The latest "ism" being expounded. Another sign of our roaring times. Salvation's on offer everywhere. From right and left, God and the new heroic producer, nation and the international, art and nature, even women.' She laughed. 'It makes me think of Werfel's "Mirrorman" ditty. I quoted it at my lecture today.

Eucharistic and thomistic
But also of course marxistic
Theosophic, Communistic,
Small-town godly churchly mystic
activistic, brassily buddhistic,
superior eastern taoistic
Salvation from this enmired time
in artistic primeval slime
fashionably mixing into one fat pot
Barricade and word, god and fox trot.'

Klaus didn't laugh. 'Weren't we like that once? In the business of salvation, I mean.'

Bettina wouldn't meet his mournful seriousness. 'Still are,' she quipped. 'Though only partial salvation, of course. The slow, steady somewhat unfashionable kind, that isn't bloated with its own instant certainties. And that only when we're not showing the weight of our years.'

For a moment, looking at him, she felt their weight and sighed again. An odd notion propelled itself to the front of her mind. Would she live to a time when she could see clearly which 'ism' history had backed? History – which was always so full of surprises, which had converted what she had experienced as a glorious flourishing time into something now recognized as the decline and last gasp of the Austrian Empire. History – which, depending on the next piece of the jigsaw, would make of this decade an epoch of competing lunacies or a fertile laboratory of the future. She must consider this more in her next article, insist on the need for clarity.

But the car was already turning into the street which bordered on the Landwehr Kanal, pulling up in front of the Flechtheim Gallery. It was hardly the moment for seriousness. Seeing the laughing, glamorous crowd milling round the gallery doors, Bettina drew back her shoulders proudly and showed her deservedly famous profile to advantage. Thomas might be here, she thought with a girlish shiver of excitement.

'If you can make your way through that mob to a picture, you're a better man than I am.' Josef Winterstein, a social democratic MP, embraced her with a smile.

'I've always been a better man than you are, Josef,' Bettina chortled, excused her way through the throng. 'And we must find Johannes.'

'He's in there somewhere. Almost bit my head off when I asked why he still insisted on painting such depressing pictures when things were obviously on the mend.'

'Serves you right for asking unartistic questions.' Bettina put her arm through Klaus's and, laughing, made her way through the doors.

Inside, the rush of a hundred voices mingled with the smoke of countless cigarettes, swirled round turbaned and jewelled and cropped and pomaded heads.

Bettina and Klaus dropped their coats, responded to a flurry of greetings and embraces. Everyone was here – nattily dressed businessmen and rumpled proletarian artists, cabaret dancers resplendent in scarlet and silver, double-chinned politicians, bespectacled critics, notorious satirists, lauded writers.

Alfred Flechtheim himself came to greet them. The perpetual thin cigar between his lips, he shook Klaus's hand vigorously and thanked him again for the loan of two of Johannes's early pictures. 'The great man is over there.' He pointed them towards a far corner of the room.

As they pressed through the crowd, Bettina spotted a slim woman in a long shimmering gown standing a little to one side of the throng. The bright aureole of hair now trimly cut to reveal smooth bare shoulders was unmistakeable. Anna. Her sister. Always beautiful, always herself. She seemed to be the only person in the room whose gaze was focused on a painting.

'I didn't expect to see you here.' Bettina kissed her warmly on both cheeks.

'I didn't expect to be here.' Her face had a wintry pallor, Bettina noticed, though it only served to emphasize the purity of its lines, the touching vulnerability of her eyes. 'But Johannes rang and insisted. I arrived this afternoon and checked into a hotel. In case . . .' She looked at Bettina beseechingly.

'No need to explain.' Bettina hugged her, then watched her sister as Klaus embraced her.

How odd life was. She would never understand how two people whose love for each other was so blatantly passionate could so flagrantly fail to make a life together. Anna and Johannes seemed neither to be able to live together nor apart for long.

Bettina had almost stopped keeping track of their comings and goings, the tempestuousness of their relations; though two years ago now, after some apparently disastrous attempts at family life with Leo, she had suggested to Anna that rather than embroil the child in the heat of their twosome and continually disrupt his schooling, the boy would be better off in Berlin with her – Berlin, where Johannes hated to be. Though he had grown to hate Ascona, too, it seemed, couldn't stand the unreality of it. Bettina shrugged.

She knew that last year, somewhere between Ascona, Munich, Seehafen and Berlin, which marked the corners of Anna's erratic trajectory, she had had an affair with another man. Anna had confided that to her, told her in dismal tones that Johannes had driven her to it, had perhaps even set it up.

Bettina didn't pry. She didn't really want to know. Passion, she had begun to think, was not a useful experience as one grew older, unless one could contain it in its proper place – like a secret delight one kept in store for oneself, a special treat at special moments, not a great hairy beast that trampled over everything in sight. Bettina smiled to herself. That was the way it was for her with Thomas, had been for a year now. Thomas Sachs, who made her understand for the first time what it meant to be young. And young in the roaring twenties. Bettina smoothed the close crop of her hair.

She should tell Anna about Thomas. Not that it would help. *Her* problem was that her lover was also her husband. Johannes was simply not cut out to be a husband.

Bettina hadn't seen much of Johannes over these last years, though he wrote to her occasionally. At the rare times when he came to Berlin, he met her in some quiet restaurant for what was always engagingly civilized conversation. She read about him of course, heard his praises sung by the critics. His work was all the rage at the moment.

Bettina glanced at the bits of paintings she could see over people's shoulders. She had schooled herself to appreciate Johannes's work intellectually, but she still felt a kind of visceral unease as she looked at his images, though she had grown genuinely to like the early pictures now. And she was particularly fond of the sketches he had done of Anna and her in 1919, when they were all together in Seehafen. 'Sisters', the series was called. She could see one of the paintings based on it. The front room at Seehafen: herself sitting upright at the small table, reading peacefully, and Anna, curled like a sleepy cat into the cushions of the sofa, her animal eyes gazing eerily out of the canvas.

Those eyes, darkened with kohl in the current fashion, now followed the line of her own, and rested on the canvas.

'Things were better then, weren't they,' Anna said softly.

'Nonsense, Anna.' Bettina was abrupt. 'Things are far better now. Just look around you. Think of the chaos after the war, the fear, the misery.'

'You're right, of course,' Anna murmured, 'I was only thinking . . .'

Her words were smothered as a large bearded man lifted her into his arms and laughed sonorously.

'I thought I'd find you here, Anna, but I was hoping you'd be wearing one of those perky little leg-revealing rags that women only used to wear under their clothes in the bad old days, not this elegant garment.' Gert Hoffman winked with lascivious humour.

'Sorry to disappoint, Gert,' Anna was wry, 'but I think you'll find the goods are amply on display everywhere but just here.' She pointed to the walls.

'Harrumph,' Gert growled. 'Johannes's green-tinged flesh doesn't, I'm sure, do justice to the real thing.'

Bettina cleared her throat.

'I don't know if you've met my sister, Bettina Eberhardt, Gert; nor my brother-in-law, Klaus Eberhardt.'

'Herr Hoffman and I go back a long way,' Klaus murmured, shaking Gert's hand.

Gert turned to Bettina and bowed, surveying her. 'Charmed, Frau Eberhardt, though I think I have met you before in one or two of Johannes's canvases.'

'Johannes's fame precedes us these days.'

'What are you saying about me behind my back?'

Johannes was suddenly upon them, his hair tousled, but his white collar and tie immaculate against the dark suit. As always Bettina was at once taken aback by and drawn to the directness of that sea-blue gaze, the electric field he seemed to generate round himself.

'Nothing I wouldn't say to your face, as you know, Johannes,' Bettina smiled, felt his lips on her cheek.

'Though it's far more fun saying it behind your back, you old scoundrel,' Gert boomed. 'But congratulations anyway. Some not too bad pictures of yours they've managed to scrape together for this show.' Gert's eyes twinkled.

'Yes, congratulations, Johannes,' Klaus echoed.

Johannes shook him warmly by the hand. Then he stopped, gazed at Anna. Silence covered them for a moment. Bettina saw Anna inch towards Gert's bulk as if for protection. And then Johannes folded her in his arms, kissed her intimately, deeply with no heed for the rest of them. Bettina shivered, averted her eyes. It made her feel as if she were spying into a stranger's bedroom.

'I'm so glad you've come, Anna,' she heard Johannes murmur.

Bettina glanced at Klaus. There was a strange boyish melancholy on his features. She took his hand.

'That's enough, you two. You'll have us all rutting if you carry on.' Gert's voice seemed to resonate through the room.

Bettina flushed, heard Johannes and Anna laugh, turned to see them hand in hand. Perhaps it was her imagination, but Anna looked transformed. Her pallor had vanished. Her eyes sparkled and there was a swing in her movements which drew the gaze of everyone she passed. Bettina shook her head. If only all these powers that Johannes so evidently possessed and liberally passed on could be harnessed for some good purpose.

Later, when the crowd had thinned a little, they all stole away. Johannes had tickets to the annual press gala at the Zoological Gardens. Klaus pleaded fatigue and paternal duty; he had promised to help Max and Leo with school projects. 'I'm an old homebody these days, you know,' he said to Johannes.

'If I could, I would emulate you,' Johannes replied with an earnestness which made Bettina wonder. 'But you'll lend us Bettina, won't you?'

'Of course,' Klaus said with an emphasis which reminded her of the old days. 'As long as you bring her back safely. She's looking far too dashing for a respectable woman this evening.'

'I'm quite capable of bringing myself back.' Bettina drew herself up to her considerable height.

'You're capable of anything, Bettina, we all know that,' Klaus smiled, and then abstraction seemed to cover him again as he donned his hat and coat.

'You should see more of him, Johannes, while you're here,' Bettina murmured as they tried to flag down a taxi. 'I think you're good for him. There's no one left from the old Munich days.'

'I will,' Johannes promised and then before she could say any more he had his arm round Anna and was kissing her hungrily.

The spacious pavilion teemed with people. Anyone who was anyone in Berlin had gathered here – actresses and dramatists and white-faced dancers, film-makers from the UFA studios and diplomats and writers, scientists and academics and industrialists.

Crowds of scribblers and gossip columnists from hundreds of daily papers would on the morrow avidly report who had been wearing what, been seen talking to whom or executing the latest dance steps to an assortment of the latest bands. It was rumoured that political as well as amorous alliances were formed and broken here, deals struck, reputations made and unmade, if only until the next column was penned.

Anna, moving to a jazzy beat in the circle of Johannes's arms, cared nothing for all that. She felt alive for the first time in months, as if a great burden of tedium had been miraculously lifted from her shoulders allowing her to stand tall, to move freely, to look straight ahead.

It wasn't exactly that she had been suffering since she had last seen Johannes. Not like after those earlier ruptures. She had carried on with her daily life this time. Ascona's ever increasing number of new arrivals had heard of her skills and not a week passed but that she was asked to undertake the design of yet another garden. And she had travelled too, been to Vienna to sort out Tante Hermine's affairs, to Paris, to Scotland to see Katarina, pregnant at last. But not a day had passed when the effort of getting out of bed had not seemed almost too great. The cough too had started again.

Then Johannes had written, had telephoned, pleading with her to come to his opening, saying it was as much her triumph as his. She knew her initial resistance was a sham, knew that against all the odds, however fearful she felt, she was unable not to come once she heard those soft suasive tones of his. And now she was here, hope as effervescent in her as she laughed into his eyes as if she had been a slip of a schoolgirl innocently about to embark on her first passion.

'Shall we get a drink?' Johannes caressed her back, drew her towards the edge of the dance floor.

'Oh no you don't. It's my turn to dance with the beautiful Anna.' Gert was suddenly upon them, pulling her laughingly away from Johannes, embarking on a complex series of hops to the band's newest rhythm. He danced lightly, precisely, despite his girth, all the while miming the melodramatic faces of a lovesick movie hero.

Giggling, Anna followed the tremulous shimmy of his hips, saw a little space form around them as people turned to watch, heard a small burst of applause as Gert executed a particularly precarious movement and she responded in kind. Suddenly Johannes gripped her arm and pulled her away. His eyes were black.

'That's enough, Gert,' he murmured.

Gert grimaced affably, let his arm fall loosely over Anna's shoulders as he followed them. 'Don't let him frighten you with his scowls, Anna. A little jealousy will fine-tune his passion. Won't it, old man?'

'Let it go, Gert.' Johannes was gruff.

'I don't think I really need any help with the anatomy of Johannes's passions.' Anna laughed her old free laugh and wound her arm through Johannes's. 'We have had a little time to get to know each other, haven't we, Johannes?'

He let out a short, sharp laugh. 'That we have.' His voice changed. 'But when I see you like this, after an absence, Anna, I always feel it's for the first time.'

'And that,' she turned to Gert, 'is because Johannes has a very convenient memory.' She said it playfully, smiling.

'Do I?' Johannes was startled.

'Yes, my dear, I'm afraid you do.'

'But I remember some things.' He caressed the inside of her arm lightly, watching her face.

'Some things,' Anna conceded, wishing he couldn't sense the pulse he had set up in her.

'What things?' A striking bob-haired woman she dimly recognized was upon them, her cigarette waving from a long gilded holder, her softly parted lips luminous red as she planted a kiss first on Anna, then on Johannes.

'Anna's been telling me I have a convenient memory, Renate.'

'I'll second that,' Renate giggled.

'Passed,' Gert concluded.

Anna let them joke as they made their way through the crowd. But it was true. She wished her memory was as convenient. But she could remember everything. Remember how after the blissful promise of life as a threesome in Seehafen, it had all gone wrong. In a kind of panic, she had abandoned Leo for Johannes, terrified that she would lose him at the very moment when he had made so many concessions to her, not least among them marriage itself. They had returned to Ascona, so that he could finish his current series of paintings. Then, in a flurry of guilt, she had gone to fetch Leo. They would try again. And try though they did, it hadn't worked. After a time, Johannes had retreated into that implacable coldness of his. He had ceased to work and gradually he had filled the house with people – anarchists, drug addicts – so that soon there was no place she and Leo could turn without stumbling on a blank-eyed body or two wrapped in embrace, Johannes sometimes amongst them. She had fled with the boy, vowing never to return.

Yet when Johannes had begged her to come and live with him in Munich, she had left Leo and gone, at least as far as Seehafen. It seemed as if the perfection of their early days together was now to be repeated. Work was pouring out of Johannes, scores of canvases, each one more powerful than the last. He even encouraged her to spend weeks with Leo. Yet after some six months, as soon as she was beginning to feel secure in the pattern of their existence, everything had broken down again.

Johannes had taken off, not to reappear for three or four weeks. She knew there were other women. That no longer seemed to matter so much. What she couldn't bear was the sense of coercion, the attempt somehow to break and soil and manipulate the fabric of her life as well. So that when Johannes had returned accompanied by two men, whose talents he began to sing to her, she had run, sensing an inevitable variation on the Janine affair. In spring she had set off for Ascona with Leo, determined to make a life for herself there.

But the little boy was unhappy with her, pined for the Berlin that had become his home, for Klaus, for Bettina. When Johannes reappeared one day without warning and Leo's fractiousness increased, she had taken him back to Berlin, intent on staying with him. Johannes, however, had pleaded with her to come to Seehafen, told her how much he needed her. And, despite her better judgement, she had come back to him. There had been months of joy after that and again she was lulled into a sense of its going on forever.

Then, when was it, about eighteen months ago now, Johannes had asked her permission to invite a young man who wanted to come and work as his apprentice to the house. It had all seemed so innocent that she had agreed. And it had been innocent at first. But gradually, Anna had noticed that Johannes kept engineering situations in which she and Kurt would be alone together. Finally he had come out with it and told her it would be good for her to love another man, particularly since he no longer desired her.

At first she had wept and resisted. Then, partly because she liked Kurt, partly because she wanted to confront Johannes with the pain of his own idiocy, partly out of a kind of weariness, she had slept with Kurt, had moved him into her bedroom and banished Johannes. She could see, after Johannes's initial sense of triumph, the jealousy taking hold of him, but she would no longer sleep with him, certainly not allow any notional threesomes.

Then one night Johannes had overpowered her, taken her brutally in the garden. She had been aghast, had told him to leave in no uncertain terms. And he had gone. She hadn't seen him since. The affair with Kurt had quickly dissolved into nothingness. Without Johannes's hidden desires to sustain it, it was a lifeless thing, like the child she had miscarried soon after. Johannes's child. She was as certain of that as she had been that Leo was Bruno's.

And yet, now, with Johannes's arm tightly round her, even though her inconvenient memory rendered every moment of her pain with crystalline clarity, that pain was weightless, the mere fluttering of a bird's wings, compared to the intensity of his presence beside her. She wondered at herself, wondered when lucidity would ever begin to dictate her actions. Wondered at the inevitability with which his caressing presence made her feel him as a gift, a present of the present. It outweighed everything else.

'Anna, Johannes,' a voice jarred her reflections, 'you must meet my friend, Thomas Sachs.'

Anna looked up to see a radiant Bettina with an elegant young man at her side. He had one of those finely chiselled faces that spoke of breeding. But it was the eyes which caught Anna's attention. They twinkled with irony, all the while assessing their object with an intelligent directness which yet had nothing of superiority about it, so that no sooner had they shaken hands and exchanged greetings, than she felt seen, understood, and accepted all at once.

'Thomas has just taken over a list at the Reinhart Sachs Verlag and he's trying to convince me that I should write a book for him,' Bettina glowed.

'The New Woman.' Thomas Sachs stretched his arm dramatically towards Bettina. 'Who better than Frau Eberhardt, who is her very embodiment.'

'And has been for some time,' Johannes murmured.

Bettina looked at him askance and then laughed brittlely, 'Johannes would have me write a book called *The New Older Woman*.'

'Closely followed by his autobiography, *The Older New Art*, no doubt.'

'Touché, Herr Sachs,' Johannes chuckled. 'It wasn't generous of me. But then Bettina and I go back a long way.'

'No offence intended, Herr Bahr.' Thomas's eyes twinkled good-humouredly. 'I was being quite serious. I was struck by the references in your work to Dürer, to Cranach, the old masters, particularly in the Ascona series.'

Johannes looked at the younger man with new interest. 'You have a fine eye, Herr Sachs.'

'Not half so fine as yours.' Sachs bowed, but his gaze fell playfully on Anna so that it was clear to her that the compliment was directed at her.

Gert, who had found a bottle of champagne and was busily refilling their glasses, boomed with laughter. 'Johannes Bahr will go down in history as much for the beauty of his models as for what they inspired him to.'

Anna could feel Johannes stiffening in anger, his arm tightening around her, but his tone was even. 'Anna far and away the chief among them.'

'But if a new woman were writing the history,' Bettina's eyes flashed, with a warlike vengeance, 'she would have to ask what it was you inspired your *models* to, Johannes.'

'And that would be difficult to determine, wouldn't it, Bettina, let alone to judge?' Johannes's voice carried a sliver of ice. 'Before the war you and I might have called it *freedom*, but now that that's so easy to obtain on the marketplace and some of us have become as responsible as our parents,' he looked at her sardonically, 'we'll just have to dip into the catechism of deadly sins. Shall we start with lust?'

Bettina bristled.

Anna caught Thomas Sachs's eye, wriggled away from Johannes. 'I don't know.' She smiled at Bettina. 'From one newish sort of woman to another, I might be able to tell the historian that Johannes had inspired me to *something*. Despite himself, perhaps.'

She saw Johannes look at her aghast as if preparing for the worst, saw Bettina stiffen with anxiety. She could read their minds. They were expecting a confession of intimacy. Anna laughed. They weren't wrong. She could tell them that Johannes had awoken her to passion, to the gift of her own body. She would inevitably die of it, but at least she had had that and it was a great deal. But that wasn't what she had in mind now. Anna gave them each a wry glance in turn.

'Johannes led me to paint, you know, encouraged me, first with oils, and then with something far less new-fangled – flowers and shrubs and vines and stone, the oldest elements.'

Johannes took her hand, squeezed it. 'And I can testify that Anna's gardens are as magnificent, as lush as her generosity.'

'They must then be very beautiful, indeed,' Bettina murmured.

'*The New Eve's Garden* . . . My list is growing apace tonight.' Thomas Sachs grinned mischievously at Anna, then bowed, and turned to Bettina. 'Shall we dance?'

She nodded brightly and he led her away.

Watching them, Anna noted that Bettina was gazing up at him with the look she usually reserved for silver-haired professors. 'I think Thomas Sachs must be teaching Bettina how to be a *young* new woman,' she whispered to Johannes.

He followed the line of her gaze, chuckled. 'Bettina never ceases to surprise me. But do I detect a note of jealousy for your indomitable elder sister?'

'Perhaps.' Anna smiled ruefully.

'And so I shall have to behave like a young man.' He drew her on to the dance floor, placed his hands on her hips, held her close, began to sway.

'I love you, Anna. More than I love anyone in the world.' He looked down into her eyes. 'You know that, don't you? Despite everything.' He kissed her.

And despite everything, she knew that it was true. She also knew that for Johannes, that love had little to do with ordinary everyday happiness. But for the moment, as she melted against him, that mattered as little as the notion that she might die on the next day.

Leo Adler stood in front of the heavy panelled door which led to the front salon of the house in Grunewald. He hesitated. He could hear the women's voices, one crisp, clear, certain of its words; the other murmuring, fuzzy, too soft. He thrust his hands into his trouser pockets. The smooth stone was there in one of them, its hardness soothing. In a trice he could fit it into the slingshot he had in his other pocket, take aim, and launch a missile. Pftoing. Splat. Like the young American brave in the Karl May novel he was reading.

And then the voices would be stilled. Silent.

He liked the silence. When he sat by the window and looked out, it had its own sounds: the laughter of the ducks as they landed on the lake, the rustle of the sooty squirrels racing through the branches of the oak. But not in winter. In winter, there was only the crackle of ice, the snap of twigs. Sometimes a restless bird.

And the women's voices drowned them out too easily. There were always so many women's voices in this house. They drowned out his dreams, too, of becoming a blood brother to Hawk-eye and Chingachgook in the virgin forest, or an officer, a soldier in the Prussian Guard, of limitless adventures and boundless courage.

Leo reached for the door knob, fidgeted and then bent instead to look through the keyhole. There they were, Bettina and Anna. Anna and Bettina. Uncle Klaus wouldn't be happy if he splatted them with his slingshot. He didn't like hurting things, killing. And Leo liked Uncle Klaus, liked him best of all. Far better than that horrid man his mother had married who wasn't his father. Though Klaus was too soft and sometimes didn't understand things. For example he didn't understand it when Leo got angry, so angry that things got all blurred and red and he had to scream or run away into the woods. He had been angry just a few minutes ago when old Martha had told him he had to stop reading, had ordered him to go downstairs.

Not so angry though that he couldn't open the door and aim his slingshot, right there into his mother's breast.

Mothers. Bettina had said to him one day not so long ago, 'You're lucky, you know, Leo. It's as if you had two mothers. Your natural mother and me.'

'Are you my unnatural mother?' he had asked her then and she had laughed, said, 'No, I'm your natural aunt,' and she had gone on to explain at length, as she always did, with too many words, so that he stopped hearing and only wished that he had no mothers. Neither the one who talked too much, nor the one who touched too much.

But then she had mentioned Corinne's name and he had started to listen again. He was lucky, Bettina told him, because he had two mothers, whereas Corinne had none and no father either. So she was going to stay with them and they would be her family.

Leo didn't want to be anybody's family, especially not Corinne's, who came into his room without knocking, touched all his stones with her dirty fingers, his collection of bullets, the birds' feathers he had carefully arranged in the shape of an Indian headdress, and laughed at him. She had horrible knobbly knees and sprouting breasts and everyone was so kind to her, especially Max, even when she said stupid things, which was every time she opened her mouth.

When he was bigger, soon, he would run away to America and live in the woods, alone, without a family, like Hiawatha or Winneton. It would be quiet there, so quiet that he could hear the snakes slithering through the tall grass.

'Leo.' The door opened suddenly and Leo stumbled over Bettina. 'There you are. I was just coming to fetch you.' She looked at him with momentary disapproval and then smiled. 'You've been daydreaming again. Come and give your mother a kiss.' She shepherded him across the room.

Leo kept his eyes on the floor. Golden wood. Polished. Hard, so that he could hear his heels echoing on it. Then the softer rug with the patterns whose end or beginning he could never find. If he concentrated on the patterns, he could almost bear the sense of that moist hand ruffling his hair, stroking his neck. But she was lifting his chin.

'My, how you've grown again.' She squashed him against her so that he smelled that rich fetid smell that suffocated him. He struggled away from her and then met those eyes, sad eyes that always seemed to want something from him, like a whimpering puppy. If only he could kick her to make her go away, make her stop wanting something he couldn't give.

'I'm only here for a few days, Leo, and I thought we might go out together today, have some cakes, ice cream, catch up on things.'

'I'm not hungry,' Leo said sullenly.

'Leo,' Bettina reprimanded him.

'No, no, that's all right.' His mother's voice was cloying. 'Perhaps a walk round the lake, then. It's lovely out.'

'I wanted to finish my book.'

'Get your coat, Leo. And don't let me hear that rudeness again.' Bettina was firm. He walked quickly from the room.

'He hates me,' he could hear Anna whimpering as he closed the door.

'Nonsense, he's just shy. They're all like that at his age. He's not eight yet, and he hasn't seen you for a while.'

Leo fingered the stone in his pocket.

It was bright out. The sun made shadows on the thin layer of crisp snow which crunched as they walked. He could see the two of them on the ground, like great skinny giants. If he moved ahead just a little, he was as tall as her, taller. He smiled.

She had her hand on his shoulder, but he could barely feel it through his thick coat. It wasn't so bad this time. He wasn't melting into her, disappearing. His coat was thick, his skin hard. It was all right.

'How is school?' she asked him.

'Fine.'

'Just fine?'

In the distance the lake shimmered coldly. He shrugged off her hand, started to run towards it. She raced after him, stopped him, laughed.

'You run quickly now. Bettina tells me you've joined a youth group. Do you enjoy that?'

He nodded. 'In the spring we'll be going off camping,' he offered.

'That sounds wonderful.'

'Look, there's Uncle Klaus.' He pointed. 'He's got Wolfi with him. You haven't met Wolfi yet. Max brought him home. He had an injured paw, but he's better now.' He bounded off.

Anna watched him. He was so beautiful with his shock of blond hair, those wide hazel eyes flecked with yellow, like her own; it made her heart ache. She trailed after him, saw him bury his face in the dog's heavy coat. He seemed happy, she thought. As long as she wasn't there.

'Anna, nice to see you.' Klaus smiled at her. 'Meet Wolfi.'

At a command from Klaus, the dog placed a shaggy golden paw in her hand.

'I've been ordered to wait here, for exactly another minute,' Klaus looked at his watch, 'and then Wolfi and I are setting off to track Max and Corinne. Will you join us?'

'Yes.' Leo answered for her. 'Can I hold his lead?'

Klaus nodded, staring at his watch. 'Five, four, three, two, one. Go.'

'Find Max,' Leo commanded. The dog sniffed the ground and then, to the little boy's evident delight, set off deliberately up the slope.

'It's our latest game,' Klaus smiled. 'One or t'other of them is lost in the woods and Wolfi has to track them, save them from the elements. It was Leo's idea originally. He's been reading about the Wild West.'

'Isn't it a little dangerous?' Anna worried.

'I don't think so. They always go in pairs and they can't get very far in ten minutes.' He laughed gaily. 'It isn't really the Wild West, Anna, not even as wild as Seehafen.'

'No, I guess not.' She looked dubious. In the distance, at the top of the slope, the woods were thick, gloomy. She pulled her coat more closely round her.

They followed briskly behind Leo and the dog. At intervals, the boy would let out a loud whoop and perform a strange little dance, before once more giving the dog his head. They caught up with him at the edge of the woods. Wolfi was sniffing the ground dutifully. Suddenly, he barked and raced off at a tangent, dragging the jubilant boy behind him.

'He's found them, he's found them,' Leo shouted, tripping happily between trees, leaping over fallen branches.

But the dog suddenly stopped. His ears alert, he sniffed the air and then again the ground. He looked confused. He set off more slowly now into denser wood, dark, despite the shafts of light, the occasional bright glossiness of holly. All at once he started to bark again, growl loudly. Leo whooped, 'We've found you, Max. Come out. Ma-a-a-x.'

But there was no answering call. Wolfi barked excitedly, ran towards a cluster of holly trees. He pawed at the ground. Clumps of dried leaves flew into the air, loose earth mixed with snow. Anna saw a startled look on Leo's face. She raced ahead of Klaus, then stopped in her tracks. There, half exposed on the ground, lay a woman, her hair mingled with dirt and leaves, her face frozen into a look of pained surprise, her mouth a smudge of scarlet, too bright against the translucent pallor of her skin.

Anna screamed. Buried her face in her hands, heard the rush of footsteps, the clamour of voices.

'We're here, we're here.'

'You didn't find us.'

'What's wrong, Wolfi?'

'Just look what he's found.'

'Oh.'

'She's dead.'

'Murdered.' Leo's voice.

All as if in a dream.

'Anna, Anna.' Klaus's voice was stern. He drew her hands away from her face. 'Take the children home. Ring the police. I'll wait here.'

She saw Max and a dark, frail girl, their eyes wide with awe. And Leo still staring, staring at that woman. A little rapt smile hovered over his lips.

She shook herself. 'Come on, all of you.' Her voice squeaked in her own ears. 'Come on,' she said more firmly.

'I'll stay with you, Uncle Klaus.' Leo was still staring.

'No, you go with Anna, quickly now.'

'Leo.' Anna reached for his hand. He resisted her.

'Come on, Leo. Quick, we have to get the police.' Max gave it an important sound, tugged at Leo's arm. 'They'll need to ask you questions. Come on, Corinne. Quickly.'

Leo cast a last lingering look at the dead woman. She looked so still, he thought. Silent and beautiful. Beautiful and silent. He let himself be led away by his cousin.

Bettina handed each of the children a mug of steaming cocoa and biscuits, and then poured out tea for Anna and herself. The police had been rung and they were waiting for Klaus's return. A fire crackled in the hearth.

'Wolfi and I found her,' Leo said self-importantly for the fourth time.

'I know, dear,' Bettina murmured. 'What a shock it must have been.'

Corinne, her thin pointed face almost as pale as the dead woman's, asked, 'Do you think she was murdered?'

'Of course she was murdered.' Leo's voice had a note of squeaking triumph.

'You don't know that, Leo. Not for certain,' Max said softly. His bright, intelligent face was troubled as he looked at his younger cousin.

'Max is right,' Bettina echoed, but she wasn't censorious.

'She looked murdered,' Leo insisted. 'She looked like a bad woman.'

Anna met his eyes. In her distress it seemed to her that he was passing judgement on her.

'You don't know that either, Leo,' she murmured.

'You certainly don't.' This time Bettina was firm. 'She could just as easily have fallen, broken her leg, and what with this weather, died of exposure, of cold.'

They heard the door open and Bettina leapt up.

'Well, I think she was a bad woman who was murdered,' Leo repeated stubbornly, though more quietly. This time he fixed his eyes on Corinne. 'Like that woman in the newspapers.'

'Stop trying to frighten Corinne,' Max rebuked Leo.

Max, Anna noted, though he was only ten, behaved as if he were older than Bettina's newest ward, older than all of them.

The girl had started to cry. Anna put her hand round her shoulder and patted her. She remembered Bettina's telling her that Corinne's mother had died only months ago. The tenement in which she lived was one of Bettina's regular visiting sites, and she had rescued the girl from being sent to an orphanage.

'It's all right, Corinne. I'm sure Bettina's right,' she murmured to the girl.

Bettina came back into the room with Klaus.

'What do you think, Uncle Klaus?' Leo piped up again. 'You know about dead people. Was she murdered?'

'I didn't examine her.' Klaus looked at them all with watery eyes. 'It wasn't my job. The police have taken her away now.'

'Will they come here to ask us questions?' Max asked.

'Perhaps. But I think I told them the little there was to tell.'

Leo looked disappointed.

'And there'll be no more walks in the woods for a while.'

'Why?' Leo asked.

'They've cordoned them off to do their investigation.'

Anna prodded herself. She was going off soon and all Leo would remember of her visit was a dead body.

'I know.' She smiled a bright and not altogether successful smile. 'We need to forget all this unpleasantness. So why don't I take you all to see a film? I've got a car. And I think I noticed that there's a new Charlie Chaplin playing.'

'That would be terrific, Auntie Anna, wouldn't it, Corinne, Leo?' Max rallied the others. 'I love Charlie.'

Leo looked at her sceptically. 'Will you let me play in the driver's seat, toot the horn?'

Anna grinned. 'Yes, Leo, on our way back.'

'And will there be a lot of dead people in the movie?'

'I hope not.' Anna tried not to shiver as she met his eyes. 'Death isn't very nice.'

'Our teacher said death was beautiful, dying for a cause was beautiful.'

'But he had to be alive to say it.' With an attempt at a playful grimace, Anna pulled the cap down over Leo's face.

'Your mother's absolutely right.' Bettina was suddenly stern. 'I'll have no nonsense of that kind in this house, Leo. I've told you before. That's the trouble with this country.' She shook her head in irritation. 'Teachers fill all your minds with romantic waffle. There is absolutely *nothing* beautiful about dying for a cause. Remember that, Leo. And tell your teacher I said so. Millions died in the last war for some trumped-up cause and there was nothing at all beautiful about it. Do you understand? They simply lost their lives.'

Leo looked at her stubbornly. That wasn't what Herr Reichler had said and he liked Herr Reichler, believed his stories about the war. After all, he had been there, had been wounded, had a medal. Bettina didn't.

'Do you understand?' Bettina repeated.

'Leave him be, Bettina, he's only a child,' Anna murmured.

'Children need to learn how to think clearly.' Bettina was unrepentant. 'Well, Leo?' she stared the boy down. Max and Corinne shuffled their feet. 'If you don't understand, let me hear what you think and we can argue it through.'

Leo looked at his shoes. Then, as if he had suddenly seen the light, his golden head shot up and he said politely, 'I understand, Auntie Bettina.'

Before Bettina could speak, Anna intervened. 'We should hurry if we're to get to the movie in time.' She shooed the children out of the house, bundled them quickly into the car.

Sitting next to her, Leo smiled. It was quite easy really, he thought. All he had to do was lie. Never tell them what he really thought. Just lie and smile. And they would keep quiet. He had always known it. He must remember it.

Later that night, as Anna lay next to Johannes on the large hotel-room bed, she mused again over the day's events. She had begun to tell Johannes about it all earlier, but love-making had overtaken her words. How good it was to be with him again, to be able to touch him and, yes, to hear him. That was perhaps what she had forgotten a little, how much she liked talking with him, feeling his particular intelligence play over the matters of everyday life.

'But do you think Bettina was right to be so hard on Leo?' she asked him now.

He traced the line of her breast as if rediscovering it and memorizing it all at once. 'I don't know,' he murmured. 'It's her way to argue things out. And she's not wrong. If the boy is being stuffed full of pernicious rubbish, someone has to present a more intelligent view.'

'But he's so young. And today of all days, after he'd found that woman.' Anna shivered and Johannes put his arm around her, held her close.

'I don't think children are as fragile as all that. In any event, they're preoccupied by the idea of death – where things come from, where they go. His father, after all . . .' He changed his tack. 'Perhaps it's better to have it out in the open, as a conversation, even an argument, rather than brooding privately, fantastically.'

He stared towards the window, which was festooned with dark, heavy curtains. 'I know I thought about death when I was young,' he grimaced, turning towards her again, 'as you must have done, particularly after your mother died.'

Anna put the thought away for later investigation. She was silent for a moment. 'You know that woman in the woods, she reminded me of someone. It's just come to me.' A shudder went through her. 'But it couldn't be her. It was just the mouth, that pale, ravaged face. Yes.' She looked bleakly towards the window.

'Who?' Johannes prodded her softly.

'I never told you about her.' She met his eyes. 'I didn't, don't, really know her, but I first saw her at Bruno's funeral. She was weeping. Like me.'

'Oh?' Johannes looked startled. Anna realized that she had never spoken to him about Bruno's death, the funeral, any of it. Funny that it now seemed possible, after all this time.

'Yes. She was a stranger and it struck me then as odd, though I wasn't aware of much else, that this stranger was weeping so copiously, that she didn't speak to me. And then – when was it? about two years ago, maybe more? – I had this letter in Seehafen, from a woman who told me that she had been a friend of Bruno's, that she was now destitute, didn't know where to turn. Would I help her? I don't know why, but when I read the letter I instantly had an image of that stranger by Bruno's grave.'

'I see,' Johannes muttered. 'A mistress.'

'How did you know?' Anna laughed sharply.

'I wasn't born yesterday, my dear.' He stroked her arm softly. 'And?'

'Well, she was, though she never said it in so many words. I met her in Vienna. I gave her money, should have given her far more, though she didn't ask. That woman, today . . .' Anna hid her face in her hands. 'I think there may have been a child,' she mumbled, wiped a tear from her eye. 'I liked her. There was a pride about her, even though she was in dire straits. I wish Bruno had told me about her. It might have made things easier between the two of us.'

'So you approve of mistresses now?' Johannes questioned wryly.

She gazed at him, apprehension settling on her features. 'It wasn't the same with Bruno, Johannes. I can't explain. I . . .' She trembled, started to cry. 'We didn't, weren't . . .'

He stroked her hair. 'I know, Anna. I think I know.' He covered her with his body and she arched against him, needing the confirmation of his flesh.

'I always want you so much, Johannes,' she murmured. 'So much.'

'Yet you're quite capable of leaving me?' He traced the hollows of her face, the pure lines.

'Not for lack of wanting you.' Her lips quivered.

He kissed her gently, met her eyes.

'Men are beasts, Anna, corrupt beasts, reaching for angelic heights. Sometimes it's in the reaching that they do most harm.'

She stroked him, only half aware of his words, but they seemed to have erased his passion.

'I think that's a little harsh,' she said after a moment.

'Perhaps.' He leapt off her, reached for a cigarette, his face shadowed. 'I'm tired. It's all these congratulations from people who spat in my face not too long ago. It's hard work being even as moderately civil as Flechtheim expects me to be.'

Anna laughed. 'The rewards of fame.'

'You know, I was offered a post in Dresden today. A good one.'

'And?'

'I refused it, of course. I'm not cut out for students.' He glanced at her warily.

She chose to smile. 'Judging by how you treated the last one, I should say that's right.'

He looked at her wonderingly. 'So you've forgiven me.'

'I'm thinking about it.' She was wry, took his hand.

'Excuse me a moment, Anna.'

He sprung from the bed. She watched him, that tall form, still lithe despite the passage of years, saw him search in the wardrobe, take a small packet from his jacket pocket, walk towards the bathroom. A few moments later he was back, burrowing into the bed beside her.

'Are you on some sort of medication?' she asked him softly.

'You might call it that.' Then, noting her worry, he laughed. 'Come here, Anna, come closer to me.' His hands travelled over her body. 'Let me love you the way you deserve to be loved, my darling.'

When the first light peeped round the edges of the heavy curtains and he was still loving her, Anna reflected that he seemed to think she deserved a great deal. That in itself made her feel supremely happy.

At noon the next day, they left Berlin for Munich in Johannes's new Mercedes.

As always, and despite all the current excitement of the place, Johannes was pleased to be leaving the city that bore the indelible imprints of his childhood, to see the last suburb disappear behind him.

He put his foot down on the throttle, felt the car leap like a large cat into powerful motion, saw, from the corner of his eye, an excited smile curl simultaneously on Anna's face. For a moment, she looked again like the impulsive slip of a girl he had once met. Yes, she shared that too with him – the sheer pleasure of speed.

How he loved it. The sense of freedom, the exhilaration of perspectives which changed by the second, making the world into a kaleidoscope of planes and angles trailing colour. The sense of being contained in an iron beast which purred and leapt at his slightest touch, and yet in constant danger, instincts on the alert for the slightest bump or veer in the road, for the presence of another.

It was like an exercise in mortality, pleasure vying with risk, gambling with fate, an excess of sensation always on the edge of its own annihilation. Speed was the sweet serene taste of life itself, only experienced in the proximity of death.

He hadn't driven with her like this before, the distance opening up before them into a seeming eternity. How lucky he was. He hadn't expected her to come back to him, not after that last time. Yet she had, a little fearfully. But then the fear was in him, too. A sense of defying the odds. Gambling. Like overtaking the car in front of him now, uncertain what lay beyond.

If only this time he could prevent that sensation of waning that came over him when they had been together for a solid stretch of time, that overarching, almost demonic, need to reinvent, to feel the new, and in the process, to punish her, to destroy.

Anna refused his love games, had even defied him over his father. She was always herself, fully, amply, giving the lie to his demands, his manipulations. That was why he had to punish her. But that was also why he always came back, always wanted her back. Her passion was her passion and she gave of it generously. She wouldn't hide her hurt, lie about it. She was integral. Strong. Stronger than him. Freer. And he drank of her thirstily, but in the drinking, drank her up.

Johannes wasn't unaware of it. When they were apart, it haunted him: her ghost, her absent presence, nibbled at him in revenge, taking a little, then more, until there was nothing left and he had to drink of her again. Slowly at first, and then more and more, until he was replete. That was when the trouble always began again. When he was replete he was no longer himself. That self was always hungry, desiring. Like an alley cat prowling dark streets.

That was why he couldn't stay with her in that paradise she had created for them in Ascona – her own embodiment of the good natural life. It made him feel trapped, a fat man imprisoned in a green and golden cage, unreal. In Ascona, the world only arrived in distant whispers, and though he no longer felt the zeal with which to change it, he still had to be immersed in its ugliness, its dirt, its teeming corruption. That was the currency of the real. That was what fuelled his work. Together with a hunger for the other, the new, the extreme. A craving, sometimes a random craving. That sustained him. But now he wanted only her.

He braked to a sudden halt, met the question in her eyes with a long kiss, almost made love to her there, on the dirt track by the side of the road. But no, it would be more tantalizing to wait, the speed whetting their appetites. He started the engine again, felt it leap into life, placed his hand on her leg, beneath the coat, the soft dress. Warm, taut flesh. He pulled her closer, felt her fingers on his thigh.

Perhaps this time it wouldn't happen. Perhaps this time they would arrive at the precarious equilibrium of tightrope walkers, always at the point of falling, but never quite. Yes, that would be the ideal. Like this driving, too fast, on the edge of a precipice. If only he had the necessary control.

Sometimes in this last year when he had taken too much of the drug – at first because the pain had come back and then simply because he preferred the dazzling clarity or swirling fog it induced to the dull throb of the everyday – he was filled with the sense that the whole country was on the edge of a precipice.

One particular vision pursued him. He had begun to paint it in the hope of exorcizing it.

A heaving multitude had just crawled out of a stinking abyss, crawled out inch by inch, their grimy feet poised on the heads beneath them, their bleeding fingers gritty with dirt. And now they were precariously balanced on a pale ribbon-thin strip of road. If there were any clamour, any loss of control, they would hurtle over into a yawning void on its other side. This second canyon was unlike its turbulent neighbour. It beckoned with a hard icy brilliance, echoed for him with the pure high longing of the overture to 'Parsifal', yet he knew with a certainty that its depths would shatter them all irrevocably.

'May I drive for a while?' He heard Anna's soft tones as if from a great distance.

'Yes, yes, of course.' He slowed the car, pulled on to the first possible verge, watched as she settled herself into the seat, confidently pulled away, driving with a swift certainty which brought the colour into her cheeks.

Yes, Anna would have no trouble manoeuvring the thin ribbon of road. He could trust her. Unless she were propelled by another, the icy yawning canyon would have no attraction for her.

Johannes half closed his eyes, stared ahead. He felt safe, the car a cocoon spun from their two bodies, warm, embracing. He had forgotten that easy, stilling warmth. The climate this last year had had a constant edge of desperation. His nerves were jagged, fraying. That was probably why he felt haunted by the voice of that mad little corporal. With Anna beside him, the voice seemed less threatening, a comedy on a distant stage.

It had been just after he had returned to Munich in February of 1924. A journalist friend who wrote for *The Times* had asked him if he wanted to go to the trial of the *putschists* at the old Infantry School in the Blutenburgstrasse. Their great hero, Ludendorff himself, was in the dock. It had all the makings of a promising spectacle. Johannes tagged along, as he might have for a beer.

And there, amidst the ten prisoners, he had seen his old acquaintance from the military hospital, the little yellow-faced corporal with the hectoring voice. He had missed the putsch itself, had been away, hadn't taken in that this very same Adolf Hitler was one of its leaders. And now there he was, engaging in unstoppable harangues, wooing court and public and the world's press alike, manipulating language so that truths became lies and lies truth.

All attention focused on him as he proclaimed himself a revolutionary against the revolution, a destroyer of Marxism; denied that there could be any high treason against the traitors of 1918; asserted his destiny, a dictator born. Evoked the eternal court of history, not a mere gaggle of judges, to pronounce sentence on these brave men and himself, who wanted only the good of their own people and the Fatherland, who wanted only to fight and die.

Johannes had a vision of almost hallucinatory strength. A new edition of his father stood in the dock, his father reborn, democratized, popularized into an earnest clown who spoke his words with a demagogic fervour. And the judges must have seen it too, for on the *putschists* they passed the mildest of sentences, whereas his own friends only a few years back had been treated as rabid criminals.

'Johannes.' Anna's soft voice displaced the histrionic rant of the little corporal which had kept pace in his mind with the roar of the car.

She had pulled up in front of a village inn, all sloping roofs and eaves. 'I thought we might stop. You look tired.'

'I am tired, Anna.' He took her hand, looked at her earnestly, as if not quite believing in her reality. 'Whatever else happens, Anna, please remember that here, now, Johannes Bahr is eternally grateful for your presence.'

She eyed him strangely for a moment, ruffled his hair teasingly. 'I wasn't planning to leave you, Johannes, not just yet. I'm far too hungry.' She laughed her old raucous laugh.

It buoyed him up, drowned out that other voice, gave him hope. In them, if in nothing else.

THIRTEEN

1931

WHEN LEO ADLER was fourteen, his daydreams were filled with glorious images of heroic self-mortification.

He was in a dense wood traversed by a cold mountain stream. A morning mist curled from the water while the ground beneath their trampling feet was still covered with a thin crust of frost. They had already marched some five miles, crossing the river by way of a rickety bridge now long lost to view. Their packs were heavy on their backs, but their shoulders were straight, their heads high like knights of old marching fearlessly into battle. Directly in front of him was Gerhardt, their leader, Sir Gerhardt, taller than the rest, his shoulders straighter, his white-gold hair glinting in shafts of sunlight, his voice stronger, deeper in the harmony of their song.

Leo marched, sang, his voice matching his leader's.

> 'Forward, forward, forward,
> Youth knows no danger
> Our flag is greater than death . . .'

He would do anything for Gerhardt, gladly follow him anywhere, die for him, if he asked, if only to have his eyes rest on him for a moment as they had the night before when they were all sitting round the campfire listening to his story of Teutonic knights guarding the purity of their homeland against the enemy from the east.

Leo's voice rose in a triumphal chorus.

Suddenly Gerhardt turned, ordered a halt. The flag. Where was the troop's banner, proudly emblazoned with eagle and sword? It had been left forgotten at the camp. It would have to be fetched. Who would volunteer to fetch it? Leo stepped forward. But he wouldn't retrace their steps, through wood, over bridge. No, it would take far too long. He would plunge instead into the icy stream and race the short distance. It would take no time at all.

Quickly he shed his thick sweater, his shirt and trousers, leaving only his shorts. He could feel the other boys' eyes on him, Gerhardt's. How good it was that his muscles had been toughened by the rigorous daily calisthenics and cold baths. He plunged into the water. Icy cold bit at him, lashed, took his breath away. But he thrashed his way to the other side, head high, clambered out up the steeper bank, raced, despite the needles and pine cones which lacerated his feet, the branches which flailed his body. The flag. He held it aloft, as he struggled back through the icy swirling water, presented it proudly to their leader. The boys cheered loudly.

'Well done, Adler.' Gerhardt's tone was laconic, almost curt. But his eyes shone on Leo with a warmth which made him forget the glacial cold of his body. And as Gerhardt dabbed at the cuts on Leo's chest with his white handkerchief, Leo felt as triumphant as if he had returned with the Grail itself. In the background, it was as if he could hear the anguished yearning strains of 'Parsifal'.

They were rudely interrupted by a noisy rattling.

'Leo, unlock the door. Get on with it, quick.'

Old Martha. Leo roused himself, leapt off his bed, wiped his brow, moist with the excitement of his dream. What did they want with him now? They were always interrupting him, getting at him, these prattling women with their mundane nonsense. In the small mirror, he caught a glimpse of his face. He stopped and looked at himself. Gerhardt had said he reminded him of that wood-engraving of Parsifal, in the book they had passed from hand to hand.

'Leo, Frau Eberhardt is coming in a moment.' Martha's voice was stern. 'Have you got your room ready?'

He had forgotten. Today was the day a boy was being moved into his room, another of those snivelling brats who had gradually filled up the house in these last months, so that there was no longer any space in which to breathe. Leo unlocked his door to let Martha in.

She looked round her aghast. 'You haven't done anything, Leo. You know you were supposed to clear that space.' She gestured towards the window where all his trophies were lined up, to the table cluttered with his whittling tools, his animals and heads.

'It'll only take a moment.' Leo began to move the figurines half-heartedly.

'Let's just carry the whole table over. Kurt's on his way with the extra bed.'

No sooner had she said it than Kurt appeared, pulling a folded camp bed into the room.

'Give us a hand, Kurt. Leo's done nothing.' She looked at the boy scathingly.

'I forgot,' Leo mumbled.

'Forgot? And the poor little boy's already downstairs.'

Poor little boy this, poor little girl that . . . That's all he ever heard any more. It had all started with the dreaded Corinne and in this last year it had grown to mammoth, disgusting proportions.

'We have to help in whatever way we can,' Aunt Bettina said, always adding portentously, as if the words were magical and explained everything, 'We're in the midst of a depression. A crisis.'

There was even no room for his mother in the house any more when she came to visit. Not that he minded that. But these ugly, dirty, snivelling, timid brats, with their watery eyes and coughs, would soon overrun them all, swallow them up. He was sure there were Jews and Poles amongst them. He could smell their sweaty glands.

Aunt Bettina had this silly sentimental idea that everyone had an equal right to happiness. A soft humanist notion about progress, his history teacher had called it. But this was 1931 and if the divine Reich of German culture was to be established one had to have the courage of despair. One had to be hard, strong. Not soft. But what could one expect of women?

That was the trouble with this house. There were no real men in it.

There had only been his room left untouched by the whimperers and now that, too, was being invaded, polluted.

He had found himself complaining to his mother on her last visit. He tolerated her now. At least she didn't laugh and argue when he told her about what he liked at school, in his youth group, the way Bettina did. But it had been a mistake to complain. She had offered to take him away with her. He didn't want that. Didn't want to leave his school, his teachers, his group. Certainly didn't want to live with her and have to suffer those constant hugs and wet kisses.

But now even his room was lost.

Aunt Bettina didn't mind. She just let all those hectoring, suited women who pawed him with their lacquered fingers into her study and closed the door on the rest of them. All those fine words, all that do-gooding made her blind to what was really going on. He had tried to tell her once, tell her that Corinne was a disgusting beast, that she had left a bloody rag under his bed, that she had come to his room one night and tried to show him her ugly body. But Bettina had merely replied, 'Poor Corinne, you have to understand . . .'

And it was the same when he had tried to point out that the spindly-legged Inge stole from the kitchen, or that she had beaten up Irena. All Bettina had said was, 'Poor Inge, you have to understand . . .'

Thomas Sachs had been there that time. Leo wasn't sure about him, he seemed less loathsome than Bettina's other friends. He stood straight and looked like a soldier, had told him his figurines were beautiful. Thomas Sachs had taken him aside and said he could understand how he felt, all that noise, his privacy gone. He had suggested to him that he might teach some of the children basic forest skills, perhaps how to whittle, be a leader to them. And Bettina had butted in, told him, yes, he should follow Max's example.

Max. Leo hated Max almost as much as he hated the noisy squalling brats. Max, who was always bringing home stray dogs and cats, with mangled paws and stinking fur, who preferred them like that. Max, who told the orphan beasts that everything in the house was theirs, who let them run all over him, helped them with their reading, their sums. And argued with *him*, Leo, laughed at him secretly, destroyed everything he believed in with his endless reasoning.

The whore reason, Gerhardt called it. Yes. Just like Bettina. Like the time when he had brought home his prize-winning essay on Siegfried and the Niebelung Saga and they had both told him to forget all that nonsense and come and help out in the soup kitchens instead. As if life wasn't about a struggle for something higher and deeper than soup, as if life was simply explained by soup. Even Uncle Klaus didn't stand up for him any more. He was too old and dotty.

A few weeks ago he had had a terrible nightmare which wouldn't now leave him. It had started off well enough. He was in the house, all alone. Bettina, Klaus, Max, they had all gone away, left him. Forever. He was happy, quiet, in control, fencing with his shadow. And then a voice had shouted, 'He's an orphan now.'

'Like us,' another had added gleefully. And then suddenly there was a great tumult, cries of, 'Let's get him,' and all the brats had appeared, their nails sharpened, dirty, and they had begun to claw at him, tear at his skin. No matter how much he thrashed and flailed his limbs, they kept at it so that he was soon bleeding from every pore. He wanted to shout for help, call for Gerhardt, but he was too ashamed and slowly the room filled with his blood.

'Leo.' Bettina's voice brought him back sharply. 'Leo, you haven't prepared.' She looked at him disconsolately. And then with that half-smile of hers which meant her mind was already elsewhere, she said, 'This is little Leo, a namesake for you. He's six years old and he's going to be sharing your room. Just for a little while, until his mother is better, is back from the sanatorium. Now show him where he can put his things.'

She urged the little boy into the room.

The boy looked at Leo with wide doleful eyes, clutched a rag dog to his chest.

Leo took the tattered case Bettina handed him and placed it on the camp bed.

'Good, now we'll leave the two of you to settle in. Leo, you bring the little one down to lunch in half an hour. And be kind.' She gave him a stern look, ruffled the small boy's hair and left.

Leo stared at the little boy, who hadn't moved since he had come into the room.

'Sit down,' he snapped, pointed to the bed, watched the boy obey. 'Good, that's the first rule. You do everything I tell you instantly. We have discipline here. Understood?'

The little boy nodded. His eyes filled with tears.

'And you don't cry. Boys don't cry. Understood?'

He snuffled and then nodded again.

'Right, the next thing is that you can't be called Leo. It's too confusing. What's your family name?'

The boy stared at him uncomprehendingly.

'You know, your father's name.'

'I don't have a father,' he mumbled, his eyes filling with tears again.

Leo looked at him. 'That's nothing to cry about either. There's lots of boys without fathers. Fathers die in wars. The Fatherland looks after us instead. And we fight for the Fatherland. Understand?'

The boy nodded, gripped his dog tighter.

'So what's your other name?'

'Walter.'

'Good, here you'll be Walter. This side of the room is mine, Walter.' Leo drew an imaginary line close to the camp bed. 'Don't touch anything here unless you ask my permission.'

He began a little brusquely but methodically to arrange the things which had been moved to his side of the room, the figurines, his collection of plant specimens. He tried to pretend the boy wasn't there. But even with his back turned, he couldn't be rid of his presence. And he could hear him snuffling.

'Don't cry,' he ordered gruffly, without turning round. 'Or I'll be forced to give you something to cry about. Put your things away.'

He heard the lock on the case snap, a scurry of movement, a repressed sob. It was impossible. He would never be able to do his morning work-out with this snivelling idiot in the room. All the disciplines he imposed on himself would come to nought. How would he work, dream? Thank God he was going away in two weeks' time, to the camp where he would see Gerhardt again. And he would be rid of the chaos of this house.

Leo stumbled over the rucksack which Kurt had moved to the centre of the room. He cursed under his breath, then looked at the bundle. Of course, that was it. That was what he would do.

'Come on, Walter.' He heaved the rucksack on to his shoulder. 'You can help me put up this tent. I'll sleep out tonight, under the stars. It's beautiful under the stars. Quiet. Lonely. You'll like it too, when you're bigger.'

The little boy followed him dutifully.

Bettina looked round the table and smiled gratefully at Max. At least he was beside her today and making a spirited attempt to keep some semblance of conversation going. They took turns on Sundays: one or two of what she had taken to calling the core family would sit with the little ones in the kitchen, while the others and the older children ate at the dining-room table.

There were twenty of them now, not counting Martha and Kurt and the changing round of daily help. Plus the stalwarts amongst her women friends, Marie and Tina, who took turns helping with the smallest ones, and coordinating lessons. They were with Klaus today, at the kitchen table.

Sometimes she felt that her old Munich nurseries had taken over her life and she was living perpetually inside them. And today, the effort it demanded was more than she could give. Still, what else could one do but help out best as one could in these desperate times?

Bettina tried to shrug away the clawing fingers of depression. They were always at her throat these days, making breathing difficult, clear-sightedness a luxury to be struggled for. It wasn't simply the sheer unabating hardship the economic crisis had brought in these last two years to those already dismal tenements she visited so frequently. It wasn't even that she no longer had any ready answers to anything – except to muck in and help out with their own dwindled resources.

The last elections in September 1930 had brought a huge rise in the vote for both the Nazis and the Communists, and as a result a parliament that could barely function. Yesterday morning she had witnessed what had so far for her only been hearsay about the ever-increasing thuggery of those contemptible brownshirts.

She had just come out of a meeting in Kreuzberg when she saw a man dragged out of a tiny local shop by a gang of five uniformed youths and beaten to a pulp. They had paid no attention to her shouts and imprecations, only one of them turning to spit out, '*Ein verfluchter Jude*'.

She had let herself be led away by a passer-by. 'They're making Germany strong,' he had said. She wasn't certain whether there had been any irony in his tone.

Brutality was the horrifying physical counterpoint to the rabble-rousing hatred the Nazi press spewed out with its search for scapegoats and empty patriotic rhetoric. She had met that unctuous little Goebbels at some gathering and scolded him about it. He had merely leered at her and pointed out that such things were not meant for a woman of her calibre.

Bettina stirred the thin soup in her bowl. Who would have thought their hard-fought struggle for a just democracy would have led to this? She would have welcomed a little censorship to still those braying voices. No, she musn't think that. Bettina fingered the coolness of her necklace with hot fingers. Still, when she read that woman's rightful place was as a preserver of the biological inheritance, of the unadulterated Aryan blood line, that the women's rights movement was a symptom of degeneracy and an invention, like democracy, like parliamentarianism, of the syphilitic Jewish intellect, she wished that there was something called liberal censorship.

Normally, she could put some of this nonsense down to the mere yapping of illiterate hotheads, no more significant than the ranting of loonies on the corner soap-box. But today she had a rare presentiment of disaster.

Beads of perspiration gathered on her brow.

'Are you all right, Mutti?' Max, ever sensitive to her moods, was pouring her a glass of water. 'You look a bit pale.'

'I'm all right, dear, thank you. It's just a little warm in here.' She tried a smile.

'It's because it's so crowded. There's no air,' Leo piped up.

Bettina looked at him, that handsome unsmiling face. She tried not to scowl. 'You could open the window then, Leo,' she said in an even voice. 'And I'll excuse you and little Leo from table, as soon as you've had enough to eat, if you're feeling cramped.'

'Walter, not Leo. We've decided he's to be Walter.'

She barely managed to contain her irritation. Yet she musn't take out her anger on Leo. She watched him cross the room, watched his long-legged grace, his air of carrying out an important mission and almost smiled. He was behaving better than she had hoped, had even taken their latest arrival out into the garden with him. And she could understand his unwillingness to share his room. It was his *general* lack of generosity which irked her, his air of superiority towards all these hapless children. Still he did well at school, had glowing reports. Bettina shrugged.

No, it was what Klaus had told her last night which was at the core of her current rage. A rage at once so hot and so helpless that it brought a paralysing depression in its train. Klaus was thinking of resigning his post at the Institute, had been brought to the point where he felt he could do nothing else but resign unless he were to turn his research to purposes which were anathema to him.

It was that which she felt with the force of a physical blow. Intelligent men, men she respected, conniving to pervert science, the pursuit of pure knowledge, and turning it to distorted ends. It was as if the whole fabric of her being, her hopes, were being undermined in that single act. For the universities to contain almost twice as many Nazis as the rest of the population was a statistic which made her bow her head in shame.

Over the last years Klaus had been carrying out research into brain pathology. Now a new head of department had arrived at the laboratory. He was a political appointee and he was putting pressure on Klaus to focus on the difference between Jewish and Aryan brains, in order to pinpoint the biological roots of degeneracy and hereditary psychopathic signs. The perversion of it shook her. The racial hygienists were winning.

Bettina pushed her chair too noisily back from the table. 'Corinne, will you see to the little ones with Martha? I need a walk.'

Corinne glanced up at her sullenly. 'But I wanted to have a talk with you.'

'It can wait an hour, my dear, can't it? Then my head will be clearer.'

The girl nodded.

Bettina looked at her for a moment. She suspected what Corinne wanted to talk to her about, had thought she had noticed a slight swelling of breasts and waistline. But she had held back from doing anything. That too was unlike her.

'Shall I join you for a bit, Mutti?' Max was looking at her anxiously.

Bettina nodded.

They walked silently away from the house, into the park where the crocuses had begun to show their plump heads. She could feel Max waiting patiently for her to speak.

'Your father is under pressure,' she said at last and hurried to explain.

'The bastards,' Max muttered when she had finished. 'The stupid fascist bastards. How is Klaus taking it?' He turned a worried face to her. For years they had talked about Klaus as if he were an innocent who needed their special care.

'As well as can be expected,' Bettina murmured. 'We'll have to pull in our belts a little more, if it comes to it.'

'He has to fight them. He has to. We'll help. Write articles, get a petition going.' Max was adamant.

'Go and talk to him. It'll give him courage.'

'Okay.' He squared his shoulders, grinned at her.

She watched him walk swiftly away, thrilled as always that this young man with the furrowed brow and deep-set grey eyes, who now towered over her, with whom she could discuss anything and always expect an intelligent, considered reply, was her son. She had that to be grateful for, at least, Bettina thought, the tears suddenly clutching at her eyes. And that, after all, was a great deal.

With sure fingers, Klaus Eberhardt sketched the anatomy of a bee for the children's nature books: the striped fuzzy body, itself almost the shape of a hive, the many-faceted eyes, the spindly legs with their curved hair baskets for carrying pollen, the long nectar-sipping tongues, the fragile wings.

As he sketched, he half listened to his son's impassioned voice, his strategies for fighting the faculty, the university, the Nazi ideologues. It was his tone that he heard more clearly than anything else, that heated, fervent tone which reminded him, which demanded things of him he no longer had the strength for, had never really had the strength for.

Klaus had cut himself off from the jangle of politics after the Munich uprising, had had to, like a convalescent whose steps are sure within the periphery of the rest home, but teeter as soon as that boundary is transgressed. It wasn't that he didn't see. He could see over the fence clearly enough. But the very seeing struck him with terror and the leap across the perimeter would blind him permanently, forcing him to crawl dumbly on all fours, aware of nothing but the difficulty of traversing the ground.

Bettina understood. Understood his fear of the fires, the bounding passions. They had never been so close, their extended nightly conversations where the world was sifted and analysed and ordered, as important to her, he sensed, as they were to him. And she had taken an interest in his work in these last years.

But now the perimeter fence was drawing closer and closer, its barbs thrusting into the cool sheltered space of his laboratory. Soon they would prick into his home. It had already started. His son was asking him to enter the fray, to do battle for what he believed in, the integrity of his work.

Klaus focused in on Max's urgent tones, waited for him to pause, then turned to his son a little sadly. 'I'll do my best, Max. I've never been a hero, will never be one, you know.'

Max looked at him solemnly for a moment. 'All I wanted you to understand is that you're not alone. Lots of us are with you.'

Klaus examined that young earnest face. 'Thank you, Max.' He put his hand on his son's shoulder. 'That helps. Thank you very much.'

If Bettina had reason to be grateful for Max's sensitivity over the next weeks, she had equal reason to be grateful to Thomas Sachs. He came that Sunday afternoon, as he had come regularly over the years for a chat and coffee. Even though they no longer slept together. Even though he now had a wife and child of his own.

She told him the news as soon as they had retired to her study.

For a moment, he didn't say anything, merely lit a cigarette and paced. 'And you're worried that he'll crack, aren't you, Bettina?' He turned to her at last.

'That too,' she murmured.

He sat back in the armchair and crossed his legs. 'You know, I was rummaging in a second-hand bookshop last week and I came across that botanical book Klaus put together. It's very good. And beautiful. I wonder if Klaus would consider coming to do some work with me, just to distract him a little. On a popular science list?'

She looked at him speculatively.

He hurried on. 'There hasn't been anything interesting since Bölsche. And we need something a little better than this accursed nonsense about the survival of the fittest. Every treatise I pick up at the moment seems bent on proving that only the ruthless, the tough, the brutal can find a chosen place in the sun. Now we have Nazi plants. And animals too.' He laughed a little grimly.

'Are you serious, Thomas? About Klaus, I mean?'

'Am I ever less than serious, Bettina?'

'Never, of course,' she smiled. 'Will you speak to him?'

He nodded, pausing to look out the window. 'I see the redoubtable Leo has decided to camp out in the garden. That's quite a tent he's putting up there.'

Bettina followed the line of his gaze. 'He doesn't like sharing his room. So he's planning to brave the elements in protest,' she grimaced.

'It won't do him any harm.'

'No, I guess not. Less than that waffle they feed him at school, in any case.'

Thomas chuckled. 'He's still a romantic, is he? Chivalric codes and great Teutonic quests.'

'You mean I still don't understand him,' she recognized his teasing, 'whereas in fact I don't approve.'

'He's just a boy, Bettina. Adolescents need their great meanings. It makes them feel less awkward.'

'And you remember this, while I don't?'

'Perhaps,' he laughed.

'I don't know.' She didn't meet him on it. 'He makes me nervous. Max was never like that.'

'Max is decidedly your son. And wonderful for it. But don't underestimate Leo. He's talented. And he'll grow out of what you call this waffle,' Thomas grinned.

Bettina looked out of the window reflectively, saw Leo pick up some earth, show it to the little boy he had chosen to call Walter, let it trickle through his fingers on to the ground. She started suddenly, remembered. 'I hope you're right, Thomas,' she murmured, turning to meet his eyes. 'You know, I'm growing into a fretful old woman.'

'A wonderful fretful old woman,' he teased her again. 'And one of my more successful authors.'

'Only because I spent twenty minutes as a member of our ever-fluid Reichstag.'

'Time always did move quickly with you, Bettina,' he laughed. 'But never mind, they were twenty minutes of glory.'

'Will you talk to Klaus, now?'

He nodded.

'Thank you, Thomas.'

He bowed, smiled. 'The pleasure is always mine.'

Bettina watched him for a moment, thinking how lucky she was in their friendship, and that perhaps he was right not to be as troubled as she was. After all, he was younger, more in tune with the times. It was a time for youth. She turned back to look out of the window. Max was tumbling with a few little ones in the distance. The two Leos had vanished inside the tent.

She sighed. She must write to Anna, catch her up on things. They were good friends again, she and her sister. It came upon them, from time to time, this closeness, she never quite knew all the reasons why. And this was one of those times.

Bettina picked up her pen. 'Thomas says I'm a fretful old woman,' she began, 'and it's true. I'm fretting about the state of the nation, about Klaus, about Leo . . .'

By the time Anna had returned to Munich to find her sister's letter, Bettina was no longer fretting about Leo. He was away at his Easter camp, nestled comfortably beneath a firmament of stars.

He had been here for four days already with boys not only from his own group but from three others, all of them between fourteen and sixteen. And Gerhardt was the second in command of them all.

Gerhardt had remembered him – Leo had trembled to think that he might not – had greeted him with the group's customary salute and click of the heels, had added, 'Good to have you back with us, Adler.' And Leo had flushed with pleasure, had dug latrines and pounded stakes with a bright energy for the length of that first day.

Apart from the treks and the hikes, the woodlore, craft, and history periods and singing, this time his own small group and a group of older boys, ten of them in all, were seconded to a local farmer. They helped him till the land and prepare the soil, learned basic farming skills, felt the magic of embedding seeds in moist earth.

Thrilled to be away from the growing chaos of the family home, Leo revelled in the austere discipline of the group, the company of his peers, the sense of single purpose which accompanied each of their activities. Gerhardt came with them to the farm and in his presence Leo felt doubly alert, his daydreams giving way to the joy of the moment. Here, he felt, was his true home, amongst boys and men, meeting the challenge of the elements.

Yesterday, there had been a torrential downpour, and after their chores they had altered their plans and retired to the ramshackle barn for a free craft period. In the woods, Leo had found a thick oak branch which he had brought back with him for just such a moment. He had begun to carve, his hands moving as they always did, of their own volition, until the wood yielded a shape which his eye could refine. When he worked, he was totally immersed in the process, all but oblivious of what went on round him. So he had no idea how much time had passed before he became aware that someone was looking at him. He glanced up to see Gerhardt. He flushed.

'No, no. Don't let me disturb you. Carry on,' the older boy murmured. 'It's good. Very good. I can even begin to see the resemblance.'

Leo looked down at his carving and back at Gerhardt, his flush deepening. He hadn't realized it was Gerhardt's face the wood had yielded. But it had – the high cheekbones, the line of the jaw, even the small zigzag of the fencing scar, were all unmistakeable. The knife fell from Leo's hand with a clatter.

'Carry on, Adler,' Gerhardt had said more severely then and walked away.

Leo had thought he was angry. But this very morning, after breakfast, Gerhardt had asked him whether he would like to be his second tomorrow, accompany him to the market town nearby for fresh supplies. They would take the jeep, of course.

Leo had been so excited he could only nod his agreement. And he had been able to think of nothing else since, not even to concentrate on the story the old soldier was telling them now round the glowing campfire.

Usually he loved this hour, when they huddled in small groups round three adjacent fires, gazed up at twinkling stars while a voice evoked distant feats of heroism. But Oberleutnant Steinecker was almost as ancient as Klaus, and Leo's thoughts had wandered as soon as he had begun his complicated narrative of the exploits of his Freikorps group in the Baltic at the time of the Bolshevik uprising.

Leo preferred the Landsknecht stories, or tales of the Wälsung and Siegfried. But he forced himself to listen now. Something about the taking of the grand Kreuzberg Castle from the Reds. It was easier to concentrate if he imagined Gerhardt at the head of the Freikorps band, himself in the ranks. And Steinecker's voice had moved now from rumbling drone to agitated gusto.

'We surrounded the castle by night. Stealthily. The Reds didn't see us. They were busy whoring with their rifle-women, pretending to the high life. We spied them through the lighted windows, kissing, dancing, the remains of their manhood dissipated in debauchery.'

Steinecker spat loudly, his voice raised in distaste.

'So that when we began our assault at the crack of dawn, it was as easy as child's play. A few well-aimed grenades, a barrage through doors front and back. We caught them with their pants down. Thrust, stabbed, throttled with disciplined savagery. The women went wild. They grabbed the guns from their men and shot at us.' He laughed. 'But Red sluts are no match for the Freikorps. By noon, it was so quiet, we could hear the birds singing.

'The desecration those Communist swine had inflicted on one of our noblest castles was unspeakable. Everything had been plundered. Venetian mirrors were covered in excrement, baronial libraries used to feed fires. The chapel altar was defaced with obscene inscriptions, the ancient crucifix riddled with bullet holes. And worse, in the grand bedchamber, we found the countess's body, raped and bloody.' He spat again. 'Pigs.

'We paid them back in kind, never fear. Not a bed in that house did we leave without a Red whore caught in death's tenderest embrace.'

Leo suddenly felt as if he were going to be sick. He took a deep breath, looked up at the stars, blocked out the man's voice, heard it again urging them to remain undefiled, pure, strong, to shun the Communist swine, to mould themselves into the iron flower of Aryan greatness. He touched the stone he always carried in his pocket. Smooth. Hard. Soothing. Yes.

The next morning, after a hurried breakfast, he presented himself in front of Gerhardt's tent. His shirt and shorts and sweater were clean. He had tied his bandanna carefully.

'Ready, Adler?' Gerhardt addressed him curtly.

Leo nodded, followed behind him.

They set off in the muddy jeep down the track road between the towering trees. The woods behind them, the sky emerged high, clear but for a fluttering of frothy white clouds. Leo sat stiffly in his seat, keeping his eyes front, daring only to glance occasionally at Gerhardt's pale elegant hands tensed round the darker steering wheel. But as they picked up speed and left the camp behind them, Gerhardt began to chat, to ask him questions about himself, first in that curt formal voice he knew so well, and then more casually, almost as if they might be friends.

He told Leo about his engineering studies at the university, about his real love, philosophy. They exchanged musical tastes, noted books they liked. At one point, Gerhardt said, 'I noticed you didn't look too happy last night when Oberleutnant Steinecker was talking.'

'I . . . I . . .' Leo stumbled.

'These old-timers' language leaves something to be desired,' Gerhardt finished for him. 'They're a little crude for our generation. But they know how to fight. That's important. Crucial. If we're to build Germany up to her former glory.'

'Yes,' Leo murmured.

'Perhaps tomorrow, you'd like to take part in the rifle practice. It's usually reserved for the sixteen-year-olds, but we could make a special exception in your case. You look tall enough, strong enough.'

Leo felt Gerhardt's eyes flicker over him, assess. An unseemly flush rose to his face. He turned towards the open countryside. 'I'd like that very much,' he said in as even a voice as he could muster, his pulse fluttering wildly in pride.

Ancient beamed houses and a spired church clustered round the busy market square in the little town, giving its inhabitants the air of characters in some medieval painting. In the centre of the square stood a fountain overseen by a painted saint, two buckets hoisted on a bar over his shoulders. A water deity, Leo thought, examining the carving.

'Do you think you could do that?' Gerhardt followed the line of his gaze.

'Perhaps.' Leo was shy.

'But you'll finish my head first, won't you? You can give it to me as a birthday present.'

'May I?' Leo met his eyes.

'Of course.' Gerhardt was suddenly gruff. 'Come on. To work.'

Leo followed him mutely as they went from stall to stall, their sacks growing heavy with provisions, only to be replaced by another set from the jeep which they had left at the edge of the town. At one stall a buxom young woman with curling hair laughed up at them. 'You're not from here, are you? But you'll come to our dance tonight.' She wriggled her hips provocatively. 'It's in the Great Hall.'

Gerhardt walked quickly away. 'Women,' he said disdainfully under his breath. 'All they think of is dancing and . . .' He scowled, looked away. 'Let's get some lunch and head back.'

But by the time they emerged again from the Stuberl's dark interior, the square had been transformed. All signs of the market had vanished and in its place in front of the squat town hall, there stood only a platform.

Then, from the four streets leading into the square as the town clock struck two, they heard the roll of drums. Within minutes the place was a sea of red banners, bold with swastikas and the bright heraldry of the Nazi Party. The men, their chins thrust forward, their uniforms impeccable, marched six abreast, meeting their opposite numbers in the centre of the square with choreographed exactitude as if they were taking part in some well-rehearsed medieval pageant.

Leo looked on awestruck. He joined in the roar of the crowd as the speaker mounted the platform, saw Gerhardt lift his arm in salute, raised his as well, listened to the pounding of words, honour, Fatherland, strength, purity, shame, Communists, Jews, corruption.

Just as the second speaker was about to mount the platform, Gerhardt tapped him on the shoulder. 'If we don't leave now, we'll never get back. Don't forget to salute everyone on the way, or someone may decide to persuade us.'

In the jeep, Gerhardt said to him, 'So, you've joined the Party?'

Leo shook his head. It had never occurred to him. Parties, politics, were what Aunt Bettina and Max talked about non-stop. He was interested in deeper things.

'I'm going to join. Soon. They're the best we've got. The party of the young, the future. A bit crude, but if the likes of us join them, we'll sort things out. And they're on the right track. They understand the old Germany, the special spiritual needs of our people, our willingness to sacrifice ourselves for the German ideal. Our heroic destiny.'

'Yes,' Leo murmured. He looked at Gerhardt's profile. It was suddenly as if he were hearing his own vague thoughts put into words.

'And they're not afraid to use force. They understand authority, the power of leadership.' Gerhardt made the jeep leap forward. 'None of this sentimental nonsense about saving the weak. In a dense forest only the strongest saplings survive to reach the light, eh, Leo, what do you say? That's the only way to build a great nation. That's what our Bund is all about, too, loyalty, obedience, strength.'

Leo nodded. He felt his heart racing. He would always be loyal to Gerhardt, strong for him, with him.

'Good,' Gerhardt murmured. Suddenly he started to sing, his voice rich and mellow over the noise of the jeep. Leo recognized the heroic strains of Siegfried: Siegfried, holding his precious Notung in hand:

> 'Notung! Notung!
> Sword of my need!
> You are fixed again firm in the hilt.
> Snapped in two,
> once more you are whole;
> no stroke again shall ever smash you.
> You broke when my father
> was doomed to death;
> his living son
> forged you again:
> for me now you laugh and shine,
> and your gleaming edge will be keen.'

They were driving through a small village now and Gerhardt had slowed the car.

'Look.' He pointed excitedly to the crest of the hill above and stopped the car short on the embankment.

Leo stared in fascination. Coming towards them he could see a group of men, boys perhaps, carrying a strange-looking person clad from top to toe in alder and hazel leaves and water flowers. His head was completely covered by a pointed cap on top of which perched a nosegay of peonies. His arms were held aloft by two young men, each carrying a drawn sword. As they drew closer, Leo noted that they all had drawn swords and for a moment he was afraid. They looked so bizarre.

'It must be a *Pfingsten* rite,' Gerhardt whispered with something like awe. 'Whitsun, but ancient. Pagan. I've read about it. Let's go after them. The others will understand if we're late because of this.'

He leapt out of the car, Leo close behind him. They followed the strange procession towards the village houses. At each house, the youths banged at the door, called for gifts. Instead, from an eave window, Leo saw buckets of water poured on the leaf-clad man. The wetter he got, the more the youths cheered until at the end of the village he was thoroughly drenched. Then they carried him to the brook which ran through the fields at the backs of the houses and stopped by a little bridge.

The whole village seemed to be gathered now as the youths waded into the water. When the leaf-clad man was in up to his waist, one of the youths perched on the bridge, lifted his sword and pretended to slash his head off. The cheering reached fever pitch.

Leo felt Gerhardt's hand on his shoulder. 'They've killed him now, killed off the old tree spirit, the dying god, to make room for the new,' he whispered into his ear.

Leo glanced at him, saw the excitement in that austere, aristocratic face, the flare of the nostrils. The hand was still on his shoulder.

'And we are the new,' Leo said, gazing into the distance. He wasn't sure whether he felt or imagined the answering squeeze on his shoulder. Whichever the case, he felt the sap rising in him, as if he too were a young tree god.

That night his dreams were wild. He was in a dense wood, a bold hero, a fearless Siegfried in search of the corrupt dragon god he would displace. The birds spoke to him in a threnody of song, telling him the location of the evil treasure horde. He held his trusty sword, his Notung, aloft.

Suddenly the trees were metamorphosed into knights, their banners bold swastikas, blood red. They urged him on, cheered. Forward. If he didn't slay the dragon, he would never be able to free his friend, his wounded leader encased in a wall of stone in a jagged cliff surrounded by fire. But he wasn't afraid.

He marched on and then he saw him: on the other side of the river, the grizzly creature, his tail a scaly mass, his mouth a cavern. And beyond, the mountain surrounded by fire. If he could lure the dragon to plunge into the depths, the water would put out the fire.

He called a challenge to him, raised his sword high, higher, jumped into the depths, heard the dragon plunge. He cried out his leader's name, 'Gerhardt, Gerhardt,' and struck, stabbed hard and again and again.

The creature writhed madly. Black blood oozed out of it. In the distance, he heard Gerhardt's answering call, pure, sweet, like the notes of a horn. So sweet. But suddenly, he couldn't move. The blood was pouring out of him too, sticky, clammy, imprisoning him in the water. He was drowning. And the men were laughing, the trees were laughing.

Leo woke with a start. The five other boys in his tent were giggling, staring at him curiously.

'That was some nightmare, Adler. You woke us all up.'

'Sorry,' Leo murmured.

'Look, look, he's wet his sleeping bag,' the small runt-like boy, who was the only one in the group he had always disliked, pointed. There was a leer on his face.

Leo looked down at his bag aghast. It was true. There was the tell-tale stain. Shame covered him.

'What do you expect from Jew scum? They're bedwetters all.'

'What did you say?' Leo clenched his fists.

'You heard me, Jew scum. Adler's a Jewish name, isn't it?' the boy taunted him.

With a single gesture, Leo leapt from his bed and landed a fierce punch on the boy's face. He had only a second to see his look of surprise before he launched another. With this one, the boy fell backward, hit his head on a tent pole. There was blood oozing from his nose. Leo pounced on him. The punching felt good, so good, he could throttle him, but the others were clawing at him, holding him back.

'You'll get sent home, Adler.'

'You know it's not allowed.'

'I don't care,' Leo said. But he let go, fought to restrain the tears which now threatened to flood his eyes. Carefully he rolled up the wet sleeping bag, packed his few possessions methodically into his sack. He wouldn't let his glance fall on the boy who lay sprawled in the corner. Or on anyone else.

No sooner had he finished than Junger, their local group head, was upon them. He stared at Leo. 'I'll deal with you later,' he muttered, then rushed to tend to the injured boy and see him off to the infirmary.

Leo waited, but not for long. Junger was soon back.

'Now what's all this, Adler? I want an explanation. A good one, or you'll be sent home. You know the rules.'

'I hit him,' Leo said.

'Why?'

Leo shrugged, was mute. He couldn't bring himself to repeat the scene.

Junger stared at him. 'It'll be a black mark on your record, Adler.'

Still Leo didn't speak. He felt the boys staring at him. On the ground he noticed some ants scurrying. He was tempted to crush them. But he didn't move.

'Well, Adler, another minute and I'll be forced to send you home.'

'I had to hit him,' Leo murmured, then fell silent again.

The minute grew into an eternity. At last Junger said, 'Right, Adler. That's it. Do I put you on kitchen duty until your parents come and fetch you or will you make your own way home?'

'My own way,' Leo mumbled.

'You've got money for the fare?'

He nodded.

'Bernfeld and Schmitt will walk you to the station. You'll have an explanation ready for me when I'm back in Berlin. Understood?'

Leo nodded again, anxious now to be off, terrified that he might bump into Gerhardt if they didn't go quickly.

But they managed to leave the camp grounds without any confrontations. That bit of luck, at least, was on his side.

On the train to Berlin, he sat and stared blindly out of the window. He would never see Gerhardt again. Never see any of them again. For a moment, he thought he could smell his sullied sleeping bag on the rack above him. He would throw it out, burn it.

But now his cheeks burned instead, with shame. That little runt. He would have liked to punch him until his whole body sagged, punched all the breath out of him. How dare he call him Jew scum?

He would never tell about the incident or repeat the accusation, never tell Junger. The whole thing was too demeaning. The other boys would keep their mouths shut as well, if they knew what was good for them. But what if they told? What if Adler *was* a Jewish name? He suddenly sat up straighter. The thought had never occurred to him before.

Leo knew nothing about his father, except that he had died before his birth, and that he was Austrian. He had always thought of himself as a member of the Austrian aristocracy, a von Leinsdorf, like his mother, his aunt. Bettina had told him about the von Leinsdorfs. He was proud of them, their closeness to the Emperor. There were generals amongst them. He had dreamt about that when he was younger. But his father? What if he really were Jewish scum? It would be just like his mother to inflict that too on him. The blood taint.

By the time Leo reached Berlin, he was racked with confusion. On top of it all, he would have to explain his presence to everyone. They weren't expecting him for another week. He should run away from home. But where would he go? To his mother who would ask him countless questions, who would attempt to pity him, to bury his head in her bosom? No. Berlin was preferable to that.

It was dark by the time he reached the house. The little ones, thankfully, would be asleep. He glanced at his watch: nine o'clock. With luck everyone would be out except Klaus and old Martha. He could cope with them. He squared his shoulders and turned the key in the lock.

Everything was quiet. Leo made his way softly up the stairs. On the first landing, he could see a light coming from Bettina's study door. Should he slink past or confront her? No, he wasn't a coward. He would see her now.

He paused at the door before knocking and, with that old habit of which he was now ashamed, listened for a moment. Bettina was talking as always. And the answering murmur could only be Klaus. He raised his hand and then hearing his name, dropped it, listened more carefully.

'Yes. About Leo. Thomas made me think of something the other day. I forgot to tell you. He said his little sculptures were really good and I was looking out of the window at Leo and suddenly it struck me. Johannes. He reminds me of Johannes. I know Anna's always said Bruno was his father, but at the time, way back then during the war, she wasn't so certain. And now all that talent, I just thought . . .'

'Soon you'll be telling me that Max . . .' He couldn't hear the rest of Klaus's mumble, only Bettina's, 'Don't be silly.'

They were silent for a moment.

Leo stared at the door in a tumult of confusion. Was Bettina implying that Johannes was his real father? She could only mean Johannes Bahr, his mother's husband. But . . .

Leo slunk away. He could hardly remember Bahr, hadn't seen him in years, only vaguely remembered as a small boy being afraid of him. He never came to the house now. Still, if Johannes was his father, then Adler wasn't. And Bahr wasn't Jewish as far as he knew. A few weeks back one of his teachers had quoted a famous jurist called Bahr. And his mother had told him that Johannes had been a soldier in the war, had earned medals.

Yes, that was it. A plan began to formulate itself in Leo's mind as he softly climbed the stairs to his room. He would go to Munich. Confront Bahr. Ask him. He would steal away at the crack of dawn. Nobody would know he had gone, or had even been back.

Leo opened the door to his room, saw a nightlight revealing a little tousled head peering above blankets. He had forgotten Walter. He put a finger to his lips, closed the door silently.

'Shhh, no one's to know that I'm here,' he whispered. 'And you're not to tell that I've been, okay?'

The boy looked at him with frightened eyes.

'I'm just going to sleep a little, change, and I'm leaving again first thing. Understood?'

The boy nodded.

'Promise.'

'Yes,' he squealed.

'Good, it'll be our secret. Look, here's one of my best stones to seal it.' He took one of the stones from his table and handed it to the boy. 'It's magic. It'll bring you luck if you keep your promise. You'll never have to be frightened again. Right?'

The boy gazed at the stone distrustfully, then, with a sudden smile, tucked it under his pillow. 'Okay,' he whispered.

'Good.'

As silently as he could Leo opened the cupboard door, threw his rucksack into it, got out of his clothes. Then he rummaged in his desk. He needed an address. There was a letter from his mother somewhere. He hadn't answered it yet and thus hadn't thrown it away. He remembered that it had borne a Munich postmark, not the usual Seehafen one. Yes, here it was. Leo tucked it into his jacket pocket, took all the money out of his savings box and put that in the pocket as well. Then he clambered into bed.

'Night, sleep tight,' he murmured to the small boy whose eyes had never left him. 'And remember our secret.'

Leo left at the crack of dawn the next day, before the house had stirred. Once again he had a sense of being a hero on a quest. After all, Siegfried had set out to find out who his father was. His mind raced ahead of a journey which seemed interminable. He hadn't taken account of how far Munich was, how long it would take him to get there. And by the time he arrived, it was late at night and he was too tired to think of confronting anybody.

He looked round the station and tried to think sensibly. A youth hostel. That was what he needed. They wouldn't ask questions. He found a policeman who guided him to an information desk and eventually, exhausted, and having lost himself in a maze of streets, he located the hostel on a cobbled back street.

In the morning, he woke with a sense of being lost. He couldn't remember where he was, and when he did finally remember he thought he must be mad. What would he say to Johannes Bahr? And would the man be able to answer? Would he know whether he was his father and if he knew wouldn't he have told him so years ago? Perhaps his mother had kept it secret.

Leo's mind reeled with the untold possibilities, with duplicities. He covered his head with his pillow. Didn't fatherhood mean anything to her? No, she was just a stupid woman, had no respect. Like Bettina, the two of them the same really, despite all the surface differences. They had no respect, cared not a hoot for men, wanted to trample them. Like those wild Red women old Steinecker had talked about. Why, just look at Klaus, what Bettina had done to him, ground him down.

From a distance he heard the wake-up bell ringing. His cheeks were hot. Slowly he dragged himself out of the bed, went to splash cold water on his face. He must pull himself together. He had come this far and he wouldn't give up now. He remembered that horrid little runt telling him Adler was a Jewish name. He squared his shoulders. No, he wouldn't be afraid. Some food. That was what he needed. He hadn't had a proper meal since the day before he had left the camp. Food would set him right.

He looked at his face in the small bathroom mirror, saw the clean lines, the square jaw, the shock of gold-blond hair. Gerhardt had said he looked like Parsifal. He must remember that, even if he never saw Gerhardt again. Couldn't see him unless he cleared his name. He took a deep breath, fought back the tug of tears. Boys didn't cry. They didn't cry.

He found a café, scoffed two buns hungrily and tossed down two glasses of milk. His money was running short. He had to be careful, but he desperately wanted another bun. He had one. After all, he could always ask Johannes Bahr for money, if need be, whatever his paternal status. The thought calmed him.

By the time Leo had located the address on the crumpled envelope, it was almost noon. It occurred to him that there might not be anyone in. That made him even braver. He crossed the small courtyard with long strides and then, on the instructions of an old man who was sitting there, sunning himself in a rickety chair, climbed the stairs in twos, till he reached the top of the building. The door to the apartment was ajar. He hesitated, knocked nevertheless, and when there was no response let himself in. There was a long dark corridor with a multitude of closed doors. At the end of it, one was open to a blaze of light.

Leo walked softly towards the light. When he reached it, for a moment, he felt blinded. All he could see were huge leering shapes jumping off the walls. Then, from the far end of the vast room, he heard a high-pitched laugh.

'We have a visitor, I think, Johannes.'

A woman was standing stark naked on a pedestal, her breasts pendulous, her heavy shanks blotchy in the sunlight.

'One of your pretty boys,' another woman laughed. She was sprawled over an old easy chair, her legs parted, so that Leo could clearly see her private parts where the tulle of her gown spread. He averted his eyes. There was a huge dog at her feet, a mastiff, its great mouth agape.

'Invite him in,' a third voice said. 'I'm tired. I could do with a pretty boy.'

He looked up from the dog to see a woman and a man lying naked on a crumpled sheet on a large tabletop, no, not a woman and a man, two women, their limbs and hair intertwined.

'Come in, pretty boy.' The seated woman beckoned to him, her mouth parted lasciviously.

'Quiet,' a man's voice barked.

Somewhere a baby began to squall. 'And now there goes that brat again. Do something, Veronica.'

One of the women on the table leapt off, came towards Leo as if she were not wearing only her smile, lifted a grey rumpled bundle from a sofa and stuck it to her breast.

The man in the centre of the room threw the brush he had been holding noisily to the floor. He veered round, stared at Leo with great bleary eyes. 'What do you want here?' he bellowed.

Leo stood as if transfixed.

'Well? Have they sent you here to pose? What is it? Have you lost your tongue?' The man came towards him threateningly.

Leo turned and ran, ran down the long, grey, corridor. He could hear them laughing behind him.

'You scared him away, you old monster.'

'Now look what you've done.'

'Such a pretty boy, too.'

Then the man's voice, shouting after him, 'Wait a minute, wait a minute.' He was running to catch up with him.

Leo raced down the stairs.

'You're not Leo, are you by any chance?' he heard him call, as he reached the courtyard. But he carried on running, ran until he could run no more. And then ran a little further, as if his life depended on it.

No, his thoughts raced, no father there. Just a filthy debauched monster, a canker on the pure white body of the Fatherland. He lost himself in a maze of streets, finally stumbled on the station, took the first train north, any train. He had to get out of this city.

As the train pulled out of the station with a great puff of smoke, Leo closed his eyes. He would wipe that scene from his mind, expunge it, tear it out shred by shred. God, how dirty and defiled he felt. He wanted to jump into a cold mountain stream, whip his body into cleanliness.

How could his mother be married to that monster? Suddenly his stomach heaved. He ran to the toilet, retched, felt his insides rise up through his mouth. He clung on to the wall of the lurching train until he could stand no more. Then, like a wounded animal, he dragged himself back to his seat, huddled into a corner, closed his eyes.

He didn't know quite how he got back to Berlin. He remembered changing trains twice, sitting on dark empty platforms, having to fight away an old drunk with foul breath. He was so tired now, so utterly weary, that he didn't care who saw him, didn't care about anything.

Bettina must have heard his tread for she opened the door of her study as he made his way up the stairs.

'Leo, whatever are you doing here?' She stared at him and then quickly came towards him, a look of concern on her face. She felt his forehead. 'You're ill, Leo. You've got a temperature. They should have called us. Someone would have come to fetch you.' She put a hand on his shoulder, guided him to his room. 'Those miserable youth movement leaders. They'll kill you with their ridiculous love of strength.' She was mumbling half to herself.

Leo was too tired to answer back. He let himself be steered, let himself be tucked into his bed, let the doctor fuss over him, accepted the broth that Martha brought, lay there thinking of nothing, staring out at the familiar oak. For five days he lay there, saying nothing, simply gazing into space, dozing. Little Walter came to sit by him sometimes. One night, he even curled next to him. Leo let him. What did it matter? What did anything matter? There was nothing to live for. He didn't want to show his face at school, confront his friends. He would die like this. Quietly. In his bed. The old oak his only comfort. And little Walter beside him.

He had given him back his stone, tucked it into his hand and whispered, 'Magic'.

On the sixth day, Bettina came up to his room and handed him two letters, before taking his temperature. 'You're mending,' she pronounced. 'Are you going to tell me what happened?'

Leo stared out of the window, felt her shrug.

'Well, if you ever want to, I'm here.'

He fingered the envelopes, tore one open randomly. His mother. Almost, he crumpled it up, but the sight of Johannes's name whet his curiosity.

> Johannes tells me that you may have visited the studio. He isn't sure. But if it was you, he wants you to know that it would have been better to have forewarned him. Then he could have welcomed you more adequately. And if it was you – this person who looked like a younger version of me with

> short hair – he's very sorry if he frightened you away. I told him it was unlikely, both because you would have let me know and because you're frightened of nothing. Am I right? I'll be in Berlin soon.

Leo tore the letter into a hundred little pieces and threw them into his waste-bin before opening the second letter. His heart lurched painfully. Gerhardt. He had never written to him before, but there was his signature in bold black ink at the bottom of the page.

> Leo,
>
> I have finally managed to extricate the story behind your sudden departure from your mates. You were right to use your fists. Honour must be preserved at all costs. And sometimes force is the only way to strike sense into the lesser representatives of the Fatherland. Especially little lying runts.
>
> You left the carving of me behind. I shall bring it back to Berlin. Perhaps you would like to finish it. If so, come and see me at my rooms. I can also then show you the book which tells the *Pfingsten* story.
>
> This was my last Easter camp in the Jugendbund. I am glad to have been able to spend a few of its days with you. I hope we will meet again.
>
> Yours,
>
> Gerhardt

Leo leapt from his bed in jubilation. Stretched, touched his toes ten times in rapid succession. Gerhardt understood. Gerhardt understood. There was no need for fathers. A Fatherland was enough. No need for mothers really either. Mother Nature would do. The oak, the dense woods, the soil in which he had so carefully embedded those seedlings. Only brothers were necessary. Brothers in spirit, like Gerhardt. He pulled a piece of paper from his desk and began, carefully, to pen a reply.

FOURTEEN

1934

JOHANNES STOPPED SHORT at the top of the staircase which led to his studio and stared. There was a crimson swastika on the door, freshly painted, dripping like blood.

So it had happened at last. The inevitable.

For a moment, he felt a rush of exhilaration. He had known they would come sooner or later. For almost eighteen months now, he had anticipated the event daily, so that the anticipation itself had taken on a kind of monotony. And in his bones, the period of anticipation had been even longer, dating back to the time of Leo's visit, when he had seen the shocked eyes of Anna's son on him; perhaps even to the period when his father had had him confined to the madhouse.

What else was it that he had railed against, warned about these last years but this very thing: the brutal intrusion of the long tentacles of authority into every aspect, even the most private, of one's life.

And even now he could turn back, flee, for a little while longer. But the door drew him like a siren.

He paused at the threshold, listened. Everything was quiet. Perhaps they had already gone. Shame, that, to delay the ultimate moment. He pushed open the door.

Devastation. The long corridor to his studio was littered with debris. Ripped clothes and books rent from their bindings lay in heaps, battled with shards of glass, the innards of mattresses, old photographs, shattered crockery. Walking was like picking his way through the wreckage of his own life. He retrieved a photo of Anna, the remains of a notebook. Everywhere there was a stink – of urine, of the sweaty excitement of male bodies.

The studio itself was even worse. He leaned against the wall, feeling his stomach rise into his throat. Paintings, drawings, had been torn from their racks, his figures blotched by tins of colour, cut, split, sliced, hacked.

Not just random vandalism but carnage. Murder. And rape, particularly rape. It was the women who had suffered most, women he had loved, held, listened to. Their bare bodies now lay spliced, kicked, defaced, defecated on. He could almost see the vandals at it, smell them in the act, the collective sexual frenzy of it, their tawdry little consciences dissolved in the name of something greater, something pure, something German. Something that was summed up in the name of Hitler.

His signature was everywhere in the epithets they had scrawled on walls, on canvases. Scum, Degenerate, Swine, Polluter, Traitor, Jew-lover. That too. His portrait of his dealer bore the words '*Entarteter Jude*' Degenerate Jew: he had effectively been disembowelled.

And they would happily have disembowelled him too, had he been here when they arrived. Or marched him off to one of their camps, which meant the same thing.

Suddenly a laugh shook him, a loud hollow laugh which reverberated eerily through the room. It was only two years since the little corporal had ascended to power and already he had happily installed himself inside people's all-too-willing minds, their most private of thoughts. What were those giant rallies, after all, but big, really big, political erections. And it was so much nicer to have thought taken care of from the outside, replaced by uplifting slogans, while one energetically went about the business of the state.

The pageantry and the fires helped, of course. Those great cleansing pyres, larger than the bonfires of the Hitler Youth which one stumbled over at every turn in the countryside, but in the same purifying spirit. First the Reichstag – blamed on the Reds, it went without saying – but did one after all really need a place where all those impure thoughts were spoken and debated?

And then those lovely medieval pyres, in city and town centres across the country, where scores of those vile, impure books written by degenerates and Jews were burned. Soon to be followed by their makers, no doubt, which would occasion even greater pageantry.

The little corporal, now their Führer, had always shadowed Johannes like a nightmare he couldn't shed, and now the very images of his nightmares had been taken over, emptied of their meaning and perverted into terrifying use.

All his artist friends had been ousted from their teaching posts, and had had their pictures removed from the museums. Many had left the country, or were planning to leave. Others – writers, political journalists – had disappeared into the hellholes of Columbiahaus or Oranienburg.

He had no post to be ousted from, so they had paid him this little visit instead. And helped themselves to some pictures, he could see, as well as to the joy of destruction in the name of the purification of the race. Some forms of degeneracy, after all, could be sold abroad to swell the coffers of the state. And they would stop at nothing to swell those coffers. Impure publishing houses could be swallowed up for gain, as well as the property of those other degenerates, the Jews.

Oh yes, he was well aware of the cynical tricks performed in the name of Aryan purification, had read the little corporal's monumentally odious tract way back in 1925 when it had first appeared. It was all spelled out there. Though not in his wildest imaginings had Johannes thought it could so quickly come to this.

The pure Aryan blood line. The great Nordic race. He laughed again. Well, unless his mother had not been telling his father the whole truth, there was no purer scion of the Aryan line than he. And yet here was his work being proclaimed impure, degenerate, unnatural. With the result that he would soon inevitably be naturally selected out of nature's natural course by a few of nature's trusty Aryan superthugs. It was wonderful the uses to which nature could be put, the way it could be called upon to legitimize any old nonsense.

He had been guilty of it himself, of course, all those years ago when he still nurtured a social hope. That was why he was always pursued by this dastardly sense that the little corporal was a perverted echo of himself, almost his father's better son. Oh yes, he too had called on nature – wild, rampant, rich, sexual, in his case – to signal his dissatisfaction with the straitjacket of the culture in which he lived, to designate his hope of freedom. Now he knew better, knew that the only naturalness in man was that he was born and died. Between those two poles, everything else was his own creation.

Johannes perched on a stool and looked at the devastation around him, at last registering the significance of it, realizing that he would never set foot again in this space in which, for the last ten years, he had worked as an artist. Rupturing old forms, trying to breathe new life into the frame.

And Hitler was an artist who had moved beyond the frame. That was the hideous, tragic, rub of it. Moved beyond even that tired old adage of living one's life with the controlled intensity of art – something that was dangerous enough, as he himself knew too well.

All of Germany was the canvas on which Hitler enacted his vision, execrable as it was, but a vision nonetheless. And like the omnipotent artist, he set out to control every detail in his bloated canvas, every effect, every figure, fashioning vast orchestrated pageants, regalia, inventing a heraldry of muscled heroes and sentimentalized peasants, brutally excising what jarred with his dream – all in order to create a *total* work of art.

To combine power, the ability to control lives, with the single monomaniacal vision of the artist was, Johannes shuddered to realize, to create hell.

As for him, kicking a bit of debris from beneath his feet, he no longer had either any visions or even the power to wield his brush to any effect.

He stopped in front of the cracked mirror over which the word 'degenerate' had been scrawled and looked at himself. The scowl, the lines of weariness, the bloodshot eyes. Yes, perhaps the word was right, but not in the way they meant it. In these last years, the only thing that had propelled his unsaleable work was hatred, an attempt to rub their noses in the shit that Germany had become. And the work was bad, empty, against the grain, a sterile recycling of old forms with only venom to give them life. There was no hope left in him. The ribbon of road which had once held at least the glimmer of a horizon had long disappeared.

And now there was the brute fact of the devastation around him. It was the signal he had been waiting for. Everything was finally over – the last of his nine lives at last trickling to its end.

Strangely, it filled him with relief. He suddenly felt lightheaded, carefree, calm, as if the Cassandra-like burden of the years had been lifted from his shoulders. He was free at last.

Grinning, he unearthed a brush from the rubble, a half-spilled tin of paint. With quick deft strokes, he covered the large glass with a caricature: a vast figure of Hitler, floating in the skies, crouched, defecating; beneath him, a multitude, their arms and eyes raised, their caps lifted to receive his gift of excrement. Above Hitler, he wrote the words, 'Aryan Purity'. Below the crowd, 'The New Man'. Then incorporating the scrawl, 'Degenerate', into his signature, he wrote in Latin, 'the last work of Johannes Bahr, degenerate painter, December 23 1934'.

With a smile on his face, Johannes made his way from the room. Half way to the door, he turned back. He had altogether forgotten the reason for his coming here. Was there anything he could salvage to bring to Berlin? The sheaves of drawings in the desk had been scattered, torn, bore the imprints of boots. He found one that was relatively unscathed, rolled it under his arm. The last thing either Klaus or Bettina would want in their home was another work by a degenerate, even as a Christmas present. But it was for Anna he had come here and he didn't want her to ask any questions, to know of this yet.

He raced down the stairs. It had stopped snowing. The old keeper was sweeping a path through the courtyard.

'They came before, Herr Bahr. Six of them. In uniform.'

'I noticed, Hans.'

'I couldn't stop them. I'm sorry, Herr Bahr.'

'I won't be back, Hans. Take whatever you want. Though they haven't left much intact.'

'I told them you had gone. Perhaps to Vienna.' He grinned toothlessly.

'Thank you, Hans. And here,' Johannes pulled some bills from his pocket, 'buy yourself some Christmas spirit. We have to drink for the Führer, eh,' he winked mischievously, 'since he doesn't. Take care of yourself and the old woman, Hans.'

He lifted his hat, waved, hurried down the cobbled street, turned a corner hastily as he saw a group of uniformed youths marching towards him.

They were everywhere now, these young men, brazen in the anonymity of their uniforms, bold in a brutality sanctioned from above. There would be a war soon, though it was denied officially. Why else all these uniforms? Policing was only the first part of the reason. His father would have approved of the policing. But now it was the young policing the old. The new men and new women working for a new Germany. Strength through joy. Hard, tough, quick. Iron youths with a steely inwardness. Blood and soil. The slogans paraded through his mind to the sound of their boots with hollow inanity.

Yes, they were clever, these Nazis, taking over the young, promising, promising, filling them with high purpose and blind obedience. What was it Nietzsche had written about young men? With an effort he could almost remember it verbatim.

> When one considers how much the energy of young men needs to explode, one is not surprised that they decide for this cause or that without being at all subtle or choosy. What attracts them is the sight of the zeal that surrounds a cause – the sight of the burning fuse and not the cause itself. Subtle seducers therefore know the art of arousing expectations of an explosion while making no effort to furnish reasons for their cause: reasons are not what wins over such powder kegs.

But they had made a travesty of the philosopher as well.

Still, that was no longer his concern. Nothing was any longer his concern, he reminded himself. Except to take a last look at these streets with their graceful pastel houses, the gardens. Streets he had nonetheless loved. And to spend a last few days with Anna.

Johannes glanced at his watch. He must hurry or he would be late. Anna would worry.

The train station was heavy with smoke and steam. But there she was now, pacing the platform, her hair lustrous beneath a new little toque of a hat, her eyes luminous. His heart leapt as if he were already seeing her in memory, a first time which was also a last. He raced towards her.

'I'm sorry I'm late, darling.' He took the cases from her, the brightly wrapped packages, helped her up the steps.

'I thought you weren't coming.'

'I'm here, you see. As promised. Despite the fact that we're going to Berlin,' he smiled ruefully. He knew she had thought he might not turn up at the last minute. He hardly ever went to Berlin with her. But this time was different. Bettina had summoned them both in no uncertain terms. And in any event, he wanted to make the journey now. Revisit the sites of his blighted youth.

They had their own compartment on the train and as soon as he had closed the door behind them, he turned to kiss her, slowly, luxuriantly.

She searched his face. 'What is it, Johannes?'

He chuckled, 'Am I not allowed to kiss you, Anna?'

She looked at him curiously. 'Have I ever refused you?'

'Oh, once or twice, as I remember it. But you look so delicious today in that little hat,' he held her at arm's length, examined her, helped her off with her coat, 'and this new dress.' He fingered the soft pale green wool which swirled at her hips, the clasp at the bodice. 'All in honour of your son, I gather. Not for me,' he teased.

She flushed. 'Don't be silly, Johannes.'

'I don't mind.' He sat next to her, close, breathed in the fragrance of that bright hair. 'Though he might get strange ideas if his mother looks more like a sister.'

'He's not like that, Johannes.' She met his smile this time.

'The more fool he.' He ruffled her hair. 'Do you remember what it was like at that age, all those juices stirring, taking you over?'

Anna laughed. 'Leo's a serious young man, not like you. Or me, for that matter.'

'Oh, I don't know. You know those Hitler Youth camps, like the one he went to last summer. I'm told they have sister camps. And the pregnancy rate amongst those serious young women is not altogether negligible.' He hummed a little tune:

> 'In the fields and on the heath
> I lose strength through joy.

I'm told that's the young ladies' version of the great motto. But then the Fatherland needs its babies. Babies for Hitler.'

He saw the frown settle on her face. He had promised her that there would be not a breath of politics during this trip. He knew how concerned she was about Leo, how she had convinced herself that he would grow out of what she called his Hitler nonsense, if only they didn't argue with him. He knew she was wrong, judging from his one more recent encounter with the boy he was certain was Leo – though no one had acknowledged the truth of that.

Johannes wrapped his arm round Anna, held her close.

'But we won't talk about that. Won't mention the great man again. Promise.'

Snow had started to fall again as they chugged through the countryside. Fat round flurries of flakes brightening the early evening sky, lulling them into dreaminess. Johannes stroked Anna's arm.

She turned to face him. 'You're behaving strangely, Johannes,' she mused. 'Has something happened?'

She had always been able to read him like an open book. He shook his head. 'I'm just enjoying the journey. Enjoying being with you.'

'You haven't taken anything?' she murmured.

'You know I haven't, Anna. Not for almost two years.'

Yes, it was true, Anna thought. She knew that. He hadn't taken any drugs since that last cure, when he had entered a clinic of his own accord just a few days after the boy he claimed was Leo had come to his studio. It was extraordinary how that event had affected him, like a sleepwalker who has suddenly been awakened. Nonetheless, she still occasionally worried that when Johannes wasn't with her, he might succumb. It was a habit she hadn't been able to drop, obviously more ingrained than his.

'I know,' she murmured. Suddenly she smiled, turned to meet the good fortune of his latest mood, to kiss him flirtatiously, nibble his ear, whisper into it, 'The surprise is that I've booked us into the restaurant car. While they make up our beds.'

Johannes groaned. 'And here I thought we could go to bed straightaway.' He took her face into his hands. 'Do you remember, Anna, in the old days we never used to eat. First.'

She straightened his tie, pulled him up. 'In the old days, Herr Bahr, I was always starving, but too timid to say anything.'

'The things one learns with age,' Johannes muttered.

The dining car glowed with the soft light of bronze lamps. They sat opposite each other, giggling into their wine, like children. Each new arrival occasioned a little portrait from Johannes, refined by Anna.

There was the stern suited man with exaggeratedly thick bifocals who held his menu at a vast distance from him and peered at it disgustedly. Johannes immediately dubbed him The Reich's Art Critic. There were the two plump thick-calved women sporting girlish blouses, their earnest faces scrubbed squeaky clean, bare of any trace of make-up, who Anna decided were the Führer's Rhine Maidens. 'Righteous Rhine Maidens,' Johannes corrected her. 'Soon to be in charge of the Reich breeding farm for muscled youths of little brain.'

Anna laughed, then stopped herself. 'None of this when we get to Berlin, Johannes.'

'Promise.' He looked at her woefully. 'Not in Berlin.' He laughed again. 'Look, here comes an undercover agent from the Soviet Union.'

Anna looked up to see a dark bearded man with rounded spectacles, looking shiftily from side to side.

'He's been sent to convince the German Communist Party that the Nazis are really on their side. Don't resist now and you can take over later.'

'Johannes,' Anna chided him.

'But he looks so worried that nobody believes him.' He raised his glass to her, his eyes wry. 'Why do you grow more beautiful every day, Anna?'

'It must have a great deal to do with the fact that you never wear your specs. A fact about which I should undoubtedly be grateful.'

He called the waiter and paid the bill. 'I'm going to put on my specs straightaway, Anna,' he threatened her mockingly as they walked back to their compartment, 'to carry out a thorough investigation of the damage the years have wrought.'

'You do that,' she giggled.

But when they entered the compartment with its tidily turned-back bunks and he had locked the door behind them, he took her instead into his arms. 'Anna, Anna,' he murmured, kissing her so deeply that the old swoon took her over. His fingers played over her back, her neck, making music thrum through her, the notes of the Mozart sonatas she had taken to playing again, over and over, their bubbling innocence blotting out the dissonance of the times.

She gazed into his eyes, saw his passion. Slowly she loosened his tie, unbuttoned his shirt. He was watching her, taking in every gesture, as if he were registering it. She ran her fingers over his lips.

'Do you want those specs?' she teased him clumsily.

He shook his head, the grey-flecked chestnut hair falling over his brow, giving him the dishevelled air of the rude young man she had first met all those years ago on one of the paths in Seehafen. 'I don't need them, Anna.'

He pulled her close again, loosened her dress, urging it from her shoulders so that it fell in a huddle at her feet. He stroked her bare shoulders, the silk of her slip, running his hands down her body, finding the bare skin where her stockings ended, rubbing. She pressed against him, her breath coming fast. It had been too long. It was always too long, when he came to her this way, with his passion clear, direct, whether it was only a day, a week or a year. But this time it had really been too long. Oppression had clung to him for months, making their love-making a mockery. Not now, not now. She lifted her lips to him.

'Look,' he suddenly said. He turned her towards the window. She saw their reflections hazy in the window, like figures coming towards them – a tall man with a strong thin face, a smaller woman, pretty, her mouth bright, her hair rumpled – coming towards them from a sleepy snow-bound village, its slender church spire etched against the night by the flickering lights of the nestling houses.

'Like our own ghosts. Pale. Beautiful. Coming from beauty,' he murmured, caressed her breasts, his lips in her hair. She turned towards him, wanting his mouth, saw the tears in his eyes.

'Oh, Johannes.' She kissed him, kissed until she felt herself melting into him so that she was sure if she turned now, there would only be one body coming towards them from that sleepy village.

It was she who pulled him down on that narrow bed, wanting him to fill her, but slowly, augustly so that time stopped as they moved against each other, the chugging and whistling of the train drowning their moans as it careened through the dark night.

She didn't know when it was in the midst of that night of loving that she asked him. 'Is it Max, Johannes? Is it because of Max that you've always refused to come to Berlin with me? I've never dared to ask you before.'

'Perhaps.' His voice seemed distant. 'Though that was only one of countless reasons.'

'Does it trouble you that you've never had any contact with your son?' The words stumbled out of her, making her flush, making her welcome the dimness of the tiny nightlight.

He laughed suddenly, a low rumble, lifted himself on one arm to examine her face. 'No, Anna. What strange thoughts go through that head of yours. You know I have no particular feelings about biological property, paternal blood lines. I'm not a good enough German for that. No, no, though I have been curious at times to see how Max would turn out. No, it's more a concern for Klaus. I've always thought he should have no competition in fatherhood. He wanted it so much. Was so good at it.' He laughed again.

'You know I'm far too selfish to be a good father. I'd inevitably turn into a replica of my own as, you've been so kind to tell me on various occasions, I was managing to do in any event. And that's another reason I don't go to Berlin. I don't like confronting those memories. It's the Justizrat's city, after all.'

She curled against him. 'Don't be silly, Johannes. You're not that selfish. Not any more.'

'Not that selfish,' he mimicked her, grimacing. 'Not any more. But selfish enough.' He looked away from her, seemed to lose himself in thought. Then he started to speak again. 'What I've never told you, Anna, never dared to confess altogether, even to myself,' he ran his finger along the line of her throat reflectively, 'is that I'm afraid of small children.

That's why I was so abysmal with Leo all those years back. Small children, the ones I used to think of as the model for all human passions, are screaming monsters of selfishness. And I saw myself in them. Saw myself in Leo. I couldn't handle that. And I had this feeling of displacement. Mother should love only me, I felt. I wanted to scream.'

She laughed. 'I know.'

'Do you?' he mused. 'It was far worse than thinking of you with another man.'

'But not with another woman?'

He considered. 'I don't know. Perhaps that too.'

They were silent for a moment.

'I think Bettina would have liked you to pay more attention to Max,' she said then.

'I think if Bettina had wanted it, she would have told me. She has never had any trouble in saying anything she thinks.'

'You're hard on her, Johannes.'

'Am I? I've always assumed that Bettina thinks all children are rightfully hers since she can bring them up better than anyone else. And heaven knows, she may be right.'

Anna laughed a little uncomfortably.

'I think what you're really saying to me, Anna, is that you would have liked me to pay more attention to Leo.'

She flinched at that, but took it. 'Perhaps.'

He sighed, stroked her hair, pulled it back from where it had fallen over her face. 'I should have, of course. I'm sorry about it now. Truly I am. But . . .' He shrugged. 'I've spent most of the last years being a wretch to everyone, including myself. In the name of what, I'm not quite sure. A few paintings. And . . .' He stopped short.

She prodded him. 'And what?'

He reached for a cigarette, passed her one, lit them, took a deep puff. 'And, I don't know. By the time Leo had grown into less of a beast than I was, and I could even exchange a few words with him, it was somehow too late. You were always so protective of him, guarded him so jealously. And perhaps the fact that you had insisted so often that he was Bruno's son, nothing to do with me, made it easy for me to pretend that he wasn't there. I don't know.'

He stretched back, looked up at the bunk above. 'I failed you in that, Anna, as in so much else. I'm sorry.'

She snuggled closer to him. 'And I failed you,' she murmured.

'Not that. Never that.'

She was happy that he had said it. But the tears crept into her eyes nevertheless. Why was it that all those years ago she had been so certain, so adamant, that Leo was Bruno's son? She had no proof, except the insistence of her conscience. Bruno had wanted a son. Bruno, who had been so good to her and whom she had repaid with the present of his death. She shivered.

'What is it, Anna? Don't cry, my darling. Life leads us all a merry chase. And we've had some good moments.' He kissed her tears, her lips, her bosom.

'We should take more journeys together, Johannes,' she murmured.

He gazed into her eyes as if he were looking into a great distance, nodded, and then with a groan which seemed compounded in equal parts of sadness and pleasure, pressed into her again, so that she forgot everything but the tender weight of his body and the lapping of her own flesh.

Bettina gazed at the tall Christmas tree which dominated the sitting room. Martha and she had dressed it lovingly just two days before, unwrapped the little silver bells and mosaic globes, arranged the candles. And now they all glowed, flickering over the freshly scrubbed faces of the youngest children, Thomas's elder son and the three little ones who still remained with her, over the presents heaped under the tree, over Klaus and Johannes and Anna and Thomas and his wife, Gretel, and their baby, sleeping peacefully in her lap. The fire crackled pleasantly in the hearth and, through the large window, she could see the trees, their branches gracefully arched with snow.

Johannes had just begun a song and the other men had joined in, their faces teasing, wreathed in smiles.

'What shall we get little Michael
For this cold Christmas feast
A bouncing ball? A drooler's bib?
A small light next to his crib? . . .'

Tucholsky's Christmas song written for the Christmas of 1919. The kindly satirist Tucholsky, now in exile, silenced.

Bettina watched the wide-eyed children, their growing incomprehension.

> 'Shall I give him a bedpan on wheels?
> Or offer him a moratorium?
> A roundly swollen piggy bank?
> Or perhaps a doll's crematorium.
> A new intelligent face for the nation?
> Now that would fill him with rare elation.'

The men were harmonizing happily, their voices rising in a crescendo.

> 'Oh dear cousins, uncles and aunts,
> Give him something, I don't know what it might be.
> You're the quick and clever ones
> Hang it for him on his Christmas tree.
> But please don't give him reaction
> He's already had that to distraction!'

Fifteen years since the warning song had been written and, despite all their efforts, things had only grown worse. Far worse.

Bettina tried to shed her gloom and concentrate on the scene. It was idyllic, almost as if she had decided to provide an illustration for a picture book. The Bauhaus chairs with their clean functional lines, the moulded table with its capacious earthenware bowl, now laden with fruit and nuts, the gleaming radio console from which the sounds of Beethoven's 'Ode to Joy' would soon spill out, the warm smell of chocolate and spices and burning logs. And her nearest and dearest nestled together in this high-ceilinged, well-proportioned room, where ideas had crackled and life had unfurled for over a decade.

Johannes looked handsome, his eyes clear, almost the youth she had once briefly loved, yet with a calm certainty about him that she didn't recognize. Klaus, a little stiff in his limbs, but gangly as ever beneath the white mien, was strangely cheerful, his old sociable self, buoyed as ever by Johannes's presence. Thomas, as quickly elegant in his movements as he was in his wit, had his perennial ironical twinkle; while Anna was clothed in that particular radiance which always signalled that she and Johannes were once again in love. Even the chattering Gretel was composed tonight, quiet.

Bettina smoothed the full skirt of her Titian-red dress and then restlessly signalled for Martha to serve the mulled wine.

Everything was perfect and everything was wrong. For one thing, the boys weren't here. She let her mind rest on the thought she had evaded.

Weren't here and should have been here hours ago, and she had no idea where they were. Not that that was unusual in itself. Max after all was rarely here except at weekends. He had just turned twenty, she had to remind herself, and was no longer a child. But still she worried, because the city had grown so hostile, becoming a battleground for opposing forces, a site for criminal warfare. Three times in this last year Max had come home trying to hide bruises, bandages.

He had taken a room in Wedding. Room was a euphemism, she shivered, more like a shared hovel at the top of one of those rank, cramped tenements, where disease was as rife as gang brawls, where the smell of sewers and stale cabbage lingered permanently in the air. She should know. She had spent enough time there, even been to visit Max's room, against his wishes.

If the room was bad enough, the reason he had taken it was worse. Oh yes, he might be enrolled as a philosophy student at the university, but in fact he was working in an electrical factory and underground for the Communists. She had known it for years, though he had never told her. Not only from the line he took in discussion, but from the publications she had found in his room at home – everything from the *Arbeiter Illustrierte Zeitung* to *Die Linkskurve* to a variety of Muenzenberg journals. She hadn't objected then. After all, she shared many of their sympathies though she had been progressively enraged since the beginning of the decade at the way the Communists refused to support the Social Democrats in Parliament. Still, far better the left than the right.

But ever since Goering's henchmen had raided the Communist headquarters, the KPD been declared illegal, all left-wing publications banned, Max was blindly endangering his life . . . Bettina let out an inadvertent sob.

'Are you all right?' Anna was instantly at her side.

'Yes, yes.' Bettina tried a smile. 'It was just the wine.' She coughed dramatically. 'It went down the wrong way.'

Anna looked at her queerly. 'Do you think Leo will be back soon?'

'In time for dinner, I expect.' Bettina put as much assurance into her tone as she could muster. Leo hadn't even bothered to wait for his mother before leaving this morning. Bettina glanced at her watch. 'We should give the little ones their presents now, then get them to bed.'

Anna looked at the little grouping by the tree. 'I've never seen Johannes so engrossed in play,' she mused.

'He's come of age at last,' Bettina muttered under her breath.

'Don't be nasty, Bettina,' Anna chided her.

'Sorry. I'm in a foul temper.'

'The boys?' Anna asked softly.

'Them too.'

In the distance they heard the brush of the front door, a call, 'Hello.'

'Max!' Bettina leapt to her feet.

Anna watched her sister stride across the room, her steps light, saw her hug Max so hard that the parcels almost dropped from his hands.

'Sorry I'm late.' He was wearing a peaked worker's cap, a thick navy jacket. 'Shall I change or do you want me as I am?' He grinned at his mother.

'As you are, Max, for the moment at least. Come and say hello to everyone.'

He took off his cap, embraced Anna. 'Happy Christmas, Aunt. Good to have you back.'

'Happy Christmas, Max.'

As always Anna felt warmed by his direct gaze, his open face. She watched him as he hugged Klaus, shook Thomas and Gretel by the hand, then Johannes. Was it her imagination or was Johannes looking at him strangely? Seeing the two of them together, she was suddenly struck by a resemblance. Was it the set of the head? The stance? Did everyone see it? She glanced at Bettina, wondering at her thoughts. But she could not see beyond the visible relief which now covered her features.

'Good to have you with us again, Uncle Johannes. It's been a long time.'

'Too long. You were just a little sprout when we last met. And now . . .' Johannes indicated the shared level of their heads. 'You're a man.'

'And longing to be a new man, eh Max?' Thomas embraced him warmly, perched Max's cap on his own head. 'A heroic worker in a just and egalitarian society.'

For a moment Anna didn't know whether the joking warmth of Thomas's tone would obviate the irony of his words. But Max seemed to take it in good stead.

'We all have a little way to grow for that, I think, Thomas.'

'Particularly given the wide success of that other form of new man, the super patriot,' Anna heard Klaus murmur.

'Klaus,' Bettina said sharply. 'We made a promise. No politics over Christmas.'

'Whoops.' Klaus lifted a small boy under his arm, took another by the hand. 'Time to get a move on, poppets. Collect all your presents.'

Amidst great cries and squeals, the children received their gifts and then, with only sleepy protests, were pressed upstairs by Bettina and Klaus, Gretel immediately behind them.

'I'll come and tell you all a quick story in a moment,' Max called after them. He took a glass of mulled wine from the tray, drank thirstily, then turned again to Johannes.

'How are things in Munich?'

'Bad for some and I can only assume good for others.'

Max laughed. 'Half and half, eh. Like the election. There's still hope.'

'That was two years ago, Max. I think the figures have changed somewhat now,' Thomas intervened. 'The trouble with your lot is that you never think beyond the cities, take account of those vast tracts of land inhabited by the great German peasant to whom our Führer has promised everything.'

A shadow crossed over Max's face, but he covered it with a laugh. 'And if you and your lot see everything so clearly, Thomas, will you please tell me why we're in this pickle?'

'You have me there, Max,' Thomas grinned. 'Unless we spend the next two hours in explanation. To which Bettina will heartily object.'

'Object to what?' a voice asked from the far end of the room.

They all turned. Leo had come in as softly as a cat. Or a spy, Anna thought inadvertently. They all stared at him in silence for a moment, that handsome gold head, that military bearing, those eyes which gazed at them yet beyond them. A palpable electric field seemed to surround him.

Anna ran towards him. 'Leo!' She raised her arms for an embrace. But he put out his hand before she could touch him.

'Hello, Mother.' He shook her hand stiffly, let it drop, greeted Max and Thomas. Then his eyes locked with Johannes's. Anna could almost hear the electricity crackle. As if through its haze, she saw Johannes step forward, heard him murmur, 'I don't believe we've met for some time, Leo.' Saw Leo turn stiffly away.

'How are you, Leo?' she said to cover his rudeness.

'Very well, Mother. I hope you've had a good journey.'

'Yes, thank you.' She flushed stupidly, in part at his stiff politeness, in part at the memory of it. 'Would you like a drink?' she asked to hide her confusion.

'Please, if there's some juice. I don't drink alcohol, you know.'

'Of course not,' she mumbled.

She poured out some juice clumsily, at a loss for words. Behind her, she heard Max speaking to Johannes.

'I hear they've removed your paintings from the Dresden Gallery.'

'Not only from there,' Johannes laughed too loudly.

'The swine!'

'You're not German enough for them, Johannes,' Thomas interjected.

'I'll drink to that.' Johannes raised his glass.

Suddenly Leo marched towards the canvas of Johannes's which hung over the mantelpiece. With a slow, deliberate gesture, he spat at it.

'Leo. You will apologize instantly to Johannes.' Klaus was standing at the door, his eyes blazing, his voice firmer than Anna had ever heard it. 'Instantly.'

The boy suddenly looked young, confused.

'That's all right, Klaus.' Johannes made a joke of it. 'I've had to deal with severer forms of criticism in my time.'

'Leo!' Klaus's eyes didn't leave the boy.

'Sorry,' he muttered at last, but the word was directed at Klaus, not at Johannes.

Anna walked over to the chair in which Johannes sat, placed her hand on his shoulder. He covered it with his.

'The children are waiting for their story, Max.' Klaus gestured to his son.

'I'll go up too,' Leo mumbled. 'I need to have a wash.'

'You do that.'

Anna gazed after him. He looked humbled, forlorn, despite the proud shoulders. There was a vulnerability in his intractable absolutism. Suddenly, she was reminded of the young Johannes. She swallowed hard. And there it was, that sense of being ripped apart between them, just as strong as when Leo had been a tiny child.

And he was still only seventeen, after all. With a little shrug, she extricated her hand from Johannes's and followed Leo from the room.

* * *

Bettina presided over the table, bright with the sparkle of silver and crystal and candelabra. With a queenly smile, she heaped goose and spoonfuls of red cabbage and dumplings on to everyone's plate.

'No goose for me, Aunt Bettina, remember.'

'No, no, of course, not.' She interrupted her gesture. Leo had suddenly decided to become vegetarian, like his Führer. Guns before butter. The new Puritanism. She sat back into her chair, unfolded the stiff white napkin with an irritated tug.

'Where have you been today, Leo?' she asked.

'To a film. With Gerhardt. It was wonderful in fact. Leni Riefenstahl's "*Blaue Licht*". Have any of you seen it?'

'Gretel and I have.' Thomas eyed the boy keenly.

'Tell us about it, Leo,' Anna prompted him gently.

'Well, it's set in this peasant village high up in the Dolomites. Beautiful.' He gazed past her into the distance, seeing what couldn't be seen. 'On the peak of the mountain above the village on nights when the moon is full, a miraculous blue light appears. Ghostly, magical. All the youngsters are drawn to it even though to reach it means to tumble down the precipice to their deaths.'

'More half-baked visionary rubbish,' Bettina muttered under her breath.

'Let the boy finish, Bettina. He's trying to describe something,' Johannes chided her.

She turned on him, as if all her suppressed annoyance had at last found a suitable target. 'Yes, you were always good at that, Johannes. Visions to blind oneself to the reality of facts.'

He chuckled good-humouredly, refusing the bait. 'You have to allow that a little vision, no matter how half-baked, is necessary to my profession. But I want to hear about this film.' He turned to Leo.

'Yes, tell him about these wonderful peasants, Leo.' Bettina couldn't stop. 'I bet their faces were noble, etched with suffering, eh? The women particularly. All those aeons of breeding children and preserving the pure biological inheritance of the tribe. What can you expect?' Her voice rose.

'In fact, the film wasn't about that.' Leo wiped his mouth carefully. 'In fact, since you're so interested in facts, Aunt, it was about an artist who destroys everything, the miraculous light, the heroine.'

Johannes laughed loudly. 'It sounds a wonderful film.'

Leo stared at him from those unblinking eyes. Then, as if he hadn't said anything, he turned back to Bettina. 'And another fact for you, Aunt, you do realize that under the new regime, the unemployment figures have fallen drastically.'

Anna, watching Bettina's face, held her breath. The growing tension in the air made it almost impossible to swallow. It was an accumulated tension, flashing with the sparks of months.

'You've stolen one of the words from my vocabulary, Leo.' Max raised his glass to him. 'I didn't know you were interested in the unemployed.'

'It's not difficult to create jobs if you turn half the country into policemen.' Bettina plunged her fork angrily into a piece of goose.

'Soon to be transformed into soldiers, whatever the treaties allow or don't allow,' Thomas muttered.

'Not difficult to raise the employment figures if you force your scientists, your university teachers, your publishers, not to mention countless others, to emigrate.' Klaus was looking scathingly at Leo.

'If they refuse German ideas, then it is right that they go.' Leo stared back at him without flinching.

Klaus slammed his napkin on the table. 'German ideas! There we have it again.' Two red spots had formed on his pale cheeks. The pulse in his forehead throbbed heavily. 'German water boils differently from other water. Aryan blood pumps differently through Aryan veins and brains. The properties of German mass and German energy are unique to Germany. True physics is the creation of the German soul. Goodbye Einstein, goodbye . . .'

'Einstein is a Jew. And like all Jews, bent on the destruction of the Aryan spirit, sapping the life force of the great German nation.'

A hush fell around the table, a silence so total that in it Anna could hear the beating of her own heart. At last, she said, her voice cracking, 'Your father was Jewish, Leo. You're half Jewish. You must know that.'

He stared through her, his face stony.

'Which must be the ultimate disproof of all racial theories, Leo.' Max tried a laugh. 'After all, as one of my girlfriends pointed out to me, you're the very model of the most desirable Aryan type.'

Leo pushed his chair back from the table with a scrape. For a moment, Anna thought he might raise his arm in salute. Instead he walked slowly away from them, his head high. Under his breath she thought she heard him mutter, 'Traitors.'

No one stirred.

Then with a sudden abruptness, Bettina rose. 'Anna. We need to talk. You'll excuse us, all of you. Martha will bring in the pudding.'

'I'll take some to Leo, shall I? He can't be feeling very happy,' Max mumbled.

'Do as you like, Max.' With a sweep of her skirts, Bettina turned away, walked with a trembling stateliness up the stairs to her study. Anna followed slowly, closing the door behind them.

'I can't take it any more, Anna.' Bettina leaned heavily on her desk. Her knuckles were white. 'I never thought I'd have to say that.' She picked up a solid bronze paperweight, clutched it. 'But I'd like to throw this at him, tear out his beautiful golden hair clump by clump.' Her eyes filled with tears. 'I thought he'd grow out of it. Wake up. Thought it was just the usual rebellion against us. Adolescent nonsense, a little ecstatic groping in cosmic expanses, all that idealism about community and leader they instil in them in the Jugendbund. But now,' she threw her arms up in the air, 'now it's the Hitler Youth. And he believes it, believes he's the superman marching to the tune of the German soul. And all that vile racial rubbish. He's never come out with it as clearly as tonight. Never dared the anti-semitism. But he believes every word of it. It's clear. Someone who has been brought up in my house. My nephew!' She jabbed a cigarette into her holder, broke it in the process. Tried another.

'And I'm afraid of him, Anna.' She met her sister's eyes. 'Yes, ever since he came home from the camp this summer, that indoctrination camp, worse than military school. I'm afraid he'll do something to us. I don't know what.'

She paced restlessly across the room.

'I'm sorry, Bettina,' Anna murmured. 'I'll try and take him away with me. I'll . . .'

'It's not that, Anna. I know you tried to convince him to come with you last year. But he doesn't care about any of us. He's only interested in his group, his friends, his *Vaterland*.' She blew her nose loudly into her handkerchief.

'Anyhow, that was only part of the reason I asked both you and Johannes to come this week. I hoped the serious conversation would keep until after Christmas, but I might as well say it now.'

She paused for a moment, met Anna's eyes once more. 'Klaus and I have decided to leave. To go to America, to take Max away from here before it's too late. We would have put all the necessary procedures in motion sooner, but Max resisted. And now I'm afraid for him too, afraid he'll get himself arrested, killed.' She dabbed at her eyes again. 'And I still have to convince him. But I'll manage that, somehow.'

She sat down, her face suddenly haggard, motioned for Anna to sit, too. 'I think you and Johannes should come as well. Things can't be very easy for him. Thomas, too, is making plans.'

'And Leo?' Anna asked softly.

Bettina shrugged. 'You can try and convince him. I haven't a chance. But Anna,' she paused, lit another cigarette, 'I don't think there's much hope.' She rose, opened the top drawer of her desk, took out an envelope. 'I fear he's lost to us. This came two weeks ago. It's the second item on the family agenda.' She handed Anna the envelope.

For a moment Anna stared at it, not wanting to know its contents. Then with a sense of dread, she glanced at the official letterhead, perused the typed sheet.

Leo had been selected to attend a special National Institute, the letter stated. A high honour. Because of the extraordinary nature of his recommendations, he could begin in January.

Anna looked up at her sister. 'Is this so very terrible?' she asked.

Bettina threw up her arms in despair. 'Where have you been living for the last two years, Anna? This is one of the Nazis' elite institutions. An offer of a place is not simply an offer, it's a command. Let's say we could even find a way, on trumped up medical grounds or whatever, of refusing the place, do you think Leo would agree? Not in a million years. He's thrilled by it all, ecstatic.'

'So he goes,' Anna said softly.

Bettina looked at her aghast. 'Anna.' She shook her by the shoulders. 'Anna. Open your eyes. Not only will they turn your son into even more of a little militaristic Nazi puppet than he already is, but what happens when their secret police get even better at their rooting out of racial lines? Oh, I know, it's never meant anything to us that Bruno was Jewish. We've never talked about it – to the point I think that Leo really didn't know – until you said it tonight. But if they find out . . .'

'Aren't you exaggerating, Bettina? It's not that bad, is it?'

A look of utter astonishment covered Bettina's face. 'Not that bad? Not that bad? My friend Petra's hair turned white in two weeks over what they did to her family. Do you want details?' Her voice rose to a near shriek. 'What do you think Klaus and I have been up to, but helping Jews get out of the country? And those poor little mites.' She sobbed, then with a visible effort restrained herself, said more quietly, 'Talk to Johannes about it, see what he says.'

'I will,' Anna murmured. 'But what you're really saying is that there's no solution but to go. To leave. And somehow drag Leo with us.'

'Yes, Anna.' Bettina began to pace again. 'It's time to go. To say goodbye to all their swastikas and salutes and raving. To make a clean break with their Aryan motherhood, their Aryan science and their Aryan philosophy. It's enough! Did you know that Heidegger has gone in with them? Heidegger!' Her voice cracked. 'It's the triumph of the little rural idyll, the small clean and mean green space inhabited only by the Aryan soul. That dreamt-of soul conjured up by blue-eyed dreamers.'

She pursed her lips as if she were about to spit. 'They hate the cities. Cities are the creation of an international Jewish and capitalist conspiracy.' She laughed too loudly. 'Why? Because cities are international and not small and mean and pure and green and can't be fitted into their horrible idea of a *volkisch* German nation.

'And do you know, Anna, the women, I can't bear it, they love Hitler, even though he's taking away their voting rights.' The tears filled her eyes again. 'I'm going, Anna. It can't be fought any more. It's like a disease gone wild.'

Anna stared at her sister in silence. Then, with an uncontainable sob, she ran and embraced her.

FIFTEEN

BROWN FOG COILED through the narrow streets behind the Ku'damm, crept round yellow lights, and up to the doors of cheap dives. Pale mottled faces appeared as if from nowhere.

Like rats crawling out of their sewers by night, Leo thought. He flinched as a cheap whore leered at him, opened her coat to reveal a bare breast.

He should never have come here, never have accompanied Max into these sordid streets where the vermin of the city lived out their perverted lives. He tried to keep his eyes straight ahead, tried not to see the bloated virago waving her fat cigar, urging them to enter the dank bar; tried not to gaze at the gartered leg the blonde-wigged transvestite thrust lasciviously in their path.

'Not tonight, Hans,' he heard Max laugh, greet the creature by name.

He glanced at his cousin in disgust.

No, he should never have come with him. But he had felt the house stifling him, felt all their hands at his throat and when Max had said he was going to meet a friend at a cabaret and would Leo like to join them, it had seemed like a godsend.

Now all he wanted to do was somehow to metamorphose these close rank streets with their smirking night-dwellers into a sweet-smelling pine forest overarched by distant stars, where all he could hear was the scurrying of furred creatures, the hoot of an owl, the burble of a cool stream.

They had turned a corner and Max was exchanging a few words with a commissionaire in a somewhat tarnished uniform. The man beckoned them through a peeling door.

The blare of a saxophone filled Leo's ears. A scantily clad cloakroom girl whisked away their coats, pointed them with a cocky smile through another door. The reek of a thousand cigarettes riding on the din of voices trampled his senses. He could hardly see through the smoky half-light. He had a momentary panic, a feeling of suffocation. Space was closing in on him.

When he made out his bearings, he realized they were in a crowded but cavernous room, surrounded by slightly raised alcoves. Beyond the clustered tables, heaving with glasses and bottles, there was a small stage, a dance floor, a band. A handful of motley couples danced desultorily, their buttocks gyrating.

'All right?' Max's voice cut through the din.

Leo nodded, putting on a brave face. After all, anything was better than the family, clutching at him, arguing. Only two weeks more and he would be free of them, off forever.

He smiled at Max, followed him to the red and silver bar on the far side of the room, perched on a padded stool, saw the sleek-haired bartender glance at him curiously as he ordered a fruit juice, was happy to have Max deflect him,

'It's all right, Frank. It's my little brother's first night out.'

He bridled a little at that but drank his juice gratefully as Max chatted with the bartender.

It had been noble of Max to come to his room after the rest of them had tried to humiliate him. Perhaps it wasn't too late for Max, despite all their usual disagreements. He was young, after all, could understand the important role youth had to play in making Germany strong again. Not like the old ones with their weary blinkered pessimism.

He had explained to Max that it wasn't true what Anna had said about his father being that Jew. Bettina could confirm that, confirm that his father was Johannes Bahr. But his mother knew he had always hated Bahr as much as the man hated him, so it had been easier to attribute him to Adler.

In any event, his mother didn't want it to be known that he had been born before her marriage to that decadent. But none of all that mattered any more. The wrinklies had had their day. As for him, just to prevent any future misunderstandings, he was going to apply to change his name to von Leinsdorf. He would talk to Gerhardt about that. The group, the Party would sort it out.

Max had still had that slightly pitying look of understanding on his face which he couldn't bear. He hated the thought that he was feeling sorry for him. So, he had told him the good news about the Institute as well. It was then that Max had asked him if he wanted to come out with him.

A loud fanfare interrupted his thoughts. The room grew quieter. A woman came out on the stage, started to move ecstatically, her legs splicing the air. A hot blush rose in Leo's cheeks. As she lifted her crossed arms he could see she was wearing nothing but tattoos round her breasts, a string round her pelvis. There were catcalls and hoots from the audience. Fat men's beady eyes glistened. They smacked their lips. Leo felt sick, turned towards the bar counter, averted his eyes from the mirror which, despite himself, drew his gaze.

What if any of his friends should see him here, Gerhardt, or one of the many Party members whose acquaintance he had made of late? He sunk down into his jacket, riveted his eyes to the floor.

At last the music stopped. There was loud applause and then came a voice from the stage. He looked into the mirror, saw a man on the platform, breathed a sigh of relief, turned.

The man was small, dapper, almost dainty, with pointed features. He was telling a story. Leo listened.

'I was feeling a bit the worse for wear this morning. You know how it is, all these late nights. So I decided to go out for a breath of air. Right outside my door, there was my neighbour, Otto, and his dog, Spitzi. Beautiful dog, all gleaming muscles and well-brushed fur. Except for his face. His face, well . . . in fact he's grown to look a lot like Otto.'

The man drew his features into a picture of utter inanity. The audience laughed.

'Well, I followed them, why not, first along the Friedrichstrasse, then down Unter den Linden. And then right by the Brandenburgtor, the noblest spot in Berlin, site of our historic Reichstag, Spitzi decided to do the necessary. And a lot of necessary it was, let me tell you. Well, no sooner had Spitzi finished, than another dog came along and followed his example, then another and another. Like an epidemic it was, I tell you. And I got scared.'

The man was running up and down the small stage with a frenetic look on his face.

'Finally I couldn't bear it any more, the sight of all that filth in front of our noblest spot. And I don't know what came over me. I'm not a very public sort of man, but there I was, turning to the gathering crowd and addressing them. "Ladies and gentlemen," I said, "ladies and gentlemen, do you realize that very soon we're going to be this high in shit?"' He clicked his heels together and raised his arm abruptly over his head.

The audience burst into roars of laughter.

Only after a moment did it dawn on Leo that the performer was enacting the Party salute.

Max turned to him, his face wreathed in smiles. 'Good, isn't he?'

Leo had no need to answer for a voice now blared from the floor riveting everyone's attention. 'Insulting the Führer! How dare you, you dirty Jew!'

There was a hush of nervous anticipation. Tension gathered in the atmosphere. The dapper little entertainer turned slowly in the direction of the outburst and shook his head sadly. 'I'm afraid you're mistaken, sir. I only look this intelligent.'

A spattering of laughter broke from the crowd, an assortment of claps and jeers. Then the band began to play a sprightly tune, drowning the rising hubbub. A slight pink-cheeked woman in an Eton boy suit appeared on stage. Rapturous applause greeted her.

In saucy girlish tones, she began to sing. Her gestures, replete with mischief, were as spiky as the dialect of her song.

'Hermann's 'is name!
'Ow this man can smooch, press, kiss.
I know many men of action,
But none make it as quickly as this
Yah, 'e's the master.
'E's called Hermann.
Hermann's 'is name!
Even took me to a ball
Last fall.
'Ow he can bend, sway, twirl,
Up and down with a girl;
Sometimes makes a pass with 'is knees,
Hermann, please.
Medals left, medals right-er
And his paunch grows ever wide-er
And in Prussia he's Gauleiter
Hermann, Heil to'm.'

It was only with the last stanza that Leo realized the old song had been adapted to refer to Goering, Prime Minister of Prussia, one of the Führer's nearest and dearest. And the audience was singing along.

Suddenly he was filled with the sense that Max had brought him here for the distinct purpose of shaming him, of making a laughing stock of him, of besmirching him in the eyes of the Party. And if anyone saw and informed on him, Max would be to blame. Max with his Communist friends. Leo's thoughts swirled.

But Max was tapping him on the shoulder, smiling genially, waving him towards the dance floor. The band had struck up a lively tune.

'Let's find some young ladies, shall we? Anita said she'd be here.'

Leo shook his head. 'I think I'll go.'

'Don't be shy, Leo. Tell you what, I'll bring some friends over.' He winked at the bartender, walked away into the milling crowd.

'Another juice?' The bartender was eyeing him dubiously.

Leo stood, unable to make up his mind whether to leave or wait for Max. As he thought of the fog swirling through the streets, the long trek home, the family lying in wait, he suddenly felt desperately tired. He leaned heavily against the counter, nodded at the bartender. There was only the music now. He drank down the juice. It tasted a little strange, but it was cool. He closed his eyes for a moment, heard the throbbing rhythm.

'Another glass?'

Leo nodded again.

The man smiled, slicked his hair back with a tender gesture, and winked at him.

'This is Greta, Leo. And Anita.' Max was suddenly upon him. 'They're just longing to dance.' He swivelled his hips humorously, put his arm round Anita.

'You didn't tell me he was so handsome.' The woman called Greta looked up at Leo with dusky laughing eyes.

Leo emptied his glass quickly.

'Let's go then, comrade.' She wound her arm through his.

On the dance floor the noise of the band swelled to dizzying heights. Leo had a sense of hundreds of heaving, perspiring bodies, closing in on him. Greta's full breasts slithered against his jacket. He could feel her breath on his chin. He held himself taut, tried to keep a distance between them, but the crowd pushed them together. Too close. He felt his head beginning to whirl, his hands grow clammy. He thrust her away, excused himself with a mumble, stumbled through the throng. Behind him, he thought he heard Max laughing.

A toilet. He closed the door, leaned against the coolness of the tiles. The relief of quiet.

Two sleek men in rakish suits were murmuring by the urinals. Startled, they stared up at him. One of them puckered his lips lasciviously. Then they retreated, brushing past him with little smiles on their faces.

On the floor near the urinals, Leo heard something crunch beneath his foot. He looked down, saw a broken syringe. That too! With a sense of helpless rage, he beat his fist against the cold tile wall. Communists, Jews, addicts, all the debauched scum the Party had to eradicate. And he was in the midst of them.

When he re-emerged, he saw Max waving him towards a crowded table. He shook his head bluntly.

He would have one more drink to calm himself down and then leave. Awkwardly, he made his way towards the bar. It felt as if all the eyes in the room had homed in on him.

His stool had been taken by a fat man, all stomach, sallow skin and double chins. Leo found another perch and ordered. If he concentrated all his attention on the sensation of the cool liquid in his throat, he could almost imagine he was elsewhere. He closed his eyes. He was outdoors, the rain thundering down on him, cleansing him, battering the jagged mountain top, the roof of his tent. The rain would swallow up the city's squalid streets, all the filthy two-legged vermin, cover the polluted rooftops. He lifted his head to the skies, opened his mouth. Cool. Pure.

The tap on his arm had become a tug before he became aware of it. The bartender pointed to the phone he had placed before him. Leo looked up at him in bewilderment.

'From one of the tables,' the man grinned.

Leo glanced behind him. He hadn't noticed the phones on the tables before. Max, it must be Max, too idle to make his way through the raucous crowd. Leo picked up the receiver.

'Hello, handsome.' He could barely make out the deep voice that purred at him. 'I like those shoulders of yours. And that tight little butt.' There was a coy laugh.

Leo gripped the phone in disbelief. Could it be Max playing a joke on him?

'You do things for me,' the voice drawled, insinuated, 'and I could do things for you. Such things. In your mouth, between those angelic little teeth. Or in the devil's gateway. Just meet me outside . . .'

Leo slammed down the receiver. Confusion rioted through him, a herd of wild beasts. He raced blindly from the room, bumped into people, found himself stopped by the saucy hat-check girl, fumbled for his ticket, tripped on the stair.

Finally, he was out through the door. His heart was pounding madly. He stopped to breathe, looked up and down the narrow, darkened street, uncertain which way to turn, walked a few steps to the right.

Suddenly a hand tapped him on the shoulder, an arm found its way through his. He turned to see a tall, striking blonde, swathed in furs, at his side.

'Hello, handsome,' she smiled, her tongue playing over her lips. 'Yes, it's little old me. Like what you see?'

He tried to shake her off, but her arm gripped him with surprising strength and she kept pace with him.

'I think you'll like it.' Her voice was sultry. She stepped in front of him, turned to confront him. Her coat fell open to reveal a short silver shift of a dress, long stockinged legs. 'Yes, I'm sure you will,' she murmured.

She took his hand and brought it to her groin, closing her gloved fingers round his, moving against him.

Hard, taut flesh. Straining. Straining. Hot. Leo shuddered, the blood clamouring in his ears, creating havoc with his thoughts. Not a woman. Not a woman, but a man. A man. Not even a man. One of those creatures. The horror of it.

He gripped the creature by the shoulders, rammed him against the wall, shook him hard, heard the welcome thud of bone on brick, the cry, brought his knee to his groin, started to punch, to batter, to flail. The creature fell to the ground and he launched himself on top of her, on top of him, hitting, hitting.

Pervert, scum, swine, Jew, Communist filth, the words poured through him in time to his blows. He felt the warm blood trickling from that nose on to his own fist. He met the creature's eyes. A woman's face, tears. He punched again and again. But not a woman. No. He hit out. It felt good. So good. He was cleansing the nation of its filth.

'Stop it, Leo, stop.' He heard Max's voice dimly in the distance. This was Max's friend, Max's fault. He pummelled that silvery chest as if he would never stop.

Then hands were dragging him off the body, Max, the commissionaire, others. He flailed out at them. Perverts, all of them, like that creature at his feet. Red scum. He landed a punch on Max's jaw, saw the startled look on his face, and hit him again. That felt good too.

The jab that came then, the upper-cut, took him by surprise. He fell backward, tripped on to the ground, saw, from the corner of his eye, Max lifting the creature; the commissionaire, half dragging him towards the door, saw the look of pity Max directed at him. Him, Leo. Saw the contempt in the faces of his cloth-capped friends and the women, Greta, Anita.

Leo leapt to his feet, brushing the dirt from his coat. Raising his shoulders proudly, he spat at Max's feet, and strode away.

At the corner of the street, he turned back. 'I'll get you for this. You and all your Commie pervert friends. You'll pay for this,' he shouted wildly. Then, lifting his collar against the night, he made his way into he didn't know what distance.

A week later, Anna sat listlessly staring out of the window of Bettina's spacious salon. It was snowing, thick drowsy flakes falling from a slate-grey sky and covering the earth in a solid blanket.

Seven days and Leo had still not come home. From the snow she conjured up a solitary figure, trekking along the path towards her, his head high, his eyes staring directly in front of him. She held her breath, willing the doorbell to ring. But there was no one.

Anna paced the room, placed a new log on the fire, watched the flames curl and leap. Then with a restless movement, she sat down at the piano. Her fingers picked out a melody, longing, mournful. With sudden realization, she slammed her hands down in a jarring chord. The *Kindertotenlieder*.

'He's not dead, Anna.' Johannes had stolen upon her softly. 'Believe me. Or trust Max, if that's more comfort to you.'

Anna rested her head on his chest. Max had told them on Christmas Day, guiltily recounting how he had taken Leo to a cabaret to cheer him up, how there had been a brawl, how Leo had gone off. Max had assured them that he hadn't been injured. Had made light of the whole thing initially, a case of boyish pique.

Then as two days of absence had grown into three and four, he had set out to look for Leo, had promised that he and his friends would find him. Anna had wanted to call in the police, but Bettina and Klaus and

Johannes had dissuaded her of that, had told her it would be anathema to have anyone looking into their affairs. And, heaven only knew, it might put a black mark on Leo's pristine record. They had advised her to leave it to Max.

She and Max had talked more since then, privately, so she thought she now had the whole story. It had increased her anxiety rather than allayed it. She had had no inkling that Leo had been speculating about his paternity, and had somehow decided that Johannes was his father. She could almost smell his confusion, that explosive adolescent mixture of alarm, righteous indignation, ruptured pride, and humiliation which could engender either vindictiveness or despair.

She had urged Max to go and see the few of Leo's friends he knew of, to alert his youth group headquarters, make discreet enquiries, leave messages. All so far had been of no avail.

Her imaginings about where Leo was, about what had happened to him, grew ever more dismal, no matter how much she sought to control them with the voice of common sense. And waiting, with its enforced passivity, was like slow death.

'You said you'd come for a walk this morning.' Johannes stroked her hair gently.

'Yes, of course.' Anna followed him to the hall, pulled on boots, coat, hat, scarf, gloves, the endless apparel of winter.

Looking at her, he smiled, kissed her lightly on the lips. 'Ready?'

She nodded.

A blast of cold engulfed them, bringing the blood to their cheeks. They plodded through the heavy snow, their hands entwined, then walked more quickly when they reached the road. It was almost empty, the parked cars heaped with powdery hats, a lone dog walking slowly, leaving ghostly prints in the pristine whiteness.

They had been out like this together every day, walking, jumping on buses or trams, exploring a new quarter of the city on each trek, almost like tourists. For her, it was a way of forgetting the waiting. For Johannes, Anna sensed, it was a journey of rediscovery, a tracing out of the map of his memory. He was strangely tender towards her, solicitous, almost as if she were a convalescent. But he was also absent, both of them as tightly wrapped in their separate thoughts as they were in their coats.

'Too cold for you?' He turned to look at her, brushed the snow from her hat.

She laughed up at him. His lashes, his hair, were covered in white. 'You look like a snowman.'

'Then I won't melt until spring.' He joined her laugh.

They had laughed a great deal together, despite everything, despite the fact that on the tail of each laugh a lump rose in her throat with Leo for a name. Despite the fact that each ramble seemed to cross the path of a patrol of uniformed youths, arrogantly strutting their possession of the city. She always found herself scanning their faces, half afraid, half in hope that one of them might be Leo.

And each walk always seemed to abut on murder: opposite Johannes's childhood home, the spot where Foreign Minister Rathenau had been assassinated; the Landswehr Kanal, where Karl Liebknecht and Rosa Luxemburg had met their end; Kösliner Strasse, where a riot had cost nineteen innocent lives. And so it went on.

Anna suddenly stopped in her tracks. They were approaching the wood where all those years ago Leo had come upon the dead woman. 'I don't think I want to go too far today. Just in case.' She looked at Johannes helplessly. 'After all, it's New Year's Day, and perhaps Leo will . . .'

'Of course.' Johannes wound his arm round her shoulder, drew her close, kissed her on the cheek. 'Poor Anna,' he murmured. 'The trials of motherhood.'

'Don't mock me, Johannes,' she mumbled, the tears rising in her eyes. The frost bit at them.

'I wasn't mocking.' He led her off the main street into a path which would take them back past the lake to the house. 'I wouldn't mock.'

They walked silently for a few minutes, pausing at the top of the incline to look at the hooded trees, the banked patterns the wind had traced.

'You know we were planning to leave tomorrow, Anna.' He squeezed her fingers. 'Obviously, you're not ready to go yet.'

There was a slight question in his tone.

'I couldn't now, Johannes.' She turned away from his scrutiny. 'I have to wait for him. But you must go, I understand that.' She was surprised at her own alacrity. But yes, she did want Johannes to go. The pretence of being able to think about anything other than Leo made too much of a demand on her.

Johannes laughed oddly.

She put her arm through his to lessen the intent of her words. 'It's just that I'm not very good company at the moment.'

'Would you like me to stay on with you?'

Anna shook her head, tried a smile which transformed itself into a grimace. She turned away from him and began to trudge down the slope. The truth was that she didn't like him to see her in her maternal disarray, compounded by the added weight of him. She had grown so used to contending with Leo on her own.

In the distance, a child shrieked happily as his sled careened down the slope. She saw him tumble off it, saw a woman pick him up into her arms and throw him gaily into the air.

'Don't cry, Anna.' Johannes had caught up with her.

She hadn't realized she was.

'I'll go tomorrow. I know it will be easier for you to deal with Leo if I'm not here. He doesn't exactly approve of me,' he chuckled.

She almost said it then, almost told him, 'He thinks you're his father,' but she bit her lips, mumbling instead, 'It will take a lot of convincing as it is, if I'm to bring him back to Munich as Bettina advises.'

They walked on, past the woman and the laughing boy.

'But you think he'll come back?'

Johannes nodded. Then after a moment, he added, 'You know, Anna, Leo's almost a man now. If he doesn't return or agree to what you suggest, it's not the end of the world. His world. It's an age for young men,' he added grimly.

She baulked at that, but kept her own counsel. There was no point trying to convey to Johannes that Leo was still just a child, stubbornly proud as he had always been, a wrongheaded boy.

Instead she said, trying to sound confident, 'And after I've dragged him back to Seehafen, we'll put things in motion, so that we can join Klaus and Bettina abroad.'

Johannes wrapped her hand in both of his and gazed into the distance. 'One step at a time, Anna. One step at a time.'

Something in his voice made her pause and look up at him. His eyes under the shadow of the thick lashes had a strange, faraway look, an unblinking calm. And she didn't know what it was that made him wrap her in his arms and kiss her, just then, in the midst of that expanse of snowy whiteness. But his lips lulled her and for the briefest of moments, she felt the brush of a butterfly's wings, sniffed the fragrance of warmed grass and wild herbs. She had a keen, sharp, image of Seehafen, that grassy knoll where they had first played out their love so many years ago.

Then the whiteness obliterated it.

'Oh, Johannes,' she murmured, clutching at his hand.

A gaggle of cars stood in front of the house gates when they returned and in the general air of activity, Anna had the sudden thought that Leo had come back. She raced through the doors, only to find Bettina and Klaus welcoming a score of friends. She had forgotten that today was Bettina's at-home and the enquiring glance she raised to her sister only elicited a forced smile and a slightly shrill, 'Come and meet everyone, you two.'

An assortment of cold foods had been spread on the polished living-room table. People clustered together in small groups, glasses perched in their hands. The hum of conversation was broken by the occasional laugh, a surface gaiety which did little to hide the general air of tension. In every group she joined, the subject of speculation was always Hitler's next move, who had left the country, or was leaving. Or worse, the news of another suicide.

'He didn't have to go as far as Paris to do that,' a plump woman giggled nervously.

'I guess he couldn't face writing in French. And whom for, in German?'

'It's better for the painters. No language problems.'

Anna gripped Johannes's hand.

'Just financial problems.'

They moved towards another group. A bald man with steely grey eyes was holding forth, 'And did you hear? The Bavarian Minister of Education has come up with the latest definition of intelligence.' He wiped his spectacles carefully and cleared his throat. 'Intelligence, according to the great man, includes, "logic, calculation, speculation, banks, stock exchange, interest, dividends, capitalism, careerism, profiteering, usury, Marxism, Bolshevism, roguery and thievery." So we're all free to be as anti-intellectual as we wish and instinctively embrace our Aryan destiny.'

There was humourless laughter.

'I'm told Schleicher has sworn the oath of allegiance and become a professor,' a tall, greying woman murmured.

'Anything to further one's career,' the bald man grumbled.

'The triumph of the dunces,' someone else declared.

'No, no, they're actually believers, idealists. The German heaven made flesh in the Third Reich.'

This time it was Johannes who led her towards another little circle of which Thomas Sachs was part. Anna pecked him on the cheek.

'Any news?' he whispered.

Anna shook her head, looked away.

A plump man, whose jacket seemed once to have belonged to someone far plumper, was saying, 'The Rosenthals are having trouble getting visas.'

'No trouble if you can pay through the nose and leave our honoured government all your property,' Thomas commented acerbically.

Johannes grinned. 'They might as well just organize a general confiscation and hand out the papers.'

'They're doing that for the Jews without bothering about the papers.' A dark woman spoke with flashing eyes.

'It's not that bad yet, is it, Hannah?'

'But it's going to get far worse.' Klaus had joined their group.

They all looked at him in silence as if a Cassandra they didn't want to hear had spoken.

Bettina was tapping Klaus on the shoulder, a question in her eyes.

He nodded.

She cleared her throat. 'Friends,' she said in a loud voice. 'Friends,' she repeated.

The room grew quiet as all eyes turned towards her.

Bettina smiled, smoothed the material of her skirt. 'It has become something of a tradition in this house to welcome you here every New Year's Day. And every year we have drunk to the next. This year, I am afraid it will take more than drink and good will to smooth the progress of things.'

There was a general sound of shuffling of feet and uncomfortable tittering.

Anna watched her sister's proud profile expectantly, the slight tremble of her lower lip.

'All of you know Klaus and my sentiments, that there is no longer much to be hoped for by staying on in Germany. Our hard-won and short-lived democracy is gone. The Third Reich is too pure to tolerate dissenting voices. Now we can only do what we can to help those less fortunate than ourselves and somehow not collaborate with the advance of this treacherous regime.

'Through friends in various women's unions in America and Britain, through colleagues of Klaus's abroad, we have put in place a ready source of invitations, of testimonials, for those who see that the day they must leave Germany is drawing near. Klaus and I wish to share this network with you – but only those of you who feel able or need to take on the responsibility of knowledge.'

Her eyes seemed to fix individually on each person in the room, assessing them, challenging. 'You can then draw on it, when we are no longer here. And on your pockets when called for.' She paused. 'And now, we raise our glasses to you in the modest hope, if of nothing else, then at least of our continuing friendship.'

Everyone raised their glasses solemnly. Then gradually, the hum of voices filled the room again.

Anna overheard two women near her, their tones low.

'Bettina's brave to say all that in front of everyone who's here, even old Griessmeyer.'

'She's clever. Calling on their consciences.'

'Watch Reinhard and Lulu. They're already out of the door.'

'With their pocket-books firmly in tow.'

The two women laughed.

Anna turned to see Johannes shaking Klaus vigorously by the hand, embracing Bettina.

'You were always the strongest amongst us, Bettina, the one who saw most clearly,' she heard him say.

There was a sudden flash of tears in Bettina's eyes.

'So you'll come, Johannes?'

Anna didn't hear his answer. Klaus had taken her hand, was urging her to finish her drink. He had been so concerned for her these last days, so caring, his long equine face all aquiver when he met her eyes, almost as if he felt he had let her down over Leo.

She raised her glass to him. 'To you, Klaus, for all you've done.'

'And left undone,' he laughed in a self-denigrating fashion.

'We do what we can,' she said softly. 'Which reminds me, though it's not the time or place, do you need money, Klaus? I've still a little left. If . . .'

He stopped her. 'You've been more than generous enough already, Anna. The last five went off with their little cases, with the safe passage of your account.' He looked into the distance as if he could see five children standing there, waving. 'Bettina wasn't referring to you. Besides, Johannes can't be earning anything these days. You must look after your own now.' He squeezed her hand.

Yes, Anna thought, gazing out of the window into the dying light. Look after her own. But one of her own was nowhere to be found.

When she looked back on the days which marked the turn of that year, Anna always thought they had passed with an almost explosive rapidity, events piling up with a doom-laden haste which defied reflection. In the midst of them, however, time seemed to move with an uncanny slowness, morning merging into afternoon, afternoon into evening and sleepless night, with only the tick of the clock to punctuate the waiting. It was especially the case after Johannes had left.

He had gone as planned, the day after the New Year gathering, the second of January 1935. He had kissed her goodbye, held her for a long moment, and then proceeded down the snow-laden path, turning only once to wave.

Looking at him, his soft hat low on his forehead, his eyes the only spot of warmth in that frozen landscape, his lips curled in a smile so tender that she couldn't remember its likeness, Anna had almost called after him, almost run to cling to him. But she hadn't. She had simply returned to her chair by the window and waited, alert only to the sound of the bell, the ring of the telephone. And these were never for her.

Then, one afternoon, she wasn't certain which one it was, Bettina had come in with a crash of the door, a thumping of bags on the floor, a piercing call which shattered the customary quiet of the house. Anna had run to her side, Klaus just behind her.

'He's gone,' Bettina had announced, looking directly at her, as if the fault were somehow hers.

For a moment, Anna had no idea whom she meant. Then it came to her.

'Max?' she mouthed.

'Yes, Max,' Bettina was screaming. 'I've just been to his room and he's not there. Hasn't been there all week.' She marched into the living room, threw a book off the chair on to the floor with a violent gesture. 'Not all week.' She swerved round again to confront them. The tears were streaming down her face. 'And he hasn't phoned, hasn't left a message.' She started to pummel Anna, then Klaus, with limp fists, impotently. 'I knew we should have left sooner, knew it.' She collapsed into a chair, covering her face.

Klaus met Anna's eyes helplessly. He put his hand on Bettina's shoulder.

'Have you spoken to any of his friends, to Anita?' he said after a moment.

She shook her head.

'Well, then . . . He could easily be with them.' He poured Bettina a glass of brandy, held it for her while she drank reluctantly. Then, gesturing to Anna, he went off to telephone.

'I'm sure he's with one of his friends.' It was Anna's turn to put more certainty in her voice than she felt. 'Max is responsible. He wouldn't do anything silly.'

Bettina looked at her with stony eyes. 'That's precisely why I'm terrified, you idiot. He never lets this many days pass without making a sign.' She leapt up from her chair, started to pace restlessly.

The tears rose to Anna's eyes.

'I'm sorry,' Bettina murmured. 'It's just that I'm at my wits' end. I . . .'

'I know,' Anna mumbled.

Bettina stopped in front of her. 'Of course you do, of course you do.' She hugged her sister for a moment. 'We left it too late, Anna. I should have bullied them, bullied them all. All this fairness, letting them find their own feet, work out their own ideas. The times are too dangerous for that. The . . .'

'Did you have any choice?' Anna interrupted her. 'They're men now, as Johannes pointed out to me all too clearly.'

'I could have forced them. Klaus wanted it. Wanted to go last year. I thought, oh I don't know what I thought. I thought I could be useful. So I was useful to everyone except our own.' She laughed strangely, a high-pitched cry. 'And because I was scared. Because I am scared. Another country. No one I know, powerless.' She dropped her glass so that it fell on the floor and crashed into a thousand pieces. 'And first Leo, now Max.' She covered her face.

'I couldn't get through to anyone.' Klaus had come in without them hearing. 'I'm going to go round to the factory. The shift should be finished soon.' He glanced at his watch. 'Then that bar, the little one in Wedding that Max always meets his friends in. Someone is bound to know something there.'

'Be careful, Klaus.' Bettina ran up to him, put a staying hand on his arm. 'Don't ask anything of the wrong people. You never know. You never . . .'

'I'll be all right.' He pecked her awkwardly on the cheek. 'Just try to stay calm.'

'I'll get you some broth,' Anna murmured.

But when she came back with the tray, Bettina was nowhere to be seen. Anna rushed up to her study, but there was no sign of her there either. Then she heard a noise down the corridor from the bedroom. She knocked at the door. 'Bettina?' She pushed it open, saw her sister throwing clothes into a suitcase, another gaping open.

'The moment he sets foot in this house, we're leaving. Even if I have to pack him in this case.' Bettina laughed shrilly. She hummed to herself in her off-key way as she flung dress after dress, jumper after jumper, into the case, then crunched it shut and started on another. 'The first train to anywhere, whatever time it is.'

Anna stared at her for a moment and then with a shrug, began to help.

Klaus was able to find out nothing that evening, except that no one had seen Max for at least five days. Bettina hardly seemed to hear what he had to say. She carried on arranging, sorting, putting things into cases, into trunks, working through the night, hardly sleeping before she woke to begin again. She was like a trapped bird, battering her head against a window pane, refusing to recognize its existence. When the house was packed, Max would return and the window would open. And if he didn't, Anna thought, wishing the image hadn't crystallized itself in her mind, she would flutter to the ground, spent.

It was two days later that the phone call came. For Klaus. About midday. She knew that because the sun had at last come out and was riding high in a cloudless sky. A Dr Hildebrandt, a former pupil of Klaus's at the hospital. Anna had taken the telephone and repeated the identification as she held out the receiver, before rejoining Bettina who was packing books into boxes.

Klaus came in to them a few moments later and mumbled something about having to go out. It was only once he had put on his coat that Bettina raised her head as if from a trance and rushed up to him.

'It's about Max, isn't it?' Her face had the transparency of old porcelain.

'I'm not sure.' Klaus avoided her.

'I'm coming with you.' She pulled on her coat breathlessly, tucked her hair beneath her severe winter hat.

'And I am, too.' Anna followed suit, unwilling to be left behind.

Klaus shrugged. 'You may not be allowed through.'

Bettina gazed straight ahead, as if she hadn't heard him.

The hospital was on the other side of the Spree, behind the Brandenburg Gate. Its old brick buildings, clustered beneath bare trees, had the hush of a convent, a quietude to dispel the pain within.

A sister with an elaborate headdress pointed them to a building on the far side of the grounds. There Klaus asked for Dr Hildebrandt. They were told to wait. The minutes ticked by until at last a thin man, his eyes hidden by thick spectacles, appeared. He shook Klaus vigorously by the hand, looked askance at Bettina and Anna, only offering them a perfunctory bow, before he drew Klaus aside, and led him towards a series of stairs.

'We wish to come with you, Dr Hildebrandt,' Bettina called after them.

'In a moment, Frau Eberhardt.' He dismissed her.

Bettina fumed, paced. But the men were back soon enough. Klaus's face had a ghostly whiteness to it. He put his arm through Bettina's.

'Max has been involved in an accident,' he murmured.

'Yes, Frau Eberhardt. An accident.' Dr Hildebrandt silenced Bettina's questions before they came with a stern look. 'I'm happy to say he's mending now.' He gestured them across the courtyard.

The icy path glimmered in the sunlight, too bright after the gloom of the building. In her hurry, Bettina skidded, held on tightly to Klaus. There was a look of panic on her face.

At the door of the ward, Hildebrandt turned towards them again. His voice was gentler now. 'Don't be upset by what you see. We don't want to excite him. And only a few minutes today.' He nodded to Klaus, held the door open for them.

They walked in single file down the long, narrow room banked by beds. Anna tried to keep her gaze on the windows, the tracery of trees and sunlight beyond. She didn't want to see the frightened faces of these supine men, but they loomed towards her, their features arranging themselves into those of Leo's. No. She fought off the thought.

At last Hildebrandt stopped in front of a door which led off the main ward. He ushered them through.

But for the eyes, the reclining figure on the bed could have been anyone. A bruised swollen face, cracked lips, bandaged head and limbs confronted them. Bettina gasped.

'I'm afraid I've had a little set-to.' It was Max's tone, though the voice was hoarse. He was trying unsuccessfully to smile. 'Soon be better, the doctor tells me, though I suspect my career as a hero has been cut short. Sorry.'

'You're not to strain yourself, Max,' Klaus murmured. 'We're happy, so happy to have found you.'

Bettina pulled a chair up to the bed, tried to take his bandaged hand, saw him flinch. 'My poor darling. My poor, poor darling.'

Max's eyes flickered, settled on Anna. He seemed to consider, then he said, 'I had a message from Leo, Aunt. Didn't get a chance to tell you.'

Anna's heart leapt.

'He says he won't be back for a while. Not to worry.' He moved uncomfortably in the bed. At a severe look from Klaus, Anna stilled her questions.

'Thank you, Max,' she mumbled.

Dr Hildebrandt cleared his throat. 'I think it would be best to leave Max to rest now. He needs his rest,' he stressed, staring down a recalcitrant Bettina.

'I'll be back tomorrow, darling. I'll bring chocolate, books, I'll read to you, I'll . . .'

'Bettina.' Klaus took her arm, turned briefly to his son. 'You're in good hands, Max. Rest well.'

It was only after they had got home, after they had greeted the little ones and shooed them off with Martha, after Anna had poured out coffee for a dazed and strangely silent Bettina, that Klaus conveyed to them what Hildebrandt had told him in confidence.

'Max has been in the hospital for some four days now. He was brought in unconscious, suffering from exposure as well as beating and burns.' He winced, lit his pipe with a shaking hand. He seemed to be about to say something else, then changed his mind. 'It appears he was found in some barn on the outskirts of the city. Without his clothes. So no one knew who he was, until yesterday when he came to.'

Bettina gasped. 'Those bastards. It was those bastards. I knew it would come to this.' She wrung her handkerchief.

'Hildebrandt recognized the name, put two and two together and rang me.' He was silent for a moment. 'But don't start fulminating about Nazis in front of him, Bettina. He's one of them. Though I think he's still a doctor first.'

Bettina got up abruptly. 'How long before he can come out of the hospital, Klaus?'

Klaus shrugged. 'A week, two. I don't know the exact extent of the damage.'

'Right then. There isn't much time. We must have everything ready. We'll go to Switzerland first, tell Max it's an enforced holiday. Or maybe England, he'll prefer that.' She started to pace in that restless way again. 'I had a letter from Lady Charlotte, you remember, Anna, mother's friend? We could stay with her, and then go on from there to America. We'll put what we want to keep in storage and then when I cable you an address, Anna, you can ship things on and join us.' Her voice had gathered in confidence.

'And Leo?' Anna murmured.

'Oh, by that time Leo will have turned up somewhere. Just make sure you have all your papers ready.'

'You'll ask Max, again, won't you, when it's easier for him to speak, about what Leo said, about . . .'

'Of course, I will, Anna.' Bettina cut her off. 'Now let's get busy. I want to spend tomorrow at Max's bedside.'

Anna gave Klaus a beseeching look, but he was studying his hands, his face distraught.

Sleep wouldn't come that night. A book in front of her, Anna tried vainly to read. Instead, her eyes focused randomly on objects in the room which had intermittently been hers for so many years: the graceful little flower lamp with its tinted petals, the cloud-blue drapes, the walnut commode, the dainty secretaire with its wealth of tiny drawers.

Max had said Leo was safe. Why was it then that she was still so worried, that Max's words had done so little to calm her? If only she knew where he was so that she could reach him.

Her eyes fell again on her secretaire. With a start she remembered the letter about Leo's new school and rushed to look for it. He could be starting there in two days' time. Yes, she convinced herself, that was precisely what he would do, go there without contacting them, without alerting anyone.

She reached for a sheet of paper and a pen, carefully chose her words, said how she hoped he had arrived safely, liked the place, and would he please write to give her news. She added that she had put a sum of money into his account, should he need to draw on it.

She should already have done that, Anna chastised herself. But she would do it tomorrow. Then she would wait for an answer. Perhaps it would come by the time Max was out of hospital, by the time the house was packed up.

It was when she returned home from the bank the following afternoon that she found the telegram sitting there, inconspicuous in its brown envelope on the hall table. She opened it with trembling hands and a little prayer to obviate the image which had leapt into her mind of Leo bandaged in a hospital bed.

There were only seven words on the sheet of paper:

'Come to Seehafen urgently Stop Frau Trübl'

Anna stared at them. Repeated them. What did it mean? Leo must have appeared at Seehafen. But then why hadn't Johannes sent the telegram or called? He must have gone into Munich. But at last Leo was found, was home in Seehafen.

Anna suddenly whirled into action. She could make the night train if she hurried. She found Klaus in his study, told him the news, embraced him, rushed to pack. Bettina was still in the hospital, but with luck she would be back before Anna had to leave.

Bettina's voice caught her unawares just as she was shutting her case.

'We may never meet in this house again, Anna.'

Anna twirled round to see her leaning on the jamb of the door, watching her. There were tears in Bettina's eyes.

'But our boys are safe, Bettina. That's the important thing.'

'Yes,' Bettina murmured. She lifted Anna's case for her. 'But once we would have taken that as given and wanted so much more.'

Anna shrugged, squeezed her hand. 'You'll write.'

'From another country.' Bettina nodded. Then, squaring her shoulders and forcing a smile to her face, she said, 'You'll come, Anna, won't you? New trees, new flowers, a new landscape in which to build your paradise.'

A little shiver went through Anna. 'I think we've had enough of building paradises, don't you, Bettina? It would be heavenly enough just to have all of us quietly together.'

SIXTEEN

HAD ANNA had an inkling of what awaited her at her destination, her haste in reaching it would certainly have been far less. As it was, the very fact of having a destination, after what seemed like an eternity of fearful waiting, gave wings to her thoughts as well as her feet.

In Munich she sped to buy chocolates, candied fruits, tiny fluted pastries and more substantial tarts – delicacies calculated to cheer and sway a young man whom she imagined as at once hungry and ill-tempered.

On the train she had allayed her own fears about Leo's physical state. It wasn't a hospital that had telegrammed her, she told herself, Max's example clearly in mind. Leo would certainly be tired, more difficult than ever to communicate with, but nonetheless safe and within her reach. She played out a hundred different dialogues which would ensure that he stayed by her side.

She didn't try to contact Johannes at the studio. That could wait until after she had seen Leo. Leo was the important one now. Johannes would understand that, already understood it. Instead, burdened with packages, she hired a taxi to propel her through the remaining kilometres.

As always the sight of the rounded twin domes of the house from the turn in the road occasioned a little surge of joy. It was Seehafen that had become her home in the course of all these years, her resting place. The curve of the land, the clusters of snow-clad bushes, the trees with their gothic tracery of branches, the nestling village above the lake and the jutting peaks in the distance, all beckoned to her. And today, too, the turn of her heavy key in the bronze lock quickened her pulse.

'Hello, I'm back,' Anna called out. She motioned the driver to leave her parcels on the gleaming hall table, and called out again, 'Hello.'

The ancient ginger cat appeared to rub itself against her legs. She stroked it absently.

'Oh, Frau Anna.' Frau Trübl came waddling towards her from the kitchen, her girth unequal to her feet. 'Frau Anna, you've come.'

The old woman's crinkled face bore an expression of utter dismay. Her eyes were red-rimmed.

Anna stopped in her tracks. 'What is it, Frau Trübl? Weren't you expecting me?'

The woman nodded, let out a sob and then threw her arms around her. 'Oh, Frau Anna.'

Anna held herself stiff. 'What is it, Frau Trübl?' she repeated.

The woman gazed at her for a moment. 'No, no, don't take off your coat. Wait, wait, I'll get mine.'

Anna's mind raced. Herr Trübl, Leo. What had happened? 'Tell me, Frau Trübl,' she said as soon as the woman reappeared. 'You must speak.'

Frau Trübl blew her nose, took Anna's arm and motioned her towards the door. 'Another moment, Frau Anna, and you'll know everything.'

They walked along the packed snow of the path towards the lake, Frau Trübl leaning heavily on her. Too many feet, Anna suddenly thought, had trodden here. Had Leo come with his friends? Had there been a raid? Her heart skipped a beat.

'Frau . . .'

'Hush, child.'

A hare suddenly bounded out of the bushes and crossed their path. Anna jumped back, watched him disappear into the snowy expanse.

Where was the woman taking her?

They had arrived at the boathouse which Johannes had once used as a studio. Everything seemed quiet and in order. Except for the thin stream of smoke curling from the chimney. But there was Herr Trübl limping round from the front. She waved to him.

And then she saw it. A pale long box perched on the rickety old trestle table. A box of palest ash. A coffin. Anna broke free from Frau Trübl's arm and raced towards it, sliding, stumbling. Suddenly she knew, knew as clearly as if someone had written it for her in blood. Red blood on white snow.

She screamed, her cry piercing the quiet of the countryside, echoing blindly through the trees.

'Johannes! Johannes!'

She heard the rustle of a bird's wings.

'Johannes,' she cried again.

Frau Trübl had caught up with her. 'A terrible, terrible accident, Frau

Anna. He must have fallen into the lake, where the ice was thin. We didn't know. We didn't know . . .'

The old woman was sobbing now, her words suffocated.

'They found him the day before yesterday.' Herr Trübl took over. 'Brought him back here.' He shook his head grimly. 'We sent you the telegram. Thought it best to keep him out here in the cold. In case . . .'

'Let me see him.' Her voice seemed to come from somewhere else.

Frau Trübl crossed herself three times in rapid succession.

'It's not a pretty sight, Frau Anna,' the old man mumbled.

'Let me see him!' She was screaming. She controlled herself. 'Please, Herr Trübl.'

He lifted the lid of the coffin.

Anna looked down, saw a figure that was Johannes and wasn't Johannes. A bloated man's face, mottled, blue. But with *his* thick lashes caressing the cheeks, *his* hair, springy, alive. Still alive. She sobbed, threw her face down to cover his. She hadn't known. Hadn't suspected. Had hardly thought of him, thought only of Leo. The sob tore through her again. She kissed him, kissed the cold lips willing them back to life, stroked his hair, tried to lift the heavy, unmoving head to her breast. 'Johannes,' she moaned.

'Let him be, my dear.' Frau Trübl tried to edge her away from the coffin.

'Leave me with him.' Anna shrugged her off forcibly. 'Leave me alone with him. Go. Please,' she added more softly.

The old people looked at each other then disappeared into the boat-house, Herr Trübl emerging a moment later with a stool.

Anna sat and gazed at Johannes. At what had been Johannes. A grotesque mask of him, executed by a bad painter. She covered his hand with hers. Cold, cracked, stiff. Sat there, holding it, until her own was as icy as his. Until the cold of her own body had blotted out her mind and the grey afternoon light had closed round them in darkness.

'Frau Anna, you must go in now. You must.' Herr Trübl was all but lifting her off the chair, closing the lid of the coffin.

'So terrible. Such a terrible accident,' Frau Trübl whimpered as they walked. 'Still so young he was, too.'

'Hush, woman, can't you see she wants quiet?'

They led her to the pastel sitting room, made her sit in the soft striped chair by the fire which Herr Trübl stoked into a blaze, brought her soup. The cat curled into her lap.

Anna was dimly aware of all this, dimly aware too that she had sat like this before, all her senses muted, as if already dead, the cold inhabiting her like a polar stream impermeable to warmth. She had sat like this for Bruno. Bruno whom she had betrayed and abandoned for the fire of Johannes. And now Johannes had abandoned her. No, no, she corrected herself. She had betrayed him too, abandoned Johannes for Leo. A son for a father. A son for two fathers. Had left Johannes to his own devices. To die. Had she been here, with him, where she belonged, he would never have gone out to walk alone. To be swallowed by the ice.

Anna shivered, glanced up above the mantel. Her mother. She had hung her picture there herself. Her mother with the bright presence, the glowing eyes, yellow like the leaping flames. A picture now, no longer even a memory. She wouldn't even be that to Leo. He would never gaze like this at an image Johannes had painted of her.

The thought startled her. She hadn't known that she was considering her own death. No, no, she musn't think of that. She couldn't do that to Leo. Her mother's death had left her with so vast, so unnameable a sense of loss, that in a way she had given herself up to filling it. Through love. But there was no more love. Only Johannes's poor cold body, which she had betrayed.

Her thoughts stumbled round, wounded creatures circling in a dark maze, drowning for lack of light.

'The fire is lit in your room, Frau Anna. You should go up, sleep. Sleep helps.' Frau Trübl was urging her up.

'Thank you,' Anna mumbled. She hadn't realized the hours had passed.

'I've put the chocolates out for you, the cakes. Perhaps . . .'

Anna looked at her blankly.

The room. Their room when they were here together. And they had been much together these last years.

Anna suddenly sobbed, threw herself on the bed, fingered the soft satin quilt. There would be no more dreams of coming together after this last rupture. The final one. She smoothed the bedclothes. If only they still bore the imprint of him as they did on those days when he rose before her, leaving her with the scent of him, of their tumbled nights. But everything was starched, untouched. Anna buried her face in the pillow.

Something crackled beneath her burrowing hands.

Paper. The thought formed slowly in her mind. With a rush, she brought out an envelope, her name written on it in Johannes's hand. As she tore it open, her ears seemed to echo shrilly with the thumping of her heart.

> My dearest Anna,
>
> Please forgive me. I am saddened by the thought that my selfish action will once again cause you pain. I have caused you enough already. But if I had been even more selfish than I already am, I would have asked you to accompany me on this last journey to the only other country left to me. Asked you to take my hand and walk into these waters with me, as we used to do. Young lovers. In perfect harmony.
>
> But I am no longer young. You have your son and I am an old man weary of the sickness of this world. My work is dead, and apart from you, it was my life. Whatever relics of dreams I may have fostered are dead too. A lifeless husk only needs a burial.
>
> Please understand, Anna. I can no longer take part in what this country has become. And this is my one remaining form of protest, the most unGerman act that I could perform: to die not for my country, nor out of any deep metaphysical and oh-so-German anguish, but out of simple selfishness, because it was enough. At some point one has to say, 'enough!'
>
> Forgive me. And remember, as I've tried to tell you before, that I have loved you far more than this ridiculous life.
>
> Do not go to the studio to sort through my remains. Our friends in uniform have already done that admirably. Leave this blighted country. Take Leo with you. He needs to go before it is too late.
>
> And Anna. I am happy. Horribly, selfishly happy. No tears. Laugh for me.
>
> Johannes

Anna gazed at the letter and then with a sudden burst of rage, she crumpled it, flung it across the room. No accident, not the work of fate, but a deliberate leave-taking. A flagrant goodbye. She wanted to scream, to shout, 'You bastard, how dare you, how dare you.' She thrust open the windows. Blackness. A sliver of a moon. A single star. A blast of cold. He wanted her to laugh, did he?

As if a demon had fired her limbs, Anna raced from her room, down the stairs, out into the night. Raced, stumbling, skidding, along the path to the boathouse.

'You bastard, Johannes,' she screamed, pounded on the coffin. 'Do you hear me, you bastard? How dare you? How dare you leave me?' She pounded and shouted and sobbed until her voice was hoarse, her fists hot with pain. Then, suddenly, she stopped.

The silence was vast. In it she felt the moon glinting down on her, a stupid woman shouting at a dead man in a box. A laugh tore through her, too loud, raucous, rending her throat, raw. The wind took it up, carried it through leafless branches, transformed it into a wail, shivered it across the lake into the hills beyond.

And if she were to follow it? Anna gazed out at the glimmering icy surface of the lake. A few steps, a little leap, a walk towards its centre, if necessary a jump, and then the water's icy embrace. She would join Johannes.

Mesmerized, she followed her own path, saw her own slight figure in the midst of that silvery expanse. And then no longer saw it. Instead another figure seemed to emerge from the distance, walk towards her with quick strides, then pause bewildered, look round. Johannes, she thought. A slender, youthful Johannes, his hair almost white in the moonlight.

But no, not Johannes. 'Leo.' Her lips moved, trembled. She rubbed her eyes. Nothing.

She turned back towards the coffin. You have your son, Johannes had said. With a little sob, Anna walked slowly back to the house.

The next day, a knock at the door startled her from fitful sleep.

'The Reverend Father is here, Frau Anna.' Frau Trübl was wiping her hands nervously on her apron. 'To make arrangements about the funeral. It's already eleven o'clock.'

Anna leapt up. She was still fully clothed, her pale blue woollen dress crumpled around her. She smoothed it, touched her hair. 'No, Frau Trübl. Send him away.'

Frau Trübl looked at her strangely. 'But . . .'

'Thank him and send him away, Frau Trübl. Johannes would not want to be buried by a priest in a churchyard.'

Anna turned away from her to draw back the curtains. The sky was high, a crisp sunny blue. It was so clear she could see the indentations of the snow on the distant peaks, almost touch the clumps of shadowy blue-green pine. Through the tracery of the elms, the tiles of the boat-house roof caught the sun. Anna took a deep shuddering breath. Then her eyes moved to the left along the curve of the lake and stopped short. Yes, she thought, yes, Johannes, there.

'I don't think, Frau Anna, that it would be right . . .'

The woman was still there. Anna veered round.

'You heard me, Frau Trübl, and ask Herr Trübl to round up some strong men. As soon as he can. Please, do as I say.' Anna stared her down.

The old woman shuffled disconsolately away.

Anna gazed out of the window. Images fluttered through her mind of Johannes and herself in those grounds, the way, a mere girl, she had stumbled over his legs as he lay sketching beneath a tree, the two of them painting, riding, lying there, the sun warming their bodies; and then later, the arguments, the storms, the pain, the departures and comings together again. And the swimming. Always the swimming, the water rippling over their bodies. She shivered.

The letter, where had she put the letter? She searched beneath her pillow. The paper still bore the marks of her rage. She smoothed it again, read, heard his voice.

She wasn't sure how much later it was that the knock came. 'They're here, Frau Anna. Four of them. As you asked,' Frau Trübl grumbled.

'Thank you, thank you.' Anna smiled a brilliant smile to console her. 'I'll be down in a few minutes. Give them a drink.'

She glanced at her face in the mirror. Pale, but calm, strangely calm. Swiftly, she pulled on a pair of trousers, a warm shirt, and then with a gesture of defiance, she ran to Johannes's room, rummaged through his drawers, found a pullover, in soft, rust-coloured wool. She sniffed in his fragrance. Yes, that would do very well.

The voices came from the kitchen. Four men and Herr Trübl were sitting at the long oak table and sipping hot drinks. Anna gestured Herr Trübl to her, took him to a corner of the room, whispered.

He grimaced. 'It's not possible, Frau Anna. Apart from anything else, the ground's too hard.'

'We'll manage.' Anna looked at him sternly. 'Of course we'll manage. There are four men, after all.' His opposition filled her with grim determination. 'Light the fire in the boathouse, boil water if we have to. Even if it takes days,' she stared him down, 'even if I have to dig myself, Herr Trübl.'

'But what about the funeral, what about Herr Eberhardt and your sister?'

For a second, Anna felt a twinge of guilt. She hadn't thought about the others. But there was no point telling them, disturbing them even more. And Max was still in hospital. It was the last thing they needed to know. In any event, Johannes was hers. Johannes would have preferred it this way.

'No, no, Herr Trübl. They couldn't come now in any event. Today. It's best today or tomorrow, if needs be.'

'As you wish, Frau Anna,' he grumbled.

'I'll meet you down there then.' She nodded to the men at the table, leaving Trübl to organize them.

Johannes's pale coffin looked strangely innocent in the midday light: a long unvarnished chest suitable for a peasant's lodging, a simple bride's trousseau. Slowly, she lifted the lid, shivered. 'Goodbye, Johannes.' Her eyes rested on the waxy effigy. With a swift movement, she lifted the gold filigree locket he had once given her from her neck. It contained a miniature, a playful copy Johannes had executed of herself as Botticelli's Venus. She placed it under his jacket, next to his heart.

She smiled to herself as she imagined the ironic curl of his lips at her gesture. 'But you'll be happy at what I've planned, Johannes. Our place,' she murmured. She closed the coffin abruptly as she heard the tread of steps crunching the snow.

The men were carrying spades and an assortment of pots and kettles. Their solemn looks did nothing to erase the comedy of their procession. Anna felt a giggle rising in her throat. She stilled it. 'This way, gentlemen. Leave the pots here. I'll come back and light the fire, if need be.'

She led them along the winding track by the side of the lake, through the break in the shrubs to the knoll, the secret site of their love. No long grass now. No fragrance of summer herbs. But the snow didn't seem too thick here. The sun warmed the place, loved it.

'Here, gentlemen.' Anna pointed. 'Just here.'

They looked at her queerly.

'There's quite enough space for several bodies, I should think. Do begin.' She stared at them fiercely, waited until the first clump of snow had been lifted, then went back to Johannes.

They lowered the coffin just at the moment that the sun chose to disappear behind the distant peaks, leaving a pale striation of soft pinks in its wake. The tears started to stream from Anna's eyes, thick, unwanted. She raised her face to the sunset, began to sing from Schubert's *Winterreise*, her voice breaking, then growing stronger.

'Ach, und fällt das Blatt zu Boden
Fällt mit ihm die Hoffnung ab,
fäll ich selber mit zu Boden
wein, wein auf meiner Hoffnung Grab.

And when the leaf falls to the ground
Hope falls with it
I too fall to the ground
Cry, cry, on my hope's grave.'

The men, gazing at her, lowered their hats. Frau Trübl began to sob. But Anna sang on, her voice rising like a shaft of pure melancholy in the cold air, now evoking Schubert's poignant hurdy-gurdy man. Yes, she thought as she sang, a fitting portrait of the artist for a Johannes emptied of all hope.

'Drüben hinterm Dorfe steht ein Leiermann,
und mit starren Fingern dreht er, was er kann.
Barfuss auf dem Eise wankt er hin und her,
und sein kleiner Teller bleibt ihm immer leer.

Keiner mag ihn hören, keiner sieht ihn an,
und die Hunde knurren um den alten Mann.
Und er lässt es gehen alles, wie es will,
dreht, und seine Leier steht ihm nimmer still.

There behind the village stands a hurdy-gurdy man,
and with stiff fingers he turns what he can,
barefoot on the ice, he hobbles here and there,
and his little plate remains forever bare.

No one wants to hear, no one looks at him
and the dogs growl round the old man
and he lets everything go as it will,
plays, and his hurdy gurdy is never still.'

As Anna crooned the final lines, almost to herself, the men, a little fearful now, began to pile the frozen clods of earth back on to the coffin.

'Wunderlicher Alter, soll ich mit dir gehn?
Willst zu meinen Liedern deine Leier drehn?

Wondrous old man, shall I go with you?
Will you play your organ to my songs?'

Late that evening Anna picked up her courage and rang Bettina to inform her that Leo wasn't here. No, no, the telegram simply had to do with a burst pipe. Silly, yes. But Johannes hadn't been available. Yes, yes, he was fine.

She couldn't bring herself to tell. Bettina would arrive, would order her away, take over her life.

And Bettina had more pressing business. Anna could tell from the high pitch of her voice how much there was, the strain she was under. But yes, Max was mending, they would soon be off.

'Has he said any more about Leo?' Anna asked at last.

There was a crackle on the line which only half explained Bettina's pause. 'Only that he assumes he'll be at that special school. Write to him there, write to the Director.' She hesitated again. 'I'll make some discreet enquiries myself again here.'

Anna could almost see her shrug. 'But don't worry too much, Anna. It's only been a few weeks. And Leo, from the sound of it, has good friends in higher places,' she raced on. 'It's Johannes you should be concerned about. Don't leave it too long.'

Anna rang off. She had left it too long. Irretrievably long.

The days passed in no particular order. She rode for hours, forcing the mare over snowy paths, or walked, never sure of her direction, wandering vaguely through the familiar countryside. She seemed unable to focus on anything except the random flitting of memory. And on self-recrimination. No newspapers came to the house. And she shunned the radio, afraid that she might accidently come upon that ranting, hysterical voice which had blighted their lives.

But she was dutiful. She wrote again to Leo at the school. When there was no response within a week, she wrote to the Head, a cagey letter saying she hoped her son was settling well. She also penned a brief note to the one friend of Leo's she knew of, Gerhardt Braun, sending the letter to the engineering faculty, since she had no other address. She toyed with the idea of going to the police, but decided to wait at least until after Bettina had left. She was fearful too of the news getting out about Johannes. There would be questions, perhaps journalists. No, better simply to wait.

Sometimes, as her mind furrowed in the strata of memory, Anna would forget why it was that she was here in this house, in these grounds, alone. To remember, she had to grapple her way up from the depths. Then the pain would knife through her, making her dizzy so that she had to clutch at the wall or crumble into a chair, or if she was riding, flatten herself against the horse's rippling back.

Every morning and at sunset, she went to the knoll where Johannes lay. She wasn't certain if she spoke aloud to him then, but often she heard his voice, coining sentences which so indelibly bore his inflection that she was certain he at least was speaking aloud.

He was kind, the Johannes of those last days in Berlin, patient, mellow, without that turbulence which had characterized so much of their life together. A Johannes, she realized, who had moved beyond hope, desire and despair. Beyond life. It was when she mouthed those words that the pain clutched at her again and she found herself on the ground, pounding his icy grave.

If mourning took her into depths, sometimes dark, sometimes glowing like a rich seam of gold, the waiting was poised at its opposite extreme, a steel-grey cloud which hovered above her, just out of her reach. It was always there, shadowing her movements, unseen but present, a dull burden which light couldn't scatter until her son appeared. Between these two poles, there was no life she could call her own.

One day when an icy drizzle fell from the skies and she had come home from her riding drenched, she found that her vague wandering through the house had brought her to the door of Johannes's room. She hadn't gone in here since that moment before his burial when she had bundled herself in his sweater. She was still wearing it. Now, impelled by a reason she couldn't name, she pushed open the door.

Nothing had been touched in the room. She had forbidden Frau Trübl to enter it. The pile of books heaped on the mahogany desk in the far corner, the gold-tipped pen, the paperweight she had given him which burst into a dazzle of autumn foliage when one shook it, were all still there under a thin film of dust. The narrow bed with its midnight-blue spread was as smooth as if it had just been made. Only the drawer which she had pulled open, and left so, provided a discordant note.

Her visits to this room had always been infrequent. It had been Johannes's private space, and now as she broached the threshold, she felt a sudden sense of trepidation. What if she should encounter a different Johannes here, one she had never met? For she knew as she crossed the space to the desk that she was about to do something she had never done before.

Between two leather book ends fashioned into wolf's heads stood a row of black bound diaries. She had never, not in her worst moments with Johannes, thought of invading these. Now, with a trembling hand, she pulled one out and opened it at random.

An undated page filled with swift pencilled script, difficult to decipher. The war.

Anna read, began to hear the noise, the blast of mines, the din of artillery. She read until the light began to fail and then read some more, until her sight grew bleary and her head sank on to the desk. The reading merged with her dreams, invading her so that when she woke with a start she no longer knew whether she was Johannes or herself and she crept into his bed with the war still ringing in her ears.

The reading began to fill her days and her nights. It was an activity which kept the waiting for Leo at bay. She began again at the beginning, and decided to ration herself, not wanting to reach the end. A Johannes she had only half understood rose out of the dense pages, a Johannes who loathed his father, a Johannes who was filled with rage and social hopes, a Johannes with Bettina, with other women, a Johannes who locked himself in his studio, who despaired, who lived at the perilous edge of existence, who loved, who cared. These various Johannes's known and unknown accompanied her on walks, spoke to her as she forced herself to eat, slept beside her. Sometimes she hated him, hated the monstrous excess of him, the remorseless anguish. Then she would come across a passage where he talked in such radiant terms about a difficulty with a particular picture, or described a burst of crocuses in spring, that she would want to melt into his arms. It was when he wrote about her that the tears filled her eyes and she began to cry unstoppably. He hailed her as a revolutionary, a supremely confident being, a pagan sensualist who knew nothing of the hypocritical morality of her time. That was early on. Later, he grew tender and irate by terms, invoking her limitless generosity, chastising her for mothering the man, rather than the child.

Anna read the diaries through three times from beginning to end and certain passages over and over until she knew them by heart, even the quotations from Nietzsche. It was in the course of the third reading that she was suddenly filled with a sense that Johannes in his death as in his life belonged not only to her but to the world, perhaps no longer a world that was, but one that might be again.

Her link with him had always been so intimate, so passionate; she herself had so little of a public sense, that she had somehow forgotten this, or at least left it to one side. Indeed, somewhere in the diaries, he had noted it about her, written that Anna had the gift of simply being, being so intensely, that she had no need to achieve anything, do anything. He had ascribed this to her magic, one of the reasons he loved her.

But now Anna felt it as a failing. A blistering stupidity. Had she had more of a public sense, she would have been more attuned to what was happening to Johannes in these last years, been more aware of the implications of the Nazi regime for him. Would perhaps have been able to prevent his suicide.

It was with this in mind that she finally ventured away from the precincts of Seehafen to go to Munich. Johannes had told her not to bother with the studio, but she now knew that she must. The scene he had described in his diary was horrific. Nonetheless something must remain of his work there to be salvaged.

She set out on a murky day when sky and earth merged into one indistinguishable shade of grey. Yet the streets of the city seemed more crowded and prosperous than ever. There were only those terrible signs in the shop windows to remind one: 'JEWS NOT ADMITTED.' Like the signs there had once been about dogs, only larger. Anna shuddered, picked her way through traffic, pausing, without quite realizing that she was doing so, to scan the faces of the many men in uniform.

It was because of an idea which had taken hold of her that week, in the wake of the letter she had received telling her that Leo Adler had not appeared at the Institute. The letter had been suspicious, full of what she read as veiled threats as if she, herself, were responsible for Leo's non-attendance.

She had hastened to reply to say that there had been a misunderstanding and made light of the whole thing. It had then occurred to her that if Leo had not gone to the school, he might have lied about his age and enlisted in one of the numerous branches of Hitler's police. So now she skimmed those passing youthful faces. They were so bland, so expressionless beneath their caps, and yet so arrogant, as if there were nothing more natural than to kick up one's heels and march through city streets in brisk bands, like so many segments of a single machine powered from a distant source.

She parked the car around the corner from the studio, and made her way a little tremulously through the courtyard to knock at the caretaker's door.

'Frau Bahr.' Old Hans peered round the edge of the door and glanced over her shoulder surreptitiously, before beckoning her in. 'I'm so glad you've come.' His expression belied his words. 'I was beginning to worry . . .' He left the sentence unfinished.

'Here I am, Hans.' Anna tried to look reassuring.

The room was stuffy, crowded. The old man shuffled over to a table and unearthed a pile of envelopes which he handed to her. 'I had the apartment cleaned, best I could.' He peered at her, then shrugged dolefully. 'Rotten mess it was.'

'Thank you, Hans.' Anna reached into her purse. 'It must have cost.'

'You're very kind, Frau Bahr, very kind.' He stared at her for a moment, then lowered his voice. 'Herr Bahr told me to keep whatever could be rescued. I'd really rather you took it away.' He looked furtively out of the small window as if afraid that someone might be spying in. 'You see . . .'

'Of course, Hans. I've brought the car.'

'Good, good.' He tweaked his ear cannily, came closer to her. 'It's all downstairs,' he pointed towards the cellar, 'wrapped in old sheets. I'll get Gunter from next door to give us a hand. Will you wait here?'

'I'll go up for a moment first.' Anna tried to keep her voice calm.

The old man's eyes narrowed. 'I wouldn't, Frau Bahr. Your husband didn't ask me to repaint and . . . well, the walls . . .'

'I want to see,' Anna murmured.

He hedged, lowering his voice. 'I don't know if Herr Bahr mentioned it to you. There's a woman staying. Frau Feldman.'

Anna stiffened. She had been certain Johannes had stopped all that in these last years. But now, there it was. Another woman. Like Bruno, she suddenly thought, like that woman, Lotte, at his funeral, materializing only at his death.

Old Hans was rambling on, nervously. 'She came with a note from Herr Bahr. Only a few days, he said. But she's still here. I don't have the heart to ask her to leave.' He shrugged. 'Perhaps, if you don't want her there . . .'

Anna strode past him and made her way slowly up the stairs.

The swastika on the door gave her pause, even though Johannes's diary had prepared her for it. Its spokes began to swirl before her eyes, like those of a giant threshing machine obliterating everything in its path.

She knocked at the door. No answer. After a further knock and wait, Anna turned her key in the lock and walked softly through the corridor. The scrawls on the white walls followed her like raucous obscenities. She stopped at the door of the large studio and looked round. Bare of Johannes's work, it had a kind of ghostly emptiness. On the long table, the vials of powder and empty jars, the brushes, were neatly ranged – as they had never been while he worked here. She picked up one of the brushes, fingered it, and then thrust it down again. No, she wouldn't take it. She would leave everything as it was. It was only the work that mattered.

But where was this Frau Feldman? Anna shivered. Perhaps she should steal away now without confronting her. No. She wanted to see her. Wanted to with the same avidity as she had wanted to read Johannes's diaries. His last woman, apart from her. Perhaps she knew something more about those final days. It was madness that jealousy could still prick her like this. Jealousy over a dead man, compounded with anger.

Anna knocked firmly at the door of the bedroom and then thrust it open.

A dark figure sat by the table beside the window.

'Frau Feldman,' Anna said firmly.

The woman turned. Wispy grey hair round a lined frightened face.

'Frau Feldman,' Anna said more softly, gazing into a creased face that couldn't belong to a mistress. 'I'm Anna Bahr.'

Visible relief spread over the woman's strained features. 'Frau Bahr.' She leapt up, shook Anna's hand. 'I'm so grateful to you, so grateful to Herr Bahr. I hope I haven't outstayed my welcome. It's just that I've nowhere to go.' Her eyes filled with tears.

Anna's expression spoke her query.

'Herr Bahr hasn't told you?' The woman frowned. 'What a shock for you to find me here then. But of course, he wouldn't want to bother your pretty head with such things.'

'Tell me,' Anna said in a low voice.

The woman scrutinized her, seemed to reach a decision. 'The Gestapo have taken my son, my Heinzl, to one of their camps.' She glanced out of the window, her face grim as if she could see what her son was being subjected to. 'They've taken the house, as well.' She turned back to Anna. 'Herr Bahr, your husband, was the only Gentile I felt I could turn to. You know Heinzl was his friend, wrote about him, bought several of his paintings.' She passed her hand nervously through her hair. 'I don't know when he'll come back.' A little sob escaped her, then, restraining herself, she murmured, 'Please say to Herr Bahr that I hope he won't mind my staying on a little longer. Until I hear something.' She sank back into the chair, her face utterly devoid of hope.

'Of course, you must stay here as long as you like.' With an impulsive gesture, Anna suddenly reached for Frau Feldman's hand and squeezed it. Another woman, like herself, sitting by the window, waiting for her son. 'Have you enough money? Food?' Anna murmured, noting how thin the woman looked.

Frau Feldman turned away in confusion. 'I paid this man, a large sum, to get news for me. To . . .' She shrugged. 'I don't need much.'

'No,' Anna mumbled. 'But I'll see that Hans brings you some supplies. To save you shopping.' She was suddenly embarrassed.

'Thank you, my dear.' The woman looked up at her gratefully. 'And please thank Herr Bahr. It was so kind of him. I didn't know where to turn.'

'Johannes is dead, Frau Feldman.' Anna didn't know why she chose to say it now, out loud for the first time. And to a complete stranger. But it was said, and like a secret made public, it brought a flush to her cheeks, and instantly too a rush of tears.

'Oh my poor dear.' The woman's frail arms were round her. 'My poor, poor dear. But how? It's so sudden. Why I saw him only . . .' She stopped herself, as if she had suddenly understood. 'Terrible times,' she murmured. 'Such terrible times.'

Anna dabbed at her eyes, nodded. 'If you need anything, Frau Feldman . . .' She scribbled the Seehafen number on a slip of paper. 'I must go now. The men will be waiting for me downstairs. I wanted to gather together Johannes's work.'

The old woman nodded. 'Take care of yourself, my dear.' Watery old eyes studied her for a moment, 'And tell your children what a good man Herr Bahr was, a great man. Don't let those Nazis get you down,' she whispered the last.

Draped in greying sheets, Johannes's canvases stood like tattered ghosts by the gates of the courtyard. There weren't many. His letter to her had warned Anna of that. But it was something. She let the men bundle the canvases into the car, put the sheaves of drawings on the front seat. In the midst of the loading, a uniformed band turned into the street. Anna felt the sweat break out on her brow. For the first time since the Nazis had come into power, she tasted the meaning of fear. She held herself rigidly still, saw the look of panic in old Hans's eyes.

But the men weren't interested in them. They marched past the car, halted a little way up the street and pounded on a door. She saw it open an inch, saw them force their way in, heard a burst of voices, a scream. A hot rage rose in her. She wanted to lash out, hit at them, anything to stop the callous brutality of that invasion.

'Go now, Frau Bahr, while they're busy.' Old Hans was tugging at her sleeve. 'Quickly, quickly.'

For a moment, Anna felt she couldn't move. Then, as she took in Hans's frightened face, she forced herself into action, swiftly thanked him and manoeuvred her way out of the street. She realized as she reached the city gates that she never wanted to return here again.

It was enough, Johannes had said. Bettina, she remembered, had said it too. Now, as frail old Frau Feldman's face flitted before her eyes and counterposed itself with the bland unseeing features of the young uniformed men, she shuddered grimly and understood in her bones what they had meant.

Yet Leo was probably amongst those men. Her son. An executioner. Somehow, she must try to communicate to him the hideous enormity of what he was engaged in, make him see.

The next day, with a sense that she was undertaking another step in a protracted rite, Anna made it her business to find an assortment of rubber sheeting, the kind the farmers sometimes used to protect their haystacks from storms. These to hand, she spent the next week gathering together Johannes's paintings and, sometimes with Herr Trübl's grumbling help, carrying them down to the cellar. The walls glared at her in their new bareness. The conservatory, which had served as his second studio, became a barren shell, only the mural he had painted of her so long ago still there to bear witness to his presence.

As she covered the huddled canvases with the sheeting in the dark cellar, the figures seemed to leap out at her, moan, refuse her stifling of them. 'For the future,' she said out loud, almost as if they could hear her, 'the future'. The words rebounded emptily amongst the columns.

The task done, there was one more she had set herself. She wanted to erect a stone to mark Johannes's grave, something which spoke of him, something of which he might have approved, but when she scoured the local stonemasons' workshops, nothing seemed appropriate. The matter preoccupied her, she knew, beyond its real importance, as if it were freighted with emotions she refused to confront.

Then one day, as she was leading her mare along a precipitous path which bordered a stream, she saw it. There, jutting from the racing waters, stood a dark, jagged stone, not too tall, its rugged jet surface like an unhewn obelisk. It was perfect. But how to excavate it from the stream? She would need help: two men with picks, perhaps three, a sledge to drag it home with. She couldn't rest until it was done.

The weather proved inclement. Driving sleet, then snow, hindered her efforts for the next days, alongside Herr Trübl's insistence that her plan was out of the question. Anna waited, unable to think of anything else, possible inscriptions going round and round in her mind and flurrying through her dreams in a bizarre series of associations about Johannes, about his father, about her son, about Germany. The proverbial '*ein Volk der Dichter und Denker*' – a people of poets and thinkers – catapulted into '*Richter und Henker*' – judges and executioners, so that Johannes, the artist, the thinker emerged as both son and father of the judge and executioner.

It was while she was concentrating intently on the matter of the stone that the letter arrived – one stiff sheet of paper, bearing an unknown address.

Dear Frau Bahr,

I am afraid to say that I have not seen Leo for some weeks. And I, too, have begun to feel concern over this. Should you hear from him before I do, please do ask him to contact me. I have a matter of some urgency to convey to him.

Yours with best German greetings,
Heil Hitler
Gerhardt Braun.

Anna's letter had evidently taken some time to reach Gerhardt Braun. And his response gave her pause. It spoke to her of a Leo about whom she knew nothing, of a young man who had urgent matters to attend to beyond her knowledge. Of a young man who could say 'Heil Hitler' with no second thoughts.

She suddenly remembered the passage about Leo in Johannes's diary. She had avoided thinking about it, had sped over it in her reading. But now it all came back, Johannes's shock at seeing those judging young eyes directed at him in his studio. Eyes which seemed to him to bear the accusing weight of the entire new Germany, with its search for a eugenic purity, its blind intolerance, its murderous suspicion of anything which deviated from that simple-minded ideal of blue-eyed strength – as if human beings were so many plants to be bred to achieve the most potent strain, the weaker varieties or those bearing exotic flowers to be trodden underfoot.

And what, Johannes had reflected, if he had had a son? Would he, too, have judged him with that eugenic executioner's bluntness? What, indeed, if this young man with the pure deadly gaze were in fact his son, whatever Anna thought? Which meant he had two sons, both of whom had been taken from him with his passive acquiescence. Cain and Abel. No, the passage finished, this was the kind of thinking that led only to madness.

She was sitting in the conservatory when these thoughts besieged her and suddenly she started to cry again. She had been dry-eyed for days, all her energies concentrated on the business of the stone. And now the tears flowed with an added impetus. She looked up at the mural. Through her tears it had the luminosity it had borne the day Johannes had painted it. Eve in her garden a day before the fall.

And the fall had come so quickly. She shivered as she saw Bruno before her: Bruno in a rage, bounding savagely into her room; Bruno thinking only of Johannes, his mind fixed on her betrayal. The scene of Leo's conception, she had somehow assumed. A conception in which Johannes had been a full if not physical participant. Or what if it were the other way around and Leo had been conceived in the following days, Bruno the shadowy third presence, Johannes the father? As it must have been for Bettina with Max.

Anna's thoughts whirled. Perhaps she had stolen his son from Johannes, betrayed him. And then Leo had tried to convince himself that Johannes was his father, had wanted to excise the Jew, Bruno, at all costs.

Anna started to laugh shrilly. A male madness. What did that small physical moment matter at all in a history which was compounded of so many days, so many other facts? Yet Leo, she knew, felt his very life depended on it. She remembered his face at that Christmas Eve dinner, when she had said to him quietly, 'But your father was a Jew.'

Yes, he felt his life depended on it. And it was probably because of that that he had never turned up at his school. The lunacy of the times they lived in. The eugenic consciousness, as Johannes called it, blood purity raised to a religion. She would have to explain to Leo when he came back how mad, how unimportant it all was.

When he came back. He had to come back. She had been so remiss, so timid in her guilt, but now she would make up for it.

Anna slept. Lay down on the divan in the conservatory and let sleep overcome her. In it, time moved backwards and she was hurled back to that summer during the war when Johannes had appeared as if by magic on the grassy knoll.

When she woke a mellow light streamed through the great glass panes of the conservatory. In the distance, she heard the chirrup of a bird. She opened the wide doors.

There was a breath of spring in the air. She could almost feel a slight stirring in the earth. It came to her with a superstitious certainty born of the snarl of her dreams that he would come now. Now that the earth was stirring, Leo would make a sign. Would come, as Johannes had come. Suddenly. To take her by surprise. But to be taken by surprise, she had to give up her waiting.

There would be the grounds to tend to soon, but it was an activity which left her mind too free to wait and to envisage disaster. She would have to find something else. Anna knelt to touch the earth. It was wet, muddy, but soft. At last, today they could try to dislodge the stone from the stream bed. Then she would inscribe it herself, chisel out each letter with care, a lover's monument to Johannes, to mark his place, their place. And then? She blotted out her thoughts and raced to find Herr Trübl.

The stone was duly lifted and brought home, not without difficulty. Anna began to practise her chiselling, hammering out the simple epitaph she had finally decided on – JOHANNES BAHR. ARTIST DREAMER 1888–1935 – in a variety of scripts on a variety of stones.

The task was harder than she had supposed, the rocks chipping differently, depending on their type. When at last she thought she was proficient enough to begin, a letter arrived from Bettina, a long letter, not those short notes she had sent from the many stopping places in their trajectory. Anna read it avidly, but was overwhelmed as she did so by the sense of the distance between them. An ocean of unspoken things.

They had at last stopped their travels, Bettina announced, at the furthest edge of the world from Germany: California. Klaus had gone on ahead. He had fallen in love with the landscape, the vegetation, and assured them that it was a better stopping place than New York, though she herself had a preference for the latter. Never mind. They had arrived. And there was a family consensus that they now wanted none of their things. Anna could sell all that weighty furniture which smelled of Germany, and use the money for her and Johannes's and Leo's journey. And if there was sufficient, for two little Jewish girls – Bettina gave names and addresses. They could do any sums that needed doing when they were all in America together.

She couldn't say that things were going to be easy for them in America, but the country was full of marvels. And there were almost no men in uniform. That made up for a great deal. She was certain that Anna and Johannes would love it here, so they must hurry and join them.

They all trusted that Leo had now been located and that Anna had convinced him of the necessity of a move. She, herself, had left him a letter in the Berlin house to that effect, which she hoped had gone some way towards this. If, by any chance, he had still not appeared, she suggested that Anna continue to stay clear of the police, since any interest in their affairs from official quarters might make departure more difficult, particularly for Johannes. He could hardly be in any better odour with the authorities, given their latest shameful attack on the arts.

There was only one thing Klaus wanted from Germany: his books on plants and flowers. They had been left in Seehafen. If things hadn't been moved round too much, Anna would find them on the right wall of the library on the middle shelves. As for the rest, they only awaited a telegram signalling their date of arrival.

Anna gazed out the window and stifled an involuntary sob.

There would be no arrival for Johannes in America. There was no Johannes at all except for the phantom who traversed her memories and dreams. As for her, everything depended on Leo. Without him, she too was a phantom with only the past to roam in.

Bettina's mention of the police in conjunction with Johannes reawakened Anna's sense that there was now really no need to avoid the authorities. Yes, that would be the right thing. To go to Berlin, sort out Bettina's affairs, take care of the children she had mentioned, and then alert the Berlin police. She could do so in the least heated manner: explain that there had been a family disagreement, make light of it, but nonetheless display her maternal worry over the whereabouts of her son.

The decision made, Anna forced herself into activity. The library first. Klaus's books. She would post them from Munich.

It didn't take her long to find them: five untitled folio-size volumes bound in thick maroon leather, each creamy page bearing careful drawings. Klaus's drawings, she suddenly realized. How odd that no one had ever drawn her attention to their existence.

She lingered over them now, entranced by their beauty, the delicate lines and curls of stamens and pistils, the filigree of petals, flowers she knew and others she had never seen. In a strange way these creamy pages reminded her of Johannes's diaries. An intensity emanated from them, a sense of private musing.

She sighed as she lifted the last volume from the shelf and set it down beside the others on the desk. But there were no drawings here. How strange, Anna thought, to open a bound book and find nothing, simply an expanse of untouched pages, their very blankness somehow calling out for markings.

Then, on the top of what should have been the first page, she discerned a few marks, pencilled in the lightest hand and then seemingly erased. She switched on the reading lamp. There was a date, 1913, and then some words: 'Male and female exist in the plant world. But do they ever exhibit a sense of sexual property? Bettina . . .' The rest was unclear, no matter how near to the light she lifted the volume.

Pondering the words, Anna closed the tome. With an indecisive gesture, she first placed it on top of the others, and then moved it to one side. What could Klaus possibly want with an empty book? No, it would be better to leave it here, just here. She moved it to the centre of the desk and glanced at it once more before leaving the library.

The trip to Munich and then to Berlin passed in a haze. She had lost the aptitude for speaking to people, for negotiating the simplest situations. There had been too much time alone, communing only with her ghosts. Everything felt bizarre and at a distance, so that her voice seemed to resound too loudly when she put a simple question to the conductor, or the storage-firm attendant or bank clerk. The house in Grunewald, where she had nurtured an irrepressible hope that she might find a sign of Leo, was empty: a tomb replete only with soundless whispers.

The police headquarters which she built up enough courage to approach on her third day felt as awesome as a temple to some monstrous deity. An alien horde inhabited it. Here the greetings of 'Heil Hitler' had grown into a barrage, accosting her at every turn.

When she finally found her way to the appropriate officer, it was as if she were performing in a masquerade, her quandary a badly scripted play in which her hearer thought her either deeply suspicious or mad. She had the despairing sense that the few notes he took would lead to no action and her voiced protest would result only in macabre comedy. How could one say one had misplaced one's son? Misplaced him some months back and only now thought to report it? What shining example of German motherhood had we here?

After the ordeal with the police, Anna wandered randomly through the streets and averted her gaze from passers-by. She felt strangely humiliated, utterly alone. If she were to disappear now, no one to whom it mattered would register the fact for months. No, she musn't think like that.

If only Katarina were still alive for her to talk to, to turn to, but she had died in childbirth, all those years back. Anna had only learned of it weeks after the event. Left a son, a son without a mother. And now here she was, a mother without a son.

It was when she looked up from the pavement that she saw him. Right there, on the other side of the road, his shoulders tautly square, the neck rising firm into that trim blond nape, that slightly stiff long-legged walk. She dashed across the street, oblivious of the traffic, dimly heard the screech of a car, a man's angry shout. But it was drowned by her own.

'Leo, Leo!' She raced after him, put a staying hand on his arm. 'Leo, at last.'

She looked in confusion at the stranger's face that turned to her, a glowering, hostile face with narrowed eyes. The man shook her hand forcibly off his arm.

'I'm sorry. Apologies,' Anna mumbled. 'I thought . . .'

'Keep your thoughts and your hands to yourself,' the man muttered and strode away.

She was trembling, her sudden burst of hope shattered as violently as if a hammer had been taken to a fragile crystal goblet.

She left Berlin that evening. The notion that she couldn't recognize her son began to obsess her. She didn't know him, not even enough to distinguish him from a stranger. And the correlative was that he didn't know her, knew nothing of her. Yet here she was, her existence propelled only by the hope that he would return, that she had somehow to save him from all that he seemed independently to want.

When she returned to Seehafen the next day and began at last to chisel away at Johannes's tombstone, it was these thoughts which continued to preoccupy her. She was kneeling in front of the jagged rock, which had been placed in the boathouse, and she found herself addressing it. 'Tell me what to do, Johannes, tell me.' But her words provoked no response. Only the chip and scrape of steel on stone was to be heard, and she laughed at her own anguished plea.

That night, looking for a world outside the maze of her own thoughts, she crossed the threshold of the library again, this room which she had always thought too severe, too forbidding. She pulled a novel randomly from the shelves and went to sit at the desk. Klaus's leather-bound volume was still there. She let her fingers run over the grain of the cover and then opened it to examine those erased lines once more. They still wouldn't come clear. It was the date that was most prominent. 1913.

Yes, how well she remembered that summer. She could almost touch that stiff white linen dress she used to wear.

Suddenly the house seemed crowded with voices, the bustle of Bettina, her friends, a bearded, gangly Klaus, Bruno, burly in his driving gear, Miss Isabel, with her slightly protruding eyes, Johannes, mellow-voiced, so seductive.

Anna gazed at the creamy page. It seemed to beckon to her. With a little shiver, she picked up the pen which stood in the inkstand and traced over the date. 1913. She had asked Johannes what to do and here was an answer. A story for Leo, a story to fill the waiting, a story she could never tell him if he were sitting there in front of her. But a story he could read, if only to make him understand, just a little, about her life, Johannes's, Bettina's, all their lives. His own, too.

Scenes from the past began to race through Anna's mind and with only a momentary hesitation, the words to fit them flowed from her pen, until dawn took her by surprise.

Her days now shaped themselves into a new pattern. In the mornings after a dreamy canter, she worked, still dreaming, on Johannes's stone. Worked slowly, as if unwilling that the process should reach an end. Then, after a stroll and lunch, she sat down at the desk and let her dream of the past find words.

When her shoulders and fingers grew stiff with the writing, she went out into the gardens. Spring was now well on its way and the crocuses poked their fat purple and white heads through the grass. There was earth to be turned now, flowers to be planted, in the ever-expanding days. Around Johannes's grave, she seeded poppies and forget-me-nots, placed little clumps of violets and primula, tiny bulbs of autumn-flowering cyclamen, some rambling roses to transform the knoll into a bower. Sometimes as she worked, she would stop to look over her shoulder, as if sensing or hoping for a presence which might imminently materialize.

In the evening, she always returned to those creamy white pages, filling them with her small, flowing script. The library had begun to grow friendly, an Aladdin's cave replete with treasures. She had only to pen the magic words and its secrets opened themselves to her, insights she didn't know she possessed, matter garnered from Johannes's diary, distant conversations with Bettina. What she didn't know for certain, she imagined – the imaginings taking on a reality as she struggled to understand, Bettina, Bruno, Leo, even Klaus, always so silent.

These pages, she realized as she wrote, were her testament. To be bequeathed to Leo, to the house, to the future. A future, she increasingly sensed, she had no place in.

They were also a way of defying time. While she lived in the past, the sense of lack which was overwhelmingly her present could be kept at bay.

When she had passed the half-way mark in that thick bound volume, it came to her that she was swiftly catching up with that empty present.

Racing towards it in fact, the material of their lives too painful to dwell on.

It was then that the pact she had made with herself but refused to voice forced its way to the forefront of her mind. 'There isn't much longer, Leo. Come soon,' she murmured aloud. The saying of it to this house which seemed to carry all their secrets made her feel lightheaded. Strangely free.

The next day, she didn't write. She had put off the laying of Johannes's stone too long, in the superstitious hope that Leo might arrive in time for it. But now, she felt it must be done, perhaps because the sky had such a limpid clarity, perhaps because the clouds floated with that particular laziness of early summer. Perhaps because she had reached that point in her narrative where Johannes's despair called out to her with a bitter urgency.

Anna summoned the men to carry the stone to the knoll. She stayed there long after they had left, fingering its cool surface, so dark as it jutted out amidst the brightness of the flowers. The layers of gold paint in the chiselled letters glinted fiercely in the light, like Johannes's eyes when he was angry.

She smiled at her own thought and gazed out on the green-tinged waters. Soon, it would be warm enough to swim. With a little sigh, she lay down on the sun-warmed grass next to the grave. 'It won't be long now, my love,' she whispered, 'when the grass grows high and the poppies bloom crimson. Our time. Not very long.'

PART TWO

SEVENTEEN

1985

A SINGLE TABLE LAMP lit the large rectangular room. In its immediate glow, a woman sat, her pale golden head all but buried in her crossed arms. She looked like a child who had fallen into innocent sleep, reluctantly but soundly.

At the door of the room a tall burly man gazed at her in consternation. With swift silent steps, he crossed over to her. After a moment's hesitation, he lifted her in his arms and carried her towards a worn leather sofa.

'Let me go.' Her eyes suddenly fluttered open. 'Let me go,' she repeated more loudly, struggling, waving long legs in the air, landing a deft kick on his.

He dropped her unceremoniously on to the sofa.

'What do you think you're doing?' She looked at him with flashing eyes, brushed the sleeves of her jumper as if his hands had been covered in dirt.

He laughed a short grumbling laugh. 'I really think that's my question, don't you?' He repeated it for her with a different emphasis. 'What do you think *you're* doing here?'

Helena Latimer glanced around her and had the grace to look at least slightly disconcerted. 'I . . . I guess I must have fallen asleep reading.'

'That much I gathered for myself.' The man's eyes were amused.

'Anna's Book.' Helena gestured towards the table. 'Finished it though, if that's all there is. Interesting. Very. Upsetting, too.'

'I'm sure Anna would be grateful for the review. But that doesn't answer my question.'

'You mean she's still alive!' She looked at him in amazement. 'I'd love to meet her.'

'No, she's not. Well . . .' He tapped his foot impatiently. 'I think I deserve an explanation. I don't usually come back at night to find a stranger curled up in the library. Did you break in?'

'Certainly not.' Helena leapt off the sofa and started to pace. Her eyes fell on the spectacle case with its broken glasses. She must collect her wits, proceed carefully. She had come here on business, perhaps dangerous business. In search of Max Bergmann. What was it that she had dreamt? Max calling to her from a dark dank place. She shook the image from her mind, turned towards her inquisitor. 'A young woman let me in, told me to wait. In here.'

'I see.' He laughed pleasantly enough. 'A long wait. Elsa can be a little forgetful.'

'You speak very good English.' Helena suddenly stared at him in astonishment. It had just occurred to her that not only were they speaking English, but that this was odd in the remoteness of the Bavarian countryside. The confusion of her dreams was still just a blink away. But at least he didn't look so dangerous now, despite his size and the strange shadows the light cast. A big man with tousled hazel hair and large hazel eyes, soft eyes. A dimple in a chin which needed shaving. A mobile nose.

'Shouldn't I speak English? I've had lots of practice.' He was laughing at her.

'Look, I think I'm still half asleep. Could I come back in the morning? To talk about the business, I mean.'

'Not if you're about to sell me double glazing. Or a fitted kitchen . . .'

'No, not a thing to sell.'

'In that case, you might as well spend the *rest* of the night here.' He gestured towards the window.

Helena looked out. Thick flakes of snow were falling from a steel-grey sky. The ground was covered with them. She glanced at her watch: two o'clock. She had had no idea it was so late.

'Not many hotels in the vicinity open at this time of night, even if you managed to find one.' He was wry. 'And there are a few rooms here to spare.'

'That's very kind,' she murmured, her hesitation visible. 'But . . . Is there anyone else here?'

He shook his head, walked towards her.

She stepped back.

'I can assure you I'm not a rapist.'

'I wasn't . . .' she protested, though that old sexual fear had niggled beneath the greater one.

'Nor a murderer.' He laughed loudly, the sound echoing strangely through the empty house.

'No, no, of course not, I didn't mean . . .'

'Still, if you'd rather brave the weather, Murnau's not that far away.'

'No, no, I'd like to stay.' Helena smoothed her jumper and her trousers, gave him a bright smile. 'Thank you, it's very kind of you.'

'Have you got a case? Shall I get it for you?'

'No, that's all right. I can get it.'

'Suit yourself. But don't forget your reading glasses.' He handed her the blue case she had left on the table.

Helena blinked, scrutinized him. 'They're not mine. I found them here.'

'Strange.' He followed her through the door, watched as she reached for her coat. 'I wonder who left them.'

'Someone who came to visit, I imagine.' She swallowed hard.

'Now why hadn't I thought of that?' He gave her a sardonic look.

She was so preoccupied with trying to read his face in the half light that she slipped as soon as she stepped out on the first marble step. He caught her. She leaned heavily against him for a moment, then backed away from the intimacy of the touch. 'Should have worn my boots,' she muttered stiffly.

'Why don't you just give me your keys.' He was eyeing her with evident impatience.

Helena dug into her pocket, handed them over, watched while he walked to the car.

Was he lying about Max's specs, she wondered? No, perhaps not. But then there must be someone else in the house, someone who had seen Max. Who? Her mind reeled, too full of vibrant dreams, of all those characters in the book whose lives intersected with this house. For it had to be this house. And the boy called Max who had spurred her reading. Was he her Max? It was too improbable. Her Max wasn't German. Yet his letter had described the lie of the land in front of her and the house so exactly . . .

Helena shook out her hair as if the gesture would give clarity to her thoughts. She breathed deeply of the cold moist air. It was beautiful outside, the thick flakes falling from the midnight blue of the sky, the trees sparkling in their white cloaks. And so still.

The muffled slam of her car door fractured it. In a moment the man was back.

'Thank you.' She took her bag from him.

'Any time,' he smiled. 'Shall I get you a cup of coffee?'

She shook her head.

'Tea, then, herb tea, I imagine, for you. A tisane.'

'How did you know?'

He laughed.

The knowingness of that laugh grated. But she followed him silently past the wide staircase, through a set of doors, then another, to a low cluttered room with a long refectory table. Funny, it was as if she had already been here. Anna's Book. She had in a way.

'Do you live here alone?' she asked.

'Sometimes.' He was non-committal as he put the kettle to boil on the old stove, warmed the teapot, brought out a tin of biscuits with practised gestures.

'You're American,' Helena suddenly said.

'That too.' He glanced at her sardonically.

'I'm sorry. Still asleep. It's only just occurred to me. That book, it's made me dizzy. Too much reading. All that painful history.' She rubbed her eyes, sat down at the table, focused on a bowl of gleaming red apples. 'May I?' she asked, biting in before he had a chance to answer. 'It made me forget to eat as well.'

'Another sterling review for poor old Anna. Here, help yourself.' He put a slab of cheese on the table, cut some slices of bread. 'Hope you appreciated my title.'

'*The Possessed*?'

He nodded.

'Yes, it fits them all,' Helena mused, looked up at him. 'Your title, you say?' Then it came to her. 'Those people in the book, they're your family?'

'Don't look so astonished. I'm not a ghost. You can touch if you like.'

She let that pass, was silent for a moment. 'Why *poor* Anna?'

'Just a manner of speaking.' He turned a chair round, back forwards, and sat astride it, examining her reflectively as he sipped his wine. 'Now that we're friends of a kind, are you going to tell me what you're doing here?'

Helena looked at him. He was what her friend Claire would call 'dishy'.

She could hear her uttering it, could see her sidling up to him, clinking glasses, and saying in her best Mae West imitation, eyes and hips rolling, 'Hiya, Handsome.'

'I'm on holiday,' she said at last.

'Sure. And you reckoned this place was a wayside hotel, so you thought you'd just step in and stay the night.'

She laughed. 'Can it wait until morning?'

'Okay. What shall we talk about now while you gorge yourself on the hotel food?'

'How about telling me who you are?'

'Now why didn't I think of that?' He rose quickly to his feet and stood to mock attention. 'Adam Peters, thirty-four years of age, sometime anthropologist. Six foot two, eyes definitely not blue. Will that do for a start?'

Helena grinned, nodded. 'And what are you doing here?'

'Working.'

'As an anthropologist?' She was sceptical.

'We're a wandering breed. Your turn now.' He deflected the question poised on her lips.

'Helena Latimer, twenty-eight years old,' she paused, wondering whether to say it, decided to prevaricate, 'writer, five foot six. Eyes definitely blue and brain definitely fuddled.'

'Hello there.' He stretched out his hand.

She took it a little shyly.

'Glad that you're staying the night. Though if we don't watch it, it'll soon be morning. Now let's see, which room shall it be?' He gestured grandly, then chuckled, 'I guess it will have to be the clean one. And don't worry, there's a lock on the door.'

It was already eleven o'clock when Helena woke the next day. The unusual lateness of the hour, the strangeness of her surroundings made her want to prick herself to see if she were properly awake.

She looked round the little room she was in. A girl's room, a maidenly room, she thought, remembering that she had had the same thought the night before. A room with bright yellow curtains tied with white bows, daisy-chain wallpaper and a narrow frilled bed.

The view as she looked out of the window was breathtaking. Young Anna's room, it came to her. The pages she had read the day before haunted her again, like a prior existence over which her own was being played out.

She snuggled back under the warm duvet. She had to think about Max Bergmann, not about those ghosts from another time with their exorbitant passions and ravaged histories. Max, like a clever Hansel, had laid out a trail for her, gleaming pebbles in a dark wood. She had only to find them and the paths that led home to him would be clear. So far, she had located only the first.

He must definitely have come here to this house. But had he met Adam Peters, who had pretended not to recognize the spectacle case?

The man was American which made things harder, meant she had to be more careful. Adam Peters would certainly know the name of Max Bergmann, sage of Orion County, campaigner on environmental issues. And so? If Max had chosen not to identify himself, had chosen not to name names and places in his letter to her, that could only mean there was danger of some kind.

She couldn't allow herself to trust this Adam Peters too quickly, however easy-going his charm: he could be anyone. He could be a CIA agent. The thought tumbled into her head with the force of a revelation.

But no, she was letting her imagination run away with her again. She must keep calm, must find out what this Adam Peters knew before giving anything away. She would check with the Greens in Munich, see if they had anything on him, on this house. Perhaps there was some kind of farm attached to it that Max had been interested in, some breeding ground for new species. And he had been caught out spying. No, that didn't hang together either. He wouldn't have had to keep that from her.

Helena rubbed her eyes, started slowly to dress.

She had dreamt about Max again last night. She was wandering through the streets of Munich, but the men were all frightening, dressed in uniform, as in Anna's Book. Then Munich had somehow merged into Bhopal – streets of pain under reddened skies, and she was stumbling amidst the afflicted. She was just a small girl and on the other side of a flaming pyre, she saw Max. She screamed out to him. And he came running. He sat her on his lap and talked to her in that special voice of his. Talked to her like a father, until the cries around her and in her ceased. But she couldn't remember his words, only that she had thrown her arms around his neck and wept.

Helena shook the image away. Arriving at the place Max had described seemed only to have made her thoughts more chaotic, her dreams more vivid, her actions more like those of a somnambulist. The disaster at Bhopal had shaken her more than she liked professionally to admit. And Max's disappearance on top of it, that uncanny notice about his presumed death, had toppled her self-control. No wonder her editor had been urging her to take a break – though she sensed a holiday was not what was in order. She knew she would only find her balance again when she had found Max.

Ever since Emily had died, it was Max who had been her still centre, the pole around which everything revolved. He was her mentor, her ideal reader, her guide. Without him, it was as if the earth had grown fluid beneath her feet. One couldn't walk on water, let alone run, which was what she preferred to do. She had to find him. And quickly, for her sake as much as for his.

Her task this morning was to discover why Max had described this house, when he had been here and where he was now. And until she knew whether Adam Peters was a neutral party, she needed an alibi.

By the time she had pulled on a fresh jumper, stolen out to the bathroom to wash, and come back to her room to put on a dab of lipstick and brush her hair, Helena had one in place. She went in search of her host.

Adam Peters, however, was nowhere to be found, not in the kitchen nor in the library. She was tempted to open some of the many other doors – doors that Anna had opened, Johannes had walked through as much as doors which might lead her to Max. But she restrained herself. It wouldn't do to be found snooping too soon.

Helena let herself out of the house instead.

A wintry sun hung like a pale lozenge in the swirling cloud-strewn sky. In the distance, the tall shadowy firs rose into craggy peaks capped with snow. There was a sublime beauty about it all; why then did she have this shiver of apprehension?

She set out down the drive, then turned off on a path banked by drooping rhododendron. It curved into another, which gave on to an ancient spreading beech. There was a child's swing hanging from one of the branches. An ancient slab of wood lightly covered with snow. But the ropes looked new. Again she had the strange sense that she had been here before. She perched on the swing. The cold air tickled her nostrils as she propelled herself through the air.

In the distance she heard the hum of an engine, the slam of a door. She swung a little longer and then, somewhat recalcitrantly, went back to the house. She wondered whether she should knock, decided against it. The door wasn't locked.

'Hello,' she called out softly.

There was no answering call and she made her way towards the kitchen. Before she got there, a door burst open and Adam emerged from what seemed to be some nether depth.

'Morning.' He waved a wrench at her good-humouredly. There were prominent holes in his thick green sweater. 'Boiler's acting up again. But the coffee's hot and I cook a mean brunch.'

'Sounds good.' She followed him into the kitchen. There was a boxful of groceries at the end of the table.

He ushered her towards a chair, busied himself, whistled scraps of unidentifiable tunes.

'Scrambled eggs, fresh sausage . . .'

'No sausage, thanks. I don't eat meat.'

Adam turned towards her, raised a single eyebrow in mocking surprise. 'Oh? For your good or the world's?'

'The world's, I guess.'

'All those poor little squealing piggies.' He skewered one of the sausages and twirled it round with a malicious laugh, before dropping it into the frying pan. 'What else do you do for the world?'

'What I can.' Helena sat up straighter, prepared to counter the challenge.

He met her eyes, rearranged the smile on his face, so that the mockery vanished. 'Sorry. Cynicism. Historical hazard. Occupational too.' He put a plate heaped with toast and eggs in front of her.

The words Helena had spied yesterday in the folder on the library desk leapt into her mind. Without thinking, she blurted them out at him. '"Just as the deer uses grass, the fish water, the bird air, so the holy man uses woman." And meat and land and energy reserves and everything else, I imagine.' She looked at him contemptuously. 'Nature's rapists. A holy profession. Quintessentially male. Adam-cult, indeed.'

He chuckled. 'So you did a little delicate prying yesterday?'

'Very delicate.' She talked to distract him from the flush which rose to her face. 'The book was lying open. I'm afraid I'm an inveterate reader.'

'So I notice. You left this in the library, by the way.' He placed Max's book of essays by her plate.

'Silly of me,' Helena muttered. She watched his face covertly, but it betrayed nothing.

All he said was, 'I gather you're interested in matters environmental.' Then he paused, studying her. 'Not so terrible is it, this cult of the Free Spirit that brought me to these parts? A little medieval pantheism. An eco-pyramid with God and godly man at the top, instead of the more modern circle which you undoubtedly approve of.'

'Undoubtedly.' Helena bit her lip. She mustn't challenge him now and give away too much, though the desire to attack this ludicrous proposition was overwhelming. She ate a little of her egg instead. 'Delicious,' she murmured.

But he wouldn't let it rest. 'I suppose, Ms vegetarian Latimer, you'd prefer it if we took man out of the equation altogether. Left just women perhaps, and the deer and the fish and the birds. Oh yes, and the grass and the water and the sweet-smelling air.' He was needling her.

'Or perhaps, since women can't really do it all alone, we could get rid of the people altogether – impure, all of them! – and just leave nature to get on with it, as some of your more apocalyptic eco-freaks and tree huggers would undoubtedly wish.' He was waving his fork around dangerously. 'Since of course we're not part of nature, we poor human specimens.' He laughed abruptly.

'Delicious,' Helena murmured again.

Adam didn't seem to hear her. 'Had one of them round here the other day.'

Helena couldn't resist. 'A poor human specimen or an eco-freak?' she asked quietly.

He focused on her, grinned. 'The latter.'

She thought he might hear the sudden racing of her heart. To this unregenerate brute, Max might easily appear as an eco-freak. She had to pursue this calmly, without a flicker of the eyes. 'Oh?' she said as casually as she could, pretending no interest.

'Yes, she would gladly have fed my parts, bit by bit, starting with the most delicate, to the darling little piggies.'

'She?'

'A former student of mine.'

'I see.' Helena tried not to let her disappointment show. 'You teach?'

He seemed suddenly to have lost all interest in the conversation. 'I've been known to,' he mumbled, rose to pour them some more coffee, offered her a cigarette.

She shook her head, grimaced her disapproval.

'Oh no, of course not, how could I have forgotten. But you'll mind if I don't. No virtue possible if it's not tested,' he chuckled sardonically, lit up.

She could have smacked him.

'So, Ms Latimer, it is Ms, isn't it? Now that we've had our breakfast, can you tell me what your business here is.'

Helena had her lines ready. She scurried over them quickly. 'I'm writing a travel piece about this part of the country. A friend, who was supposed to meet me in Munich and who didn't turn up for some reason, told me about this place, said the artist Johannes Bahr had once lived here.'

The explanation didn't seem to thrill him.

'The piece is for *Harper's and Queen*,' she added, as if it would make the difference.

'Am I supposed to be impressed?' He stubbed out his cigarette, added, 'I have a horror of living in a museum.'

'But Bahr . . .'

'I know, you're going to tell me it's my responsibility to art, to the world. And the local inn-keepers will love me.' His lips curled maliciously. 'But do you really want all those rampaging tourists polluting these innocent green meadows?'

She glared at him.

'Okay, okay, you've come all this way. What do you want to see?'

'Everything,' Helena murmured. 'The . . .'

A loud ring interrupted her.

'The telephone here sounds like a fire engine,' he muttered, vanishing through the door.

Helena relaxed. She had learned nothing yet, but at least her alibi was in place. The rest would follow soon enough. She could ask him casually if he had read Max's book. That would be a start.

When he came back into the room, he had a preoccupied expression on his face. 'I have to go out. Sorry.'

'Oh.' She was crestfallen.

'I didn't realize I'd been that charming,' he smiled, meeting her eyes.

There was a moment's silence between them. In it, Helena had the sudden sense that she had been touched, caressed.

It passed as quickly as it had come. All at once he was in a hurry. 'Feel free to look around. There are pictures here and there – everywhere except on my desk,' he chided her for a second. 'The grave is by the lake. Don't dig up any bodies. And you're welcome to come back, if you need to see more.' He gave her an open charming smile.

But as he turned to go, she heard him mutter under his breath, 'Third snooper in as many weeks. What is this place coming to!'

She was sorely tempted to run after him, ask him about the others. Max, she was suddenly certain, had been one. What had he told him? She would have to come back. Otherwise, it would be too obvious.

And she would clear up. It wouldn't do to be a bad guest. Quickly Helena washed pans and dishes, and scrubbed the table clean. A quick tour round the house was in order. Max hadn't described the interior, but she wanted to see it in any case.

She found the conservatory through which the trees rose like columns, contemplated the pictures by Johannes Bahr which had been hung there, felt them through Anna's eyes. She had wanted to question Adam Peters about Anna as well, but that had to be a secondary consideration. Nonetheless, she looked into the salon, where so much life had passed. The room needed a coat of paint, but its essential grace was still there, the rococo flair of dusky rose, soft blue and white, and more canvases by Bahr. She paused in front of one she was sure must be of the two sisters and felt a shiver run through her. Ghosts again.

Helena prowled, traipsed down into the cellar just to still yesterday's fears. There was an assortment of wine racks, an array of dusty furniture, an ancient boiler. But no signs of Max or any rough and tumble. Her conversation with Adam Peters had already put paid to those imaginings in any case. She went up to the first floor, opened doors, shunned the room with an unmade bed which must be Adam's. A restless sleeper, she thought, a maddening man. But she didn't go beyond the door. Nor did she climb the stairs to the attic floor. She didn't want to arouse his suspicion in any way. Then, having tidied her own room, she put her bag in the car and set out towards the lake.

Max's letter had mentioned the tombstone, the boathouse. Why? What was it about them that was significant? Helena gazed out across the lake, hoping to catch sight of some factory towers billowing their pollutants into the sky, excreting them into the lake, but there was nothing here except the mountains, the trees, a church spire, and a cluster of houses on the other side.

She would have to follow the rest of the trail. Max must have stayed somewhere near here to detail the area so precisely. And she would come back to Seehafen. Adam Peters wouldn't run away. His bad politics apart, she was now almost certain he was just a little too welcoming to be an agent of any kind.

Two villages away, Helena struck lucky. In a little slope-roofed inn set back from the road, she was greeted by the buxom pink-cheeked owner, who seemed only too happy to settle into a chat.

'A friend of mine passed through here,' Helena began after a series of preliminaries about the charm of the spot, the idyllic view, the pleasantness of the inn. 'An older man, tall with white hair.'

'Herr Hillman,' the woman burst out. 'A charming gentleman, so soft-spoken. And no bother at all. He complimented my cooking. Said it reminded him of his youth,' she giggled. 'He stayed for almost two weeks. Went out walking every day, just like a young man. Had a spot of bother though. Lost his passport, poor man.'

'When did he leave?' Helena asked with growing excitement. She had picked up the trail again. Max had simply transposed 'Hill' for the German 'Berg'.

'Oh, let's see. About ten days ago.'

Helena's hopes faded a little. 'Did he say where he was heading?'

The woman considered for a moment. 'I'm not sure, Fräulein. He did talk about going further into the mountains. But he left in a great hurry. Even forgot his letters. I posted them for him,' she added with a touch of pride.

Helena's pulse raced. 'One of them may have been to me.' She laughed too loudly. 'In London. Do you remember if one of them was to London?'

The woman looked at her askance. 'I . . . I think so. But I don't pry you know,' she said hastily.

'No, no, of course not. And the others? You couldn't possibly remember whom they were addressed to? It might help me find Herr Hillman more quickly.'

The woman shrugged. 'There was only one. But no, I don't remember.'

Helena couldn't tell whether she was lying or not. 'Well, if it comes to you, do let me know,' she urged the woman without insisting. 'Meanwhile, I'd like to stay for a day or two, if you have a room, that is.'

The woman suddenly beamed. 'You can have Herr Hillman's room. It's the prettiest, best view. I only have one other guest so far this evening. A young man. An American.'

'Oh?' Helena stilled her instant suspicions. 'I'll need a phone to check in with my office.'

The woman looked at her with something like injured pride. 'In your room, Fräulein. A completely new system.'

The room, as austere as a monk's cubicle and as neat, looked out on the gleaming lake. From it, Helena thought she could make out the bend where the house was. She scanned Max's letter again. Yes, this was right, the cluster of oaks, the double dip of the valleys. But however hard she stared, there was no clue here as to why Max had considered any of these details significant. Though he would have liked this room. Helena sighed with an impatience bordering on despair. Perhaps she had been on the wrong track all along and James Whitaker was right. Perhaps Max was in no trouble at all, but was simply here to enjoy the view, to escape, to retreat. And wanted none of them to find him. Not even her.

'Speak to me, Max.' She addressed the letter. 'You've always spoken to me before when I've needed you. Tell me.' But the letter was as silent as the hills, as silent, she suddenly thought, as if she had been addressing the father she had never known. It came to her that she was behaving like Anna, invoking her missing son, entreating the dead Johannes to speak.

Helena shrugged the silly notion away. She had a sudden desire to work in order to regain her bearings. Writing always soothed, made order out of chaos. She had brought a file full of notes with her, for a piece on pesticides she had been researching for some time. She rang her office, spoke to the Environment page assistant, checked on post and telephone messages, then had a word with Carl Sykes, her immediate editor. Yes, it would be wonderful if she could get the article done. But it would wait a week. She was meant to be on holiday.

Some holiday, Helena thought. She found her file, the accumulated notes of a long investigation, together with a preliminary draft of her article.

By the time Helena had written her piece, she felt better. Night had fallen. A drink was in order and perhaps another little chat with her garrulous hostess, who might be prodded into remembering something specific.

Downstairs, the inn had taken on an altogether different allure. The dark-beamed bar was abuzz with voices. Men with square weather-hardened faces sat at the long oak tables now laden with beer tankards and dishes of pretzels.

There was a momentary silence as Helena walked towards the bar. She could feel the eyes on her back, curious, suspicious. She was tempted to turn towards them and rail, 'Have you never seen a woman before?' But she kept her counsel, asked the barman for a glass of wine and a sandwich, looked up to see a fair young man at her side.

'Hi, Frau Bauer told me there was a fellow foreigner here,' he grinned. 'Doing a spot of out-of-season tourism?'

It was interesting, Helena thought, as she nodded. As soon as this young man had claimed her, the voices in the room had started up again. She was made safe, tamed by a man's presence. How ridiculous it all was. With Max, and that too was something she so valued about him, there was never any question of the accident of her sex.

'Nice place,' the young man said. 'I'm Bob Rawthorne, by the way.'

'Helena Latimer.'

'You're from England.'

She nodded.

'I've been living in Munich for some six months. Work in pharmaceuticals.'

Helena pricked up her ears, offered her newest identity. 'I'm writing a travel piece about this part of the country.'

'Oh? There's some good walking. I could show you tomorrow. And some picture postcard chalets to rent. Thought of doing it myself.'

She hadn't considered that. Helena kicked herself. Of course. If Max had wanted to be invisible for whatever purpose, a chalet would be far better than a hotel. She started to chat animatedly with her new friend. One never knew where one's leads might come from.

Over the next days, Helena pursued these with the tenacity she brought to her investigative journalism. She drove further into the Alps, visited monasteries with lavish baroque chapels, questioned hotel keepers and estate agents.

One in Oberammergau had rented a chalet to a man of Max's

scription, but there was no one in the tiny wooden house when Helena went to visit. Peering through the windows revealed nothing. She left a note naming the guesthouse where she was staying. Then she sat in a local tavern watching people come in and out, hoping against hope that Max would walk through the door and she could hear the comfort of his voice.

It was from Oberammergau that she sent Claire a card, telling her that she was hot on Max's trail *and* having a holiday, despite everything. But she wasn't; she was tired, too tired.

On Friday, she went to see the two firms she had made appointments with on the advice of the Munich Greens. She grilled the Public Relations man in the chemical plant mercilessly on toxic waste and its disposal. His smooth manner irritated her, but she could find little fault with what he said; nor did his face flinch when she mentioned the name of Max Bergmann or indeed Herr Hillman. He had heard of neither. On the other hand, he was quite prepared to have an assistant show her round the plant. The *Sunday Times* was a paper he respected.

At the timber firm, the red-faced manager was a little less suave, a little less comfortable, but she quickly determined that whatever it was he was hiding had nothing to do with Max.

Helena travelled back to Munich, went to Green Headquarters again, burrowed through files and clippings, asked about Adam Peters, but to no particular avail. On the off-chance, she rang Max's deputy, James Whitaker, in New Hampshire, to see whether he had had any news. He hadn't, but he told her the Bavarian link might mean something. Apart from the woman from Berlin who had openly confronted Max at the Oslo conference, there had also been a delegate from Murnau and Max, for some reason James hadn't been able to fathom, had been troubled after he had spoken to him.

'His name wasn't by any chance Adam Peters?' Helena asked with bated breath.

'Hold on. I've got the list of delegates somewhere. Here it is, Gerhardt Stieler.' He gave her an address.

Stieler, when she saw him the next day, was effusively cordial, but no help at all. He sat prodding a tiny scar on his cheek and told her what a wonderful, wholly admirable man Max was.

Downcast, Helena returned to the little inn where Max had stayed. Perhaps if she remained here long enough, Max might magically appear.

The buxom Frau Bauer was visibly pleased to see her. As if in reward for her return, she said to her the next morning at breakfast, 'You know, I think I've remembered where that other letter I posted for Herr Hillman went to. It was something like Sudhafen or . . .'

'Seehafen,' Helena prompted her.

'Yes, that could well be it.'

Helena could have hugged her. She didn't bother to change out of her jeans, simply donned her bright jacket and raced to the car. She had known it all along. Her instincts had told her that the house and Adam Peters held the keys she needed to Max's whereabouts.

Fifteen minutes later, she was turning into the drive which led to the house, letting the knocker fall loudly on the door. The young woman who had opened it to her last time was standing there again.

Helena remembered her name. '*Guten Tag*, Elsa. Is Mr Peters in?'

Elsa looked at her askance. Helena wondered if Adam Peters had reprimanded her for inviting strangers in, but before she had a chance to say anything, Adam Peters appeared behind the girl. He was wearing a loose-fitting dark suit and it gave him a formality she didn't remember.

'Ms Latimer, how very nice to see you again.' He ushered her in. 'Though only for a few moments, I'm afraid. I'm rushing some friends up to Munich. Your travel piece going well?'

It was odd confronting him. They were strangers, yet they had shared the intimacy of a house, of breakfast.

Helena cleared her throat. 'I need to ask you a few more questions.'

He led her towards the kitchen. 'No time now, really.' He glanced at his watch. 'But come and have a very quick cup of coffee and meet my friends.'

Two short, muscled men with jet-black eyes and inky hair stood as Helena entered the room.

Adam Peters addressed them in a language she couldn't understand. The men nodded sagely, grinned at her.

'Roman Barriga and Moses Palcazu are from Amazonia. They've been representing the Union of Indian Nations in Geneva, and since they'd already flown so far, I invited them here, to make some speeches, see some journalists. About the rainforest and land rights.'

Helena looked at him in astonishment. It was a little difficult to tally this information with the cynical image she had constructed of Adam Peters. She was about to launch a series of questions at him when she remembered herself: she was still playing the part of the slightly scatty travel writer. She cursed herself for a professional opportunity missed, made some comments which sounded inane to her own ears and finally asked Adam, 'Are they here for long?'

'One more interview and then I'm afraid it's the airport. In fact we must be going.'

The man called Barriga said something to Adam Peters which brought a smile to his lips.

'Roman says you should come and write an article about their part of the world. Before it changes beyond recognition.'

'I'd love to.' The warmth in her own voice made Helena realize that it was the first thing she had ever said whole-heartedly in Adam Peters's presence. The thought made her flush. She smiled brightly at the two men to hide it.

Adam was eyeing her oddly. 'Well, come back on Monday and I'll answer your questions *and* tell you how to get hold of Roman and Moses. That's if you're still in the neighbourhood then.'

'Yes, yes. Monday will be fine.' She shook hands with the two men, wished as she waved at Adam Peters from the door that she could be part of their little group; then, as if in deliberate self-contradiction, wondered if the two men's appearance here could have anything at all to do with Max.

Suddenly she felt like crying. It was a strange sensation: it had been so long since she had cried. She was getting nowhere fast. And everything seemed to grow increasingly confused. Where was the Helena Latimer who had a reputation for cool trenchancy, for ferreting things out at great speed?

Monday took too long to arrive, but when it did, she dressed carefully for her meeting with Adam Peters. He wouldn't catch her napping this time: a trim pale grey suit, silk blouse, stockings, the armour of the professional woman she was. She looked at herself in the mirror. It came to her as it had before that being a woman was in itself a masquerade. It was only when she was seen or seeing herself, after all, that she considered herself as that other creature, a woman.

And today, she was going to be the sophisticated version, par excellence. The luminously red lipstick, the black clasp holding back her hair, the loose crumpled-silk coat that Claire had insisted she buy, the box-like black briefcase, were the finishing touches. Female armour to intimidate the mere male that Adam Peters was.

It was a bright crisp day and the snow on the low-lying hills had started to melt, revealing bursts of wetly green grass. She could hear the jingle of cowbells in the distance as she turned into the drive of the house.

Adam Peters opened the door to her himself. He looked at her in perplexity for a moment. His hair was ruffled, as if he had been running his hands through it ceaselessly. It gave him a slightly disreputable air, which was hardly erased by the low whistle he greeted her with.

'Well, well. Dressed for work today, are we? You're sure you've come to the right place?'

'You did invite me back, as I remember.'

'So I did. It was you, was it?' He was laughing at her. 'Well, come on in then. Though it can't be the kitchen today.' His eyes skimmed over her, landed with an ogle on her briefcase. 'Perhaps the sitting room.' He opened the door, then shook his head. 'No, forgot. I've started painting the walls in there and we wouldn't want to be responsible for any damage to that coat. Might get sued for more than I'm worth. Can't be the library either. Might start reading my papers again, while I offer you some tea. I know, it'll have to be the conservatory. Then you can gaze on Johannes Bahr in all his glory.'

'That was quite a speech,' Helena muttered as she plumped her coat into his arms.

'Was it? I must be babbling overtime. All that interpreting.' He smiled a disarming smile.

She followed him through the left wing of the house into the conservatory.

'Will it be tea today, Ms Latimer? Or something stronger?'

'Tea would be lovely.'

'You're rather lovely.'

'It must be the suit.'

'No, no. It's the briefcase.' He winked at her. 'Sugar?'

She shook her head, watched him stride away. Ridiculous man, she thought to herself.

She looked out of the glass expanse at the back of the spacious room. There was a fluffy cat prowling through the shrubbery, a robin perched in absolute stillness on a branch as if he were enticing the cat closer.

Helena observed them for a moment, then walked slowly round the room. She paused in front of the mural she had read about.

Anna had indeed been a remarkably beautiful woman. Those softly rounded limbs, that head bent back with a swaying grace, that lilting expression: it was as if she were giving herself up, giving herself away to the elements. The notion suddenly made Helena uncomfortable.

'Yes, you can see it now, can't you?' Adam Peters drawled behind her. 'The queues lining up to gape. The "wow"s and "awesome"s and "wicked"s; the men grumbling, "My five-year-old can do better than that"; the women preening, "She's a bit fat, isn't she".'

Helena veered round to face him. 'I'm not writing a guide to Disneyland, you know.'

He chuckled, placing a tray on the wrought-iron table. 'What you are writing is *exactly* what I do want to know.' He was carrying a newspaper and he now waved it at her threateningly. 'I've just read a rather long piece by you, all about something called "The Dirty Dozen", a little travel guide to DDT and paraquat and chlordane and other such chemical wonders of the unnatural world.'

Helena examined her hands. It had never occurred to her that he would read an English paper here.

'Well?'

'Well, I'm on holiday,' she looked up at him brightly, 'doing a little freelancing to pay my way.'

'You're sure you haven't been taking soil samples or testing the lake while my back was turned?'

'Would that be so very terrible?'

He scrutinized her for a minute, stepped menacingly close. 'Well actually, no.'

Then, as if it were the most natural gesture in the world, he suddenly put his arms round her and kissed her hard on the lips. For a moment, Helena was so surprised she forgot to struggle. When she pulled away from him, she was angry, at herself as well for not having seen it coming. She looked at him severely. 'That wasn't necessary.'

'No, perhaps not. But it was quite nice. Only quite. And you owe me one. For misrepresentation . . . Besides, I warned you,' he skimmed her cheek with his fingers, 'I can't resist a woman with a briefcase.'

'I'd better get rid of it then,' she grumbled, tucking the case under a chair.

'Some tea?' He was laughing at her again.

'If you behave as one does over tea.'

'The perfect host.' He handed her a cup ceremoniously. 'Now what can I really do for you, Ms Latimer?' His voice now carried a formal propriety which erased anything else that might have passed.

'First of all you can tell me who else around here has been snooping, as you so plainly put it, apart from me?' Helena plunged right in, her discomfort over that stolen kiss adding an edge to her voice. 'I don't want to find I've been scooped.'

'I shouldn't think *that* happens too often. In any case, no journalists as far as I know.' He looked away from her through the glazed door. 'Just an old man, out there. Right out there,' he pointed.

Helena sat very still.

'I caught him at it. He told me he was an admirer of Johannes Bahr. Obviously Bahr's admirers like turning up in unconventional ways.'

Helena let the aside pass. She cleared her throat. 'And? Who was he?'

Adam shrugged. 'Some man with a lot of time and no concern for the waste of another's.'

She was about to press him when she simultaneously realized the thrust of his remark and that she was showing far too much curiosity about someone who was obviously not a potential rival. Helena put her cup down with a clatter.

'All right, I take the hint, just the minimal guided tour please.'

Adam showed her round the house, giving her information about pictures, a little potted lecture about twentieth-century German art.

'You make a wonderful guide,' she told him.

'Yes, my future cut out for me after you've written your fabulous piece. A new career. Just what the bank manager ordered.' He said it with a hint of bitterness.

'Surely the bank manager needn't worry. All this belongs to you, I presume.'

He looked at her askance. 'You mean I could sell the lot and be a rich man. Now I'd never have thought of that.'

It was a rebuke and Helena fell silent. They were walking down the path that led to Johannes Bahr's grave. When they arrived at the sheer black slab, Adam said in a flat voice that was too loud, 'And this is where they're buried.'

'They?' Helena looked up at him in consternation. His eyes were dark, angry. 'I'm sorry. You don't like coming here.'

'No, no, it's not that.' His tone softened. 'It's just the waste.'

'They?' Helena asked again.

'Of course, you don't know. Anna's here beside him.'

'I see.' Helena let the thought sink in. There was a host of questions she wanted to ask, but the set of his face forbade it. Something in it made her want to reach out and touch him. She did so, impulsively, softly.

He raised a querying eyebrow, smiled. 'Had enough?'

She nodded.

It was as they strolled back to the house that Helena suddenly decided it.

'Look, I haven't been altogether honest with you.'

'You don't say?'

She let the edge of it pass. 'I do say.'

'Well, tell me another story now.'

'This is the story. I'm not a liar. It's only because of the extraordinary circumstance.'

'Go on.'

'Well, first of all, I'm not writing a travel piece.'

'That's good, because you haven't looked at the scenery once or asked me about the name of that bruiser of a cliff over there or about the fish in the lake or . . .'

'All right, that's enough.'

'So?'

'So I'm looking for someone. Someone who has disappeared. A man by the name of Max Bergmann. Do you know him? Does the name mean anything to you? He might be calling himself Hillman.'

They had come round to the back of the house. Through the conservatory windows she could see the wrought-iron table, the tea tray, the spot where he had snatched a kiss from her. Max could have been standing right here just a few weeks back. It came to her again that trusting Adam might be the wrong thing to do. But she had no choice now.

He was gazing at her reflectively. 'The short answer to all that is no.'

He opened a narrow door at the side of the house, held it for her. There was a challenge on his face. 'Does that mean your business with me is finished or are you going to take up just a little bit more of my time?'

Helena walked brusquely past him.

'Who is this man? Your lover?'

She turned on him, anger lodged in two pink spots on her cheeks. 'Why is it that a woman can't look for a man, ask after a man, without the instant imputation that he's her lover?'

'I'm sorry. You're right. I have an occasional affinity for those creatures you don't like to eat.' He looked genuinely shamefaced. But then he grinned, 'So he isn't. Your lover, I mean?'

Helena stamped her foot with irritation. 'No, Max Bergmann is not my lover.'

'Good, I'm glad. It's just that you had that fiery look in your eye when you said his name.'

Had she had something to throw, Helena thought, she would have thrown it.

'Wait a minute. Bergmann, isn't he that environmentalist whose book you had with you? The prophet of natural disasters, the apocalypse-monger.'

'You *would* call him that.'

'Now, now, don't get me wrong. I'm interested in apocalypses. Winged horsemen, writhing serpents, rough beasts slouching, polluting plagues, winds, floods, fire, ice. Hot or cold, wet or dry or any variety of visitants from outer or inner space, ancient or modern,' he chuckled. 'You could even say I'm something of an expert on them.'

'Which undoubtedly accounts for your sweet temper.'

'Undoubtedly.'

They glared at each other for a moment.

'So why are you here? And here again?'

She didn't answer him immediately.

He uncorked a bottle of wine, passed her a glass. 'A peace offering. And the truth please.'

Helena took a deep breath and told him about Max's disappearance, the worry over his possible death; told him about the letter she had received with its descriptions, one of them of this very house.

To his credit Adam looked genuinely puzzled. 'And have you been to the local police?'

Helena shook her head. 'I can't do that.'

'Why ever not?' Suddenly he let out a low whistle. 'I see. You think he may be up to no good. Or to good, from your point of view,' he grimaced, altering his tone as he looked at her face. 'Well, I wish I could, but I don't see how I can help you.'

'That man who was here, the one you said was snooping . . .'

'The older man, you mean?'

She nodded.

'You mean Bergmann is not a dashing young prince. Well, well, well . . .'

Helena scowled. 'What did he look like?'

'Let's see, weather-beaten face, white hair, tall, quite prepossessing I guess, if he hadn't been a snooper.'

'It could have been him, in fact I'm almost certain it was,' Helena murmured. 'Can you remember exactly what he said?'

Adam Peters shrugged. 'There wasn't much more than I've already told you. I don't usually talk to snoopers, unless they happen to have exceedingly long legs and golden hair and deliciously blue eyes,' he grinned, mouthed 'Sorry', then hurried on. 'We talked a little about Johannes Bahr. He asked me whether I liked the work. Quite genial really. And he had an *echt* Berliner accent. I always like hearing it. So different, so much quicker than what's spoken around here.'

Helena looked puzzled. 'I didn't know Max had German,' she murmured.

'Well, maybe this wasn't your Max.'

'I think it was,' she said softly. 'Was he wearing glasses?'

'Those. Of course,' he shrugged. 'He came back. Or at least I assume it was him.'

'You didn't tell me that.'

'I haven't had a chance yet. I'm telling you now.'

'And?'

'And I wasn't here. Elsa told me about it. Said he'd presented himself as a friend of mine. Asked if he could look around. She was rather taken with him, so she let him. This Max of yours, if it is him, obviously has a way with women.'

'And what did he tell her?'

'I wasn't curious enough to ask, I'm afraid.'

Helena leapt up. 'Is she here now?'

He shook his head. 'Not till Wednesday.'

'Wednesday!' Helena felt a tug of desperation. 'Could I go and see her today?' She couldn't bear the thought of waiting any longer.

'You could. Though if they spy you in that get-up they may not open the door.' His eyes skimmed over her playfully. 'I'd come with you, but I have this nagging sense of an impending deadline.'

'I wouldn't want to put you out any more than I already have,' Helena murmured, meeting his eyes. 'But . . . but I'd be grateful.'

'Now *that* is exactly the kind of encouragement a man needs,' Adam chuckled. 'Come on. It's not very far. If you drive and let me hold that briefcase of yours, I'll sit back and show you the way.'

'What more could a woman ask!' Helena muttered, not altogether sure it might not have been better to try her luck on her own.

EIGHTEEN

IT WAS AFTER they had turned into the fourth steeply banked and fiendishly narrow country lane that Helena Latimer began to feel not a little grateful to the man at her side. Not only had Adam Peters directed her with thorough equanimity through the sudden driving rain, but she hadn't seen him stiffen once when she took particularly dangerous curves too fast. A man who allowed a woman to drive without offering a single comment was a rare creature indeed.

To top it all, this decidedly mercurial man seemed now to have taken her search altogether to heart. She had told him more about Max, implied something of what he meant to her. Told him a little about her work, too; about being in Bhopal. And he had spent the rest of the drive itemizing the possibilities for any Green action in the immediate vicinity and instantly discounting them. It was a quiet part of the world, small traditional farms, timber, tourism, a few new high-tech plants, nothing he concluded which could warrant covert action, unless Max Bergmann had a particular animus against pig and dairy farmers.

'Certainly not.' Helena glanced at him curiously. 'If I didn't know better, I'd say you sounded like a friend of the earth today.'

'More of a distant cousin,' he chuckled, and returned to his subject. 'Now in the northern tip of Bavaria, near the Eastern frontier, it might be different. And just outside Munich, there's an atomic research centre. But you say the letter led you here. Perhaps you're on the wrong track; perhaps there's another place that in prose sounds exactly like Seehafen.'

'No.' Helena was adamant. 'Max Bergmann has definitely been around here. Several people have confirmed that.'

'Which leads us to Elsa.' Adam sat up straighter. 'Next right and we're there.'

'By the way, I was told he wrote a letter to you.'

'To me? Not as far as I know. Never had it in any case.'

'Well, to someone at Seehafen. Does anyone else live there?'

'We're here.' He pointed to a small shabby concrete house. Beyond it there was a ramshackle barn. 'Park on the verge.'

They ran through the heavy rain, heard chickens squawking, a dog's frenetic bark. It loped towards them, a large black hound growling through bared teeth.

Adam knocked.

A pair of eyes peered through a yellowing net curtain. 'It's Adam Peters,' Adam called out. 'I've brought a friend.'

The door opened slowly. Elsa was wearing the frock Helena had first seen her in. But she looked different. It was the expression in her eyes. She seemed frightened.

'Can we come in, Elsa? Only for a moment. Look, I've brought a bottle.' Adam pulled one magically from his jacket pocket.

The low, darkly cluttered room had a hot fetid smell, the odour of bodies too close together, of eternal cabbage and persistent poverty. Something in Helena recoiled. She perched on the edge of her chair, felt herself grow dizzier with each rancid breath. There was a pot on the table in front of her, meat swimming amidst flecks of fat.

It was Adam who addressed Elsa. 'My friend here is looking for the man you told me visited while I was out. Can you remember what he said, Elsa?'

She looked at him vaguely, mumbled something in that thick accent Helena couldn't make out.

Suddenly there was the sound of a door opening. A small blunt man with thick arms and tiny mean eyes stumbled into the room. He was slowly buckling the belt of his trousers.

'What does he want, Elsa? Is he bothering you?' he grumbled.

Helena saw the girl shiver, shake her head. From the room behind them there was a loud cry, a crash, then a baby's squawl. A radio or a television blared persistently.

'Afternoon, Herr Kiener,' Adam said politely.

As he spoke, another figure emerged from the shadows of the room, a big man, no, not a man, a stubby, overgrown boy with a squat forehead and a mute violent expression on his square face. He pulled up a chair close to Helena's, so close that she could smell the sour sweat of him. He was staring at her.

Helena moved her chair to one side.

He edged his closer, smiled at her inanely. She moved away again, tried to concentrate on what Elsa was saying in that incomprehensible speech of hers. But the overgrown boy had tipped closer once more.

Suddenly she noticed that he had his hands in his pockets. He was rubbing himself furtively, his leg pressing against hers, the bulge in his trousers growing larger.

Helena felt her stomach rise to her throat, her head begin to swim. She was suffocating, the room closing in on her. She jerked her chair away from the table. 'Excuse me,' she mumbled, fled towards the door. It wouldn't open. She panicked, rattled it, rattled and pulled until it gave way. She raced into the rain, skidded in the wet mud, almost fell. By the time she reached the car she was sobbing, great shuddering sobs.

She leaned her head against the steering wheel. It was all there. All still there inside her, despite the passage of years, despite Emily, despite Max, despite the life she had made for herself.

She saw the low dank room, the fly marks on the greasy old wallpaper with its endless procession of faded rosettes, saw the three cramped beds, felt her old nightly revulsion of getting into hers. For no sooner were the lights out, no sooner had the breathing in the bed next to her own grown even, than he was there pressing against her, his hand against her mouth, that heavy pungent smell of him, like old gym shoes stacked in a damp changing room, robbing her of breath, robbing her of everything including the desire to live.

Every night since his fourteenth birthday, their fat only son, with his beady bully's eyes, the bristle sprouting on his sallow skin, clambering against her, threatening – 'If you tell, if you breathe a word, I'll say it's your fault, tell how you undress in front of me, wriggle those whore's hips, what's a lad to do, and who d'ya think they'll believe, me, their darling only son, or you, the whore's child, who's only here 'cause of the monthly dosh?'

And Helena hadn't told, had known he was right, had simply struggled against his hideous weight, and kicked and clawed, only to find that thin stream of sticky cum marking her thigh, had scrubbed it off the next day, would have scrubbed all her skin off if she could.

She discovered that her kicking and clawing excited him more, made him thrash about, hit her. And she didn't want to wake little Sandy, with her tiny waif's face and her terror-stricken eyes. So she stopped struggling, learned. It was easy enough, though it made her retch each time.

All she had to do was clasp his testicles in her hand and the sperm would spew out of him.

And then it stopped being enough. One night he tried to put that thing into her. Somehow, she slipped away from under him, stumbled down the stairs, locked herself in the freezing parlour. They let her come in here sometimes. To escape the noise. God, how she hated that noise – the violent brawls, the swearing, the blaring radio, the television game-shows. They had first let her stay in here when the note had come home from the headmistress, telling them she was clever, that she needed quiet in which to work. Sometimes they would forget about her and she would stay in here, the door locked, all night. But Billy spoiled that. He would remind them she was there. In the parlour.

It was in the parlour that they saw the social worker on her irregular visits. Mum, as she was forced to call her, powdered over her bruises for the social worker, pulled on that grey dress which puckered stiffly over her bosom. She would put on her sweetest smile then, and say how well Helena was getting on, brilliant reports from school. Once Helena had said to the social worker, right there, in front of Mum, 'I'd like to go back into care.' But Mum had stepped in with that false hurt look and said, 'Don't be silly, Helena. You're so happy here. We all love you.' And the social worker had picked up her case, and patted her. 'There, there, Helena.'

She was never allowed to see her alone.

It was after Billy had managed to put it into her one night and she had seen Dad's eyes flickering over her once too often that she started to hide in the school after hours. In the locker room, behind the showers. She had grown thin, so that she could see her bones jutting out at odd angles when she looked into the yellowed mirror.

For almost two weeks, bar the weekend, she managed to stay one step ahead of the cleaners and remain undetected. On her tenth day, she all but collided with Miss Latimer.

'Are you still here then, Helena?' The woman had looked at her with her kind eyes. 'Don't you want to go home?'

Helena had burst into tears.

'Come on, my dear. I'll get you some tea and sticky buns and you can tell me all about it.'

She hadn't told her all about it, in that little café with the white net curtains just off the High Street. She couldn't bring it up through her lips, but somehow Miss Latimer had understood, had dragged something out of her which let her understand.

'Would you like to come home with me for the weekend?' she had asked. 'I'm sure it can be arranged.'

Helena had looked at her with wide eyes and nodded quickly.

She had been agog at the house, the beauty of it. But she couldn't sleep, even there. The nightmares always came back: Billy suffocating her, making her gag. Even after Miss Latimer had adopted her, had become Em, they came back. And then gradually they stopped. Vanished. Until today. Helena shuddered.

'Helena, what is it?'

For a moment, she didn't know to whom the voice belonged.

'Come on, move over. I'll take us away from here.'

Adam Peters urged her gently away from the driver's seat. She refused his eyes, made herself small against the door. He put the car into motion, sped them away, glancing at her every few moments.

What had happened to her, he wondered? The silky hair tumbled over her averted face, hiding everything but that wave of a nose. A bare hour ago, she had been cool and proud and possessed, even bold, and now she was shivering, as vulnerable as a child whose pain couldn't find words. Still proud though. And beautiful, so beautiful that it was hard to keep himself from staring at her, as if he were afraid of missing a single moment in that shifting stream of expressions. She made him think of one of those breezy spring days when fluffy clouds romped across the sky, cast playful shadows on the fields, only suddenly to give way to bursts of shower. And then with equal suddenness, the clarity returned, crystalline, pure, almost painful to the gaze.

Fool, Adam Peters, scolded himself. Fool, to wax lyrical over a chance passer-by. Fool, to allow the equanimity he had attained here to be broken.

It was as a fool that he had met her. She didn't remember that, hadn't recognized him without his carnival mask. But he had seen her beauty then, the purity of that profile and the shifts from poise to confusion to rage. She was good at rage. It fuelled her, fed the litany of her beliefs, gave them that fiery certainty that he had never been able to find in himself. Angered him, too, those certitudes, that assumption that one particular moral perspective was the correct one. But then everyone seemed to have certitudes these days, except him.

He glanced at her again. She had composed herself now, was looking straight ahead, wondering, he imagined, what story to spin for him. He didn't mind. If it kept her here for a while, a respite from his imposed solitude.

'They're not exactly a prepossessing family, the Kieners.' Adam cleared his throat. 'I'm sorry if they upset you.'

She didn't answer for a moment and he tried to reconstruct the scene. Was it when they had heard the child's howl that she had raced out?

He tried another tack. 'I've thought of doing up the little house in the back for Elsa. To give her a chance to get away from there.'

'That would be a good thing to do.' She was suddenly emphatic. 'A very good thing.'

'Done,' he smiled. 'And just before I bring out hammer and brush, shall we stop and have a bite? There's quite a nice hotel restaurant not too far from here. You look as if you could use a pick-me-up.'

'All right.' Out of the corner of his eye, he saw her shiver. Then she said, 'And I'm sorry. Sorry to have rushed out like that.'

He shrugged. 'It happens. Do you want to tell me about it?'

'Not really,' she murmured. After a moment, she added, 'The place just reminded me of something. Dank, dirty. I had to get out.' Her voice had a quiver in it.

'Well, this will make a change.' He pulled the car into the drive of a gothic structure which looked as if it might have had its origins on Ludwig of Bavaria's drawing board. The rain was still pelting down grimly, great sheaths of it from a darkened sky. 'Shall we make a run for it?'

He put his arm lightly round her, more firmly when she didn't edge away. They dashed for shelter.

'The food's better than the architecture,' he whispered as their coats were taken. Her face was still tear-stained, her eyes too large for it.

'Excuse me a moment.'

He waited for her by the ornate wooden fireplace in the bar, watched the flames rise, then turned to watch her cross the room. Long legs moving gracefully in the trim skirt, her lipstick brilliant again beneath the shadowed eyes, the hair still ruffled from the rain. There was a boldness about her and a rectitude. He had heard that when she had talked about her work. But there was something else, too, something he couldn't quite describe. What was it? A kind of alertness, like the vigilant stillness of a forest creature sensitive to any sound. In any event, he wasn't the only one to watch.

'Is it hard being a beautiful woman?' he asked her when they had sat down.

She laughed at that, the first laugh he had had from her in hours. 'Easier perhaps. I don't know. We only get the one skin. Ask me again in ten years' time and I'll tell you what it feels like when the men neither stand to attention nor aggravate you with their advances.'

'That bad, eh?' He raised a querying eyebrow.

'That bad,' she smiled, but there was that shiver again, the storm gathering in her eyes. She looked out of the window at the side of their table. There was a little valley below them, a stream and then beyond, lost in cloud, the mountains. She turned back to him suddenly, as if everything else had lost its importance. 'Tell me what Elsa said about Max.'

He waited for the waiter to pour the claret, warmed the balloon of a glass in his hands. 'I don't know that it was worth the misadventure, but here goes. Elsa found the glasses by the way, stepped on them accidentally. In the conservatory. Apparently the man, let's call him Max since it pleases you, was exceedingly polite, asked her a few questions about Johannes Bahr, which, needless to say, she couldn't answer. Also asked her about his wife, the family, all to very little avail. Then he went into the conservatory and sat. Sat and stared at the mural of Anna. She knows this because when she brought him some tea, that's what he was doing, just gazing at it. And when she peeked in on him later, he was still there, just staring. Do you think your Max is just a dirty old man perhaps?'

Horror spread over her features, seemed to jerk her hand so that she involuntarily struck a glass. Red wine spilled on the white cloth, a brilliant splash of it.

'Sorry,' Adam murmured, dabbing at the stain with his napkin.

She moved her chair away, seemed about to get up and flee. There was a stricken look on her face.

'Helena, please, I'm sorry. It was just a joke. Silly.' He put a staying hand on hers. Her fingers were icy.

Then it came to him, as if he had registered it without seeing it at the time, Elsa's brother on the chair, moving closer and closer to Helena, the jiggle of the worn plastic cloth. 'Was it Elsa's lout of a brother who offended you?' he asked softly.

She stared down at the stain on the table, nodded almost imperceptibly. He kept her hand in his, felt as if he were a blind man in big clumsy boots treading on eggshells.

'It's all right now.' She looked up at him with a little forced smile, retrieved her hand. 'Tell me the rest. But no more jokes. Max is very special to me.'

'So I'm beginning to realize.'

They ordered: a pasta with asparagus for her, a steak for Adam. They watched the waiter spread a new cloth on the table.

'And then your Max apparently asked Elsa about *me*,' Adam laughed, his eyes crinkling.

'Why is that so funny?'

'Why on earth would he want to know about me?'

'You tell me. I don't know anything about you.' As she sat back, Helena realized how true it was. She watched his face, the irony filling his features, the full lips curling.

'I should think you know a lot more than Elsa,' he chuckled. 'Let's see, why would your Max want to know about me? Perhaps he's read my books, my travels into deepest Amazonia, doesn't find them Green enough, and has decided to do away with the author. Or . . .'

'No more jokes, remember.'

'Yes, of course. Well, from what Elsa could remember, he wanted to know who I was, how long I had lived at Seehafen.' He paused, suddenly serious. 'Perhaps he wants to buy the house, turn it into another of his model farms. Anna would have liked that. Or,' the twinkle was back in his eyes, 'perhaps he wants to create another of his male retreats, boys together in nature, beating the drums of their psyches, a paramystical fraternity. The Germans are good at that.'

Helena looked at him in amazement. It was edged with renewed suspicion. 'So you know a lot more about Max than you let on.'

He winked at her from those hazel eyes. 'Memory's always there in scraps. Like shreds of paper in a vast dustbin, waiting to be retrieved or chucked out. All that about Max Bergmann's just come back to me. One of my graduate students last year wrote a paper about male initiation rites. I think that's where I got it.'

'But none of that explains why Max chose to disappear. To use a different name. To write me that strange letter.' Helena gazed out of the window. The rain had stopped. A swathe of grey-blue light crossed the darkening sky. The branches of the trees were thick with glistening droplets. All at once, a man stepped out from the shadow of an oak trunk. His mane of a head was held high, lifted to the skies. He was stretching out his arms towards her. 'Max,' Helena whispered.

She ran from the table, found a side door which led to the back of the hotel, raced along the path. He would catch her in his arms, embrace her, stroke her hair, as if she were a little girl. Like he had in her dream. Max found again, so firm, so comforting. She shouted his name, 'Max, Max, it's me.'

There was no answer. There was no one sheltering beneath the oak. Perhaps she had mistaken the tree. She stared at it. Something about the place was familiar. That moist smell of withering leaves. It was as if she had been here before. But she hadn't. She blinked, raced along the incline, towards another tree and another, went round in circles. 'Max,' she called again, more softly.

'Helena.'

She turned at the sound of her name, collided with a different figure.

'You'll catch your death, Ms Latimer.' Adam was standing over her.

She shrugged away from him. 'I was sure I saw him.'

He looked at her sceptically. And then he spied a figure walking up the slope at some distance from them. He raced after it, was back minutes later, almost forcibly urging a man along.

Helena stared at a tall ageing man in a Burberry, and shook her head in shame. 'I'm sorry. Sorry. Thought you were someone else.' She turned away, rubbed her eyes.

'*Wahnsinnig!*' the man muttered.

Adam put his arm loosely around her. 'Come on, we'll have some coffee and strudel. It's good here. Then we'll check the hotel register. Do some detective work. Okay?'

She nodded. Get a grip on yourself, Helena, she ordered herself. You're behaving like a madwoman today. *Wahnsinnig*, indeed.

The strudel was as good as Adam had promised, flaky and tart. She finished her second glass of wine with it. It loosened her tongue. 'You know, I think I'm beginning to hallucinate. I need to get back to my cats.'

'Only your cats?'

'And some plants, who talk to me. Though not quite so much as my friends.'

'I think I want to know more about you, Ms Helena Latimer. Even if you make it up as you go along.' He was looking at her with that slightly sardonic expression.

She grimaced at him. 'Isn't much to know if I don't make it up.'

'Well, let's start with the simplest bits. Family English?'

'I haven't a clue.'

He looked at her in consternation.

'No, really. I'm what you'd call the genuine article. Little orphan Annie. No father, no mother – at least none that are named or that I've ever bothered to trace. A free woman,' she laughed, quoting Em.

'And your childhood?'

'I didn't have one,' she quipped at him. She had all these lines ready-made, had used them on various occasions.

He scowled. 'You mean you don't like to remember it.'

'That too. But actually, I don't remember much. Institutions, a couple of foster homes.' She sped over it. 'And then I struck lucky.'

'A man,' he filled in for her.

'You call that luck?' Helena laughed again, let him pour her more wine. 'No, a woman. A wonderful woman. She adopted me. Gave me her name, her knowledge. A home.' She gazed into the distance. 'She's dead now.'

'I'm sorry.'

They were silent for a moment.

'Now it's your turn.' Helena looked up at him. 'All those questions Elsa couldn't answer. What are you doing in Germany, for one?'

'Having a sabbatical. Finishing a book.' He smiled wryly. 'Well, writing one, anyway.'

'And why here?

'My adepts of the Free Spirit, remember them? There were lots of them around here. And carnival. That comes into it. Not quite anthropology and not quite anything else.' He gazed at her a little strangely, then turned for a moment towards the window.

'And I'm interested in Germany, not only because my family disowned it.' He paused to reflect. 'It's a country of excess and excessive monotony. It's all Europe in one, overburdened with its terrible history and the suppression of that history. It's got an almost wholly homogeneous population and it still worries about being polluted from without. Will that do for a start?'

'That'll do.' She looked at him curiously, trying to assimilate what he had said. 'You like contradictions.'

He laughed. 'I don't even mind ambivalences.'

For a moment Helena thought he was going to chuck her under the chin, that he had been referring to her. She countered him. 'I prefer things clear so that one can act upon them.'

'I've noticed.'

'And the house?'

'Let's say it's come to me.'

'From the people in Anna's Book. Your family.'

He nodded. 'Unlike you I have rather a lot of them, mostly dead, mind you.'

'And you had a childhood.'

'That too. I even remember mine,' he smiled.

'Where was it?'

'In sunny California. Father, a lawyer, mother, a mother. A good enough one. And sometime illustrator.'

The waiter was hovering round their table with an air of veiled impatience. Helena glanced at her watch. It was ludicrously late, almost five o'clock. 'We'd better go.' She reached for her bag, took out her purse.

Adam stayed her hand, 'My treat. It's been a pleasure.'

He was looking at her with a strange intentness. Helena averted her eyes and stood. The room whirled for a moment. She had drunk too much, somehow lived through too much in too few hours. She steadied herself against the table.

'I think you'd better drive,' she said a little peevishly.

'And the hotel register?'

'Of course. How stupid of me.'

She let Adam do the questioning, watched his easy manner as he asked whether Herr Bergmann or his American brother, Mr Hillman, had checked in yet, saw the shake of the clerk's head. It wasn't, Helena told herself, as if she had held out much hope.

In the car, he turned to her. 'Where to, Ms Latimer? What's the next step in the search for the great Max?'

'I don't know.' She was too tired to counter his irony, though it made her bridle. 'Just drop yourself at your place and I'll find my way from there.'

After a moment of peering blearily into the gathering darkness Helena closed her eyes. It had all been too much today, the visit to the squalid house, that memory overtaking her, trapping her in its claws, so that all those old scars started to bleed afresh. And then the ludicrous hallucination, imagining Max emerging from behind a tree, stretching his arms out to her. The scene played itself out again on her eyelids and suddenly she saw herself running; herself but not herself: a thin little girl in an ugly blue frock. And the man, that tall man with the mane of hair emerging from behind the tree, and calling, 'Coo coo, here I am,' swinging her up in his arms, holding her.

Helena opened her eyes abruptly. Where had that scene come from? Had she dreamt it or remembered it? Who was that man if that awkward little toddler was herself?

And then the thought coalesced in her. She closed her eyes again, rubbed them hard. Had Claire been right? Was it a father she saw in Max? Or was Max her father?

She clenched her fists tightly. Everything was running away with her again. She tried to envisage where that scene had taken place, *if* it had taken place. The convent orphanage perhaps: she knew she had been in one in the Hampshire countryside, before it had closed down and she had been moved to London, and from there briefly to the Willoxes and then finally to the Moores. Em had been through all that with her.

A toddler's game of hide and seek. With a man. A father perhaps. A father whose wife had died or left him or whom he had left. A father who had given her up only to recognize her again all those years later, tell her how special she was, write to her when to all intents and purposes he had vanished into oblivion. Max, her father.

Helena tasted the notion. It had a sweetness to it. But did it have any truth?

There was a simple enough way to put paid to all those fancies, before they ran rampant and drove her mad. Max had a past, even though she had never bothered to find out about it. It could be checked on. A trip to the States, a little digging if it wasn't all already clear to someone who had bothered to find out where she hadn't. And she had to do it quickly or these visions would overwhelm her. Em had been right to nurture her sense of independence, to suggest that buried family histories were best left to rest.

As soon as one let them, emotions, the past, ran away with one. But now that they had started to run, she could stop them, with cold, clear facts – as clear as the properties of chlordane or paraquat.

Helena replayed her last meeting with Max in the light of her present imaginings.

The conference had taken place in a large hotel just outside Oslo. It had been an enervating gathering, with delegates from the four corners of the globe. Max had spoken forcefully, his words gathering in resonance as he flatly stated that the biosphere could no longer absorb the effects of human beings' polluting activities.

The global environment, he pointed out, was being changed more now than it had changed at any previous time since the end of the Mesozoic Era, sixty-five million years ago. The Bhopal disaster was a warning. Toxic waste, global warming, drought, soil depletion would mean that the vast populations of the South which didn't die off would be forced to migrate northwards. In the next forty years, the world population would expand more than it had in the last several hundred millennia. Too many people equalled too much pollution, too much destruction of natural habitats, and an end to the diversity of species and the earth's life support systems. We had to begin to think of the earth first!

In the discussion period, after the rush of applause, a German woman had spoken, regal in her authority. Wasn't Mr Bergmann's call of 'earth first' an affluent Northerner's luxury? Her sisters in the South wouldn't thank him. Wasn't he, with his ethical niceties about plants and animals and the wild, really making a plea for the greening of the North? And the greening of the North was merely a recipe for exporting the environmental crisis to the third world. Did Mr Bergmann in his worries about the exploding population of the South take into account that the United States alone consumed thirty-three per cent of the earth's mineral and energy resources, though it only had five per cent of the world's population?

There had been no time for Max to answer. But afterwards in the bar when they were all milling round, the woman had been right behind her and Max. Helena had heard her say to another woman, draped in a magnificent sari, 'He reminds me a little too much of my country's ghastly history, that man. It's fine and well for him to worry about your population. He's had his two point two white children.'

Max had looked back at the woman with the first scowl she had ever seen on his face. It was in response to that, that she herself had turned, said politely, 'I think you ought to check the accuracy of your facts.'

How clearly it now came back to her. Max had put his arm loosely round her shoulder then and guided her outdoors. 'Let's get away from that overbearing woman, Helena,' he had murmured, 'and breathe a little air. I can't stand her voice.' Then he had chuckled, 'Perhaps she thinks you're my daughter.'

'Sleeping?' Helena heard a whisper.

She realized that the car engine had come to a standstill. She sat bolt upright. 'No,' she shook herself, 'just dreaming.'

'Nice dreams?'

'Just dreams.' She looked around her. Night had fallen, starless, bleak. Only the house in front of them shed any light. 'I guess I'd better get back. Thank you for your help.'

'Look, I think it would be better if you didn't drive now. You're not in a fit state. You can stay the night here.'

His voice was soft, but something in its tone annoyed her, as did the proprietary caress of his hand on her hair.

'Stop treating me like a child, or like some helpless *woman*.' She said the first thing that came into her head, took her irritation out on him.

'Was that what I was doing?' He laughed that ironical laugh. 'I'll have to go to a school for manners. A very special one. Run by the new woman. But suit yourself.' He leapt out of the car, poked his head back through the door. 'Bye, then. I could say it's been nice knowing you. But that too might offend.'

'Oh, don't be so pompously male.'

Adam Peters nodded once abruptly and left her.

Helena moved over to the wheel, turned on the engine and lights, watched him unlock the door. She lurched the car into motion, swung wildly round the drive, then jammed on the brakes as shrubbery loomed in front of her. She stared at it uncomprehendingly, realizing she was indeed in no condition to drive.

She sat there for a few moments in the dark, her head swimming, and then with an effort got out of the car. It would serve her right if he didn't open the door now. She had been insufferably rude.

She walked up and down the drive, talked to herself as she would talk to one of her friends. 'I don't believe it. You were too afraid to knock, so you crashed the car. Pull up your socks, woman. What's the matter with you?'

Taking a deep breath, Helena finally confronted the door. It took Adam a while to open it and when he did, he looked at her as if he had all but forgotten who she was.

'So you've changed your mind?' he said at last.

She nodded.

'Right, well, you know where the room is, and the kitchen. If you want anything, help yourself.'

Helena murmured a barely audible 'Thanks' and ran up the stairs. She didn't see him glaring after her.

Adam Peters sat back in the worn leather chair and looked for a moment at the familiar clutter on his desk. Funny, he hadn't expected her to be like that. He had been blinded by her beauty, no doubt. But there it was, another instance of what he had termed for himself 'the representative woman'. The individual standing for the whole gender, enshrining herself as victim, and therefore wholly within her rights to treat any man as the oppressor, the enemy.

God, how he hated this triumphalist victimhood. It made him fume.

What did these women want? Once they had identified themselves as victims, they could behave as badly as they liked and be indiscriminately rude, blatantly selfish. The world owed them. Nothing was their own responsibility.

Well, he'd had enough of that, enough of being guilty of the sins of his entire sex.

Too much, really.

And the terrible thing was that it was infectious, this triumphalist victimhood. Almost everyone it seemed had now become part of a victimized group, wearing their victim status proudly like a uniform. The simple-minded group slogan on the sweatshirt absorbed all identity, regardless of any personal history. 'I'm a victim. Treat me right. Let me hit you over the head.' Women, Blacks, gays, ethnic groups, and soon it would be men, too, whole national cultures, children, dogs, cats, seals.

Everyone loved victims, wanted to be one, speak on behalf of one, with all the self-righteousness it permitted.

It wasn't that there weren't real crimes, formidable atrocities, inequalities, genuine and terrible suffering – all of which had to be battled against. He was only too aware of that. It was the wholesale absorption of the person into a public collective identity which drove him frantic; the Whole swallowing all its richly disparate parts, smoothing them out – a standardizing in the name of the almighty victim.

And the righteousness of it, the high-pitched moral whine!

He lit a cigarette, puffed deeply and then laughed at himself. He was ranting, and without an audience to boot. He hadn't indulged in that particular form of lunacy for a long time. It was that woman who had driven him to it, that Helena Latimer he should never have allowed into the house after the first lie. A narrow-minded feminist puritan with a one-track mind chasing the guru she had somehow misplaced. A little fanatic who happened to be endowed with beauty. He was a fool. Only fools allowed whimsical hopes to take root so quickly.

Adam shrugged her image away, turned to a pile of photocopied papers and began to read. He had almost finished his section on the heresy of the Free Spirit and the golden millennium they envisaged – a mystical anarchist paradise where state and hierarchy had given way to a kind of pagan communitarianism. Funny, how so much of it reminded him of Johannes Bahr.

Johannes Bahr: his grandfather, if Anna's Book and the hints within Bahr's own diaries were to be believed. He had read both several times and he had no reason to disbelieve them. But he had never dared to confront his grandmother Bettina on the question directly, let alone his father. Neither of them had ever returned to Germany and nor had Klaus – though he had no way of knowing that for certain, since Klaus had died when Adam was still a babe in arms. They refused the place – had voided themselves of it, as if it were an illness to be shed and never thought of again.

Yet Bettina had never sold the house.

He was twenty-one when she told him about it in that straightforward unsentimental way of hers, her over-precise English issuing from her lips in clipped phrases. 'I possess a country house in Germany, Adam. Probably very dilapidated now. I am giving it to you for your birthday. You can sell it, use it, do with it as you will. If you decide to keep it, I will cover the taxes on it until you can do so yourself or until I am dead, whichever comes first.'

He had looked at her in astonishment. It was the first he had ever heard of a house in Germany. He couldn't remember what he had said to her, probably 'Gosh' or 'Gee', followed by a bewildered, 'Thanks'. A horde of questions crowded his mind, but before he could ask them, she had gone on, that familiar wry smile crinkling her lips and eyes even more.

'It is hardly an exciting present for a twenty-one-year-old, I know. The exciting part of the present is that I shall pay for you to go to Europe this summer, on the condition that you visit the house and place some flowers on my sister's grave. On the grave of her useless, if brilliant, husband, too. Now that is better, isn't it?'

Adam thought he had probably danced with joy at that. In any event he remembered bending to kiss her dry cheeks. She was already smaller than him then, though he still thought of her as hugely tall and as stiffly straight as if she were somehow corseted in the bones of the last century. And he was a little afraid of her, though very fond. She always listened to him so carefully, made him say things he hadn't known he had yet thought, only to clarify them with a little twist of that precision instrument which was her mind.

Bettina Eberhardt – as unusual a character as ever there was, to be washed up on the once lazy shores of California by the waves of history.

Over a plate of those Viennese cream cakes she still ate with relish, he asked her, 'But don't Dad and Mum want the house?'

'Your father? Ha! He thinks I am a crazy old woman to have kept it this long, though he is pleased with himself for having indulged what he sees as my secret sentimentality. No, Max has never wanted anything to do with all that. Ever since the war, he has been two hundred per cent American. He even dropped his family name, as you know. Max Peters, short and simple. No Eberhardt to be found. It is a good thing I didn't name him Max Wolfgang or Max Sigismund, then he might have had to use his imagination. As for your mother, has she ever contradicted your father over anything?'

If any of Adam's university friends had heard Bettina talk of his father in this offhand way, they would have been astounded. For Max Peters was something of an idol then, a vigorous civil rights lawyer who had defended draft resisters and free speech protesters, Black activists and

Chicano farm labourers, a man who addressed the anti-Vietnam demonstrations Adam and his friends went on. But Adam knew well enough that Bettina was inordinately proud of his father, of his military record, his legal work, all of it, whatever her quips. His mother was another story. The old woman had never forgiven her for letting her mind and her degree go to nought and for merely staying at home and raising himself and his sister.

He had asked Bettina then, since she seemed for once to be prepared to talk about the past, nonetheless phrasing it carefully, 'Did your sister die in the war?'

'You mean like a good Nazi should?' she laughed, her irony quick as fire. 'No, Anna decided not to bother to wait for the war; in her wisdom, she decided to follow in her husband's footsteps.' And then Bettina had grumbled beneath her breath in German, 'I should never have let them out of my sight.'

Adam had heard her, had understood. Bettina and his father had always spoken German to one another and he had picked it up, the sound and rhythm of it perhaps more than any extensive vocabulary. Later, but that was after that first visit, he had studied it.

And so in that heady summer of 1972 he had travelled to Europe, first to England, then to France and Italy, and finally to Austria and Germany. He was there in the wake of the Baader-Meinhof round-up, but the scenes of armed warfare that students he struck up conversations with in Munich and Frankfurt described to him seemed a million years away from what confronted him at Seehafen.

The tangled, overgrown gardens, the silent house when he first saw it, had for him the aura of a ruined summer palace, a decayed remnant of an extinct branch of some royal family. It breathed of a time out of time. And he had fallen in love with the grace and romance of it, as well as with the roll of the hills and the valleys, rich mellow greens and clear blues of a texture and colour altogether different from those he knew.

Bettina must have arranged for someone to clean up a little, for the house was not in as parlous a state on the inside as the overgrown gardens had led him to believe. Later, he learned that it had been occupied by some Nazi dignitaries during the war; relatives of the now dead Trübls had lived there after that, until the mid-sixties.

He had stayed for a few weeks, familiarizing himself with the countryside, rummaging through rooms, finding clothes that would have sat happily on some hippy market stall. And he had cleared Anna and Johannes's grave, laid flowers for Bettina.

But it wasn't until the following summer when he returned with two friends that he came across the store of Johannes's paintings in the cellar. They were in remarkably good condition and he and his friends had dusted them off and hung them throughout the house. It was that summer too that he had come across Johannes's diaries and Anna's Book. His reading German really wasn't up to the effort and it was only by dint of speaking the words aloud that he was even able to discover what it was he had found. He had brought Anna's Book to Bettina. She had taken it from him with something of a disgruntled air, then returned it some days later.

Her manner had been imperious. 'Put it back in the house,' she had ordered. 'That is where it belongs. One day the historians will come and look at it and understand nothing. But it is the best of my sister. The best and worst of our lives.' She had paused then, added more softly, 'I never knew she had grasped so much. My little Anna.'

Spurred on by the manuscript, the house, Adam had studied German that year in the course of his graduate work in anthropology. And then, with growing amazement, he had read Anna's Book, twice from cover to cover. He wanted to talk about it with Bettina, wanted to test the truth of it, but she always deflected him, and he didn't know how to be direct with her. After that, he had gone off to Amazonia.

When he came back she was bedridden, dying. There was a nurse in the house. On the second evening when he replaced his father by Bettina's bedside in the austere bedroom he had rarely visited before, she suddenly opened clear grey eyes to him. They were huge in that wizened face. She started speaking very quickly, softly, in German. He bent closer to her. 'I never believed in eugenics, Adam. Blood lines, race, the *Volk*, national character or family character, that's all Nazi rubbish. A politics of origins and essences is a politics of disaster. Life is what we make of it. Your father knows that. You know that.' Then she had closed her eyes and whispered, 'You're a good boy.'

A day later, she was dead.

He had pondered Bettina's words, that sudden quickfire German, the old formulations. He decided that whatever wisdom they bore, they were also a warning. Bettina didn't want him to show Anna's Book to his father, didn't want him to stoke old embers, question Max about Johannes and Klaus, that minor matter, at least to her, of paternity. Was Bettina right on that score? He couldn't judge that, though he certainly couldn't imagine his father getting stirred up by the ancient question.

So he left it.

It was only when he came back to this house that it ever raised its head. Yet he felt comfortable in Seehafen, cocooned in a history which fed his imagination as much as those extents of time spent in tropical climes; full of an energy which at home in America was sapped. And during these last months he had spent here, his first winter in the house, he had sensed Johannes's presence with particular strength, the battling excess of him. Perhaps because everything seemed to dovetail with his research.

Adam worked, his concentration now total.

Only after he had turned out the lights and was climbing the stairs did he remember he wasn't alone in the house. That irritating woman was here, though there was no irritation left in him now, only a residual sadness, almost a sense of loss for what might have been.

He had to pass by her door to get to his room and as he did so he paused. A distinct but muffled sound of sobbing reached his ears. It was the sound of a child crying inconsolably in the night.

He hesitated, then knocked softly. There was an interruption in the sobs. He knocked again. 'Can I get you anything?' he asked. 'A night cap? A glass of brandy?'

'That's very kind.' Her voice quivered. 'But no, thank you. Thank you very much.'

She sounded utterly desolate and for a moment, he was tempted to open the door and urge her up. But she would only chastise him.

'Well, if you change your mind, I keep some in my room, at the end on the left. There's a fire in there.' It suddenly occurred to him that she hadn't brought a bag with her, that she might need some things. 'And there's a spare robe in the bathroom on the right and an extra toothbrush. Goodnight.'

'Goodnight.'

He put a log on the fire, Mozart's mournful String Quintet in G Minor into the tape deck and stared at the leaping flames. It was better this way really. He had become something of a recluse over these last months. The work benefited. And he loved dreaming in this spacious room, his burrow, the only one apart from the library and the small bedroom he had done any work on. It doubled as a bedroom and a sitting room with its two deep blue chairs inviting one to sink down and meditate by the fire. He did so now, but then shrugged at the direction of his thoughts and picked up the thriller he had been reading erratically.

He couldn't have read more than a few pages before he heard an awkward, 'May I come in?'

'Please.' He turned to see her standing by the door. She was wrapped in his old burgundy robe, only her feet and that blonde head visible. She looked strangely fragile, not at all the woman who had knocked boldly at his front door not so very many hours ago.

'I thought I could use that drink after all.' She attempted a pert little *moue*, but there was a tremble in her lip.

Adam poured her a brandy.

'I'm not usually like this, you know. I don't break down and cry and frazzle.' She shook her head impatiently so that her hair tumbled about her face. 'Nor do I repay generosity with rudeness.' She was staring into the flames.

He didn't say anything, just looked at her. He couldn't stop himself looking at her.

'Believe me?'

He smiled. 'I believe you. I won't call for the references.' He handed her her glass, felt the cool flicker of her fingers.

'Good, though they'd be sterling, I'm sure,' Helena laughed with no evident mirth.

He wanted to take her hand, touch her, stop her feeling that she had to justify herself. He had been wrong to berate her.

'Won't you sit down?' He pointed to a chair.

She curled into it, tucking her feet beneath her. 'This is nice,' she murmured.

'But you were crying.'

'I was.' Her voice caught.

'Tell me about it. I'm good at listening. They teach us.'

'I'm not very good at self-revelation.'

He waited. The shadows of the flames flicked over her face.

'Can I touch you?' he asked. 'Would you like me to touch you? Sometimes it helps.'

She looked up at him abruptly, her pupils vast, velvety. 'I don't know,' she murmured. 'I never know.'

It was true, Helena thought, though she hadn't put it into words before. She never knew whether she would like to be touched, didn't think she liked being touched very much at all. It wasn't on the whole why she went to bed with men. And perhaps she only did because occasionally one somehow had to. Though there were other more complicated reasons: they had to do with helping or pleasing or easing a working relationship. She had no qualms or guilts about that and she liked the helping and the pleasing or the easing, though she didn't do it very often any more. It wasn't necessary. She preferred other methods. And in bed, she preferred to do the touching, the initiating, to be in control. Of herself as well.

Adam Peters was staring at her, his eyes brooding. 'Sometimes it's easier. To talk, I mean. Afterwards.'

'Is it?'

He stood up. She could hear him pacing behind her. He was fed up with her, right to be. She should go. She was no use to anyone today, least of all herself.

But before she had extricated herself from the chair, his hand was on her head, ruffling her hair, smoothing it gently, lifting it from her shoulders, so that his fingers skimmed her neck. Soft. She shivered, turned to him. He traced the line of her cheek, the arch, the curve, her lips. He had big blunt fingers, but soft, intelligent, so that she could almost read her features from his touch. And his eyes . . . She looked away, something in her afraid, despite the gentleness.

'I'd like to know you better, Helena. I don't quite know why, since . . .' He cut himself short, lifted her to his lips, kissed her. It wasn't like it had been this morning, that hard snatched kiss. She could cope with that. But this soft exploring, this desire to know, to search out, his hands on her back, touching, touching, smoothing . . .

'Please.' She turned her face away from him.

He let her go. There was a flicker of yellow in those hazel eyes, an anger. But his voice when it came was light.

'She likes being touched and she doesn't like being touched. That's all right. I'm a master of contradictions. Remember? I like them.'

Helena tried a smile that didn't quite work. 'I'm a little shaky tonight.'

'Only tonight?'

'Mostly tonight.'

He walked over to the bed, sat down on the edge of it, patted the space next to him. 'Come on. It's big and comfortable and you're tired. And it's warmer in here. I won't touch. I'm a big boy, you know. I've learned all about self-control.'

'Which you rarely have to exercise,' Helena tried to joke along with him, ease the tension in herself, in the room.

'And why would that be?'

'Because I imagine they all tumble over your big feet. The women, I mean.'

He laughed. 'Of course, they do. But not always the right ones. I can't imagine it's any different for you.'

'I guess not.' That made her happier, equalized things a little.

She sat down cross-legged on the vast bed, leaned against the headboard.

'This is a lovely room.'

'It has a very lovely person in the midst of it. But then you've heard that before.'

'I've heard that before.'

'It's hard to be original with beautiful women.'

He sipped his brandy, scrutinized her. 'What is it, Helena? What's happened?' The banter had evaporated.

'I think Max Bergmann may be my father.' It came out bluntly. Just like that.

He whistled beneath his breath. 'Found only to be lost. Or is it lost only to be found?'

'I don't know. Don't make fun of me.'

He took her hand, kissed it softly. 'I'm not making fun of you. The words only tumble out like that sometimes.'

She didn't know why, but tears came into her eyes at that. Perhaps it was because he was looking at her so protectively. 'You look like a good father now,' she mumbled, searching for humour again.

He let that pass. 'So what are you going to do?'

'Look for him, find him, check out some facts.' She said it with a kind of desperate determination.

It was strange, Adam thought, how they had filled their separate spaces that evening with parallel questions. The spectre of paternity, more powerful as spectre he sometimes suspected, than as the everyday lived experience. The lost father more significant than the existing father. No, he musn't think of that. Must think of her.

It was terrible the way she had stretched out so seductively now. It made it harder to think. And he needed to know. What was it that had brought her to this conclusion? Or had it been there all along and she had simply kept it veiled from him? No, he suspected it had something to do with that visit to Elsa's. That was when the trouble had all started.

'Helena, may I kiss you again?'

'You may kiss me again.' She felt easier now that she had said all that about Max out loud.

'Will you kiss me back?'

'I'll try.'

'No, don't try.'

He switched off the bedside light.

'No!' There was a sudden note of panic in her voice. 'No, I must have the light.'

'For the kissing or the sleeping?' he asked softly.

'More the first than the second,' she murmured.

'Trust me, Helena, trust me,' he whispered against her cheek. 'I don't want to see you now. I want to feel you.' His hands were running over her body, gently rubbing the rough towelling of the robe against her bare skin, finding the skin itself, tentatively, delicately. She felt his hardness against her, tried to still her panic.

Suddenly, he rolled away from her. 'It's no good,' he murmured. 'Let's get some sleep. Here, get under the blankets, I won't touch.'

She heard him get up. She didn't want him to leave.

'Please don't go, Adam. Just hold me.'

He came back. He had undressed. She could feel a matching robe. She snuggled up to him. 'Thank you,' she murmured.

He lay very still, the warm bulk of another being. Here in the present. Protection. Against what? That momentary eruption of the past? Why was it that she trusted him so soon? Before she could answer the question to her own satisfaction, Helena slept.

She woke or thought she woke before her eyes opened. The dreams still played themselves out. Em youthful, smiling, a tall handsome man at her side. The man turned. It was Max, she was certain of it. Why were they together? Em and Max, a mother and a father just for her, dignified, stately, not like the sordid, brawling Moores, that other parental couple. Stupid to allow her dreams to fulfil her hidden wishes.

But then she saw a different image, not a dream, but a memory: Max and her walking in the woods in Norway during the conference. She had been telling him about Bhopal, about the sheer human horror of it, but also about how the management of the plant hadn't ensured adequate safety; hadn't informed the staff adequately of the dangerous substances they were working with. Max had listened, had given her more background on Union Carbide, the parent company, had told her she should visit their plant at Institute in West Virginia.

Then in the midst of it all, he said, 'I heard you speaking German before, Helena. I didn't know you could.'

She had answered, laughing, 'I'm a woman of hidden talents. Em taught me.'

'Em?'

'Emily Latimer, my adoptive mother. She was a headmistress, and a wonderful teacher.'

'Oh.'

Did she now imagine the look of consternation on his face, the furrowing of the brow? Or had it been there? Had she struck a memory in him?

Helena opened her eyes abruptly. She was clutching at air, particles of memory with no visible substance to them, as wavering as the flickering shadows playing on the wall in front of her. But where was she? She sat bolt upright.

Adam Peters's room. There he was beside her on the far corner of the bed. He was sprawled on top of the bedclothes. That was her doing, it all came back to her. There was a gutting candle on the night-table. That, too, for her. A kind man with a rare thoughtfulness. She gazed at him: tousled dark hair, thick lashes, an arm curled under his head – a stranger, who hadn't insisted, though she was palpably in his debt.

He must be cold, Helena suddenly thought. She lifted one of the two blankets she had lain under and folded it over him gently, tucking it round his shoulders.

He stirred beneath her. She arched away as if she'd been caught in an unthinkable act.

'Hello there,' he murmured.

'I thought you might be cold.' She stumbled over the words.

He met her eyes, a warm brown gaze, questioning.

'I am.' He stretched out his hand to her. She took it hesitantly.

He pulled her towards him. 'It's very nice to see you,' he said. He was looking up at her as if she were an apparition. 'It is you, isn't it?'

'It is me,' she laughed.

He lifted her hand to his lips, his touch feather-light.

She rested her head against his chest, felt his fingers in her hair. She touched him, that bare stretch of throat where his robe was open. Cool, smooth, and then the roughness of hair. She heard the rush of his breath.

When she looked at him again, his face had that hunger in it which she recognized from other men's faces. She knew how to assuage that, how to fill that brooding expectation. And he deserved it. He had been so patient, so kind; there was nothing to be afraid of. She smiled a little, removed the barrier of blankets and robes. He was handsome, those broad shoulders tapering into the tautness of his stomach, pale against the blackness of his briefs, and then those long, strangely elegant legs. She slipped astride him, played her lips against his throat, ran her fingers along his chest.

Adam felt her, and watched in fascination. It was as if his body were the site for some strange ritual to which he was a mere spectator. He had a sixth sense that if he moved too abruptly, held that ministering priestess just a little too hard, she would flee. Or finish him off.

Yes, that was it. A bizarre thought leapt into his mind. Finish him off like some skilful prostitute in a remote Brazilian outpost might. For the moment she was playing him like some new instrument she had yet to get the measure of, but as soon as she had, she would be in her stride, thrum over him skilfully, perhaps even find the condom and slip it on him, then finish him off, give him his pennyworth of pleasure, complete the rite. And smile sweetly, averting her eyes, before she rushed off to wash.

He arched against her nonetheless, his body running away with the pleasure of her, those quick sensitive fingers, that silken hair tumbling against him, those long smooth legs clutching. He cupped her small firm breasts, watched that wide-eyed smile. Did she close her eyes when he kissed her, he wondered, and kissed her. So sweet. There was a flicker in her gaze and she put her hands to his groin.

Should he let her? Did he really want to stop her now? Stop that delicious rubbing, that whisper in his ear, that expert roll of the plastic over his cock, followed by the cool fingers, and then that taut yet soft grip of her bringing the moan to his lips?

He pulled her down to him, so that he could look into those wide blue eyes. So distant. Somehow virginal. A Diana. She was somewhere in her own world. Did he exist there? An edge of anger grew alongside his pleasure.

'Helena,' he whispered, turned her over, so that she was beneath him, moved slowly inside her, pinning her arms back, kissing her, lapping against her. 'Helena,' he murmured again, searching her eyes. And then he rolled off her.

'What is it?' she asked softly.

He didn't answer, got up instead, strode to the other end of the room. She watched him. Watched him pour out the brandy, light a cigarette. He didn't want her, she thought. It made her despondent. She covered herself, appalled that she had been so wrong.

'Don't you like me?' she murmured, as he handed her a glass.

'I like you,' he said abruptly. 'But for some reason, that isn't enough.' His eyes were black. She could feel the controlled rage in him.

'I'm sorry,' she shrugged, making herself small in her corner of the bed. Then with a gesture of irritation, she rose, looked for her shoes.

'Sit down. I want to talk to you.'

He saw her shudder.

'Please,' he said more gently.

There was a look of trepidation in the face she turned to him and for a moment he thought he had been wrong about everything. 'Please,' he said again, stretched out his hand.

She sat stiffly at the edge of the bed.

'Is there someone at home you're attached to? A man you particularly miss . . .'

She swung round to face him. 'Whatever do you think of me?'

'Or a woman, perhaps?'

'No, not that. Why do you ask?'

'Do you like sex, Helena?'

She laughed loudly at that. 'You mean, do I like it with you?'

'Maybe that's all I mean.' He strode over to the window and looked out at blackness.

'Actually, I do prefer work. The struggle against pollution, the battle for the earth, averting a self-inflicted apocalypse. It really is rather more important, don't you think, than a little self-indulgence?'

She was sneering at him.

He veered round, his movements suddenly violent. 'Do you know what

I think? I think that if I hear the word "pollution" used in that tone one more time, I'm going to take that person and rub his or her face in mud, good earthly mud, or better still, shit, that wonderfully pure and natural human or animal excrement that used to float happily in the water supply in the good old Green days and still does in some places to spread those wonderful natural ailments like typhus or cholera.

'And do you know why? No, don't give me that look of disdain. Do you know why?'

She shook her head once, abruptly.

'Because the idea of pollution presupposes that there is something called purity. And oh that wonderful mentality of purity! Purity of the water supply, purity of the environment, purity of the air, purity of nature, and let's extend it a little to its other obvious ramifications, purity of the blood, purity of the race, purity of the nation, purity of the gender. Let's worship purity! And in order to keep purity pure, we really must get rid of all those irritating pollutants, those poisons, toxins, acids, Jews, Blacks, foreigners. And men, of course, those ultimate sexual and environmental pollutants. Get rid of the pollutants. Keep the world pure. Keep Helena pure. Avert the apocalypse.'

'You're raving.' She was pacing now, as angry as he was.

'Yes, I'm raving. And you can go back to London and tell your pure friends that you met a dirty unregenerate raver, who tampered with your body and with your emotions. No, no, what am I saying? It's quite the reverse. That's my line. I tell them, this pure little Green and feminist miss came along and tampered with my body and my emotions and remained quite pure, untouched. Like all those uncaring male swine purportedly do.'

She had come to a halt in front of him. Her eyes flashed wildly and for a moment, he thought she was going to hit him, the way she had hit the man in the tavern. But she didn't; she simply hissed, 'I think you're talking about someone else.'

He took a deep breath, forced into silence by the possible truth of that. He gazed at her, the robe tightly belted at her waist, her colour high, her face proud, only a tell-tale tremor in her lips. 'Am I, Helena?'

He kissed her again, hard, too hard, oblivious to her struggle, wanting something back from her that wasn't mechanical, controlled, distant, even if it was her rage.

Helena felt herself beginning to suffocate, to drown. She pulled at his hair, pummelled his chest, but still those hands pressed down on her back, her hair, pressed her close to him, too close, kept her lips on his. And then alongside her panic, something within her leapt and took fire, bounding over her controlling sense of herself, making her cling to him as she beat at him; kiss, in a way she didn't recognize, so that she was breathless when he let her go, riven with confusion.

He had moved back from her, was staring at her with those dark, soft eyes of his. She took a step towards him, wanting him close again, suddenly wanting the risk of him, the risk of obliteration which was also a freedom.

And then she wasn't quite sure what happened, wasn't sure if he was making love to her or she to him, whose gestures were whose, whose breath or kisses or fingers or lips or limbs were hers or his. All she knew was that after a great deal of time and no time at all, she heard his cries and hers echoing through the silence, as mingled as their intertwined legs and the moisture of their bodies.

Then he was staring at her, something like wonder on his face. 'Well, well, well,' he murmured.

'Don't joke. Please don't make a joke of it.' She felt the tears spring into her eyes.

'I wasn't. Wouldn't.' He stroked her damp hair, touched her breast. 'My darling.'

And again that flame she didn't recognize leapt in her, so that she turned a face to him which was molten in its beauty. 'Am I?'

He nodded, loving her once more, this time with a mixture of passion and gratitude that he had long ceased hoping would ever be possible again.

Afterwards, before they fell asleep, she said to him, 'I hadn't planned for this.'

'Life is what happens to you when you're busy making other plans,' he laughed a little wryly. He looked into her eyes. 'You'll stay, won't you? Please stay. Your Max is as likely to turn up here as anywhere else.'

'Mmm,' she murmured against him, having for the moment utterly forgotten what had brought her here.

Helena woke first. A thin stream of light played through the shutters, fell on the man at her side. He was sleeping soundly, his hair ruffled against the pillow, his arm stretched across her in a proprietary gesture.

From somewhere deep inside her, there was an unfamiliar tremor. Its presence confused her. She frowned, found herself tempted to wake him with a caress. No, she would wash first, make breakfast, bring up a tray. Surprise him.

She slipped silently from the bed, wrapped herself in the heavy robe, tugged it firmly round her, padded towards the bathroom.

What a graceful room this was, with its vast fireplace, the deep blue chairs, the lofty French windows, the bed in the arched alcove. The bed: she looked back at it shyly, then went on. The recessed shelves in the corner held all his musical equipment, tapes, records. She paused to examine them, get a sense of his tastes. She knew him so little.

On the top shelf, there were some framed photographs. A large one in black and white of an old couple, a woman with an oval face that must once have been handsome. Her eyes gazed out at one with an unmistakeable authority, which was also an irony; next to her was a hatted man with a close-cropped beard and a faraway expression. Bettina and Klaus, Helena suddenly thought. It had to be them.

She scanned the other pictures, hoping to see Anna and Johannes Bahr. There was another couple, but the woman was dark, American she thought, judging from the palm tree in the background. Adam's parents, perhaps. She looked for a resemblance, could see nothing in particular. Next to it there was a coloured portrait of a young woman with dark hair and eyes, a calm expression on her face. Was she a friend of Adam's, a former lover? She found the thought strangely irritating. She would have to ask him.

Then her eyes alighted on a photograph that had been pushed back a little, a threesome. Helena leaned heavily against the wall. It was Adam, Adam looking dashingly handsome in a pale dapper suit, next to him a woman with brightly flowing red hair. He had his arm round her shoulders and between them stood a child, a toddler with hair as bright as the woman's, the dimple in its chin, the shape of its eyes unmistakeably Adam's.

Helena stared at the image, transfixed, saw another beside it, a little red-headed girl on her own, a winsome look on her face. Adam's child.

He had a wife and child.

She felt as if she were about to gag.

'Good morning.' His voice reached her from the other end of the room, soft, almost a caress.

‘Morning.’ She didn’t look at him. ‘Your family?’ she queried, despite herself, gestured towards the photographs.

‘Mmmm . . .’

‘They look nice.’ Her tongue felt thick. ‘Very nice.’ She paused, giving him a chance to explain.

But he only laughed evasively. ‘All families seem nice from the outside.’

She waited.

‘Come here, Helena.’

‘No. I must rush. I’ve got an appointment. I’m late. No, no, don’t get up.’ She raced from the room, blotting him from her sight, afraid that if she were to focus on him, she would start to shout, to rail, to throw things at him.

She pulled on yesterday’s muddied tights, didn’t bother to tuck her shirt into her suit, fled down the stairs.

No wonder he had reviled purity. He didn’t have a shred of it, had lied to her, misled her, cajoled her, bullied her, forced her to trust him. To feel. The worst kind of seducer. She loathed him.

The most important thing now was to get out of here while a shred of her pride remained intact.

And he had made her forget Max. Max who had written to her, who had called for her help, who was in trouble, somewhere. Helena sat in the car for a moment and looked at the house, the grounds. In the distance, she could see the arch of the beech, the strands of morning light glittering over the lake. By its side, those two people lay buried. She shuddered.

It was a nightmare. The whole place in its very stillness was like a nightmare, pulling at her, turning her topsy turvy, making time formless, tumbling the past into the present, casting shadows into the future. It was this place, with its ghosts, that had made her certain yesterday that Max was her father. She had clutched at him, then clutched at that man. The stuff of dreams.

Helena started the car, revved the engine, sped down the drive.

She didn’t pause to see the face peering at her from behind the curtains.

NINETEEN

SNOW STILL COVERED the meadows and rolling hills around Orion Farm. Against the high crisp blue of the New Hampshire light, the rambling clapboard house with its twin pointed gables seemed suspended in time. The outlying barns, the distant greenhouses, had an eerie quiet to them as if Max Bergmann's disappearance had robbed them of active life.

But the high fortress-like gate opened automatically as Helena nosed her car towards it and when she turned off the engine, she could hear the barking of dogs. They were soon at her side, two golden collies, closely followed by a burly man in a red-checked lumberjacket.

'Helena. Good to see you.'

'Hello, Sam. All well?'

'As well as can be expected.' He looked at her as if he were about to pose a question, then changed his mind. 'James is expecting you.'

He led her to a side entrance, down a narrow corridor, past a series of doors each clearly marked with their uses, past the office she knew as Max's.

It was odd to pass by it. The last time she had been here she had been ushered straight in to see Max, whose warm voice had embraced her. But now everything was quiet and the hush felt slightly eerie. Funny how what she had previously experienced as calm and order now exuded an almost regimental hostility.

But James Whitaker put paid to that. He was a slender reserved young man with sandy close-cropped hair and a narrow face which seemed impassive until he took off his rimless spectacles and turned his blue eyes on you. Something about that impassivity reminded her a little of Andy Newman, the man she had once shared her life with.

James was sitting in front of a computer screen. Stacks of bound files and a printout lay spread on the desk next to him. He rose eagerly when Helena came in, as if she were offering salvation. It occurred to her for the first time that the whole business of the Farm, Max's enterprises, now lay on his shoulders.

'Am I glad you're here!' He shook her by the hand. 'But you must be exhausted. Can I get you some coffee, tea? There'll be lunch soon.'

'Tea would be lovely.'

He gestured to Sam, who closed the door softly behind him.

'And so, what have you found? Tell me everything.'

'I don't think it's much.' She brought out Max's letter which she had photocopied. 'I'd like you to read this properly first, in case it means anything to you.'

He looked over the letter quickly. 'Max's style. I'd recognize that anywhere. As for the rest . . .' He shook his head a little hopelessly. 'But you said on the phone you'd found the track.'

'The track perhaps, but not him. He's definitely been in Bavaria. Where he is now, I have no idea. Still, we know he *is*.' She said it emphatically with a hope that the saying would engender the reality.

James gave her a look which was all bleakness. 'I don't know how much longer I can manage without him. Sure, I do all the daily routine, the rotas, the accounts, but as for the rest, the finances, the spirit . . .' He shrugged his shoulders in a way that said it all. 'And I've rung everyone. Even those I think I wasn't supposed to know about,' he grinned so that behind that narrow impassive face she saw the mischievous boy. He vanished quickly. 'You're the only one who's had anything from him.'

Helena allayed the sudden suspicion she read in his face. 'And I can't think why.' It was only half a lie. Since she had left the shadowy terrain of Bavaria, the sense she had had that Max Bergmann might be her father had become overlain with common sense. Yet the need to find him was as acute as ever and had now been joined by the need to find out more about him, if only to disprove the disturbing intuitions that had come over her.

She waited for Sam to deposit the two mugs of tea before continuing.

'I suspect there was another letter, besides the one to me. Have you really been through all his papers, James? Checked for any contacts neither of us might have known about?'

James shrugged. 'I think so. All the business papers are in here and next door. Max always kept his own office locked and I haven't been in there. He's a very private man, you know. Anyhow, I put it off and then when you said you had received that letter, I put the thought out of my mind altogether.' He looked at her a little petulantly. 'Anyhow, he never kept anything in there. It was as bare and tidy as a cell, except for the lecture or book he was currently working on. Sam typed those, so I've looked through the last texts. No clues there.'

'You're sure?' Helena studied him.

'You can read for yourself.' He opened a drawer and pushed a sheaf of papers at her. 'Everything he wrote before we left for Norway just before Christmas.'

'I still think we should go in there,' Helena murmured. 'Look, I have this hunch, it's no more than that, that his disappearance may have nothing at all to do with what we know of him. It's something else. Where did Max come from by the way?' She slipped the question at him as if it were an aside.

'Sweden.'

'I thought it was Norway.'

'His passport says Sweden.'

'I see.' Helena swallowed that, let it ride for a moment. 'And you don't think he's vanished for . . .' she scrutinized his face before going on, 'for financial reasons? This place isn't bankrupt, is it?'

'Not yet. The endowments will keep us going for a while. Max was good at the financial side, though you wouldn't think it to read him or look at him. But the place will fall apart without him sooner or later.' He glanced at her sadly.

'I think we should go into his office.'

'Fine.' He hesitated. 'As long as it's clearly your decision.'

'My decision. I'll take the flak. I just hope there's someone to take the flak from.'

'So you think he might be dead after all.'

'No, I don't think that.' She was emphatic. 'Though I didn't contact the police in Germany. I presume you still don't want them nosing around?'

James took off his spectacles and wiped them slowly on the bottom of his pullover.

Strange, Helena thought, how he was transformed without them. Quite handsome, but also oddly naked.

'I consulted with the Trustees at the Board Meeting Max didn't turn up for. Which was when, by the way, I realized something was wrong. Max has never missed a meeting before. He's punctilious about that. In any case, we discussed it. We agreed that to call in the police prematurely would end up with publicity which was bad for the movement, whatever the real story is. The money would dry up. You know that as well as I do. So far there have only been two small notices in the press, one here and one in England.' He paused. 'Anyhow, Max is police-shy, for all the reasons I presume you know.' He looked at her meaningfully.

'Because of direct action?' She said it blandly.

James twitched, glanced involuntarily over his shoulder, nodded once abruptly. 'I'm not supposed to know,' he mouthed at her.

'Neither am I,' she grinned, mouthed it back.

They gazed at each other like two childish conspirators.

'In any case, we should go into his office.'

'After lunch,' he put it off, 'which is just about now.' His watch beeped a moment later.

'Do you know when Max came to the United States?' Helena asked casually as they got up.

'In the fifties I presume, perhaps a bit earlier. He never talks about his early years. Too long ago, I guess.'

'Yes,' Helena murmured. 'But I think we should find out more. Will you introduce me? To his oldest friends I mean. I don't really know any of his contacts at this end.'

'I'll make you a list. Though I have talked to everyone.' He gave her a somewhat querulous look. 'You won't push them too hard though, will you? I don't want anyone withdrawing support while we still need it.'

Two long tables were set in the high-ceilinged dining room, around them a motley assortment of men in woollen sweaters and tweedy jackets. Not unlike a dining hall in one of the lesser Cambridge colleges, Helena thought. She looked automatically towards Max's place only to find it empty. The room didn't have a centre without him, and indeed, the men looked shabbier than usual, disheartened. And they stared at her with less veiled an interest. Or perhaps it was her imagination.

James sat in the place next to Max's and gestured her beside him. Then he stood and quickly said the grace Max had invented and was wont to recite in resonant tones.

'For the food and drink placed before us, we, her children, thank Nature, whose bounty we work daily to replenish and in whose keeping we remain.'

The food was all vegetarian and Helena ate quickly, unthinkingly. Without Max here she had a greater sense than ever of being an interloper.

And the spirit had definitely gone out of the place. The man beside her had developed an inordinate fascination with her crotch and however she crossed her legs or moved her chair, his eyes focused only there. Meanwhile, the two men across from her were bickering, their insults flying like electricity, so that soon the whole table seemed to be immersed in petty squabbles.

'I'll see you in half an hour,' Helena whispered to James, and tried to move invisibly from the room.

There was a rack of snow-shoes by the back door. She put on a pair over her boots and walked pigeon-toed out into the afternoon. The weather had held and the air was as bracing as a cold morning shower. She breathed deeply, made her way towards a little copse of trees she liked to wander in at the crest of the meadow.

She had brought Andy Newman here two winters ago, almost, she now thought, in order to get Max's benediction. That certainly hadn't been forthcoming. Max had been polite, of course, but he had somehow contrived not to notice Andy's presence, continued to talk as he always did, but over his guest's head. If their relationship had been different, she would almost have thought he was jealous. But perhaps that was how a paternal jealousy manifested itself? She had no way of knowing.

It was strange how she could hardly remember Andy any more. His features wouldn't coalesce into a face. Yet for the ten months or so that they had been together, she had been more than happy to have him around. It solved certain problems, living with a man.

Helena smiled into the trees, as she suddenly remembered having read the same thing in Anna's Book about Bettina. Perhaps things hadn't changed that fundamentally, despite all their surface casualness and freedoms.

She had slipped into the relationship with Andy from one day to the next almost without thinking. He was a tall thin man, with a narrow equine head and a penchant for Fair Isle sweaters. He was preparing a film for the BBC on the environment and had come to her with some queries. They had started to talk and the talk stretched, growing more passionate as they found a fund of common interests. He had asked her if she would act as a consultant on the project and she had accepted happily. And then somehow, the talk extended into the evenings and one night he simply stayed over.

It hadn't been a particularly memorable night, but then sex was hardly in her experience what it was cracked up to be either in books or in some of her friend's tales.

Helena suddenly flushed, remembering her night with Adam Peters. It *would* take a deceiver to prove her wrong. She shunted away the memory violently, walked more quickly, forced herself to look at the trees. Instead, her mind presented her with those poisonous scenes from her childhood which had engulfed her in Germany. She picked up some snow and formed it into a ball, hurled it into the distance. She didn't want to think about all that, not now, though she knew there were links there that one day she might have to confront. That was the problem with navel-gazing. Once one started, there was no end.

It wasn't long after they had been to see Max – whose presence so excited Andy that he had to take off his specs several times in rapid succession to wipe the steam from them – that Andy had walked out on her, just like that. As unemphatically as his coming.

They hadn't exactly had a row. They didn't row. He had merely turned to her in bed that night after they had performed their little act and said, 'You know, you make me feel two feet tall. I'm getting tired of your favours.' His aristocratic nose had quivered a little. And that was that.

Helena hadn't thought she was doing him any favours. Then she had thought contradictorily and with a burst of resentment that a lot of people would queue up for her favours. And that if he felt two feet tall, maybe he was. But she hadn't really known what he meant.

It came to her with a sinking sense that perhaps now she did. If nothing else, her encounter with Adam Peters had given her an intuition of that.

Helena had left Germany the very day she had fled from Adam Peters. There seemed to be nothing more she could do in Bavaria, short of sitting and waiting for Max to appear. And the word 'waiting' wasn't in her vocabulary. Another strategy presented itself, one which wouldn't bring her into Adam Peters's vicinity. She would go to America. She had been planning to go for some time in order to do some more work on Union Carbide. And en route, she would try to talk to some of Max's friends, sniff around Orion Farm. She was certain that once there, she could unearth something of the reason for Max's disappearance and reasons, like a plot line, would lead her to Max. Then too, she hoped that she could put paid to that sequence of imaginings that had begun to haunt her about Max's paternity.

She had only stopped off in London long enough to tend to cats and plants, sort through the post, say hello to Claire and check in at the office to pick up her Bhopal files. Her editor, Carl, had suggested once she was already in the US, she should fly to LA. The LA police force had just set up an anti-pollution squad. It would make a good article. She also suspected he thought it would make a good holiday.

'Twenty-five pounds for your thoughts.' A voice from behind startled her.

Helena turned to see a man of about forty on cross-country skies skid to a halt directly beside her. He had dark curly hair and laughing brown eyes that crinkled in a pleasantly attractive face. A bobble hat sat precariously on his head.

'Wait a minute, how much *is* twenty-five pounds?'

She smiled, despite herself. 'A lot more than my thoughts are worth.'

'Oh?' He looked at her curiously. 'I thought you might be thinking what a bunch of stinkers that lot in there are. I'd pay quite a lot to have it shouted bright and clear.' Suddenly, he shouted into the trees, '"Lousy lot of rotten fakes." There, I feel better. Can I walk with you? Ski with you, I mean.'

Helena shrugged.

'Please.' He lifted his hands in prayer, clattering his ski-poles. 'I saw you in there. Said to myself what a relief it is to feast one's eyes on a woman. Even a beautiful Englishwoman who's pretending to be a boy.' He looked down at her baggy jeans and shook his head scathingly. 'Men really shouldn't be allowed out on their own. It's bad for their souls, you know.' He laughed merrily.

'Why did you come then?'

'That's what I've been asking myself for the last ten days.'

She giggled. He had all the mock drama of a New York comedian. 'And the answer?'

'Still haven't found it, though I've looked everywhere. It's all that Max Bergmann's fault, you know, the fellow who runs this place. Though I notice *he* manages to stay away. He convinced me it would be good for my soul or some other invisible part. Told me I'd find myself. Frankly I'd much rather lose myself at the moment.' He looked at her with frank lasciviousness.

'You're a writer?'

'That's what my agent keeps telling me.'

'So you're not a writer.'

He grinned. 'I'm a writer. But I'm a better procrastinator. Rafael Santucci's the name.' He put out his hand.

'Helena Latimer.' She took it. 'And you've brought your typewriter?'

'Yup. I've brought my typewriter. Brought my paper. I've got all the necessary. My soul. Nature. Peace and quiet. Only one thing wrong.'

'What's that?'

'Everything.'

She laughed.

He gestured her over to a fallen tree trunk, patted some snow off it, and bowed to make way for her. 'So what are you doing here?'

'Passing through.' Helena was non-committal.

'From somewhere to somewhere.'

'I like this place.'

'You like this place?'

She nodded.

'That's either gotta be because you're crazy or 'cause they don't allow you into the men's group. Have you ever spied on one of those groups they hold here with that priest or therapist or whatever he is?'

Helena shook her head.

'No, of course not.' He took the bobble hat off his head and twirled it round and round on his finger. He looked at it reflectively. 'Well, I tell you something. It's taught me.'

'Taught you?' She was suddenly curious.

'Ya, before this I used to think only women really knew how to complain. But now I know that men are better at that too.' His face was suddenly wreathed in smiles.

'Ya gotta hear men complain to hear the real thing.' He started to count on his fingers. 'My cock's too big; my cock's too small. I can't get it up. She won't let me get it down. My father didn't love me. My mother didn't love me. No, she loved me too much. I make too much money to have time to have a soul. I have too much soul to have time to make money. My girl competes with me. My girl puts me down. I can't feel it when I do it. I can't do it when I feel it.' He stopped, looked at her. 'Enough?'

'I'm riveted.'

'Good. You staying long?'

'Probably only until tomorrow.'

'Even better. Will you give me a lift outta here? To anywhere. I'll tell you some more stories.'

Helena laughed. 'I've never met an American without a car.'

He looked sheepish. 'I was dropped here. My own choice. Thought I wouldn't stay the course otherwise. Run off and chase the whisky bottle, not to mention the wine, women and song.'

'But now you want to go in any case?'

'I've gotta go, nice lady,' he met her eyes seriously, 'or I'll end up by beating some smug motherfucker up. And I'm not a strong man.'

They made their way back to the house. Helena noticed that for all his antics, he handled his skis with professional grace.

'Do you write comedy?' she asked him.

'Me?' He glanced at her caustically. 'I'm America's most serious writer. That's why I don't write too often.' His eyes crinkled and he waved her off. 'I'll be waiting for you, so don't think you can vanish without me.'

Helena went back to James's office with a smile on her face. It vanished as soon as she saw him. He was palpably nervous.

'My responsibility, remember?' she urged him on.

He handed her a ring heavy with keys. 'All yours. It has to be one of these.'

Helena tried the keys, beginning to despair as she reached the end of the ring. None of them seemed to fit.

James shrugged. 'That's all there is. Obviously he doesn't want anyone in there.'

'Are these the cleaner's keys?'

He shook his head. 'Mine.'

'Well, the cleaner must have some,' Helena persisted.

'I don't like to ask.'

'James, this is serious. We're not going to steal anything. Just say Max asked you to do something and forgot to give you the relevant file. Say anything,' she said encouragingly.

He went off with a hangdog expression only to come back some minutes later with a grin on his face. 'He wasn't there. So I borrowed them.'

'Good.' She resisted the urge to pat him on the back.

At last the office door opened. They stood there for a moment as if Max might suddenly materialize behind his desk. But the room was empty.

The old pine desk glowed in its coatings of beeswax. The books were neatly lined on the shelves, just as Helena remembered them. She scanned the shelves first, as if they might provide a clue she had missed – the volumes of Nietzsche, Jung, Heidegger, Rousseau, poetry by Whitman and Frost, two volumes of Goethe, she hadn't remembered those, and then scores of more recent specialized books on farming and soil preservation, as well as the standard environmental texts that replicated her own.

She leafed through the Goethe quickly, volumes on the morphology of plant and animal life, on geology and meteorology, was struck for a moment by a tone which reminded her of Max's writings; but there were no clues here, no marginal notes.

Then, while James watched nervously, she started to search the desk. She wasn't too sure what she hoped to find. Old passports perhaps, a stack of love letters. But aside from a ream of paper, some empty notebooks and a packet of paperclips, the first drawers yielded nothing.

'I told you,' James mumbled.

Helena let it pass, continued her search. An image of Adam Peters's cluttered desk flashed through her mind. There would be no shortage of clues there to anything and everything. She banished the thought and opened the final drawer.

There was a book in it. She pulled it out. Another volume of Jung's writings, in German this time. Curious. Perhaps Max had been working on something in it just before his disappearance. A sheet of paper was folded into the volume, and next to it a letter clipped to a brochure. She glanced at the sheet of paper first. Max's writing. She read: 'The leader must be able to be alone and must have the courage to go his own way. But if he doesn't know himself, how is he to lead others? Every movement culminates organically in a leader, who embodies in his whole being the meaning and purpose of the popular movement.'

And then, underlined in heavy black ink, in English this time: 'Emphasize leadership to action groups.'

A note Max had made to himself, Helena thought, unsure whether it was a quote from somewhere or not.

Then she read the letter and whooped aloud. 'This is it, this is it, James.' She felt like hugging him. 'Look, an invitation to speak in Berlin. From the Green Party. With a choice of dates.'

'He never told me,' James murmured.

'Perhaps he hadn't made up his mind. Or he wrote to them himself. He had German. But look, the letter is dated 1 December. One of the possible dates they've invited him for has passed, but the others are all still to come. Let's ring them straight away.' Helena was jubilant.

James glanced at his watch. 'It's too late. Everyone will have gone home. We'll have to wait until tomorrow.'

'First thing then.' Helena examined the brochure. It was printed on coarse recycled paper. The images had a sienna-like feel. Did they correspond to anything she had seen in Bavaria? It was so hard to tell. The trees and mountains, the young people holding placards. She would have to let the images sink into her.

The telephone call to Berlin confirmed that Max Bergmann was scheduled to speak there in April. Helena felt a great weight slip from her shoulders. Soon everything would be clear – why Max had chosen to disappear, why he had written that strange letter to her. And perhaps why she had these odd notions about him. She kissed a flushing James on the cheek, danced from the room. 'I'll see you in Berlin in April then, if not before.'

'Guess so.' James had a taciturn look. 'It still doesn't make sense. Why didn't he tell me?'

'Perhaps I can find something out from these people on your list. I'll let you know.'

'Do that. And Helena . . .'

'Yes?'

'Thanks.'

It was only while she was driving with Rafael Santucci towards Boston that the euphoria wore off and she realized James was right. It didn't make sense. And she had omitted to ask the Berlin organizer when he had heard from Max. If it had been before his disappearance, then the promise of a lecture on a particular day might mean nothing at all. Helena shrugged away the threatening cloud.

With Rafael Santucci to entertain her, it wasn't so difficult. He kept up a ready stream of chatter for the length of the journey, gave Helena what he dubbed a short guided tour of his life with peeks into sewers and monuments. He asked for the same from her, but she stalled him, asked instead whether he knew Bradford Summers and Charles Raymond, two of Max's closest friends in Boston.

'Oh yes, beautiful lady, that I do. In fact, to repay you for your impeccable chauffeuring, I can even introduce you to Brad tonight. He's throwing a book party.' Rafael lowered his voice in conspiracy. 'He can afford to. It's his first.'

'And you'll take me along?'

'I'll do better than that, I'll take you along *and* help you leave. So that you can have dinner with me.'

'That would be very nice,' Helena smiled. 'And by the way, since you know everyone, have you ever come across an Adam Peters?' She didn't know what had made her ask it.

'Adam Peters? You mean the anthropologist who writes too well by half for anyone with a bunch of initials after his name?'

'I think that's him.'

'Don't think I can help you there. Though a friend of a friend of a friend might just . . .'

'It's not that important. Tell me about Bradford Summers first.'

He prepared her, told her how Brad Summers had recently been dubbed a 'Green dream' and 'a king of bio-diversity' by *Vanity Fair*; how he had put millions into an experimental mega-greenhouse in the desert; told her about his first venture into print, *Wild and Pure*; about his business interests, his three marriages, his mistresses. He prepared her so well that when she was introduced to Bradford Summers, she felt that twinge of discomfort which always shadows a meeting with someone one has heard too much gossip about.

The house reeked of wealth ostentatiously displayed. It was there in the designer labels on the fake indoor columns, the movie set bar with its flow of champagne, the pale plaster busts which popped out between the jungle growth of the vast conservatory where the party largely unfurled. It all came as something of a shock after the austerity of Orion Farm, and in her jacket and trousers, Helena felt grossly underdressed.

Bradford Summers himself, with his tanned face, curly head and open-necked shirt, looked, Helena thought, like a slightly ageing paratrooper who had forgotten to shave off his beard. He was half sitting on the edge of a table stacked with copies of his book.

Rafael propelled her through the crowd which milled round him.

'Good to see you, Raf.' Summers rested his large hand on Rafael's shoulder. 'What do you think? Quite a place my wife's rented while the house is being done up.' He gestured round him and then winked comically.

Rafael introduced Helena, mentioned that she wanted to talk to him about Bergmann, if he could spare a few minutes.

'I'll try,' Summers chuckled. His gaze focused on Helena with an intent blankness which made her think he was doing a data base check on her. 'Helena Latimer, wait a minute, didn't I meet you once with old Max? Yes, yes, it was in the winter of eighty-two. I was passing through and I remember asking him whether you were his granddaughter or whether I was allowed to flirt with you. He gave me short shrift on both counts, needless to say. You don't recognize me, of course. I didn't have the beard then. I've gone natural.'

'It suits you, I'm sure.'

His eyes narrowed and Helena smiled warmly to take the sting out of her words.

'Yes, well . . . Here, have a copy of my book. I'll inscribe it for you. Any friend of Max's, as the saying goes. I quote him a lot. Though I'm more of the pure American Wild type myself; take my model from the wolves and the bears rather than the saints.' He curled his fingers into claws and pawed the air in front of her.

Helena didn't know whether she was supposed to laugh. Instead she asked, 'Have you known Max long?'

'Forever. Well, since sixty-three, in any event. My first wife's family lived down near Orion Farm. He had just bought it then, convinced some people it was a good thing to do. Max has always had a way of convincing people – even when his ideas weren't as fashionable as they are now. I've set up an endowment for the place myself. Though the credit all goes to him. He worked like a demon in those early days.' He looked at her astutely. 'You're trying to find out where he's got himself to, aren't you?'

Helena nodded. 'And before the Farm?'

'Worked for the forestry department, as far as I know.' He deflected her. 'You know what my hunch is? I've told that James of his. Once back in Scandinavia, Max just took himself off into the forests of his childhood. He always had a way of looking at a tree as if it were a woman. Often wished I were more like that myself.'

Rafael laughed, 'Keep working at it.'

'I am. And he's probably still there. Simply forgot to count the days and let us know. He'll turn up.'

Helena swallowed hard. 'Did he ever have a wife?'

'Max! No, not since I've known him. Handsome devil though he was. My first wife used to speculate about it. She had this notion that he'd been through one of those devastatingly romantic affairs in his youth which had turned him off women forever. Not that we ever talked about it though. Max isn't the kind of man you can ask about these things. Too lofty. But that's what we all like about him, isn't it?'

'Brad!' A large woman with copious red hair suddenly flung her arms around Summers. 'Congratulations.'

Helena stepped back, opened the book Summers had given her and glanced down the contents page. *Wild and Pure*. For some reason an image of Adam Peters bounded into her mind, Adam fulminating about purity. The rotter. A poisonous man, insinuating himself into her life, her body, her imagination.

'Shall we head off, or do you want to mingle some more with the good and the great?' Rafael whispered in her ear.

'Let's go.'

The next day Helena forced her attention away from Max Bergmann to the Union Carbide Corporation. She told herself that he would have wanted her to do that.

Shares in UCC had plummeted after the Bhopal disaster and the executives were squirming, changing their PR with each passing week as the threat of claims grew imminent. The corporation's initial line had been one of humane compassion. They wanted to be seen as caring. They had insisted that safety standards at their plant in India were the same as at their plant in West Virginia. They had even made the ludicrous gesture of flying Mother Theresa in to bless the orphans and the wounded. Helena had seen her, had noticed that few knew who she was, that the miraculous medals she presented meant nothing to the Hindu and Muslim recipients. But it made good footage for the cameras.

Then the line had shifted subtly. UCC now claimed they were not the parent of the Bhopal factory, but that it was a mere affiliate, that safety equipment was different, in short that the disaster was the Indian company's own responsibility.

What Helena wanted was to see at first hand was just what safety and storage equipment there was at the plant at Institute, and to unearth how many of the Indian team had in fact been trained there. She spent three days at Institute, knew that she was being given the run around and being fed a line. Whatever the greater degrees of safety, she had a dire sense that a leak could as easily take place here as in Bhopal: there were so many variables and so many holes in the system. Then too, it was clear that routine emissions of toxic chemicals were taking place. The entire Kanawha Valley was plagued with them.

What was needed was government regulation on these vast corporations which inevitably put profits first; a set of tight standards for controlling hazardous air pollutants, treacherous gases. There were lobbies at work, she knew. Why then did Institute fill her with an apocalyptic sense of gloom, rather than that anger which fuelled energy and work which would have been hers just a few months back? She seemed once again to be walking the stricken streets of Bhopal. To be immersed again in the despair which had paralysed her when she had first read the notice of Max Bergmann's death.

Her editor was right. If she couldn't have Max straight away, she needed that holiday which would make time speed past until she saw him again in Berlin. And her worry about that had now become more than a niggle.

The frothy blue of the Pacific danced and soared before the house in an endless expanse. On the pale sands to the side, gulls paraded their plump bellies and leapt into flight. A lone lean swimmer tested the water.

Sitting on a sofa of infinite white in a living room whose golden floor seemed to stretch and stretch only to abut into thin air, Helena reflected that she had suddenly landed herself into the midst of someone else's dream of Los Angeles. She liked this house with its stark furnishings and clean, geometric proportions, as much as she liked the warm Californian light which burned away her gloom.

An article in *Mother Jones* had propelled her here. She had picked up the magazine in Boston, but had only had time to open it on her flight from West Virginia.

The lead piece was about a trial in Northern California. Some environmentalists had placed an injunction on hunting grounds. In interview with the writer, they quoted Max Bergmann on the overriding need to preserve natural habitats. Their lawyer, a man who had come out of retirement specially for the case, was called Max Peters. The article gave a brief bio of him. Helena was certain the man was Adam's father.

With the logic of chance, and as if to provide the incontrovertible proof, there was an article in the same issue by Adam Peters. Helena had stared at it, not wanting to see. She had a sinking sense that the man she most wanted to forget was pursuing her. 'Yet another version of the apocalypse', the title beckoned, and she read, despite herself. The experience was oddly like talking to him, a conversation more finely honed in prose.

As the plane winged her across the continent, she pondered the chance concatenation of names. With that intuition which had always served her so well in her journalism, she felt certain that there was a link between them, which she somehow couldn't see. Max's letter had led her to Adam and now his name occurred in a piece about Adam's father. If Adam had lied to her about his wife, had omitted to tell her, she corrected herself, why then he could just as easily have lied about everything else. He did know something about Max, or even if Adam didn't, then perhaps it was Adam's father that Max's letter had intended to lead her to. How she wished she hadn't slept with Adam so that she could pick up the phone and simply ask him whether his father had recently been to Seehafen. But she couldn't. Swift, sharp breaks were best in such matters, not that she had any direct experience of quite a comparable matter.

So she had come to see his father instead, on the pretext of an interview. There were the makings of a story in a novel use of the law for environmental ends. This consoled her.

Helena smoothed the creamy linen skirt and jacket she had treated herself to in a sumptuous arcade yesterday, just round the corner from the newspaper library where she had looked out clippings on Max Peters. The warm weather had caught her unawares, as had the humour of the head of the anti-pollution squad she had seen later in the day.

'Ms Latimer?' The plump kind-featured housekeeper who had seen her in was calling her from the door. 'Mr Peters will see you now.'

'Thank you.' Helena sped after her, through an archway, up a few stairs.

The woman knocked, opened the door for her.

She was in another spacious room, this time with walls lined with what looked like legal texts, but again with that vista which wouldn't release the eye. In front of the vast expanse of glass, there was a long glazed desk, silver paper trays neatly ranged on it.

'Ms Latimer.' A lean bronzed man with the lined face of an ancient Roman senator appeared from the side of the room. He stretched his hand out to her, waved her impatiently towards a chair, then studied her for a moment.

Helena murmured something about the view.

'Yes, the view is wonderful, Ms Latimer, but I'm a busy man and unfortunately an old one. I have little time left, let alone for the ardours of publicity. I am only seeing you because you argued your case so persuasively on the telephone. And you have come a long way, though if I may say so a preliminary letter would have been more in order.'

The rebuke was tempered by the sudden smile which lightened his face. It was a smile of great charm and without the evidence of any other resemblance, Helena instantly thought of Adam.

'I won't take too much of your time, Mr Peters,' Helena began, then explained hurriedly that she wanted to do a profile of him as part of a series of articles on law and the environment. His recent defence of a band of eco-warriors, his use of an injunction to prevent hunters entering a stretch of land where the native species could be said to be in danger of extinction, would stand as an example to British lawyers.

'Ms Latimer, I am neither an environmental campaigner, nor am I a hero.' He turned his steady gaze on her. 'It is those young people I defended who behaved, if I may say so, with somewhat foolish heroism. And you should know,' he smiled that melting smile again, 'that I only undertook the case as a favour to my son who is the young man's friend. They have no money, you see, and I came at a premium rate.'

He stopped her possible intervention. 'Nor is that heroism or particularly charitable. I have earned more than I deserve in my time.'

Helena took a deep breath. 'And your son – Adam Peters, isn't it – is an environmentalist?'

He didn't question the name, simply chuckled. 'My son is not easily susceptible to labelling, though he makes a fine friend. And he has been known to take up the cause of the Yanomamo and their land rights in a receding rainforest. But it is neither my family nor my personality which is in question here, Ms Latimer,' he looked at her severely again, 'you want the issues, the case.'

Helena forced herself to concentrate. She looked down at the questions she had prepared and started in on them.

At one point in the course of the interview, he chuckled at her again and said, 'You would have made a fine lawyer, Ms Latimer.'

She smiled at that, returned the compliment. 'And you have, from what I've read, been a great one.'

He bowed slightly in old-fashioned acknowledgement. They went on and then, as if he had just looked at an invisible watch, he stood up. 'One of the secondary reasons I undertook this case, Ms Latimer, is that I am interested in a curtailment of this country's far too generous gun laws. I mention it because you come from a more sensible country, so it may not be instantly apparent to you. Please make that clear in your article.' He smiled formally. 'I believe you have enough to work with now.'

'Thank you.' Helena bundled her notebook into her bag, chatted in a lighter tone, while she did so. 'You do visit Britain occasionally?'

'I have only been there twice and that many years ago. Before you were born.'

'But you are European? German?'

He laughed. 'No longer. Europe is a very distant place.' He gestured expansively at the Pacific Ocean. 'And I have had quite enough of that history. Though my son seems to have developed a fascination with it,' he grimaced slightly.

'You don't approve?' Helena dared to ask.

'No, no, Ms Latimer, no insult to Europe intended. It is simply a personal matter.'

'And you have grandchildren?' She slipped it in and he seemed relieved to change the subject.

'Two fine grandchildren.' He gestured towards the desk where she saw there were two framed photos.

She went round to look at them. A little girl with flaming hair stared out at her from one of them – the same little girl. Helena's mouth grew dry. There was the tangible proof. Was that too something she had come for?

'Lovely children,' she murmured.

He smiled, 'Always even lovelier to their grandparents.'

Helena looked down at the desk, away from those perceptive eyes. On top of one of the silver paper trays, she spied a hand-written letter.

How strange, she thought to herself, only half registering the notion, the writing had the thick, heavy curves of Max Bergmann's. It *was* his.

'By the way, Mr Peters,' she said, trying imperceptibly to read the letter, not succeeding as he moved towards her, 'do you know of a Green philosopher by the name of Max Bergmann?'

'Can't say that I do.'

Helena paused for a moment. 'Oh. His name was mentioned in close conjunction with yours in an article about the trial.'

He looked at her impassively.

'I think he might interest you.'

He didn't comment on that either, simply stretched out his hand. 'It's been more of a pleasure than I supposed, Ms Latimer.'

'Thank you.' Helena took his hand, shook it, she later thought, with perhaps too much warmth to cover what had been altogether too ostensible snooping.

TWENTY

WOMEN, ADAM PETERS TOLD HIMSELF in another sequence of the dialogue that had run obsessively through his mind for the last week, are no longer interested in love. The life of the passions has been lost to them. They have wanted to approximate men and they are achieving it fast. The problem is they have chosen the worst men as their models; the hit and run, fast track variety.

Nonsense, his other voice protested. The reason women are not interested in love is men themselves. And quite right, too. They're either violent brutes who kick first at what's closest to them or blindly arrogant brutes who don't notice what's closest to them. What's more, you, my dear ageing male, are becoming the worst form of misogynist. The whining closet variety. A few little disagreeable episodes and wham, bang, a whole sex is at fault.

– No, just a regional phenomenon.

– Name names.

– Bah!

With a violent gesture, Adam Peters flung the creamy white paint on his roller angrily at the wall. He watched the thick rivulets form, lazily edge their way downwards. Then with a mutter he corrected the damage and spread the paint evenly on the wall. Up down, up down. But for the ceiling, it was almost done.

A cold breeze whipped up the terrace and round the open door of the Seehafen drawing room. He looked out disconsolately and wished with a desperate fervour that he might see Ms Helena Latimer walk in. He could then shout at her rather than at the wall, the paint, himself.

What had induced her to leave like that, without so much as a word? They had fallen asleep with their limbs entwined, their eyes locked in caress. If anyone had asked him then would he wager his life on her smiling at him when he woke, he would have done so gladly. The taste and smell of her had engulfed him like the sweetest of dreams. Still did.

And like the sweetest of dreams she had dissolved moments after he had opened his eyes.

But why?

Adam sloshed more paint thickly on the wall, covered the outlines of picture frames, ancient marks, like ghosts of other lives.

He had asked himself that question at least a thousand times in the last eight days. Days in which he had been good for nothing, unable to concentrate, to sit still, to sleep; days in which he had thrown himself into physical labour which left his mind too free to roam.

Was a shared passion, for it had been shared, he was certain of that, worth nothing at all, not even a goodbye, it's been nice knowing you? Was he so hopelessly out of touch? Or had it all been a sham, a masquerade?

No, he could swear that wasn't the case as certainly as he could swear that he was standing holding this roller of dripping paint in this room somewhere in Germany.

Adam put it down, went to gaze out the window. The view was no solace today. The mountains were covered in low-lying cloud. He could barely see the lake.

Was it something he had said? For he knew that he had said far too much. He had derided her, mocked her. But it wasn't her he was mocking so much as the fact that she had chosen to stand for something, as if all of her could be subsumed in that. Words said in anger, to provoke. Directed at someone else, he had thought as soon as he had said them. For she had come to him after that, met him so beautifully, so fully. He could still see those eyes, darkly blue, with something of astonishment in them, gazing at him, wide open at the height of her passion.

With a curse, Adam Peters threw the pack of cigarettes he had dug out of his pocket on the floor. Perhaps he should have told her he loved her, thought he had fallen in love with her at first sight. It wouldn't have been a lie.

Yet no woman wanted to be told of love any more. No man either, he suspected. It was a dirty word, much worse than its four-letter kin.

Perhaps it was simply that he no longer understood anything of women, was no good to them.

'Stupid self-pity,' he lambasted himself out loud, sank into a deep chair draped in a dust cloth. 'You're soon going to join the Victim Brigade,' he sneered at himself, stared into the empty hearth.

It had started well enough, his life with women – after the first few inevitably clumsy overtures, more like the tuning up of an orchestra really. The overture itself had taken place right here. That was probably why he always liked being here. Had taken place the very summer that he had read Anna's Book. Perhaps that romantic great aunt of his had inspired him.

He had met the girl, Olga, in Munich, had invited her to join him and his friends at Seehafen. She had come, a blowsy young woman of his own age, with soft lazy eyes and a fierce tongue. They had talked unstoppably about Marx and Freud, Vietnam and America, Red Army Factions and alternative societies. She knew far more than he did, innocent Californian that he was. About love as well. And she had taught him, right here under the trees for the length of that summer. It was a lesson well worth the learning.

Olga still wrote to him occasionally, and he to her, and he had seen her not so long ago, shared that laughing conspiracy of one-time lovers, playing with but never quite reviving the flame.

He had liked women then, continued to, really, despite what he sometimes named for himself as the 'hiccough' of the last few years when everything had gone wrong. And there had been many women after Olga, friends and lovers, any number of which he might have settled down with happily enough. But the women seemed to want it no more than he. The times weren't about settling. They were about falling in and out of love. Everyone was in a hurry, hungry for more and different, relishing the freedoms that freedom brought. There was pain, of course, but few seemed to sink with it.

Perhaps they were all merely young and callous.

Certainly, as the decade grew older things shifted, imperceptibly at first and then with a vengeance. He had been in Brazil with the Yanomamo for some eighteen months and when he returned to Berkeley, the university he was by then attached to, there was a new woman in the department.

He first met Samantha Grey at a departmental meeting. He was riveted by that clear precise voice which argued so logically, so concisely, as much as he was taken by that mane of flaming hair, the green eyes, the pert suit over her trim body. He had always liked strong women who spoke their own mind, had always liked to argue – Bettina's legacy, undoubtedly; and there had been no one to argue with in the Amazon. So when she approached him after the meeting, invited him to lunch, emphasized how much they had to talk about, he was delighted. He still remembered how he had had his hair trimmed, gone out to buy a new shirt and trousers, had presented himself punctually at twelve thirty at her office door.

They had gone to a small Japanese restaurant near the campus, sat at a table outside by a little makeshift fountain. They had talked for nearly two hours, talked shop – kinship systems, myths, barter economies. They had dropped names, exchanged CVs and bibliographies. It had all seemed strangely exhilarating, like some first meeting with a tribe he had long forgotten. It was only in retrospect that he realized the only questions she had asked him about the Yanomamo were about the women.

It was a busy season. There were notes to write up, courses to organize, trips to various campuses for pre-arranged lectures, as well as visits home to his parents. So except for brief exchanges in the corridor, he hadn't seen her for some weeks when she invited him home to dinner. He had gone willingly, fascinated by the punctiliousness of the little card she had sent him. The dinner was a more formal affair than he had expected, an assortment of colleagues and strangers around a carefully set table, complete with candelabrum. She had presided with all the cool of a practised hostess, though once he had heard her bark at the little Mexican maid in a voice which made him shudder. He ought to have known then.

But that was always the story one told oneself in retrospect, Adam acknowledged, still staring into the empty grate. Stories which had endings were always different from those one lived.

At the time, he was quite taken with her ways: an Easterner, he thought to himself, amongst this casual gaggle of Californians or those who had acquired its lazy ways. So when she had asked him to stay after the others had left, he had stayed, more than willingly.

Going to bed with her had a whiff of high excitement. Although she had effectively invited him, it was as if there were a host of trials he had to endure and overcome, a book of rules he had to learn, before he was considered suitable for the ultimate race.

At one point she had said to him, her pretty lips formed into a perfect pout, 'Unless I initiate, it's rape, because I'm the weaker one.'

'I hadn't noticed,' he had laughed, assumed a joke. And when she had said to him, sitting astride him, her wild mane of hair covering him, 'I don't like penetration, except sometimes, when I'm on top,' he had simply buried her words in a kiss.

And so they had gone on for some months, merrily enough, enjoying the astringency of their professional arguments, not exactly engaged on a love affair, but lovers nonetheless, though the four-letter word itself never reared its head.

During the summer, he had gone back to Brazil to finish up some work which would provide the finishing touches to his book. He hadn't thought about her much then, had assumed without quite putting it into words that it was over, the matter of a season.

It was when he got back early in September that she told him. She had invited him to lunch at her place. He could see the expanse of the Bay from her window, the curve of the Golden Gate Bridge, had been gazing at it dreamily, when she said, 'I'm pregnant. It's yours.'

His first reaction was to protest, 'But I thought you were on the pill, you never said . . .' He didn't. He knew there was no reason to make that assumption. So he stilled his thought, said instead, looking into those green eyes, 'Do we get married or . . .' She hadn't let him finish his sentence, had simply kissed him and declared proudly, as if he had passed another test, 'I knew you'd do the right thing.'

It was strange how she always knew what the right thing was, about everyone and everything, as if there were a moral guide book imprinted on her mind which she read off at any occasion.

They rented a house together in the hills overlooking the city, had a wedding party of which all he could remember was his mother's tears; started their lives together.

She was as meticulous over the pregnancy as she had been over staff meetings and dinner parties. Everything was by the rules. He could understand her not wanting to be touched, her fear of harming the baby. What he couldn't abide was the way she perched herself next to him every time he started to work and complained that she couldn't concentrate. 'Look, I would carry the baby for you, if I could,' he said to her, meaning it, 'but I can't, so please let me earn our keep.'

She never forgave him that, repeated it to their friends, as if it were the ultimate in male malevolence.

He started to curtail his working to office hours, relishing them as he had never done before, loving his book, writing it speedily. But he was fascinated, too, by the baby's growth, wished she would let him touch it.

She kept him away from the birth, preferring her female friends. Yet as soon as he saw that puckered little face with the clear unflinching gaze, a sense of wonder overcame him. And a gratitude. The intensity of it surprised him. He held the tiny bundle in his arms. It was not unlike being in love. 'Thank you.' He kissed Samantha, who averted her face. 'Thank you. She's beautiful. Like her mother.'

'You don't mean that.'

'She's beautiful,' he repeated firmly.

The sense of little Janey's beauty, the awe that she was there at all, never altogether left him, not in the face of Samantha's growing hostility nor in what now became her constant jibes. There was a new rule book, a timetable of who was responsible for the baby in what hours, who did the shopping when. Samantha wrote it, assuming that was her natural right.

He would gladly have done more than his half share.

Before Janey had come along, he had always thought that the great anthropologist Malinowski's description of the behaviour of Trobriand Island fathers was an idealization – one of those little sleights of hand common enough among anthropologists. In order to emphasize the lacks in their own culture, they painted a rosier-than-thou picture of the other. So Malinowski, product of a strictly patriarchal Europe, where the division of labour put children firmly in the mother's camp – though they were the father's property – evoked an idyllic Trobriand Island: a matrilineal society, where fathers tended to their babies with a natural fondness, fed and changed them, carried them around for hours, gazed on them with pride and love, talked about and exhibited their virtues and achievements untiringly. And because of this, the children, when grown, in turn had a duty towards their fathers, even though these same fathers had little authority or property power over the generational line.

With Janey, Adam felt he could have entered the idyllic condition of a Trobriand Island father – if only Samantha had permitted it.

It was her clock-like precision which drove him mad, the fact that nothing was ever spontaneous or allowed to take its own time. So that on the dot of four, whether he was in the midst of a game or feed or more rarely a paragraph, the shift ended.

Yet whatever he did, however malleable he made himself, it was either not enough or too much. It came to him after some months that Samantha resented the baby with a barely containable passion, could neither forgive Janey for being there, nor him for wanting her there and enjoying her presence. He knew the first was not altogether unusual, so he waited for it to pass. He hoped that once it did, her resentment of him might diminish as well.

In May, when Janey was five months old and Samantha had already proudly been back at work for three, his wife announced she had accepted a post at Tufts outside Boston. She had given him no prior warning.

For once he had voiced his rage. 'And what am I supposed to do?' he had shouted.

'You can come with me and be a house husband. Or you can stay here. Janey comes with me, of course.' She had looked at him smugly. It was in that look that he had started to hate her.

He knew that he was part of a generation living an experiment. The roles were being reversed and he had been cast as old-fashioned wife. Would he have minded so much if he had felt the casting had more basis in love and less in vengeance? He didn't know.

In any event, he had gone with her, unable to be parted from Janey, at a loss as to what else to do. He didn't have a set of rules ready-made to apply to the situation. He arranged for a leave of absence, found odd bits of lecturing to do on the East Coast; and for a year he had written articles, made inroads on a new project and looked after Janey except for those five afternoon hours when the minder he had hired came to the house.

Strangely enough, he had enjoyed it. Janey sustained him, her gurgling laugh, her first running steps, the babble which wasn't quite speech; as did the favourable notices for his first book when it appeared, the promise of a post at Princeton. There were a few friends too, though the oldest one, met again here, told him he was becoming a martyr to the women's movement. Adam didn't feel like a martyr.

He was both too much in love with his daughter and too angry with his wife for that. The anger had come again after his book had appeared.

Ever since the new year, Samantha had taken to having regular meetings with her women friends in the house. He thought he didn't mind, but the voices raised in complaint would sometimes fall irritatingly on his ears. It was always the same tone and when he bumped into the women, they would look through him, like he imagined the Victorians had done to their servants.

Had women felt they suffered from this invisibility? His mother? Bettina? He certainly couldn't imagine the latter ever being invisible.

But perhaps it was the case, and he was being made to pay for historical crimes.

Then one day, he had heard Samantha's voice, raised over the others, mocking his work, complaining of how that piddling little achievement had prevented her from finishing her own. He had stolen her ideas, she claimed. It was the last which sent him into a fury.

They no longer shared a room, rarely sat at the same table. But that night he had sought her out, his fists tightly clenched lest he raise them to hit her.

'I don't like it being said that I've stolen my work from you. There isn't a grain of truth in it and you know it.'

'Isn't there? You've stolen my life.'

He looked at her aghast. 'Stolen your life?'

'I have your child now. I'm trapped.'

'Trapped?' He could only echo her stupidly.

'Yes, it's your doing.'

'You're not trapped. You can go when you please.'

'I can't leave my child.'

'She was mine a moment ago.'

'She's mine. I carried her.'

'I am not responsible for biology, Samantha.' He had hissed that.

'I should never have allowed you to seduce me.'

'I never seduced you. Who invited me out, invited me home? Who got me to marry her in a contemporary version of the shotgun marriage? You're so completely enmeshed in your cruddy ideology that it's driven you mad. Tell me: is there anything I can do which is right?'

She looked at him blankly.

'No, nothing,' he had answered for her. 'Because I owe you. By the very fact of my sex, I owe you. Right?' He was screaming by then. 'It's biologically determined.'

'Right!' So was she.

'Okay! Since I can't do anything right, I'm going to start to do everything wrong. Next week, I'm going to walk into your Victim's Brigade and announce that they're not to set foot in this house again while I pay my share of the rent. That'll give you all something tangible to moan about.'

'Don't you dare,' she had spat at him.

He had gone on, his venom spilling over now that he had started, 'I don't understand how relatively attractive, supposedly intelligent women, all of whom have more than their coats on their backs, can carry on in this idiotic fashion. You daughters will grow up to loathe you, let alone your sons.'

She had shrieked at him then. 'I want a divorce.'

'Good, file for one.'

'Go and have an affair with someone. One of those young dimwits who looks up to you in lectures with gooey eyes.'

'I thought you respected women.'

'I'm taking Janey.'

'No you're not.'

Their exact words were now lost to him, but the pattern of the row, repeated so many times over was eternally engraved in his mind. It had gone on, horrible, hateful, for days, months.

Until the summer, when Samantha had come to him with a self-satisfied smile on her face and announced that her friend Sarah had invited her to accompany her to France. She wanted to go. He could have Janey for the summer.

She was happier when she came back, a little easier, as was Adam. He suspected that she was having a lesbian affair, but he didn't pry, didn't care. His move to Princeton was imminent and he would have liked to take Janey with him.

There was no question of that, Samantha was adamant. But he could visit every weekend.

He did. It drove him frantic, that little face lighting up when he arrived and then asking him every few hours with a mournful gaze when he had to go. He was stricken with guilt and a sorrow he didn't know how to assuage.

That was over three years ago now.

There had been other women in that time, though not many: he had grown cautious. Yet he had too much intellectual self-respect to allow himself to universalize from the particular and attribute to all women what he had experienced in one. Then, too, after the first period of resentment, he had admitted to himself that the whole marriage had been a mistake from the start, on his part as well. He had been too easy-going, too willing to treat his own existence like some exotic spectacle to be observed, experienced and then wrapped up in commentary before he moved on to the next. As if life were a never-ending stream of riches that carried one lazily on from one lavish possibility to the next.

He was a wanderer by nature; Janey had put a stop to that, made him want to dig deeper, take stock.

And this year, he had at last stopped hating Samantha. He could talk to her with a degree of courtesy, appreciate her competence. He had almost forgotten the pain and felt he had a new fund of hope.

But perhaps that wasn't the case.

Adam stared at the empty grate in the empty house and buried his head in his hands. Didn't so many of the things he had said to Helena Latimer, had defensively felt, have their origins in Samantha? In his own fear of repetition where he least wanted it? Not in her, the woman who had shown him so much vulnerability, so much generous passion, alongside her boldness, a woman who in her loving was utterly unlike Samantha.

That was perhaps why she had run away.

A fool. Always the fool.

He stood up slowly and with an effort started to slosh paint on the wall. He would have to see her again by hook or by crook. Get her back here. How he wanted her back here. Explain.

He knew that she had left the little inn she had told him she was staying at. Whether she had left Germany, he had no idea. He had written to her care of her paper in London, but there had been no reply from there. Probably wouldn't be. If she had decided to go, she wouldn't bother to answer his letters. Then too, she was presumably still looking for that man, Max Bergmann.

That was it, of course. Adam held his brush in mid-air and stared at it as if it were a magic key. He would have to find Max Bergmann for her. Somehow.

Finding a person who may not want to be found is no simple matter. But Adam Peters threw himself forcibly into the task. Activity, any activity, was better than this passive mooning and endless introspection.

Over the period of his various stays in Seehafen, he had met a number of people in the area, and now he went to see them one by one, chatted, asked, gleaned. He looked through the register of deaths; by any means he could, got descriptions of the deceased.

He followed false leads. There had been a murder in a town some twenty kilometres away. Adam did what Helena had not dared to do. He chatted to his local policeman about it only to find that the victim was a young man, and in the course of the chat learned about other crimes in the area which had led to imprisonment.

He visited the regional hospital in a search for accident victims, conscious and unconscious. Since he had never met Max Bergmann, he ordered his books from a bookshop in Munich, in the hope that one of them would have a photograph. Then he did the hospital rounds again. He put ads of various descriptions in local shops and papers, 'Helena Latimer wishes to contact Mr Hillman of New Hampshire, please write to, etc.' or 'Would the elderly gentleman interested in information about the painter Johannes Bahr please contact . . .' The latter resulted in two letters about Bahr which he answered dutifully. But as for the rest at the end of three weeks, he had only one distant hope. There was a man in the hospital in Murnau who could at a pinch be Bergmann. The police had brought him in and he had no identification on him. He was old, confused, rambling, said his name was Otto Stroheim, but no one had been able to ascertain that.

It was something. Adam Peters set off for London, the lecture he was to deliver for the LSE in his bag and next to it, the photograph he had taken of Otto Stroheim.

Screens flickered along the rows of desks in the crowded, brightly lit newspaper office. Telephones rang incessantly, hung from shoulders as fingers tapped. Voices were raised and lowered. Men and women with intent expressions stared into hardware or space. Paper cups with dregs of rancid coffee littered tabletops.

'It's him again.' Lynn, the assistant to the Environment section glared at Helena. She was a fresh-faced, tow-haired young woman, not long out of university and prone to unstoppable chatter. 'Fifth time in two days. What do I say this time?'

'Tell him the same thing again. Or tell him I've gone to Timbuctoo.'

The woman made a face at her, then pressed a button on her phone. 'I'm afraid she's gone into another meeting. Can I take a message please.' Her voice rang out in efficient tones. She scribbled something on a pad. 'Yes, I will. Thank you.'

With a grimace, she handed the message to Helena. 'If you don't go to this lecture tonight, you're a first-class rotter. The man's in love.'

'The man's a pest.'

'Sounds pretty nice to me. And given the excuses, exceedingly patient.' She grinned. 'So what's the story?'

'The story is what's up on my screen and not getting written.'

'Okay, but I'm putting a bomb under your chair. It explodes at seven. And if you're not out of here by then, bye bye.'

'You haven't given him my home address?' Helena looked at her askance.

'Would I break the golden rule? "I'm afraid that we are not permitted to give out . . ."'

In exasperation, Helena threw the crumpled message at her, then smiled. 'Keep it up and I'll get you an extra special birthday present.'

Lynn made eyes at her. 'A cuddly toy boy.'

'If you ladies would please try to concentrate on something Green, I might get this page together for next week.' Carl Sykes, their section editor, looked over from his desk, lightening his words with a laugh. 'And I need your article, Helena.'

Helena focused on her screen and tapped out a rapid paragraph, then, checking her notes, another and another.

'Coffee?' Lynn called out behind her.

'Tea, please,' Helena murmured.

While Lynn was off and about, Helena glanced down at the invite which had been waiting in her tray on her return from California.

Department of Anthropology, London School of Economics. Guest Lecture by Professor Adam Peters (Princeton) and then, the title: Hybrid Lives. There was a note appended to it. 'Please come. And join us for dinner afterwards. Please.'

For a moment she pondered the 'us' and wondered whether it included his wife. No, he wouldn't be that callous. He had undoubtedly left his wife at home as men so often did. At home in Princeton.

There had been a letter from him too, sent earlier. She had chucked that out, flushing as she read it. A mixture of amorous twaddle thinly veiling his anger at having been left. Served him right. He had lied to her, lied doubly. About that letter from Max as well. She could recognize Max's writing anywhere. And there it had been on Adam's father's desk. He was a liar who wanted her to be the other woman. She had never been the other woman. It wasn't fair on the first or the other. Women needed to have solidarity.

When her profile of his father was printed, she would send it to Adam and attach her own cool little note, telling him how pleased she had been to learn of his child's existence and how angry to find that letter.

Helena tried to concentrate on her article. She had had so much to catch up on since her return, though it had been a real pleasure to come back, to be greeted so warmly, to be surrounded by the familiar faces, to dawdle over a companionable drink in the evenings. But the matter of Adam wouldn't leave her alone. Perhaps she ought to go to that lecture, ought to tell him face to face. After all, she had nothing to be ashamed of. The shame was all his. And he couldn't rape her in the midst of a crowd.

No, no, that wasn't right. He hadn't raped her. Rape was what had happened to her in childhood. She had to be clear about that now. Quite clear. What Adam Peters had done was to seduce her, with her active compliance. The problem was he had seduced her into something she didn't quite recognize as sex.

'Tea.' Lynn plopped a paper cup down beside her.

'Thanks,' Helena said absently. She picked up the phone and rang her friend Claire's number. 'Fancy going to a lecture tonight? At the LSE?'

'Don't think I can.' Claire hesitated. 'It's Nick's and my weekly night out. The one you persuaded us into, remember? To stimulate our marriage to new heights? Alone together, no kids, just a candle and dirty memories between us. On the other hand, a lecture and you between us might make a stimulating change.' Claire laughed her familiar ironical laugh, rushed on. 'What time?'

'Seven thirty. The New Theatre.'

'We may be a little late. But we'll be there. Grab some seats.'

'Good woman.' Lynn was grinning at her. 'I couldn't have coped with another day of messages. I'm proud of you.' She was examining Helena with her prize-winning student's expression. 'You know, my father tells me – he's a shrink – that men have very fragile egos, at home that is. In public, they're ripe for trampling.'

Helena glowered. 'Maybe I should go out with your father then.'

The lecture hall was already crowded when Helena arrived, a steeply raked room that looked as if might have been used for one of Charcot's exhibitions of his hysterics. Not a fortuitous analogy, Helena chided herself. She looked round for some seats where she might sink into invisibility, found three by the windows on the side, not too far from one of the exits.

Being here, seeing that spectrum of faces both eager and dramatically bored around her, the chalky blackboards, the large institutional clock over the door, reminded her of her Cambridge days. She had enjoyed doing her degree in Modern Languages, had enjoyed her college existence as well, the endless trials and tribulations of a dormitory full of students who led high-velocity lives.

It was towards the end of her second year that the creeping realization came on her that her own internal life was a calm space in comparison to the drama-packed goings on around her. She was the one who was always called in at the moment of crisis, the shoulder to weep on, the negotiator, the peace-maker, sometimes even the bully. Like Em, she realized. And she relished that; she preferred it that way round, excitement on the outside, calm within.

It occurred to her now as she gazed at the empty demonstration table where Charcot might have stood that it was probably those turbulent early childhood days she didn't like to remember that had prepared her for that. Life was always on the outside, better kept at a distance, safer, and her role was to tidy and make safe, to clean up. Armour had to be kept on for those external battles so that she could remain intact. The mess musn't be allowed in.

'Why Helena, it is Helena, isn't it? I haven't seen you for so long.'

An old woman with papery cheeks was looking up at her from the seat diagonally below her.

'My, how beautiful you've grown. How glamorous.'

'Mrs Fenton. How lovely to see you.'

Mrs Fenton was an old friend of Emily's and Helena was filled with guilt at the thought that she hadn't visited her in perhaps two years. 'I thought you had moved down to Sussex.'

'I moved back,' the old woman smiled whimsically. 'I got bored and missed dear grubby old London. There were no lectures to go to in the country. And no young people. Only the flowers to tend. And winters are very long, you know. So I moved back into a flat close to my old address, just round the corner in fact. You must come and see me sometime.'

'I'll do that.'

'You know Emily and I were students here just before the war.' She lowered her voice conspiratorially. 'She was madly in love with one of the younger lecturers. We used to come here, right in this theatre, and listen to him. Then he was killed in the war. She never got over it.' She shook her head sadly.

Helena stared at her. Well, that put paid to one of her other German fantasies. Emily and Max, a mother and a father. What a fanciful idiot she had been, a bereft child in search of a family. And yet . . .

'Helena, there you are.' Nick Foster, Claire's husband, was waving at her vigorously from the bottom of the stairs. He strode up them two by two, pulling his long scarlet scarf off all the while. She smiled at the tall dramatic figure he cut, with his sleek black hair and pirate's eyes, and returned his embrace.

'Hello, gorgeous. You're a sight for tired television eyes.'

It was when he sat down that Helena noticed Adam Peters had just come into the room, preceded by a small vivacious woman with a round doll-like face.

'I came straight from the office. Claire must have been held up by the kids. Which means I get two whole delicious minutes alone with you.'

'In a vast crowd and just as the lecture is about to begin.'

'Drat. Foiled again,' he chuckled.

Helena didn't take up the familiar banter. She was sinking down into her coat, making herself small and watching Adam Peters. She had forgotten how handsome he was. The suit emphasized it, a chunky herringbone tweed which fell smartly from his broad shoulders, a bright blue shirt, and a tie with something yellow in it that brought out the warm hazel of his eyes. But it wasn't only the suit.

Her face grew warm and she sank deeper into her coat.

'There's Claire.' Nick stood to wave again.

If Adam hadn't seen her before, it would be a miracle if he didn't see her now, Helena thought. But she smiled at Claire, petite and vivacious, and as darkly dramatic as her husband. It was always a pleasure to see her, though when they had met on the evening of her return from California, Claire had been stern with her, had criticized her for running herself into the ground for Max Bergmann.

The woman was introducing Adam, paeans of praise about a list of books and publications Helena hadn't known about. Meanwhile he was scanning the room, assessing his audience. Or looking for her, Helena suddenly thought. She had an almost irresistible desire to run. Then his eyes rested on her. His lips curled into a smile which a second later had vanished.

He walked to the podium, looked out at them all for a moment before beginning. The silence grew expectantly.

'In the West, we have a tendency to locate our hoped-for future somewhere in a golden past. Our paradises, those moments of essential purity, of authenticity, are always lost. And always somehow to be redeemed. It is as if we could only walk towards an imagined future by looking backwards into an imagined past.

'For Christians, that golden age is Adam and Eve's garden before that fiendish alien, the serpent, inveigled his way in and propelled the Fall; for certain feminists and sexual reformers, a matriarchal society before Fatherright usurped its just place; for Greens a pagan or medieval countryside before industrialization brought its evils; for the Nazis the age of the great Nordic heroes, set to music by Wagner.'

There was a titter. Adam went on.

'For libertarian capitalists, a time before the welfare state imposed its restrictions on almighty freedom. For native Americans, a time before the plundering white man arrived on their shores. And for the English, a time, I imagine, before the Empire had struck back to deliver the colonized peoples into this green and pleasant land.'

There was some laughter from the audience accompanied by an uncomfortable shuffling of feet.

'For anthropologists, the golden age is too often the primitive peoples we study with such attention. They are our very own dreams of innocence. So that when we find the serpent even in this garden, we would prefer to gloss over it. Paradise must remain pure, an authentic clime.

'What I would like to explore today – and I will draw on a number of ethnographic examples – is what would happen if we rid ourselves of that fearful symmetry of loss and redemption, of sin and salvation – with its intermediary notion of apocalypse. And don't forget that the discourse of the apocalypse is now both scientific and religious: environmentalists use statistics to evoke the late great planet earth, while presidents talk of Armageddon and God's wrath.

'It seems to me that there is little basis in the modern world for an essentialist and moralizing language of lost or future purity. All our cultures, from that of the Yanomamo Indians in the Amazon to the United States or Afghanistan, are hybrid, heterogeneous, mixed, diverse, impure

– whether through the movement of peoples, global media or harder currency.'

Helena listened, her concentration so intense that when Adam glanced at his watch and noted the passage of the hour, she was taken altogether by surprise. He was smiling now, that ironical smile of his.

'And as a parting word, my grandmother once told me that she couldn't bear living under the weight of those twin burdens, "the sins of our fathers, the purity of our mothers". "I want to invent the present," she said to me, "the past is an outworn invention."'

There was a burst of applause. The woman next to Adam was glowing with pleasure as she rose to thank him and invite questions. Nick popped up instantly. Helena wished she could vanish as she saw Adam focus first on her, then on Nick, then back at her.

But he answered his question politely and fully, turned to another.

Helena rose as quietly as she could, whispered to Claire, 'I have to go to the loo. Meet you outside.'

'Let's stay and talk to him.' She raised ogling eyes to Helena, 'He looks and sounds decidedly interesting.'

'I'll see if I can get back in,' Helena prevaricated, smiled quickly at Mrs Fenton who had turned to look at them. 'I'll ring you,' she murmured.

Then she fled without looking back at Adam. When she reached the safety of the women's room, she was breathing as hard as if she had run for her life. She felt as if Adam's lecture had been directed specifically at her, as if he had set out to rumble the very underpinnings of her life, to cast a dazzling and annihilating light on the man she most valued in the world: Max, whom he had once called an apocalypse-monger, a prophet of disaster.

'We should have gone and chatted to him,' Claire proclaimed when they had all gathered outside. 'I thought you knew him.'

'I've met him once or twice.' Helena kept her voice flat.

'Well, you should meet him again.'

'Don't listen to her. She just wants another bod to mosey in on our delicious threesome. And one who's made it on to every American high-brow's pick of the year list.' Nick hugged his wife.

'I didn't know that,' Helena mumbled.

'That's why you have me here.' He put an arm around each of their shoulders. 'I've booked a table at Joe Allen's. A brisk walk to whet the appetite, ladies.'

'I've told you. I'm not a lady,' Claire grumbled, then grinned, 'Lead the way, Sir Galahad.'

The restaurant, beyond its almost invisible facade, was as always abuzz with voices and laughter. At the long crowded bar, suited bleary-eyed men and glossy-haired women clinked glasses and rubbed legs. The unostentatious red-checkered tables groaned with the weight of wooden salad bowls and heaped plates of traditional American fare.

They were shown to a table in the wide second room. For once Helena turned her back on the merry crowd.

'Tired?' Claire asked her.

'I've got masses of catching up to do.'

'And you're probably still jetlagged. All this galloping around the world can't be good for you. Though it would be great for me,' she chuckled.

'Poor old downtrodden wife.' Nick patted Claire's head playfully. 'Did I tell you I'm taking her to Paris next weekend?'

'Because I threatened to go on my own.'

Helena let them banter. She couldn't seem to concentrate. Going to the lecture had been a distinct mistake.

It was when they stood to leave that she saw him, right there, at the other end of the room, sitting at a table with some six other people. The woman who had introduced him had her hand on his arm.

Claire saw him too. 'There's that Adam Peters. Shall we go and tell him how much we enjoyed the lecture?'

'They're all busy talking. There's no point.'

But Nick was already at the other end of the room, was shaking Adam by the hand, greeting what seemed to be an acquaintance, gesturing to them to join him.

'Never let it be said that my husband is a slouch,' Claire muttered.

'Guess that's how he gets all those programmes made.'

Adam was standing when they reached the table, gazing at Helena sombrely.

'Will you excuse me,' he mumbled to the others. He took her arm and physically propelled her towards the bar. She could feel Claire's eyes on her back.

'Take your hands off me,' she hissed.

He loosened his grip. 'I've been trying to reach you for days,' he sought her eyes, 'weeks, in fact.'

She wouldn't meet his gaze.

'Let me get you a drink.'

She shook her head. But he had miraculously found a single empty stool at the far end of the bar and, short of making a scene, she couldn't refuse it. 'All right, a glass of wine,' she said. She had told herself she wouldn't be afraid. And there was no reason for it, except for that touch on her elbow. She edged her arm free.

He was sipping his whisky and staring at her.

'There's a man, isn't there? You lied to me.'

'I lied to *you*?' She was incredulous. Then she remembered Nick, with his demonstrative kiss, his arm around her in the lecture theatre. She laughed. 'I guess lying is in the air.'

'Is that why you ran off, Helena? Look at me.' Adam raised her chin, scrutinized her face.

'I met your father,' she said as evenly as she could.

'You met my father?' It was his turn to look incredulous.

She nodded.

He laughed abruptly. 'How? Why? Did you enjoy it?' There was an obtuse air on his face.

'I went to interview him. Yes, I enjoyed it. In a manner of speaking. He told me about his grandchildren.' She paused expectantly.

'Yes, he's very fond of them.' He looked into the distance for a moment.

She waited for him to say something. He would have to tell her now. But all he said was, 'Look, I want to talk to you, see you. Alone. Can we go somewhere? My hotel?'

Helena flinched.

'I don't mean that. Anywhere. Anywhere quiet. I have something to show you.'

'You can show me here.'

He shrugged. 'I'd like to talk to you, Helena.' He took her hand.

She kept herself very still. Yes, he would talk to her, would tell her that it didn't matter about his wife. Would smooth-talk her into anything. She was suddenly angry, and pulled her hand away.

'So it didn't mean anything? Just another little fuck in a distant country?' He was scowling at her.

'Don't be crude.'

'The holier than thou always brings out the crude,' he threw it at her contemptuously. Then he turned and strode away.

Helena leaned shakily on the bar, sipped her wine. She had to compose herself for Claire and Nick.

But in a moment he was back. He unbuckled his briefcase and then thrust a photograph in front of her. 'There, is that your Max Bergmann?'

Helena stared at the picture, saw an old man, confusion in his eyes. She shook her head slowly. 'No, that's not him.'

She looked up at Adam. It didn't make sense. A few minutes ago, she would have sworn he knew Max – that lecture, that letter on his father's desk. She cleared her throat. 'Was this the man who came to the house?'

'No, but that's all I came up with after three weeks of scouring the vicinity.'

'Oh.' She swallowed hard. 'I've located him in any event. I should have let you know. I didn't think.'

'No, you didn't think.'

She couldn't bear that contempt on his face.

'And you lied to me about that too,' she suddenly hissed at him. 'You did get a letter from Max. I saw it on your father's desk.'

'Snooping again, were we?'

She flushed. 'That doesn't alter the fact that it was there.'

'Another drink, sir, madam?' The barman smiled at them sweetly.

'Whisky please,' Adam nodded, as Helena shook her head.

They were silent for a moment.

'So where did you find your Max the father?' he said at last.

Helena ran a hand through her hair, looked into the bar mirror, saw Adam's face reflected there. She turned back to him. 'I haven't exactly found him, I just know where he's going to be on April the twentieth,' she murmured.

'I see. Well, I guess I should say I'm pleased for you.'

'Thank you.'

He met her eyes for a long moment. 'So I guess that's that.'

'That's that,' she echoed him.

He gulped down his whisky.

'Shall we go back?'

She nodded.

She had just stepped off the bar stool, when he suddenly stopped, 'Wait a minute, I've just thought of something. There *was* a letter. I sent it on to my father. A letter in an old-fashioned script addressed to Eberhardt. I assumed that someone in the neighbourhood must have thought the old ones were still alive, so I posted it on.'

'You didn't open it?'

'It never occurred to me.'

They walked slowly back to their table. Helena suddenly felt an overwhelming wave of sadness engulf her. 'I'm sorry it can't work,' she mumbled at him, then planting a bright smile on her face, she nodded at Claire and Nick. 'Shall we go?'

They rose, said their goodbyes. Just before Adam took his place again, Helena said, 'By the way, I'm not certain you've been properly introduced. My friend Claire Stanton, her husband Nick Foster. Thanks for your help, Adam.'

He looked after her with utter bewilderment written on his face.

TWENTY-ONE

IF ADAM PETERS in his lecture had suggested that people stumbled into the future while looking backwards into the past, Helena felt over the next weeks that she had obliterated any notion of the future. She was trapped into grubbing around in the swamp of her personal history.

It was only partly intentional. The process having started, she now found herself subject to shards of uncomfortable childhood memory which cut across her line of vision, no matter how hard she concentrated on work. And she worked like a demon, putting in long hours in the office, arguing at editorial meetings, rooting out stories, placing word after word on the screen. She knew that she was also trying to wipe out Adam, overlaying with words and activity the presence which loomed in the forefront of her imagination. Yet despite it all, whole swathes of his conversation would erupt on her, ironic phrases that had begun to displace Max's uplifting tones which had always served as her guide to the future.

To make matters worse, she had had notes from both of them.

Adam's had come first – in response to the article on his father she had sent him. It was a formal little message, thanking her for the piece, saying how he had enjoyed it. And then had come that postscript, 'I thought I was falling in love with you. Still can't get you out of my mind. Or my body. Odd really, given the circumstances. But there we are.'

It came to her that no one had used the word 'love' to her since an admirer at university had sent her reams of not very wonderful poetry.

She took the letter home, put it into her top drawer.

Two days later the cards had arrived from Max, three of them in an envelope, on which the postmark was altogether obliterated. She gazed at the pictures. Glacial mountains beneath a pristine sky. The Grosse Hundstod, the inscriptions on the backs of two of them said. And then another card of a quiet lake nestling amongst hills, too quiet, perhaps a reservoir. Some kind of building was visible in the distance. Sylvenstein-Speicher, the print announced.

There was no message on the cards, simply Max's name. A statement that wasn't a statement. She rang James to ask him whether he too had heard something and James in turn rang the list of friends. Her cards were the only ones. Again she was confronted by the sense of her specialness and again those notions of Max being her father took up their refrain, as resonantly as they had while she had been in Germany.

What did it mean to have a father? She wasn't quite sure. The only person she had known who fulfilled that role had been Tom Moore, whom she had been schooled to call 'Dad', but whom she had never considered as such. He was someone to be feared and avoided, his temper always unpredictable, blows as likely to erupt from him as words, though there were perhaps fewer of the latter. Not at her, though. She didn't remember him ever hitting her. Yet she lived in fear, tiptoeing round him, trying to make herself invisible, sensing the violence in him even when it was held at bay.

And then, as she grew older, the threat of him took on an added dimension. 'Like father, like son,' Mrs Moore had been wont to repeat either in pride or anger; and the words for Helena – particularly after Billy had begun his sexual bullying – had taken on an aura of intolerable menace.

That had been her only direct experience of fathers. There had been indirect ones, of course. She had met, during her grammar school years, the fathers of friends, kind men with a slightly absent look in their eyes, whom their daughters would treat with an offhand respect or tease and cajole. It was the latter which most fascinated her. It struck a note she had never heard, a note which was at once a signal of underlying trust and its opposite – an address to another who had to be appeased, pacified, flattered.

It came to her now, as she meditated on these things, that this teasing and cajoling was something which spilled over into her friends' relations with men. She herself had rarely if ever been capable of it: this blithe coexistence of contradictions, an ability to trust and yet to recognize the danger in the person one trusted. The danger, she sensed, had something to do with sexual excitement as well as with power.

She had refused both trust and danger. Or kept them at bay in discrete packages tied with innumerable safety knots, though occasionally festooned with ribbons so it looked as if they could be easily opened.

But all of that led her to Adam again and not to Max. It was Max she needed to think about.

When she had moved in with Emily, the world had begun and ended with women. Oh, of course there had been the occasional male visitor, and the occasional physics master at school. But those apart, the only men were those august presences who peopled the shelves of the library, the Dickenses and Tolstoys and Trollopes whose names stood out boldly from the spines of books. There was Virgil, too, chanted over breakfast with metric aplomb in the Latin whose hard sounds bore a distinct relation to Emily's German pronunciation.

Sometimes, it was true, Emily talked of her own father. She always spoke of him or quoted him in that tone of mingled reverence and gratitude, not unlike her citations from Virgil, so that in Helena's mind his image fused with the austere face of the ancient poet who looked out blindly from the frontispiece of the *Aeneid*.

Perhaps it was the residue of that image that she had transferred to Max when she had first met him shortly after Emily's death. Certainly the awe in which she held him was not so very different from Emily's for her dead father. And it came to Helena that she quoted Max in much the same way that Emily had quoted not only her father, but the old masters in her library. A received image, given flesh by Max's presence.

Helena debated with herself whether she should fly out to Germany early to try to find him, but decided it would be another fruitless chase. Better to wait until the appointed date in Berlin. Max, as Bradford Summers had said to her in Boston, might simply have chosen to have a period of solitude.

Meanwhile, she decided actively to fill out the geography of her childhood memories. She was a big girl, now, she told herself. She could take it. But she started, nonetheless, with the easiest point of entry: Emily's close friend, Mrs Fenton.

Mrs Fenton had moved into a pleasant first-floor flat close to the Soane Museum, just behind the LSE. The front room into which the spry old woman ushered Helena was filled with the memorabilia of a lifetime. Photographs of children who had long fled the coop and a cluster of grandchildren vied with images of the Aldermaston marches, old theatre programmes, and the plunder of travels – Javanese puppets, a nest of beautifully painted Russian dolls, an assortment of lacquered boxes.

‘I had to get rid of a great deal when I moved again,’ Mrs Fenton smiled ruefully, as she watched Helena’s gaze move over the room. She was pushing along a trolley laden with Wedgwood china and a plump ginger cake. ‘But one acquires far too much in the course of a lifetime. Emily was far better than I in keeping herself unencumbered. Sugar, my dear?’

Helena shook her head.

‘I’m so pleased that you’ve come to see me. I know how busy you must be. All these wonderful things you young people do now, I’m quite in awe. We never thought of the health of the planet in my day. Oh yes, I’ve been reading your articles.’ She looked at Helena with bright eyes. ‘Emily would have been so proud of you.’

Helena made a modest murmur and then added, ‘It’s Emily I wanted to talk to you about, Mrs Fenton.’ She paused for a moment. ‘Do you know what ever made her adopt me?’

The old woman smiled. ‘Now that, my dear, is a very easy question to answer and a very difficult one.’ She looked out the window as if she could see her old friend there. ‘Emily always wanted something of her own, you know, apart from the school. And after Rafi Lever died, her great and only love, well, there was the occasional man here and there.’

Helena listened intently, not daring to move.

‘But she really wasn’t interested. What she was interested in was having a child. Well, you know Emily, she was such a rationalist – the most rational person I’ve ever met – she convinced herself that there was far too much risk in having one’s own child, even if there were a man to have one with. And there was an equal risk in adopting a baby. One never knew if one would like them when they grew up. She hadn’t been all that fond of her own mother, a silly, slightly tittering woman. Her father was a different story: she idolized him, claimed he taught her everything she knew, but he died when she was still in her teens.

‘In any event, when you appeared on the scene, it was the answer to her deepest dreams. You were such a frail little thing.’ Mrs Fenton looked at her as if it were almost impossible to put together what she could see before her with the image she held in her mind.

‘But fierce, too. And obviously intelligent. Emily had told me about you well before you arrived at the house. She thought you were wonderful and she saw that she could only do good by taking you on. You were the answer to her dreams.

'Another cup of tea, my dear? Some more of this cake?'

'Please.' Helena nodded. 'I've been wondering,' she cleared her throat, 'did Emily find out anything about me, about my parents, that she might not have wanted to tell me?'

The old woman scrutinized her carefully, rearranged a stray lock of white hair behind her ear. 'I don't think so. Emily believed in honesty, and if there was anything to tell, she would have done so. At an appropriate time, if necessary. Why? Have you discovered something?'

Helena shrugged, then decided to come out with it. 'Just this stray fancy that she might have been my real mother.'

Mrs Fenton sipped her tea. Shrewd eyes looked out at Helena from above her cup. 'Well, anything is possible, my dear, though I think I would have known. Let's see, when were you born.'

'1957,' Helena prompted her.

'1957,' Mrs Fenton reflected.

She looked, Helena suddenly thought, as if she were trying to determine whether it would be best to encourage Helena in her speculations or dissuade her.

'1957. We were in Australia around that time.' She shook her head rapidly. 'But I don't think so. It would have been totally out of character. Even if she had managed to keep such a major event from me, she would certainly have held on to you, whatever the circumstances. She was a brave woman. No, my dear.' She paused, looked into Helena's eyes and held her gaze. 'You know, Emily would have far preferred you to have sprung fully formed as you did, like Athena from the head of Zeus, than to have you leap from her womb. That was far more her style. And she certainly considered you no less her real daughter than if you had.'

Helena smiled. It wasn't the reassurance she was looking for. She had no qualms about Emily's love.

'And Emily was really rather opposed to any arguments from heredity. Though she did like to think she was like her grandmother.'

'Her grandmother?'

Mrs Fenton nodded. 'I met her once or twice, in the early thirties it must have been. Tall dignified woman. Not unlike Em in some ways. Though rather more eccentric, I suspect. Or perhaps just Viennese. You know what those Viennese were like.' She tittered, putting her hand over her mouth with the gesture of a naughty girl. 'But tell me about you, my dear, you're not spending all your time worrying about your ancestors, are you?'

'No,' Helena laughed. 'Just a little of it. I suddenly felt I should know.' She started to gather up her things.

'It's a strange old world,' Mrs Fenton sighed. 'Those that have their families spend much of their time wishing they weren't there. And those that don't, spend it wishing they were. Still, you'll come and see me again, won't you?' She smiled as Helena stood. 'And tell me if you discover anything.' She looked at her with a little frown. 'It's too bad those Sisters of Ste-Marie were sent off to the four corners of the world. I know Emily tried to find out more about your parents at one time. She was fretting about this very eventuality. Though she herself was quite adroit at cutting herself off completely from her own mother, soon after her father's, or was it her grandmother's, death. Because of Rafi Lever, I guess it was. He was a Jew, you know.' She tsked under her breath. 'All so long ago.'

Helena bent to kiss her. 'I'll come back soon. Oh, and I almost forgot. I thought you might enjoy this.' She dug in her bag for an invitation she had received to a lecture at Conway Hall.

'Thank you, my dear. If it's as good as that last one I met you at, I shall enjoy myself enormously. What a clever young man he was.'

As she cycled slowly home through the early evening drizzle, Helena tried to digest what Mrs Fenton had told her about Emily, her parents, her Viennese grandmother. She had a sudden image of a vast string of generations doubling up over each other – like the lamp-posts on the street reflected in their wavering and fractured puddles. Each generation was haunted by the spectres previous ones had battled with. Each somehow lived out prior dreams or fears with unexpected twists.

Emily had co-opted her into a chain, even if she didn't quite belong there, and she carried that strong-minded woman with all her rebellions and evasions within her more fully than any parents she had never known.

She shivered away the notion that Emily, through her Viennese grandmother, had brought her back to Adam rather than to Max Bergmann.

Nonetheless, now that she had begun, she wanted to plumb her own childhood further.

Sunday dawned with the soft brilliance of early spring. As soon as she pushed open the shutters, Helena knew that today she would make the trek. She shooed the cats away, rushed up to the library and pulled open the drawer she had had more than one occasion to rifle through of late. There it all was, in Emily's neat hand, the bare rudiments of her trajectory. And the list was topped with the relevant address.

At a whim, Helena rang Claire, told her of her destination and asked if she could borrow her car for the day.

'You sure you want to do this alone?' Claire asked a little querulously.

'Positive.'

A little after nine, Helena was already easing her way across the Thames, over Barnes Common and on to the motorway which led towards Hampshire. The traffic was light and she made good time in Claire's little Citroën, still relatively new despite an interior which crackled with the remains of crisps and an assortment of chocolate wrappers.

As suburbs gave way to gently rolling country, her spirits lifted. Here and there, clusters of almond in glorious bloom burst on her line of vision. The copses were a pale feathery green, their buds plump, on the cusp of leaf.

Close to Winchester, she turned off the main road to skirt the city and parked in a lay-by. Her map in hand, she traced the route to Farley Chamberfayne. It wasn't far. She was there within half an hour: a village that had exceeded its limits to become a countrified suburb. What had it looked like twenty-five years ago? She had no recollection.

She even doubted now that she would recognize the premises of the Sisters of Ste-Marie Home for Children, but it felt odd to pull up at a garage or a pub and ask. She drove through the narrow High Street, past a little wooded incline, and was just about to retrace her steps when she saw the beginnings of a long brick wall. She followed its curve to an opening. There was a sign: FARLEY SCHOOL FOR GIRLS.

With a quickening of the pulse, Helena turned into the gateway. What could be more logical than that the orphanage, the convent, should have become a girls' school? She passed a playing field; a number of girls in brown gymslips were engaged in a desultory game of field hockey. They looked up as she drove slowly by.

The road after that was bordered by an old yew hedge, thick and dark, so dense that when the house came into view, it took her by surprise.

It was a Victorian building of no particular beauty, rather squat and solid with a bow towards gothic excess in its turreted central part. She remembered nothing of it, not the broad steps which led towards the main door, nor its heavy wood which creaked slightly as she pushed it open. The front hall was strangely empty. But a door to the side bore the sign 'Common Room' and, taking a deep breath, Helena knocked.

There was no answering call, but suddenly a voice behind her asked, 'Can I help you?'

She veered round to see a stern woman with greying hair, in a checked skirt and twinset.

'It's not a visiting day, you know.'

'No, no, of course not,' Helena mumbled, reminding herself that she had lived so long with a headmistress that she really ought not to feel that little twinge of pure terror which went through her.

'I've really come with a different kind of visit in mind.' She tried a smile, tried to keep the tremor out of her voice as she quickly explained how she had been here as a child, in the home, and wanted really to speak to anyone who had been here for a long time, twenty-five years to be exact.

The woman scrutinized her carefully and Helena breathed a sigh of relief at the thought that she had at the last minute decided against her jeans and put on a pair of sensible navy trousers and a good matching woollen jacket.

'Well, you might as well wait in here.' The woman opened the door to the Common Room. 'Everyone's at chapel, but Mrs Fisk, our music teacher, might be able to help. She comes from the area.'

Helena's profuse thanks were met with only a nod. She settled herself under that watchful eye in a chair by a window, but it was only when the woman had closed the door behind her that she dared to look out.

She was confronted by a rectangular courtyard, shadowed by the sides of the building. One corner of it was a chapel. In the centre of an expanse of lawn stood a fountain. She gazed at it, hoping for memory. But again, there was nothing. Perhaps she had come to the wrong place.

The girls were pouring out of the chapel now: brown girls, in brown blazers over brown tunics, the occasional woman amongst them.

Helena waited.

At last the door opened and a tiny white-haired woman poked her head in.

'Mrs Fisk?' Helena asked.

'Are you the young woman who wants to know about the Sisters?'

Helena nodded.

The woman had a cherubic smile in a face that was all pink cheeks and crinkly blue eyes.

'Well, how can I help you, Miss . . . ?'

'Latimer. Helena Latimer.' Helena took a deep breath. 'Though I believe I was Helena Stevens when I was a child here, some twenty-five years ago. And I wondered whether there was still anyone here who might remember that time. Might know something about how I had got here. Who my parents might be.'

'Oh dear, oh dear.' Mrs Fisk shook her head sadly. 'Wasn't all that in your file?'

'No,' Helena murmured.

'No, well I don't suppose files were kept so strictly then.'

The woman gave her a puckish smile and then settled into an armchair.

'There isn't much in a name, in any event. I imagine a lot of people gave false names.'

'Did you work here then?' Helena asked.

'Only in a manner of speaking. Sister Richard let me play the organ in the chapel. I lived in the village, you see. And it was the only one. Then I started to do music classes with the children. Singing mostly. My own were off at school and I was a little bored, to put it bluntly. Sister Richard was very kind. Strict, mind, but very kind. We became great friends. I was so sorry to see her go. We corresponded for a while and then . . .' She lifted her hands in a dramatic gesture.

'My adoptive mother told me that I may simply have been left, on the doorstep, or . . .'

'In the chapel.' The woman suddenly looked up at her queerly. 'There was a babe left in the chapel sometime around then. A few years before the place closed its doors. A girl. It could have been you.' She smiled winsomely, and Helena had the sudden sense that the woman might be inventing all this for her benefit.

But she was rushing on now. 'I can't remember the name they chose for her. All the Sisters fussed over her. They saw it as a benediction. At Christmas, it was. A sweet little girl with a tuft of white-gold hair. And there had been a death a few months earlier. One of the big boys had drowned himself in the pond. Horrible. So this was a benediction. Even Sister Richard was quite besotted with the child. She was so quiet, you see, never cried. And she'd come in a beautiful basket.'

The woman leaned towards Helena with a mischievous air. 'And all the Sisters had fanciful notions about where she'd sprung from, whether it was from some poor estranged love-sick snip of a girl or a great lady trapped by an illicit passion.' Helena suddenly had a vision of a gaggle of nuns in long habits and elaborate headdresses preoccupied only with her romantic origins. It all seemed a little exaggerated.

'My own pet notion,' Mrs Fisk couldn't be stopped now, 'was that the poor little creature was the babe of a young woman in the village, Hetty Musgrave. She had gone off to America a few years before, all hoity-toity and full of herself, but she came back around that time, very pale, wouldn't speak to anyone. Only stayed a few weeks and then vanished.'

'Did anyone ever come to visit this foundling?' Helena intervened.

'Oh, I couldn't tell you about that, my dear. I wasn't here all the time.'

'Did men ever come here?' Helena realized the absurdity of the question as soon as she had voiced it.

'Oh yes. It wasn't that kind of a place. Though the Sisters' quarters were off limits.' Mrs Fisk pointed across the courtyard. 'It was all very busy and quite jolly, really. There were about a hundred children. Perhaps more. Almost no tiny ones, though.' She examined Helena again. 'My, my, just imagine if Sister Richard could see you now. I'm sure she'd be able to recognize you.'

She stared at her again with those bright blue eyes. 'I wish I could say I remembered you. But I don't. Never was much good at babies.' She laughed at herself. 'And everyone else from those days has vanished. Still, there we are. You seem to have done well for yourself.'

Helena smiled politely. 'Do you think I might wander round a bit?'

'Feel free, my dear. The classrooms are that way. The girls' rooms over there, though I don't imagine Mrs Prendergast would like you in there.'

'And the chapel, the grounds?'

'Oh yes, I can't see any harm in that. I'll show you the way.'

The old woman rose nimbly.

'You know, in all the years I've had a link with this place, there have only been two other people who have come back to have a word about it. Strange that, really, if you think about it. And it wasn't a bad orphanage, as they go. The Sisters were very good to the children. A lot of prayers, mind. But as for the rest . . .'

'Well, thank you for your time.' Helena stretched out her hand to Mrs Fisk, as she pointed out the door to the courtyard. 'It's all given me a lot to think about.'

Had it, Helena wondered as she made her way towards the chapel. None of it felt quite right. Nor did it hold any resonance for her. No sooner had Mrs Fisk mentioned this Hetty Musgrave as the prospective mother of the foundling she purportedly was, than she knew she had absolutely no interest in tracing her, or indeed anyone else.

She had read about orphans and adopted children who had obsessively pursued their biological parents, sometimes, though not always, with dire results. As she imagined herself confronting this Hetty Musgrave or any other putative mother, she had a sense of mingled awkwardness and disinterest. It wasn't a mother she wanted. She had had that in Emily and had no desire to see her displaced.

In fact, except in order somehow to place that feeling she had about Max, she had no particular interest in another father either, a Mr A or B or C. Or indeed in the story of her origins, whether romance or tragedy or simply tawdry, mundane tale. What her search was about was a source for that hallucination which had taken her over in Germany, that sense that Max was her father.

Or was she deceiving herself out of a fear of what she might find?

Helena gazed at the fountain in the centre of the courtyard. A muscular Neptune, surrounded by nymphs shaped by a not particularly dextrous hand. Hardly an appropriate set of characters for a convent or a girls' school.

She walked on quickly, pushed open the heavy door of the chapel.

It was strangely quiet in here, dark, but for the shafts of splintered sunlight which fell through the high stained-glass window. The altar was spare: a wooden Christ, a white embroidered cloth. To the side, a painted statue of the Madonna looked somewhat out of place. The ceiling was vaulted, graceful, and there, on a balcony, she saw the organ that Mrs Fisk had presumably played.

She sat on one of the unadorned benches and imagined a basket, a baby within it, placed on one of these benches, imagined a man gazing at it, fleeing; then a nun entering the chapel and finding the child. Nothing. The scene unfurled before her like one of those melodramatic silent films, eliciting no emotion except humour mingled with a kind of archival enjoyment. She had no connection with it.

Helena rose slowly, let herself out of the door and walked into the grounds behind the chapel. It was prettier here. An ancient mulberry tree arched its gnarled branches over a smattering of crocuses. Beyond, there was a little copse, and a drop in the terrain. She walked towards the crest of the hill, made her way down a path and across the still moist ground.

It was when she got to the first oak that the shiver ran through her. There was something about this spot, the lie of the land, the gothic tracery of the branches, spreading, soaring. A sense of vertigo suddenly overtook her, made her dizzy. She leaned against the tree, dropped slowly to the ground and looked up through the fan of dark oak to the sky. She felt it then, as certainly as she had felt nothing before. She had been here. Here in this very spot, her hands on this prickly earth, on these stubby clumps of grass. And that smell – moist, slightly sweet. She breathed it in.

In the distance, up the hill, she could see the roof and top floor of the school. It looked massive, solid. Too big. And from the neighbouring tree came a whiff of something like excitement, danger and pleasure at once. As if some presence both expected and unexpected were about to emerge. She felt it so fully that she was certain it would materialize.

It was then that she remembered that image she had had: a child playing hide and seek amidst the trees; a big man with a mane of hair. It was here that the scene had unfolded, on this very spot. And was the man who had caught her in his arms Max?

She could have no proof of this until she saw him.

Slowly, she continued her tour of the grounds, but no other memories besieged her. But for that one spot, it might as well be as if she had never been here.

That Thursday evening, Helena left the office early. She knew that if she didn't, she would allow herself to get entangled in work and the moment for which she had steeled herself would be put off yet again. She was afraid, she acknowledged that. Her palms were moist as she dug for her tube pass.

The journey in the rush-hour train amidst a sea of tired faces seemed to stretch out endlessly, as if London no longer had any boundaries. When her stop appeared, she was a little surprised, yet her feet carried her automatically up the escalator and round the corner. The bus stop was still there. Nothing had changed. No, that wasn't true. In the old bomb site round the corner, where Billy and his friends had once chased her through brambles and dusty foxgloves, there now stood a sleek supermarket, signal of the eighties. The old council blocks round it, however, were still there, if anything more dilapidated, their sooty brown brick punctuated by the eternal net curtains.

Helena leapt off the bus, walked past the apartment buildings, turned into a street of shabby terraces, then another.

Last week on the off-chance, she had looked up both her foster families in the telephone directory. She had rung all the R. Willoxes and met with no success. But the Moores were still at the same address, though there hadn't been a phone in her day. She hadn't used it now either. She had a feeling they might refuse to see her if she announced herself.

The light had grown dusky by the time she reached the street. She could see the changes though, the signs of middle-class incursion in the stripped pine doors with brass knockers, the tidy front gardens.

She stopped before pushing open the gate to number thirty-nine. The forsythia was still there, vast now and straggly, but its outer branches laden with golden bloom. She had a memory of herself in the parlour. She was standing by the window, staring out through the net curtains at the burst of gold, as if the shrub might take her off and away, swallow her into itself. She must have been small, perhaps six or seven.

For a moment, Helena had a palpable sensation of her own unhappiness then: an awkward lonely child, an outsider whom no one particularly wanted, thrust into a cramped alien world of loud, hostile voices. She remembered gazing for what seemed like hours at a ladybird who had somehow made its way on to the empty fire grate and chanting over and over in her mind,

> 'Ladybird, ladybird
> Fly away home
> Your house is on fire
> Your children they will burn.'

She had felt the flames beginning to envelop her, welcome flames. And then, Mum's voice, angry, piercing, 'Barbara's asked you somethin', 'elen. Answer her.' And then that grumbling whine, 'We made a mistake. I told 'arry, it was a mistake. She's a loony 'un. Just sits and stares into space. Never cries, mind. Just sits there. Like a cabbage.'

It had been better at school. They left her alone there. And once a week they went to the local children's library. She couldn't remember learning to read, only remembered the joy of turning those pages filled with bright pictures, and then the stories. They were allowed to take two books home with them. But Mum didn't like her reading. 'Lazy good-for-nothin',' she would lash out at her and snatch the book away. But that must have been later.

Helena straightened her shoulders and went to ring the bell. A dog barked angrily. There was a series of muffled cries and then the door opened.

A young woman stood in front of her. A crown of close-curled red hair that had come out of a bottle, bright lips, a hard, pretty face. She was pregnant and her long blue sweater clung closely over her stomach. There was a hand placed assertively on her hip.

'Ya?' She looked at Helena brazenly.

'I'm sorry, I must have come to the wrong place. I was looking for Mrs Moore.'

'You found her.' The young woman's eyes narrowed suspiciously. 'You from the council or somethin'?'

Helena shook her head. In the background, she could hear a television set, other voices. 'The Mrs Moore I'm looking for would be older,' she murmured.

A toddler came up behind the woman and tugged at her sweater. She lifted him into her arms, but otherwise didn't budge, the two of them a solid barrier against entry.

'What d'you want?'

'I . . . I used to live here. A long time ago. My name's Helena. Helena Stevens.'

The woman stared at her, moved the child on to her other hip, then shouted without turning, 'Mum, there's a Miss Helena Stevens here for you.' The 'Miss' was said in a tone of derision.

Helena heard the shuffling of feet. An emaciated woman with frizzed yellow hair appeared at the door and looked up at her warily.

'Well, well, if it ain't the Madam herself.' Her lips curled into a little cunning smile. 'Come to see the old home, have you?'

'Hello, Mrs Moore.' At a loss, Helena stretched out her hand.

It went unheeded.

'I told you about her, Sarah. She's the foster girl who found herself a better place. Caused us a right lot of trouble, she did.' There was that glint of old hostility in her eye, but Sarah was now looking at Helena with open curiosity.

'You gonna invite her in?'

'May as well. Dad'll wantta lay eyes on her. Always said she'd be a looker.'

'I've brought you something.' Helena pulled a bottle of wine out of her bag, realizing as soon as she did so that a six-pack would have been more appropriate. But Mrs Moore took it with a nod of the head.

'So you made something of yourself with that rich headmistress of yours?' Mrs Moore was truculent. 'We weren't good enough for ya.'

'I'm a journalist,' Helena mumbled.

'A journalist?' Sarah's tone had changed. 'Is that good fun then?'

Helena nodded, smiled.

They were in what had once been the parlour, but a television set and a vast three-piece suite now dominated the space. There was a Black child playing with a fire engine on the floor. Sarah put the toddler down beside him. 'This is Seth, our neighbour's little 'un, and this here's my Billy.'

She had taken over. 'Turn down the telly, Dad, we got a visitor. Look at her. Remember her?'

A pallid man with beetle brows looked out from the wings of an armchair. His features showed not the slightest interest.

'She's your Helen,' Sarah shouted, whispered to Helena, 'He's gettin' a bit deaf.'

His eyes flickered for a moment. He grunted something like a greeting and then sat back into the chair, his eyes glued to the television.

Looking at him, Helena suddenly realized that the terrifying ogre of her memories was in fact a feeble ageing man, old before his time, tired out. She couldn't imagine him raising his fist to hit anyone now, nor perhaps even his voice.

'It looks nice in here,' she said, for lack of anything better.

Mrs Moore's tone had altered, in tune with her daughter-in-law's. 'Ya, there've been lots of changes, what with Sarah and the little 'un here, and Billy earnin well.' Her voice rose in pride.

'We're gonna get our own place, soon,' Sarah interjected huffily. 'As soon as this next one arrives.' She patted her stomach comfortably. 'You got any yet?'

Helena shook her head.

'Leavin it a bit late, ain't ya?' Mrs Moore stared at her. 'You must be twenty-eight or -nine, now.'

Helena nodded.

'Don't wanna leave it too late. That's what I did. Never could have more than Billy. That's why I took on you lot.'

'Whatever happened to Sandy?' Helena thought of the frightened little girl whom the Moores had taken in some years after her. She had always tried to protect her from the others. With a dizzying clarity, she suddenly remembered how the two of them would go off and lock themselves in the loo, when Mrs Moore was out and Billy chased them. She would tell her stories then, to stop her crying. Once they had stayed in the corner shop for hours, pretending to be choosing a comic book, until Mr Moore had come in and dragged them home. Helena remembered trying to explain to him then that Sandy was afraid when Billy was rough. She must have been about eight, Sandy four.

And then Helena had abandoned her, had gone off with Emily. A pang of remorse suddenly shot through her.

'Bad lot, that one. Even harder than you. You were pretty good up till the year you got . . .' Mrs Moore lifted her hands to her breasts. 'But Sandy, she went completely wild. Ran away when she was fifteen. Never seen her since. Beverly was better. Remember her? No, no, course not. She came after you'd gone. Grown up now, got a job. But comes to see us regular. A good girl that. Weren't she, Dad?'

Mr Moore grunted, his eyes still fixed on the telly. Then suddenly he turned. 'Helen were the best. The prettiest. Clever too. Always told ya that. A lady.' His eyes rested on her for a moment, before he turned back to the screen.

'Dad's always had an eye for the pretty ones.' Sarah winked at her suggestively, put some more toys in front of the children who had started to squabble over a red car.

Helena smiled, liking her.

'Mrs Moore, I wanted to ask you. Did anyone ever come to see me or ask about me after I'd come to you? A man, perhaps, from the old days?'

Mrs Moore lit a cigarette and gazed at her cannily. 'Lookin' for your lost parents, are ya? Like that girl we saw on the telly?' She sat back in her chair and took a long puff.

'No, there was no one,' she said smugly. 'We were your only family. That Mrs Latimer, she grilled us about that, too. Didn't she tell ya?'

The neighbour's child had started to cry, and Sarah picked him up to comfort him. 'They'll be wanting their tea,' she said, moving into action.

'I'd better get along then.' Helena rose. 'Thank you for seeing me.' She stretched out her hand to Mrs Moore, who took it this time with a condescending gesture. Then she did the same to Mr Moore, who looked at her blankly, before responding with evident discomfort.

'Bye, then,' he grunted.

Helena stared at him for a moment, smiled. 'Bye.'

For the briefest of seconds, she thought she saw his lip curl.

'Don't you want to see Billy? He'll be back soon, if he doesn't stay for a second pint.'

'No, no, I'd better go,' Helena said, realizing she was being a coward. 'Thanks again.'

'And ta for the wine,' Sarah winked at her when they got to the door. 'It'll all be for me,' she laughed brazenly and waved her off.

Helena walked quickly towards the bus stop. She was shaking.

An ordinary family, she scolded herself. It was she who was the odd one out. Mrs Moore had almost said the proverbial lines: giving yourself airs and graces, think you're better than us, do you? She could hear her scolding tones in her ear; had – it came to her – heard them all those years ago, saying just that as she towered over her, watching her scrub the kitchen floor. But Mr Moore had stood up for her today. Odd, that. She couldn't remember it ever happening before. But then, what did she know? She had been a mere child who had been sent on from another family who didn't want her once a fourth of their own had arrived. Emily had found that out.

Yes, she had been a frightened, lonely child who saw the world in her own distorted way. Not even that frightened, perhaps. She had stood up for Sandy.

It was Billy who had been the demon. Billy, whom his mother idolized, Billy who could do no wrong. And the terror of his abuse had gone deep. Too deep. It had made her wilfully blot everything out.

Helena hurried on. The streets were dark now, the lamps casting only their little pools of yellow light. Suddenly, she saw a man illuminated in one of them – a fleshy ruddy man, swaggering towards her. It was Billy, exactly as he had always been, except bigger. For a moment their eyes locked and she saw those moist plump lips shape themselves into a whistle, saw those piggy eyes. Then he was past her.

Helena broke into a run, ran until she reached the bus stop. She was perspiring, as if she had barely eluded a terrible danger. With relief she leapt on to the approaching bus, with even greater relief she felt it pull away with her safely on it.

She stood looking out of the window, her hand taut round the seat handle beside her. How could that nice Sarah bear to be with that man, allow herself to have his children? The very thought made her gag with disgust.

'Would you like to sit down, dear? You've gone very white.' A hatted old woman looked up at her.

'No, no, thank you, I'm all right. That's very kind of you.' Helena forced a smile to her lips.

'Here, have this one. My stop's coming up.' The man next to her slid out.

Helena murmured her thanks, edged into the seat. She was making a spectacle of herself.

'These buses do swing around so,' the old woman smiled at her sweetly, then chuckled. 'Whenever I offer my seat, the men always remember.'

Helena grinned.

'Feeling better?'

She nodded.

'Well, bye now. This one's mine.'

They were crossing Vauxhall Bridge, the wide expanse of the Thames separating her from the shadows of her childhood. Helena relaxed into her seat, but her hands were still tightly clasped.

It was ridiculous that seeing Billy after all these years should have so distressed her. She had been prepared, after all. Yet she had fled, would have found it hard, she realized, to shake his hand had he been in the house when she arrived. Far harder than the others. Yet that nice, spunky woman had married him, seemed happy enough. Perhaps it was only the powerlessness of childhood that had made her see him as a monster.

Helena sat and tried to be sensible. From one point of view, what had Billy been then but an ungainly adolescent taking advantage of a situation which offered him sexual release? It was just too bad that she had been there to provide it, a girl in the next bed who wasn't even his sister. Mrs Moore should never have allowed them in the same room. But there hadn't been another.

Helena consoled herself. She would never have run away, if it hadn't been for Billy. She would never have found Emily. She should write Billy a thank-you note.

Helena smiled at the thought. The very fact of the smile made her feel suddenly better.

They had arrived at Victoria station. She leapt off the bus and made her way down into the underground. She felt pleased with herself now. She had done it, had gone to visit that part of her past. The ghosts could be laid to rest.

But she wasn't any wiser about Max. It was funny how she swung between thinking that her notion of his being her father was a total fantasy and a decided reality. She knew now that she *wanted* him to be her father, this wonderful saintly man whose vision of the world she so profoundly shared.

She remembered having read somewhere that children whose fathers were violent and abusive often defended them against any accusations. It was as if to keep the terror of the real father at bay they had to block it out completely and construct an ideal figure whom they wholly believed in. Was that what she had done by displacement? Obliterated all the men in her childhood in order to replace them with Max?

Too much navel-gazing, Ms Helena Latimer, she scolded herself and pushed her way to the tube door. She had almost missed her stop. Another few weeks and everything would be clear. There was really no more need for her to try and excavate her past, either the one she carried within herself or the one whose fossils lay scattered around her, on a road that seemed to lead nowhere.

The next day Helena got to the office early. She had slept more soundly and dreamlessly than she had in weeks. It was as if the visit to the Moores had marked a turning point. She had fretted over it so and now that it was accomplished, she felt as if a great weight had been lifted from her. She could settle down to the work at hand and make certain that everything was clear for that week of absence she had promised herself with Max in Berlin.

It was just after ten and she was in the midst of a telephone interview with the manager of a new wind farm, when Lynn placed a piece of paper in front of her.

Helena read it swiftly. 'Adam Peters, from Germany. Has to speak to you *urgently*. Do I tell him to hold or ring back?'

'Ring back,' Helena scrawled.

Some fifteen minutes later, she confronted Lynn.

'What does he want?'

'Who?' Lynn looked at her with a blank expression.

'Adam Peters.'

'Oh.' Lynn scrambled through the papers on her desk. 'Here's the number. You're to ring him, as soon as poss. It did sound urgent.' She made a face at Helena. 'It's about your Max Bergmann.'

Helena gasped audibly. She picked up the telephone instantly and punched out the number.

'He's found the way to your heart this time, has he?' Lynn was chuckling.

'Quiet,' Helena scowled at her.

Adam's voice when it came frightened her. It was formal, almost punctilious.

'It's important that you come. Straight away.'

'Has he asked for me?'

'Just come. There's a plane from Heathrow at twelve twenty. Another at four o'clock. I'll meet you at Munich if you like.'

'That won't be necessary. Where shall I go?'

'Come here. To Seehafen.'

'Does he want to speak to me now?'

'Look, I can't talk.'

'This isn't a ruse, is it?'

'Don't be stupid. Just get here.'

He hung up on her.

Helena looked at the dead receiver. Her heart was pounding. And on top of it all, she had managed to be insufferably rude again.

She glanced at her watch and then at Lynn.

'Book me a ticket on the twelve twenty to Munich, will you. And then ring Adam Peters and tell him I'll be catching that plane.'

'Jawohl, mein Fräulein.' Lynn saluted and grinned at her comically. 'Got a story about Bergmann up your sleeve?'

'Perhaps.' Helena was noncommittal.

She had a quick word with Carl, then hurriedly gave Lynn a list of the things which would have to be done in her absence, including a call to Claire about the cats. But her mind was already racing ahead of her, was already in Seehafen and the rush of fearful possibilities that awaited her there.

TWENTY-TWO

ADAM PETERS PACED the length and width of the freshly painted room for the hundredth time.

The house was finally in order now. The white sheets had vanished from sofas and chairs. Johannes Bahr's paintings hung on the walls in a sequence Adam had long debated. The conservatory had acquired tiles and cane chairs. The hall and the vast formal dining room glowed and the kitchen walls were pristine, as were a smattering of the upstairs rooms.

All this in the time since she had last been here. Almost two months now.

It had been wise to hire the decorators or the business would have gone on interminably. It had perhaps been less wise to bury himself in the Archives in Heidelberg after his return from London. There might have been a faint chance then of preventing all this.

But the memory of her was still too strong in the house, as if they had spent weeks here together. And he had wanted to flee. Particularly now that he knew there wasn't anyone else. She had made that quite clear. It was simply that she didn't want *him*. Fair enough, he had said to himself, but nonetheless he had fluctuated between cursing her as a cold bitch and subsiding into a state of utter incomprehension. That was the worst.

He had thought – and he was hardly a fledgling in these matters, he assured himself – that something rare had passed between them, not just sex, a tawdry one-night stand, but a whole gamut of sexual emotions which were partly subsumed in the word 'love'. He had written the word to her and there had been utter silence.

The ground beneath his feet grew unstable, wavered like water. When a man can't trust his feelings any more, the world becomes a leaking boat, he told his image in the mirror, attempted humour. One has to bail out. But his face stared back at him with a look of dour incomprehension.

And so he had gone to Heidelberg, bailed out into that other world of musty papers and inquisition documents. He had succeeded well enough. But then he had come back to all this, that slight sense of nagging self-reproach, even though there was no justifiable reason.

Adam stepped out through the French windows. The sun was just beginning to set, rosy behind the distant white peaks. But the grounds before him had that soft glow of early spring. Everything was busy, in flux. He could feel it in the earth beneath his feet, in the chattering of the birds, in the glimmering greens of the trees and shrubs. The border of primroses he had planted just a few days ago was bright with purples and yellows and in the woods where he had walked this morning, he had found clumps of snowdrops. He would have liked to walk again now, but she should be here soon, was in fact already late. Perhaps her flight had been delayed. It would take time to hire the car.

Stubborn woman, not to let him go and fetch her. And what would he tell her?

He heard the car pull up just as he was pouring himself a glass of whisky. He was already at the door when she rang the bell.

When he opened it to her, his carefully prepared speech left his lips. She was so beautiful. He had forgotten the sheer physical impact of that: the arch of her cheeks, the full lips, the deep blue-grey eyes beneath the cluster of corn-gold hair, longer now. Against the pale cream of her suit and tawny blouse, her skin looked even finer, purer. And that look in her eyes, a kind of fearful wistfulness. He could sense her tension, see it in the white grip of her fingers on her bag. Almost, he put out a hand to ease it.

But she broke into quick-fire speech and the moment passed.

'I got here as quickly as I could. The plane was delayed.'

'Come in.'

'Where is Max?' She strode past him.

'He's not here.' He showed her into the salon, took the coat that was draped over her shoulders, gestured her towards an armchair.

'But you said . . .'

'I asked you to come.'

She glanced at him angrily. 'Where is he?'

'A drink? Some white wine?'

'Where is he?' she repeated stubbornly.

'Sit down, Helena.' He was brusque.

She met his eyes, her own blazing. 'If this is some kind of trick . . .'

'What do you take me for?' he lashed out at her, then controlled himself. 'Now will you please sit down.'

She perched at the edge of a dusky rose chair. 'A glass of white wine, if you have it.' Her voice was taut.

'There's some cold in the fridge. I'll just be a moment. Make yourself at home.' He said it quietly, smiled.

When he returned with a tray, she was standing at the back of the room, looking at one of Johannes's canvases. She turned quickly at the sound of him.

'It looks lovely in here. You've been working.'

'Decorators,' he murmured.

He handed her a glass.

'Thank you. Now tell me, Adam, please. I've been worrying myself silly.' Her voice was soft now.

He watched her sit down, cross her legs. He took a deep breath.

'He's dead, Helena.' There was no kind way of saying it.

The glass tumbled out of her hand, rolled on to the rug. Her face had an almost transparent pallor.

He put his hand on her shoulder. She didn't move, but he could feel the pulse beating heavily beneath the fabric.

At last she murmured, 'Dead, dead? No, not that.' It was almost a whimper. Then shrugging his hand away, she leapt up. 'How do you know?' She turned towards him, suddenly savage. 'How do you know he's dead? You don't even know him.'

'No. That's why you're here. That's why I rang you. Someone has to identify him.'

He saw the sudden hope in her face and erased it quickly. 'But I know it's him. From the picture on his book.' He went over the details quickly, almost surgically.

'A man was found, drowned in the lake, probably suicide the police say, though it could have been an accident. Everyone around here knows I've been looking for an old man. It's a small place. So they called me in and I called you, to make what is known as a positive identification.' He shrugged. 'I thought you'd want to know. And I couldn't think of anyone else. I'm sorry.'

She stared at him, incomprehension in her eyes. 'So it's not certain?'

'No, it's not one hundred and ten per cent certain.' He let it go. He couldn't dissuade her of her hope if she wanted to cling to it.

Helena slumped back into the chair, the fire gone out of her. She looked wretched, like a small girl who had been utterly abandoned. He would have liked to hold her, comfort her, but he suspected she would lurch away from him.

'Would you like that glass of wine now?' he asked softly.

She gazed at him as if she couldn't remember who he was. 'Wine?' she repeated mechanically, then her eyes focused. 'Shall we go and see this person now?' She stood abruptly.

Adam glanced at his watch. 'It may be too late. But we can try if you like.'

She nodded.

'My car?'

She nodded again.

They drove in silence, the night darkening around them, the headbeams cutting holes through the banked road.

'When did you learn all this?' she asked at one point.

'Yesterday afternoon. But I don't have your number at home.'

He could feel her eyes on him for a moment.

'And when did it happen?'

'On Easter Sunday probably. Just after I got back.'

'You've been away?'

He nodded.

'To see your family?'

Her voice had an odd ring to it.

'No. In Heidelberg. Research for the book.'

'Can you really tell from a picture?'

'Perhaps not.'

The police station in Murnau had a sleepy nighttime air about it, as if crime only took place in regulation hours. But the officer in charge found someone to accompany them to the mortuary.

Their footsteps echoed hollowly on the stone stairs and the key in the locked door clattered, too loud. Inside the air was chill. One in a row of fluorescent lamps flickered on and off as if it were engaged in a struggle for life. It emitted a high-pitched sound.

Adam saw Helena shiver, saw the officer cast her a worried look.

'She won't faint, will she?' he whispered to Adam. 'He's not pretty.'

Adam put his hand on her shoulder as the man pulled open the numbered vault.

There was a heavy translucent plastic sheet covering the body.

Helena leaned involuntarily against Adam. Her entire being was focused there, in that plastic sheet, moving slowly backwards away from a snow-white head, a pallid face strangely smooth, like the plastic, except for the blue and yellow blotches. It was Max and wasn't Max.

She stepped forward, wanting to touch him, shake him awake, somehow breathe expression back into that blind face. She touched his cheek lightly. Like wax. Her finger left an imprint.

A host of dizzying contradictory thoughts and emotions whirled through her.

How could she have let him die, when he had written to her, called out to her? Her father perhaps. Now she would never know. She should have found him somehow, prevented this. It was because of Adam that she hadn't persisted, had fled. Suicide? No. Someone had done this to him, had pushed him. Someone who was against him. Some corporate executive interested only in profits. Some nuclear cabal. She should have found him, helped. Why didn't the body move? Emily's body hadn't moved, but she had said goodbye to her. There was repose on her features. Not here. Not in Max.

Helena let out a single angry scream, part sob. It beat against the walls of the cavernous room.

Then quiet.

She felt rather than saw the officer looking at her expectantly.

'This is Max Bergmann,' she whispered.

He pulled the plastic sheet up quickly. 'You'll sign the form upstairs?'

Helena nodded.

Later, she was dimly aware of Adam manoeuvring her towards a noisy overheated bar, putting a glass in her hand. The brandy seared her throat. She couldn't meet his eyes.

A wind had come up. As they drove in silence, clouds scurried across the sky. The moon emerging from their passage was as bright as a neon light. Trees and hills stood illuminated for a moment and then vanished into darkness. Once, she thought she saw a child standing bleakly in front of a small house wave at them.

Then they were back at Seehafen.

Helena couldn't summon the energy to leave the car. She forced herself to put one foot in front of the other, found herself in a chair, Adam hovering around her.

He put a plate of scrambled eggs on the table in front of her.

She pushed it away.

She heard his voice as if from a great distance.

'He was an old man, Helena. Let him have his death.'

'What do you know about it?' she lashed out at him.

He shrugged. 'Nothing. I don't know anything.'

The way he said it gave her pause.

'I'm sorry,' she murmured. 'I'm upset.' She met his eyes at last.

'I know.'

'Would you like to be alone, lie down?'

She nodded.

He made her a pot of tea, found her bag, brought all of it and her up to the little lemon yellow room.

'If you need anything, just shout. I'll be across the hall.' His eyes rested on her for a moment and then she was alone.

The next thing she knew, she was lying in bed, her head buried in a pillow. It was wet. Her face felt streaked. She had been crying. Why had she been crying? An image of plastic leapt into her mind, a corpse wrapped in plastic with a pale plastic face. Max.

Helena sat up, cradled herself. The room was dark. She couldn't remember getting undressed, going to bed, switching off the light. Couldn't remember anything except Max's dead body.

She grappled for the bedside lamp, saw the pot of tea untouched on the table. She glanced at her watch. It was three o'clock. She had slept. And now she was awake. And alone. So alone, the twin poles of her universe gone. Emily gone. And now Max gone. Gone forever. The very thing she had dreaded just those few months back when she had read the notice about Max Bergmann in the paper. 'Feared dead.' And now he was. It was almost as if she had misplaced him and by doing so, left him to his fate.

But Max wouldn't commit suicide. The Max she knew respected life too much. She had seen him, bent over his tiny seedlings, separating one from the other with delicate gestures so as not to bruise or damage. No, he wouldn't wilfully take a life.

An accident then? Adam had said there had been a boat. But that made no sense either. Max was physically adept, at the worst, knew how to swim. He had tried to save her that once. And they had often swum together in that small lake, murky with its own vegetable life. Max would strike across it with a young man's vigour. No, no, not an accident.

Suddenly Helena was afraid. A cacophony of voices seemed to have sprung out of the walls to rail at her. Her fault, they screeched. She hadn't investigated to the source, hadn't dug deeply enough, hadn't sought the proper help, had let her own stupid fantasies of Max-the-father blot her vision.

She hid under the duvet. But the voices were still there and that waxy corpse, wrapped in plastic. They would suffocate her. Helena leapt up. Adam. She would go to Adam. A live presence. Any live presence.

She knocked softly on his door and was met by silence. She pushed it open. Everything was dark, but he had left the shutters open and the stars cast a faint light into the room. She could see the bed, the outline of his shape sprawled beneath the white sheets. She groped her way towards it.

It came to her that he might be angry with her. She shunned the thought. He was alive, warm. What did anything else matter? She looked at him for a moment. His face, half buried beneath his arm, was turned towards her like it had been that last time. Was she doing the wrong thing?

She let the thought fade, slipped quietly beneath the sheets. It was warm. That was what she had wanted. And she could hear his breath, even, reassuring. A bulwark. She touched his arm. That too was warm. It moved beneath her fingers. Not wax, not plastic. Alive. She turned to sleep, snuggling just a little closer.

He stirred. His arm encircled her. She felt safe, protected.

Then there was a muffled sound in her ear.

'Helena?' His voice was husky with sleep.

'I was frightened. I snuck in. I hope you don't mind,' she mumbled quickly.

'My poor darling.' He stroked her hair, held her more tightly.

Something in her moved, a fluttering of birds in her womb. Like the last time. An ache. She held herself very still. He was smoothing her nightie down over her, his hands light over her breasts, her legs.

'Sleep, now,' he murmured.

She could feel him hard against her back, his skin warm, firm. She didn't want to sleep. She wanted him. Had never really wanted anyone before. Only him. It came to her in words, like a declaration echoing through her mind. One more time wouldn't make any difference. Not here, in this house, far from everything. One last time, like a wake.

She shivered.

'Are you cold?'

He reached for an extra blanket at the base of the bed.

She stopped his hand, brought it to her lips.

He leaned over her, his face dusky, posing a question.

She ran her fingers through that tumble of hair, brought his face down to her lips.

The kiss swept her up, seemed to lift all of her, carry her through time, so that the weeks that had separated them were obliterated as was everything that had passed within them. There was only this moment, stretching indefinitely over the landscape of their bodies. All she was aware of within it was the pounding of her heart in her ears, the sound of life itself. And the smell and touch of him in every nook and corner of her body, a cleansing, like a flood rushing through the stables of her self, sweeping away cobwebs of fear and the dry grass of old couplings.

At some point, she thought she heard him murmur, 'Told you I was in love with you.'

She didn't know whether she said anything in return, but in the morning when she woke to see the sun, already high, pouring through the window, the trees shimmering in its light, she had a sense that she was someone else or had entered a new joyous world.

The feeling didn't last long.

At first she flushed to see the tumble of sheets around her. Adam was already up. Making breakfast, she imagined, and smiled at the thought. She fingered the sheets where he had lain, felt that strange trembling within her womb again. She lay back for a moment to wonder at it and then leapt up. It wasn't right that he was always serving her. She would go and help him. In any event, she wanted to be near him.

It was as she was pulling on her nightie, smoothing it over this newly sensitive body of hers, that she remembered what she had forgotten. Max was dead. How could that grisly fact have evaded her? And here she was . . . Helena shuddered. She made the bed quickly.

As she padded towards the door, she looked up to see the row of photographs on the shelf-top. It was still there. Portrait of a Smiling Family. She had a sudden urge to smash it against the floor. But she reminded herself, as she stood under the shower, that last night's little escapade had been all her doing.

She quickly pulled on jeans and a jumper, pushed sockless feet into her boots and with her hair still wet, went downstairs.

Adam was in the kitchen, as she had expected. He was tossing pancakes like an old hand.

'Regulation American breakfast for special days,' he grinned at her. His eyes were warm, flecked with gold. He turned back to the stove, flipped the pancake on to a dish already heaped, and slid it on to the table.

'That'll do for a start.' He walked towards her with open arms.

With an effort, Helena stood stiffly within his embrace for a moment, then moved away.

He gave her a curious glance as he poured coffee into mugs, motioned her towards a chair.

'I'm sorry if I used you last night,' she said. Her vocal cords felt taut, over strung.

He scrutinized her. 'I don't feel *used*, if that's what's bothering you,' he said at last. 'Love does sometimes take place in a pre-capitalist register.'

She didn't know what he was talking about and she gave him a stony look.

'Let's just call it primitive barter, shall we.' His voice took on an acid tinge when she didn't answer. 'I have something you want. You have something I want. They may not be equivalent in absolute terms, but since the absolute currency doesn't exist, we make do with a satisfactory trade. Okay? But thank you for mentioning it nonetheless. Now what's really bothering you?'

He piled pancakes on their plates, poured syrup over them, glanced at her, then dug in.

'You are going to eat the fruit of my labours, I hope.'

She nodded, ate. 'Delicious,' she murmured politely.

'What is it, Helena?'

She met his eyes fiercely, 'Max is dead.'

'I haven't forgotten.' He chewed deliberately, gulped some coffee. 'Look, it's going to sound crass, but the perennial human reaction to death is sex. The books are full of it and I'm sure I could even dig up the relevant statistics without trying too hard. Does that make you happier?'

She scowled at him.

'You're the one who's so keen on the natural. This is nature itself making a bid for the preservation of the species. So stop glowering at me.' He ruffled her wet hair. 'You look nice.'

Helena swallowed hard. 'Please don't touch me.'

'Why?' He paused.

She couldn't answer.

'Because you like it?'

She nodded.

'Well, it's good to see you confirm it, because I was beginning to think I'd spent last night with someone else.'

Suddenly he was at her side, lifting her from her chair, kissing her, kissing her. She struggled against him, pummelled his chest. 'It's not night now, Adam.' She pulled away from him.

'Well I may be available to be used again tonight. Or I may not. Never count on it,' he growled, but he smiled as he said it, looking at her with such open warmth that it was only with an effort that she reminded herself of the situation.

'There's so much to be done,' Helena mumbled once he had sat down again. 'I'll have to phone James at the Farm. I'll pay, of course.'

Adam grunted.

'And then arrange for the obituaries, the funeral. So many people will want to come from everywhere. I don't know where to start with the funeral business here. In England . . . Or perhaps he should go back to the United States, where he belongs.'

He interrupted her. 'Whoa. One step at a time. The inquest will be on Monday.'

She looked at him blankly. 'Inquest?'

'Well, it's purely formal. But they don't know how he died. Suicide . . .'

'They don't know that.'

'That's why. That's what they'll try and ascertain. Look.' He stood up suddenly, began to busy himself with more coffee, dishes, talking all the while. 'I know the last thing you probably want is my advice. But here it is, free. I don't think you or anyone else should try and organize a big funeral here. The less people who come to this place, the better. You don't want journalists prying, digging things up. If he decided to die, that's his business. The suicide won't do your cause any good. So just have him buried here, or cremated, and get the ashes back to the States. Have a memorial service there, and in England, and wherever else people think it's proper.'

Helena looked at him in open astonishment.

'Why are you so certain Max committed suicide?'

He shrugged.

'He wasn't the type. It's not like him.'

'Wittgenstein once said, "Death isn't part of life".'

'I don't care what Wittgenstein or anyone else said. I knew Max.'

'Helena.' He tried to take her hand, but she avoided him. 'I know this is hard for you. But the story goes that a little boy, just a few miles from here, let Max have his row boat for a few hours in return for a couple of marks. The boy came back at the appointed time. No Max, and he saw his boat empty, floundering about in the middle of the lake. He eventually told his parents, next day I think it was, who told the police. Both Max and the boat were washed or brought ashore some time after that.'

'It could. Perhaps that's what you should tell the press. Yes, emphasize that. Otherwise you'll get headlines like, "Green visionary takes his own life in despair". But maybe that's what you want. In any event, just keep the snoops away from here.'

'Someone could have pushed him.'

He stared at her in disbelief.

'You don't really think that!'

'I do.' She set her face stubbornly. 'Max did a lot of things people in power weren't too pleased with.'

'Well, suit yourself.' He started to wash the dishes, broke into a whistle.

'You just don't give a damn, do you? A man is dead and you don't give a damn. An important man. A man who may have been my father. I would have found out in just a few days.' Her voice rose and suddenly cracked into a sob. She buried her face in her arms.

'Get it out of your head, Helena. Max Bergmann was not your father. It's a story you tell yourself because you like the sound of it.' Adam's voice was soft but insistent.

It infuriated her. 'You know everything, don't you?' she jumped at him. 'You muck about with your dusty books and you think you know everything.' She scraped her chair back from the table noisily.

'What my dusty books tell me is that the whole edifice of Max Bergmann's ideas – those ideas you're presumably so enamoured of – is based on soulful shit. No, shit's too nice. Have you really read him? Have you?'

'Yes,' she raged at him. 'And maybe you should tear your crumbling books up and look at the world for a change. Max did things. He . . .' A sob overcame her words. She raced from the room.

Behind her she heard him mumble, 'I'm sorry. I shouldn't have said all that.'

Helena got as far as the drive, then she turned back, wiping her tears. She poked her head through the kitchen door. 'Look. I didn't mean all that about your books. I'm just distraught. I'm going for a walk. To clear my head.'

He looked at her soberly. 'If all this is too much for you, Helena, I'll handle the funeral arrangements.'

She shrugged. 'We'll talk about it later. I have to phone the States first.' She glanced at her watch. 'Another hour should do it.'

The lake was as calm as a looking glass. Surrounded by dappled meadows and picture-postcard mountains, it hardly looked like a site for anything more extravagant than a little Sunday fishing amongst the swaying reeds.

Yet the voices clamoured in Helena's head. This is where it had happened. Right here in this lake, Max had drowned, his body bloating, taking on that waxy pallor. By his own will? She didn't know.

Beneath a clump of distant willows, shimmering yellow in the crystal sunshine, she saw some people fishing. Perhaps the boy who had lent his boat to Max was amongst them. She must go and talk to him. And to the police.

But there was something else bothering her. Something about Adam, something that went beyond the pettiness of the row she had instigated. She should never have slept with him.

Why was he so hostile about Max? A difference of ideas alone, didn't breed that kind of hostility. And why should he be so worried about journalists? Snoopers, as he called them. Why was he so certain that Max had taken his own life? Why should he want to convince her of that? And that extra certainty, about Max not being her father. He had been so insistent about that. Adam knew something. Something he wouldn't share with her. She had long suspected it. It had confronted her at every turn.

She ruminated on this as she walked along the shore, past the boathouse and the grave with its new border of primroses. Something was eluding her. She looked up through the budding trees and an idea came to her.

Adam had worked with the Yanomamo Indians in the Amazon, had defended their land rights. His father had pointed the latter out. Max too had been to the Amazon, had written about the rainforest, the annual loss of some twenty million acres. Had the two of them met, squabbled over something? Adam had originally pretended never to have heard of Max, and then suddenly he had seemed to know a great deal about him. And she had felt that his lecture implicated Max. Her mind raced.

By the time she arrived at the arching beech with its empty swing, she had concluded that Adam was somehow involved in Max's death. Why else should his house have featured so prominently in Max's letter to her? Why else should Max's body end up with Adam? She shuddered. But what was the link?

She found Adam in the library. He was ensconced behind his desk which burgeoned with an increasing array of papers.

'Could I use the phone now?'

He nodded.

Was it her imagination or was he looking at her strangely?

'There's one right here,' he pointed to his desk, 'and one in my bedroom. Take your pick.'

She felt the heat rising in her face despite herself.

'Here?' He unearthed the phone and brought it to the table she had sat at on that first night. 'I guess you'd like to be on your own?'

'I'd prefer it,' Helena murmured.

She dialled the number quickly. It took some time to rouse James, but eventually she heard his somewhat fuddled voice at the other end.

'Sorry to be so early, James. But it's very bad news.' She waited to give him a chance to prepare himself, then she told him, told him too that he should make his way here, in time for the inquest if possible. She asked his advice about the funeral, repeating in part what Adam had said.

James whistled. 'I'll have to think about all that. I can probably get a plane this evening, tomorrow at the latest. I should sort out things this end. Alert the lawyers. I imagine there's a will somewhere. God only knows what will become of this place. Where are you?'

She gave him the phone number, told him she would come and meet him in Munich.

'I'll ring you at twelve thirty, my time. Will you be there?'

'I'll make sure I am. By the way, James,' she turned towards the window, lowered her voice, 'if you can, if there's time, run a check on a Professor Adam Peters for me, will you? He's based in Princeton.'

'Helena, this is hardly the moment . . .'

'Try.'

She rang off.

For a moment, Helena fingered Anna's Book absently. Then she glanced at Adam's desk, so full of papers that there was an overflow on the floor. If only she could look through that mass. But it was hardly the right time. She reached into her bag instead, found a twenty-pound note and placed it on an open periodical.

The name Max Bergmann leapt out at her like an assault. It was the very article she had been thinking about. On the rainforest. A numbness seemed to settle over her. She walked slowly into the hall, didn't call out, 'I'm finished,' until she had reached the door of her room.

She changed quickly, willing herself not to think for the time being, not until she was out of the house.

Her suit was too crumpled to put on. On the spur of the moment, while the taxi had waited for her in London, she had packed her black dress. As if in premonition, she thought now. She slipped it on. It would do admirably for the police, though when she looked in the small mirror, the dress seemed to have a little more slink in it than she remembered. She brushed her hair out and on reflection, clipped it into a smooth bun. Only the waves at her brow persisted.

She bumped into Adam at the base of the stairs. He was carrying a pot of coffee into the library.

'Like some?' His eyes flickered over her.

'No, I'm off now.'

'Going somewhere special?'

'The police.'

'Would you like some company?'

'I thought you were working.'

'I was. Deadlines . . . sorry, the calendar beckons. But if you like . . .' He was scrutinizing her.

'In fact, I'd rather go on my own.'

'Will you be all right?'

'Of course I'll be all right.' She was brusque. Too brusque, she realized as she saw his face. She was overreacting, letting her suspicions run away with her. And he suddenly looked so vulnerable.

'Adam, it is true that ninety per cent of suicides leave notes, isn't it?' she asked more softly now.

He shrugged. 'My dusty books haven't provided me with that statistic.'

'I apologized about that.'

'So you did.' He met her eyes for a moment and then turned away instantly. 'Yes, it is meant to be the case that most suicides leave notes of some kind,' he said tersely.

'And Max hasn't?'

'I don't know. Perhaps they haven't found it yet.'

'I'm going to find it, if it exists.' Her voice had a note of triumph. She brushed past him. 'And I'll be back at six thirty. I'm expecting a call from the States.'

'Your butler will undoubtedly be waiting, Ms Latimer. Drive safely.'

She didn't. That last remark of his had infuriated her and for a brief moment it passed through her mind that the reason she was so suspicious of his involvement with Max was his general duplicity. And the fact that he enraged her. But she chased that from her mind. He knew something. Something he wasn't telling her. And if it implicated him in Max's death, she was going to find out about it.

She put her foot down on the accelerator and drove too fast, taking the curves in the road precariously. She realized that if she let her mind move into that dreaming trance that usually accompanied driving, all she saw was the plastic sheet over Max's body. And the tears would start to blur her eyes. So it was better to stay alert, angry.

The business at the police station took far too long, an exceeding politeness masking an exceeding inefficiency. The officer in charge of the case wasn't available and no one else could tell her anything. She waited, uncomfortably aware of the fact that Max lay close by in the plastic winding sheet.

When the officer – a middle-aged man with a dour face – finally arrived, he seemed to be willing to do little more than offer his condolences.

She grilled him, told him she was a relative and wanted to see the file on the case, which he said was impossible.

Irritated, Helena flashed her press card, impressed on him Max Bergmann's importance, and finally he gave her a narrative of the events.

It was little more than Adam had told her, but at least she knew for certain that the police had no suicide note. She also had the name and address of the little boy who had rented Max his boat.

'And where was Max Bergmann staying at the time? I hope you've searched the place.'

The man's temper was rising. 'Not only did we search it, but we had to search it out. Not easy, I can tell you. A chalet, rented out by Schluss, eight miles from the lake. But there was no car; that puzzled us. He was an old man, after all. He wouldn't have walked.'

'And what did you find in the chalet?'

The man looked at her suspiciously. 'It's all in the bag. It'll be handed over after the inquest.'

Helena smiled her sweetest smile. 'Thank you, officer. It's a relief to know that everything has been properly handled. One worries so, you know.'

She could feel him looking after her as she strode out of the office.

Outside the day was waning. Helena cursed the fact that she had risen so late, held herself back from blaming it on Adam. There wouldn't be time now to drive out and find the little boy's place or an estate agent. It would have to wait until tomorrow.

The affluent little town had a sleepy air about it. Only a few strollers were visible on the high street near the stone fountain with its youthful Madonna. Beyond, there were the district hospital precincts, loudly sign-posted, and a small hotel complete with heraldic arms set into its turrets. On a whim Helena thought she might check in for the night. She could ring James at the appointed time and set about her business early tomorrow. She would avoid Adam that way.

How was it that he could tempt her to transgress against all her principles? And more than that, Helena stilled the sudden ache inside her, despite all her suspicions.

No, she would have to confront him. And she wanted to ask him some more questions, search the library, perhaps even his room if the opportunity arose.

She drove back to Seehafen, her pace slowed by the gathering darkness and the steady stream of weekend traffic. Somehow, she managed to miss a turn and had to retrace her route.

By the time she arrived, it was already six thirty and she raced up the steps, certain that she could hear the telephone ringing. She prodded the bell fiercely.

'Right on time, Ms Latimer.' Adam opened the door to her. The lazy smile played round his lips. 'There's a Mr James Whitaker on the phone for you. Max Bergmann's Chief Administrator.' He bowed ceremoniously.

Helena rushed past him.

'James, sorry. I got lost on my way back here. When are you arriving?'

'Nine on Sunday. It'll give me another day to sort things here. I've rung round the Trustees. Haven't been able to get hold of Brad or two of the others, but I've managed to reach Jerome and Charlie. They think the funeral itself should be in Germany. Simpler that way. Memorial service here in New York. Maybe Boston. Ashes here, if that's feasible. I'm preparing the Press Release now. We've agreed not to mention suicide, since it's not certain. Just "died tragically while vacationing" – something like that. They're both going to try and come to the funeral, as soon as you name a time. By the way, they're a bit perplexed about you.'

'So am I,' Helena muttered.

'I've spoken to the lawyer's office. There is a will. Max was very correct, as we know. But all that will take time to unravel.'

'You will ask them if there's anything about all this in the will? A letter or something,' Helena said on the spur of the moment.

'Jesus, Helena, I've got enough on my hands here to cover the next three weeks, let alone twenty-four hours.'

At that, she almost let her last query drop, but something prodded her. 'And you'll check out Adam Peters?'

She could almost see him slamming his fist on his desk.

'What is this, Helena? You chasing a murderer or something?'

She blanched, but kept her voice even. 'Don't be dramatic, James. Just do it.'

Adam was pacing between the hall and the front room when she emerged. For a moment she thought he might have been eavesdropping.

'I didn't want you sneaking out on me as you're wont to do,' he grinned at her so that the dimple played in his cheek.

Helena smiled back. The straightforwardness was irresistible. 'I wasn't planning to at the moment.'

'Good, because I've used the payment you so kindly left me to buy some very good champagne. And there's a salmon waiting to be cooked. I thought we might try to have a friendly evening. No rows, no tiffs, no unwanted ironies, no . . .'

'Sex,' she finished for him, blushed.

She saw the spark in his eye, saw him control it. He performed a little pirouette.

'What? In my best suit?'

Helena laughed, noticed for the first time that he had changed, was wearing a loose linen suit in some tawny shade, a fresh blue shirt.

'I'm afraid I'm wearing the only dress I brought.'

He eyed her up and down with a comical expression. 'It'll do admirably. I don't think I could get you out of that if I tried. Whoops, sorry.'

He gave her his arm formally and led her into the sitting room.

There was a soft glow of lamplight in the room. It played over the pinks and dusky rose, the burgundies and clarets and smoky blues of the chairs and rugs. For a moment the scene of her arrival yesterday flashed through her mind, the thought of Max, the spilled wine. She banished it, said instead as he handed her a glass, 'I saw the officer in charge.'

'Oh? Learn anything you didn't know?' He sat down in the armchair on the other side of the hearth.

Helena watched him carefully. 'No, only that they hadn't found a suicide note. And about the chalet where he had been staying. I'm going to go there tomorrow.'

He sipped his champagne.

'I haven't had a chance to tell you yet, but Bergmann came here while I was away.'

Helena tensed, moved to the edge of her chair. 'What for?'

He glanced down at the carpet for a moment, then reached in his pocket for a cigarette. 'It's not clear. The decorators were here. Apparently they showed him into the library. The only room that didn't have wet paint in it. Elsa found him in there.' He lit up and blew a smoke ring into the air. 'He was looking through Bahr's canvases. They were all stacked in there. I assume he wasn't planning to walk off with one.'

Helena baulked at that. 'He wouldn't.'

'No, of course not. Did he ever mention Bahr to you?'

Helena shook her head.

'Well, in any case, it seems he told her he wanted to have a last look before he moved on. So she left him in there.'

'Is that all?' Helena tried not to scrutinize him too openly.

'That's all. Elsa as you know is not the most forthcoming of speech makers. Now if it had been you . . .' He changed the subject rapidly.

'I've been reading your articles, you know. They're good. Well written. Well researched, I imagine. You could try your hand at a book.'

'I enjoyed your lecture, too.'

'I wasn't being patronizing, Helena.' There was a flicker of anger in those hazel eyes. 'But I'd forgotten, you don't approve of dusty books.'

'That's nonsense.'

'Only of *my* dusty books, then,' he laughed, but there was no malice in it.

'That's not true either. I haven't read them yet.'

'Well, that's honest enough.' He refilled her glass. 'Will you keep me company, while I get dinner ready?'

'I'll even help.' She stood, followed him through the door. 'It's probably about time I did.'

'You can chat to me. It won't take long.'

Everything in the kitchen seemed to be ready. There was a plate of cold asparagus on the table, a salad, bright with an assortment of leaves, a dish of hollandaise. He simply lit the gas beneath the saucepan of new potatoes, and lifted the salmon into the fish kettle.

'There.' He turned to her.

'You knew I'd stay.' She glanced at him with accusing eyes.

'No I didn't. I hoped. It's not the same. And I thought to myself that if the beautiful Ms Latimer fled my presence yet again, I'd settle for the young woman in the village round the corner.'

Helena felt her heart skip a beat. She smoothed her skirt. 'It's not too late, you know. If her favours are . . .'

'Don't be silly.' He cut her off. 'I'm teasing. Don't you know about teasing?'

'Perhaps not.' Tears suddenly gripped her eyes. She turned away from him.

'I thought we might eat in the conservatory. Special evening. Table's all set.'

She walked in front of him, too aware of his presence behind her. She felt herself growing confused again. She had been so sure this afternoon, so certain that there was something suspicious about him, some complicity in Max's death. And now . . .

Helena gasped audibly as she looked into the conservatory. There was a lamp flooding the garden beyond and the room seemed to stretch and stretch directly into it, the two trees which served as columns marking a false point of entry to the outside. These, too, were illuminated somewhere at their base, as was the mural of Anna. The table complete with an ornate silver candelabrum was set beyond the columns, so that it seemed to be outdoors, yet in.

'It's beautiful,' she said softly.

'I'm glad you approve. You're my first guest since the overhaul.' He placed the asparagus on the table, uncorked a bottle of white wine.

He raised his glass. 'Shall we toast your Max?' he asked softly.

She nodded. Her voice had a quiver in it as she murmured, 'To Max.' Tears filled her eyes.

He turned towards the window. 'To Max,' he echoed.

She told him then what James and the others had said, how it tallied with what he had originally suggested.

'I'm glad of that. I took the liberty this afternoon of ringing round. I thought you might not have the time, with everything else. And tomorrow is Saturday. I hope you don't mind. There's a crematorium in Munich that could do a service on Wednesday. You can arrange the contents of that. I booked it in provisionally. If the inquest is straightforward, then we can confirm.'

'That's very kind of you,' she smiled in an attempt to erase her tears. After a moment, she asked, 'Why are you doing all this, Adam?' She scanned his face.

He laughed a little edgily. 'Because I'm a kind-hearted man. Or haven't you noticed?'

She didn't respond.

'Or maybe because I like you.' He sought out her eyes. 'And I live and pray that one day you may actually decide you like me, rather than simply resenting the fact that you like making love with me . . .' He stopped himself as he saw her face.

'You're a fool, Adam.' She looked away from him.

'That too. I'll happily testify to that. You don't know, may not even remember. But one night during *Fasching*, you were walking through Munich with a suitcase in your hand, when a lady or was it a man in blond curls . . .'

'The jester in motley.' She stared at him in amazement. 'You?'

He nodded.

'I'm grateful.' She paused. 'For everything.'

'At your service,' he grinned. 'And now, if I don't hurry, that food will be dry as old rubber.' He raced from the room. 'Don't disappear.'

When he came back, she was standing and gazing at a large intricate doll's house which she had somehow missed in the far corner of the room.

'Your daughter's?' she asked as he disburdened the tray.

He nodded.

'You must miss her.'

'I do.' He looked into the distance.

Helena waited breathlessly. He would say something now. Had to say something. But he didn't, simply arranged the food attractively on their plates.

'Now, tell me what you're working on these days.'

She told him about the wind farm, the attempts to think and put through a new energy policy, the campaign against a nuclear reprocessing plant in Cumbria which far too much public money had gone into. She found herself warming to her subject as he plied her with questions, expounding on it.

'And when do I get to read all this?'

'In a few weeks.' She gasped suddenly. 'I forgot to ring the office today.'

'Not even to dictate an obituary?'

She shook her head in dismay. 'I didn't think of that either. Should it be me?'

'No one better. After all, you knew him well, admired him. And a tribute always helps.'

'You're right, of course. I'll alert the paper tomorrow. And write it. James can help with any missing facts when he arrives.'

'And when is that?'

'Sunday morning. I'll stay over in Munich tomorrow. So as not to be late for the plane,' she added lamely.

He was watching her carefully. 'So that's that then. You don't want to stay on here? With me?'

Helena avoided his eyes. 'I couldn't,' she murmured, and smiled. 'Thank you for a delicious and delightful dinner. I'll wash up.'

Adam shrugged.

They carried the dishes back to the kitchen together. Helena rolled up her sleeves.

'Leave it. They'll wait for the morning.'

He sounded grumpy.

'All right.' She turned to face him. 'Adam, why are you so certain Max wasn't my father?'

He looked away, shuffled some plates around on the table. 'I don't know. Instinct, I suppose. But believe what you like.'

'Well, goodnight then, thanks again.' She stood on her toes to kiss him lightly on the cheek, felt that flutter inside again.

But he didn't prevent her going.

In the little yellow room, she couldn't sleep. Her mind was racing. She tossed in the bed and tried to compose Max's obituary, but the words jumbled themselves, danced a mad meaningless dance around the image of his dead body. And there was so much she still didn't know. Why had he disappeared in the first place? Why had he written only to her? Why did she have this sixth sense that Adam – Adam whom she had to admit she more than liked, despite his duplicity – knew something, was behaving suspiciously? Why did that image of Max being pushed from the boat reappear? Why? Why? Why?

And beneath it all that fluttering, that ache, like a double bass plucked somewhere inside her, when she heard Adam walk past her room, when the image of him in bed came to her. She decided that must be what people called desire.

After what seemed like hours of tossing she leapt from the bed. She had to do something.

She tied the burgundy robe she had taken from the bathroom tightly round herself and looked out into the hall. Everything was dark. There was no light seeping from under the door of Adam's room.

Carefully, she crept downstairs, opened the door to the library, switched on the light. If he found her here, she could always say she had come in search of a book.

She looked at the mass of papers on the desk, afraid to disrupt their order even if there didn't seem to be any. She scanned the page in the typewriter. His manuscript. Next to it sheaves of notes, all in his hand. She read hurriedly, but there was nothing of instant interest here.

There were two letter trays at the far end, half covered with more notes. She lifted them to glance beneath. And then she saw it. Max's writing, a single sheet, half covered by a note in another hand. She scanned the note swiftly, her heart thudding.

My Dear Adam,

I've answered the enclosed, since you were kind enough to forward it. Obviously the sender finds your presence in the family vault a suspicious one.

There is no return address, but for the name of an inn. If you can find it, send it on. If not . . .

Helena heard footsteps at the door. She leapt away from the desk and in a flash picked up the telephone.

He looked huge in the doorway. Angry. His eyes whisked across the room, landed on her.

'You've taken up snooping again.'

'Don't be silly.' She tried to keep her voice cool. 'I was just phoning.'

'At this time of night?' He was incredulous.

'There are people who don't mind the time of night.'

'Who?'

He was standing directly in front of her now. She could see the muscles taut in his throat.

Helena gestured evasively.

'Lovers.' He spat it out.

'If you like.'

'You said there wasn't a lover.'

She shrugged, babbled, 'Not *a* lover. But there are always one or two.'

'So you prefer to perform telephone sex under my roof than engage in the real thing?' His eyes were savage.

'Don't be ridiculous.'

'Ridiculous? You make me ridiculous!'

'Adam, please.'

He had gripped her arm. 'And if you can have one or two lovers, you can have three. It's easy enough.'

He pulled her to him, kissed her too hard, so that her lips felt bruised with the resistance of it. She could feel the tension in him through the length of her, the smell of him, and despite herself the lapping started up in her, mounted, flowed. Her mouth opened to his, her arms found their way to his back, stroked, stroked. She no longer knew if he was pinning her to him or she was cleaving.

He moaned against her, lifted her in his arms, so that she sat astride him. He was looking at her with something like hatred in his eyes.

'So which lover shall it be tonight, Ms Latimer, the one who does it on the table, on the floor, on the sofa? Perhaps against the dusty bookshelves?'

'Don't humiliate me, Adam.' Her voice cracked. She was rocking against him.

'It seems to me that I'm the only one who gets humiliated around here.' He dropped her unceremoniously on the sofa.

She felt cold, destitute. 'Please, Adam,' she whispered, held out her hand to him. 'Please.'

He looked at her for a moment. His face was suddenly haggard. Then he dropped to his knees, wrapped his arms round her. She ran her fingers softly through his hair, over his chest, untied his robe. He was kissing her, caressing, her face, her neck, her breasts. She arched against him.

'Say you want me, Helena. Say it,' he was whispering in her ear. His hand was on her mound, rubbing, pressing.

'I want you.' She was crying suddenly, the tears streaming down her face. 'I want you more than I've ever wanted anyone in my life.' She coiled her fingers round him. Smooth, taut skin. She felt the rush of his breath in her ear.

'And you hate yourself for it.' He pulled her head back, looked into her eyes.

'And I hate myself for it,' she was sobbing. 'But I don't hate you. I wish I hated you.' She buried her face in his chest.

'Don't, please don't.' He was stroking her hair, suddenly gentle, lifting her, edging her on to him, so they were both on the floor, clutching each other, rocking, their eyes as tightly locked as their bodies. The waves shuddered through her almost instantly, little moans of them, and then great surging cries.

He carried her up the stairs, tucked her into the little bed like a child. He looked at her for a moment. 'I don't understand anything, Helena. I told you that before. Perhaps when you've stopped wishing you hated me, you can explain to me.' He kissed her softly. 'But give it time. Don't run away.'

TWENTY-THREE

As it was, Helena didn't need to run. She simply left. It happened quite easily.

She woke feeling bruised, humiliated, hating herself, hating Adam, wishing Max were there, alive, strong, pure, to point the way to something bigger, greater than this tremulous, vacillating creature she had become.

Adam could turn her into a mass of quivering jelly in seconds. A being without a spine. It had been better before, when she felt nothing. She had had invulnerability then, pride, and a clear straight sense of what was right.

How could she have loved him, with Max's letter there beside them, just a few feet away – a clear indication that he was lying about Max as he had lied about everything else? The treachery of it. And of herself.

She longed to speak to Claire, to anyone who would reflect a different sense of herself. Claire had laughingly called her Joan of Arc when she had first set out in search of Max. She should see her now.

Helena went downstairs, her small case determinedly in her hand. She would throw it, she thought, if he stepped near her.

There were voices coming from the living room, Adam's and someone else. She sighed with relief, poked her head round the door. He was standing with a suited stranger, clipboard in hand.

'Don't want to disturb you,' she made her voice light, 'but I'm off now.'

'Come in,' Adam turned towards her, 'come and meet Andrew Wright. From London. There's coffee on the table.' He motioned towards the window, but she could feel him scrutinizing her, looking at the case. 'Helena Latimer, Andrew Wright.'

Helena shook the man's hand. He had a certain flamboyance about him, lazy hooded eyes above a prominent nose, a dazzling bow tie against a dark shirt, an indolence of gesture.

'I believe we've met somewhere before,' he drawled.

'London's really just a village,' Helena smiled. If she hadn't already met him, she knew his doubles.

Adam handed her a cup of coffee. 'Andrew is doing a feature on the German art show at the Royal Academy. And I stupidly forgot he was coming to look over Johannes's pictures this morning.' He gave her a lopsided grin, passed his hand over unshaven cheeks.

She avoided his eyes, focused on Andrew. 'Oh, when is the opening?'

'End of May. But I wanted to have a better look at these. Don't know them. They're something of a revelation. Look.' He put his hand lightly on her shoulder, guided her towards a canvas and gestured enthusiastically. 'The brushstrokes . . .'

Adam watched them, saw the easy camaraderie, the way she clutched her bag firmly in the midst of it. She was going. She wouldn't come back. He sensed it as a certainty now. He had found her only to lose her again.

A demon had taken him over and he had humiliated her. Humiliated her when she was most vulnerable, made her say things, painful things. He had lost his temper, his control, his heart. Like some stupid, callous yet yearning adolescent. And he had started out wanting to protect her.

Of course she had lovers. So she should. He was hardly the only man in the world. But he had seen red then, been overtaken by a passion he couldn't counter and he had forced her and tried to force truth from her. As if in love one could grasp at some tidy truth.

What was it Freud had said somewhere? Truth might be a goal of science, but love was a goal of life and had its own logic.

What had drawn him to her from the very first was that fierce impetuosity in her, an integrity which had nothing to do with truth. She had lied to him from the first, easy, obvious lies, which didn't touch any depths. And the depths were there, vulnerable, accessible – unlike so many people he had known – and he had stamped on them. Like . . . like a man.

He scowled at himself. Perhaps the women were right.

He watched her, laughing easily now, extricating herself from Andrew's hand. She was going. He had lost. It was a loss he didn't know how to repair.

'It's goodbye then, Adam.' She was looking over his shoulder. 'Thanks for all the help. No, don't come to the door. I'll see myself off.' She waved at them both.

* * *

Helena sat very still for a moment before starting the engine. Her heart was beating too fast. She took a deep breath. She had escaped. And now she could focus on what needed to be done. She would find out the truth of Max's death, even if she hadn't been able to unearth the whole truth of his life. Adam Peters wouldn't prevent her.

She glanced at her map, traced the route and drove away, her thoughts keeping pace with her speed.

Adam had held back from telling her that Max had been to the house again. They troubled her, these visits he had made, usually it seemed during Adam's absence. Why? What could he have been looking for? She had never known him to show any particular interest in art before. Perhaps it had something to do with Adam's father.

By the time she had reached her destination, her speculations had decided her upon the necessity of a thorough search of the house. If she couldn't carry it out, then the police would have to. James and she would talk to them tomorrow.

It took Helena some time to convince the bossy grey-haired woman behind the desk at the Schluss agency that she had both a perfect right and a familial responsibility to visit the chalet in which Max had spent his last days. But at last, the woman handed over the key and traced the directions on the map.

'The key must be back with us by two o'clock at the latest. I do not have anyone to send with you now, so you must leave me some identification. *Ja*?'

Helena searched through her purse, decided on her British Library card.

The woman examined it dubiously. 'A passport or a driving permit would be better.'

Helena plunked her passport on the desk.

'So, that is good.' Her thin lips formed into a stiff smile for the first time. 'Now I have some insurance. Till two o'clock then, Fräulein.'

'And Fräulein Latimer,' the woman was leafing through the passport, 'you will not speak of this to anyone. It is not good for business for one of our best chalets to be associated with a death.'

'Not to anyone,' Helena muttered.

* * *

The chalet was remote, perched half way up a steep incline. Around it, the tall firs cut out the sun. Behind, the ragged mountains loomed, granite-hard, topped with snow. Helena walked, her boots crackling over a carpet of prickly cones. It was colder here, gloomy. She drew her coat more closely round her.

In the distance, she could hear the rush of a brook against stone. Closer to, a flurry of bird calls.

She opened the door with a sudden sense of apprehension.

The room was square in shape, utterly functional – a bare wooden floor, two chairs, a table, a small stove, and next to it a tiny paraffin cooker. A ladder led to the loft. She climbed it, saw two camp beds and a chest of drawers, nothing more. A hiker's cabin, she thought, providing only the bare requisites.

She looked out of the window through the ruddy bark of the trees. There was a glimmering on the horizon, a cold hard light. It took her a moment to realize it was the lake. She shuddered. She could feel Max, standing here, on this very spot looking out on that cold, glistening surface, staring through the trees into the light.

Quickly, she opened the drawers one after the other, knowing she would find nothing. She checked under the beds as well, then clambered downstairs and sat at the rough bare table.

She could imagine Max here, day in, day out, alone, meditating, writing. Or perhaps he had passed beyond writing, beyond the desire to communicate, to a sparer communion with the elements themselves. And then walked all those miles to sink himself within them. She stared out at the trees, wishing they could speak to her.

Suddenly she jumped up. Writing! Surely the officer in charge would have said something about a manuscript that had been found here, would have read through it to see if it contained an indication? But in English?

She was suddenly filled with excitement. She locked the door to the chalet and with an acute sense that she was literally treading in Max's footprints, she climbed down the hill some way, skidding between the trees on the wet ground. Then she came back doing a full circle round the cabin before returning to the car.

From the road, unless one knew it was there, it was easy to miss the cabin, its dark wood all but obliterated by the surrounding trees. It occurred to her that as well as a site for meditation, the cabin served as a perfect hideaway. The thought disturbed her. A hideaway from what?

When she examined her map, she realized she wasn't far from the site of one of Max's postcards to her: Sylvenstein-Speicher. She sped along the route, stopped in a little hamlet to ask about the place, was told by a talkative waiter that the Sylvenstein was a vast reservoir, a technological wonder. Roads and settlements had made way for eighty million cubic metres of water. He looked at her with pride.

What could the dam have meant to Max, Helena wondered? That kind of information couldn't be gleaned from a visit. It would take research, digging into files. That would have to come later.

She retraced her steps, headed back to the agency with the chalet key, before moving on to find the little boy who had rented Max his boat.

The house was on the side of the road which bordered the lake. As she should have known, the boy in question was at school. His mother, somewhat defensively, reiterated the story Helena already knew, only adding in a scolding tone that her son should have told them sooner about his missing boat.

'He was afraid, of course.'

'Poor child,' Helena commiserated.

The woman accompanied her over the road and down the curving path which led to the lake. The boat was there, tied to a tree stump by a thick rope.

'Could I go out in it?' Helena asked the woman on impulse.

The woman looked at her with fear in her eyes. 'I think it is better not,' she murmured, turning away.

'No, no, of course.' Helena didn't try to persuade her. The woman's anxiety was too evident.

Helena would have liked to be left here on her own, but she had missed her chance. The woman hovered around her nervously.

She paused nonetheless to gaze out to the centre of the lake. There was no wind and the waters were glassy, an aquamarine stillness. To her side, around the bend, she suddenly noticed the unmistakeable contour of the grounds at Seehafen and beyond the trees, half hidden, the domed roof of the house. Why the house, again? It was uncanny.

'Thank you for letting me look.' She turned to the woman, who was visibly relieved to see her back to her car.

* * *

The police station in Murnau offered no joy, however hard she pressed. Officer Weiss was not in. They told her to come to the inquest. She drove to Munich, checked in at the hotel where she had stayed two months ago, and walked: past the stately buildings of the Residenz, past the blondly elegant university, through a small stretch of the English Gardens and then up into the busy narrow streets of Schwabing. She thought for some reason of Johannes and Anna and Bettina, and then of Adam.

He had told her that he had seen her that first night she had come here. That night of Carnival. Adam the fool. What had he said to her then? She couldn't remember now. She had been too upset. But he had guided her. And now he had led her astray.

Useless thoughts, she scolded herself. She stopped in front of a bookshop, went in on impulse and asked whether they had anything on the construction of the Sylvenstein-Speicher reservoir, was handed a thick glossy book. She paid for it, walked on, backtracked, towards the Marienplatz and into the market square.

From somewhere music echoed. A crowd had gathered. In its centre stood a young tow-haired man with a girl's face and a pure skin-tingling tenor. He was singing to a backing tape: Cavaradossi's last aria from 'Tosca'. Emily's favourite. She stopped to listen, felt the tears biting at her eyes.

> '*Svani per sempre il sogno mio d'amore*
> Vanished forever is that dream of love
> Fled is that hour
> And desperately I die
> And never before have I loved life so much!'

The music followed her across the square. She fled into a Stuberl to escape its longing, sat at a long narrow table, ordered a sandwich, a glass of wine.

The cover of the menu showed a thin gangling figure, bent like a question mark. The comic, Karl Valentin. A sophisticated clown. His sayings littered the menu. *'Die Zukunft war früher auch besser.'* 'The future was better before too.'

Helena smiled, thought of Adam's lecture. Adam.

With sudden determination, she took a notepad from her bag and started to make three lists: Suicide/Accident/Other.

* * *

She showed the list to James Whitaker the next day. His plane had been only a little late. He had had time for a kip and a shower and they were lunching together in the Hofgarten Café. Through the windows she could see the bright ochre facade of the colossal Theatinerkirche where the Wittelsbach kings lay buried. Helena shook herself. She was finding death everywhere.

'Well?' She turned to James.

He handed her list back to her. 'Have you gone crazy, Helena? I know you're a brilliant investigative journalist, but this time you've gone mad.' His voice was hushed. 'Tear it up. Put it away.' He looked covertly over his shoulder and then turned his scrubbed face to her. His eyes beneath the spectacles were red-rimmed like a rabbit's. 'You're not really imagining that Max was murdered?' He wiped his mouth carefully as if to remove an obscenity.

'It's possible.' Helena put more certainty in her voice than she felt. In the quiet formality of this room, the basis for her suspicions seemed strangely inchoate, out of place.

'Well, put it out of your mind. If the police haven't suggested it, have no evidence, there isn't any. And can you imagine the scandal of a murder, what it would do to our reputation, to endowments?'

'Since when have we been on the same side as the police?' Helena muttered.

'That's not the point. If any of your suspicions get out to the public, we're sunk. You know very well that murder rebounds on the victim. The press would have a field day. And you have proof of nothing. Only doubts. That house Max wrote to you about, a fragment of a letter. A couple of pictures he sent you. A reservoir. This man you keep harping on about who you say has shadowed all your movements here. And Max's. But it's just coincidence. None of it adds up. None of it.'

'Did you check him out?'

'I put the call through. Despite my better judgement.'

'And?'

'And nothing. I'm here, aren't I, not by my computer.'

Helena pushed the food around on the large white plate.

'So despite all I've said, you think Max's death was an accident?'

'I prefer to think that. Jerome and Charlie would prefer to think that.' He evoked the eminent figures who had provided the backdrop to their entire conversation. At Helena's scowl, he went over it all again, as if for a child.

'Look, Max obviously wanted to be alone, away from us all. Like a monk in need of solitude. So he went off. That's altogether in keeping with his character. There's nothing suspicious about it.'

'That's not what you said back in January.'

'That was early days and there's been no buzz of any kind from the activists since then, no rumours. And I've been thinking about it a lot, re-reading him. It makes sense to me now. A lot more sense than what you're suggesting. The next thing you'll be telling me is that the Stasi were after him or the CIA, that the redoubtable Max Bergmann was about to blow up some nuclear installation or put a hole in some dam.' He flushed as he realized his voice had risen, quickly gulped his mineral water, steadied himself. 'I know it's hard coming to terms with the death of someone we loved and admired, perhaps even worshipped, but there's no point engaging in paranoid fantasies, Helena.' He met her gaze earnestly.

'So now you're telling me I'm deluded.'

'No. Only that you have an active imagination. Mine is very prosaic. Max tripped, slipped off the boat, somehow. There was no one around to shout for. Or maybe he decided to go for a swim and the water was too cold for him to bear. He used to do that, you know, go for dips in the early spring, when the pond had just melted. Ritual purification, I used to think.'

'With all his clothes on?' Helena intervened caustically.

'No, perhaps not.' James looked a little sheepish. Suddenly he leaned towards her and a different expression came over his face, a look of reverent awe which sat oddly on his thin features. 'In my heart of hearts, Helena, what I really think is that it was suicide. A grand gesture. The retreat, the isolated chalet you told me about, Max had reached the end of his tether and decided to merge into the elements before there were no more elements to merge into. But the money men don't want that. It's too extreme, kooky. And as I see it, my job is to keep the Farm alive, to keep Max's work going.'

'At the expense of the truth.'

He nodded, wiped his spectacles again.

'So after all I've told you, you won't ask the police to search the house.'

He gestured at her impatiently. 'Let's wait for the inquest, shall we.'

* * *

The small courtroom had been recently refurbished, a conference hall rather than a palace of justice, with red padded seats and solid tawny furniture. The giant of a public prosecutor presided with brisk efficiency. Helena had trouble following the list of precise questions and expert answers. She reminded herself that this was not so much a problem of German as of legal language as a whole.

On the other side of the room, amongst a cluster of people she suddenly thought might be reporters, she could see the straight-backed woman from the Schluss agency and the small boy's fearful mother. Seated amongst a row of policemen was Officer Weiss who refused her glance as assiduously as she refused Adam's.

He had arrived shortly after them. Somehow, she hadn't expected to see him here. There was no real reason for him to come, unless the apprehensions she harboured and James had so derided had some basis. Helena stared resolutely in front of her, declining to acknowledge him, though she was all too palpably aware of his presence.

Officer Weiss's testimony followed the lines she already knew, but she learned that other people in the vicinity had been questioned, and that no one had been seen on the lake apart from Max.

To Helena's surprise, the name of Adam Peters was the next but one on the clerk's lips. So that explained his presence. She listened intently, watching that mobile face for any sign it might give. But Adam was terse, answering questions briefly and exactly, explaining how the deceased had come to his house on three occasions to look at the work of Johannes Bahr; how he had suspected the deceased might be Bergmann because of a contact in London who had come to search for him; how he had got in touch with the person in question when he had heard of the death.

So she was now a contact in London. Helen grimaced at the designation, almost missing the sound of her name in the process. She walked awkwardly to the stand, confirmed she was a journalist, heard herself being asked whether the man who had identified himself to the Schluss agency as Max Hillman was to the best of her knowledge Max Bergmann. She nodded, was asked to speak up, and clipped out her 'Yes'.

Did she have any knowledge as to why Herr Bergmann might have used a false name?

Helena shrugged, found herself mumbling something as to Max wishing to be alone, untroubled by acquaintances or press. Or perhaps he was evading hostile forces. He was a well-known figure in the Green Movement in America.

The prosecutor looked at her sternly. What kind of hostile forces did she have in mind?

Helena felt James scowling at her, though he could only have guessed at her words. She shrugged. 'It's only an intuition,' she murmured.

Contempt settled on the prosecutor's features. 'Thank you, Fräulein Latimer.'

She thought he was about to gesture her off the stand, but he continued. Had Herr Bergmann suffered from depression? Had there been any intimation that he might want to take his own life?

Helena shook her head abruptly in response to both questions.

Had he to her knowledge latterly suffered from fainting spells, moments of unconsciousness?

'I don't think so. I don't know.' There was so much, she thought, she didn't know.

'That will be all, Fräulein Latimer.'

It was as she returned, a little shamefaced, to her seat that Helena met Adam's eyes. They were warm on her, too intimate. She stiffened her shoulders and saw his lips curl into that ironical smile. He was laughing at her, a laugh of triumph, she suddenly thought, as suspicion gripped her again and with it something like rancour. She slid hastily into her place.

The interrogation of the pathologist lasted longest. The intricate technical terms, the impersonal tone of voice, left Max utterly to one side. What was under investigation was a pulmonary condition, a fibrosis of conductant tissue. In the midst of it all, Helena heard the word cardiac arrest.

'Which could in a man of Herr Bergmann's years whose conductant tissue was fibrosed be caused by the shock of icy water?' the prosecutor asked.

'Certainly.'

The verdict, though it came some time later and after the question of suicide was raised and discounted, was clear for her from that moment on: Max had suffered an accidental death.

She had only had a moment's time to relay this to James when amidst the general hubbub of the court rising, she heard her name called again.

A clerk gave her a slip of paper. She could go and pick up Herr

Bergmann's effects now and leave instructions about transport of the body.

The body. Suddenly, the room in front of her swam into opacity and in its place Helena saw Max's waxy face on that slab, the stiff cold sheath of plastic. The smell of chemicals rose to her nostrils, like the high strong whiff of formaldehyde that had emerged from the plastic sac of yellowy rats they had been forced to dissect at school. Billy had once chased her with a dead rat through the old bomb site. Held the rat by the tail and swung it in front of her face while his jeering friends looked on. She must have been small then, because she couldn't run very fast and she was crying as he cornered her. She could feel the jagged wall against her back, could taste the tears and then her scream as he lifted her skirts and flung the creature at her.

'Helena. Are you all right?' There was a steadying arm on her shoulder. The room regained its outlines. Adam was gazing at her.

'Yes, yes, I'm fine.' She shrugged off his hand, saw James emerge from the huddle of people. She stepped towards him.

'James, this is Adam Peters. James Whitaker.'

The men shook hands, assessed each other.

'We're to go and collect Max's things now. Give them instructions about . . .' She stopped herself.

'The funeral arrangements,' Adam finished for her. 'I'd better come along. I have all the details here.' He took a small notebook from his breast pocket. 'It's this way to the police station.'

James eyed her curiously and Helena forced herself into composure. This was the moment she had been waiting for. There would be something amongst Max's effects, something the police had missed. She was certain of it.

The police station, a short block away, was busier than she remembered it. Her slip of paper was taken unceremoniously and a plastic bag handed over, together with a small old-fashioned brown leather suitcase that she would have known anywhere as Max's. She reached for the case, let James handle the plastic, saw Adam murmur something into his ear.

'Let's go and have a bite to eat.' James ushered her towards the door. 'Your Adam Peters tells me there's a restaurant round the corner.'

Helena hardly heard him. 'I want to look through these straight away.' She blinked at the bright noonday light, looked round for a moment to get her bearings and then walked swiftly in the direction of the court house.

'Wait for me,' James grumbled. 'Don't know why we have to do this now.'

She didn't answer him, rushed instead towards the car park.

In the back seat of the car, she sprung open the locks of the case. The clothes were neatly folded: shirts, socks, two sweaters, a jacket, a pair of dark blue trousers, the same soft grey suit Max had worn in Norway. She was almost afraid to touch it, had to force herself to burrow beneath. But there was nothing else, not a notebook, not a slip of paper.

James took the suit and trousers from the case and rifled through the pockets. Part of her wanted to stop his hands: it felt like a travesty.

'Nothing,' he murmured.

Helena folded the clothes carefully back. She felt a sense of desolation she had kept at bay beginning to overwhelm her. There was no notebook, no message. Nothing. Just the unresolved silence of death.

'And the bag?' She gestured impatiently at James.

He held it upside down and spilled the already glimpsed contents gently on to the seat. There were the rumpled clothes Max must have been wearing, a watch, water-soiled. Helena looked at it. It had stopped at five past twelve.

'High noon,' James muttered.

She shivered, picked up Max's thick black pen, an ink bottle. She forced herself to focus on it. The bottle was almost empty. That could only mean that he had written something. Letters, notes. But where were they? Almost angrily, Helena looked at the single book, a volume of Hölderlin's poems, shook it to see what might flutter from its pages. Nothing.

James was checking through pockets again. 'He must have had this on him.' He waved a brown wallet in the air. 'Plastic is intact, but the money's a little the worse for wear. What's strange is that I can't find his passport anywhere.'

'He lost that ages ago. An inn-keeper told me.'

James looked at her in surprise.

She didn't explain further. 'What I can't understand is why there are no papers, no notes, not even a diary.'

'I kept that for him, remember? Come on, let's get out of here.' James crumpled everything back into the sack. 'These things give me the creeps. I think we should chuck them in the nearest bin or drop them off at an charity shop.'

'James!' Helena was scandalized.

'All right then. You take care of them. But Max wasn't interested in *things*.' He jumped out of the car.

'Don't be so sanctimonious,' Helena murmured after him. She sat there for a moment and fingered the clothes in the case. An image of Max, stalking between the trees outside that remote cabin, came to her; another of him rowing out into the centre of the lake, his face set in the lines of his customary austerity. Slowly Helena snapped the case shut. Perhaps she was wrong and James right. Perhaps Max had wanted simply to disappear into the elements and leave no trace of himself, not even the reminder of a few words on paper.

Or perhaps he had taken a notebook with him and it was lying engorged somewhere at the bottom of the lake. Or someone, someone who had pushed him, had already appropriated his notes.

Her thoughts began to swirl again with a menacing fury.

'Are you coming?' James had opened the door on her side of the car and was tapping his foot impatiently on the ground.

She gazed at him unseeingly and then with a shrug slowly got out. 'All right, let's get rid of everything. Though I'd like to keep his pen. Perhaps the book.'

They walked in silence. Then, as the police station loomed in front of them again, James said in a new low voice, 'I'm beginning to realize it's different for you. I was so used to seeing Max every day that I think I must have done my mourning in those first months after his disappearance. So all this now seems somehow anticlimactic.'

'Whereas he wrote to me and I had counted on seeing him in Berlin.' Her voice cracked and she coughed to hide it. 'I must ring them. Where are you taking me, James?'

'That restaurant's meant to be somewhere around here.'

Helena pointed.

'That's it.'

The room was dim, heavy with oak tables and the warmth of thick soups. Helena only had time to take in its general size and shape before she saw Adam waving to them from a back table.

'You didn't tell me we were meeting *him* here,' she snapped at James.

'Funeral arrangements, or have you forgotten already?' He gave her a queer look. 'You'd think you'd be pleased to have me check out your prime suspect,' he grumbled.

Helena stilled her visceral fears. 'Get him to tell you about Max's visits to his house.'

But she found it difficult to meet Adam's eyes and when he took her coat and brushed against her, she was enraged at the flush which rose to her cheeks.

She was doubly angry when, after the waiter had placed a large pitcher of wine on the table, Adam said to James, 'I hope you don't mind my sorting this funeral business out. Helena was a bit overwhelmed by events and it seemed the least I could do as the bearer of bad news.'

'What do you mean, I was *overwhelmed* by events?' she lashed out at him.

His eyes rested on her and she suddenly remembered how she had come crawling into his bed, how he had held her, how . . . She scraped her chair away from the table. 'Excuse me.'

'I didn't mean it as a criticism, Helena. It would be odd in the circumstances if . . .'

Helena, rushing to the ladies' room, didn't hear the rest of his sentence. She stared at herself in the small mirror, unable to recognize the troubled wide-eyed face which looked back at her. With a grimace she splashed cold water on herself, dabbed on bright lipstick.

Of course, she had been overwhelmed; she had suffered a shock. But she was quite capable of thinking now. She brushed her hair fiercely. And what she thought was that no man, no married man at that, would take the time and trouble Adam had taken over all this simply for the fleeting favours of a woman who was reluctant to return them. And any woman who thought the contrary was pulling the wool over her own eyes and would suffocate in the resulting tangle. Which simply left her with the added certainty that there was something else behind Adam's actions. But how was she to find out?

If the police had been handling an enquiry they would have ascertained where Adam had been at noon on the fatal day; they would have checked out his links with something more than Princeton – not that she had done even that. They would also have looked for a motive. But that was where all her instincts came unstuck. She couldn't begin to construct a reason why Adam would want Max dead – though she could think of several why she wanted Adam dead, Helena smiled grimly at her reflection.

The men were talking earnestly when she returned. Adam gave her a smile, which turned into something else half way, when she didn't return it.

'Better?' James was looking at her with a superior certainty which he could only have gained from Adam's presence.

'I didn't know I was poorly,' Helena muttered. 'So, have you gentlemen sorted everything out while the poor little woman was powdering her nose?'

'Everything,' Adam grinned. 'Though we thought it would be appropriate to wait for you before confronting the small matter of the funeral service. Wouldn't want to unbalance the fair division of labour.'

'Yes, leave the emotional work to the women.'

'You have it in one.'

'But we don't want it too emotional.' James had missed their ironies. 'Max was a restrained sort of guy. I thought I might ask Charles if he would say something. He's meant to be coming. In fact I should ring him in about an hour.'

'We can go back to my place, if you like. And you can make all your calls from there.'

'That would be very convenient.'

Helena grimaced, then suddenly found herself blurting out the first thought that came to her mind. 'What's your interest in Max Bergmann, Adam?'

The waiter chose this moment to place the bowls of steaming soup in front of them. She couldn't see Adam's face, but she heard him mumble, 'I've told you. And I would have thought your vaunted intuition would have made it doubly clear.'

She glared at him, aware that he was deliberately using the word that had slipped out of her during the court proceedings, but quite unaware of where her intuitions were meant to lead her.

The funeral took place in an ornate baroque building on the outskirts of Munich. Only Charles Raymond had flown in from the States. She hadn't met him before and his relative youth and effusiveness surprised Helena, who had imagined a different man of Max's own years. It was he who led the service. He spoke of Max's life-long dedication to nature, his work in forestry, begun in Sweden, continued in America, his new home; his setting up of Orion Farm. He evoked Max's single-minded dedication to the Green cause, his ascetic life, in terms of an almost political zest. His speech was interlarded with smatterings of German aimed at a gathering which surprised her by its size.

The notices Adam had penned for James and inserted in two daily papers had done their work, together with the phone calls to Green Party Headquarters. A network had been put in motion, and its members now sat there, bound by their common interests and their common reverence towards a man who had been a leading light in their movement.

From her pew on the platform, Helena looked at their upturned faces, indistinguishable to her but for one at the very back. Adam. Even his posture set him out from the others. There was nothing of reverence in it. Despite the distance between them, she could make out that cool, assessing gaze. He cared nothing for Max.

Why had he bothered to come? James had invited him, of course, that day when they had all gone back to the house together. But a casual invitation was hardly an imperative, and she certainly hadn't reiterated it.

Helena had stayed close to James that afternoon, away from Adam, pretending to herself that he wasn't there, that these rooms weren't charged for her with a significance that part of her refused to forget.

She had looked through the books in the library as James made his phonecalls, not daring to glance either at the spread of papers on the desk in case James reprimanded her or at anything else.

It was then that she had found the passage that she was now to read. The book had leapt out at her, the same volume that they had found in the bag of Max's remains. A collection of Hölderlin's poems in an old edition. She had read them through, had suddenly understood why Max had the volume by his side: that deep longing for a golden nature, eternally lost. Helena read.

> 'O Nature, in the beauty of your light
> The kingly fruit unfold with love
> Effortless, unconstrained
> Like the harvests in Arcadia
> Dead is now what raised and nursed me
> Dead is now the youthful world
> That breast, which once filled a heaven,
> As dead and needy as a stubblefield
> Oh, the spring still sings my cares
> As it once did, a friendly comforting song,

But my life's morrow is already here
My heart's Spring ceased flowering.'

As she walked back to her pew, her eyes fell on the coffin. She had been avoiding it. Max lay in there: still, unhearing, dead, only living on in their memories. And so few here had known him, would now never know him, as she would never know, never be able to solve the mystery of his possible paternity. A father found only to be lost. Adam had said that to her.

Despite herself, the tears started to stream down Helena's face.

She wouldn't see Adam any more after this either. Max had brought him into her life and he would leave it with Max, whatever suspicions she might still harbour. Or guilty desires.

Through bleary eyes, Helena watched Gerhardt Stieler stand now, the single German amidst their number who had known Max, however briefly, and whom they had invited to take part. He extolled Max as that very special being, a natural leader. Then he read a passage from one of Max's books. Odd to hear those phrases in translation. Their resonance was somehow different, somehow in keeping with what she herself had read.

It was James's turn last. He was low-key, spoke about the Farm, Max Bergmann's greatest concrete achievement, his pioneering work in the preservation of endangered plant species, expressed his hope that his project would be able to continue in America without him, the greatest tribute that could be paid to him. Looking at James, Helena wondered whether he might ever take on Max's charismatic stature, decided against it, derided herself as ungenerous for doing so, found herself seeking out Adam's face and then, ashamed, looking back at the coffin.

From somewhere the high clear tones of plainsong filled the room. Max's coffin started to move slowly down the ramp and suddenly the back of the room dissolved and in place of a wall, a garden took shape before her eyes, a softly glimmering vision of ancient trees and mellow light. For a breathless moment, Helena thought she was hallucinating a paradise. Then she realized that the wall was a series of sliding doors, open now on to the outside where Max's coffin vanished.

People began to file from their seats, gather at the doors, spill out into the courtyard. Hushed voices rose into chatter.

Helena, walking with the group from the platform, whispered to James, 'I'm going to disappear. See you back at the hotel.'

She had managed to make her way invisibly to the wrought-iron gate when a voice stopped her.

'Running away from here, too?'

She looked up into Adam's face.

'You could call it that.'

'But I thought this was your group.' He was blocking her path, preventing her from leaving. 'I'd have thought that you'd want to extend your homage to the great man, your great leader.' He drawled the words, twisted them into their opposite sense.

'Don't be so contemptuous,' she snapped at him. 'I don't know why you bothered to come.'

'Anthropological interest, I guess.' There was a bitter edge to his laugh. 'I'm fascinated by the phenomenon of leaders and followers. What is it about someone like your Bergmann that allows him to mould people into a group, halve their critical intelligence, turn them into sanctimonious or slogan chanting half-wits . . .'

'Stop it,' Helena hissed at him.

'Okay.' He raised his arms as if she'd held a gun to him and suddenly smiled disarmingly. 'You're right, this is hardly the moment for spleen. I liked the poem you read, though I'm not quite so fond of other sides of Hölderlin, that patriotic longing for the Fatherland, for instance. You know he suffered from something that might have been schizophrenia.'

She wasn't listening. 'Let me through, Adam.'

Dark eyes scrutinized her, searched. 'May I come with you?'

Helena shook her head. 'I need some time to myself.'

'So is this goodbye?'

'I guess so.' She put out her hand, 'Goodbye, Adam.'

'You might add, it's been nice knowing you.'

'I might.' She met his gaze and then turned away quickly before he could see the tears which suddenly pricked her eyes.

The old table lamp with its copper globe base cast a circle of light over the long pine table in the kitchen of the Kensington house. It was set for two with merry striped place mats, peach-yellow plates and plump balloon glasses. But its far end held no food. Instead, it was spread with an assortment of photographs. Helena sat and stared at them.

The package from the Murnau police station had arrived that morning just as she was setting out for work. She had cut open the string with clumsy fingers and an excitement she could hardly contain. It was here, the missing link: the hidden story which she had known all too well they had overlooked.

Inside, wrapped in heavy plastic, there was an old-fashioned Leica. Max's camera. She knew it as soon as she saw it, though it was not what she had expected. A letter accompanied it, from Officer Weiss, telling her that Frau Dieter, the small boy's mother, had found this in his room on the day after the inquest. It had been given to him by Herr Bergmann and Frau Dieter had dutifully turned it over to the police who thought that, as the recipient of Herr Bergmann's effects, it should come to Helena.

She had examined the camera swiftly: there was a roll of film in it, almost at its end. Its contents, developed during the day, were now spread across the table in front of her in the order they had been taken. Helena scanned them for the hundredth time, trying to unearth the story they might be telling.

The roll began with two photos of a small snowy clearing surrounded by trees. The land was flat.

She could attach no significance to these pictures, could not remember seeing the site, nor could she make out if there might be anything wrong with the trees.

Then there were several photographs of a more familiar Bavarian landscape, snaps any tourist might have taken as mementos: rolling hills and idyllic meadows, craggy mountains with awesome peaks.

These were followed by photos of the artificial lake he had already sent her a card of. She had read the book about the dam's construction already. It was hailed as a marriage between nature and technology. There was nothing in the book, of course, to suggest that the dam might have intruded into the eco-balance of the region in a significant way. But had it? Was that what Max was interested in? Did this explain why he had gone to the area? She would write to the Green Headquarters in Munich and find out more. At least it was something to go on, though she felt she was grasping at straws when what she needed was a power digger.

Then there was a sequence of snaps of the house and grounds at Seehafen and the lake, including one of Johannes Bahr's mural of Anna. The photos made her feel a little queasy, reinvigorated her suspicions and simultaneously brought Adam vividly into her mind.

Finally there was a group of photos which could have been taken from and around Max's last stopping place, the isolated chalet in the hills: a close-up of earth rich with pine cones; clusters of trees tall against a blue sky.

Repeated scrutiny of the photographs had filled her with despondency. There was either too much here that she couldn't begin to understand or nothing more than they all already knew. Perhaps she should just, like James, resign herself to the fact that Max had suffered an accidental death.

The doorbell only cut into Helena's concentration after several rings.

'Hi there, hon.' Claire hugged her, then stood back to examine her. 'You poor old thing. Feeling wretched?'

Helena grimaced. 'That too.'

'I am sorry, you know. Even though I wasn't exactly fond of him. Horrid to spend all that time looking, only to find him dead.' She squeezed Helena's hand. 'Here,' she dug into her bag and brought out two bottles of wine, 'to drown your sorrows.'

Helena uncorked a bottle, filled their glasses.

Claire raised hers. 'To Max.'

They drank, settled into the capacious sofa at the front of the room.

'I want the whole story, you know. From the beginning.'

'I *want* to talk, Claire. There's something nagging at me about this whole business. It doesn't smell right.'

Claire tucked her feet under her. 'Slowly then, from the top. I've had an afternoon full of kids and my powers of concentration are at a new low.'

Helena smiled. 'It's good to see you, Claire. I need an injection of common sense. My mind's reeling.'

Claire waved her on. 'From the beginning.'

'Okay, but I'm not sure where the beginning is. Though for me, it's somewhere around the house.' She leapt up and fetched some of the pictures which were spread on the table.

'That's it. That's one of the first places I traced Max to, way back in February. These photos were taken by him.'

Claire glanced at the photos then looked back at Helena expectantly.

'Well, the man who summoned me to Germany this time, the man who told me Max was dead, is the man who lives in this house.' Helena paced, told Claire how Adam, though he claimed only to have met Max once, had taken an inordinate interest in the case, had a letter from him in the house which he had lied about. Told her how Max had been there on several occasions for no good reason. Told her of the purported circumstances of Max's death, the inquest verdict which she didn't trust, the lack of any notes though she was certain Max had been writing.

Her voice rose as she gathered momentum and her face grew warm as she pointed out how Adam seemed to have been stalking her movements from the very beginning. And stalking Max's. How she felt he was somehow implicated in Max's death. That there was something in the house.

'And the whole thing is uncanny,' Helena finished. 'But I don't have anything except hunches to go on. And nowhere to turn. It's driving me slightly mad.' She met Claire's eyes. 'Do you think I am?'

Claire surveyed her for a moment, then rose. 'Let's eat. It helps me think.'

'Oh God, and I've probably burned all the food.' Helena ran to the kitchen. 'Only slightly charred.' She placed a dish of lasagna on the table, tossed the salad.

'So?' She sat down and looked at Claire.

'So, based on experience, your hunches usually have something in them.'

'Well, that's a relief to hear – even though the public prosecutor didn't seem particularly impressed.'

'But . . .'

'But what?'

Claire made a great play of digging into her food, exclaiming on the wonders of charred lasagna.

'But what?' Helena repeated.

'But I also have this hunch that you just don't want to let Max die and you're masking grief, your anger and disappointment at his death, with detective work,' Claire said too quickly. 'It's a way of mourning.'

'I see.'

They were quiet for a moment.

'Who is this man anyway?' Claire said at last. 'The one in the house.'

'Adam Peters,' Helena mumbled. 'You remember, the man whose lecture we went to.'

'*That* man! You mean the anthropologist!' Claire gazed at her in consternation. 'Helena Latimer, if that man has been stalking you, as you so emphatically put it, it's because he's interested in you. Why, the way he was looking at you in the restaurant . . . If anyone looked at me like that, I'd be half way to the bedroom.'

Helena emptied her glass hastily.

'You *have* slept with him.' Claire was staring at her.

'He's married.'

'Others have been before him.'

'I don't approve.'

'What? Of his marriage?'

'No, of sleeping with him, silly.'

'I didn't ask you whether you approved. I asked you whether you had. Or wanted to.' Claire pressed her. 'Helena Latimer, the only time I have ever heard you speak so passionately about a man, he was a purveyor of DDT or some other noxious substance. Apart from Max, that is. And I presume you didn't sleep with him.'

'Of course not.'

'Well then, what about this Adam Peters?'

Helena flushed. 'Yes, I went to bed with him. I didn't know he was married. I . . .'

'Sssh.' Claire put a finger to her lips. 'I'm not getting on a moral high horse and trying to trample you into the dirt.'

'That's a relief,' Helena mumbled.

'You do that quite well enough without any of my help. But let's look at this whole thing again calmly.'

'The fact that I may have slept with Adam has nothing to do with Max's case,' Helena interrupted her, 'unless he was deliberately trying to pull the wool over my eyes in that instance, too.'

'It was nice, was it?'

'Claire!'

'Okay, shush now. I'm thinking.' She poured some more wine into their glasses, then rose to look at the photos at the other end of the table.

'I suspect you wouldn't be half so adamant about this anthropologist's implication in Max's death if you hadn't already judged him duplicitous,' she said after a moment. 'Right?'

'Maybe,' Helena grumbled, 'but the fact is that he's been involved at every turn. Why, even when I landed in Munich . . .'

Claire overrode her. 'And perhaps you're suspicious of him only in order to clear your conscience about seeing him again, despite little wifey back at home.'

'That's utter nonsense.' Helena was sharp.

'All right, all right, I was just speculating.' Claire helped herself to salad. 'But in any event, it seems to me that if you're going to think clearly about the circumstances of Max's death, you'll have to imagine your Adam as some neutral figure, some matron of middle years, or wizened clerk, doing all the things he did or didn't do. And then assess the links. After all, you can't condemn a man as a murderer just because he's broken his marriage vows.'

'I wasn't talking of murder,' Helena protested.

'Just a little amorphous non-sexual foul play, alongside the sexual?'

'Be serious, Claire.'

'I am being serious. But now I'll be blunt as well. All right, I generally trust your hunches. In this instance, I'm not so sure. First of all, the whole thing is overdetermined. You'd begun to think Max might have been your father. Which makes his death far more difficult to accept than the death of an old man who was a friend, even a very good friend.

'Secondly, the man you suspect is a lover. Well, we're all rather prone to be suspicious of lovers. Finally, you have nothing to go on except an absence. An absence of explanation, of notes, of everything. And we tend to rush to fill up absences with imaginings.'

Helena got up, began to clear dishes from the table.

Claire put a staying hand on her arm. 'That having been said, if Max's ghost won't let you rest, you'll just have to go to the source of your suspicions and play Mata Hari.' She suddenly grinned. 'And from the sound of it, that shouldn't be too difficult.'

'It's impossible.' Helena's voice cracked.

Claire scrutinized her carefully. 'As they say back at home in the USA, I think you've got it bad, sister. I've never seen you like this. Come on,' she squeezed Helena's shoulder, 'let's take it all over from the top. I haven't been listening carefully enough. And you're such an adept at hiding yourself.'

TWENTY-FOUR

IN THE DUSTY PINK GLOW of early evening, Manhattan rose from a curve in the road like some vast many-tusked beast with a thousand glinting eyes. A huge bloated greedy beast, who stripped the earth of its resources and whose days, like those of its kin – Tokyo, Sao Paolo, London – were numbered, Helena thought.

Nonetheless, seen like this, from a distance at night, the city never failed to work its magic on her. It was awesome, beautiful in the way that a great fire is, despite the havoc it leaves in its trail.

For the first time since she had promised James that she would attend Max Bergmann's memorial service, Helena was pleased that she had done so.

She had spent the last month in something of a twilight zone, a hazy world of indistinct shapes, never quite obliterated by the dark night of sleep or the bright clarity of day. It was like a waiting state, though she couldn't quite grasp what it was she was waiting for, except for the haziness to be dissipated.

She had worked of course, if anything more fiercely than usual. But it was more like a desperate holding on to what wasn't lost than a pleasure energetically engaged upon.

She hadn't returned to Germany. Claire's analysis of her suspicions had taken their toll on them, so that she mistrusted her own motives. And if Claire had latterly been vociferous in urging her to confront Adam Peters, to do *something*, anything, Helena had increasingly seen the impossibility of it all. From Adam, of course, there had been no word. She had hardly expected any.

The obituaries had appeared in two British papers and a score of American ones. Their collective weight, their unanimous assertion that Max Bergmann had died tragically in a boating accident, created a wall of right thinking which it now seemed impossible to scale. Then too, her enquiries into the sites that Max had photographed had rendered no clear clues. The photos might as well have been holiday snaps.

The cab curved round Columbus Circle and pulled up in front of the awning of the Mayflower Hotel.

Helena pushed her bills through the slot in the grimy plexiglass window which shielded the driver from her and waited for the door to unlock. In London the internal window denoted privacy; here, imprisonment. Nonetheless, the buzz and hurry of the street, the striking assortment of faces and styles and walk, was like an electric jolt and for a moment that ever-present internal haze seemed to disperse.

Helena hoisted her bag over her shoulder and went to register. James had had the room booked. Apparently several of the out-of-towners were staying here. She had done so herself once on a previous occasion, but was happy to see that this time her room was on the tenth floor and overlooked Central Park.

She gazed out of the window for a moment at the dark crests of trees and the graceful expanse of Central Park South. She would take a shower, then go for a stroll there, have a bite and tuck in at a reasonable hour so that jetlag didn't have her wide awake at three in the morning.

It was when she had returned to the hotel and was making her way through the restaurant that she heard a familiar voice.

'Helena Latimer, my angel of mercy, I thought it was you.' A man with dark curly hair and laughing brown eyes leapt up from a table and hugged her forcibly. 'But I wasn't sure. I've never seen you dressed as a woman.'

'Only when I'm in New York. Don't let it go to your head.' Helena chuckled.

Bumping into Rafael, the man who had entertained her all the way from Orion Farm to Boston, was like walking into a warm frothy bath after a month of cold showers.

'It isn't my head you have to worry about,' Rafael chortled. 'Now, sit down. I was just about to order and I can treat you to New York's hundred and first best dinner. And a good bottle of wine. It's the least I can do for my angel of mercy.'

'Now that sounds like a very good idea,' she smiled at him.

'Don't look at me like that, lady, or I won't vouch for your chastity. And I imagine we're both here on solemn business.'

They talked about Max, ate toasted goat cheese and sole in a lemon sauce, drank an exquisite Montrachet. The wine took its effect and Helena found herself telling Rafael about how she was still haunted by the notion that Max's death wasn't an accident. He listened intently, his mobile face mirroring her fears. When she had finished, he was quiet for a long moment.

At last he said, 'Well, it has all the makings of a good thriller. But we're dealing in the real, which is a very unfortunate genre. Even if Max was tipped overboard by the long arm of the big guys, you won't prove anything for years. If ever. Not that I would put a little high adventure beyond him. He was a cagey old soul.' He studied her face. 'Whatever the case, Helena, you musn't lose sleep over it. He'd scored a good many runs, our old friend, and at some point you have to strike out. Right?'

'Right,' Helena sighed. But she felt strangely better for having confided in a stranger. 'You're good to talk to, you know,' she smiled at him.

Rafael's eyes crinkled. 'I'm trying. But since you're kind enough to mention it, what do you say we retire for a little more conversation to the comforts of my suite. Oh yes, a suite.' He gestured grandly. 'Some loons have bought a film option on my last book and I'm a rich man for a week.' He winked at her humorously. 'There's a huge TV; we'll get the gremlins to bring up another bottle of wine. And I should tell you that I give the best back rubs this side of Fifth Avenue, not to mention the fact that I'm a really sweet guy.'

She was about to demur when she suddenly thought, why not? Why ever not? She liked Rafael, liked his quick gestures, the humorous face, the dapper air. One man to wipe away the memory of another who continued to haunt her.

'You've almost convinced me,' she said aloud.

'Only almost? Well, I always did like a gamble,' he grinned ruefully.

The suite was neither in the best of taste, nor the worst, but it was capacious and the TV as mammoth as Rafael had promised. On the desk next to a bucket of chilled wine lay a bulky typescript.

'Yours?' Helena asked.

'My latest. I'm just reading it through before delivering it to the most important man in my life.'

'Who is?'

'My agent, who else? Uh uh, no peeking. But I'll read you a bit, if you're very good.'

Helena sat down on the leather chesterfield and crossed her hands with a great show of primness. 'Good enough?'

'Better if you cross your legs as well. Inspiration.' He poured her a glass of wine, then cleared his throat with mock portentousness and began to read in a dry clipped voice.

'No one lived in the town of Shoobin, Missouri. Not any more. Not since Ebenezer . . .'

Helena listened, found herself smiling, beginning to giggle as a tall tale unfolded, filled with fierce satirical portraits and flights of incisive fancy.

He stopped after a few pages. 'Like it?'

She nodded. 'Very much.'

'Good,' he beamed, 'because this is the moment at which – according to the stories they told me when I was a mere novice – the ladies are supposed to fall before my feet, murmur genius, and raise their hands to the height of my phallic power.'

'I'm not the falling at feet kind.'

'No?' He glanced at her with overblown exasperation only to wink comically. 'Give us a little kiss in any case then.' He stretched his hand out to her and pulled her close.

Their eyes were on a level and he looked into hers intently as he stroked her hair back from her face. 'You're a very fine woman, my angel of mercy.' He kissed her lightly, tasting her lips, nibbling, as if the banter of conversation could now continue in a different mode. Then he let her go, smiled, refilled their glasses.

'I know a very good remedy for jetlag. All you have to do is kick off your shoes and stand right here in front of me. Promised you a rub, didn't I?'

He started to massage her shoulders, gently at first and then more deeply, his body wiry against her, his thumbs pressing into points of tension.

'You have nice hands,' Helena murmured.

'And as they say in the vampire films, you have a delicious neck.' He kissed her on the nape, wound his arms round her bosom, caressed.

It was pleasant, Helena thought from a long way away. Like being a child licked by tall grasses in a sunny field. He turned her towards him. His mouth now searched for hers, his tongue probed, too forcefully, as he pressed hard against her, rubbed. A shadow covered the sun. She felt cold, her skin clammy.

The shadow took on a shape. A face, hazel-eyed, lips curling in irony. No. She chased it away, held on tightly to the man in front of her, saw through the fuzziness of proximity his curly hair, the line of a brow.

He was unzipping her dress now, reaching for bare skin, manoeuvring her towards the couch. A taut light body covered hers. The shadow loomed larger, started to laugh bitterly, then turned away. Helena felt a gag rising to her throat.

'No.' She pulled away from Rafael. 'No, please, I can't go through with it.' Her voice broke with a sob.

'Hey, lady. That's not part of the code.'

'I know.' She was crying now. 'I'm sorry.'

'And what am I supposed to do with this straining erection?' he growled. 'Whoops, well it was a moment ago.' He smiled suddenly, ruffled her hair. 'You gonna tell me about it? I might be able to use it somewhere.'

Helena tried to smile through her tears. 'I don't know,' she mumbled. 'It's not you. It's me.'

'Well, that's a rare enough beginning. But I know it's not me. I'm the wunderkind of sexual sensitivity. Haven't you read my PR? So what is it?' His face was suddenly serious, as if he genuinely wanted to know.

Helena shrugged, 'I read somewhere recently that every sexual act, however new, brings in its train all others. Well, the baggage compartment was carrying the wrong luggage today.'

'I like it.' He took her hand, stroked it softly. 'Though I didn't have you pegged as Lady Broken Heart.'

'Just a little crack.' Helena grimaced.

He had a reflective look on his face, as if he hadn't heard her and was talking to himself. 'I guess I had you pegged as an early sexual awakening and early blotting out lady. All that surface sexiness and then you blow cold. Sex in the family does that sometimes.' He turned towards her. 'Now that's the version without the psychobabble. If you want the latter, it's a hundred dollars for a fifty-minute hour and the couch is right here,' he grinned.

'I think I'd better go,' Helena said uncomfortably.

'I wasn't suggesting you needed it.'

'Still friends?' Helena asked, realizing it was important to her.

'Of course. How could I say anything else to those wide velvety eyes? But watch who you try it on with again. This is some mean city.' He squeezed her hand. 'I'll see you tomorrow.'

Helena was crying again by the time she had reached her room. With a fierce gesture, she kicked off her shoes and sent them flying across the room. It was ludicrous. Her behaviour was ludicrous. The feelings which overcame her were ludicrous. She couldn't even sleep with a man she liked any more. All because of that duplicitous male who had taken a hold on her. And she had spent more time crying this blasted year than in the last ten put together. She was like some rudderless boat, the tears sweeping over her like storm waves, carrying her any which way.

Savagely, she unzipped her dress, was about to pull it off when she noticed a red light flashing on her telephone.

Message service, the notice beside the light said. She pressed the relevant number and heard a recorded voice telling her that an envelope was waiting for her downstairs. She was about to put her shoes on again when she thought better of it, dialled the porter instead and asked for the letter to be brought up.

Minutes later, there was a knock.

'Porter, Mam.'

He handed her a thick manila envelope.

Helena stared at it in consternation, then recognized James Whitaker's handwriting. She tore it open.

Inside there was a wad of typed sheets and a quickly scrawled letter.

Dear Helena,

Hoped to give you this in person, but you weren't in.

A request on bent knees. Please, please, will you say or read something at the service tomorrow? At the last minute we realized that there wasn't a single woman amongst the gathering of tributes. Typical, I know, and hideously late, but it only goes to prove that in Max's company you were a singular figure. I've already taken the liberty of adding your name to the program. Please don't take the lateness amiss. Things have been chaotic at this end, to put it bluntly.

We gather at ten forty-five at St John the Divine (on Amsterdam and 112th St).

I enclose a selection of possible material, which may or may not prove helpful.

Give me a ring before midnight on 212 427 6310. Or in the morning before nine thirty.

Until then.

Yours as ever,

James

ps Amidst the chaos, I forgot to forward the enclosed. About your prime suspect. I think you'll now agree that there was nothing there to go on.

Helena read through the letter twice with a sinking feeling. This, on top of everything else. She skimmed through the pages of photocopied poems: a lot of Walt Whitman; fragments of Thoreau's *Walden*. Finally, she was confronted by two sheets of paper headed by the name Adam Stephen Peters.

Reluctant to read them, she put them down on the night-table and prepared herself for bed. Only when she was ensconced beneath the cool sheets did she pick them up again, her curiosity winning over her sense that the last thing she needed, now that the moment for detective work had passed, was to immerse herself in the story of Adam's life.

The top paragraph read like a shorthand entry from *Who's Who*.

> B. Los Angeles, 1952. Father: Max Peters (b. Eberhardt), lawyer. Mother: Eva Levi Peters. Studies – Anthropology, UCLA (BA 1973); Stanford (PhD 1978). Fieldwork Amazon Brazil with Yanomamo Indians. University Posts: Berkeley, Princeton (Associate Professor). Mar. Samantha Grey, 1979. Div. 1982. 1 child Janey Augusta.

There followed abstracts, summaries of publications and a brief note on links with Green issues: nothing evident either pro or contra though the work with Yanomamo bordered on rainforest preservation.

Helena gazed at those three letters 'Div' with incomprehension and then started to laugh. The laugh was not unlike a cry. It echoed through her like great repeated gusts of wintry wind scattering the mouldiest leaves, revealing the naked brittle ground beneath. God, she was a fool. Her archetypal duplicitous male was a figment of her own prejudices. Not Adam, but in his place, a type. A type to prevent her from feeling what she had begun to feel, a barricade against emotion, against risk, a nascent need.

Within that barricade she could be strong, independent, a woman without baggage. Pierce the barricade and she shored it up with whatever came to hand, the sticks and stones and cobbles of more prejudice, of principles, suspicion, doubt – created a demon, even a murderer, anything to push away the emotion which threatened the tightly constructed armour which was her self.

But there were other selves than the smoothly functioning, well-oiled, quintessentially independent Helena Latimer. She had glimpsed them, even been forced to confront them over the last months. She couldn't control those so well and they leapt at her from the dark – the little lost girl looking for a father; the frightened brutalized child at odds with a sexuality which could only be assumed when it was contained, controlled. The yearning woman whom Adam had somehow found, awakened from the sleep of the senses.

With a shudder Helena switched off the light. In her mind she relived her relationship with Adam, saw how at every turn she had misconstrued, had behaved rudely, stupidly. She started mentally to compose a letter to him. But there were no appropriate words.

'I mistook you,' she could say, 'assumed you were married, were using me for a little light relief. I was too English or too stupid to ask.'

The words were at once trite and not quite true and they had at their base the premise that he would care, would want to see her again; while it was quite clear to her that if the roles were reversed, she would be filled with contempt for a man who had been at once so presumptuous and so ungrateful.

Helena slept. She dreamt.

She was in a rowing boat on a lake. The waters had the limpid clarity of turquoise. She could see the shoreline, the droop of willows with cascading leaves. There was a figure on the shore: a tall man with tousled hair. He waved to her. She recognized him in the gesture. Adam. She reached for the oars, but they had vanished and a wind came up tossing the boat, carrying her in the other direction. The gusts grew fiercer, created a whirlpool. She was cold. Cold and wet. A hand was dragging her down. She was drowning. Max was down there. She could see his face. Bloated, ghastly. Terrible.

Helena woke with a start. She was covered in perspiration. From the corners of the window blind, she saw a dim grey light. Suddenly a scene came to her from somewhere in her buried childhood. She must have been seven or eight. She had been sent home early from school for some reason. The house was quiet, seemed empty and she had walked up the stairs to her room to change. A voice beckoned from the bathroom. Dad.

'It's only me,' she called back.

He ordered her to him.

He was lying in the bathtub, his hair shiny from the water, little droplets clinging to his face and chest. She had never seen him naked before, had never seen that pink glistening thing sticking up from his middle above the line of the water, had never seen that strange expression on his face.

'Come in then. Time you had a wash,' he said to her and when she demurred, he growled out the word, 'Now!'

She had undressed quickly, seen from the corner of her eye how his hand was round that stick. When she tried to find a space in the lukewarm water where their bodies didn't touch, he pulled her down on top of him so that the stick was lying between her thighs, bright pink, throbbing, like the pig's snout snuffling in the trough when they had gone to visit the zoo. She drew her legs together to shut out the sight of it, only to hear Dad moan as if she had hurt him. Then he went very still.

She turned to look at him. His eyes were half closed, drowsy. There was something sticky on her thighs and scum rising to the surface of the water.

Dad passed her the face cloth, leapt out of the tub. 'Not a word about this to anyone, you hear? Not a word, or . . .' With a lunge he pressed her face into the water, held it there until she was certain she was drowning.

It was the drowning which had frightened her above anything else. The rest had made no particular sense until now.

Helena glanced at the digital watch on the night-table: five forty-eight. She rose slowly to shower away the night. Odd, that that memory had come back to her now. As far as she could remember, nothing of the kind had passed between her and her foster father again.

In retrospect, she realized that she had made certain she was never alone in the house with him. He was usually at work in any event. But he had never hit her, as far as she could recall, even though there had been bruising rows between him and Mum and he had walloped Billy over the ears often enough.

By six fifteen, Helena was sitting at the little desk and trying to decide if she should compose something for Max's memorial service or read one of the passages James had chosen. She was rather taken aback at the notion that she was to act as the token woman. Perhaps that was what she had been to Max, the token woman in the monastic circle he had created. It had struck her as odd before, this lack of women, yet she hadn't made much of it, only cherished her specialness.

The thought had never before crossed her mind that Max might have been homosexual, but now that it did, she rejected it. He seemed so far removed from things of the body that the question didn't raise itself with any credibility. He was old, after all.

But in the past, had there been anyone? Her preferred daydream took flight despite herself. Max and her mother, whoever she might have been. And after her mother, no one. Repentance. And redemption through asceticism.

Suddenly Adam's lecture came to mind, his attack on the language of loss and redemption, of sin and salvation. But Max belonged to that language.

Helena began to write.

'I first met Max Bergmann at a conference on the environment. He struck me as that rare thing: a being who was totally dedicated to, indeed a being who embodied, the very causes he stood for. He saw the planet as a vital organism, a vast feeling earth of which we humans were only one, if an important, part. Our role was to be its stewards, but more often we behaved as despoilers. And so Max flagellated us with the purist's cudgel, but just as often, I suspect, he wielded it stringently at himself.

'Over the years I came to see in him something of an ideal father, something of a saint . . .'

Helena wrote for over an hour, attempting to capture the essence of her experience of and encounters with Max. Then she crossed out, redrafted, managing even to incorporate one of the shorter passages from Walt Whitman.

The great granite and stone interior of St John the Divine reverberated with the mournful chords of Bach's Adagio in C. The nave was a sea of strangers, men in impeccable suits, fresh-faced youths, a smattering of elegant women, their brimmed hats shielding their eyes. Amongst their number in the front aisles, Helena recognized a few notables. She was grateful for James's presence next to her, his familiarity in itself a solace.

As the proceedings unfurled, tributes followed by music, followed by more tributes, Helena had a strange sense that Max was being taken away from her, becoming amorphous in the gathering tide of public respect. Her own comments, in comparison, seemed too personal, too intimate for this august gathering. But she persisted in them, her voice gathering in strength as the words she had written evoked Max's presence for her and this in turn made her brave, confident.

The words gone, so was he, dispersed into the great unfinished arches of the cathedral. Helena looked silently into the vast nave, found she was trembling, made her way back to her seat on shaky legs. In the sweep of music which followed she found herself feeling utterly alone, like a small child abandoned in a cavernous railway station; a child uncertain of its direction, afraid.

The sensation lasted only for a moment. The service over, she was swept off by James, then by Rafael, in a tangle of activity. But it left its residue, followed her home to London, to her house and her cats, made her aware that she now had to construct her life again stone by stone.

Instead of going straight into the office, she worked in the garden. It was a maze of May colour. Bright crimson clusters of tulip, sweet-scented narcissi, vied with purple azalea and a late-flowering cherry. Helena weeded and trimmed and tied, willing thought away, until the labour dispersed it of its own accord. In mid-afternoon, she rode her bicycle to Kensington Park and jogged until she felt she would drop. Then she turned her attention to her interior, hoovering and washing, clearing tables and desks of paper and bills and envelopes, throwing away and filing.

Order had to be created. A new order. With a little heave of the shoulders, she took a pristine blue folder, wrote the name Max Bergmann on it, and placed in it all his letters to her in chronological sequence, finishing with obituaries and finally the memorial service programme together with her own tribute. Only after she had done that did she go to bed.

The next morning, on her way to the office, she stopped in her favourite boutique on Kensington Church Street, found a dress in a vibrant electric blue with a matching fitted jacket, its shoulders slightly padded. She donned it straight away, pleased to see a different Helena looking back at her, at least from the mirror.

Her desk, when she arrived at the paper, was a clutter of post and magazines. But on its corner stood a glass vase, crammed with white tulips. Next to it there was a bottle of champagne, a bow round its middle.

Lynn and Carl hugged her in unison.

'We thought you needed a little brightening up.' Carl looked sheepish.

'At least a little,' Lynn chorused.

'But don't let it go to your head.' Carl cleared his throat. 'Editorial meeting, as soon as you've looked through your post.'

'Yes, sir,' Helena grinned. 'Do I have five minutes or ten?'

'Fifteen.'

Helena began to sift the post quickly – the usual run of press releases, invites to press conferences and television screenings; a personal note from the Director of Friends of the Earth which accompanied a set of papers on Ozone depletion. At the bottom of the pile, there was a package which looked as if it might contain a book. It bore no stamps. Adam's writing, Helena suddenly thought. Her heart skipped a beat. She tore it open with clumsy fingers.

Inside, there was a loose-leaf folder and a letter. It didn't bear her name or a signature and seemed to have been scrawled hastily.

> Since love's logic is no longer in question, truth may as well prevail.
>
> I hoped to give you the enclosed in person, since I'm here for the opening of the German Art Show. But I'm told you're away. I trust that's not a euphemism.
>
> Whatever the case, once you've read the enclosed, I think you'll understand why I may not have wanted to give it to you sooner or even at all. The sins of the fathers weigh more heavily on some than on others.
>
> The original of the enclosed arrived on the day before I learned of Max Bergmann's death. It was addressed to, 'Max, Seehafen'.
>
> It is Max Bergmann's journal.
>
> You know where I am should you wish to reach me.

'Fifteen minutes, Helena.' Carl's voice interrupted the last line of the note. She put it down. A flash of foreboding prevented her from lifting the cover of the folder.

She didn't do so until late that evening. It had been a long busy day, too full, and now she sat on the sofa, her feet tucked under her, a glass of milk at her side, the package from Adam on her lap. She read the letter once more, pausing on the first sentence. Her throat felt constricted.

No, love was no longer in question. How could it be after the way she had behaved?

She opened the folder quickly, was astonished to find a text in German rather than the English she had expected. The entries were sporadically dated.

Helena read, wonder and horror seizing her by turn. It was, she realized, the elusive link she had been looking for.

TWENTY-FIVE

Berlin – January 1985

I am here. Only half a city, but the half is a half too much. Like that half of myself.

I have known and not known for so long that the not-knowing merged with the knowing. I am the same man and have become another man who has forgotten the sameness. And not forgotten. For now that I am here in this clime as familiar and as foreign as the dreamscapes of She, *the language springs to my lips without my bidding.*

Why am I here? She *sent me here. That woman. She-who-must-be-obeyed. We used to call Bettina that secretly. That German woman in Oslo reminded me of her. She had her hectoring, implacable certitude. The-voice-that-must-be-obeyed.*

It began to come back then, random heavings of scenes long buried. The earth churning. As if the plateau of my life were a volcano newly awakened.

My life. Has it been my life? Or a figment in the dreams of that youth who vanished beyond the gates of the city?

Berlin – January

There was a boy in the woods near the house today. A slim blond youth in a brown cap. He had a bow and arrow in his hands. I followed him at a distance. As if I had been following myself.

The woods have grown smaller. The city has eaten them, tree by tree, a hungry careless beast that knows no predator.

The boy led me to the spot where we found the body. An ugly woman gashed out of life. I was happy that day: she was frightened. I could see she was frightened, as if her own death confronted her in that whore's body. My mother was a whore who respected nothing. She only knew how to seduce and how to laugh.

Berlin – January

Did I write those words? No. It was him. I could feel him inside me churning with hatred and furious indignation. Yet he was good. When he was with the group he was good.

Berlin – January

The school is still there, its bulk solid despite bombs. Perhaps they rebuilt it. I look into its windows and see myself looking out. I am dreaming. I dream of the open air, the whistle of the wind through trees. I am happy. Soon I will be with the group.

The group is a body composed of all of us. It doesn't matter if the names change. We melt into one another. We have no boundaries. Our arms are interlinked like the branches of a single tree and we gaze up into the stars. The stars are us. The sky is us. The earth is us. We have no boundaries.

I lived for the group. My being merged with it. Merged with the leader who was all of us, but better. Like the father I never had. My mother robbed me of my father. She killed him. I heard her say so once. She laughed one of her little laughs when she said it. But perhaps he wasn't my father. That was why she laughed.

In the group there are no guilts, no niggling individual fears. It cleanses us, makes us strong, bold, unafraid. The group does not listen to their reasons. Without the group I was at their mercy.

Berlin – January

She-who-must-be-obeyed never let me dream. Words and reasons poured out of her. Her mouth was like a beak endlessly pecking, churning up the earth, tearing at any flesh it contained, destroying.

Berlin – January

A boy at school sniggered and called the Führer, He-who-must-be-obeyed. We beat him up, left him, his nose bloodied, in a dark alley. We were cleansed, proud.

Laughter, Gerhardt once said, is permitted to the few, not the many.

Berlin – January

Why am I here in this dusty hotel overlooking a dingy blind alley?

A tiny scar on a man's cheek, a second Gerhardt. A crack which opened into a chasm.

And those sentences: 'The leader must be able to be alone and must have the courage to go his own way. But if he doesn't know himself, how is he to lead others? Every movement culminates organically in a leader, who embodies in his whole being the meaning and purpose of the popular movement.'

Over there I was a leader.

But do I know myself? I am learning.

Berlin – January

A gaggle of schoolgirls were skating in the park today, their giggles cluttering the air, taxing the snow's quiet.

That summer our group joined with a girls' group. We were no longer one, but at odds, each of us distinct in his carapace. One of them was sent to gather firewood with me. She chattered and giggled continuously. When we reached the riverbank, she caught me by the shoulders and brazenly stated, 'Give us a kiss, then.' She foisted her fat lips on mine before I could escape. Then she ran. If she hadn't run I might have hit her as I wanted to hit my mother each time she smothered me in her embrace.

Women cannot be led. They welter in their secrets, disturb, provoke. And they talk when they have nothing to say.

That summer, one of the boys quoted the custom of the Amahaggers, of killing off the old women in the tribe as an example to the younger ones. Men without women are free, he said.

Berlin – January

I am a hateful old man. And hate still lives inside me. I hadn't realized it still churned. This city of my childhood brings it back.

Berlin – January

I have stumbled on the clearing at the edge of the city. It was waiting for me.

It is still bounded by its trees, the single lopped oak at its centre. The city has not eaten it. They have put a picnic table at its edge.

Now I know why I am here.

The memory took me by surprise. So strong that I could smell the excitement and the fear. It bent me over double. I had to lie flat in the snow to get my breath back. But still it almost failed to come. I had to grab it by the throat and force it.

I had a brother once. A cousin technically, but a brother in fact. I bear his name: Max. I do not know by what act it has come to me.

In spirit and body, he was the incarnation of She-who-must-be-obeyed. Her creature. His father was nowhere in him. The father was kind to me. His was the kindness of the weak.

It was a few nights after Max had taken me to that den, a mire of filthy words, filthy thoughts, a democracy of filthy bodies. He wanted to cover me with that filth, pull me down into the polluted pit in which he lived. I loathed him. Germany would have become that vile pit, but for the strength of a few.

Can I still think that? History has a way of putting the lie to experience.

Gerhardt had rounded up the others, the nearest and dearest, four of us in all. We were to avenge my honour. Cleanse the nation of filth.

He – my cousin, my brother – was already known to them, as were various members of his cancerous cell. A Communist, a traitor against the nation, a swine, a believer in equality and licence. A degenerate.

The words ring hollow now. At the time they were fuelled by passionate vision.

We waited for him to emerge from the arms of his co-conspirators. The narrow street was empty, dark. We threw a blanket over his head and dragged him into the waiting car. We bludgeoned him when he struggled. He didn't struggle for long.

Gerhardt drove, his profile silver in the moonlight. He whistled something from 'Siegfried'. We didn't speak. We knew our parts. We were engaged on a heroic mission.

After the walk through the dark woods, the clearing emerged white, glistening, the snow untouched. We had our black hooded masks on then. We undressed Max, left him with only his shirt and pants, tied him to the trunk of the tree. The cord was thick around his middle. We lit two torches, placed them erect in the ground. The trial was set to begin.

Gerhardt carried out the interrogation, his voice strong amidst the silence of the stars. Did he believe in equality or blood? Was the Führer equal to Jew scum? Was he selling the proud German nation to the Slav hordes?

Max refused to answer. At each refusal, we jabbed and prodded him, each in turn, with our fists, our boots. The thuds rang through the night air like birds falling to the ground after a pigeon shoot. When my first kick landed in his groin and I felt his flesh give, I was filled with a frenzied excitement. That one was for Bettina, I thought, and with each subsequent punch or kick I vented my daily humiliations in that house where everything was soft and sickly except the shotgun verbiage of their reason.

Max had begun to cry out, 'Nazi swine, Nazi swine' over and over again like a chant. The blood was pouring from him. His hands flailed weakly. The shouts incited us. We ceased to wait for Gerhardt's questions. We simply hit and kicked randomly, until Gerhardt stopped us.

In the silence filled only with the harshness of our breath, he took one of the torches and flourished it over Max's body, brought it to rest inches from his face.

'Admit your crimes. Repent of your sins,' he said in a low voice.

Max said nothing.

Gerhardt seared his shirt, brought the torch closer to his face.

A single word burst upon the stillness, reverberated through the trees in a dizzying circle. My name. 'Leeeeeoooo.' Max was looking straight at me. His eyes dark, accusing. Then his head dropped on to his chest as if it had snapped, his body sagged.

I don't know why, but my stomach started to heave. I was retching. I ran, ran to the echo of my name, ran from the clearing, ran and ran until I could run no more and then I continued running. I ran from the knowledge. I had murdered my brother. The woods were aflame. Each tree bore his charred body.

I ran until there were no more trees and no more bodies. I ran until there was only a numb blankness.

Berlin – January

I was seventeen years old and I murdered my brother.

Are murderers permitted language?

I have not written for days.

My mind is empty. As empty as it was then.

I will die here.

Bavaria – January

The snow covers the ground. Two lines break its infinite expanse. To their side, the tracery of a bird's progress. Nothing else.

The snow has covered the markings. It falls thickly.

Bavaria – February

The church steeple is claret red. How does the frail white-capped cross at its peak withstand the wind? I am propelled by its gusts. I move through the landscape like a wraith.

I walk. I walk without a sense of time over a world of whiteness. I walk like a pilgrim in search of the excess that was my self.

Bavaria – February

I have found the farm. It sprang out at me from a turn in the path on the other side of a pine-strewn hill. A low-lying clapboard house with a red-tiled roof. Next to it a sloping barn. It is the farm and isn't the farm, just as I am and am not what I was then.

The house has freshly painted green shutters. The facade glows, each plank in place. The rickety structure I remember has been manicured and when I steal a look through the windows, I see a re-upholstered interior. Time has given it a new pampered life. Like me. But the old structure is still there.

When I knock, no one answers. But someone hails me from the barn, a young woman in jeans and sweater.

The barn is now a workshop. It has a kiln and rows of pots, russet red and deep blue, sometimes overlain with painted flowers. Shelves rise from where the cows used to lie. The woman thinks I have come to buy. She and her husband, she tells me, have moved here from Berlin and set up as artisans. I mention that I used to know the place many years ago and she offers to show me round, take me on a tour of their transformations. I prefer to be on my own.

I used to sleep in the barn. I had slept in many before, one indistinguishable from the next. The hay returned warmth to my body. There was only the hay and that prickly warmth. And the rich fetid smell of the cows. Sometimes they lowed.

Here the woman offered more than a cup of milk, an egg, a slab of bread, in return for coins or a day's work. Her son was in the army, her daughter had abandoned her for the city, her husband was dead. She needed a hired hand. I came cheap.

There were cows, a few pigs and chickens. There were fences to be mended and tiles to be repaired. When the snows melted, there was earth to be turned.

We worked side by side. She rarely spoke, was more mute than her animals, as silent as the earth we dug and as ageless, her face a mass of ruddy crevices. I worked and thought of nothing. I was moved from the barn to a tiny room in the house. It was colder here.

I cannot remember her name. Perhaps I never knew it.

On Sundays we went to the church with the slender steeple. I kept my eyes on the ground, slipped out before the rest of the congregation, shunned the village, escaped into the hills. I walked.

It was on one of those walks that I came across the house. It astonished me. I had had no idea that I was so close to it. The house where I was conceived. She had told me that. My mother.

I did once have a mother.

Bavaria – February

Once found, the house drew me like a magnet. I returned there every Sunday, slipped through the grounds unseen. The snows had gone by then and the earth squelched beneath my feet.

One day I saw her by the water's edge, a tiny figure, smaller than I remembered her. She was digging, planting flowers in a neat rectangle. For a moment, I had the eerie sense that the rectangle was a grave.

She turned and seemed to look straight at me. I held my breath. She was close enough for me to see the colour of her eyes: tawny. Deep and still, like an animal's. Like my own.

Bavaria – February

One night, after the silent evening meal of thick soup and bread we now took together, my peasant woman stood when I did and reached for my hand. Her touch was dry, gritty as crumbled earth on a hot summer day. She led me to her room. It was dark, a cave with shadowy outcroppings beneath the eaves. The only light was from the tallow candle she carried. She placed it on the window ledge, untied her apron, then let her thick skirt fall to the floor and stepped out of her clogs.

I wanted to bolt, but it was as if something had nailed me to the spot. She lifted the heavy eiderdown on the bed, then looked at me. For the first time I noticed that her eyes were a watery blue. She gestured me towards her and when I didn't move, she smiled so that I could see the gaps between her teeth. She came towards me, swiftly unbuttoned my trousers, pulled me towards the bed, down on top of her on that crackling mattress.

But for her hands she could have been part of that mattress. Her hands did something to my buttocks, to my penis, so that it arched and I found myself inside her, her crinkled, matted hair against the skin of my groin. She smelled of onions. I remember nothing else, except thinking that I was dying and was grateful for the death.

I had never been with a woman before. But I had seen them at it, seen my mother and that man who was not my father. It came back to me in those weeks as it comes back to me now.

My mother was on top of him, writhing, her blonde mane covering his chest. He was moaning, crying out. Good, I thought, she's killing him. His eyes opened and he looked at me with the stony gaze of a statue. I wanted to laugh.

But the next day, he was still there.

Coupling is a little murder carried out by women against men. They take you and they spew you out as children.

I wanted to die to merge finally and fully with the elements of which she was one. I went back to her whenever she signalled, but the final death refused to come.

The big murders are left to men.

Bavaria – February

In America I became a father without recourse to women. I reincarnated myself in my sons, replicated myself in the boys who came to me, clean, strong, their minds avid for the filling. Our only mother was mother earth. I taught them how to husband her, how to respect her riches. I achieved generation. They were part of me, their leader, their teacher, their father, and I part of them, my disciples, my sons. Women were extraneous, unnecessary.

Is this not a suitable dream for a Green Faust?

The laughter tears at me.

I had my Helena, too, saved from the waters. Pure as ice. Almost a boy. She knew how to listen, how to be silent, for all her beauty. It seemed to me that I could replicate myself in a woman. The ultimate feat.

Bavaria – February

I dared to confront the house with the twin domes today. Seehafen. My mother's house.

Except in patches, the grounds are overgrown. I wanted to get a scythe, a spade, restore their order. But there is someone living in the house. I could see that through the windows. I could also see the paintings. Those hideous paintings which make a mockery of man and nature, executed by her husband.

A man caught me looking through the windows. He was friendly enough. I told him I was a devotee of Johannes Bahr's work. He showed me round.

Bavaria – February

I have not been able to write for days. When today, I looked back over my last entries, I couldn't remember the act of penning them. Pages of detail to keep the presence of death at bay. Minute descriptions of the house, the terrain, in order to avoid the issue. All in English.

I had a sudden desire to send those pages to Helena. I have done so. It is strange how she seems clearer to me than all those others from my afterlife. Perhaps it is because I have been circling round a woman, so like and yet so unlike her. My mother. Today I must confront her.

The apples were already beginning to cluster like nuts on the branches when my peasant woman tersely announced that her son was about to return. I was glad. Those trysts under the eiderdown were beginning to disgust me. The small deaths had become harder to achieve. Her smell engulfed me for days, even after I had immersed myself in the stream's icy water.

I had no clear idea where I was going. But it didn't seem to matter. The journeying was all. She gave me a big round loaf and a hunk of cheese wrapped in a cloth. She said, 'Grüss Gott, *Max.' I still don't remember ever telling her that was my name. Perhaps she read it on my lips one night when I was dying.*

I found myself at Seehafen. I must have wanted to say goodbye to the house. It was early morning. The sun was just rising over the peaks. Everything was still, but for the chattering of the birds.

Sheltered by the trees, I walked across the grounds and came to the spot where I had seen my mother digging. A black stone jutted out of the earth. I saw his name there, etched in gold: Johannes Bahr.

So he was dead. I still remember the glee that knifed through me, as if an act of divine vengeance had taken place. The stone marked the place where degeneracy had met its end.

It was then that I heard the crackle of a twig, the light padding of feet. I crouched behind the shrubbery.

She was wearing some kind of white shift. Her hair gleamed in the sunlight like a golden mantle. I couldn't see her eyes, but her profile was pure as if nothing she had done had ever touched her. She bent towards the stone, embraced it. I could hear her murmur, 'Goodbye for now, Johannes. I'll be with you soon.'

She turned towards the lake and gazed out at it. She was only a few metres away from me and her voice reached me, distinct, without a tremor. 'Goodbye, Leo, my little one. Forgive me.'

I could have rushed out to her then, taken her hand. Could even have caught her shift as she waded into the water. Could have plunged in after her as she swam, reached her while she was thrashing, or even after she had gone down and the little whirlpool formed with its froth of bubbles. Could have towed her back, my arm under her chin as they had taught us.

But I did nothing. Simply stood there watching, as if I had grown thick tangled roots. I think I called out once, 'Mutti' *– at least my lips were arched in the shape of the sound.*

Then I was free. I ran.

Bavaria – March

They taught us to be strong, pitiless in the service of the nation. I was strong. I was pitiless. I was no one. Some ragged outcropping of a flinty mountain. I was a man. A hero with a stony stare. My darkness had no heart.

I was a murderer, twice over.

Austria – March

I don't know where I ran to. I can remember mountain trails and cold nights and a cave. I had never had a father, only ghosts with whom to wrestle. Now I had no mother. Like Parsifal's, she died when I left. I was free to be reborn.

When did the rebirth start? Had it already started? A rebirth from the ashes and water of a double death.

I must have gotten to Austria. I cannot recall a border or a crossing. But I was there, on a farm again, one farm after another. And then somewhere along the line, I must have acquired papers.

I recall a youth, my age, perhaps slightly older. We shared a barn. He was on a walking tour. He had come from Sweden. He gave me his name, his address, told me to come and visit him. He had sandy hair which fell over sea-blue eyes. Perhaps that was when the idea took hold of me.

The lying came easily. It was no longer even a lie. I had lost my papers. I acquired new ones. No one ever questioned anything I said. I always looked straight at them, particularly when I crossed borders. I must have crossed many for the next thing I can see clearly are the long days of the North.

I never looked up the youth who had given me his address. I worked the farms, gradually acquiring snatches of the language. Its strange music worked its way into me. But it was the silence which healed, the silence of those empty expanses. In it I was simply a pair of hands.

When the snows came, I found work with a forest ranger, a man with a gaunt face and steely eyes. We understood each other. Words were only used when there was need.

He taught me everything I know. He became my father. I learned to feel the land in a new way, to hear its murmurs, to shepherd its resources, to commune with its vastness. I began to see the intricate web which bound earth and stars and species.

One day, he told me he had nothing left to teach me. I must go off to the university, study soil engineering, forestry. I could come back to him in the holidays.

I listened, as I did to everything he said and gestured.

When I returned for my fourth summer, he was dying. He refused medicine, hospitals. Everything, he told me, had its term. I was with him when he died. I cried then as I had never cried for the others.

He left me his bible, his rifle, his skis, his jeep and his name. Bergmann. I took the first and the last with me to America. I lived a life in his image, austere, simple, touched by heroism. I sent my angels of purity out to rescue the planet from the ravages men like me have inflicted.

This is the only time I have looked back.

Bavaria – March

What does it mean to be a man? I have no single answer. I am perhaps too old for answers.

He was a man. The one who chose me as his son. He knew how to be alone, how to be at home in the world, how to be strong when nature demanded it, how to succumb when the end had come.

Hitler taught us how to be men too. Men bound in a group which allowed them to transcend the confines of their small selves. Men in pursuit of an ideal, strong, single-minded, capable of cruelty. The meek do not inherit the earth, let alone the nation. Though perhaps they inherit heaven.

But it was an excessive ideal, obsessed by obliteration. It had no respect for the fine balances which nature demands, even in its violence.

Yet I understand again the need it filled in us: the need for service, the need for purity, the need for meaning unbounded by the meagre limits of our daily lives.

As I write them, the words disperse before my eyes. Lies, like the flimsy veils of my life, hiding what I was unable to confront.

A murderer in the service of nothing but my petty vengeance.

Bavaria – March

I am still here. The place draws me in like a vortex, its centre radiating magic. From my tiny window, I can see the sloping roof of the pines, and in the distance the glimmer of the lake where I let her die.

What does it mean to be a woman? Since the surfeit of my childhood, I have spent so little time in their presence that I really do not know. Then they were clammering beaks, arms which smothered like waxy feathers, hot treacherous smells. My head in clouds of song and story, I escaped them. The stories sang of their ineffable purity or their traitorous sexual magnetism. I was happy to sing along, though the experience was not mine.

Does the violence some men enact on women find its core in a sense that their own murder, their own death, lies in women's sexual power? So the proposition becomes: their death or mine. I have only gone to women when I wanted to die. My violence was all in the past, buried with that first life.

I have always preferred sameness, homogeneity. Difference was what separated me from the plant and animal spheres. Here I worshipped diversity. Is it that which marks me as a creature of the time and place I left behind me like an outworn mask?

Bavaria – March

In the village where I go for my few supplies, an old chattering woman mentioned the Eberhardt house to the shopkeeper. It is the second time I have heard the name. I have a faint recollection of writing it down. Did I send a letter to Bettina? The past is clearer to me than the present, except for the tang of the pines.

Trust Bettina to outlive us all. She was always the strongest. I should have been born a woman. Like that girl, Helena. She defended me from that latter-day incarnation of the-voice-that-must-be-obeyed.

Will I see her again? I think not.

I have sent her some pictures to remember me by.

Bavaria – March

I dreamt of an apocalypse. A great flood wiping the earth clean of its parasites, leaving behind only the peaks, the highest pines.

I walk. I read Hölderlin. I gaze out at the lake. I wait for the end.

I will visit the house one more time. It beckons to me like a cave replete with hoary secrets.

Bavaria – April

I have been to the house again. The visit has rendered me wordless until now.

All the veils have fallen from my eyes. Her fire has burned them away. Anna's fire. My mother's fire. The fire of love. It has shown me that it is I who am the chattering monkey, the shivering beast, a mere parody of a man. Nothing more.

I am not the hero reborn from Max's ashes, the leader battling for the regeneration of the Green world, the murdering saint who engaged on a dark night of the soul and a life of atonement. Yes, yes, even if I may have had the humility not to write them down, those images have all played before me.

But now I know. I am less than nothing: an arrogant parading youth strutting his hours on a tawdry stage, juggling with outworn images even as he and they crumble into senility.

I read my mother's words. Her book. She understood me better than I understood myself. She understood my visceral loathing of women. My panic. My desires. Yet, she loved. She forgave.

Max was not murdered. Even that act of mine was a charade. Yet he never told them of my act. His silence is a greater accusation than any other.

Max was not murdered. I am not Max. I am no one.

To lie one has to know truths. I had none. I have none.

It is time to make an end.

The child will be my boatman.

The waters will enfold me.

I come. Mother, I come at last.

TWENTY-SIX

CRIMSON AZALEA CLUSTERED by the sides of the road. Beyond, the rhododendrons were a mass of colour, pinks and purples and scarlets resting on glossy greens as if there had never been a winter. The countryside had become a garden. Through the density of the foliage, the lake was invisible, a memory rather than an existing landscape.

Perhaps she shouldn't have come. Two months had passed since she had last been here. Two long months in which her world had been transformed. She might have left it too late.

Helena hesitated before turning the car slowly into the drive at Seehafen.

She had written to Adam, of course, to thank him for sending her Max Bergmann's journal, had added that she would like to discuss it with him one day.

Everything else had been left unsaid. She hadn't told him how the horror of the journal's revelations had made her feel that the foundations on which she had constructed her life over these last years had been undermined. Neither had she told him how the very existence of the journal in Adam's hands had finally assuaged all her suspicions about his actions. Nor had she said how it saddened her that love's logic no longer prevailed between them.

She hadn't, in fact, been anything more than formally polite. Yet some small part of her had waited for the response that never came.

The greater part had had more pressing business. How to come to terms with the fact that Max wasn't Max? That the man she most admired had been a fascist who had set out to murder, a man whose saintly identity was a fabrication? What implications did that have for the crusade he had led and of which she had felt herself part? Did his person tarnish everything she believed in, all the principles she had always assumed they held in common? And what of her vaunted instincts?

It was almost as if she had been seduced and betrayed. And it was Max who was the seducer, not Adam, whom she had so hastily cast in that role.

On the pretext of a story, she had gone to spend a few days at Greenham Common. The women's vigil at the cruise missile base seemed a suitable site for reflection. A suitable site too, for purging herself of her shame – the shame of her association with Max.

As she marched up and down with her placard in front of the wire mesh fence and stared directly into the guards' eyes, she wondered whether she had fallen prey to an apocalyptic mind set which turned thought to frenzy and saw disasters in everything: from cigarette smoking to industrial pollution; from the massacring of seals to cruise missiles. Was the desire to control the bad simply the desire to control?

The state Max had once believed in had championed purity and nature, as she did. Adam had lectured her on that.

It was one of the things that had prevented her from coming to Seehafen sooner – the thought of the contempt he must feel for her, with her overweening admiration, her near obsession with a man who was a wholesale fraud.

Helena pulled into the drive. The chestnuts were in bloom, covering the lane with a lush shade she didn't recognize. The house was almost obscured by them and for a moment she was filled with a fear that no one would be there, a ghostly paradise abandoned by its key players, nothing remaining of them but a grave.

She should have written to announce her arrival. She hadn't. She had been a little afraid that he wouldn't want to see her.

After her sojourn at Greenham Common she had returned to London chastened, but at least still certain of that particular cause. Yet her depression didn't lift. For the first time in her life, she found it difficult to put sentences together on a page. Her syntax unravelled before her eyes; her words sprang out at her with an opposite meaning. She was tempted to ask for leave, but she didn't dare: the thought of not having an office to check into filled her with trepidation.

In the midst of it all, a man whose name she didn't recognize rang her from New York. He was a publisher. He wanted to launch a new eco-magazine. He had read her work, had heard her at Max's memorial service. And she had been recommended to him not only by Max, but by his friend Rafael Santucci. He was coming to London and he wanted to talk to her about the magazine.

After their second meeting, after they had talked for the length of two evenings about markets and format and content, he had offered her not simply a job, but the post of editor, an opportunity, as he put it, to think through an entirely new and radical publication.

It was as if a window had opened on a stifling room overburdened with heavy furniture to let in a fresh breeze.

But the room was still in disorder. Helena had asked for a little time to think it over. It was while she was thinking that she realized she had to see Adam, whatever his feelings for her. He was the only one she could talk to about Max. The journal, it now occurred to her for the first time, had as many implications for him as it did for her. After all, it was his family history.

Then too she wanted to re-read Anna's Book so that she could get Max's – or should she say Leo's – story straight.

There was no second car in the drive and as she slammed the door of hers, Helena was suddenly filled with dismay. She really should have written or had the courage to pick up the telephone. Then in the distance she heard the distinct sound of a laugh. It was quickly followed by the sight of a little girl in jeans and sweatshirt who came dashing out of the shrubbery. She stopped short when she saw Helena.

The flaming mass of hair was unmistakeable.

'Hello.' Helena tried to keep the quiver out of her voice. The child would soon be followed by her mother. But she bent to the girl's height and put out her hand. 'I'm Helena. I'm a friend of your father's.'

The child touched her hand hesitantly with her own grubby one. 'I'm Janey,' she said solemnly, adding with a burst of excitement, 'We just found a hedgehog. Come and see.' She tugged Helena along and then, remembering herself, put a finger to her lips and announced in a stage whisper, 'Have to be quiet. Not to scare it.'

'Okay,' Helena murmured.

She followed the child along a path which led to the midst of the rhododendron grove. A man in light trousers and blue shirt was standing half-hidden by glossy leaves. He turned as they approached. She would have recognized that craggy senatorial face anywhere.

He looked at Helena with evident surprise, then pointed Janey towards the thick of the bushes. The child sprawled down on her stomach and wriggled snake-like along the ground.

'It's asleep,' she proclaimed in a loud voice after a moment, then quickly repeated the words in a whisper.

'Not for long.' Max Peters winked at Helena.

She peeked through the bushes, saw a small prickly form curled into a ball of non-existence.

'Perhaps if we got it a bowl of milk, a few snails or caterpillars, we might tempt it into action,' she murmured to Janey.

'Okay.' The child leapt up. 'I'll get the milk. You get the snails.' She screwed her face up with evident disgust and raced off.

'Afternoon's work cut out for you,' Max Peters laughed, then stretched his hand out. 'I'm sorry. I haven't said hello.'

Helena smiled. 'You probably don't remember, but we've met before, Mr Peters.'

'I do, now that you mention it. Ms Latimer, isn't it?'

'Helena, please.'

'I trust you haven't come all this way to interview me, Helena?' He gave her a sardonic glance.

Helena flushed despite herself. 'No, no. I had hoped to find your son.'

'So the two of you have met now?'

The flush wouldn't go away. But she let the question pass. 'Is he here?'

'No.' Max Peters was studying her.

'Oh, I'm . . .'

'But he should be soon.'

'Is it all right to wait?'

'I can't imagine how you'd get away with anything else.' He gestured down the path towards an encumbered Janey. She was balancing a carton of milk in one hand and a bucket in the other.

'Got everything,' she said proudly, 'and a bucket for the crawlies.'

'Let's get to work then,' Helena grinned.

It was while they were foraging in flowerbeds for snails that Janey suddenly leapt up and dashed away.

'Daddy, Daddy, I didn't hear you. We found a hedgehog.'

Helena turned and saw Adam lifting the little girl off the ground, throwing her up in the air, holding her close. She stood up, feeling uncomfortably like an intruder on an intimate scene, brushed off her dress.

'Not quite the garment for a snail chase.' Adam was staring at her.

'Hello, Adam.'

'But we've collected lots, Dad.' Janey wriggled out of her father's arms. 'Look!' She thrust the bucket at him.

'So I see.' He focused on the child.

'Now, we're going to make a nest for hedgehog out of leaves and things. Then we can come and visit him every day.'

'And what if he already has a nest?'

Janey looked at him in consternation, then up at Helena. 'Ours will be better, won't it?'

'I hope so,' she murmured.

'Come on, then.' The child tugged at Helena's hand. 'It's under the rhodos, Daddy. We left it some milk already.'

'I'll help you make the nest, Janey.' Max Peters had just rejoined them. 'I suspect Helena has come here to see Adam, not to play with hedgehogs.'

The child looked with sudden suspicion from Helena to her father. 'But she said she would and . . .'

'Janey.' Max Peters was firm.

'Of course, it'll be hedgehogs first,' Adam intervened. He didn't look at Helena as he reached for his daughter's hand. 'It'll only take a few moments. And Ms Latimer has always believed in nature first.' He raced ahead with Janey.

'My son has left his manners in the city, I fear.' Max Peters walked beside Helena. 'We've only been here for a week and he's devoted to the little one. He's missed her terribly. It would perhaps have been better if you had come after bedtime.'

'Yes.' Helena swallowed hard.

'Are you in Germany for your newspaper?'

'Not really.' Helena took her courage in hand. 'I wanted to talk to Adam about Max Bergmann.'

He shot her a quick assessing look. 'Unfortunate business, all that.'

From his flat tone, Helena couldn't determine whether Adam had shown him the journal or not. It occurred to her for the first time that Max Peters would be more disturbed by it than any of them. In fact, it had been addressed to him. What a near-sighted fool she was becoming.

They had reached the grove. Adam and Janey were crouching by the spot where the hedgehog had been sited. Adam was loosening the earth with a twig.

'Is this the right way?' the little girl called to her.

Helena stooped. 'A perfect start.' While they were collecting snails, she had explained in great detail to the child how to construct an attractive nest.

'You've made fast friends in my absence.' Adam looked up from the ground and suddenly smiled at her with such warmth that the colour rushed into her cheeks.

'Helena knows everything about hedgehogs,' Janey proclaimed seriously.

'I can't say I'm surprised.'

'Now for some dry leaves – and some hay, if we can find it.'

They scrabbled round for leaves, coming up with only a few handfuls.

'I shouldn't have done so much tidying,' Adam grinned. 'We could try the compost heap round by the stables.'

'I'll tell you what, Janey,' Max Peters suggested, 'you and I could walk over to Frau Berta's. We said we'd come and look at the horses. And there's bound to be hay there.' He looked meaningfully at his son.

'Horses!' Janey was full of enthusiasm. She took her grandfather's hand without so much as a backward glance, only remembering to call out after a moment, 'See you later.'

'My daughter loves horses.' Adam looked after them with a bemused expression.

'So I see.'

Silence fell between them, stretched itself so that the absence of speech became palpable. The chattering of birds grew disproportionately loud. When Helena dared to glance at him, he looked sullen, leaner in those pale jeans than she remembered him, rugged, somehow more dangerous. The eyes in the tanned face were unusually hard.

Finally he made a move and they walked desultorily, still without speaking, towards the house.

The living room, devoid of Johannes Bahr's paintings, was strangely bare, despite the warm pinks of chairs and rugs, the mellow light pouring through the windows. Adam didn't ask her to sit, simply stared out at the grounds.

'I wanted to see you, Adam. I know I've behaved badly, contemptibly. But I wanted to talk,' Helena blurted out at last.

'You took a little time over it.'

Helena swallowed. 'Don't make it harder than it is, Adam.'

He veered round. 'You don't look as if it's been very hard.' His eyes skirted over her.

Helena smoothed the fabric of the electric-blue dress she had bought on her return from New York, then perched at the very edge of an armchair. 'Surfaces deceive,' she said softly. 'I should know. I was taken in by them.'

Silence covered them again. He paced for a moment, then sat down opposite her. 'All right, where do we begin?'

She could read the anger in his eyes. She didn't know what prompted her then, but she touched his hand and said first of all, hurriedly, as if to get that initial misapprehension out of the way, 'I thought you were married.'

'I have been.' His expression didn't change.

He didn't understand, Helena thought, aghast. Or perhaps he no longer cared about what she thought, what she felt. She was suddenly incensed. 'I have principles about these things, you know. I try not to double-cross my sisters.'

Adam's gaze was blank.

'I thought you were lying. Deceiving me.' She had started to babble. 'I saw that picture of the three of you. Of Janey and her and I thought . . . Oh, what does it matter what I thought?' She leapt up, turned away from him. The stupid tears were biting at her eyes. She stared out the window, tried to blink them away. She should never have come.

'Helena, may I kiss you?' His voice was suddenly soft behind her.

She nodded, yet felt unable to confront him. His lips were on her hair. He turned her in the circle of his arms and kissed her, tentatively at first as if they had never tasted each other before and then more searchingly, deeply, so that when he finally let her go she neither remembered why she had come nor why she had ever left.

She gazed up into his eyes. They were laughing now, teasing.

'What I like about you is the way you live up to your principles.'

'You're *not* married?' She stared at him, suddenly apprehensive again.

'Haven't been for three years, longer unofficially.'

'What do you mean then?'

'When did you begin to think I was married, Helena?' He drawled the words.

She flushed. 'After that first night. I . . . I couldn't help myself the next time. I . . . you . . .' she stumbled.

He smiled at her. It was a tender smile. He ruffled her hair. 'That's precisely what I like about your principles. They give way to life. Sometimes, at least.'

'Don't laugh at me, Adam. I'm not feeling very strong about my principles.'

He kissed her again. She was flying.

'I've been such a fool,' she murmured into his lips.

'That makes two of us. I could never manage to keep you here, talk to you, without this getting in the way,' he stroked her face, 'without him getting in the way either.'

'Max?'

He nodded. 'When you came, after his death, I wanted to protect you. Couldn't bear the thought of your hopes for a father disintegrating in Max's journal. I thought you'd hate me for being the twofold purveyor of bad news. And the nephew of a Nazi to boot. But you hated me already.' He drew back from her.

'I didn't.' Helena shook her head adamantly, wanting his warmth again. 'I was just suspicious, didn't trust you, because of . . .' She waved her hands at a loss. 'I thought you knew things, were somehow implicated in his death. You did know things, but not what I thought.'

He was gazing out the window now. The sun had begun its slow descent behind the mountain peaks.

'Did I look as if I needed protection?' Helena asked, not sure whether she had liked the sound of that.

'You did. To me. Then.' He shrugged, then turned to confront her. 'When did you find out? About my divorce, I mean?'

'Just before I received the journal. When I was in New York. I'd asked James to have you checked out,' she said, ashamed.

'And you waited all this time? Over a month?' There was astonishment in his voice and something else. Indignation.

'I . . . I didn't think you'd care after . . . after the way I'd behaved. My stupidity.' She gestured helplessly. 'And I had to sort things out. About Max. About what it meant.'

'And is it all sorted now?' His eyes were suddenly black. He reached for a cigarette.

She shook her head. 'That's why I came.'

'For Max? For Leo, I should say. For him again. Even now that you know!'

'Not only that.'

'Not only that,' he echoed her.

She stepped towards him, met his eyes, the tears biting at her own.

'Do you care, Adam?'

He turned away from her, walked blindly towards the drinks cabinet, poured them each a whisky without thinking.

He had wanted her for so long and had talked himself out of her for so long, that he was loath to let either desire or pain run away with him again. The kisses, the passion, whatever it was that her body, her emotions seemed to convey, meant so little to her, that she had been ready to throw them away without even bothering to ask him directly about his wife and marriage. As if what they had experienced together were just so much flotsam and jetsam thrown up by the tide, rather than the sea of life itself. And there it was, she had only to walk into the room and he was caught up in the rhetoric of romantic excess.

No, this time he had to temper it until he knew with a greater certainty. And the timing was so bad. Janey had just arrived, he was so enmeshed in her. And his father. All those shadows from the past to be confronted, re-examined.

He handed Helena the whisky, willed his eyes into neutrality. She had that deceptively vulnerable look which came over her from time to time. He remembered it too well. But each time it was he who had ended by needing the protection.

The sun had clambered behind a distant peak, leaving streaks of pink and pale yellow in its wake like a glorious memory.

'Will you stay?' he asked.

'If I may, if it's not difficult.'

He hesitated visibly.

'There's plenty of room. It's only . . .'

There was a knock at the door.

'Only?' Helena prompted him.

Elsa came in. Her hair was cut smartly short and in what was evidently a new flowered frock she looked distinctly pretty. She smiled at Adam shyly, glanced at Helena in surprise and then with faint recognition. 'Will you be having an early supper with the little one, Herr Peters, or . . . ?'

'Early, please, Elsa. You remember Fräulein Latimer?'

The girl nodded. 'Four places?'

Adam looked at Helena. 'You'll stay?' he asked without enthusiasm, almost rudely.

Helena swallowed. 'No, no. I don't want to intrude. I'll find a hotel. I have the car.' She pretended cheerfulness.

'Are you sure?'

She bit her lip, nodded.

'Three then, Elsa. In the conservatory.'

The girl closed the door behind her.

'Elsa's staying in the cottage. She seems much happier. Brighter, too.'

'Evidently.' Helena turned away. She had a sudden suspicion that there were more reasons for that than instantly met the eye.

'Helena.' He touched her arm. 'It's not that I don't want you to stay. It's just . . .'

'That it's inconvenient. I know. I should have forewarned you.' She was blithe.

'We can talk . . .'

'Tomorrow,' she finished for him.

There was a burst of noise in the hall and suddenly Janey came racing into the room. 'I've been on a horse. I rode a horse, Daddy.' She leapt into her father's arms.

'That she did.' Max Peters was just behind her. 'And we've collected enough hay for a dozen hedgehogs.' He looked at Helena humorously.

'Tell us all about it, Janey.' Adam's eyes were only for his daughter. He stroked back the mass of flaming red hair from her face, wiped a streak of grime.

That's what it meant to have a father, Helena suddenly thought.

'Well, first . . .'

'Well, first, you go off and have a bath, young lady, and get your dad to make you spic and span for dinner. I need a little adult conversation.' Max Peters winked at Helena.

'Good idea.' Adam patted her on the bottom and shooed her away. 'Gramps has had quite enough of you for one day.'

'*He* went on a horse, too. His was black and big as a mountain with a fat tail. Mine . . .'

Max Peters poured himself a drink and sank back into an armchair. 'She's a lovely child, but she has a little too much energy for a man of my years.'

'I can't believe that,' Helena demurred.

'In another week, she'll have exhausted Adam's as well and we'll have to find her playmates of her own age. It's always like this. For two weeks, he can't have enough of her and then things settle down to a more usual pace.'

'Like a love affair,' Helena muttered before she could stop herself.

'Like and altogether unlike,' Max Peters eyed her shrewdly, 'though, I must say, you hadn't struck me as the cynical kind, Ms Latimer.'

'Helena, please.'

'Helena, of course.' He sipped his drink. 'It's one of the eventualities of divorced lives, I guess,' he continued as if she hadn't spoken. 'Still, I'm rather pleased that Adam is a man who is interested in his child. My daughter, on the other hand, manifests an altogether remarkable disinterest,' he chuckled. 'So I guess we can conclude that interest in one's children is neither gender-based nor a matter of genes, nor perhaps even of early family formations and deformations, though the last remains a little imponderable.'

He cleared his throat and Helena had the distinct impression that he was trying to tell her something.

'Janey seems a lovely child,' she said a little inanely.

'She is that.' He paused, glanced out of the window for a moment and then straight back at her as if he might catch her unawares.

'My son tells me that he sent you a copy of the journal Max Bergmann, or should I say Leo Adler, directed to this house before his death. The two of you seem to be closer than I'd imagined.'

Helena swallowed. 'Circumstances brought us together.'

'And was it the same circumstances that led you to interview me?'

'In part,' Helena stumbled, unsure of his sense. She had a feeling she was being interrogated. 'But not really. I had no idea that Max Bergmann was . . .'

'No, of course not.' He took another sip of his whisky, then abruptly turned that jagged senatorial face on her. 'You should know that I am not pleased that my son sent you the journal. It is a family matter and like most family matters intensely private.'

Helena flushed at the implication. 'You don't believe that I would publish the story?'

'I would hope not,' he scrutinized her, 'but I don't know you very well and journalists sometimes think they have a duty . . .'

'You mean a duty to expose Max Bergmann as a Nazi. A fraud, a fake, a deceiver?'

'There you are wrong.' He was definitive, almost, she thought, angry. 'Max Bergmann was not a fraud, except for the small matter of a change of name. I have read his books over the years and they are a direct progression of what he believed in as a youth. In fact I would characterize him as a Peter Pan. All those attempts to recreate those boyhood summer camps, those idylls of boys alone together, pure in the wild, and turn them into a way of life in America, a country so different. Bah, it's a farce. He hadn't read his Marx, or he would have realized that. You remember Marx's insight about historical repetition? The first time the great events may appear as tragedy. The second time they can only be farce.'

He seemed to be carrying on an argument with himself.

Helena looked at him open-mouthed. 'When I asked you in California whether you knew of Max Bergmann . . . ?'

'Permit me my little deceptions. I thought it simpler at the time not to engage in philosophical discussion.' He gave her a charming smile. 'No, I have known of Max Bergmann for many years.'

'Known that he was . . .

'My cousin? Yes. My mother was the one to spot him. She saw his photograph in the paper. Sometime in the sixties, I think it was. She went to hear him lecture, came back and announced in great excitement that she was certain she had discovered Leo. Asked me what I wanted to do about it. I wanted to do nothing. As I want to do nothing now.'

Helena began to pace, her hands locked tightly behind her back, so that she would resist the sudden unnerving temptation to bite her nails.

'I don't understand. He tried to kill you.'

'Bah. Adolescent pranks. Of a particular nastiness, I grant you. It was a violent time. But Leo wasn't evil, just deluded, resentful, his head in the clouds, more a victim of the propaganda of his times than one of its inane heroes. The proof is that I am here. He was not altogether up to the violence he worshipped.' He spread his arms in a grand gesture. 'Nor would the Nuremberg Trials have had anything to accuse him of.'

'Did you ever check him out?' Helena murmured.

He nodded. 'My mother insisted. She thought I was erring on the side of generosity. Or perhaps simply trying to repress buried hatreds. God knows, we all had enough of them. So I eventually managed to ascertain that Leo had arrived in Sweden in 1936. It wasn't that difficult. We tried a permutation of names. He used Leinsdorf,' Max Peters chuckled. 'He had always had a predilection for the aristocratic side of the family.'

'And you never went to see him?'

He smiled ruefully. 'I was never quite generous or brave enough for that. Though I did accompany my mother to a lecture once. The usual high-sounding patter, the rhetoric of prophecy. Can I get you another drink?'

Helena nodded.

It had grown darker as they talked and he switched on the table lamps before handing her her glass.

'I still don't see how you can be so moderate about it all.'

'A frenzied man of seventy would be a distinctly comic figure, my dear. Passion is for the young.'

'By that logic, I should expose your cousin.'

'Touché, Ms Latimer. But I hope you too will in this be moderate.' He looked at her severely. 'All it would result in is the glare of publicity for my family. We would all suffer for it, personally, I mean.'

'And you think Max Bergmann did nothing wrong?'

'In law, under the name Bergmann? Nothing. Or no more than any other self-styled guru.' He gazed at her astutely, then shrugged. 'I am a great believer in the rule of law, Ms Latimer, and in freedom of expression. Though not in vengeance or the sliding logic of morality. I have also come to believe that that particular chapter in European history is best buried, at least on an individual level. Otherwise, we shall all be at each other's throats again avenging historic wrongs, engaging in blood feuds. Which is why I would be prepared to attack Max Bergmann's ideas and yet not expose Leo Adler as a Nazi youth. You are quite free to disagree with me, of course,' he smiled. 'My son seems to now. My mother certainly did, though only for a short while.'

'What did she disagree with you about?' Adam had just come into the room, a freshly scrubbed and pyjamaed Janey in his arms. He frowned at his father and gave Helena a suspicious glance.

'Oh, nothing important. Is it time for dinner?'

'I'd better get going.' Helena rose.

'Aren't you joining us?' Max Peters asked.

'No, that's very kind of you.' Helena smiled at him brightly. 'I need to find a hotel.'

'But . . .'

'I've booked you a room,' Adam intervened, 'at the Waldheim, you remember, where we once ate? It's only a few minutes away. First right, then carry on for three kilometres and it's on your left.'

Max Peters looked from one to the other of them and shook his head in evident disapproval.

'I wanted Helena to tell me another story about hedgehogs,' Janey suddenly blurted out.

'Tomorrow.' Helena smiled at the child.

'Promise?'

She nodded.

'And we'll continue our conversation then.' Max Peters shook her hand. 'Though why you can't stay here, I . . .'

'Goodbye.' Helena waved at them. She let herself out the door without meeting Adam's eyes.

Under the twinkling stars of a balmy summer night, the hotel seemed less of a gothic monstrosity than she remembered it in the driving rain of February and more like a Hollywood set. Her room was capacious. Even the regal four-poster bed and the giant tapestry with its medieval lady and stylized apple tree did nothing to dwarf it.

Helena looked out of the window, saw a small terrace and opened its doors to let in the night air. She stepped out. Below her, just above the little brook, was the very spot where she had hallucinated Max, dreamt a father. She scoffed at herself.

Adam had been kind that day. Too kind. Now he had lost all patience and all interest in her. She could hardly blame him, had hardly expected anything else. There was a kind of justice in it. She had been too busy stumbling through the realm of shadows to recognize what was close at hand.

With a shake of the head, Helena went in to shower and changed into a summery black evening dress with thin shoulder straps which she had packed with heaven only knew what fantasies in mind. She dabbed on some pale eye shadow and bright lipstick, brushed her hair till it shone, and draped a shawl over her shoulders.

'Always look your best,' she suddenly heard Emily's voice, 'and hum a little tune to yourself. It's a great pick-me-up. Particularly Mozart. That's what my grandmother used to say.' Helena gave herself a watery smile. She would have done far better to keep Em's voice clear in her mind than succumb to Max's more seductive tones.

The dining room was crowded: men in trim suits sitting opposite bejewelled women with gleaming hair, merry parties with hearty voices. She was happy that the desk clerk had thought to ask her if she would be wanting dinner. A little table was waiting for her by the windows. There was a single rose in a slender glass vase at its centre. The silverware sparkled.

Perhaps after all, it had been a good idea to come down here and not to be trapped in Adam's rejection. Yet he had kissed her. The glossy menu slipped from her fingers.

As it fell, she met a man's stare. He was sitting alone diagonally opposite her some tables away. The intentness with which he was looking at her made her think for a moment that she knew him, but the thin elegant face, the jet-dark eyes, the sleek black hair were decidedly unfamiliar. Helena studied her menu again, ordered a spinach salad, poached salmon, a glass of wine, gazed out of the window at the shadows of trees, the refracted candlelight.

Within moments, the waiter was back, bearing a silver bucket. From it he drew a half bottle of Dom Perignon. She was about to protest when he signalled at the sleek-haired man opposite, popped the cork and poured the champagne into a crystal flute. The stranger raised his glass to her.

Helena gave him the coolest smile she could manage and giggled inwardly. A male from another world, or he wouldn't have dared.

He stared at her through the length of her first course and when inadvertently she met his eyes, he smiled a little and nodded as if he were carrying on a conversation with her.

When the waiter cleared her plate away, he was suddenly at her side, bowing formally.

'I thought, since we are both alone, that you might give me the pleasure of allowing me to sit with you,' he said in heavily accented German. It was as if he had perfected the sentence in his mind for the length of the dinner. Helena smiled, unable to place the accent, intrigued. She gestured towards the empty chair.

'Where are you from?' she asked.

'Buenos Aires, Argentina.' He said it with an aspirated G.

'And I am from London. So we are enemies,' she chuckled.

'What are the Malvinas between a man and a woman!' He gestured grandly.

Suddenly a large figure in a pale creamy suit loomed behind the Argentinian.

'Adam,' Helena breathed. He was scowling.

'I'm sorry. My friend . . . I wasn't expecting . . .' Helena mumbled.

The Argentinian stood. 'No, no, it is nothing.' He bowed.

'Thank you for the champagne,' Helena called after him. She met Adam's eyes, and gestured towards the vacated chair.

'Are you sure you prefer me?'

She nodded.

'That was quick work,' he grumbled.

'I'm a quick sort of lady. Or hadn't you noticed?'

For the first time she noticed the flash of pain behind the shrouded hazel eyes.

He signalled to the waiter, looked at the label on the champagne and ordered another bottle, a large one.

'So who was that?' He turned to her.

'I haven't got a clue,' she laughed. 'Just a man who was dazzled by my scintillating intellect.'

'I'm not surprised.' He suddenly smiled, his eyes growing warm, the dimple playing in his cheek. He touched her bare shoulder.

She stopped his hand.

'Look, Helena. I was rude. My father even bothered to point that out in no uncertain terms, so that now I feel like a chastened fifteen-year-old. But . . .' he shrugged, paused, 'it's difficult for me with Janey here. Then, too, I never know where I am with you. You dump me without the least ceremony. I finally manage to get over being the raging bear I was for a couple of months, force myself to be human so that I can give Janey the love and attention she needs, and you turn up again out of the blue. And I'm in danger of becoming the raging bear again.'

He laughed in self-deprecation, downed a glass of champagne in a swift gulp, stared at her. 'The trouble is, Ms Latimer, I get such confused signals from you.'

'I'm a confused woman,' she murmured, played with the food on her plate. 'You once told me you didn't mind ambivalence.' She looked at him brightly.

'For a little while. Not forever.'

'It's hardly been forever. Besides, I thought you were married.'

'You might have asked. We've hardly lacked speech in our brief relations.'

'It's not only that . . . the marriage. It's . . .' she reached for his hand, 'it's that I don't know how to deal with these things. In myself. Can you understand that?'

'What things?' he growled, but his hand was soft on hers.

She gestured vaguely. 'I don't know. Emotions. Sexual emotions. I . . .' She was about to say something about her childhood, then changed her mind. 'I've only realized it in these last weeks, since I last saw you. I . . .'

'How many men have you slept with since we last met?' he suddenly asked.

'None.' Her eyes blazed at him. 'I tried with one. It didn't work. I couldn't.'

'Why not?' He was being brutal, interrogating her.

'You appeared. In my mind's eye, that is.'

A short sharp laugh emerged from him as if it hurt. 'It's nice to know you think of me at appropriate moments.'

'And inappropriate ones.' She finished her glass, put it out for more.

'What did the man say? When you stopped, I mean,' he asked as he poured.

Helena gazed at him silently for a moment, her lips beginning to tremble, despite herself. 'He offered me a session on the couch. He was sweet. He said something about early awakening and early blocking. Said I was a sex-in-the-family lady.'

'We all have sex in the family. Of one kind or another. Sex isn't just a matter of private parts.' His voice was hard. 'Where do you think we learn it?'

'I guess mine was bad. So I learned badly.'

Tears bolted into her eyes. She rushed from the table.

'Helena.' He was right behind her, his arm round her. 'I'm sorry. But I need to know. To know about you. Please don't cry. I'll make it up to you. I'll beat them up. I'll . . . please.'

They had reached the lobby and he turned her round and kissed her gently, so gently. But the arms which held her were firm.

'Now please, shall we go and finish the champagne? Or take a walk?' She looked into his eyes. They were warm. 'I care about you very much. You must know that,' he whispered. 'If only it were that simple.'

'Both.' Her lips broke into a smile. 'The champagne and the walk.'

'So we take the champagne for a walk. But you come with me to get it, or you might vanish by the time I get back.'

'I won't. I'll just powder my nose the way women were once supposed to.'

'And then you'll talk to me?'

She nodded.

'And you to me?'

'That won't be quite so hard,' he grinned.

They walked. Guided by a plump moon, they strolled beneath the shadowy trees until they found a little wrought-iron table in a bower where they sat, finished the champagne. And all the time Helena talked. Stumbling at first, and in no particular order, she told him of the memories that had leapt upon her, here, while she was with him in Germany, shameful, shaming memories of her early life, of Billy and how she had escaped, of the tangled undergrowth of emotions and the struggle to control them, and how everything seemed suddenly to conspire to make her lose that control – him, too, perhaps primarily him, though not only. How she had held on to Max as one holds on to a fetish of order, a principle that protects, yes, a father. How she needed him, particularly after the experience of India. But it wasn't only that. How she had tried to find out, give his fatherhood a real basis, explored her buried past, visited, snooped.

The darkness helped the talking. Everything suddenly seemed clear and as she spoke it occurred to her for the first time that she was in love with him, that love was in part being able to speak and be heard.

He didn't interrupt her, only kept his arm tightly round her shoulder, encouraging her when she faltered.

When she seemed to have finished, he murmured, 'Poor Helena.'

'No, not poor,' she demurred.

'Also poor,' he corrected himself, 'mostly brave.'

They strolled down the little incline towards the brook.

'What I still don't understand,' he said softly after a moment, 'is why *Max*?' He couldn't keep the contempt out of his voice as he breathed the name.

'I've thought about that too. That's been almost as hard as the rest.' She tried to look into his eyes, but they were shrouded in the darkness.

She took his hand, held it. 'It's not only Max's big ideas I was enamoured of, I think. I've never really understood his more philosophical writings, though I tried. It was his tone, that very apocalyptic dread that you're so critical of. It raised my own fears to a grander level, generalized them, grounded the everyday hysteria in something bigger. Made it something shared. I don't quite know how to explain it. But even as I try, I can feel its seductions. And dangers.'

He brushed her hair with his lips, held her closer.

She felt it as an affirmation, rushed on, 'Yet I still stand by Max's environmental campaigning, for whatever reasons he engaged on it. I don't think the two are the same.' She waited for his challenge.

'Of course not,' he murmured. 'As long as you keep the language of purity out of it. It has a way of rebounding on the social fabric. But go on.'

She faltered then, took a deep breath. 'But that's just it . . . I think what drew me to Max in the first instance was his saintliness, the lack of anything bodily about him, the asceticism. He felt pure. And certain within that purity. Certain of everything. That held me together.' She paused.

'Like a god.' Adam let go of her hand, confronted her.

'Not quite, though a little I guess, from your vantage point.' She tried again. 'It's simpler than that. He was one of the few men I have ever met who never looked at me as if I were a woman.'

'Because he would have preferred you to be a boy.'

She took that, matched her step to his as they walked. 'Perhaps. But for me it wasn't like that. It was simply the lack of anything sexual. And in a man I admired. He made me feel at peace. Strangely whole.'

They had stopped at the brook's edge. He was staring into the water, an unreadable expression on his face.

At last he said, 'I think I can understand that, too. But it hardly leaves much room for me, Helena. I'm not a saint. I can't even find a single aspiration in myself that points in that direction.' He laughed a little grimly. 'I don't even think I'm much good at being the vaunted new man. I haven't quite mastered the veneer of saintly diffidence. Probably never will.' He picked up a pebble, flung it into the stream, started to walk away from her.

'Adam.' She caught up with him. 'Adam, I'm here. With you.'

'And?'

'And perhaps I'm done with fathers,' she laughed, uncomfortable at his sudden coldness. 'Claire told me months ago I was getting a little too big for them.'

'Claire?'

'My best friend. You met her in London briefly. That night of the lecture.'

'Not a good night.'

'No. But she thought you were rather wonderful. Thinks so still.'

'It's nice to know I have a fan somewhere. Does she know? That you went to bed with me, I mean?'

'She guessed.'

He wasn't looking at her. He picked up another stone, made it skim over the water's surface.

'Will you ask me again?' she murmured.

'Even though I'm not a saint?'

'Because you're not a saint.'

'I'm not sure I want to be a sinner either. Judging from our past, that will send you off in search of another saint.'

'So you don't want me any more,' Helena said, her tone flat. 'I've left it too long.' The desolation of it shook her. She drew her shawl more tightly round her. 'I was afraid of that.' She tried to control the sob which rose into her throat. 'I'm sorry.' She moved away from him, putting one foot carefully in front of the other.

'Helena, don't go.' He called her back hoarsely. He was beside her in a moment, folding her into his arms, kissing her, stroking. 'Of course I want you, I've never wanted anyone so much. Can't you feel it?' He took her hand, put it beneath his jacket, so that his heart beat through her fingers. 'And here.' He pressed her buttocks close, made her aware of the penis jutting against her, rubbing, caressing, hard and soft at once. She drew in her breath at the sensation of it and at the pulse beginning to bound within her.

'And if you weren't such a high-minded lady who believed in saints and sinners, I'd prove it to you right here.' He was smiling at her now, a little sardonic smile. 'We'd make the proverbial earth move for us, as it does in the books. But . . .'

'Right here?' she smiled, stretched out on the sloping ground, pulled him down on top of her.

'Yes, right here.' He was looking at her strangely. She traced the lines of his face, his neck, his shoulders. His pelvis started to move against her, so that she arched to the rhythm of it, moaned in the tangle of his hair.

Suddenly he went very still. She could hear the sound of her own breath in that stillness, the eerie hoot of a distant owl. He was leaning above her, searching her eyes, his dark head illuminated in the moonlight. 'But I'm afraid, Helena. I never used to be afraid. But now, with you, I am. Afraid of the recoil. It hurts, you know, when I wake and see you hating me, suddenly despising me.'

'Try me again, Adam,' she murmured. 'Please.' She lifted her lips to him.

Through the clamour of that kiss, she thought she heard another sound, a voice angry, footsteps too close.

'I tell you it was somewhere around here. My best diamond earring.'

Adam put a finger to her lips, smiled, stroked her hair. Then the beam of a torch irradiated them. They sat up abruptly.

'Well, I never!'

A large woman frowned down on them, turned on her heel. She was closely followed by one of the hotel staff in a maroon jacket.

Helena started to giggle.

'What kind of establishment do you run here?' she heard the woman say in a loud voice, followed by the man's, 'It's a lovely night.'

'But the earth is proving a little recalcitrant,' Adam was chuckling. 'I think you had better invite me into less natural quarters.'

'Will you come up with me, Adam?'

'I don't think I could go if I tried,' he smiled, a little wistfully.

'And I don't think I'd let you.'

They gazed into each other's eyes. And then urgency took them over. Step in step they walked quickly to the hotel, their bodies moulded to one another, grateful for the empty lift where they could kiss and touch, more grateful for the door of her room at last closed behind them, so that she could lean against it and he could press into her fiercely, without ceremony, as savagely as she wanted him. There, there inside her where she had never known emptiness could lurk. She came so suddenly, felt the burst of him so nearly, that the room seemed to spin with the pounding in her ears, the door give way behind her.

When she could on the crest of a breath, she said, 'The room moved.' She laughed into his eyes.

'Is that all?' he smiled, caressed her cheek. 'I imagine we can do better than that.'

He carried her to the bed then and made love to her more gently, more subtly so that she felt she was on a voyage of discovery where their bodies were the uncharted land – a land filled with high vistas and new arrangements of stars and lush vegetation, bordering on a sea where the waves lapped and thundered in turn.

At one point, unable to stop herself, she asked him, faltering a little on the big word he had twice used to her though only ever in writing, and using instead its kin, 'Do you like me, Adam?'

'What do you think?' He grumbled a little at that, then mischievously took her hand and placed it on his penis so that she felt him growing hard against her fingers.

'I didn't mean that.' She looked up at him through the tumble of her hair on his chest. 'I mean after I behaved so stupidly. I really don't intend it coyly, but it's hard to understand what it is you saw in me.'

He didn't answer immediately and she moved away from him a little, sat up so that she could read his face more precisely.

'That's because you can't see yourself,' he teased, refused her gravity.

She frowned.

'No, don't protest.' He put a finger over her lips, started to chuckle. 'Just imagine a rather fetching young woman whom one minute you see blatantly slapping a man across the face and the next discover curled in sleep, innocent as a lamb, in your own house. And you don't even know her name. And then on top of it all, you find she really is Snow White, poisoned by wicked stepfathers, wicked stepbrothers – not mothers in this story – and is waiting, just waiting, to be wakened by a prince. Well, what's a man to do?'

'And if she doesn't wake straight away?' Helena smiled.

'That's because the prince is still just a little bit of a frog and things take time. But she did wake.' He looked at her seriously now, brought her hand to his lips. 'She just didn't like to acknowledge it or show it. And that's because she was poisoned not by her stepmother, but by the wicked stepfather, who after all shares a sex with the prince. So it's all a little more difficult.'

She gazed at him thoughtfully and then suddenly asked, 'What's your mother like, Adam?'

'My mother?' He paused, looked away from her, out through the window where dawn had begun to glimmer. 'She died. Just after Janey was born. The birth made her very happy.' He turned back to her. 'She was a good woman, too good to us really and a little put upon by my redoubtable grandmother who could never understand why she wanted to devote all her time to the family. It was simple enough really. Her own had all vanished into the camps. Czech Jews, they were. They sent her to the States in the thirties, a child alone.'

'An orphan, like me,' Helena murmured.

He shrugged. 'My father understood, defended her, worshipped her. Perhaps in part, as an act of reparation.'

Helena gazed at him. 'Is that why you feel so fiercely about Max, I mean Leo?'

He rose then as if he hadn't heard her, pulled on his clothes swiftly, paused only to caress her cheek. 'I must go now, Helena. Janey . . .' He gestured vaguely. 'We can talk about Leo later.'

'Shall I come with you?'

'No, no. Rest. Come for lunch. A late lunch, if you like.'

'Adam, I only have until tomorrow . . .'

He looked at her for a moment in seeming incomprehension, then with something like panic blew her a kiss and was off.

Alone in the room, Helena felt as rebuffed as if he had abandoned her for the wife he no longer had.

Later, when she came to the house, she was told by Elsa that the family were down by the lake. The family, Helena thought, once again feeling herself the intruder. But she needed to see him, needed to above and beyond her pride and her renewed fears.

She made her way past the copper beech with its old swing, down the gravelled path amidst a profusion of flowerbeds. In the distance she could hear a child's shouts of glee.

Max Peters, a panama shading his head, was sitting on a deckchair near the boathouse. He rose as she approached.

'Helena, how nice to see you. I was growing a little weary of my reading.'

She glanced at the tome in his hands.

'Anna's Book,' she breathed.

He looked at her shrewdly. 'So you have read that, too?'

Helena nodded.

He raised his arms with a mixture of dismay and consternation. 'And you know more about the history of my family, the true story of my paternity,' he scowled, 'than I did until yesterday?'

Helena felt the colour rising to her cheeks. 'You didn't know?'

He shook his head. 'It's a wise child that knows its own father. It seems I had two, if Anna is to be believed.' He prodded open another chair for her, gestured her beside him.

'And I had none,' she smiled wistfully.

'Yes, Adam has told me that, told me how you thought Leo might perhaps have been.' He gave her that shrewd look again. 'I can't of course provide concrete evidence, but I have doubts on the score of Leo's paternity. Many more than I have on his fraternity. I really do imagine from this,' he waved the fat volume in the air, 'that he was my brother. Cain and Abel. This family of mine has a lot to answer for.'

'The book has made you angry,' Helena murmured.

He gazed past her towards the house. 'Yes, I believe it has. Or at least angry at my mother, and also a little at Johannes, at Klaus for having kept it from me. Funny, I think I find it harder to forgive my mother her duplicities than Leo his.' He laughed in self-deprecation. 'You will tell me that is just like a man.'

'I wouldn't presume.'

'No, of course not. Still, here I am burdening you with all this ancient history when you have more immediate cares.' He scrutinized her with those clear grey eyes. 'Am I not right?'

'Gramps, Gramps,' a shrill excited voice broke into their conversation. 'Come see, I'm swimming. Come.'

He didn't rise instantly. 'My son, I imagine, may be a little recalcitrant and modern in these things, my dear – he's had his own rather difficult episode in scaling the heights of the newest form of manhood – but if you are still in search of a father, I would be happy to provide my services.' He chuckled.

Helena flushed visibly, faltered, 'I couldn't think of anyone nicer.'

Max Peters laughed again.

'Graaammmmpaaa.'

'Come,' he put his arm lightly over her shoulder, 'let's go and see what my granddaughter has achieved this morning with the help of her doting father.'

They walked through the break in the shrubbery, past the grave.

Adam was standing waist-high in the water, one hand under a thrashing Janey's midriff.

'Gramps, Helena,' she waved at them, 'watch!'

Adam raised his arms in the air, stepped back and sure enough Janey executed a profusion of great splashing strokes before squealing herself back into his arms.

Helena looked at his bronzed rugged form, felt that tremor within her, and shifted her gaze deliberately to Janey. For a moment, in the child's thrashing, she had an image of Max Bergmann, jumping to his death, right here, in this lake. Then, as she caught Adam's eyes on her, the thought vanished.

'Come on in.' He gestured to her.

'I haven't brought my swimming costume.'

'And it's time for lunch, in any event,' Max Peters grumbled a little.

'I'm starved,' Janey concurred.

Adam looked at Helena over his daughter's shoulders. It seemed as if she had grown even more beautiful in the few hours since he had left her. That simple white dress, the golden hair, that pensive look on her face.

Throughout the morning he had had a residual fear that she wouldn't come. A reversion to a prior state. Despite everything she had said, despite the cogency of her self-analysis. Then, too, he had left her so abruptly, had felt so torn, suddenly in a panic. A panic that Janey would leap sleepily into his bed as she did each morning and not find him there, would search through the house, would think he had abandoned her. A double panic at the thought that if Helena came with him, the child might find the two of them in bed together. And he had promised himself that he would never subject Janey to that, to the changing flow of sexual partners like some of his friends did, not unless he was certain of continuity, of some kind of permanence.

So he had abandoned Helena instead, had banished her from staying in the house. Rightly perhaps, if one looked at it with the cool light of reason, since she had said she was leaving tomorrow. But it hadn't felt right. She had been so honest with him. So open, at last, despite the pain of her words. And it still didn't feel right, since all he wanted to do now was to take her in his arms.

Yet he had had to go then, had felt compelled to take the risk.

'Put me down, Daddy.' The child bounded towards Helena, reached for her hand a little shyly. 'The hedgehog came,' she said in an excited voice. 'We didn't see it. But the snails were gone and the hay all funny.'

'We'll have to go and look. When you're dry. After lunch.' Helena's voice was soft.

'Hello, Helena.' Adam ruffled her hair, bent to kiss her a little clumsily on the cheek.

She met his eyes. Was it fear he read in them? A challenge? If only he could take her in his arms and kiss her properly. He touched her shoulder, left his hand there, hoping the others wouldn't notice.

'Here, get into your robe,' his father called Janey away, 'and run, fast as the wind, till you're dry.'

Did he imagine the wink his father gave him? He hadn't had any sleep. His imagination was overwrought. It didn't matter. He dried himself cursorily, pulled his jeans over his trunks. She was watching him. They were alone.

'It's difficult for me, Helena. I'm sorry. Darling.' He wrapped her in his arms, found her lips, soft, only a little resistant. He held her tightly.

'I was afraid you wouldn't come.'

'I'm here.' Her voice sounded strained.

'I'm so, so glad.' He kissed her again, wanted to make love to her, here in the garden, in the bright noonday light. Told her.

She smiled, that wonderful lush smile, the nighttime smile in the full light of day.

They walked slowly towards the house. Adam paused for a moment as they approached.

'My father's in a bit of a state, you know. We'll have to be kind to him. He didn't want to come back here in the first place, but I convinced him. Told him he was old enough. Told him things had changed. Told him he had to bring Janey. And then, last night, he read Anna's Book. Perhaps I should have hidden it. But having shown him Leo's journal, I really couldn't,' he shrugged. 'Just by way of warning. In case he snaps.'

'He said to me he was quite prepared to forgive Max, I mean Leo. But not your grandmother.'

'He spoke to you? I'm amazed.' He held her closer. 'I imagine it's because he's had longer to come to terms with Leo.'

'It's not just that,' Helena mused. 'Paternity is a delicate matter. I've learned that much in these last months if nothing else.'

He was about to ask her whether she understood then about Janey and him, but they had reached the arbour where the table was spread with cold meats and salads. And his father was looking at them with an indecipherable expression.

'Gramps said I could start, 'cause you were so slow,' Janey mumbled through a mouthful of sandwich.

Adam stroked her hair and smiled.

'Gramps, as I'm now known, is a little bad-tempered. He's had an overdose of unpalatable history,' Max Peters grumbled, but there was a playful look in his eyes.

'What's unlapatable history, Gramps?' Janey gazed at him earnestly.

'It's what you'll look back upon when you're older, as if you'd never lived it, as if you'd never sat here before. And what they'll teach you in school as if *no one* ever lived it.'

Max poured white wine into Helena and Adam's glasses.

The child frowned, perplexed. After a moment, she asked, 'Have you sat here before, Gramps?'

'I'm afraid so,' he chuckled. 'When I was even smaller than you. I may even have been conceived here.' He winked at her.

'It's hard to think of you as smaller than me.'

'I should think so too!'

They all burst out laughing.

'Can I go and play now? I'm finished.' She looked up at Adam. When he nodded, she scrambled off her chair, raced off, her arms spread like an airplane. She was singing.

'Captain Planet
He's a hero
Brings pollution
Down to zero'

Adam gave Helena a mischievous glance. 'Her favourite TV programme, it seems.'

'Probably our Leo's as well,' Max Peters grumbled. 'He would have been very happy as Captain Planet, rushing around in a cape or whatever it is heroes wear these days instead of jackboots.'

'But you were defending him, yesterday?' Helena said, just as Adam burst out, 'I'm glad to see you're venting a little spleen at last.'

Max Peters stared them both down. 'Anger towards the dead is not a useful emotion. The clear hard light of reason is what we need, have always needed.' His voice was stern. Then he coughed, laughed with a dismissive gesture. 'I'm afraid I'm feeling a little trapped in Anna's story. Not that I believe it all, by any means. On the other hand,' he paused and looked beyond them towards the mountains, 'it's brought it back to me, that particular atmosphere, the passionate embrace of ideas, our flounderings as we tried to shape the world into the image of our ideals.'

'But that was just the problem,' Adam challenged him. 'Still is. You can't constrain reality to fit your brand of absolutes. That's what Max did, your Leo, I mean. Get rid of impurities and we have the perfect world, the perfect state. Everything answered. Nature called in as witness and executioner.'

'I know, but we lived like that, somewhere between the clenched purity of the ideal and the capacious impurities of the everyday. Johannes and Klaus, even Bettina, when they were young, Leo, myself. All of us.'

'Not Anna,' Helena demurred softly.

'No, perhaps not Anna.' Max Peters looked at Helena as if he had suddenly remembered her presence. 'I think I never quite gave her enough credit.'

'Yet we need ideals.' Helena gazed at Adam, as if the conversation were now between them. 'The world is a far from perfect place.'

'Ideals, yes, but not half-baked absolutes to prescribe to others, an orgy of right-thinking, a nostalgia for invented perfection.' He was severe and she flushed. But he had already turned back to his father. 'You have to make distinctions: Johannes was simply rebelling against his father. His dream crumbled between his fingers. He didn't, like Leo and his cohorts, try to impose it on anyone else.'

'Except Anna,' Helena intervened.

Max Peters chuckled, 'And there's the rub. The small matter of our sexual relations. Men constraining women into the mould of their own ideas.'

'And women, men,' Adam said with an edge in his voice.

'That, too, perhaps.' Max looked from one to the other of them.

But Helena was focusing on Adam. 'You're not going to tell me that men and women are the same in . . .'

'Not the same. Different. But equal. In that too.'

Max Peters was laughing audibly. 'The two of you are hardly going to resolve that here. Off with you.'

Helena smiled at him, didn't move. 'Your son is trying to tell me that men and women have equal power over the shape of things. It's hardly a realistic assessment.'

'I think what he's trying to tell you, my dear, is that even though he's finished his book, he doesn't feel he has quite enough power. Power over you, perhaps.'

'That's not what I was saying at all.' Adam's eyes blazed. 'What I was saying was that women, since they raise the children, have as much influence over the way we see and feel the world, see and feel sexual roles, as men. Why do you think Leo was so terrified of women? Bettina . . .'

'Bettina was my mother,' Max Peters murmured, 'and I've always rather liked women . . .'

'But you had a father who didn't grow magical through his absence.'

'Which is why you're loath to let Janey out of your sight,' Helena found herself saying.

Adam flashed her a look of consternation. 'And you have a residue of admiration for an old Nazi who masqueraded as a holy man,' he lashed back at her.

'Off with you.' Max Peters was sterner this time. 'Leave an old man in peace.'

They rose reluctantly, relieved to have Janey suddenly appear from behind a shrub and whisk them into games.

It wasn't working, Helena thought to herself a little later. She didn't know quite what she had begun to hope for in that long night they had spent together, but whatever it was, it wasn't working. Adam was once again engaged on a swimming lesson with Janey and she might as well be in London as here, for all the attention he was paying her. Nor would he forgive her her association with Max.

Helena shielded her eyes from the sun and gazed out at the lake, the slight mist that robed the mountain peaks. She imagined herself flying back to London, opening the door to her house, feeding the cats, sitting down by the typewriter. She shivered.

'I'll say goodbye now, Helena. I'm off to Munich.' Max Peters's voice startled her from her reverie. She scrambled up, took the proffered hand.

'I trust I'll see you on my return tomorrow.'

'I don't think so,' Helena murmured. 'I'll have to be getting back.'

'Oh? Well, another time then.' He held her hand.

She hadn't heard Adam and Janey coming up behind her.

'Enjoy yourself with Dr Simmel, Dad.'

'Bye, Gramps.'

'You keep Grandpa company up to the car, Janey.' Adam wrapped a towel round the child. 'Run along, now.'

He turned towards Helena. He was frowning, his eyes dark, little angry glints of yellow in them. 'You're not really going to go tomorrow, Helena? It doesn't give us enough time. And I have to stay here with Janey tonight.'

She avoided his face. 'They're expecting me at work, Adam.'

'And us?'

She shrugged. 'I suspect you haven't the space for me. Your life is full now.' She gestured towards the retreating figures of Janey and his father.

'Is that what you really think?' He gripped her arm, dropped it when she winced.

'Okay, I understand.' He turned away from her.

'Adam!' She called him back. 'I . . .' The look of open misery on his face shook her. 'You could invite me back. I'd come. Or you could come to London. I'd like that, like you to see where I live, who I am when I'm not here. We hardly know each other,' she finished lamely.

'Don't we?' He had composed his face and now he grimaced at her. 'Well, if we don't now, I imagine we never will. You might as well go right away.'

This time he loped down the path. She raced after him, the tears biting at her eyes.

'I don't want to go, Adam.' She touched his hand. 'It's just that I'm not sure you want me here. I . . . I feel like an intruder. You have your family and I . . . It's like when I was little.' She gazed up into his face, saw it soften.

'Silly.' He put his arm round her, held her close, continued to hold her as Janey raced back to them.

'Shall we invite Helena to stay here tonight?' he smiled at his daughter.

'Oh yes,' the child said instantly, then looked from one to the other of them with a glimmer of suspicion. 'As long as she tells me a story.' She addressed her father fiercely.

'Two, if you like,' Helena suddenly laughed. 'One straight away. About a hedgehog called Mrs Tiggywinkle.'

Janey giggled, 'Come on, then.'

* * *

Later, while Adam was tucking Janey up for the night, Helena sat in the library and started to re-read Anna's Book. Adam's family, she thought, with a cast of characters who had walked into her life and taken her over, even when she had been least aware of it.

She was so absorbed in her reading that she didn't hear him come in, steal upon her, until his hand was on her shoulder.

'This is how I first found you here,' he murmured. 'Except that you were asleep.' He stretched out his hand to her, drew her into his arms. 'And I've wanted to hold you like this ever since.'

'I'm not asleep now.'

'No. I prefer it that way.'

He kissed her, slowly, luxuriantly, wiping the figures of Anna and Bettina and Johannes and their tangled passions from her mind so that she was only aware of him.

But she drew away from him after a moment, before the sensation of him engulfed her completely. There was still so much to be said, she was still so uncertain. She laughed a little nervously. 'They were rather wonderful, your Bettina, Anna. So brave.'

His eyes played over her. 'You remind me a little of both of them. You have Bettina's high-mindedness and Anna's impetuosity, though I can't work out which is uppermost. Your Max must have sensed it too,' he chuckled, relaxed now that they were alone. More like he had been when she had first come here.

'Which makes me suitable bait for Johannes.' She said the first thing that came into her mind.

'Of whom you don't approve.' He sank down into the sofa, looked at her seriously.

'But to whom I most probably would have succumbed,' Helena laughed, certain of at least that, as she said it.

'Lucky his grandson got there first.'

She hesitated. 'Have I succumbed, Adam?'

'Haven't you?' His tone was light, cajoling, but his eyes had grown wary.

She avoided his scrutiny, gestured at his newly immaculate desk. 'And what are you going to do now that the book is finished?'

'I'm due back in Princeton in September.' He rose abruptly, started to pace. 'I could wangle another term off. Get something at the LSE. But Janey . . . It's too long.' He seemed to be talking to himself and then suddenly he turned to her, gripped her arm. 'Helena, why did it matter to you when you thought I was married?'

She looked at him in incomprehension. 'I told you. I just don't get involved in things like that.' The floor seemed to sway beneath her feet.

'What I mean is, do you have designs on my future?'

'Designs?'

He groaned. 'I'm not putting this very well. Look, it's simple.' He kissed her fiercely with a hard passion that took her breath away. 'I'd wish us like this, Helena, together. Always. But I don't know how to arrange it. There's two thousand miles of ocean. There's my child. You won't even stay an extra few days, take time off work . . .'

'Have you asked me?'

'To stay? I thought I had . . .'

She shook her head. 'No, how to arrange it.' A smile played over her lips. She touched his cheek, traced the line of it, the dimple, tasted the wave of happiness that swept over her. 'Well, ask me?'

'How, my darling?' he whispered.

'I've been offered this job in New York. I was thinking . . .'

He twirled her round the room, didn't let her finish, kissed her, kissed her, whispered, 'Wait.'

He was back in a moment. He bowed to her formally, took her arm as if they were to engage in some arcane waltz. He led her up the stairs to his room and at the threshold lifted her off her feet. 'It's a good thing you're wearing white,' he whispered.

'Obviously part of an intricate design,' Helena smiled.

The room was exactly as she remembered it, except that on the low table in front of the fireplace, there was a bowl of flowers, a bucket of champagne and two tall fluted glasses. She walked round while he popped the cork, the memory of what she had experienced there racing through her. She paused in front of the row of pictures, examined them.

Adam was by her side, following the line of her gaze. He hesitated and then with a visible effort took down the picture which included his former wife.

'You have to understand, Helena. I keep it there for Janey. That delicate matter of paternity, remember? What would she think of a father who completely denied her mother? I never look at it. But it's a fact. A fact of my history. Just like that manuscript you were reading downstairs.' He shrugged, made to put the picture in a drawer.

She stopped him, placed the photograph back on the shelf, smiled a little impishly, sought out his lips.

'If I'm going to forgive you behaving like a father, you'll have to forgive me dreaming Max was mine. He brought us together after all, brought me to this place.'

He laughed. 'At the moment I'd forgive you anything. Except walking out of this room.' He raised his glass to her.

'Yes.' Helena glanced out of the window, thought she saw the glint of moonlight on Anna and Johannes's grave. 'Max brought me to this house. Where the children, it seems, are only conceived when another man is present.'

'I don't want any other man here, Helena, not even a ghost,' he growled playfully.

'I came in search of a father.'

'And you've found a lover with a history too full of them. And what some might call their sins. Won't that do?'

'Very well,' she smiled at him dreamily.

'Though I must say I do find it difficult to combine the two in one. Father, lover, what's a mere man to do?'

'A mere man might call on a mere woman,' she laughed up at him.

'Now why hadn't that occurred to me?'

He pulled her towards him, down on to the bed, gazed into her eyes. 'Would you like a child, Helena? To equalize things a little?' There was that old irony in his eyes. And something else.

'I think so. With you. Sometime.'

'Janey would be jealous,' he chuckled.

'She might not be the only one,' Helena smiled down at him. 'These new-fangled doting fathers. It's just not natural.' She shook her head with mock ferocity so that her hair tumbled over him.

'Nothing's natural, Helena, except what we make of it.'

'I'll buy that, Professor Peters,' she murmured as she felt him moving beneath her, 'for tonight at least.'